Bathed in the Blood of Ravens

A Destiny of Blood & Magic: Book 1

R.L. Parker

Enhanced Edition

Written by: R.L. Parker

Edited by: Kristina Parker

Visit the official website:
https://ayrelon.com

Published by Ayrelon Press
https://ayrelonpress.com

Cover Art by: Charlotte Mallory
https://www.charlottemallory.com/

ISBN-13: 978-1-7366221-2-4

For the creative & loving,
Kristina Parker

You are my everything.

Timeline / Reading List

PROLOGUE

Ris'Kitthu, Danufyr 9th, 1119 of the 1st Era

THERE WAS a faint sucking sound as Drakahl dragged his sword out of the Griffin Guard's back; a moment he'd been waiting for since before the war. No longer would he suffer through every tongue in the land professing the man's prowess and honor. The wheezing of his victim—struggling to breathe despite the gaping hole in his chest—pleased him greatly.

The guard fell to his knees, grasping frantically at his chest; trying in vain to close the wound and survive just that little bit longer. Smiling, Drakahl knelt before the dying man and peered deeply into his eyes; filled with fear and pain. Beyond it all, the true glory of the look he saw on his rival's face was shock at being betrayed.

Across the field of battle, Orluhnd's army was winning the day. One man's death would change nothing; the war was over. Drakahl pondered, for a moment, what his victim must be feeling.

We're on the same side! Our army is the victor. Orluhnd will be king, he thought mockingly.

When the once-famed Griffin Guard rapidly gasped in the throes of his last breath, Drakahl leaned in close to feel the rush of the man's final exhale upon his cheek.

As Orluhnd's army finished the last of his tribe, he mounted his horse and rode north. Cries of treason called out behind him, but none dared follow. He towered over every man in Orluhnd's army. The only one that had shown him no fear—their champion—had just died by his hand. He turned northwest as he left Engle Plateau, leaving the bloodshed of the final battle of the 'War of the Wilds' behind him.

Orluhnd's father, Arkhan Vaelin, had once imprisoned him. Decades of forced servitude and constant suffering had taught him to hate humankind. Upon gaining his freedom, his sole purpose had been defending his Toor tribe and getting revenge upon the Vaelin family.

The Toor had waged war on Arkhan's forces at his command. Both sides suffered heavy losses, and the cost to the land and its people had been tremendous. Had Arkhan's second wife not murdered him as he slept, the Toor would have been driven into extinction. Instead, one woman's act had allowed the Toor to retreat.

They had carried Drakahl to safety that day, heavily wounded and with little chance of survival. The tribe's shaman tried every treatment they knew, but their efforts were not enough. Funeral rites were already being prepared when Arkhan's wife arrived in their camp. None could recall her approach or determine how she had found them. She was suddenly—and without explanation— among them.

Several guards tried to protect their chief, but their attacks could not reach her. A force they did not understand kept them from touching her, allowing her to enter the tent and save his life with strange magic. For several years she remained at his side, instructing him in the ways of the world; its past and its future.

Initially, he tolerated her presence because he owed her his life. When she first predicted the impending demise of his people, his reaction was disbelief. However, one by one her predictions came true. Over the years, even the tribe's shaman came to rely on her visions. Where to hunt, where to harvest, where to live; every facet of their lives revolved around her words.

The second time she told him of her prophecy for the demise of the Toor, he listened. He knew without a doubt that she spoke true.

She then asked one simple, terrible question. 'Will you die with them?'

That question had changed everything. Even if he fought alongside the Toor, their destiny as a species was death. It was his choice whether to die with them, or fight against them, but he could not avoid the war. If he fought against them, she explained, he could play a part in Ayrelon's future.

'Ayrelon is but a steppingstone,' she had explained.

So it was that when, Orluhnd followed Arkhan's dream and sought to unify the lands under one rule, Drakahl had volunteered his services. He spent years in Orluhnd's army; fighting the Toor and founding allegiances with the Afyr and the Ekthri.

'When the final battle nears its end, slay his champion and return to me,' she had instructed. 'It is only then that our path toward destiny will begin.'

He rode through the night without knowing his destination—following the urges of a familiar but unseen force—before dismounting in front of a small, dilapidated shack. When he entered, an old woman turned to greet him. Her wrinkled skin sagged as if it simply didn't have the life to remain attached to her bones any longer.

She walked toward him, straightening from her hunched position as she approached. Her skin tightened, smoothing and shrinking to fit tightly around her frame. The gray hair upon her head darkened to a deep black, softening into silky, seductive locks. Her wrinkled face smoothed and gained the sharp, crisp features of youth.

As she arrived, she put her hands on his chest and begged him to lean down and kiss her. Her small body pressed firmly against his seven-foot, muscular frame as they kissed. He stood upright again, and placed his hands on her upper arms, looking deep into her eyes.

"The task is complete," he stated pridefully.

"Then it begins," she said, smiling.

BATHED IN THE BLOOD OF RAVENS

A DESTINY OF BLOOD & MAGIC: BOOK 1

LEGACY

Ris'Anyu, Oghenfall 13th, 113 of the 2nd Era

When battle doth wage,
And the raven is slain,
True power will reign o'er
The sundered isle.

Night's Writ, Parable 5

AVING FINISHED his morning chores, Laurence returned to his room and flopped onto the bed to take a break. His mind was racing with the possibilities of the life that lie ahead of him. One more night at home and he would be off to Fel'Rechaun, Arkhania's warrior college; just as he'd dreamed for as far back as he could remember. With the day so close at hand and anticipation building, his departure was the only thing he could focus on for more than a few seconds.

"Laurence!" called Arcturus. "Come down here, boy, we need to talk!"

With a sigh, he got out of bed and made his way toward the shop below. The stairs descending from their residence above creaked and groaned as he begrudgingly complied.

"Pap, we've been over this," Laurence retorted. "I've wanted this my entire life! My mind's made up. There's nothing to talk-" His voice caught in his throat as he rounded the corner and caught sight of his uncle Gaerin.

He'd been raised by his grandfather Arcturus in their two-story house, many miles north of the town of Mooncrest. Acting as apprentice, he helped operate the alchemy shop and tend the herb gardens that supplied much of their ingredients. His duties often occupied most of the daylight hours.

Gaerin owned a farm a few miles south and was a trained, experienced warrior. Laurence would often slip away at night, or for entire weekends, to have Gaerin teach him swordplay and combat. That training had been a point of contention between the three of them for as long as Laurence could remember.

He wanted nothing more than to be a great warrior like his father, Tolrin; something Gaerin understood. Arcturus—who didn't want Laurence to die the same way Tolrin had—disapproved of Laurence's pursuits, and made his opinion frequently known. After years of arguments, they had finally agreed that Laurence was allowed to train with Gaerin, but only after he had completed his work with Arcturus each day.

Those arguments had resurfaced in recent weeks, as his departure to Fel'Rechaun drew near. After hearing the tone in Arcturus's voice, he'd instinctively expected another round of heated debate on the subject. Rounding the corner of the shop and seeing Gaerin gave him pause. The last time they'd all three been in the same room to discuss Laurence's chosen path, it hadn't ended well.

"If you're quite done," sighed Arcturus. He turned and walked to the middle of the shop, past rows of shelves filled with vials, herbs, and tiny chests. When he reached Gaerin, he stopped and pointed reluctantly to a large, strapped chest on the floor between them.

Laurence walked toward them hesitantly, unsure what was about to happen. *Has Pap finally accepted my decision?*

"Laurence... you know where I stand on the issue. I've always supported you; much to the chagrin of my father," Gaerin said, jutting his thumb casually toward Arcturus. "He has his reasons for not wanting the warrior's life for you, and yes—to your earlier point—that debate has run its course. Since he cannot dissuade you, he asked me to retrieve this," he concluded, pointing at the chest.

Gaerin knelt, knees popping, and unlocked the chest with an old, rusty key. After undoing the straps that held the lid tightly closed, he stood and backed away, smiling.

"What is it?" asked Laurence as he knelt in front of the chest.

"Open it and see, lad," responded Gaerin, smirking.

The hinges creaked loudly as he lifted the lid. He reached in, carefully hefting the metallic contents. "Where did you get this?" he asked in awe.

"That was your great grandfather's armor, Laur. If the blasted school had let me have it decades ago when I originally asked them for it, your father might still be alive today," answered Arcturus with distaste. He walked over to his desk as he spoke, frustration lacing his words. "Since I cannot talk you out of this nonsense, you may as well have the protection my father had."

The armor, composed of highly polished metal rings, was the finest Laurence had ever seen. It gleamed with silvery luster in the dimly lit shop. The left side of the armor was distinctly different from the right, having black plates mounted in layers atop the maille.

The plates extended from the neck, over the shoulder, diagonally down the left side and over the left arm. The plates, in their long, form-fitted rectangular scales, interlocked when flexed to shift the entire left side of the armor into a shield-like structure. They moved fluidly atop the silvery maille as Laurence inspected the sleeve.

"This is heavy, isn't it? It looks... damaged. Right here," Laurence said. He ran his finger along a nearly unnoticeable seam down the front center of the chest piece. The seam was slightly jagged, four inches wide and of a different quality metal. The repair had a faint blue tinge when viewed at certain angles.

Gaerin had never seen the armor. His father used to tell stories of how Gahl lived and died. The tales often included exhaustive ramblings about the armor he had once worn, and how Fel'Rechaun had kept it from the family. However, seeing the armor in person was a different matter entirely; the stories had not done it justice.

"That, my lad, is where your great grandfather, Gahl, was run-through," answered Gaerin.

Arcturus left the room, apparently done with the conversation.

Gaerin knew it was up to him to fill in the details. "Gahl was a Griffin Guard for the first King of Arkhania, during the War of the Wilds. He died on the battlefield, betrayed by one of the King's generals. You'll find the same damage on the back of the armor."

Laurence turned the armor over and laid it across the chest before him. It was heavy, and his arms had grown weary of holding it. *That weight will take some getting used to*, he thought.

"According to the tale, he was stabbed in the back during the final battle on Engle Plateau. Orluhnd the First had selected him to become Lord Commander of his Legion once Arkhania was claimed, but—for obvious reasons—that didn't come to pass."

Gaerin turned the armor over again so that the front was once more on display. He pointed to the plate that covered the left breast, and specifically the silver engraving that adorned it.

"That was once our family crest. Note that it differs slightly from the one you grew up seeing. This one is simpler, and yet says much more; a raven gripping arrows in one talon and a sword in the other. Your great grandfather was known as Gahl the Raven. When your grandfather was born, that became Gahl of House Raven. His exploits in battle caused his reputation to spread across the land. Tales of 'The Raven' inspired countless men and women to join Orluhnd's forces.

"In your grandfather's time at court, he went by the title Arcturus of Raven's Crest. By the time your father and I were born, Arcturus had retired from service and moved here to Mooncrest. He dropped the declarative, taking the simpler surname Ravencrest," explained Gaerin. "We later adventured together, which resulted in your father's death. After which, we all lived in Vellenheim for a time, in service to the King. Our presence at court caused more turmoil than the King could afford, so we returned to Mooncrest when you were four."

"Why was I never told how Gahl died? That seems something worth teaching, doesn't it?" asked Laurence, wrinkling his brow.

"Arcturus remembers his father well, and no longer enjoys speaking of him... not since Tolrin's death. He was young when his father died, and they never captured the man that murdered him. Well... that and the school enshrined his armor and weapons and wouldn't let Arcturus have them. It was all rather dramatic and political. Then his oldest son—my brother—dies in much the same way and the whole subject has been off limits ever since. As you can tell by his absence, the whole situation still upsets him."

Laurence felt for his Pap. He hadn't known his own father and often mourned the lack of potential memories and experiences. How much worse would it be to know your father well, have him taken from you, and then get caught in decades of political turmoil trying to reclaim your father's belongings? He lifted the armor and sat it upon his lap, staring at the crest; lost in thought.

"We can talk about it more later. I just," Gaerin paused, struggling for words, "it's a lot to process." He stopped for a moment and opened the chest again. "There's more to a suit of armor than just the breastplate. Why don't you go through the rest and try some things on for size, okay? I'll go tend to your chores." Gaerin stood and exited, leaving Laurence to his thoughts.

Laurence sat the armor aside so he could more easily retrieve the rest of the chest's contents. He removed everything, piece by piece, and laid the items out across the floor to his right and left, matching the side of the body they belonged to where possible.

The left gauntlet was of the same black plate on top with soft leather on the palm. In contrast, the right gauntlet was supple black leather, hardened on top and soft underneath.

Beneath the gloves he found a pair of blackened leather pants adorned with shiny steel plates affixed at the thigh and knee. Digging deeper, he found a padded leather shirt, two belts, boots with metal shin guards, and a dagger.

"This is amazing," gasped Laurence. He looked over at his grandfather questioningly as the old man came back into the room. "How did you get the armor back? You said you asked the school for it decades ago and they refused."

"I did, Laur. However, when I sent payment for your schooling, I also sent along a very lengthy letter detailing exactly what this old wizard was about to do if they didn't comply with my decades-old request."

"Surely they don't take threats seriously from an old man like you," joked Laurence as he stood.

"Surely they've been led to believe I've not lost my powers," Arcturus defended. "Lest you forget, I was once the King's Archmagus. In all seriousness, I simply needed to ask the right person. There are many who owe me favors, especially after the death of Tolrin, and my accomplishments in the King's court. Since none of the family were adventuring anymore, I didn't have a good reason to cash in those favors... until now. I can't very well have you run off to find fame and fortune unclad, can I? I'd put it off as long as I could, but... it's time to stop pretending I have any say in the matter."

"I'll be fine, Pap," assured Laurence. "Uncle Gaerin taught me well."

Arcturus sent a scolding glance toward the rear of the room—where Gaerin had exited—which would have looked more menacing if it weren't for his years. His prickly, balding, gray hair and dark, wrinkled brow just didn't hold the same imposing facade he'd used to his advantage for half a century.

"You'll find the rest hanging in the barn, boy. You can spare a few moments to go see those pieces and have Gaerin help you learn to put it all on. After that, I expect you'll see to your duties one last time."

"Absolutely!" Laurence agreed, moving toward the back door.

Gaerin entered a few moments later to grab the forgotten suit of armor for his nephew.

"Keep the boy safe, Gaer," demanded Arcturus. "I trust your training has been exhaustive enough to bring him home safely."

"If it eases your mind, he leaves for Fel'Rechaun more skilled than his father and I were upon graduation. I even tried to convince him they had nothing left to teach him, but he's a true Ravencrest; once he has his mind made up, there's no changing it. The only thing he lacks is discipline."

"I hope you're right, son. I hope you're right. This family has been through enough in my lifetime."

"To be fair, the entire world has been through enough in your lifetime, old man... you're older than our Kingdom," Gaerin quipped. He smiled as he carried the armor outside in the chest it had arrived in. His father meant well. They had not always agreed on their approach for raising Laurence, but his heart was in the right place.

He had to admit Laurence had turned out better under Arcturus's care than he probably would have under his own. The boy's life would have been far less disciplined, and recklessness more the norm. In child rearing, there was little they saw eye to eye on, but the combination of their efforts had been very successful.

∴ ∴ ∴

LAURENCE WAS in the backyard swinging a sword around wildly. It was a sight that Gaerin remembered from their earliest days of training, so many years prior. Gaerin thought it was ironic how he'd just finished thinking about Laurence acting recklessly and had come outside to see that very thing taking place.

"Laur, come show me what you've found!" yelled Gaerin. He slowly descended the back steps into the yard, hefting the weight of the chest carefully.

Laurence stopped swinging the sword, panting heavily and smiling as wide as his face would allow. Gaerin sat the chest down as Laurence approached, holding the sword before him like a prize.

It was exquisite in every detail. A gold raven sat perched at the center of the quillon, beak pointed towards the handle and wings spread wide and upward toward the blade. The blade bore several minute scratches and minor nicks.

"Very nice. Quite an impressive sword, lad. Better than any I possess, to be sure."

"There's a bow and quiver too, but no arrows. That's fine, though. I can make some on the road. It'll give me something to do at night," Laurence proclaimed, still smiling and gasping for breath.

"You've come a long way, lad. Few boys your age would be as dismissive at the thought of fletching arrows on the road to the kingdom's military college."

"Well, those other boys didn't have you to teach them, did they?" He said, smirking.

"I've got one more thing to teach you, boy. Stow that blade and let's don this armor. From the looks of it, I think you're nearly Gahl's height. The challenge for you is that he was apparently of mountainous strength whereas you—"

"Yeah, not so much. I'll bet I'm quicker than he was, though."

"That very well may be, unarmored. But in this thing, you may find movement to be harder than you think," he answered as he held up the hauberk.

Laurence took his shirt off. His brown skin glistened with sweat from his frantic, imaginary swordplay. His muscles, while not overly impressive, were athletic and firm. He was lean and very fit; more than capable of handling himself in battle should the day come.

Gaerin smiled reassuringly as Laurence slipped on the cotton shirt. The shirt laced tightly at the neck and wrists but was baggy everywhere else.

They worked to get the blackened leather padding on next. Every other suit of leather padding Gaerin had seen was unattractive, scarred and not meant for show. Gahl's leather padding, however, looked very much like a piece of armor unto itself, though softer. It laced up on Laurence's left side and again at the neck and wrists. The hardened wrists were easily thick enough to deflect a small blade.

"I could probably wear this around town by itself, don't you think?" asked Laurence.

Gaerin took a step back to get a good look. "It could work well for general scuffles too, if push comes to shove. I wouldn't rely on it instead of the full armor, but in a pinch you could get by. Keep in mind that leather armor damages easily in blade fights, though. It would be a pity to replace custom work like this just because of a reckless bar fight."

"Right... me, in a bar fight," Laurence joked as Gaerin hefted the hauberk. It slid down over his head and into place rather easily. "It's kind of loose, don't you think?"

"It is. Like I said, he was much larger than–" his voice stopped for a moment. "Aha!" Gaerin exclaimed.

Laurence asked, "What is it?"

"Lift your left arm," Gaerin replied. Laurence complied and Gaerin immediately began unhooking the metal plates from atop the maille hauberk. "These little hooks on the edge of the plate go under like this," he explained. Laurence tried as best he could to watch while holding his arm up. "That attaches the plates to the maille. Ah! You could wear just the maille, or attach the plates for tougher battles. This design is splendid! Underneath all this, there are leather straps to tighten it all down!"

"They thought of everything!"

"Either Gahl was rich or Orluhnd loved him. This armor is unlike anything I've ever seen."

Gaerin finished lashing the side of the hauberk tight, then reattached the plates to the side of the armor. He stepped back to watch while Laurence put on the pants, boots, belts and gauntlets. "Amazing, lad. You look formidable. How does it feel?"

Laurence stood before him proudly. The silver maille of the hauberk sparkled brightly in the mid-day sun. Black plates of armor locked together as Laurence flexed his left arm, creating a shield-like barrier. The thick, black leather boots and leggings bore small, shiny steel plates at strategic points. Gaerin was certain that had he run across someone dressed in that armor during his adventuring days, he'd have thought twice about testing their mettle.

Laurence moved around, trying to decide how to answer. "I can barely feel it on me."

Gaerin gave him a perplexed look.

"Seriously, Gaer, it's like I didn't even change clothes. It was heavy at first as you were helping me put it all on, but now it's... it's like I'm not even wearing it. I mean, it's bulkier, sure, but I can't feel the weight at all. Not even a little."

As if to prove his point, Laurence ran full speed back to the barn to retrieve the sword, now complete with scabbard and sword belt.

Gaerin watched in amazement.

"How does this thing go on? It's got a different style belt than I've ever seen," asked Laurence as he returned.

Shaking off his disbelief, Gaerin answered, "That's a hand-and-a-half-sword, and since Gahl was a griffin rider, he couldn't very well wear a longer sword like that on his waist. At least not while riding a beast with wings."

"It goes on my back!" Laurence blurted happily. He was ecstatic. After years of Gaerin insisting that he should never back-draw his weapon, he had just received a suit of armor that required him to do so.

"Here, let me help," Gaerin said with a sigh. "It looks like this gets worn at an angle." Gaerin helped him don the sword. He then knelt and fastened the dagger to Laurence's right calf, just over the boot's top. "And we're done."

"I wish Gahl were here to thank. This is more than I ever could have wished for. I didn't even know armor like this existed." Laurence was having a hard time hiding his excitement.

"Well, it mostly doesn't. This is unique, as far as I can tell. I've never seen this tradesman's mark before," he said, pointing at the little symbol on Laurence's left gauntlet. "Maybe someone at the school will have a better idea of where this all came from and what it really... is. It's apparent to me it's enchanted, considering how light you say it feels. Perhaps your grandfather can answer that question later tonight, eh?"

"Oh! Maybe!"

"As for tonight," Gaerin said, "sleep in this."

"Why?" asked Laurence.

"You won't want to take this thing off on the road at night. If you get attacked in the middle of the night, you'll want to be ready. So, sleep in it tonight in a normal bed before you get on the road and see how it feels. If you can't handle it in a bed, then you won't be able to handle it in a bedroll. That means you definitely shouldn't travel alone, because you'll need protection while you sleep and help to get this thing on and off."

"That's a good idea, uncle. A great idea, in fact," said Laurence excitedly.

"Well, I'm off now. Lyla will absolutely lose it if I'm not home for dinner. Will you be okay to do your chores in this armor?" Gaerin instantly regretted getting him fully suited. *I should have returned after dark to do it*, he thought.

"Oh, he just wants me to label some flasks for him and muck the stalls. I can do that easy in this armor. Take my gauntlets off for one, take my boots off for the other. I'll be fine. Besides, as you said,

I need to get used to wearing this."

Gaerin hugged Laurence and clapped him on the shoulders proudly before leaving.

∴ ∴ ∴

ARCTURUS FOUND it amusing when he saw Laurence carefully labeling flasks in a full suit of armor. He found it even more amusing when he mucked stalls, using leather waders and an apron to keep his armor clean. The entertainment value dissipated when Laurence sat down for dinner, still wearing the armor with a sword on his back.

"What's the rule about wearing armor at the table?" he asked. His dark brow wrinkled notably above his bushy, white eyebrows.

"There isn't one, Pap," Laurence answered curtly.

"Well... there should be a rule," quipped Arcturus.

They ate for a time in awkward silence. Both realized it was to be Laurence's last meal at home. Neither knew precisely what to say under such circumstances.

Laurence noted that his Pap had prepared the thirty-year-old, aged, salt-cured venison that he'd been saving. It was the most delicious meat he'd ever tasted; the side dishes didn't even matter. It wasn't until his fourth helping of venison that Arcturus spoke again.

"Your father, Tolrin, caught that venison," stated Arcturus.

The bit of meat that Laurence was swallowing caught for a second in his throat.

Surprise must have shown on his face, for Arcturus continued, "It's okay, I still have a little more. If any occasion calls for a special meal, though, this would be it. As much as I might dislike your chosen life—and as hard as I've tried to change your mind—it is your choice and I must both respect that and help you celebrate it. You've earned this meal, Laurence, and I can only apologize for not being more supportive as I raised you."

"I... thanks?" Laurence stammered. He wasn't sure how to respond. He'd never heard Arcturus be apologetic about anything. Ever.

"Your father, my eldest son, died in my arms. He was a warrior, much like you wish to be. He trained at Fel'Rechaun, much like you're about to do. I buried my father over a century ago, who died the same way. He was also a warrior. He also trained at Fel'Rechaun.

In fact, he was part of Fel'Rechaun's founding class; mere months after Arkhan Vaelin and his Ekthri advisers established the school.

"For my entire life, I have suffered memories of those who have trained at that damned school, only to die by the very arts they thought they'd mastered. Your uncle Gaerin is the only exception to that experience, and that came at a price... a heavy price. Your father died saving Gaerin's life. I forbade your uncle from adventuring the moment we returned from that damned trip. That journey took both of your parents, my wife Fraela, my brother Octarian and countless others."

Laurence looked at his grandfather with tears in his eyes. He had knots in his throat and chest. He struggled to find the right words to respond.

"None of that should be your burden. You're only seventeen. You are not the cause of those events, and it isn't fair for me to hold them against you. My regret is that I didn't come to this conclusion until today," Arcturus finished, the words nearly catching in his throat.

"It's... it's okay, Pap. I know you meant well. You always had my best interests at heart. I realize that, and I love you for it. But... my father was a warrior. I never knew him. The only 'self' I can cope with is one that honors him by trying to be the best warrior that I can be. Some of our greatest ancestors were warriors and knights; honorable ones. I want to follow in their footsteps and bring that honor back to our family. Especially now. More so now than I ever did."

"It's not just about that girl?"

"Tylee?" Laurence laughed. "Sure, she likes me, I suppose, but it's not like she's running off to school with me." If he was being honest, Tylee was a constant presence in his daydreams of glory and fame. He didn't think Arcturus needed to know that little detail. At least, he didn't intend to share it.

"Fortune, fame and glory are not something that the honorable seek. If you truly wish to do justice to your family name and 'bring back our honor', as you say, then you'd best keep that in mind. A powerful man should have no desires toward praise. Neither should he seek rewards for his actions. A hero performs as he knows he must, for the good of those around him."

Arcturus continued as he cleared the table, "I may not agree with your choice, Laurence, but if you're doing this with honor in mind... *that* I can abide. However, that is a harder road than you might think, lad. A much harder road, indeed."

Those thoughts loomed over Laurence for the rest of the evening. He couldn't shake them.

Am I doing this for the right reasons?

As he nodded off, he fought back thoughts that challenged his own motivations in self-defeating circles.

∴ ∴ ∴

THUMP, CAME a sound from downstairs, startling Laurence from his slumber. Try as he might, he could hear nothing more than the gentle rain outside. As he nodded off again, another *thump* came from below, followed by his grandfather's steps descending the stairs to go inspect.

"Blasted shutter!" Arcturus grumbled as his creaky bones carried him down the stairs.

He listened as Arcturus passed through the door into the shop below, its hinges creaking wildly. They had often discussed oiling them but neither of them had ever remembered to do so when they had oil in hand.

With all the various oils in the shop, why have we never–

The lock on the shop door clicked shut abruptly, if not violently, echoing up the stairs.

He never locks that door!

Laurence sat upright in bed, straining his ears to hear. Muffled speaking resonated through the walls and floorboards from below.

Someone is in there with Pap!

So intense was Laurence's thought, he paused for a moment to make sure he hadn't yelled it aloud.

As he took his first step out of bed the metal plates on the left side of his armor clinked together. He froze, horrified.

After a few seconds—once he was certain they hadn't heard him—his tension faded. Realizing he was still wearing the armor, he turned back to his bed and grabbed a blanket. Draping the blanket over himself to muffle any sound his armor might make, he crept slowly and carefully toward the stairs.

Thank the gods I snuck out so much as a child, he mused.

His feet carefully and silently found those familiar spots on the steps that made the least noise. He made it to the bottom, arriving in the kitchen, and walked up to the shop door without notable changes in the muffled words beyond. Carefully, he leaned over and pressed his ear to the door, listening intently.

"You think that will free you from this? You applied the curse, old man. You shall lift it!" growled a man's voice angrily. He sounded mature but young.

"As I told you, I cannot cure the incurable. I created the blasted curse to be *quite* permanent. If his damned witch can't cure him, what makes you think I can?" retorted Arcturus, his voice wavering.

Laurence quietly tried the door latch as slowly and carefully as he could.

A very heavy pair of boots entered the shop from the front entrance. They rumbled through the shop slowly and methodically, shaking the very foundation with every impact upon the old floorboards. The floor and walls around Laurence trembled with each step. The door he leaned against rattled on its hinges.

What in the hell is-

"Arcturus," resonated the horrific, raspy voice within the shop. It seemed strained, as if the speaker were trying to speak softly. "This curse-"

"I cannot cure it, Drakahl. I-" Arcturus stammered. His voice was trembling, and his words were catching in his throat.

Laurence tried the door again with more force. It still wouldn't budge.

"You misunderstand me, old one. I do not seek a cure. Quite the contrary... I mean to inflict this gift upon others. I simply came verify for myself that you couldn't undo my work before I began."

The voice paused for a moment before unleashing a deep, hollow laugh that shook the building.

Laurence took advantage of the noise to run toward the back door, only to find it barred from outside. He cast off the blanket he'd been using to muffle his armor and ran up the stairs as fast as his legs would allow.

This man will not get what he came for!

Once he reached his bedroom, he could hear the men below rallying to charge up the stairs behind him. He grabbed his weapons from atop the footlocker at the end of his bed. There was only one way out that didn't involve trying to wield a longsword in a narrow stairwell. He quickly made his way to the window.

His weapons slid wildly across the muddy ground below as he tossed them a safe distance from the house; everything but his sword, which he held tightly and safely at his side. Pushing back the fear that welled up inside him, he sat on the windowsill and swung both feet out.

The door to his room burst open.

The ground was soft, thanks to the rain, and provided minor cushion for his fall. He survived the jump with nothing more than a twisted right ankle. Resisting the urge to crumple up in a ball and grasp it painfully, he gathered himself and limped towards the front of the house as best he could. Knowing what lie ahead, he pulled the sword free and dropped the scabbard behind him.

When he reached the front corner of the house, adrenaline coursed through him anew. Two men were guarding the front yard.

The closest one noticed him, turned, and charged forward. The man's leather armor bore several scratches, gouges and abrasions, as did his bronze bracers. It was clear, to Laurence, that his opponent had survived many battles.

The massive two-handed battleaxe he was wielding came screaming down from the sky above. Laurence pushed toward the man with all the might that his good leg could summon. He drove himself as fast as he could toward his foe's right side at a sharp angle. He didn't want to deflect his attacker's powerful blow, nor contend with the weight of the man's axe. The risk to his own arms and sword were too great, so he chose instead to get beyond the blow, under the arc of the man's swing.

Laurence was faster than his attacker had expected. Not only did Laurence narrowly avoid the downward strike, he ripped his longsword through the man's side as he slid between him and the front of the house. With their combined momentum, Laurence's blow had split the man wide open at the hip. It was a lucky strike, but he was in no position to argue with luck.

His second opponent wore a mixture of chainmaille and plate. After donning a set of field-plate himself, Laurence knew that his only chance was to either work his blade between protective plates, strike a less protected area, or bludgeon him to death inside his armor. Fighting back against his fear, Laurence closed the distance as fast as his right ankle allowed.

His opponent seemed astounded by his speed. Wearing similar armor, the boy moved quicker than should have been possible under such weight. He raised his shield and held his sword ready, braced to meet Laurence's charge.

Seeing the man's stance, Laurence attempted to come to a stop. He failed. His feet went out from under him, sending him into a slide past the man. Mud collected beneath the plate armor on his legs, slowing him to a stop.

The man jumped out of the way just in time, avoiding a collision. Laurence came to rest several feet behind where his opponent had originally stood, looking up at the man's lower left side. Peering back, he could see a gap beneath the man's hauberk, just above his left hip.

Laurence drove his sword toward that gap as fast as he could. His blade pierced through the man's gambeson, deep into his torso, and stopped in the middle of the his ribcage. He fell backwards, ripping the sword from Laurence's grasp.

His adrenaline rush fading, Laurence barely reached his feet and retrieved his sword before his next opponent rounded the corner of the house on the far side. He knew that adrenaline and luck were keeping him alive, and hoped that it would last long enough to save Arcturus.

An elf, clad in black brigandine, raced toward him wielding two curved short swords. His pointed ears and tightly bound hair enhanced the angry scowl upon his chiseled, angular face. It was the first time Laurence had seen an elf in person, and it wasn't the set of circumstances he had always hoped would provide that experience.

The elf closed on him far quicker than should have been possible in the mud. His blades were a whirl of steel, moving at an impossible pace.

Laurence turned his left side toward the opponent, clenching his arm as his uncle had shown him. He did his best to deflect as many of the elf's blows as he could with his sword.

It wasn't long before the elf had disarmed him. A series of quick strikes battered the interlocked plates on his left side, sending him reeling backwards in pain. His backward progress sent him over his second opponent's corpse, onto the ground. Everything above his waist on his left side was throbbing in pain, feeling broken and bruised.

"Enough!" roared the voice from the door. "Let me see this fool before he dies."

"Lord Drakahl," said the elf in recognition. He backed away with a twirl of his blades, exposing the path between Laurence and the door of the house.

A seven-foot-tall man came into view. His armor was comprised of black and blood-red plate. It seemed to writhe in the moonlight as if it were alive. Strategic points of his armor bore spikes, spines and horns. So gruesome was the appearance of the armor itself, and the horrific skull helm that sat atop it, that the face within the helm came as a complete shock. His face was strong, mature, and rustic, yet strikingly beautiful.

The man's crystal blue eyes and piercing gaze amplified the contrast in his appearance. If it weren't for the man's face, Laurence would have described him as a demon.

Laurence then noticed the man was holding his grandfather like a rag doll over his left arm. The horror that Laurence felt deepened. He was too shocked and terrified to scream. His mouth opened as he tried, but no sound escaped. All he could hear was the beast-man's breathing.

"Ah... it has been ages since I've seen Gahl's armor. Oh, this should be delectable." He dropped Arcturus perpendicular on top of Laurence's legs, leaning over to look the boy directly in the eyes.

"I will enjoy this very much," he laughed. The ground trembled beneath Laurence. The elf held his hands to his ears and backed away, smirking evilly.

Drakahl turned to the elf and spoke in a notably softer tone; something which seemed to require a great deal of effort. "This game is just starting. Leave him for now."

"My Lord, I have what we need," a young human in leather armor pointed out from the house.

Laurence recognized the new man's voice as that of the first person he'd heard talking to his grandfather. Tears welled up in his eyes.

"He killed Ulger and Dison," said the elf.

"I am aware of what he has done, Soth. Gather the others. We are leaving." He looked down at Laurence as the elf and the human walked off to do their master's bidding. "This isn't our time, boy. We will have our day... when you're ready."

Drakahl stomped on Laurence's right ankle, breaking several of the bones within. "But, as I can't have you wasting my time just yet, I leave you with this."

Laurence wailed uncontrollably. Between the pain in his left side, his shattered ankle, and the death of his grandfather he could no longer control his emotions.

His cries please Drakahl greatly.

Six men emerged from the house carrying various bottles. Flames erupted behind them as they crossed the lawn, collecting their fallen comrades. Each one of them looked down upon, spat into the face of, or laughed at Laurence as they passed. A very dirty man with a tangled, braided black beard and several missing teeth relieved himself on Laurence before departing.

Once mounted, they rode north. Laurence lay beneath his grandfather for several moments in severe pain, wishing his adrenaline would return and wash some of it away. The house was burning fiercely, and the rain was growing in intensity. He knew it was just a matter of time before he ran out of options.

∴ ∴ ∴

DIFFICULT AS it was, Laurence finally freed himself of his grandfather's weight, rolling him off his legs as carefully as he could. With tears filling his eyes, from both pain and sorrow, he tore a square of cloth off the back of his grandfather's robes. He rolled onto his stomach, draped the rag over his head and, using just his arms and left leg, he crawled toward the house while dragging his right.

Once at the house Laurence lifted himself carefully up the stairs, trying his best not to use his right leg, which was sending shooting pains into his hip and back with every single movement of his body. Flames danced playfully across the ceiling and most of the walls. The fire had not overtaken the floor yet, and most of the lower shelves appeared to be safe in the alchemy shop.

Carefully, he dragged himself inside. He knew that many of the dangerous flasks and vials were on the upper shelves, so that children couldn't reach them. However, that also meant that they were closer to the flames above. He was certain that he wanted to be clear of the building before they finally caught fire and exploded. He paused for a split second at the thought of what might happen when polymorphic, poisonous and curse-laden vials all exploded at once. With a greater sense of urgency he pressed on, biting back against the pain in his right leg as he did.

The heat from the flames above him made itself known. The rag atop his head grew warm and the leather of his right gauntlet had begun to steam. As quickly as he could, he reached the first set of shelves and found what he was looking for; healing potions. He looked left to glance over his shoulder as he went to back out of the aisle and leave the shop when his eye caught something he instantly knew he couldn't leave without; one of his grandfather's tattoo kits.

Pushing the vials and the tattoo kit with his chest as he moved, he slid across the floor, dragging himself with his arms and pushing with his left leg. Back out in the rain, he worked his way back across the lawn as quickly as he could. Small pops, bangs, and explosions began ringing out behind him in an eerie, morbid chorus.

Once he reached what he considered a safe distance he stopped, turned onto his back and sat up. The pain in his leg was dulling to a slow throb. If his grandfather's teachings were correct, the change meant either a fresh rush of adrenaline or he was entering a state of shock. Laurence glanced around, searching for his sword. Upon seeing where it lay, he sat the equipment he'd gathered on his lap and dragged himself in a seated position toward it.

The house began falling in on itself as he moved.

Adrenaline, shock; whatever had been dulling his pain left abruptly as he carefully removed his right boot. Slowly, he unlaced and rolled up his right pant leg. Struggling at such an awkward angle, he eventually revealed his entire shin, ankle and foot. His shin sagged horrifically, many of the bones shattered into what he could only assume were shards and dust.

He wiped the blade of his sword as clean as he could, using the rag he had worn to protect his hair from the fire. After a few seconds of battling himself internally and searching for the will to proceed, he slid the sword across his shin, vertically, slicing through flesh and down to what remained of his bones. He never screamed so loud in his life as he did in that moment.

The pain was more than he ever could have imagined... his vision went dark.

By the time Laurence awoke, the house had reduced to an oversized bonfire. None of the structure remained.

It was still pitch black out. He squinted as he peered at the sky, trying to block out as much of the light put off by the fire as possible. Using the position of the moons and the few stars he could see, he guessed there were still a few hours before the first light of morning would emerge. Aside from the pain in his leg, which had changed little, he felt weak and lightheaded. He was fairly certain he was losing too much blood. Then again, he hadn't planned on passing out after preparing his leg.

He sat back up, collecting one of the healing vials he had rescued from the shop. As he uncorked it, the welcome smell of duskberries and lavender surrounded him. Arcturus had designed the odor to calm the recipient of the elixir. It was one of his grandfather's specialties.

He'd helped Arcturus perform his next task several times, but always on other persons. Never once had he considered he'd have to repeat the task on himself, without help. Left with no other options, he clinched his teeth and pressed on.

Using his left hand, he gently spread the skin and meat of his leg as much as he could bare. He growled with the pain, hoping that would help him fight off the urge to pass out again. With his right hand, he carefully poured the healing fluids into his leg, aiming specifically for his bones. The thin stream of violet liquid ran down across the bones, binding them back together bit by bit.

He slowed the trickle of fluids carefully and, emboldened by the numbness now washing through his leg, he shoved his left hand into the wound and pushed the bones into alignment. As he proceeded, he adjusted the stream of fluids so it would strike each new seam.

He finished the healing of his leg by dumping the rest of the liquid onto the muscles and sinew, then using both hands to press the flesh back into position. His newly healed leg was numb, his foot responding slowly as he tried to move it. Potions were never as good as a healer or proper medical treatment, but he would at least be able to walk.

Slowly, carefully, he rolled his leather pant leg down, laced the shin together and clipped the plates back into place. He held his foot up to the rain now, sitting cross-legged in the mud, and rinsed it off a bit before donning his boot. Cautiously he stood, favoring his left leg.

Limping to protect his freshly healed limb, Laurence walked around the house and gathered a shovel.

He went to the side yard and dug a shallow grave beneath Arcturus's favorite tree. It was all he could manage while in pain, in the rain, but it would have to suffice.

He limped, once again, over to his grandfather and dragged him methodically toward the grave. Sorrow faded slowly during the chore. His mind was awash with Drakahl and the other men who had attacked.

Sadness gave way to anger, hatred, and the need for revenge.

DEPARTURE

Ris'Nammlil, Oghenfall 14th, 113 of the 2nd Era

A young boy's tears shall mark the path,
One generation gone.
The old man's death shall form the seal,
And with it make none one.

Night's Writ, Parable 2

A S LAURENCE carefully placed the last bit of soil on Arcturus's grave, the image of Drakahl consumed him. Consciously reminding himself to favor his left leg, he retrieved the tattoo kit and returned to the mound.

He lowered himself to the ground and removed his gauntlets, then placed the tattoo kit in his lap and opened it. Inside was a fine-tipped writing quill; a steel quill with three very fine tips set in a row; two inkwells, one filled with very special ink; several small strips of cloth and a small vial of healing liquids.

One of Laurence's primary duties in the alchemy shop was labeling flasks. He'd grown skilled at drawing detailed pictures, because not all of their customers could read. In addition, he'd occasionally helped in the application of tattoos. Most often they'd been applied to the elderly to provide moderate improvement to certain ailments. He briefly wondered if fate hadn't given him those skills in preparation for the task before him.

Retrieving the normal quill, he dipped it in ink and went to work. Carefully, he drew Drakahl on his left palm, hunching over to protect his drawing from the rain. He began with the intricate details of the man's face, fading in complexity as he drew the horrid helm he'd been wearing.

Happy with the detail he'd achieved, he set about tattooing that face into his left hand permanently. He picked up the steel quill, dipped it into the special inkwell and carefully stuck it deep into his flesh along the lines he'd just finished drawing.

Tiny droplets of blood formed along the dark, ink filled lines in his palm. Try as it might, the rain could not wash them all away. He winced as the quill bit flesh again; not from pain, but because that's what his subconscious mind had convinced his face to do. After all, every other man he'd seen get tattooed had winced in pain.

His mind was a blur of purpose, anger and remorse; every thought laced with memories of a life that now seemed distant. Drakahl had sent his world crashing down around him in a pile of flaming timbers. As he jabbed the quill into his flesh again, he could feel no pain; he had no room left to feel.

He spared a moment for another glance at what remained of his childhood home as it burned before him, sizzling in the rain. Coldly, with tears of anger joining the rain upon his cheeks, he dipped the quill into the inkwell again.

The rain hadn't made it any easier to bury his grandfather, and it wasn't helping with the tattooing process. Easy or not, he had to ensure that the tattoo was complete while the image of that man's face was still fresh in his mind. It had to be now.

Laurence ran the evening's events through his head repeatedly as he worked. Every face, every piece of armor, every weapon and everything they said. He wanted the exacting detail of every single moment to plague him for days, weeks, months... even years. He didn't want to forget, for he would have his revenge on every single one of them. Most of all, he would have his revenge on Drakahl.

Why did he leave me alive? Why not end this? He has to know I'll come after him. In fact, he most likely expects me to. But why?

Unable to figure out Drakahl's motivations, he turned his thoughts back to re-playing what happened. He was seeking any minute detail that could shed extra light on what had taken place.

∴ ∴ ∴

HOURS LATER, as the first rays of sunlight streaked through the sky, he decided he had completed the tattoo. The remains of their house smoldered in a blackened heap and Arcturus lie buried in the mound beside him.

After studying his hand for a moment, he withdrew the thin cloth strip from the kit, uncorked the vial of healing elixir and dabbed a little out of it. Using the cloth, he cleaned the top of the tattoo, healing the surface of his skin and sealing the artwork safely beneath.

Laurence stood, stretching off hours of tension and working his joints; loosening them up from the ordeal of the night he'd just survived. With a mournful sigh, he collected the few belongings he had left. Afterward, he used the horse trough to clean the mud out of his armor. As he donned his weapons and gauntlets, he lamented the animal corpses in the barn next to him.

He would have to walk.

With nothing left for him at the remnants of his former home, he started south. Not only did Gaerin need to know what had happened, but hopefully he would have a horse that Laurence could use to get back on track. If he was to seek revenge, he would need a lot of training and practice; of that he was certain.

The event had taught him well about his position in life, and he was aware he had been ill prepared to face those men. Regardless, he was distraught at his inability to save Arcturus's life, and blamed himself for his grandfather's death.

Fel'Rechaun was still to be his destination, he was certain of that. To add to his problems, the ordeal had set him behind by at least half a day. As it was, he'd barely left himself time to get to the school before the next class began its training.

Though Arcturus had already paid for his spot, he wasn't sure how long they would hold it open for him if he was late. He needed their training more than ever. He had a new purpose, rather than just childish desires.

Being late was a risk he could no longer afford to take.

∴ ∴ ∴

LYLA AND Gaerin were in the kitchen preparing breakfast when they heard a knock at the back door. As Gaerin stepped into the mudroom to answer it, he muttered toward Lyla, "I told Laurence not to waste time saying goodbye this morning. He'll be late getting to-"

Gaerin's words trailed off as the door opened and he caught sight of Laurence. Covered in dirt—his hair caked with mud—the boy smelled of cinders and earth. The bags under his eyes revealed that he hadn't slept. Something was horribly wrong.

Lyla, hearing her husband's voice stop mid-sentence, removed the plate she was cleaning from the soap-filled bucket. She dried her hands as she turned to join Gaerin saying, "Well now, let the boy in."

Gaerin backed up and held the door open to let Laurence walk past.

Laurence barely glanced at his aunt as he entered the room, choosing instead to cross directly to the table at the far side of the room. He sat down and said, "I need you to join me." He patted the table calmly, inviting them to sit across from him. As he waited in silence, he removed his gauntlets and placed them on the seat next to him.

His face was puffy from crying, and he was sure they had noticed. His eyes were painfully dry, and likely bloodshot if his assumptions were correct. There was no easy way to say what he needed to share with them, and it was all he could do to choke back the knot that was forming in his throat.

Gaerin and Lyla gave one another concerned looks. He joined Laurence at the table while she stopped by the wood stove and grabbed the kettle of coffee. Seeing her actions, Gaerin got up and retrieved three mugs. The three of them remained silent until Lyla had served their coffee.

As Laurence reached for a mug with his left hand, Gaerin caught sight of the tattoo.

"By the gods, Laur!" gasped Gaerin. "What have you done to yourself?" Confusion and concern laced Gaerin's voice.

Lyla's face went pale and her eyes widened, as if she knew what was coming next.

Their nephew finished his sip of coffee and returned the mug to the table. Afterward, he held up his left hand so they could both see the tattoo clearly.

It was Gaerin's turn to go pale.

Lyla let the words, "Oh my," escape her lips before covering her mouth with her fingertips in disbelief.

"This man murdered Arcturus and destroyed the entire farm while I looked on, horrified. His name, according to his men, was Drakahl." Laurence finished his sentence and then put his palm within inches of his own face, staring at it. "I will see his world *destroyed* and his head upon a stake before I'm done."

"Dra-" began Lyla, visibly shaking.

"Drakahl," finished Gaerin, barely able to contain his anger. "I told Arcturus we should have killed him! 'Let me go back and finish this now,' I pleaded. 'No, Gaer, I've lost a son already this day,' he responded. I should have stood my ground!" Gaerin punctuated his sentence by slamming his fist down into the table, using the force of the blow to help himself stand. A single tear fought past his anger and cascaded down his cheek, betraying his true feelings.

Laurence looked up at his uncle, "And that must be why he strode into the shop last night demanding a cure for some curse... which he enjoys having and wants to share among his men." He fought hard to hide his feelings, but the hatred inside him was so thick he could taste it.

"He what?" exclaimed Lyla, her dark brown skin slowly going pale.

"First, his men demanded the cure to a curse. When Arcturus couldn't produce it, Drakahl strode in, laughing, and declared that he just wanted to be sure there wasn't a cure before he gave it to some of his men," said Laurence, exacerbated.

"But that doesn't-" began Gaerin, pausing. He wiped the tear from his cheek and sat back down, perplexed.

"It doesn't make any sense," concluded Lyla. "Arcturus assured us that the curse would drive Drakahl insane and that his fate would be worse than any death. He assured us it was, in fact, over. Yet... the betrayer lives."

"He doesn't just live, he thrives. He looks younger than both of you by half, or more, and is more powerful than any man I could have imagined until now." Laurence paused for a moment to let his words sink in. He once again fought to choke back the knot in his throat. His emotions kept swinging wildly from anger to sorrow; the process was taxing.

"Betrayer?" asked Laurence. "What, or whom, did he betray? How was he involved in my father's death? How did Arcturus come to curse him? And why, if he's old enough to have killed Tolrin, does he look like he's in his mid twenties?" Laurence asked frantically. There were too many questions and not enough time to have them all answered. I'll take frustration over what I've been feeling.

"Let me see your palm again, lad," requested Gaerin. Laurence removed his gauntlet again, his frustration showing in his actions. As he held up his palm, Gaerin inspected it again. "Yes, that is definitely the same man I remember. That's not the armor he wore back then, but... it's been a while."

"Well, when we met him, Gaer, it's not like he looked that much younger than when we left him some ten years later. Thinking back now," she paused, thinking, "I'm not sure I could confidently say he aged, even then. Ten years we knew him. Ten years of that same face staring back at us. Why did we never question it?"

"More importantly... how has he come to relish and embrace a curse that makes him see the world decay around him endlessly?" asked Gaerin. He stood and started pacing back and forth across the kitchen as he spoke; a nervous pace that Laurence had never seen from him before.

"Either tell me what's going on here or I'm just going to go find out myself when I hunt him down," Laurence demanded, his patience exhausted. He rose to his feet, hands resting angrily on his hips.

"Nearly thirty years ago, we set out to seek... well, fame and fortune, I suppose," Lyla explained. "We were young and foolish. Tolrin and Gaerin had just graduated from Fel'Rechaun and had heard many tales of their grandfather, Gahl.

"They wanted to be like he was, so we went adventuring. Arcturus, Fraela and Octarian were still young enough to travel and Arcturus was a powerful wizard, so they went along to protect us. It was like the perfect dream."

"We met Drakahl in Gusarski Cove, a port town north of the capital city of Vellenheim," continued Gaerin, calming himself and sitting back down. "With his added strength and prowess, we felt like we could take on anything. Soon we were slaying bands of orcs for this town, clearing out goblin hordes for the next. Before long, we were facing more and more powerful foes until finally we killed a fierce, ancient hydra for the people of Uldenheim, much further north.

"It was about that time that we got word of a horrible tyrant on the Isle of Pelrigoss to the east. He ruled with an iron fist, slaughtering anyone who disagreed with him in even the slightest way. Supposedly his rule was rife with unsavory acts; exploitation, unjust imprisonment, high taxation, you name it," stated Gaerin.

Lyla jumped in, adding, "Aye, two men from that isle traveled to Gusarski Cove, pleading for aid. Not only were we promised more gold than we'd ever dreamed of, we were told that if one of us were honorable and sought to rule their people fairly after we dispatched King Pahn, that they would get us the support we needed to do so. They'd been so beaten down by Pahn that they had no leaders remaining, and no ability to revolt or fight back any longer."

"I still remember the look in Tolrin's eyes when he heard that bit of news," added Gaerin.

Laurence wondered why he'd never been told any of the story before, but didn't want to interrupt. He needed the information, and knew that if he interrupted he might not hear it all. As frustrated and impatient as he was, he forced himself to wait and listen intently. Calmly, he took his seat and drank more of his coffee.

"He would have been a great King, I'm sure of it," assured Lyla.

"Well... when we arrived in Pelrigoss, King Pahn's forces attacked us at every turn. We lost Fraela and Octarian before we'd been there a week. Both died defending Arcturus during a night ambush by enthralled minotaur," noted Gaerin.

"They were horrid beasts," added Lyla.

"Aye, and it took nearly a month of fighting, hiding and scouting to find Hoalfast; a small town that was free enough of Pahn's influence to get a good night's rest. Ah... The Bloated Goat." Gaerin's voice trailed off as he reminisced briefly.

"I'm sure it was lovely, but I've still yet to hear how Drakahl betrayed the family," grumbled Laurence. He was at his limits and no longer concerned with trying to hide it.

"We're coming to that part, Laurence. The Bloated Goat was a critical stop in our journey," chimed Lyla.

"The Bloated Goat was the source of every pleasant memory we have of Pelrigoss, Laur," continued Gaerin. "It is also the reason you exist."

Laurence looked back at him, perplexed.

Gaerin continued, "Your mother, Myrindia, worked there as a bar wench."

Lyla gasped and slapped Gaerin's shoulder.

"Okay, okay, waitress..." mocked Gaerin, coyly. "That's where Tolrin fell in love. That love caused us to stay for some time. About three months, in fact."

"Drakahl was none too happy with their union, that's for certain," added Lyla.

"Indeed. That was when we first saw his dark side. While we took advantage of our brief respite to investigate and gather information about our target, Drakahl spent his days stalking Myrindia and, apparently, plotting against us.

"We eventually left Hoalfast and set off to find a magical blade, with pregnant Myrindia in tow. After months of searching, we found this black-bladed sword in the bowels of an undead-infested crypt. We'd been told that we absolutely had to have the sword to defeat Pahn. When we finally found it, only Drakahl could touch the damned thing. It couldn't even be near Myrindia without her doubling over in pain, cradling her abdomen."

Gaerin paused, took a sip of coffee, and let their story sink in for a moment. Lyla had started quietly weeping. Gaerin knew that she was weeping more for the memory of Myrindia than Arcturus. While she had loved his father, there had been a special bond between her and Myrindia.

"By that time, it had been nearly ten months since we'd arrived in Hoalfast. Lyla was helping tend to Myrindia with her healing ways. Myrindia could use her magic from a safe distance, but we knew that it was risky taking her with us. However, Pahn's guard had overrun Hoalfast while searching for us. Really, we had nowhere to leave her. So we pressed on.

"Weeks after leaving the crypt, we arrived at Pahn's fortress. We gained entry through a sewage grate and set fire to the barracks while most of his men were sleeping. Both tactics came from Drakahl. After hours of fighting, exhausted and dangerously low on magical support from Arcturus and Myrindia, we finally breached Pahn's throne room.

"That's when his treachery struck." Gaerin stopped for a moment to catch his breath and take another drink.

Laurence immersed himself fully in their tale, his mind no longer racing with memories of the previous night's events. His yearning to be off towards Fel'Rechaun was now the focus of his subconscious mind. His conscious mind wanted nothing but the conclusion of Gaerin's story.

"Tolrin charged for Pahn's commanders, encircled around him protectively. I flanked them from the right. Drakahl was to flank them from their left. He, instead, stood back a safe distance and watched anxiously as we dispatched them. It was an arduous task.

"Myrindia used what spells she could muster to shield us from attacks, but she was quickly losing strength. Arcturus was... well, you never witnessed your grandfather in battle, but rest-assured he was being his usual mischievous self. The man was never really happy unless he was ruining some poor fool's day in the heat of battle.

"Lyla was trying her best to keep Myrindia up and active, but her supportive spells just weren't keeping pace," Gaerin said.

"It was as if she was sucking the power to wield magic from

her very bones, in desperation. We were honestly out of our depth. Drakahl knew it," Lyla added.

"Aye, that he did. As the last of Pahn's guards fell, we noticed that Drakahl was engaged with Pahn himself, clashing blades mercilessly. It didn't take long at all for a fully rested Drakahl to dispatch an exhausted, ill-prepared Pahn. The magical blade Pahn supposedly wielded? Pure fabrication. The oracle who'd sent us after it, a liar... likely a co-conspirator of Drakahl, now that I think of it," remarked Gaerin.

"That witch was horrid. I trusted not a hair on her head. I told you all as much, but you were so bent by purpose that nobody took heed," added Lyla.

"Aye you did, my love. And I regret not listening to you to this very day. Though, part of me says they would have just found another way to make us do their dirty work." Gaerin paused for another sip of coffee. Lyla topped off his cup and sipped some of her own. Laurence was so enthralled in the story he hadn't touched his cup in several minutes.

"As Pahn hit the ground, Drakahl stepped over him and charged Tolrin without skipping a beat. Poor Tolrin was panting and hunched over, hands leaning on his legs. And there came Drakahl, fierce, full of energy and wielding a powerful magical sword," continued Gaerin.

"The trails," muttered Lyla fearfully in recollection.

"Trails?" asked Laurence.

Gaerin smiled at his wife, reassuring her that it was okay to continue.

"Black, wispy trails of..." she paused for a moment, trying to find the right words. "Magic," she finally decided. "They were streaming between his sword and Pahn's corpse as he ran toward Tolrin. They kind of floated off and faded like wisps of smoke. When the wisps touched the sword they pulsed, growing more solid and... darker. They ran up his arms like tendrils. He grew visibly stronger on just that short run across the room. It was mortifying."

"By the gods," gasped Laurence. "His blade drank power from Pahn and fed it to him?"

"Souls, Laur," corrected Gaerin. "She was too far away to hear the faint screams emanating from the black smoke. It was Pahn's soul being drunk by the blade to empower Drakahl. We don't know whether the effect was temporary or permanent, only that it gave Drakahl the edge he needed to make Tolrin look like a toy."

"He laid into Tolrin with a ferocity I'd never seen before. He had skills we'd never seen. Skills born of long years of war and a great deal of experience. He had been playing us from the very first day he met us, nearly a decade prior. It was as if he and that witch had planned the entire adventure up to that very moment.

"He was seconds away from beheading your father when I reached him. Tolrin's right arm, left leg and chest already had deep gashes in them and black tendrils were already beginning to stream between he and Drakahl. I blocked the fatal blow to his neck, but it shattered my sword and left wrist to do so," said Gaerin.

"I ran in as quickly as I could to help. I-" she stopped short, crying.

"She didn't realize that Myrindia had run into combat, trying to save Tolrin," Gaerin said, finishing her sentence for her.

"What about Arcturus? What was he doing during all this?" begged Laurence.

"Channeling a very long, powerful spell. One that it turns out he'd nearly invented on the spot out of desperation. That's how powerful he was—something else which he hid from you all these years, I'm sure," answered Gaerin.

"I assume that was the curse?" guessed Laurence.

"Indeed, it was. But something very critical happened before that spell finished. Lyla made it just in time to pull me clear when she saw my sword shatter. Myrindia arrived just behind her and dove between Drakahl and Tolrin," said Gaerin. He paused for a moment as he saw the look of dread on Laurence's face. There was no simple way to tell him about the slaughter of his parents, but the lad needed to hear the conclusion of the tale.

"Drakahl drove his blade through Myrindia's right shoulder and upper chest, then into Tolrin's neck in one thrust. He'd been aiming for Tolrin, to be sure, but Myrindia's frantic dash to save her lover had placed her in harm's way. Had she not done as she did, Tolrin would still have died and she might have become Drakahl's prisoner for decades to come, who knows. That's where his motivations seemed to lie." Gaerin shrugged unknowingly. It was a guess, but he was fairly certain it was an accurate one.

"That's when Arcturus's spell hit. Drakahl instantly doubled over in anguish, shrieking. His eyes began glowing an eerie blue, and he grasped for his face, dropping his sword. Myrindia, gasping for life, broke her amulet violently on the floor with as strong a throw as she could muster and, in the blink of an eye, we found ourselves standing on the shore near where we'd docked."

Laurence looked at Gaerin with surprise in his eyes, "How?"

"Tolrin had told her where we'd docked and she'd apparently prepared a teleportation spell to take us there in an emergency," answered Gaerin.

"But not Drakahl?" asked Laurence.

"No, I..." Gaerin stammered, "I guess not!"

"She must have known all along!" exclaimed Lyla.

"Wow... it... never dawned on me," gasped Gaerin.

"She knew Drakahl was a problem before we even left Hoalfast! I remember Arcturus mentioning during our very first camp with her, after we left, that she should *'turn down the brightness on that silly neck lamp so the rest of us could sleep',*" Lyla exclaimed, chuckling.

"I remember that joke," Gaerin said. "Trouble is, none of the rest of us could see it glowing. Just Arcturus."

The three of them sat around somberly for a bit while Laurence mulled over their story. He now knew more about his father, his mother, his grandfather, his uncle and aunt, and the man who'd wrecked more than half his family.

Laurence broke the silence, peering inquisitively at Gaerin, "That still doesn't explain how he knew I was wearing Gahl's armor."

"He what?" gasped Gaerin, a hint of fear in his voice.

"He looked down at me and said, *'Ah, it's been awhile since I've seen Gahl's armor,'* before he crushed my leg, gathered his men and rode off," recalled Laurence.

The look on his face must have been very saddening.

Lyla looked at him and started crying.

"But we never even... I mean... I never saw Gahl's armor until Arcturus unveiled it for you yesterday. They locked it away the entire time we were in school. It was waiting on someone to repair it, they said. Something about finding the right smith. We figured they were just dodging us. Truth is, I don't think a soul set eyes upon it at all from the time Gahl died until your grandfather gave you the chest. Well, except for the man who repaired it on route to us two weeks ago," responded Gaerin.

"Two weeks ago?" asked Laurence.

"Yes, I remember Arcturus complaining about the cost. Something about a 'Joril' charging too much, I think it was. I was shoeing a horse at the time and not really paying attention, I fear. Farm life has dulled my sensibilities lad, I'm sorry," apologized

Gaerin.

"So if he recognized Gahl's armor, and you guys say he didn't noticeably age for the past thirty years... then it stands to reason, as bizarre as it sounds, that he might have known Gahl," reasoned Laurence.

"Well, yes," answered Gaerin. "I suppose that makes sense. Though, if you'd suggested that to me yesterday, I might have laughed in your face for being mad," Gaerin added. He sat back for a moment to think. "If you're right, then-"

"He could be the one who killed Gahl," Laurence finished. After a moment he asked, "So that was the last time you saw him? Just before the teleportation spell?"

"We tucked tail and ran at Arcturus's bidding. Your mother gave birth to you, after a long struggle, six hours later and promptly expired. Lyla could not save her. Drakahl's sword's wounds are—for all we can tell—permanent."

Laurence took a few moments to drink his coffee, which had become cold, and process the full story. It was much more than he'd expected. He wasn't sure that knowing the story would have changed anything about his life, much less the previous night. However, he was a little upset that he hadn't been told any of it previously.

What, precisely, were they waiting for, another tragic death in the family? My grandfather had to die in order for me to learn anything about my father's death? He sighed as he shook the thought away. *I'm sure that wasn't their intention.*

"Well, I must be off," stated Laurence, frankly.

"Absolutely not," jumped Gaerin, putting his hand on Laurence's arm. "You might well make it to Fel'Rechaun quickly if you leave now, Laurence, but you won't pass the entrance trial in the state you're in. Only solid rest will get you back on track before your journey."

"You may well be right, Gaerin. In fact, I'm certain I agree with you—as much as I wish I didn't. I was on the verge of being a late arrival as it was and then... this crap happened," lamented Laurence.

"Aye, this is pretty much the worst thing that could have happened to you. You need time to adjust, rest, and mourn," assured Lyla.

"That may be, but I must travel to Fel'Rechaun. Not only am I certain I need their training, but I'm also certain that they have information I need for my quest. Either way, I don't plan to spend my last night here," concluded Laurence firmly.

"What?" responded Gaerin, shocked.

"I'll see Tylee once more before I depart and, gods permitting, we'll spend the night together before I set off. I'll not venture out on this journey with her not knowing how I feel about her. Too long have I played the shy boy in her presence. Sad to say, I think my naivety wore off with a single blow last night. Besides, who knows when I'll be able to return. I'll get my rest in her arms."

Lyla blushed knowingly.

Gaerin responded, "Oh. Well then, you do as you must, lad!" He clapped Laurence on the shoulder approvingly.

Lyla gave Gaerin a disapproving look—half in jest—to which he smirked.

"I'll saddle Onyx for you, lad. Meet me outside after your aunt has packed you some lunch."

∴ ∴ ∴

TYLEE SAT in the front room of her family's house staring bored out of the front bay window; her coffee cold on the sill beside her. Her only care was whether Laurence would visit before he left her forever. She had never heard of anyone moving away from Mooncrest and returning; she was no fool.

She sighed depressingly as she realized it meant she would have to choose another, less interesting suitor. None of the other boys in town had his promise or his allure. *Maybe papa is right? Maybe it's just because he isn't actually from Mooncrest? Maybe I just need to find another country boy!*

She didn't really want to find another boy; the tear that slowly caressed her right cheek revealed as much. She'd never felt as strongly about anything in her life as she did in that moment for Laurence. *Perhaps I should join him. Maybe I can join in on his adventures and we'll find a nice, new city to call home. Anywhere is more exciting than this dull place.*

With that thought, her mind was made up. It would be another year before her father would let her leave without a husband. She would do so, if need be, to follow Laurence to the ends of Ayrelon and be with him forever. *Assuming he even likes me.*

Silly boy. How many times had she practically thrown herself at him without response? *'Oh look, I have a bite!'* he'd respond as she leaned in, alluringly.

Was he blind, she asked herself, too short-sighted to recall that they'd been fishing in the creek.

"Tylee, darling, why must you sit there as if your world is ending?" her mother asked, entering the room. Her mother was attractive enough for her age, Tylee decided. Delriahna was a beautiful name and her mother had been a beautiful woman in her prime, Tylee was sure of it. Just as she was also certain that she didn't want to end up like her mother; hidden away from the world and tending house while her husband spends all day traipsing around town in ironed robes pretending to be important.

"He will come to see me, mother. I know he will," she said stubbornly. *How could he not be here?* Her legs were sore. Her rump was hurting. Her feet were asleep. *How long have I been sitting here?*

"Well, you've been sitting there all day, dear," her mother stated in a snappish tone, answering her unspoken question.

There's my answer, mulled Tylee.

"Yes, mother, and I'll keep sitting here until the world ends if that's what it takes," she pouted.

"Dear... if he hasn't arrived by the time your father returns from council you must join us for dinner, regardless. It will not please him to know you wasted your entire day's lessons waiting for a boy that didn't show up," her mother warned.

"Lessons? What lessons?" she asked as she got off of the window seat, stood and turned to face her mother. Her intentionally dramatic momentum nearly carried her full circle and down to the floor. *I really hope mother didn't see me stagger.* "Do you really think it matters if I learn a new stitch, read another poem or bake another tasteless hunk of bread?"

"It's only tasteless if you're no good at it, dear, which is why you need more practice and thus more lessons," her mother answered sharply. Tylee scoffed. "Scoff if you must, but these lessons are not a waste. They will serve you well when you find a proper, more suitable man to wed."

"Proper? Proper!" she let her anger flow through her words, and her stomp. "Proper like Constable Welsh? I'd rather marry a toad!" she ended dramatically.

"Oh no, dear. Constable Welsh withdrew his proposal when he heard of your nasty response to his offer. He would have made you happy and your future would have been secure in his home. Our family would have greatly-"

"You mean father would have greatly benefited from our bond, not our family! Certainly not me! With the Constable in his pocket the council would have swayed more easily to his whims, would it not? That's all you care about... not love." Tylee was upset and very, very weak. The latter of which her mother did not need to know.

"Call it what you will, child. You'll be hard-pressed to find an honest, 'proper' man to marry you with that tactless mouth of yours," her mother chided. She stormed off, leaving Tylee alone again.

Oh, I'll hear about this later, I'm sure, she thought as she returned to the window seat in a huff. *I don't want to marry some crusty old Constable, or his friends. I want my Laur*, she thought with a frown.

It was hours before there was a knock at the door. The knock was firm and loud. It awakened Tylee, crumpled up at one end of the window seat, fast asleep. Nearly every joint in her body popped as she stood, many of her muscles knotted and resisting her movements. It took everything she could muster to force her body to jump out of the window seat and race to the door.

It has to be him!

Tylee whipped the door open a little too fast in her excitement, hitting herself square on the forehead. Laurence rushed through the rebounding door and caught her as she stumbled backward, groaning in pain. The scene might have been romantic if not for the rosy red knot forming on her forehead, the tears running across her cheeks, and the obscenities streaming from her mouth.

Laurence couldn't resist a chuckle. It was the funniest thing he'd witnessed in what felt like forever.

"There's my little klutz," he chuckled. "Should I lay you down and go fetch some ice?" The scene had totally taken the morose mood out of Laurence, albeit temporarily. His thoughts were not on Arcturus, or Drakahl. They were wholly on the woman he held in his arms.

"Don't you ever let me go, you twerp!" she belted, rubbing her forehead stubbornly.

"Twerp? Is that the kind of language your lessons are teaching you? Should I just go?" he asked jokingly, thumbing toward the door.

"I'll crochet a rope and tie you down faster than you could say 'Fel'Rechaun', you jerk!" Tylee was about to continue when Laurence, smiling wider than he ever had in his life, leaned in and kissed her squarely on the lips. What his subconscious had intended to be a quick peck became something else entirely.

The kiss was as much a surprise to him as it was to her.

∴ ∴ ∴

ANDOR COLVIN was a portly man; his hair neatly groomed and clothes crisply pressed. His outer robe and sash identified him as a very important man; a member of the town council. He was proud of his position and it had taken a lot of hard work to get to where he was in life.

He had very little time for anything that didn't yield results. Town law, politics and social intrigue were the only things to which he granted mental effort. It was important for him to remain focused, sharp of mind, and quick of wit. He prided himself on his powers of observation and his deep knowledge of every member of his community.

So it was quite a surprise when he passed through his front gates to see a young man in a full suit of expensive armor leading his blushing daughter through his front door. He was, in fact, so taken aback that he involuntarily stopped in his tracks with his jaw open and eyes wide; something he never allowed himself to be seen doing.

"Sire Colvin, I am taking your beautiful daughter on a sunset ride this evening, as it is my last night in town," Laurence declared.

"Aren't you the lad she goes fishing with at the Reincrik whilst avoiding her studies?" asked Andor in a condescending tone, pretending not to recognize the boy he and his wife barely tolerated.

"I am," Laurence answered confidently. He didn't like Andor's tone and decided he no longer needed to put up with such an attitude. "I will also be the man who marries her, should she have me?" he added, casting her a questioning glance.

"Oh yes! Yes, yes, yes! So much yes!" Tylee squealed aloud.

"You'll what?" barked Andor.

"My grandfather was murdered last night, and my house burned to the ground," he explained. "I am setting out to train, with hopes of eventually hunting down the men who killed him. The only part of this town I wish to take with me is holding my hand as we speak. So, you can give this your blessing or not, but it's happening... because it must," Laurence insisted.

Tylee's eyes grew wide in horror. She couldn't process how he must have felt, or what he'd been through.

Andor's face contorted, stunned by both the reality of the situation, and Laurence's sudden change in tone.

Laurence had never spoken like that to anyone. He never

expected he'd have to. He'd always dreamed of wedding Tylee, but had pictured the process being more romantic. With recent circumstances, he didn't feel he had the time, or patience, to follow normal ceremonies and rituals. *It has to happen now*, he thought with certainty. His adrenaline was rising in anticipation of Andor's impending rebuttal.

"I-" stammered Andor, finding himself oddly at a loss for words.

"We'll just handle this ourselves father," declared Tylee. She grabbed Laurence's hand more firmly, walked past him and began dragging him toward the church.

"What's all this, then?" inquired Delriahna from the porch.

Andor calmed himself and let the air settle between them a bit before responding. Putting his arm out to indicate Tylee should stop, he gave Delriahna a look to put her at ease and let her know he had a plan. He understood that Laurence had been through a traumatic experience and decided he wouldn't hold the boy's outburst against him. Further, he was a man who could recognize opportunity when he saw it.

"Do you still plan to attend Fel'Rechaun?" he asked.

"I do," answered Laurence with a nod.

"When are you leaving, *son*?" asked Andor with genuine concern and care in his voice. Calling Laurence 'son' had been a strategic decision. It was a brief quip, and one easily dismissed. His wife, however, would know exactly where his mind was going.

"Tomorrow morning," answered Laurence. "I planned to stay at the inn, or camp just outside of town, one last time before I left. I haven't decided which."

"Do you plan to serve the kingdom once you graduate?" Andor continued.

"All things permitting, I do. Though, I have things that must be resolved beforehand. I'm sure you understand, given the circumstances," Laurence responded.

Andor looked to the sky as if checking something, and then to his wife. She nodded, answering an unasked question, and headed back into the house with haste. After watching her leave, he sighed and turned back to the couple; staring straight into his daughter's eyes.

"Is this your wish?" he asked in a very serious tone.

"Yes. So very yes," gasped Tylee, returning to the moment. She stepped back to stand directly at Laurence's side.

"I am truly sorry for your loss, son. Arcturus was a great man, and he did quite a lot for the people of Mooncrest over the years," said Andor, returning his gaze to Laurence. "You've his passion, that's certain. And you are, as much as I might approve or disapprove, quite possibly the most perfect match for my odd, daydreaming, and willful daughter."

Laurence, feeling his adrenaline wane and his fears dissolve, responded, "She is the only thing left in my life that I can't imagine being without." He freed his hands from hers and turned to face her, adding, "I couldn't go off to Fel'Rechaun without her knowing that."

"I can't very well have her sitting here day after day, unwed and rotting away on our bay window... waiting for your return," said Andor.

Laurence and Tylee turned to look at him, intent on responding.

Before they could, he added, "That's why Del is off to fetch Priest Thomasen as we speak."

The teens both turned toward the house to see Delriahna closing the door behind her, a shawl draped over her shoulders.

"Let me by, boy, so I can see about making you our son," she chirped at Laurence as she approached.

He stepped backward off the walkway as she neared to make room for her.

"Is this?" Tylee gasped. "Can this really be real? Are we really going to be married? This isn't fake, is it? Am I still sleeping?"

"I didn't expect you to be so accepting of this," Laurence admitted to Andor in shock.

"You've been through quite an ordeal. It's obvious my daughter loves you, and if I were to deny your request I'd not only be losing you as a prospective son, but her as my daughter," Andor explained. "As far as the marriage goes, don't be so quick to thank me. With no father and no grandfather, marrying my daughter makes you my legal son by Kingdom law. While that will allow me to look after you and to step into legal matters on your behalf, Tylee can tell you herself that I'm no prize parent. You may yet live to regret this decision," he stated, half-jokingly.

"I doubt that very much, sir," answered Laurence.

"Now, obviously, this isn't the ideal scenario nor the best-planned wedding. This will be legal, to be sure, but this isn't final. I expect you to return to Mooncrest and finish the job with a proper wedding at the town chapel as soon as you've graduated," demanded Andor.

"Absolutely, sir," answered Laurence.

"Anything you want, father, but I'm going to Fel'Rechaun with my husband," declared Tylee.

"Oh, I fully expected you would want to, my dear. We must secure housing in Raven's Nest for the three of you while Laur attends school. There's much to discuss and plan," said Andor.

"Raven's Nest?" asked Laurence. He had never heard of such a place.

"The three of you? I'm not three people, father," Tylee retorted.

"Del and Bronsin will accompany you, Ty, and that is not up for debate," answered Andor. He turned to Laurence, "Raven's Nest is the former city of Englevauld. It sits atop the southern cliff bordering Engle Plateau and looks down upon the outer courtyards of Fel'Rechaun, across the Western Reach. It is most commonly used by family, friends and support staff for those attending school. Housing there will suit this situation well."

It surprised Laurence he hadn't heard of the city from his grandfather, or uncle. He also found the name curious. He had to assume they named it in tribute to Gahl.

"A lot has changed since your father's graduation. It's been nearly three decades, after all. In fact, many of the new recruits bring brothers, sisters, or spouses along to train as squires. They often stay in Raven's Nest. Obviously, Tylee should not take part in such training. I educated her as a lady of standing and I would have her remain so," said Andor.

"Oh, I don't want to be a dirty ole squire, father. If I can be near my love I'll do whatever you please," she said smiling.

She pressed her body against Laurence, allowing him to envelop her in his armor-clad arms. She loved the feeling of the armor pressed against her. It made her feel safe. She couldn't have imagined such a day and was having a very hard time getting her mind focused enough to converse sanely.

Tylee blinked hard, trying to wake up... just in case.

∴ ∴ ∴

ALBERTUS THOMASEN was a reasonable man. It took a reasonable man to succeed as the only priest of Galrath in a small town. His church was small and understaffed, yet quaint. The chapel could only hold a few dozen attendees, which suited him fine. In reality, the chapel saw more use by the town council than it did during sermons, so its size was never a limiting factor.

Confessions occupied most of his time, if one could call them that. The residents of Mooncrest brought their troubles to him and relied on him for counseling. Therefore, he considered himself more the town psychologist, and less their priest.

He loved the people of Mooncrest, as his position dictated he should. However, if he was being honest, he thought most of them desperately needed help he was unqualified to give. Their troubles ranged from cheating spouses to the mundane. He often wondered if they thought of him as some form of entertainment; seeing how far they could push him before he snapped.

Such was often the case with the Colvins; particularly with Delriahna. Any little thing that upset her during the week became his problem to solve. It didn't shock him at all to see her burst through the chapel doors on a random afternoon. He merely wondered, *what is it this time?*

The shock came when she explained the purpose for her visit. After years of complaints about a young boy distracting her daughter, she stood before him demanding their immediate bond. No courtship; no dowry; no negotiations... just a wedding.

Her request was abnormal by any measure. The church did not perform such weddings. He knew the people of Mooncrest too well to let Delriahna take such actions. The entire affair would be scandalous; casting a light upon her family that she would not enjoy.

When he tried to protest, she glared at him in a way that only Delriahna dared to. Within seconds she pressed the seriousness of the matter by presenting him with a small purse filled with silver coins. Donations to the church came frequently from the Colvin household; especially when Delriahna wanted something done.

Begrudgingly, he agreed to perform the wedding. He was sure that his choice would backfire in the coming weeks. However, he could tell that Delriahna was sure of her actions. As they walked, side by side, to the Colvin home, her sense of purpose convinced him that the situation was serious.

When they entered the Colvin home a short while later, he expected to find a happy couple waiting patiently. There was no joy in their residence that day. Andor and Tylee were crying, and Laurence was pacing in frustration.

Laurence had just completed telling Andor and Tylee about Arcturus, including what he'd learned from his visit with Gaerin.

The gravity of the scene hit Thomasen a few feet inside the door. He wasn't sure if he should marry them or counsel them.

Delriahna stood beside him for a moment. She could sense his inner debate taking place. Deciding it was best to proceed as planned, Thomasen gave in and approached the table with several scrolls.

"These scrolls signify a covenant between Laurence Vendric Ravencrest and Tylee Amber Colvin," he explained. "One notes this covenant before the church of Galrath, our divine lord of justice. The other, crested with the Kingdom's royal seal, proclaims this marriage lawful in the eyes of the court."

He handed one quill to Laurence and another to Tylee. "Please sign here," he said to Laurence, "and here," he said to Tylee. As they finished signing the church's scroll, he slid the royal scroll before them and continued, "and do the same here, and here."

The two of them finished signing and backed away to make room for Delriahna and Andor. After all had signed, the priest led them to the backyard, into the evening air.

Tylee and Laurence stood, hand in hand, before Priest Thomasen, his back to the sunset. The moons of Aygos and Provoss were rising to the east and fireflies drifted through the air, flitting in erratic patterns.

Tylee's mother, father and two of their house servants gathered around them in silence. The priest withdrew a small scroll from his robes as Tylee stifled the thought, *where does he keep getting these scrolls from, I wonder? Are there pockets hiding beneath the fabric?*

Priest Thomasen read from the scroll as he had many times. His voice was unwavering as he began the traditional wedding prayer.

"*Secundum tuam sanctam legem, ego obsecramus te. Locum tuum, et benedictionem super hanc unionem.* Galrath, we ask that you shine down upon this marriage with all the blessings you deem worthy of this bond and-" his words cut short in awe. A faint blue beam of light descended upon the teenage lovers before him.

"I've never," gasped Delriahna. Having attended dozens of weddings, she had never seen Galrath's light descend in such a manner. Surprise had gotten the better of her, causing her to forget that family and guests were to remain silent.

Priest Thomasen shared her surprise. He looked at Delriahna inquisitively. Her response showed that she was also experiencing the event for the first time. In all his life he'd merely heard, or read, the words out of habit and as a matter of routine. Never had he seen a beam of light descend from the heavens.

Laurence and Tylee looked about themselves in awe. They didn't know the event was abnormal. They heard mention of Galrath's light and saw the beam of light fall upon them. To them, it was natural. They smiled, happily and blissfully unaware.

Priest Thomasen cleared his throat and continued reading more carefully than he ever had.

As he pressed on, the light about them slowly grew brighter. Small golden particles of what Laurence could only describe as dust drifted down in slow spirals around the perimeter of the blue light. The specs of gold landed atop and about them, each pulsing brightly before going out completely.

Laurence and Tylee took turns repeating the matrimonial oath to Priest Thomasen. Tylee struggled to focus. She wanted the ceremony to be over so that Laurence could sweep her off her feet and they could ride off into the sunset.

As the ceremony concluded, the blue light and golden sparkles faded. Priest Thomasen blinked, trying to shake off the layer of disbelief that had crossed his face. Walking toward Andor and Delriahna, he tried to put on the familiar air of confidence the public often associated with a priest of Galrath.

Delriahna stood for a moment, tapping her foot impatiently. She wanted a word with Laurence and Tylee, but the pair wouldn't stop kissing long enough to pay attention. Eventually, she stepped in and pried them apart by their shoulders.

"You are one, now. I'll remind you that this bond is permanent and can never be broken. It is not to be taken lightly. This, Tylee, is not some fantasy. Nor is it a plaything to be tossed aside lightly when you tire of it," she scolded.

"I won't, Momma," reassured Tylee. It was hard for her to focus, amid the dreaminess of what had just happened to her.

"He is now your husband and he will provide for you. You may visit on occasion, however, you are to be with your husband. For now, that means traveling with him to Fel'Rechaun. After that... who knows. Nevertheless, you will abide by the laws of our land, by the oath that you just swore and by your professed love for this man and do as he asks of you."

"Mother, I-" Tylee started, but her mother wasn't listening anymore.

"And you," she said to Laurence firmly. "I do not care for the way this transpired, but I understand that these are troubling times for you. I also understand that our daughter would have no one else. Take care to treat her with compassion and respect, or I will hunt you down myself," she swore.

Laurence thought for a moment about proclaiming that he would protect her as if she were his own flesh and blood. However, considering the previous night's failure to protect his grandfather, he decided instead to smile and nod.

"You are also now, legally, our son—having no living father of your own. According to the laws of the Kingdom of Arkhania, that makes us as responsible for you until you come of age as we are of her. As such, I will be escorting you to Fel'Rechaun—as will one of our servants—to help watch over Tylee during your training. We will also pay for any extra expenses that your grandfather wasn't able to cover before his passing. That will be our wedding gift to you," she concluded.

"Thank you, my lady," responded Laurence, fighting back against the tears welling up in his eyes.

"Now be off with you," ordered Andor. "Consummate this bond. We expect you early on the morrow. A carriage will be waiting for you at dawnfry."

Laurence held Tylee's hand and led her eagerly through the house, out into the front yard and to his horse, waiting by the front gate. After they had gone, the servants set about their nightly chores while Andor, Delriahna and Priest Thomasen had a last few parting words.

"The light... what did it mean?" asked Delriahna.

"I'm not sure, Del. I've never seen that happen. I've been a priest for nearly three decades and was raised in the church. I've never even heard of an actual light descending upon the betrothed," said Thomasen.

"I can only think of it as a blessing, your worship. Del," Andor began, placing a hand on her arm, "we must turn in. We've things to discuss." Turning back to the priest, he concluded, "Thank you for your services, your worship. Responsive and supportive, as always. Our donations to your church will be tripled this month."

"Thank you, Andor. I'll withhold a few of my arguments with you during council in coming weeks... as usual," replied Thomasen with a nod.

∴ ∴ ∴

LAURENCE AND Tylee reached the banks of the Reincrik as the sun completed its descent. Aygos, glowing light blue to the east, combined its light with Provoss, glowing slightly orange from the southeast, to cast a very soft and calming light across the landscape.

Mooncrest towered above them to the southeast, sitting high atop the cliffs. The Reincrik flowed from the Mythaeil River to the northwest, ending in the rocky cliffs below the city.

It had only taken them an hour to reach the creek by horseback. It was the only time they'd ever used a horse for the trip. Neither of them was certain how long the journey had taken them on their previous trips. They just knew that they'd always had to take an entire day to walk down, fish and walk home.

Laurence remembered that he'd always walked back to his grandfather's house late at night. Often, he would make it halfway and stop at his uncle's house instead. It had been the source of many arguments.

"I can't believe it took you twelve years to admit that you loved me," scolded Tylee, half teasing.

"I was a nervous little boy and you," he started, "you're a beautiful woman and always have been. You're intimidating. I half expected you to belt me when I mentioned marriage. Had you not kissed me at your front door, I don't think I would have had the nerve."

"I kissed you? You know damned well you kissed me," she teased.

"You'll be happy to know, thanks to your constant temptation and flirting over the years, that when everything came crashing down last night... the only thing I could think about was you. Getting to you; seeing you... I couldn't imagine leaving without you or ever losing you," Laurence said as he stared into her deep, blue eyes.

She didn't respond verbally. It was a night she had dreamed of and hoped for her entire life. She knew the day they met that her parents would never approve of him. He would never be proper or upstanding enough for their political motivations. He would never live up to their expectations. Maybe that was part of what intrigued her.

Her whole life, he was the only boy that hadn't tried to win her heart. He let her be her goofy and uncoordinated self without judgment. He stuck by her, defended her, and never left her side. Everything about her entire life, in her eyes, had built to one perfect moment.

Laurence dismounted, reaching up to help Tylee. As her feet touched the ground, she leaned in to kiss him, savoring the feeling of his arms around her. He wasn't very muscular, or even particularly strong, but she felt safe in his arms nonetheless.

With his guidance, she worked carefully to remove his armor, piece by piece, her clothes following closely behind. They lay together on the ground, atop her outspread gown. She wept lightly at the dark bruises and abrasions that colored his torso.

He brushed her tears away and kissed her cheek. "Your tears hurt more than my wounds, my love."

"I can't stand to see you hurt," she whispered timidly.

He pulled her closer and whispered into her ear, "There will be more pain in my future. It is part of the life that I have chosen. I accept that, and I need you to accept it also."

"Whatever you say, my love," she whispered back as he kissed her neck.

Kissing her gently, he rolled atop her, letting her feel his weight. She caressed his back and sides gently, enjoying the sensation of his skin beneath her fingers. In playful frustration, she pushed him and shifted her weight, rolling him onto his back and landing atop him.

She sat upright and smiled down at him as she released her hair from the pins that held it bound. Golden locks enveloped his face as she leaned in for another kiss. Her milky white skin was a stark contrast to his brown complexion as their bodies entwined. The light of the moons glistened off his tight, well-defined frame... enticing her.

It was an evening she had dreamed of since she'd come of age.

∴ ∴ ∴

THE MORNING sun woke Tylee as it poked through the buildings that lined the edge of Mooncrest above. A light dew covered her skin, cooling her in the gentle breeze that welcomed the day. Memories of the previous evening flooded her mind as she reached beside her, seeking Laurence.

A warm, empty space greeted her fingertips. She opened her eyes and looked around, seeking her new husband. Laurence stood near her, donning his armor. She moaned a bit as she stretched her back and blinked sleep out of her eyes playfully.

He looked down at her and smiled.

"I never knew armor was such a chore," she joked as she looked up at him.

"Perhaps if you get your naked ass up here and help, I'd be inclined to help you with your insanely complex seven-layer dress with two thousand laces and support in areas that shouldn't need support, or whatever that heap is," he joked back, pointing at the pile of clothes that had accompanied her dress.

She laughed and got to her feet as she answered, "Silly boy. It's a petticoat, a bodice and a very expensive dress which is now ruined having been stained with grass, mud, and gods know what else last night."

He chuckled at his wife as she helped him don his armor. She asked quite a few questions about the pieces and how they went together. He gladly answered, more than a little intrigued by the sight of a naked Tylee helping him put it all together. He could tell she was enjoying learning more about the armor, most likely because it was part of who he had become.

When it was her time to dress, he returned the favor; helping her into her petticoat, bodice, dress, and everything else that she bade him to assist her with.

"We'd better get going," he said. "We've a lot of ground to cover and I'm already a day late."

"So much for the honeymoon, eh?" she teased.

He helped her onto the horse behind him. She wrapped her arms around him tightly and put her head on his shoulder.

"Honeymoon?" he snorted. "Does anyone even do that?"

"Well, aside from the dangerous countryside full of goblins, orcs, bandits, and other baddies that are all trying to eat you up, I hear honeymoons can be quite nice at the right time of year," she responded, nodding playfully.

"What on Ayrelon have I gotten myself into?" he sighed rhetorically as they set off.

"If you knew that, you'd be trying to magic your way through time right about now, my love," she teased.

The ride back seemed to go much quicker than the ride there. Laurence didn't yet smell the morning meats being fried, morning breads being baked, or anything else he would have normally associated with early morning. That told him it either wasn't yet dawnfry, or they'd missed it entirely.

A carriage was being loaded in front of the Colvin house when they arrived. Servants were buzzing in and out of the house, carrying all manner of things, while Delriahna orchestrated the whole affair, as she was apt to do.

Andor stood idly by sipping coffee, as he was apt to do.

Laurence stopped Onyx behind the carriage. He dismounted, helped Tylee down, and bid her to tie up the horse for him. She did so with a puzzled look on her face. She was about to challenge the request and demand that it not become a trend when she noticed that he was walking directly toward her father.

A servant ran up to Andor as Laurence made his way over.

"Andor!" called Laurence.

"Call me Father," answered Andor. He finished signing the scroll that his servant presented, then returned it to him. The servant tucked the quill into a wooden tube on his chest and rolled up the scroll as he walked away.

"Father," continued Laurence awkwardly; he'd never directed that term at anyone. "I am now two days late for my arrival at Fel'Rechaun." He glanced back at the carriage and then continued, "I really can't afford to be any later. In fact, if I can make up time on the road, that's what I should be doing. All this-" he said, gesturing toward the carriage.

"-Is necessary, I assure you. Bronsin will handle the carriage. There will also be spare horses along to share the load and allow you to rotate between them. That should keep you going for longer stretches between rests. With Bronsin along to assist, there will be less trouble at night when you make camp. Everything should go much smoother than you traveling alone," answered Andor, reassuringly.

"That's fine, but-"

"In addition... I've taken the liberty of sending a pigeon to Fel'Rechaun, explaining your circumstances and the reason for your delay. Mooncrest happens to keep a few on hand that are homed to the school. We need them for handling matters of state, and I didn't see any harm in using one for this purpose. Relax," he said, placing his hand on Laurence's shoulder, "things are in order. Take a breath. All will be fine. I said you were our responsibility now, and I meant it."

"Thank you," said Laurence. His mind eased by Andor's plan, he allowed himself to relax.

"Now, come inside and eat. We've got time," Andor suggested. "Del and Ty are off to procure more appropriate attire for their time on the road. We can't have 'bodice this' or 'petticoat that' causing further delays as you travel."

"No, we certainly can not," he muttered, recalling the morning's dressing routine. "Those things are just... why?"

"It's said that they do it for us," Andor explained as they walked through the house toward the dining room. The smell of morning meats struck Laurence, reminding him he hadn't eaten. "Honestly, I just don't see the point. It makes things so much more dramatic, in situations that don't require drama. My wife, for example, has a dress that makes it impossible to navigate doorways without strategy."

"Hah!" laughed Laurence.

"But... matters of state often require a bit of show, and those dresses make for a good show. So, we do as we must for impression's sake to sway those around us. It's a side of life that you've had little exposure to, growing up outside town," explained Andor.

"Dresses... politics... all I'm concerned with right now is getting trained. Drakahl's men easily bested me," Laurence remarked as he inserted a bit of sausage into his mouth.

"Nonsense. You stood your ground. You killed two of them. That's two more than anyone else your age would have accomplished, I wager," assured Andor.

"Perhaps, but I got lucky. I'd love to rush off and just handle this situation immediately, but Pap raised me smarter than that... and Gaerin made sure I had a mind for tactics and strategy. I know very well that I was outmatched. It wasn't even a contest, really. I shouldn't have survived the night. I should be dead right now," he added.

Laurence nearly choked on the knot that was forming in his throat.

Andor wasn't sure what he could say to be more reassuring.

"I know what I have to do. I need more training. I need more experience in combat, and the Kingdom can give that to me better than anyone. Fel'Rechaun was once but a boy's dream. Now, it's an absolute necessity. I can't miss this class. I can't wait a year for another to start."

"We'll get you there. Worry not," declared Andor.

∴ ∴ ∴

ANDOR, LAURENCE and Bronsin had settled into chairs on the front walk, just inside the gate, sipping spirits while waiting for the women to return. Everything was prepared and there was nothing else left to do. Laurence had resorted to pacing the front yard in frustration. Andor had pulled out a bottle of brandy as much to calm Laurence as to save his lawn.

To Laurence, it had been an unhealthy amount of time to wait. Had it not been for Andor's firm resolve and Bronsin's quiet patience, Laurence would have raced off to find Tylee and get on the road. Instead, they drew him into debates about whether dragons existed, the true skin color of goblins, and whether kobolds' sense of smell was any better than dogs.

"What I really want to know is whether kobolds sniff each other in the arse when they meet like normal mutts," blurted Bronsin.

"Asking the important questions... that's why we keep you around," chimed Delriahna from the street.

Laurence looked up, studying Tylee's attire. Her leather pants, riding boots, below-the-bust leather corset and gloves were black. The brown shirt beneath her corset was puffy on top, short-sleeved and draped lower down her left thigh than her right. Belted to her right thigh was a small pouch and a long-toothed dagger.

Tylee had completed the look by tying her hair back in a loose braid, held together with a strip of red ribbon. Delriahna had copied Tylee's ensemble, but in Laurence's opinion didn't do the look justice. A quick glance told him that Andor didn't agree.

"Are you ready then, my lovely, lovely wife?" asked Andor as he got up from his seat and crossed the yard to greet her.

Tylee rolled her eyes at them as she continued to the carriage, showing the servants that had gone with them where to stow their new baggage.

"We should be off," declared Laurence. "We have wasted half the day and we've nearly a week's journey ahead of us." His frustration had returned and his tone did nothing to hide it.

Tylee climbed onto the brown mare beside Onyx. "Well?" she inquired. "It's you we're waiting on."

Rolling his eyes, Laurence climbed into his own saddle beside her. The two of them waited while Delriahna and Bronsin took their seats at the front of the carriage. With a few parting pleasantries, they made their way out of town, onto the open road.

Laurence wasn't sure if they would run into any trouble along their route. The Southern Reach was once a well-protected highway that ran from Vellenheim all the way to Southwatch. Portions of the road were dirt, others cobblestone, but it was a well-traveled road often described as being easy to traverse.

Tylee liked to joke of goblins, orcs, bandits, and other such randomness. Such banter was often a source of humor while they were growing up. Laurence knew that all those things possibly stalked the highway in search of easy prey. He planned to keep a keen eye on their surroundings, to watch for any threats.

He hoped with all his being that his watchful efforts would be in vain.

PASSAGE

Ris'Kitthu, Oghenfall 15th, 113 of the 2nd Era

Ravens fly by light of day,
Believing in their might,
One made two, and two again,
But only one is right.

Night's Writ, Parable 6

DRAKAHL'S HORSE groaned and whinnied, gasping for breath. Each of his men's horses cried out similarly, as they all came to an abrupt and final halt on the shores of the great Hystari ocean. The riders leaped from their mounts and discarded them.

The horses wheezed and fell over, gasping in the throes of exhaustion-induced death. Having ridden straight through after leaving the alchemy shop, the mounts could take no more. The magic that had sustained them was waning, and their lives became the price that their riders' haste had wrought.

As the men stood upon the shore, dragon-prowed dinghies made their way in to greet them. Six muscular, oft-beaten men rowed each of them, wearing nothing more than leather codpieces and tattered skin. Their scars glistened proudly in the sea spray and sunlight, each a badge of honor; a symbol of pride noting their labor and service to the great Drakahl, King of Pelrigoss.

Waves crashed upon the shore, kissing the sand and daring to glance against Drakahl's blood-red boots. The water sizzled and hissed, becoming steam where it touched the vile lord's armor. The sound pleased Drakahl.

A very confident, beautiful, blonde man joined Drakahl on the edge of the beach, awaiting the dinghies' arrival. His fierce green eyes beamed as he gave Drakahl a side-long glance. The man's face tensed with pride as he looked upon his master and then back out to open sea.

"We shall set about the rituals with haste when we return, your majesty. Now that we know none can stop us, we need but find suitable hosts for our... blessings," he said with great pleasure. "An army with your powers? We'll have this world subjugated; driven passive by horror before they can plead for mercy."

"The world," mocked Drakahl. His voice caused the sand about him to tremble noticeably. "I care not for Ayrelon. It is but a means to an end. I've seen beyond this plane, Ahm. Ayrelon is just a steppingstone."

Ahm reveled in the vibrations caused by his master's deep, powerful voice. The armor he'd helped create, coupled with Drakahl's power, amplified by the souls collected by his sword Strambáneur... it was a combination that made Ahm tremble with desire. It was all he could do to contain himself.

"Whatever you desire, my lord, it shall be yours. We will need a lot of souls for this ritual, which," he added carefully, "I am certain you are aware. Have you any thoughts which province we should... how should I say," stammered Ahm, searching for the right words, "ask for tribute?"

"Triblunds," answered Drakahl.

"Which of the Triblunds, my lord?" asked Ahm.

"All of them," responded Drakahl, coldly.

Ahm looked upon his master once more, attempting to detect any sign of jest or uncertainty, though he knew he'd find neither. Drakahl's armor seemed to smile back at him, knowingly. Ahm gave a firm, obvious smile at Drakahl's armor, also knowingly.

"Grohm, Soth and Thorgen will depart as soon as we return, unless... you've other designs," finished Ahm, leaving it open for his master to say otherwise if he chose.

"Send thirty men with each. Leave nothing to chance. If they succeed and their efforts yield enough supplies, they will be the first three gifted with my powers. That should be sufficient motivation," added Drakahl.

Having obtained his answer, Ahm left Drakahl to his thoughts. He walked over to Grohm, Soth and Thorgen, informing them of their master's plans. As Ahm expected, they were delighted beyond reason.

As the dinghies ran ashore, the men boarded. Four of the oarsmen from each dinghy jumped out of their boats and pushed them back into the water before jumping back on board themselves. They executed the maneuvers without a word, as if they'd all performed their role a thousand times.

It was the way of all things involving Drakahl. He valued order, control, and absolute dominion. He demanded perfection of all who served him, regardless of his presence. He had no tolerance for those who needed reminders or constant instruction. For those who followed, and obeyed without question, his rewards were plentiful, and so most within the Kingdom of Pelrigoss prospered.

So it was odd that when they rejoined their fleet, Drakahl seemed to ignore the councilman who stood upon his vessel. The man had no business upon The Dread Tide, yet Drakahl strode past him as if he hadn't noticed, or didn't care. Such a turn of events should have caused great concern in the man. Instead, he felt relieved.

He had left Drakahl's cabin a mere instant before Drakahl stepped onto the deck. Several crew members had witnessed the man's exit from the cabin. It surprised them to see Drakahl ignore the event, and the man's presence.

That surprise faded when invitations were delivered to the other ships in the fleet, inviting all councilmen to dine aboard Drakahl's capital ship that evening.

∴ ∴ ∴

"LOOK," LAURENCE argued, "I just don't want our nightly camps to take hours to set up and hours to tear back down. If it's not raining, let's skip the tents. Okay?"

"You've made your point, son. I don't have to like it, but you've made your point," Delriahna muttered.

She leaned back against the carriage, arms crossed, in a huff. Nothing about Laurence's plan was agreeable to her. Sleeping out in the open had never been appealing. It was bad enough she didn't have a proper bed, but being deprived of a roof?

Still frustrated as night fell, she refused to help as her companions laid out four bedrolls and prepared rabbit stew. The stew had nearly gone cold before she gave in and joined them at the campfire. Her stubbornness had not won the argument, and the group had carried on without yielding to her whims. She slurped her stew angrily, realizing that Laurence wasn't like Andor; he wouldn't change his mind just to please her.

The argument had started as they passed the first Waystation, a few hours prior. Laurence had been adamant that they should not use them. He feared that the permanent shelters were nothing more than beacons for bandits. Bronsin had briefly offered his support to Laurence's point, stating, 'Things just aren't the same since the King withdrew the guards that were garrisoned in them.'

While valid, his point hadn't pleased Delriahna. Their argument had spoiled her entire evening.

Laurence's only concern was that he could no longer say whether anyone had followed them. The argument had been too distracting for him to keep watch.

Aygos and Provoss were crossing the sky, and the sun had long since kissed them goodnight. Laurence and Tylee were the only members of their party that seemed comfortable beneath the stars.

As Tylee gathered their dirty wooden bowls, a crossbow bolt slammed violently into one; ripping it instantly from her grasp, sending it off into the distance.

"What have we here?" came a strange man's voice.

∴ ∴ ∴

THE DREAD Tide was a ship that very few living creatures desired to board, and fewer still survived. It was abnormal for Drakahl to host a dinner for all his commanders and councilmen at once. It was odder still for that dinner to follow a non-military campaign on foreign soil. Still, to refuse such an invitation was suicide.

Inconvenient as it might be to ferry between vessels, none ignored the invitation. All arrived promptly and took their seats. Most waited patiently, and quietly, for Drakahl to join them. Only one stirred nervously. Only one had reason to.

Drakahl strode into the room nearly an hour after the appointed time. His armor stowed, he wore nothing but a red silken shirt, black leather pants and red leather bracers. It was not a version of Drakahl that many ever saw, and his unarmored presence instantly put the entire room at ease, including the one that should not have been.

His muscles rippled noticeably beneath the thin silk shirt as he crossed the room. Thin black tattoos covered his arms, chest and back. Visible through his translucent shirt, they hearkened back to his time as a tribal leader among the Toor.

He walked to the head of the table where his personal chair, made of carved bone and iron, sat waiting. Ahm occupied his usual place at Drakahl's left. Drendon, the councilman he'd pretended to ignore earlier that day, sat to his right.

"Begin," ordered Drakahl as he sat, a smirk upon his face.

Ahm was finding it hard to contain himself, but knew that he must.

Small iron wheels creaked as they sprang to life in the distance. Iron tracks on the ceiling groaned under the weight of the meal that hung from them. Spanning the distance between the center of the dining table and the kitchen, the tracks allowed for easier transport of large, roasted meats.

Drakahl liked to see the carcass of the animal he was consuming. Only Ahm knew that it was because he reveled in the visions caused by his curse. Whatever beast Drakahl desired was roast, hung, and wheeled above the table. If one wanted to eat, they could carve off whatever portion of meat they wanted.

That evening, Drakahl's guests watched in horror as the chef wheeled in a roast human corpse, hanging neck down. What disturbed them most was the tantalizing aroma emanating from it. As Drakahl stood, leaned over, and carved off a piece of the man's flesh, a chill ran through his guests.

Drendon's skin went stark white, his face drained of blood. He gasped for breath in shock and horror while trying hard not to scream. His eyes drifted instinctively to the right calf of the cadaver, hanging above them; the only portion of the roast which still bore unblemished skin. The tattoo of a gargoyle seemed to glare back at Drendon eerily, as if it knew what was going through his mind.

"Eat," demanded Drakahl, gazing firmly at Drendon.

Drakahl smiled wickedly.

Drendon quietly pissed himself.

∴ ∴ ∴

LAURENCE WAS on his feet in a flash, sword drawn. He looked out into the darkness trying to find their assailant but could see no one. The campfire was making it hard to see beyond its boundaries.

"Ah, ah, ah... we'll have none of that, lad," said the voice. "Put that sword on the ground and step away from it."

The voice sounded calm and confident. Whoever was out there, Laurence was certain they were using a tactic they'd grown comfortable with. He was also certain of the voice's point of origin.

The slow crank of a crossbow was barely discernible, yet unmistakable in the distance.

Knowing it would take time for the archer to reload, Laurence sprang into action. He ran as fast as he could in the voice's direction. He knew he had to reach them before they could reload. Adrenaline rushed through him, accompanied by anger. *I'm not letting it happen again!*

"Fool!" belted the voice.

The sound of swords sliding out of scabbards rang out to the south. Laurence had chosen wisely and was nearly upon them. As he gained distance from the fire, his eyes adjusted enough to see his enemies.

The man directly ahead of him raised his crossbow, dropping a bolt into place. As quickly as possible, Laurence curled his left arm, allowing the plates of metal to interlock protectively. The bolt fired with a violent snap as the string released from its clip and the string returned to its resting position.

The bolt careened off the plates in his upper arm and wedged itself between his bicep and forearm. The tip of the bolt nearly pierced his chest before stopping, having caused only minor scrapes to the surface of his armor.

It fell harmlessly to the ground as Laurence's left arm once again stretched out before him. He grabbed his sword's handle in both hands for a violent overhead swing. Arms tensed and driving the blade downward with all his strength, he brought the sword straight toward the archer's head. The man tried in vain to parry Laurence's blade with the crossbow.

The thickest part of the sword cut deep into the man's left forearm and down into the wooden stock of the bow. The end of the blade found the man's face, cutting through on its way into his upper chest.

Laurence's momentum carried him over his foe; the blade's deep gouge making him spin as he leapt to avoid the collision. He wrenched the blade free as he turned through the air, blood trailing his sword in a thin stream as his feet came to rest behind the corpse.

Two men were barreling down on the camp. Bronsin stood firm between the charging men and their party's two women, his back to the campfire. In his hands was one of the larger logs from the fire, still aglow in the middle and flaming at the far end. Small wisps of smoke squeezed past his white knuckles, revealing that the entire log was still blazing hot.

Snapping back into action, Laurence ran toward the camp, his sword at the ready before him. Bronsin swung the log wildly at the man approaching from his left. His target was dual-wielding a sabre and main-gauche, the other brandished a wooden club and shield. Bronsin had selected his target wisely.

The bandit's sabre knocked Bronsin's attack away with ease. However, the man's blade ruptured the side of the log. The man reeled backward in pain as pieces of glowing ash erupted from the log and flew into his eyes.

The other assailant drove his club squarely into Bronsin's back, right between his shoulder blades. Bronsin lurched forward in pain and fell to the ground with a grunt. The club-wielding man spun to look for Laurence just in time to see Laurence's blade erupt violently through his comrade's chest from behind.

Laurence pushed his victim off his sword, staring directly into the club-wielder's eyes.

"How?" whimpered the man in desperation. He raised his shield as Laurence stepped over his friend's corpse.

Laurence drove his sword toward the bottom half of the man's round, wooden shield. The man instinctively lowered his shield to block the attack. The impact forced the shield to tilt down and back, wrenching his wrist.

Terrified, the bandit swung his club at Laurence's face. He didn't notice that Laurence's jab had been the start of a maneuver, and not a simple strike. It was too late when he realized his mistake, as Laurence's sword arced upward swiftly, striking his weapon arm just above the wrist.

He reeled back as Laurence stepped into him, driving his shoulder into the shield. Stumbling from the impact, he fell backwards onto his rear. Laurence continued forward, stepped over top of him as he fell, and sank his blade deep into the man's exposed throat.

Laurence placed his foot on the man's chest, extracted his blade, then turned back toward the darkness. He took a few steps away from the campfire and peered into the distance.

Everyone in the party looked on in both awe and horror. None of them had ever watched a man die. None of them had ever seen

Laurence fight. A sense of dread swelled up within his companions, recalling the tale of Arcturus's fate. If Laurence could so easily best three bandits, how much more powerful were Drakahl's men?

"Anyone else?" Laurence called into the darkness.

∴ ∴ ∴

DRAKAHL SMILED at the horror on Drendon's face. Ahm found it difficult to contain himself. Everyone else at the table calmly stood, carved off a piece of flesh and sat back down to consume it. It wasn't normal to eat human flesh aboard The Dread Tide. Nor was it normal to eat human flesh anywhere in the civilized portions of Pelrigoss.

However, it wasn't wise to question Drakahl. Whatever he served at his table, his guests knew to eat. Soth expressed no hesitation, carving the largest portion of any guest. He licked his fingers dramatically and sent a wink to the chef. Ahm made a mental note to have words with him later.

"Why do you not dine, Drendon? Does this feast not please you?" challenged Drakahl.

"I... I-" stammered Drendon. He couldn't tear his eyes away from the tattoo on his brother's calf.

"Not interested in the meal?" teased Drakahl.

"I-" Drendon continued to mutter.

"Fine. It so happens I've set aside the best delicacy, just for you," said Drakahl, smirking. He clapped his hands twice, summoning a servant.

An unclad elven woman with blazing red hair and bronze skin entered, seeming to float across the floor. She held a silver platter, topped with a silver dome. Upon reaching the rear of Drendon's seat, she removed the dome and sat the platter before him.

Drendon's eyes moved down from his brother's tattooed thigh. His gaze drifted slowly down his brother's charred, carved corpse to the human head that sat before him. It was nearly unblemished, save for the thin red line across its forehead.

The servant reached over Drendon, her breast grazing the side of his cheek as she moved. Clutching the hair, she lifted the top of the skull away and placed it inside the upturned dome. As she exited, several guests gasped at the dish, unable to control themselves.

Drendon closed his eyes, trying to squeeze the vision of his brother's exposed, pink brain out of his mind. Try as he might, the image would not go away.

"Why?" he pleaded feebly, speaking so weakly that only Drakahl could hear him.

"When you sent your brother ashore to sell us out to King Orluhnd's navy—in some vain attempt to dethrone me—you must have known there would be consequences for your actions. Don't play dumb now that I have thrust those consequences before you!" Drakahl spat angrily. "Dine!"

"I-" began Drendon.

"You will consume every speck of your brother's poor excuse for a brain. If you do not," explained Drakahl, pausing for dramatic effect, "I will hand you over to Nightweaver to do with as she pleases."

Drendon slowly scooped up a spoonful of brain and held it in front of his mouth.

"She is known to torture her victims for decades, nothing more than her magic to sustain them. I would eat up if I were you, and thank your lord for his mercy," added Ahm.

Drendon closed his eyes, shoving the spoon into his mouth with forced determination.

Horror set in. Not because of the loss of his brother, or the failure of their plan; it was from the realization that the meal was pleasing to his palate.

He wasn't sure if it was a natural reaction, or if his subconscious was trying to save him, but he nearly vomited. A growl from Drakahl encouraged him to choke the bile back.

There was no part of Drendon's personality that survived his meal.

∴ ∴ ∴

LAURENCE LISTENED closely, standing still and holding his breath. No sounds came back to him from outside their camp. He flexed his left arm a bit, trying to work out the kinks and knots that were forming from the impact of the crossbow bolt. Cautiously, he walked out to the crossbow wielder, cleaned his sword on the man's shirt and sheathed it. After placing the crossbow and the bandits' satchels on top of the corpse, he grabbed the man's feet and dragged him back toward the campfire.

Bronsin finally made it to his feet. Delriahna stood behind him, checking his back.

As Laurence dropped the man's feet to the ground with a thud, Tylee ran up to him.

"Laurence!" Tylee gasped.

A strange mixture of fear, adrenaline, and pride contorted her face into a ball of beautiful confusion. Nothing could have prepared her for what she'd just witnessed. She wasn't sure how to react, or what to say.

Laurence found no such conflict within himself. Killing those men had felt natural. He wasn't sure if that should grant him comfort or concern. *How is a person supposed to feel after killing someone in self defense? Perhaps I should have negotiated, rather than letting my anger get the better of me?*

"Check their pockets," Laurence called over to Bronsin, shaking off his second thoughts. He knelt to go through the bags he'd placed on top of the archer.

"What? Are we thieves now?" demanded Tylee, crossing her arms.

"I need to know who these men were. Did that bastard Drakahl send them to kill me, or are they simple bandits? I need to know if we're being tracked... or if this was all just coincidence," Laurence explained.

"I guess that makes sense," she muttered. She still wasn't sure if she approved of digging through a dead man's pockets.

"Besides," he added, "if these men were just bandits and they've been robbing people along this road, then it would be in our best interest to know the contents of these bags. That way, should we encounter any of their previous victims, we can return their stolen property easily. On that note," he said, turning to Bronsin, "is there something we should take to prove we've slain them?"

"Hard to say," answered Bronsin. "When the Legion used to visit Mooncrest, they would talk of bounties. But, they usually had a drawing or description of the men they were after. These guys don't seem to have any common, identifying feature... like a sash or insignia. I don't think they were part of a larger group."

"Well, I'm not rolling north on the King's highway with a pile of corpses atop our carriage," snarled Delriahna.

"Absolutely not!" added Tylee excitedly.

"We're not taking corpses with us," declared Laurence.

He dug through the first satchel. Inside were dried meat, nuts, berries, bits of rope, tattered pieces of cloth, a whetstone, an oilstone, and other assorted odds and ends. Setting that bag aside as something he should keep handy, he opened the second.

Laurence struggled to keep the bag's contents contained. Necklaces, rings, bracelets, and other jewelry spilled from the opening. With a knowing sigh, he pushed the contents back inside and closed the latch.

"Bandits!" shrieked Tylee, as if they'd just arrived.

"Yes, love, they were bandits," he stated with finality and a sigh. "Not someone sent by Drakahl." He stood up and handed the loot-filled satchel to Bronsin. "Can you please put this somewhere safe? We'll turn it in at the first guard post we find."

"Good idea, Laur," answered Bronsin.

"So, am I finally going to hear about this Drakahl person?" asked Delriahna. That was when Laurence realized she had not been around during the previous telling of his tale.

"Let Bronsin and I clean up this mess and then we'll talk, okay?" suggested Laurence.

Bronsin and Laurence spent the next hour clearing the camp. They placed the bodies a short distance away, buried the blood-soaked grass around the camp under a thin layer of dirt, and stowed the few things they scrounged from the bandits' belongings.

Once their chore was complete, Laurence returned to the campfire. He blended the story of Arcturus's death with the details he'd gleaned from Gaerin. The story ended with his arrival at the Colvin house the previous day.

She listened intently, soaking in every detail.

"So, you've yet to reach Fel'Rechaun, and you've already slain five men?" asked Delriahna.

"Seems so," answered Laurence. *Not that I'm proud of it. Some of them were the wrong men.* His thoughts went back to the elf that defeated him, and the man that urinated on his face before leaving. He could feel his face getting hot with rage, closed his eyes and tried to calm down.

"That's what you got from his story, mother?" challenged Tylee.

"It's okay, Tylee. I'm not sure how I feel about it myself. I mean, I always dreamed of becoming some grand warrior and coming home to marry you," he added, smiling. "I never once considered that my dreams might include killing anyone. I didn't plan to have five notches in my hilt before I even reached school."

"You're notching your hilt?" gasped Tylee.

"No, silly. It's a figure of speech," teased Laurence.

"Actually... it's not," corrected Bronsin.

"Hmm. Well, I guess it probably wouldn't be a figure of speech... not out here," agreed Laurence.

"Real world now, lad. Not some fancy tale," stated Bronsin.

"Right, well... being that this is the 'real world' and bandits have already attacked—on our first night outside of town—why don't we set up a watch rotation?" proposed Delriahna.

"Obviously the goal of which would be to wake young sir Laurence, as he's the most capable among us. But I dare say that's a risky prospect, considering how long it must take to don that armor," said Bronsin.

"Actually, I sleep in my armor. I mean, I *have* slept in this armor. It was designed to be slept in. So, I don't think that'll be a concern," responded Laurence.

"Why don't Bronsin and I take turns on watch, since we ride on the carriage. We can nap during the day if need be. The two of you can't very well nap on horseback," offered Delriahna.

"That's a wise proposal, from a certain point of view," responded Bronsin.

"I like it," said Tylee.

"In that case, why don't we get some sleep. Bronsin, can you take the first watch?" asked Laurence.

"Certainly, lad. Get some rest. I've the feeling we'll be needing your skills more and more on our journey," Bronsin stated.

Laurence hoped that Bronsin wasn't correct. As he laid down to sleep and closed his eyes, images of the archer's shocked face kept flashing into his mind.

∴ ∴ ∴

TWO UNEVENTFUL days had passed since their scare with the bandits. The group was growing more accustomed to traveling. In fact, everyone but Laurence was completely at ease. He, meanwhile, stayed tense and often had lines of worry stretched across his face.

They had bypassed several dirt roads along their way; most leading to small farms, tiny villages, or fishing towns. None offered amenities for travelers, so they considered none of them to be a worthwhile detour. The lack of lodging forced the group to camp in the open, which had not lent itself to improving Laurence's peace of mind.

"I don't think we'll be seeing any more trouble, love. Mother told me last night that she thinks we're nearing the southern villages surrounding Vellenheim, which means guards, city folk... all sorts of people, really. Crowds are a good thing," said Tylee, attempting to reassure him.

He shrugged in response. He was too tired to debate their guesswork and optimism. None of his companions knew that he hadn't been able to sleep the previous two nights. Every time he nodded off, he saw visions of bandits attacking while he slept and everyone dying. He stayed awake at night, secretly listening for signs of trouble even though Delriahna and Bronsin had been diligent in their watch rotations.

Dusk was eminent, and they hadn't selected a location for their campsite yet. Up ahead, Bronsin could see a large wooden bridge spanning what he assumed was the Sacton River. Squinting his eyes in the failing light, he could barely make out a small Waystation on the opposite side of the bridge. His party wasn't comfortable using them, and he didn't think they had enough light to travel far enough beyond the station to give Laurence comfort.

"We'll camp along the shore beneath the southeast end of the bridge. The carriage should make it down and back just fine. The bridge should provide sufficient cover through the night to obscure our party's size and belongings!" yelled Bronsin over his shoulder.

"Fine," agreed Laurence. His exhaustion was becoming unbearable. All he wanted was for their journey to be over.

They stopped a few yards from the bridge and worked to get the carriage down the incline safely, closer to the water below and partially obscured by the bridge. Laurence tied the horses to one of the bridge supports and helped Tylee prepare dinner. Bronsin and Delriahna started a campfire, then laid out the bedrolls.

That night Laurence barely made it through dinner before he was nodding off. At one point he nearly fell forward in front of the fire. Tylee helped him remove his scabbard and laid him down. No sooner was his head touching his bedroll than he was out, gently snoring.

"The stress is exhausting him," she said, concerned for his well-being.

"He's the only one of us with the skills to defend our camp. We should have hired guards," lamented Delriahna.

"Regret will buy us nothing. We all thought the roads were safer," countered Bronsin. "I guess rumors of the King's withdrawal of funding for the Southern Reach are more true than we suspected.

The lad's done an amazing job; let him rest. If it weren't for his skills we'd have been robbed blind days ago, and sent back to Mooncrest with our non-existent tails tucked between our legs."

"True enough," admitted Delriahna. "Honestly, it could be worse."

"Well, I don't like that they forced him to kill. It's changing him," pouted Tylee.

"Did you think he'd never have to?" asked Bronsin.

"We're seventeen. He's barely a man, and I'm barely a woman. Most people grow up in a town and stay there until they're old enough, or crazy enough, to travel the wilds. Nobody has ever left Mooncrest this young; certainly not without someone older—and more seasoned—to defend them. At least... nobody that's ever returned," she whined.

"You're fine, lass. We're halfway to Fel'Rechaun and closing in on the foothills around Vellen Crescent, which hosts not one but five small towns. Each of them offers more than enough protection from the likes of those bandits," comforted Bronsin. "One day, maybe two, and we'll be able to dance naked down the road throwing gold coins like rain—if we like—and still have nothing to fear."

"I'm not dancing naked for you," stated Tylee firmly, her left eyebrow raised as she scowled at him.

Delriahna snickered.

∴ ∴ ∴

LYLA AND Gaerin had made good time. It'd been far too long since they'd been on the road together, and the trip was already more hassle than they'd remembered—yet somehow relaxing. They'd been riding nearly nonstop for days along the randomly overgrown roads of the Elbermire Way.

After Laurence left them for Mooncrest, they'd spent a few hours mourning Arcturus. Now—with a mission to occupy their minds—they felt more free than they had in a long while, even if the roads were bumpier than their aging rumps preferred.

The road was winding and led across rough terrain. It snaked up the side of mountains and down through the bottom of ravines. It was an old elven route that humans had overrun and expanded during the reign of King Orluhnd I, and skirted the eastern edges of Ekthri Wood. The road seemed to dance and play with the Mythaeil River, which the road crossed at various points. At times the river was to the east, and others to the west. Sometimes directly beside them, and others it at the bottom of a deep crevice nearby.

Their biggest reason for choosing the Elbermire Way was to approach Fel'Rechaun from the west. The road joined with the Western Reach in the northwest, which led east toward an alternate route atop Engle Plateau. Their path would take them toward Port Vaelin in a way that made it impossible for them to collide with Laurence in their travels.

Lyla had pushed Gaerin to take the journey. She knew the Ravencrest men well. They were often stubborn, but had kind hearts. More importantly, they were men of action; mission-oriented men that once they had a task to perform, concerned themselves with nothing else.

Gaerin's initial instinct was to let Laurence attend school and then—in a few years when he graduated—talk him out of seeking revenge. Gaerin remembered Drakahl's ferocity all too well, and didn't think it wise to seek the man out.

Lyla was certain Drakahl wouldn't stop with just one attack. If he'd come after them nearly two decades after leaving Pelrigoss, what would stop him from doing so again?

"Besides, love, if he's not aging... the longer we wait the more advantage he'll gain," argued Lyla.

Their argument had been over for days. In fact, the couple hadn't even been talking. Lyla had been running the argument back over in her mind and had thought of something new she'd liked to have added on the first go around. So, in typical Lyla fashion, she blurted it out blindly.

"Something on your mind, wife?" jabbed Gaerin playfully.

"Oh shush you," she sighed, realizing she'd spoken aloud.

"If I didn't know you better, I'd think you'd lost your mind; arguing with yesterday's version of me in your head while today's version of me escorts you on your quest, having already lost to your skillful tongue."

"Bah!" she scoffed.

"It's not like you lost the argument initially, is all I'm saying."

"Listen, I-"

"Shhh!" he shushed.

"Don't you-"

"Shhh!" he shushed and pointed, stopping his horse.

Ahead of them stood a copse of trees. Barely visible inside the treeline were two massive, spiked logs. They were tied to the sides of several trees, and had spikes protruding from them. Gaerin's alert gaze was returning, and thankfully he'd caught sight of the trap before they rode into it.

"Is that?" she began.

"Kobolds," he sighed.

"How could you-" she started, but then caught their scent on the breeze. "Ah, yeah, that. Can't mistake that. Blech-"

"Shhh," he shushed.

"Stop shushing me. I don't remember ever being worried at the sight of kobolds. I mean, they're just kobolds," she said, exacerbated.

"Just kobolds?" he asked.

"Yes."

"Tell me... when did you last fight a kobold, love?" he challenged, raising an eyebrow.

"That isn't the point," she argued, wrinkling her brow.

"Wrinkle that brow all you want," he said pointing, "but we're a little off our game here, and we're about to face a large enough number of kobolds to build complex traps-" he started.

"-and survive their construction," she concluded, realizing his point.

Kobolds were small, dog-like creatures. They stood three feet tall, covered in brown fur, and bore many canine features; pointed ears, snouts, tails and similar hind legs. They walked upright and had hands with opposable thumbs. However, their wild, crazy eyes were a clue to their limited capacity for critical thinking.

Kobolds were a menace for unprepared travelers. They weren't the brightest creatures, but fancied themselves clever. Their clumsy attempts to build traps often backfired. A traveler was just as likely to discover a pile of kobold corpses as they were a kobold ambush.

"Precisely, dear," he confirmed.

Alert and curious, they dismounted. Gaerin pulled a hooked stake from his saddlebag and drove it into the ground with his warhammer. They tied the horses off and then carefully proceeded on foot.

"They've likely seen us already but maybe if we're cautious and spring their own traps on them we can gain the advantage. Going around would take days and-"

"Why leave this for other travelers to fall victim to, eh Gaer?"

"Right, love."

They tread carefully as they approached the trees and entered just as carefully. Gaerin kept his eyes down, looking for tripwires and pit traps. Lyla kept her eyes forward and slightly up, looking for dangers from ahead and above.

As they neared the log traps they'd seen from the road, a faint high pitched yapping, almost cackling sound, echoed from high in the trees. Gaerin saw the tripwire ahead of them, plain as day.

"Hold," he whispered. Kneeling, he picked up a medium-sized stick.

"What do?" a small, raspy voice whispered above them.

Gaerin stood.

"Don't know," answered a smaller, raspier voice in a less effective whisper.

Gaerin tossed the stick so it would land across the tripwire. Several gasps came from above as the stick landed. One end of the stick planted firmly on the ground, the rest lay across the tripwire, gently bobbing.

"You've got to be kidding me," sighed Gaerin quietly.

Lyla laughed a little too loudly.

"It no funny-" began a small, raspy voice from above.

Several loud snaps rang out as the stick finally made the tripwire fall to the ground. The log traps swung into action, descending toward the road; one from their right, and the other from their left. Small spikes protruded from the logs, hewn from their branches.

As the logs swung, the pair watched with horror and amusement. Half a dozen kobolds in rusty chunks of metal armor were riding the logs. When they collided over the road, the spikes from each log impaled the kobolds atop the other.

With a deafening crash, the logs rebounded; the opposing log's Kobolds stuck to them as if they'd exchanged riders. Many disappointed cries rang out from above.

"Shit!" Gaerin exclaimed, realizing kobolds surrounded them.

Arrows rained down from above, careening off their armor, shields, weapons, the ground nearby, small rocks, branches, tree trunks and nearly everything else within sight.

"They suck so much," sighed Lyla in both amusement and frustration.

"Take cover in case one doesn't, all the same," belted Gaerin.

They ran ahead and, quite to their amusement, took shelter beneath the two log traps that were much too high to hit a rider on horseback, let alone someone on foot.

"Maybe they were hunting hill giants?" snickered Lyla.

"While you're laughing, I distinctly remember you requesting one as a pet not too long ago."

"I was joking," she explained.

"You pestered me for weeks."

"Okay, I was half joking," she responded, laughing.

The arrows stopped as abruptly as they'd started. The impact of fleshy bodies began all around them. Lyla looked around and saw a brown, furry lump fall to the ground a few feet away.

"They're, um–"

"Jumping down to fight us," he said, sighing. "I almost want to start a school to train them, I feel so bad."

"Uh. Don't look now, but–" she trailed off, pointing behind him.

Dozens of kobolds were running down the road toward them, from the exact direction they were heading. Gaerin and Lyla readied their weapons. They stepped out from under the log traps to face the ground forces, just as the logs snapped free and fell to the ground.

One log clipped Lyla's right shoulder as it fell, dislocating it and rupturing the skin as it knocked her to the ground. She screamed out in pain.

Several kobolds cheered.

Gaerin glanced back, confirmed she wasn't mortally wounded, and turned to face them.

"I'll hold them off!" he yelled.

Lyla began healing her injured shoulder. "This will drain my healing spells for the day."

"Do what you must," he yelled back as he met his first foe.

Gaerin's weapon got stuck in the first kobold's skull. The second and third to arrive bounced their weapons off his shield while he struggled to pull it free. When the fourth arrived, he gave up and swung the kobold along with his warhammer.

The only saving grace in all of it, from Gaerin's point of view, was how small the kobolds were. Standing only three feet tall, their body weight was barely more than his shield. While he was sure there was a certain amount of humor in using one kobold to bash in the brains of another, he knew he couldn't swing around that kind of weight around all day.

By the time Lyla was ready to aid him, nine kobolds lay dead at his feet and the remaining six were fleeing.

Gaerin gave chase.

"Damn it, Gaer!" she yelled as she brought up the rear.

They followed the kobolds out of the copse, up and around a small hill to the right. Their path led to a small stone tower, which was barely more than rubble. They hadn't been able to keep up due to both their age and the fact that kobolds were faster than humans. That allowed the kobolds to get into their tower without the pair seeing how.

"Great," Gaerin declared in frustration. The remnants of the doorway before them seemed to taunt him. "How do we follow?"

"We don't have to?" she said, wrinkling her face.

"We do. You know we do. We don't want to, but we have to. If we don't, then someone less equipped to survive will die here, and then we'll feel bad. I mean, if we find out about it we'll feel bad. And in the off chance we might find out about it-"

"-we have to. Gotcha," she concluded, smiling.

Gaerin glanced back with a smile of his own. Complain as they might, they were both enjoying their adventure. After searching outside for a few minutes, Gaerin noticed a small path leading to the left of the door, around the tower.

The entrance to the tower was a small opening in the rear. It was a small bit of wall that had crumbled away during a siege, or with time, or both... they weren't sure. It was tall enough for a kobold to enter while standing, but anything larger had to crawl.

After crawling through, the room they found themselves in was dimly lit. The only source of light was the small bit of sunlight peeking through the cracks in the walls. All about the room were piles of hay and kobold waste. There were no doors leading out of the room, save one.

The doorway opened to a ramp that spiraled up the tower. According to the discoloration on the walls, the ramp had been constructed by flattening the tower's stairs. Gaerin took a few moments to imagine a team of kobolds with chisels and hammers, whittling away at the staircase to make a ramp.

As they approached the ramp, cautiously, they noticed small rusty spikes and a single round metal disk with a hole in the center. Both lay at the bottom of the ramp in a pile of hay along with matted, bloodied kobold fur. There was a small trail of blood leading up the ramp.

"I must have wounded one," stated Gaerin.

"Is that a wheel?" asked Lyla.

"Don't know... don't really see that it matters," offered Gaerin with a shrug.

"Don't be a shit. This is a ramp, and that's a wheel. Maybe they like rolling something down it? Some form of attack? That could be what those spikes are," she explained.

"Fine. Hug the inner wall. If they roll something at us, maybe it'll whiz right by? There aren't really many choices," answered Gaerin.

Cautiously, they ascended the ramp. Old archery slits lined the walls. Several places along the once-stairwell were once landings. These areas were noticeably less steep, but sloped none-the-less. The floor of the ramp was slick, forcing them to walk with care.

"I think the room at the base was a small garrison, and this staircase was for the guards. These are arrow slits, or at least they were," he said as they crept past one that had collapsed shut. "I'd bet anything at the top we find a weapons room with murder holes for pouring oil down on invaders entering through the front, and probably the entrance to the rest of the tower."

"Should we go back and look for a hidden entrance, then?" asked Lyla. "I doubt they wanted to go up this ramp every time that-"

A strange sound cut her short, vaguely similar to distant thunder. Realization washed over Gaerin's face. While Lyla was more than a little worried at the development, she still found the will to mouth the words, 'I fucking told you,' at him.

Suddenly, a kobold whizzed past them, coming within inches of Lyla's leg. It wore what looked like a rusty bucket; with holes cut out for its arms and head, and spikes driven through from the inside. It rode on a flat piece of wood with small wheels mounted to the bottom. Little steel wheels of kobold death.

As Gaerin expected, the cart favored the outer wall as it screamed past them. However, the little ball of murderous fur yelped, "Kalahee!" as it rolled by. Gaerin and Lyla hurried, unsure what to expect next.

They didn't get far before the next kobold cart was upon them. The kobold was sticking its foot out; its rusty armored boot grinding against the outer wall to force itself closer to the inside. He collided, hard, with Gaerin's shield.

The collision rattled Gaerin's shoulder, disrupted his footing, and sent him sliding down the ramp into Lyla. They both grunted in pain. The kobold continued past. The sound of him colliding with the previous kobold below was almost satisfying.

The next kobold came soon after, whirling small daggers in all directions. Gaerin and Lyla had switched to the outer edge of the ramp and saw him just a split second sooner than the last. Gaerin braced for the collision and drove his warhammer into the whirling ball of rusted steel. The kobold's head exploded, leaving its bloody chunks following the cart down the ramp.

Before the next attacker could launch, Gaerin had reached the top of the ramp. The room contained nearly a dozen kobolds, half wearing buckets, the other half preparing karts. The outer edge of the room bore remnants of old iron pots and fire pits. There were murder holes in the floor, barely visible beneath matted blood and offal-smeared hay, and a single door on the far side of the room.

Gaerin and Lyla pushed into the room and started swinging. One after another, the kobolds fell in a furry frenzy. The pair stepped over and on their corpses with determination. In a matter of seconds, they reached the other doorway, and the stairs leading down beyond.

The rest of the tower was empty, save one sleeping kobold in the room below. Lyla woke him, waved and mouthed, 'morning,' as her husband drove his weapon through the creature's head. They found a pile of goods in the corner which the kobolds had stolen, a lot of trash, and remnants of old kills. The rest of the tower had collapsed.

"Well, that was fun," remarked Lyla.

Gaerin was slightly less thrilled, but he had to admit he'd enjoyed the adrenaline rush. "I suppose it was. Slowed us down though, eh? Now we have to go back, collect the horses, travel back through the forest, pass this tower again, and find a place to camp."

"Yeah, and we should probably collect ears and burn the bodies, no?"

"Do places still do that?" he asked.

"Burn bodies?"

"No! I mean reward adventurers for kobold ears, love," he clarified.

"Oh... how should I know? But wouldn't it suck to get there, find out they do, and not have any to show for it? I mean, if we get the ones in the forest too, we're looking at thirty or forty kobolds. That's sixty to eighty ears. Hell, that could almost pay for our voyage."

Lyla knew she was right.

Gaerin knew she was right as well.

"Well then, we're definitely camping as soon as we're done. That's gonna take the rest of our daylight. I think we should light that kobold bonfire as we leave, though. We don't want to smell that."

Their decisions made, the pair went to work... but not before Lyla rolled down the ramp on a kobold cart.

COMPLICATION

Ris'Enliss, Oghenfall 18th, 113 of the 2nd Era

Do not fear, oh poisoned one,
Your fate is not this day.
You've work to do, so get it done,
Your fate was yesterday.

Night's Writ, Parable 9

T WASN'T yet morning when Laurence awoke. An indiscernible noise caught his ear as he drifted toward awareness. It had almost sounded like the pop his hand used to make when it touched a metallic door latch, after dragging his stocking feet across his grandfather's sitting room rug as a child. Though the noise that woke him had been much louder.

The sound came again. Unlike before, his eyes were wide open and he saw the source. Blue arcs crackled through the air like miniature bolts of lightning, discharged from a globe of white light.

Bronsin was on watch and had seen the event too. He was on his feet, backing away.

"What was that?" asked Bronsin, his voice betraying his fear.

"I haven't the slightest idea," answered Laurence. He made his way to his feet and grabbed his sword, walking toward where the ball of light had been.

Suddenly the light reappeared. It quickly grew to nearly the size of their carriage. The outer edge of the mysterious light stretched into erratic streams of blue energy, sparking across the open air wildly.

Tylee and Delriahna, awakened by the noise, ran away from the strange light, trembling in fear. They gathered behind Bronsin, giving Laurence room to do whatever one must in response to such a bizarre situation.

None of them were certain what actions to take, if any.

The center of the mysterious occurrence darkened. Its border became more akin to the frame of a painting and was no longer shaped like an orb. At first it looked as if they were seeing through the center to the other side of the camp. That misconception was fleeting. They quickly realized it wasn't their camp they were seeing, but somewhere else entirely.

"By the gods!" gasped Laurence.

Laurence fought back the urge to cover his ears. The sounds of static, pops, and fizzes was deafening. He wanted his sword at the ready, but the noise was becoming unbearable. Nervous, he took a few steps back.

Two warriors flashed into view in the center of the strange field of energy. The first warrior wore scale armor that seemed to drip a vile, green, oily residue. The other wore a suit of soot-blackened plate and was holding a large, ornate shield. Neither was wearing a helmet. Their swords clashed together repeatedly, sending sparks flying in all directions.

The scale-clad warrior snarled fiercely beneath his matted black hair and ill-kept beard. He rushed toward his foe and attempted to tackle them to the ground. Laurence assumed the oily residue on the man's armor to be poison.

After deftly dodging the other warrior's charge, the knight sent him reeling with a well-timed shield bash. As the knight spun to face their opponent, hair whipping through the air, their face came into view; the second warrior was a woman. Jet black hair, brilliant green eyes, dark tan skin and slightly pointed half-elvish ears; she was stunning to behold.

The strange light collapsed into itself and vanished with an audible crack.

"What's going on, Laurence?" demanded Tylee at the top of her lungs, terrified. Neither the pitch nor tone of her voice did anything to hide it.

"I don't think he knows either, dear," responded Delriahna.

In his mental frenzy to find a course of action, Laurence hadn't heard them. He studied the warriors, trying to decide who to assist, and if he *should* assist. Other than the scale-armored warrior's penchant for poison, he had nothing to inform his decision.

The female knight arced her sword downward toward her foe, aiming for his unarmored head. He raised his shield at enough of an angle to deflect the blow without having his arm shattered and rose to his feet, thrusting his sword toward her exposed abdomen.

The knight took a half step to her right as her blade glanced off the man's shield, allowing his sword to glance off the side of her armor. He pressed his attack, swinging in wild, erratic patterns. His movements practiced, and of singular purpose; he drove the knight backward.

Using a combination of shield blocks, parries, and dodges, she kept control of the situation; deftly maneuvering him around the camp. While defending, she managed to maintain a safe distance from his armor, keep him focused on herself, and steer him away from bystanders.

Laurence raced toward the combatants, sure that the woman deserved his assistance. She fought with honor, while her opponent did not. As he arrived, he thrust his blade toward a crease in the man's armor.

The scale-clad man spun quickly, deflecting Laurence's attack with ease. His follow-up kick to the chest sent Laurence to the ground. He spun back around to face the knight, yelling, "Wait your turn!"

"Stay back, father! Daelar is mine!" she yelled.

Daelar sprinted forward, his sword ready to thrust. She leaned toward him, braced for his attack. As he neared, she dodged to her right a split-second before impact, and turned to stay facing him. He buried his right heel, slid to a stop, and parried her counterattack.

"How many times must we have this dance, Wyk'Kydarian? How many times before you realize you can't best me?" he insisted.

Daelar slashed from the left, turning the blade mid-strike to thrust toward her neck. He repeated the attack rapidly from the right and continued alternating; trying to force her to defend predictably. Regardless, he could not break through her defenses. In frustration, he locked his blade with hers, pushed her back and thrust with all his might.

Wyk'Kydarian dropped her defenses, let his blade slip through, and used her shield hand to lock it in place. She quickly lunged her body toward him while pulling his blade toward herself—to close the distance between them—allowing his blade to slip under her left pauldron.

He yanked at his sword, attempting to free it. In the same moment, she slid her sword under his left arm, down into his ribcage. He frantically ripped his blade free, stumbling backwards. She released her sword and let it fall to the ground with him. Two fingers from her left hand skittered across the ground near Laurence.

As he lay gurgling, gasping for breath in the dirt, she dropped her shield and wrapped her right hand around her left, wincing in pain. The strange light reappeared, pulsing and growing in size. Knowing she had precious few seconds remaining, she turned to Laurence with a few parting words, "Burn him, father. Burn h-"

As suddenly as she'd arrived, she vanished. The flash of light pulsed once and dissipated with an audible crack. Only Daelar's body, their weaponry, and the faint smell of burnt hair remained. Laurence made his way to his feet as the air settled back into a semblance of normalcy.

"She... she called you father," gasped Tylee.

"Pardon my crudeness but... what in the hell just happened?" asked Bronsin.

"Not hell, I can assure you that," responded a voice from above.

Each of the companions glanced upward, seeking its source. A dark figure with bright, white hair stood atop the bridge looking down at them.

"Obviously, it was a temporal anomaly; likely caused by a collision between Time and Paradox elemental magics. Both are expressly forbidden, so to see their effects by mere happenstance on the side of the road is quite a treat. Though, I admit it odd that this would occur when we are nearby. It would seem the participants, either those casting or combating in melee, are in some way linked to a member of your party... or to me," offered the voice.

"You can either come down here, or I can come up to you... either way you will speak plainly. I'm at my limit for 'random mysterious shit' at this point, and my patience is gone," belted Laurence bluntly, sheathing his sword.

"I'll... be right down," said the voice.

∴ ∴ ∴

LAURENCE KNELT and picked up Wyk'Kydarian's fingers, still wrapped in the leather of her gauntlet. He couldn't find anything remarkable about the gauntlet fragments that would help him identify the woman. As he was about to put them aside, a glint of gold caught his eye.

Squeezing gently to push the fingers out of the leather, he retrieved a golden signet ring. On top was an engraved golden raven. Its talons each held a gem. One gem was a small ruby, the other a sapphire.

In the raven's beak was a bar, holding small scales to either side. The symbolism, as far as he could tell, was a blend of his family crest and the scales of justice, signifying the Holy Order of Galrath; god of justice, law, and war.

He made a mental note to study the ring later and placed it into the small pouch on his belt, just beneath his hauberk. He stood back up as the man from the bridge arrived in the camp.

Their visitor wore black robes, trimmed in silver embroidery. A thick plate of hardened leather was affixed to his chest, the center of which bore the sigil of Fel'Vizsiour.

He appeared young, and human, but his hair flowed long and silvery-white down his back in a loose ponytail; a style and color that was decidedly elvish. His faintly bluish, almost white irises shone brightly in the growing light of morning.

Laurence stood at the ready.

"Who are you?" asked Bronsin.

"Mordechai," the man answered curtly. "And you are?"

"His name is Bronsin, and this is my daughter Tylee. I am Delriahna, and the man before you is Laurence. As he explained, we've lost our patience for mystery. Too much has happened to us in the past few days. To say nothing of this... this..." she stammered, pointing wildly at the air about her.

"Temporal anomaly, lady Delriahna," confirmed Mordechai in a soft, explanatory tone.

"I believe I said speak plainly," corrected Laurence.

"Well, I... hmm," he pondered.

"Don't look at me," said Tylee. "Laurence grew up with an alchemist, so he's fairly studied. If he doesn't know what you're talking about, I don't know who would."

"I see," muttered Mordechai. "Do you have any coffee? This might take a while to explain, and I could use a cup."

"Sure. Why not?" asked Tylee rhetorically, tossing her arms into the air in frustration.

Mordechai sat next to the campfire as Delriahna stoked it back to full flame. Tylee dutifully prepared a kettle full of smashed coffee beans while they waited.

Using a bit of rope, Bronsin and Laurence carefully dragged the corpse out of camp. They had no interest in potentially poisoning themselves by trying to check his pockets.

As they moved to bury the man, Mordechai chimed in, "I believe she said to burn him."

The two looked back at Mordechai as if to ask if he was serious. His expression indicated that he was.

"Don't worry, I'll handle it for you before we set off. For now, just be thankful you didn't touch his armor. I'm not sure I have a cure handy," he said.

Bronsin took a few moments to store Wyk'Kydarian's weapon and shield with Laurence's belongings before returning to the fire.

∴ ∴ ∴

AFTER A time, Tylee served fresh coffee to everyone but Delriahna. She chose, instead, to sample some warmed wine. Normally Laurence would have protested, considering they were soon to be back on the road. However, under the circumstances he withheld his protest.

Mordechai closed his eyes and breathed deeply, inhaling the vapors rising from his cup. After blowing on the liquid gently for a few moments, he took a single sip and looked around the group.

"I suppose I should start by explaining that magic isn't always what it seems. In fact, mystery is the very nature of magic. Casting spells is an effort in optimism. You pull magical energies from a source, recite a few words and hope that what you wanted to happen... happens.

"Few excel at it. Those that do usually accomplish their mastery through endless—almost fanatical—study. As with anything, there are those who have a natural gift... but they are exceedingly rare. By the looks of what happened, I would say the casters who caused this event are both studied and gifted.

"I'm an accomplished spell caster, but what we witnessed just now is beyond my capabilities. I've casually attended Fel'Vizsiour for several decades, but I spend most of my time doing research-" explained Mordechai.

"And this is how you seem to know what we just experienced?" asked Delriahna, interrupting him.

"I would say that my studies give me a more informed

perspective. I do not study the schools of Paradox or Time, but I've read about them. I believe both were at play in what we witnessed here. I can't be certain without attempting the same spells, but...

"The kingdoms of eastern Gargoa outlaw both schools of magic. In fact, Melrindia—the goddess of magic—forbids their use. So in reality, I don't believe anyone could give you an exact answer about what has just transpired," he explained.

"So how do forbidden schools of magic cause... this?" challenged Laurence, pointing at the corpse just outside camp

"Try not to over think it. To do so would be folly for someone not trained in the arts," he answered.

He took another sip of his coffee. Noticing it was growing cold, he caused his left hand to produce heat and placed it beneath his cup. Within a few moments, the contents were once again steaming. He blew a tuft of steam away and took another sip.

Smiling, he looked up from his cup and saw the looks in their eyes. Realizing he'd just used magic as a convenience in front of the uneducated, he sighed and continued his explanation.

"My study of Time Elemental magics suggests that its usual benefit is to produce slight time pauses—or shifts—to sway the momentum of battle. Such an effect would allow one party or another to gain an advantage. A simpler version of those powers would be a basic haste spell.

"Some surmise that more powerful magics of this ilk could bend or pause time completely. Which, as you might imagine, could be a very extreme advantage in battle if done correctly. Ultimately, time manipulation could lead to time travel, changing history, and other such things which could damage the fabric of reality," he explained.

He paused for a moment to take another sip of his coffee, holding up a finger to halt their questions. Once he finished drinking, he resumed his explanation.

"Paradox magics focus on twisting the outcomes and causality of events in time. We know little about the practical applications of Paradox magic, aside from its potential in countering Time magics. I don't think Time magics alone would have caused what we witnessed. At least, not from my understanding of them.

"I, therefore, am left to assume that Paradox magics were at play. However, I cannot see how Paradox, by itself, could cause what we witnessed either. This leaves me to deduce that someone wielded Paradox to counter someone else that was wielding Time.

"The collision of those magics would cause unpredictable

outcomes. In fact, Paradox would almost always produce unpredictable results. I don't think the battle was going how the Paradox caster was hoping, and his spell was used to counteract a Time spell in desperation.

"The collision of the magics likely occurred right on top of the martial combatants, sending them along the temporal curve of one of them... ultimately sending them to you, Laurence; someone that at least one of them seems to be linked," concluded Mordechai.

Seeing their blank stares, Mordechai quipped, "As expected, you do not understand. Shall we simply say, 'mysterious shit' happened?"

"Remind me never to ask him a question," Tylee said to Laurence, pointing her thumb at Mordechai.

"I'm sorry I can't make this easier to understand," admitted Mordechai.

"So, they landed here because it would be a paradox if Wyk'Kydarian met me here?" asked Laurence. "I mean... she knew who I was."

"A 'potential paradox', would be more accurate. Paradox magic plays upon the negative possibilities related to Time... in this case, it was likely a collision between the two," he said.

"He's doing it again," complained Tylee, rubbing her left temple.

"Nonsense," proclaimed Delriahna boldly.

"Pardon?" asked Mordechai.

"Paradox? Time? I've never heard of such magic," she submitted. "I've heard of Unfylyx the Scorcher, flame wizard of the north. I've heard of Garfax the Grand, ice wizard of the southern isles. I've even heard of Deledroth the Ancient... necromancer of the lost lands. Never, not even once, have I heard of anything you've said here."

"To be fair, m'lady," offered Mordechai, "the men you've just mentioned would be similarly confused by this conversation. While they've earned their share of fame, none of them are capable of the kinds of magic we just witnessed."

"Blah, blah, blah, magic, blah, blah, blah," mumbled Bronsin. "What are you doing here? It's a little too convenient that you just happened to be present to explain all this, isn't it?"

"I would call it a fortunate turn of circumstance, not a convenience," retorted Mordechai. "I was nearby for other purposes and was lucky enough to have a once-in-a-lifetime chance to witness the after-effects of forbidden magics; wielded by what I can only assume to be true masters of their craft."

Bronsin shrugged but maintained his stubborn, demanding gaze.

"The event likely has more to do with the ring Laurence retrieved. My estimation is that he was meant to have it now and pass it to Wyk'Kydarian in the future. In true paradoxical fashion, this event is how he acquired it. A ring that should not exist, which has no singular origin; passed down through time, only to return to this moment and repeat the cycle in an endless loop," said Mordechai.

Laurence withdrew the ring from the pouch at his waist. His companions saw it for the first time at that moment, glinting in the fire's light.

"It has what appears to be a version of my family's crest upon it," stated Laurence. He reached around the fire and placed the ring in Mordechai's outstretched palm.

"So it does," confirmed Mordechai. He studied it for a moment and then added, "this crest is very close to the one you bear. However, it symbolizes someone in your house as a member of the Holy Order of Galrath; a member that appears to be of great standing.

"Though... I don't think anyone uses this crest at this time. We have a list of registered crests back at the school, and you can find them documented in state offices across the Kingdom. This isn't a crest I've ever seen, and I've studied them all.

"Another pertinent question is why she would refer to you as 'Father'. Are you a priest? Surely you're not old enough to have spawned a child of her apparent age," Mordechai stated. He raised an eyebrow then added, "Then again if I'm correct about the usage of Time and Paradox magic, she is likely from your future... or your past. Do you remember ever meeting her before?"

"No, I would remember someone like her," said Laurence.

Bronsin grunted in agreement.

"Laur!" gasped Tylee, offended.

"She was the first half-elf I've ever seen, Ty. I'd know if I'd met her. You wouldn't very well forget meeting a half-elf in Mooncrest," he defended.

"I... I suppose you're right," she admitted. "But why did she call you 'Father'?" she asked, noticeably confused and biting her lower lip.

"Could be that he fathers her at some point, or if I'm to believe this ring, he could turn to priesthood," stated Mordechai.

"Or neither," said Laurence.

"Or neither," agreed Mordechai. "But you're probably a priest," jabbed Mordechai, trying to lighten the mood.

"Great, I married a priest," declared Tylee in a huff.

"Tylee, love, I'm not any of those things. I killed three men this week defending you. I'll kill a thousand more before I become a priest and abandon you." He tried to reassure her, but she wasn't budging. "Tens of thousands," he added, attempting to comfort her. He walked over to her, sat down, and put his arm around her.

"I don't want no crusty ole priest," she said in a huff, crossing her arms dramatically.

"You don't have a crusty ole priest," comforted Laurence, playing along with her obvious ploy for attention.

"Oh, for crying out loud," snapped Delriahna.

Bronsin chuckled.

Mordechai walked over and handed Laurence the ring.

"To answer your question, friend," he said to Bronsin, "I was on the other side of the bridge studying the interior of the Waystation. There are two corpses inside. I've been searching for a group of bandits along this road, so I was gathering evidence before moving on," explained Mordechai.

"How far south would you say these bandits are active?" asked Bronsin.

"There are likely several groups the entire length of the highway but I'm seeking, specifically, a trio in possession of a finely crafted crank-action crossbow. They assaulted a rather important caravan, from which they stole the crossbow two weeks ago. It happened near Dunforth. They were last seen heading south," answered Mordechai.

Laurence smiled at Bronsin knowingly, stood and went to the carriage. Mordechai watched with interest as he retrieved a bulging satchel from within. He brought it over and presented it proudly.

"Looking for this, I presume?" said Laurence.

Mordechai opened the satchel and had trouble keeping the contents from spilling out. On top of the pile were the broken remnants of the crossbow he had referred to; the black pearl was missing from its stock.

"Well... it seems you've done my job for me," said Mordechai. "Pity this didn't survive," he said, holding a piece of the weapon.

"I'd rather you'd caught them before we did, but it ended well enough," stated Laurence.

"Outstanding work for someone your age," said Mordechai.

"Thanks, I guess?" answered Laurence.

"No offense meant, Laurence. However, you've accomplished something that two initiates of Fel'Rechaun failed to do. You should be proud," explained Mordechai.

"As someone on his way to train at Fel'Rechaun, I find your report less than inspiring. I held the school in higher regard," he said disappointedly. "That said, there's only one man I'll ever be proud to kill," he declared.

Laurence pulled off his left gauntlet as he walked around the fire, back to Mordechai. He showed the tattoo to the wizard and began his tale. Mordechai sat in silence during the entirety of it. The rest of the group used the time to make breakfast and prepare the corpse for burning upon their departure.

The tale finished just as the group finished packing their belongings and cleaning the camp. Bronsin was calmly adjusting bridles and preparing their horses. Delriahna was listening intently, it being only the second time she'd heard the tale. Tylee had just finished washing their cooking and dining wares in the river.

Mordechai studied his thoughts for a moment and then met Laurence's gaze. He could tell the boy was shaken by the tale, even though he'd told it several times. The ordeal had forever changed him and set him upon a path that Mordechai could only assume would have extraordinary outcomes. He was sure of only one thing; he wanted to be a part of it.

"Laurence," said Mordechai, "when the time comes that you set forth to seek your revenge on Drakahl, please be sure to extend an invitation. I feel there is a fair bit more at play than you're aware of, and you'll need all the help you can get to overcome this."

"I'll consider it... I still haven't decided whether you're one of his lackeys," answered Laurence.

"Fair enough," said Mordechai. "Tell you what... since you're traveling to Fel'Rechaun, and I just completed a task under their employ, I will accompany you. I have been consulting with Lord Commander Fahrul in recent months and I will offer to stay as adviser to your class on magical studies and combat techniques. During which, you may test—or question—me to your heart's content, until I have earned your trust."

"Very well," Laurence agreed.

.˙. .˙. .˙.

AFTER SETTING fire to the corpse and returning the carriage to the road, the group crossed the bridge on their way to the Waystation. Stone blocks comprised the lower third of the first floor, held together with crumbling mortar. Wooden beams and walls stretched three stories high, forming what had once been an inn for weary travelers.

Mordechai walked calmly inside with a sense of purpose. Bronsin followed. The two emerged after a few minutes with a corpse and laid it alongside the carriage. As they returned for the second, Laurence and Delriahna wrapped the first in a blanket. Once the corpses were bound, Bronsin and Laurence tied them to the roof of the carriage.

"Didn't I say we wouldn't be strapping corpses to our carriage? I'm pretty sure that was something I said," said Delriahna, scowling.

"Mordechai has to take the corpses for inspection and burial," said Bronsin.

"Well, that gives us a sense of urgency if we didn't have one before," stated Delriahna.

"How so?" asked Laurence.

"They already smell of death. We can't have that stench permeate all of our belongings... food... water," she complained. She stopped speaking abruptly as Mordechai looked her in the eyes.

"Not to worry, m'lady," said Mordechai. He calmly walked away and mounted his white horse. "Their smell will not offend you," he offered. A faint green glow surrounded the corpses and faded from sight. Delriahna could no longer smell them.

"I... um... thank you?" stammered Delriahna.

"That settles that, I reckon," agreed Bronsin as he took the driver seat. The rest of the group prepared to leave.

"But when did he... I didn't see him... a spell?" Delriahna stammered.

Bronsin shrugged, seemingly unconcerned.

"Salvation Shire lies a half day's journey north. We'll find lodging there, but do not let your guard down," warned Mordechai.

"Sounds pleasant," chimed Tylee excitedly.

"Naivety is a charming shield, my dear, but one soon shattered," answered Mordechai.

"What does he mean, Laur? Should I be mad?" asked Tylee.

"What he means, my love, is that Salvation Shire is an ironic name and that the town is anything but salvation. Keep up your guard and be wary," answered Laurence.

∴ ∴ ∴

THE ELBERMIRE Way was notorious among frequent travelers as being inhospitable. Very few settlements remained along its route, and the wilds had mostly overtaken it. That fact was even more true as the route reached its end in the north, where the road met with a crossroads; joining with the Ekthri Fjord and the Western Reach.

Named for the deep channel that allowed the Mythaeil River to cross beneath it, the Ekthri Fjord continued west into Ekthri wood. The Western Reach continued east to the Vaelin Crossroads. The Ekthri Crossroads was the intersection between the three roads and had once been a major trade thoroughfare.

Trade with the Ekthri empire ended during the rule of King Orluhnd III. Relations had slowly deteriorated following the death of Orluhnd Vaelin II, as Orluhnd III was not as friendly or compassionate as his father. The elves eventually withdrew into isolation. Humans who continued to travel into Ekthri lands often found themselves imprisoned for trespassing, even with the efforts of Orluhnd IV making strides to repair their relations.

As a result, the road had fallen into ill repair, and the crossroads had become a ruin. The Waystation, and the few shops that had once surrounded it, stood crumbling and overgrown. Tales spread far and wide of trolls having claimed the area as their home. Many travelers had vanished after attempting to pass through.

Lyla brought her steed to a stop beside Gaerin's. She gave him a look, raising a single eyebrow inquisitively. She wasn't one to trust in rumors, tales, and flights of imagination. The crossroads that loomed ahead of them hadn't even crossed her mind as a concern.

"We might be safer to camp here," Gaerin pondered aloud. "Then again, this might not be far enough away."

"This is the first Waystation our route has taken us past, and you want to avoid it? I, for one, could use a roof for the night," countered Lyla.

"Are you seriously suggesting we camp inside the ruins?" Gaerin asked, surprised.

"Why not? You don't think there's really anything to worry about, do you? Surely you don't believe tall tales you heard in a tavern?" Lyla quipped.

"Maybe we should," he answered. "Kobolds? That's one thing. Trolls? They're something completely different, and you know it."

"Surely the King has made sure that his roads are clear."

"Kobolds! We literally just fought through a horde of kobolds yesterday... on his roads," he retorted.

"Scared?" she challenged. She was intent on not sleeping under the open sky, if she could help it, and neither of them had the patience to build a temporary shelter.

"I'm trying to be practical, dear," he answered.

"Practical is the storm that's brewing, and the value that walls and a roof would provide. Even crumbling walls are better than nothing, once the rain and wind get started. You want rested mounts, do you not? You want a rested wife?" she asked firmly.

Gaerin knew that once his wife made up her mind, there was nothing he could say to change it. His wife knew that he knew that about her.

Lyla tapped her mount with her heels, sending it into a trot.

Gaerin stared blankly at her for a moment before following suit. He had to admit the air felt like a storm was incoming. With the faint smell of electricity in the air, the damp chill in the breeze and the clouds in the sky, all signs were pointing to a rather nasty thunderstorm. He regretted that they hadn't owned tents to bring with them.

The crossroads were eerily quiet. As they entered the clearing around the buildings, they studied the Ekthri Fjord and Western Reach. Not a soul was in sight, and there was no visible evidence of recent passage.

Lyla dismounted and approached the primary structure on foot, reins in hand. The station was far from intact. The former two-story stone inn for weary travelers appeared less than a story tall in the front. Its sides tapered upward toward the rear left corner, where it reached half of the original second story's height.

Green moss had overgrown much of the stonework, and small plants clung to cracks in the facade. The mortar between the stones had crumbled away, providing purchase for vines. Lyla wasn't sure if the walls were holding up the plants, or the plants were holding up the walls.

Gaping holes stood out upon the front face, where windows had once existed. The entryway appeared more like a cave entrance than it did a door. The surrounding buildings, all smaller than the station, were even worse for wear.

The smell of earth, moss and greenery permeated the air. It mixed with the smell of the oncoming storm in a way that made Lyla both uneasy and oddly comforted. The Waystation somehow made her feel closer to nature than the wilds of the Elbermire Way. She turned to Gaerin with a smile before entering.

Gaerin tied the horses to the remains of an old stone post a few feet from the entry. He stepped inside to find her staring up through the remnants of the second story's floor at the sky above. She was in love with the place, and it was obvious.

"I clearly spent too much on our house," he chirped.

"Oh stop," she scoffed. "This place is amazing. It's like some kind of fairy tale." She twirled around slowly with her arms out, enjoying herself.

"Fairy tale? You do remember how most of those end... don't you?" he asked.

She put her hands on her hips and looked him squarely in the eyes. "You're welcome to sleep outside in the rain. I, for one, plan to lean my bedroll against the wall, under cover and protected from the wind."

"I'll... gather some firewood," he offered with a sigh.

She smiled back at him playfully and started clearing space on the floor for their bedding and a fire. Their horses clopped around on the cobble outside, happily nibbling at the moss and weeds on the stone wall before them.

∴ ∴ ∴

SALVATION SHIRE was a small town. There were only a few dozen buildings at its center, and less than a dozen along the outskirts. Nestled between hills, the only thing nearby worth mentioning was the highway from which it sprang. Where a Waystation once stood was now a sign pointing east toward 'Salvation'.

The town was visible if one stood next to the sign, making it convenient for those passing through. At its center was a single street lined with old, wood-plank buildings. Two inns, each across the road from one another, signified the center of town.

Mordechai pointed at the road between the inns and explained, "This is as far into town as you'll want to go. While they give the appearance of being welcoming, the locals don't like visitors. They're more interested in what you brought with you, and how quick you'll be leaving. The constable hopes you'll spend everything you own before you leave. The residents, however, seem to find newcomers to be a nuisance."

"Lovely of you to bring us here," stated Tylee.

"There are few populated stops along your trip, m'lady. If this doesn't suit you, camping outside of town is an option. That is... as long as the constable doesn't catch you doing it. There is a strict policy against camping along the northern stretch of the Southern Reach, and Salvation Shire will use that policy to soak you for gold.

"It's best, therefore, to lodge in secure rooms across the street from the constable's Salvation Inn and deprive him of his coin," explained Mordechai.

"I think we could all use an actual bed. Bedrolls just aren't the same. I'll remain in my armor, of course," offered Laurence.

"I don't think that wise, Laur," injected Bronsin.

Everyone who saw Laurence, or the carriage with the corpses on top, was ogling them. Residents were lining the streets. They were barely inside town and were already causing a scene.

"It's just armor," retorted Laurence.

"Fancy armor," corrected Tylee.

"Fancy armor with bits of dried blood on it," added Mordechai.

"Well, yes. I suppose there is that," Laurence admitted, studying his chest.

"Don't worry. This inn will serve our purposes. We can purchase keys for the locks on the doors, and I can seal them magically so that only we can enter. Your belongings will be safe," assured Mordechai.

"What of our carriage?" asked Delriahna.

"You needn't ask. It carries two important bodies, and a bag of evidence. It is as critical to me as your safety," added Mordechai.

She nodded her approval with a smile.

The group stopped briefly in front of the Turnabout Tavern while Mordechai went inside to secure lodging. Several townsfolk gathered around them, gawking. A short, rotund man made his way through the crowd angrily, heading for the front of the carriage.

"What is the meaning of this?" he demanded, waving his arm toward the blanket-wrapped corpses.

His portly frame jiggled as he waved his arm in dramatic fashion. He reminded Tylee of the men her father did business with in Mooncrest. The major differences being the general dirtiness of his clothes and the smudges along the front of his shirt.

"We are escorting these unfortunate souls to Fel'Rechaun," explained Delriahna defiantly.

He seemed to perk up at her mention of Fel'Rechaun. As he turned to address Laurence, she recognized the scheming behind his demeanor. It was a look she had seen on many councilmen in Mooncrest, many times before.

"I expect the school will compensate for your disruption of our peace?" he demanded.

"You can expect nothing of the sort," retorted Delriahna, offended that she'd lost his attention. "You and your residents will afford us respect and safe passage. I'll not have you disturbing my guard with such matters. He has a job to do. Kindly let him do it," she insisted.

Politics were her game, and Laurence wasn't about to protest her declaration that he was her guard.

"You have mistaken my intent, my lady, I-" he started. She was quick to interrupt.

"I have mistaken nothing. You are Constable, and you have a duty to the Kingdom. Today, that duty is to ensure that your citizens do nothing to hinder our efforts. If that is too much for you to handle, I'm sure the King can find a suitable replacement," she challenged.

Tylee looked toward her mother in awe. Seeing her boss Andor and the servants around was normal. However, she had never seen her speak with such authority in public. It was an impressive sight to behold and gave her more respect for her mother.

"Beg your pardon, my lady, but on whose authority do you make demands? Do you have proof of your mission? Your station?" challenged the Constable.

Just then, Mordechai exited the Turnabout Tavern and made his way to the carriage. He called out, "Constable Harek, are we to go through this dance again? I am here on official business, and my presence is all the proof you need."

"Lord Mordechai, I didn't see you. I-" said Harek, stumbling for words.

His face flushed as he turned, walking away without further discussion. He waved the small crowd away from the carriage, insisting they return to their normal activities.

"We need to stable our horses in the rear. We can park the carriage alongside the tavern," said Mordechai as he mounted his horse.

"Is he always like that?" asked Tylee, referring to Constable Harek.

"No," answered Mordechai. "Must be a good day."

∴ ∴ ∴

THE INTERIOR of the Turnabout Tavern was dimly lit. The lack of light did little to hide its peeling paint, worn wooden floors, and antiquated furniture. It wasn't the type of establishment that a person of higher standing would frequent.

Delriahna wasn't sure it was safe to touch anything.

Laurence and Tylee found it to be warm, inviting and homey. They didn't mind that the boards creaked as they walked, or that the walls showed their age. To them, it felt lived in, inviting, and not at all off-putting.

Tylee had never liked her mother's insistence on keeping their house in immaculate condition. She never felt that her childhood house was actually a home. There were too many rules about where she could sit, what she could touch, and which guests were allowed into which rooms. She loved the inn, and she loved the room she and Laurence were told to share.

Bronsin seemed oblivious to the state of the place. He was content to have a bed, a ceiling, and a door. It wasn't a bedroll, and he wouldn't get rained on. That was what mattered. He took one look at his bed and promptly began removing his traveling clothes to get some rest.

Mordechai had helped them to their rooms, and at the doorway of each he waved his left hand as they entered. There was no glow of energy, no muttering of strange words, or anything else to indicate why he was waving his hand. It frustrated Delriahna to no end. With each passing room, she grew more frustrated. When they finally arrived at her room, she couldn't resist protesting.

"And... that's it? That's all you've got?" she questioned.

"Pardon?" he said, taken aback.

"A brief wave of the hand, and that's supposed to scare people away? Keep us safe?" she pressed.

"Would you feel better if you saw my hand glowing some strange color while I muttered in unknown languages under my breath? Decades of training, honing my skills and endless study... and what matters is showmanship?" he challenged.

"Am I supposed to just... take it on faith?" she started.

"Indeed. That's what magic is; faith and optimism. Or maybe... realize that not all magic is visible. Not all casters require verbal components. Not all casters require reagents, gestures, runes, potions or scrolls. In fact, me waving my hand at all was a gesture for your benefit. These kinds of spells, when I cast them, require nothing from me but a simple thought," he defended.

"You can cast spells without speaking?" she asked. She found herself both confused and intrigued.

"Depending upon the spell, yes. It's not so far-fetched as one might imagine. I'm not the only caster to achieve such a thing. In most cases, I'd have sealed the rooms without my traveling companions even being aware of what I'd done. However, since you were so concerned with safety, I felt you deserved a simple gesture; to prove I had followed through.

"This particular spell doesn't produce a visible effect for the untrained eye. It takes years of training to see magical energies like this. I, for example, can see the entire doorway glowing with runes of protection, and the windows beyond that. To you, it appears a normal door lined with wood, and it will always seem to be such.

"What I can't do is produce two spell effects at once. So, I can either wave my hand and make it glow... which would be one spell. Or, I can wave my hand expressly for your benefit, while I focus my thoughts on sealing your room with protective runes... which is another spell," he concluded.

She stared back at him blankly.

"For future reference, which would you prefer?" he inquired.

He was fairly certain she would continue to be difficult in areas that concerned magic. She was still staring back at him with a blank expression. To appease her, he waved his hand and muttered strange words under his breath while his hand emitted a faint blue light.

Delriahna put her right hand on her hip, tilted her head, and looked him squarely in the eyes with the most unimpressed look she could muster.

"I have things to attend. Please ensure your companions stay close to the tavern," he requested as he departed.

Delriahna stood in the hallway for a moment longer, still unsure how to respond. She was out of her element in every way. The town she was in, the state of the tavern, the lack-luster room that splayed out behind her, magic... it was all too much.

She hoped her husband appreciated her tribulations. He owed

her. He didn't know it yet, but he really owed her.

Along the hall, each of their doors closed and latched. It was still light outside, but they hadn't seen beds in several days and they were all exhausted. Even Laurence and Tylee, who had been waiting for a chance to share a bed together, were too tired to act on their desires.

∴ ∴ ∴

THE FIRE hissed gently whenever rain found its way around the walls or through the holes above them. Gaerin had to admit the shelter had been a wise decision. He leaned against the wall with a sigh. Lyla leaned over and placed her head on his chest. It wasn't a location he would have sought for a weekend getaway, but he was happy living in the moment.

The responsibilities of tending farm, instructing Laurence, and helping Arcturus had consumed them over the years. He wasn't sure when it happened, but they'd lost sight of what was important. It had been too long since they spent quality time together, with nothing to worry about but themselves.

As he resigned himself to enjoying an evening with his wife, he heard a thud from the rear of the building. Lyla heard it too, released herself from his grasp and sat upright.

A smell wafted in through the cracks and holes in the wall. It was a smell they recognized from their past; an odor that caused immediate concern.

She looked at him with worry in her eyes.

'I fucking told you,' he mouthed.

She sighed, knowing he was right.

They got to their feet and grabbed their weaponry. There was no time to don armor. A fresh wave of regret washed over Gaerin as he glanced at their pile of gear. They had allowed themselves to relax and were now threatened in nothing but their night clothes.

Warhammer and shield equipped, Gaerin readied himself for the inevitable.

"Crap," she exclaimed in a whisper.

"What?" he whispered back.

"We can't actually do this," she gasped.

"How do you figure?" he asked, looking back at her.

"What permanently kills trolls, dear?" she challenged, rolling her eyes.

"Fire," he answered.

The campfire hissed a short distance away, as if reminding him of the storm all around them. Realization set in.

"Oh, crap," he exclaimed. "Yeah. This'll be fun," he sighed sarcastically.

"Wet trolls," she said.

"We'll *have* to lure them inside to the campfire," he said.

The sounds of movement increased behind the structure. Vines rustled, and twigs snapped. Fleshy feet impacted the mud-covered cobblestone while a meaty fist thumped the brittle barrier behind them. Chunks of debris fell from the floor above, and a new crack formed in the wall over their armor pile. The remaining vertical beams groaned under the weight of the saturated structure, gently swaying and struggling to stay upright.

"Crap!" she exclaimed.

"Crap!" he agreed, no longer whispering. "They're gonna bring this thing down on top of us. We can't wait for them to come inside."

"Gods damn it!" she exclaimed, readying herself.

Nothing about the encounter was ideal. *No armor, in the rain... sure, let's fight a troll,* thought Gaerin. He moved first, barreling through the entryway into the dark night beyond the reach of the fire.

Holding his shield at the ready, and his war hammer low to his right, he searched for their foe. He was ready to strike upward, knowing trolls were significantly taller than he. His memory had not betrayed him.

A nine-foot-tall troll suddenly emerged from the darkness and slammed its huge fist into Gaerin's shield. The impact was hard enough to send Gaerin sliding backward several feet across the muddy ground. He was adept enough to stay upright, but the feat was challenging. The pain that radiated through his left arm and shoulder was excruciating.

Lyla stepped into the doorway and called for Galrath's power. A bolt of energy arced between her outstretched palm and the troll's chest. Howling in pain, the beast stepped backward.

Gaerin kicked off the wall to increase the momentum behind his lunge. With a powerful swing, he drove his hammer into the troll's side, just below its ribs. The troll released a deep roar that sent chills through both of them. Gaerin's blow had broken its skin.

Movement caught Gaerin's eye to their left. Two trolls barreled around the eastern side of the building, running straight for him. It was of little comfort to Gaerin that they were shorter than the first. A troll was a dangerous foe, regardless of its size.

The second troll was fatter than the first. It was seven foot tall with long, scraggly hair. Gaerin nearly laughed at the way the creature's belly sloshed and flopped as it toddled toward them.

The final troll was six foot tall, making it the shortest. It grinned wickedly as it closed on Gaerin, sure of its next meal.

"Shit! Fuck!" barked Gaerin. He repositioned himself to keep all three trolls in view.

"Two more? Crap!" Lyla yelled back, unable to see them.

Knowing each other's ways had always been one of their strengths. They had learned long ago to communicate using simple words in quick bursts. In their adventuring days, they'd been able to act in anticipation of each other without speaking a word.

Gaerin knew there was precious little time to act. He stepped close to the first troll, repeatedly crushing his hammer into the beast's side, hoping to crack ribs and rupture internal organs. It tried to deflect his blows, protecting its side with a gangly left arm.

As the hammer repeatedly slammed into the beast's left side and arm, it clawed at Gaerin with its right. He held his shield up with all his strength, wedging it between the creature's right arm and torso. The angle was just enough to protect him, but difficult to maintain. As Gaerin attacked, he attempted to turn the troll to keep its body between himself and the two new additions.

Lyla stepped into the opening and began casting another spell. Seeing the new trolls, she wondered if the smaller one was a child. *Do they have children, or just cut off a piece of themselves to grow a new one*, she wondered.

Her spell burst forth as a blaze of holy fire. It struck the second tallest troll in the torso, causing minimal damage but giving it pause. Fire was something they instinctively feared.

However, that was Lyla's last attack spell and Gaerin knew it. She stepped completely into the open, prepared to engage in melee. The smallest troll pushed past its stunned counterpart, flailing with its claws in her direction.

Lyla deflected the first blow with her shield, and the second with her mace. The third slammed into her shield. The force of the blow pushed her out of position, spinning her toward Gaerin and exposing her left side. Its fourth blow struck the top of her left shoulder, ripping into her flesh and cracking the collarbone. She dropped her shield as she stumbled into the back of the first troll, crumpling to the ground behind its feet.

Gaerin pulled back his shield, braced both of his arms beneath it, and drove it upward into troll's stomach with all his strength. It lurched backward, tripped over Lyla, and crashed into the smaller troll. Both fell to the ground in a heap. Gaerin helped Lyla up quickly as the mid-sized troll charged toward them.

Lyla, struggling through the pain, knelt quickly and swung her mace low toward the troll's left knee. Gaerin uppercut the troll with his hammer simultaneously, landing his hit directly on its vile, green chin. The creature spun to the right, head lurching backward, and toppled over the other two trolls.

Gaerin ran back into the building, dropped his weapons and grabbed their armor. Lyla followed, slightly confused. She looked at him inquisitively. He looked at her and then at the floor above them. She followed his glance as he started tossing their gear out through a small window at the rear.

His plan made sense. She turned and started making noise, coaxing the trolls to finish their attack. The trolls worked to untangle themselves and get to their feet.

By the time the trolls had gathered themselves enough to make a lunge at her, their belongings were lying in the mud at the rear of the building.

"Now!" Gaerin grunted. He picked up his hammer and shield, charging back into the battle.

She stepped backwards quickly as Gaerin stepped around her. He taunted them and clanged his hammer off the face of his shield; coaxing them further inside.

Lyla raced to the back of the building and tossed her mace atop the pile of equipment. She climbed through the window, favoring her good arm. Outside, she inspected the wall for a way to climb to the second floor.

The trolls reached for Gaerin, trying to attack while avoiding the campfire. As they inched closer, he stepped further back. He needed them beneath the remnants of the second floor.

Troll blood and guts lay strewn across the ground behind them. The tallest of them clutched desperately at its side with its shattered left arm. Angrily, it shoved the smallest troll toward Gaerin with its meaty right hand. Gaerin jumped back.

Lyla was halfway up the wall, clinging desperately to vines while searching for footholds. Climbing with one arm was difficult. Climbing vines growing out of a crumbling wall in the rain was worse. Twice during her climb, pieces of the wall broke away and hinted at the structure's desire to cave.

"Now?" begged Gaerin. The trolls were in position, growing bolder around the campfire.

"Now!" Lyla yelled as she reached the landing.

The wooden floor and beams sagged as Lyla crawled over them. Small bits of stone broke free of the outer wall, tumbling to the room below. The walls sagged inward lightly, pulled by her weight on the floor.

Gaerin made his way toward a weak spot in the wall at the back of the structure, where the troll had punched it earlier. The beast's punch had formed new cracks, revealing the wall's readiness to collapse.

As the trolls closed in on him, Gaerin slammed his bodyweight into the wall as hard as he could. It cracked. The second floor dipped under Lyla's weight. A piece of the upper floor broke free and fell into the fire, sending a cloud of embers and ash into the air.

The trolls panicked and moved to the outer wall, right underneath Lyla. Gaerin slammed into the wall again, driving with all his strength through his shield. Chunks of wall pushed through, falling into the open air beyond. As the middle of the wall caved outward, its top came crashing down toward the center of the ruin.

Gaerin ran and dove through the window with a physical prowess he didn't know he still possessed. Stone ground on stone, the wooden beams gave way, and the top of the building came crashing down atop the trolls. Lyla rolled away from the walls, attempting to fall clear of the rubble.

The center of the other wall buckled under the shifting weight from above and collapsed inward. Wood and stone buried the trolls, trapping them... for a time. Lyla crashed to the floor, just beyond the larger pieces of debris. Several pieces of the higher portion of the wall fell atop her legs, hip and lower back.

Gaerin jumped over a section of the back wall and skirted the pile of debris to grab Lyla's outstretched arm. He dragged her free of the pile and into the clearing outside. Moaning, she rolled onto her bum and began casting healing spells. She had several serious injuries.

Gaerin was confident she could overcome the pain and restore herself. His respect for his wife and her courage had never been higher.

The rubble shifted. The trolls were trying to dig their way out.

∴ ∴ ∴

NOISE FROM the tavern below slowly woke them, one by one, as dusk fell. Each one stopped at the final landing, peering through the crowd for their companions. The first to wake had selected a table in the far corner. The crowd was much denser than they'd expected, being such a small town.

Tylee approached her group's table with wonder in her eyes. When she reached them, she blurted, "This must be, like... everyone." She pointed at the crowd, just in case anyone misunderstood what she meant.

"It is," answered a woman standing behind her.

Tylee squealed in surprise and spun around to see who was behind her. It was a woman wearing a leather apron, carrying several tankards of ale in her hands.

"Oh," gasped Tylee, backing into her seat beside Laurence.

"You've caused quite a ruckus, coming here. But to be fair, every time Mordechai visits he draws a crowd. Everyone seems to want something from him." She sat the drinks in front of her guests and extended her hand toward Tylee. "I'm Wendy. This is my tavern."

Tylee shook her hand happily. "They all want something from Mordechai?"

"Well, yeah," she answered, releasing Tylee's grasp. "He's pretty well known round these parts. Saved us from a pack of gnolls a little while back, so now they seem to think he can do anything."

Wendy looked over her shoulder. Someone across the room had called her name. She nodded at the companions with a smile and walked away to handle her other customers.

A platter of roast fowl lay at the center of the table. Surrounding it were small bowls filled with potatoes, corn, buns and various other local side dishes. Each place setting had a plate, a bowl, utensils and a fresh tankard of ale. Tylee cracked her knuckles and started piling food on her plate. The other companions were already in the middle of their meal.

"This must be what Mordechai meant, when he said he had matters to attend," remarked Delriahna. She placed another piece of meat in her mouth, dabbed her lips with a cloth and began chewing daintily.

"I haven't seen him since we settled into our rooms. If the locals are all here, where is he?" inquired Bronsin.

Just then, a man arrived at the end of their table wearing dirty burlap farming clothes. He was moderately tall, well-built, and carried himself with arrogance. He smirked at Laurence with a grin on his face that revealed several of his missing teeth. His blonde, unkempt beard bore several flecks of partially consumed food.

The foam at the corner of his mouth made it clear what he'd been drinking. His breath struck Tylee rather abruptly.

"Where's that fancy armor, boy? You sposed to be some kinda knight?" The two men that had followed him over chuckled. Neither of them was any better for wear.

"No... are you?" Laurence retorted.

The man scowled at Laurence.

"Best not to rile the locals, Laur," suggested Delriahna.

"Oh, locals, are we?" responded the man.

"You aren't from Salvation Shire?" asked Delriahna, in mock apology.

"Course we are, but you ain't!" declared the burly man.

Laurence nudged Tylee so she would move then slid out of the bench and stood in front of their guest. His eyes met evenly with the man, which seemed to come as a surprise. Apparently the man had expected a smaller, less eager victim for his bullying. He cleared his throat nervously.

"We're just passing through, good sir. Why don't I buy you an ale, eh?" Laurence suggested.

Laurence was wearing the leather that went beneath his armor, which looked imposing in its own right. He placed his hand on the man's shoulder reassuringly, trying to calm the situation.

"You suggestin I can't afford my own ale?" he retorted angrily.

He shook Laurence's hand off his shoulder and threw a left towards Laurence's gut. The punch landed firmly, causing Laurence to flinch slightly. His attack had been obvious, and Laurence had prepared himself for the blow; managing his breathing accordingly. Beyond the flinch, he didn't move, and the punch didn't seem to affect him. That gave the man pause.

"We're just here to eat, rest, and move on," Laurence added.

Laurence gently tried to usher the man away from their table. He hadn't taken the opportunity to return the man's attack. He really didn't want to fight—or worse—take another life.

The man reeled back dramatically and threw a right punch. Laurence dipped out of the way, landed a left under the man's rib cage, and a right across his jaw. He fell to the floor.

Memories flooded Laurence of his fights with the street rats in

Mooncrest; when he used to play around town with Tylee. Being attacked by bullies as a child was the original reason Gaerin had finally agreed to teach him combat.

The man's friends looked down at him, then back at Laurence in disbelief.

"Cletus, you causin trouble again?" yelled Wendy from across the room.

His friends looked back at her, then knelt to help Cletus to his feet.

"My offer still stands," said Laurence.

Cletus glared at him, still half out of his wits. One of his friends looked Laurence in the eye, nodded frantically, and then helped drag Cletus back to their table.

Laurence sat on the outside of the bench, letting Tylee sit next to the wall. As he settled in, Wendy approached.

"Sorry bout that. Cletus is just jealous. He always used to talk about being a knight when we were kids, and I guess he never got over it. We don't get many warriors in these parts, wearing fancy armor. When we do, it's usually an entire group of em flying the King's banners."

"It's fine... we expected something like this might happen. Can you send them a round of ale on us?" Laurence asked.

"Certainly," answered Wendy. She seemed surprised by Laurence's generosity and turned immediately to deliver the drinks.

"That was odd," decided Tylee.

"You handled that maturely, son," offered Delriahna.

"I just did what came natural. I didn't want us having more trouble than we needed, and couldn't let a bar fight spill over to the rest of you," explained Laurence.

After an hour of drinks, dining and merriment, the tavern went silent. They looked toward the door, following the eyes of the crowd. Mordechai was standing in the doorway with an elven woman at his side. She wore exquisite armor similar to Laurence's with the symbol of Arkhania emblazoned on her breast.

∴ ∴ ∴

"I'LL HANDLE this," he remarked as he strode back into the crumbling Waystation. Pieces of the wall were still falling intermittently as the rest of it gave way. They'd narrowly escaped the encounter with their lives, but he knew their victory wouldn't last if the trolls broke free.

Burying them was a delay tactic and would only hinder the regenerative creatures for so long. Gaerin knew they would run out of time if he didn't take further action. He watched patiently next to the pile as they struggled to dig themselves out. Lyla sat in the distance behind him, muttering healing words in rapid succession. The faint glow from her magic was his only source of light.

The wall had buried the campfire and the rain was increasing. Water had saturated everything around them. Fire was not an option.

A large stone shifted and fell off the pile. The largest troll's right arm shot through the opening, rooting around to remove more of the debris. Gaerin smashed the beast's underarm with his warhammer, driving the joint in the wrong direction and rendering the arm all but useless.

The beast twisted its torso, using its limp arm to create leverage. It poked its head through the opening and roared at Gaerin angrily.

Gaerin stepped onto the pile and wedged his shield down into the opening. He pushed and shoved it from the top, driving one edge downward. The shield shoved the creature's head out of the way and connected with the its neck.

He pounded the top of the shield repeatedly with his weapon, driving it downward. The lower edge of the shield grated horribly against the rubble around the opening, denting and shredding as it pushed its way through.

The clanging of the warhammer on the edge of the shield rang out through the night, echoing off the ruins nearby. The crunch of stone as the shield pushed its way through the rubble amplified the horrid scene. The troll panicked and wailed in excruciating pain.

Through the din, Lyla could easily discern the faint gurgling sound as the troll gasped for breath. With an audible pop, the shield brutally severed the troll's head from its torso. Gaerin tossed the shield, rendered useless by his assault, toward the back of the ruin.

He rejoined Lyla, panting heavily. Kneeling, he placed his hands around her face and pulled her into a kiss. They looked at each other for a moment, then back toward the pile.

"Crap," stated Lyla, exacerbated.

"Aye," agreed Gaerin.

"How long do you think we have?" asked Lyla.

He could see the exhaustion and pain in her eyes. She was out of spells and needed rest. He knew they couldn't stay, and he knew she would struggle to travel.

"Not long enough for it to stop raining," he answered.

"Well, that's no good," Lyla answered. "We've no horses."

"What?" barked Gaerin, shocked.

"Apparently they were the appetizer while we were nodding off. I think the campfire was the only thing that saved our asses."

"How far to the nearest town?" Gaerin asked.

"On foot? I think it's two or three days to Telon's Respite," Lyla answered. "Though I don't like the idea of leaving them here. Headless there," she added, pointing with her mace, "will mean four trolls for the next traveler, not three."

"We don't really have any options, love. Not unless you wish to wait out this storm." He glanced for a second at their one remaining, functional shield. Hefting it toward her he added, "We'd probably need a few more of these."

"Let's get our things," she sighed.

"No mounts. No rations. No waterskins. No bow or arrows for hunting. One shield, a mace, a warhammer, an injured cleric, and a worn-out warrior. Fine way to start a vacation," he quipped.

She chuckled and allowed him to help her to her feet.

The rubble was shifting again as they crested the first hill to the east.

∴ ∴ ∴

MORDECHAI AND his guest walked over to their table. He grabbed two stools along the way and placed them at the end, then sat and invited her to do the same. The rest of the tavern slowly returned to their banter, releasing the group from their attention. Everyone waited patiently for Mordechai or his guest to speak first.

"This is the lad I spoke of," he started, pointing to Laurence with a flick of his finger.

"Impressive," chimed their guest.

A smile crossed her face that Laurence found quite intoxicating. He wondered if all elves were as beautiful, then quickly looked to Tylee and smiled reassuringly. He couldn't have her getting jealous; she didn't handle competition very well.

"What is this about?" asked Laurence, returning his gaze to Mordechai.

"I arrived in town a few moments ago. Fel'Rechaun sent me in search of the missing initiates after Mordechai didn't report in," she answered.

"I was delayed," Mordechai responded. He waved his hand at the group, signaling that they were to blame.

"I saw him as I passed overhead and came down to investigate. He explained everything, including your recent tragedy. My condolences, young Laurence, that isn't the way anyone should enter adulthood," she said.

She smiled reassuringly. Her eyes caught Tylee's, and she turned her gaze instinctively. Tylee was staring her down.

Tylee wasn't sure who the woman was, but she didn't like her smiling at Laurence. The woman was breathtaking, and it wasn't fair. "And you are?" she inquired curtly.

"Apologies, my lady. I am Kyrilis of House Nandari. I'm a Griffin Guard in service to Arkhania; assigned to Fel'Rechaun. The school dispatched Markus and Thorsten to handle a few bandits recently. When they didn't return, Mordechai volunteered to investigate. When *he* didn't return, they dispatched me to find the lot of them," she explained.

"You're an elf!" chimed Bronsin.

"Figure that out all on your own, did you?" quipped Delriahna with a sigh.

"Yes. My people are the Afyr from the northernmost reaches of Arkhania, near the border with the Kingdom of Tellrindos. I serve Arkhania as part of our peoples' peace agreement, and to protect the schools of learning we and the Ekthri helped to build," said Kyrilis.

"You're a Griffin Guard? Is it... outside?" Laurence asked excitedly.

"She's circling above town," Kyrilis answered, smiling.

"This boy is late for his studies, Kyr. If you wouldn't mind, I'm sure he would very much enjoy accompanying you on your trip back to the school," suggested Mordechai.

"He's... nope. Uh-uh. No, no, no," demanded Tylee. Her face wrinkled in frustration. She tried to look angry. It wasn't working.

"My love, I have to get there as quickly as possible. I'm already several days behind and we're still several days away by horseback," he tried to explain.

"How much quicker can she get you there, anyway?" she asked.

"If we leave now, I can have him there by morning. It doesn't take that long when you can travel in a straight line," said Kyrilis.

"It's settled then," stated Mordechai.

"Nothing's settled," retorted Tylee, waving her hands in frustration.

"Listen. I'll visit you in Raven's Nest as often as I can, but I must get to Fel'Rechaun as quickly as possible," said Laurence.

"What about tonight?" she asked.

"Well, I–" started Laurence.

"Have your night, my lady. I need to feed Bah'Shiri anyway. She needs to land and rest. We'll depart in the morning, and I'll have him at Fel'Rechaun before evening trials," Kyrilis offered.

Laurence stood and gently placed Tylee's hand in his. He pulled gently, suggesting that they should head to their room. Begrudgingly, she slid off the bench and joined him. She made sure to scowl at Kyrilis before she left.

Morning came too soon for the young lovers.

∴ ∴ ∴

THEY'D BEEN walking for hours, and it was still raining. Their decision to leave the ruins had been the wiser of their options. However, Lyla couldn't shake the feeling that they'd doomed the next unfortunate traveler who ventured there. As muddy ground sucked at their riding boots, and sheer exhaustion begged them to find shelter, she questioned whether she should try to convince Gaerin to turn back.

Gaerin was less conflicted. He was normally the one insisting that they clean up their own mess. In their current situation, he was certain that doing so wasn't possible. They didn't have the means to handle trolls... in the rain, without spells, and with only one shield between them. He was being practical; responsible; wise.

The trees that lined the southern edge of the road sagged under the weight of the deluge. Branches creaked and moaned, swaying in wind gusts as they passed. Wet, droopy grass covered the meandering hills and plains to the north. Daylight played and flickered across the blades, the puddles, and even the distant air. That told Lyla the rain was nearly over, or at least they'd be walking out of it shortly.

"Ya know... say what you will, but I didn't get bit by a single mosquitoe at all last night," he joked.

They'd walked in silence since leaving the ruins. An unbearably long time for him to remain silent, and a miracle for his wife. He recognized the situation for what it was. They had remained silent because of the gravity of their situation.

Gaerin knew Lyla well enough to realize that she was stewing over the trolls. That was the reason for her silence. Lyla stewing over a subject was never a good thing. The least he could do was lighten their mood.

Lyla knew what he was trying to do and played along. "Well, that will all change when they evolve and adapt to all this rain... and learn to swim through the sky," she retorted.

Gaerin laughed and shot her a smile.

She stopped walking and gently grabbed his arm, bidding him to join her. They stood in silence for a moment, staring directly into one another's eyes. He could see the pain in hers; the sorrow. She was far more upset than he'd expected.

"We should handle this, and you know it," she insisted.

"With what?" he demanded.

He tried to be gentle with his tone, but was sure his words had come out harsher than he intended. The exhaustion was getting to him. They hadn't properly slept in two days.

Suddenly the rain stopped. The sound of gentle pattering that had surrounded them all night vanished abruptly. They hadn't realized how loud the rain had been until the silence filled its void. Gaerin popped his ears as they adjusted, wincing oddly.

"Oh, thank fuck!" Lyla yelled.

A doe that had been watching them panicked and fled deeper into the wood, alerted by her outburst. They barely noticed.

"Look... you need rest. We can't do anything without your spells. We also need fire to do the job properly, and everything is still saturated. Worse... I doubt they stayed put, which means tracking them down. All of that will take time. So... that means food, water... supplies," he explained, his hands on her shoulders.

He pulled her into his chest and held her for a moment. She protested briefly, but then nuzzled into his arms and closed her eyes. Whether or not she liked the idea, she knew that he was more in tune with her exhaustion than she was.

"We'll handle this. Let's get our wits about us, rest a bit and see what we can come up with. Okay?" he asked.

"I love you sometimes," she answered.

"Sometimes," he agreed, holding her tighter.

∴ ∴ ∴

MORDECHAI FOCUSED his mind, leveraging decades of study and practice toward lucid dreaming. He focused his eyes on the inside of his lids, then pushed his focus past them until tiny specks of light appeared amidst the blackened void. He brought forth the memories of the event, and focused his mind on a singular point.

As the dream state took hold, he found himself standing in silence at the center of the Waystation's main room. Its wooden floor gave way to cobblestone foundation in several places. Weather-worn walls surrounded him, and there was a faint smell of general mustiness in the air.

Small gusts of wind whirled throughout the building, stench and decay wafting about in bursts. The scene and its ambiance would have made most people sick, but Mordechai was not most people. He had an unfortunate level of experience in matters of death.

With a sigh, he studied the corpses before him. Small remnants of bolt shafts protruded from their chests, tearing through the cloth and leather of their ineffective armor.

Were they out of brigandine? The school should have equipped these lads better, he wondered.

He withdrew a small wand from under his robe and used it to manipulate their clothing. The bolts had hit them from relatively close range. Major bruising around the entry wounds, cracked ribs... all signs indicated they were close to their attacker.

No other readily visible wounds, no signs pointing to poison... it didn't seem like the product of an ambush. They knew their attackers. In fact, the wounds didn't appear to have been instantly fatal. There were no drag marks entering the station. It wasn't a dump site... the boys had walked here.

Dried droplets of blood led into the structure, from the entrance to where they were laying. The puddle beneath them confirmed his suspicion. They had somehow survived the attack long enough to seek shelter on their own.

Markus, the larger of the two boys, still leaned against the wall. Thorsten had slumped into Markus's lap. It seemed likely to Mordechai that Thorsten had expired first. Markus had held his friend as he died. *Shame*, he thought.

A crackle of energy interrupted his investigation. He stood and looked for the source. Another burst of energy came a few moments later, brightening the area just outside the door. Curious, and on his defensive, Mordechai stowed his feeble wand and walked outside.

A protection spell shimmered across his form as passed through the doorway.

Magical energies descended from the leylines above the clouds, disappearing below the cliffs at the northern edge of the Sacton River to the south. Strange light glowed from the area below, pulsing and growing in strength.

He stepped out onto the bridge and looked down at the mysterious occurrence. Runes cut through the air, forming a very large doorway. The runes shown an iridescent blue, with faint purple flames licking about their edges. The line of runes held steady in the shape of a large square, while white light filled the void between them.

A *portal*, he recognized.

The portal moved, abruptly, toward him. The inner light stretched behind it, forming a cube of smoky white light, floating over the shoreline. Suddenly the portal closed, and the light dissipated.

Mordechai had studied magic for as long as he could remember. In twelve-hundred years of study, he'd never experienced forces like these.

Two combatants spilled out of the cube of energy as it faded. He watched as they battled their way around the camp. It was an impressive display of skill. The occupants of the camp stood watching, many of them terrified.

As the events progressed below him, Mordechai withdrew into the recesses of his mind. With focus, he slowed the visions. The exit portal was imminent, and he wanted time to study it. He had sensed energies beyond the portal at the time of its occurrence. However, there hadn't been enough time to reach into them as they occurred.

None of the people below wielded magic. That told him the energies were from elsewhere. Since the event involved portals, he was certain their source was on the other side.

As the final portal opened slowly beneath him, he reached out with his mind. Time slowed almost to a halt at his bidding. He could see the individual particles of energy flowing toward the portal so slowly they appeared to hover in mid air.

He closed his eyes and pushed his essence into the field, seeking its source. There were several sources of magic on the other side. The first seemed more powerful than the sum-total of all casters at Fel'Vizsiour.

Whatever it was, the power it held was raw and unbridled. It hadn't played a part in creating the portal. Its presence was blinding, forcing him to shy away. He withdrew his inspection and moved his focus to the others.

Two other sources of power came into view. He closed his eyes tighter out of reflex, pushing his mind to reach them. The primal forces of Paradox magic radiated from the first. He could feel similarities between the caster and the portal's energies.

Shifting his focus, he pushed his mind toward the third source. Time magic rolled out of the being in waves. The source seemed familiar.

What are you, he wondered.

Casting aside the rest of the vision, he narrowed his mind on the source of the Time magics. Biting back against the pain, he forced himself deeper. He pushed harder, thrusting his mind further, until he became one with the being.

Its form was familiar. He felt its hands extended outward in positions he often used. Its stance was familiar, as was the weight of the robe and chest-piece it wore. Everything about the man's form felt natural, as if he belonged to it.

By the gods... you're- "Me!" Mordechai blurted aloud as he awoke. "I caused it!"

He shot upright in his bed, his lucid dream concluded. Blood trickled from his nose, across his lips and down his chin. He had pushed too hard in search of answers. Pain radiated from his head, through his neck, and into his torso. His body would take time to heal.

What he had seen concerned him.

How far into the future did I just see? What could have driven me further into Time casting?

He needed to know more.

He needed to return to Fel'Vizsiour and research the revelation further.

∴ ∴ ∴

TYLEE WOKE to the smell of dawnfry. Her eyes still crusted with sleep, she reached to her side in search of Laurence. The space beside her was empty.

She sat upright and opened her eyes, checking the room for him. He had agreed to leave in the morning, but she hadn't expected that to happen before she woke. She'd hoped for one last hug, or kiss... a proper goodbye.

Instantly depressed, she flopped back down onto the hay mattress. A gentle knock followed closely after, breaking the silence of her room.

"Go away," retorted Tylee angrily. She was in no mood to begin her day.

"The quicker we get to Raven's Nest, the quicker you can see Laurence again," offered Bronsin from the hallway in muffled tones.

She didn't want to get out of bed. She didn't want to travel without Laurence by her side. Unable to think of a viable argument, she moaned in protest.

"Your mother insisted that I 'see to it' you got dressed and came downstairs promptly. So either you come out and join me, or I'll be forced to... uh... 'see to it,'" he explained. He paused for a moment, listening, and then added, "Please don't make me 'see to it', m'lady."

"Fine!" she said, displeasure in her tone. She crawled out of bed in a huff and thumped her feet onto the floor sternly. Mother always sent Bronsin to do her dirty work.

He listened through the door as she dramatically stomped across the room and rifled through her things. Hearing her compliance, he sighed in relief and stepped back from the door, leaning against the wall on the other side of the hall to wait. She emerged a few minutes later wearing her traveling leathers.

"It's all yours," she stated snidely.

Tylee turned on her heel and proceeded downstairs. The mess in her room was to be his problem. Releasing a sigh, he stepped into her room and packed her belongings.

She descended the stairs and looked out across the dining room. Mordechai and Delriahna were already seated at their familiar table.

"You folk should come more often! Business is crazy!" Wendy remarked. She whipped past Tylee in a hurry on her way to the kitchen.

Tylee made her way between tables, stools, and people. When she arrived at their table, she threw herself onto the bench next to Mordechai in a huff. The table jostled a bit as she landed, spilling some of Mordechai's coffee. He gave her a stern look.

"Does it matter, mother? He's in class, I won't see him for weeks. Or months. Or years," she whined.

"He'll visit Raven's Nest often, dear," her mother remarked, coldly.

"Every Ris'Enliss, at least," added Mordechai.

A single tear rolled down Tylee's cheek. Delriahna took notice. "I'm sorry, hun," she said. She reached across the table carefully, dodging the bowls of meat and eggs, and placed her hand on top of Tylee's.

"I-" she started. "I dreamed of being his wife for my entire life and when it finally happens, I get less than a week with him and share a single bed? How is that fair?"

Tylee knew that her usual antics were over the top. She found humor in the responses that her actions drew. Taking things too far came naturally, as did pretending she was ignorant.

Drama had been her primary source of entertainment as a child. Growing up as an only child in a small town with protective parents made her feel trapped. Over the years, acting out and causing a scene had become part of her personality.

She couldn't hide her emotions behind a defensive barrier. She couldn't hide how she was feeling. Laurence's departure made her realize that she'd never learned to cope with her emotions. She wasn't able to process what she was feeling. Her feelings flowed freely down her cheeks.

"Oh, hun," said Delriahna, gripping Tylee's hand more firmly.

Delriahna saw the pain in her eyes. It wasn't normal 'Tylee' behavior. She knew her daughter's antics were a way of getting attention. Her dramatic scenes were often humorous, but also frustrating.

Tylee's usual antics revealed her own failings as a mother. In their efforts to protect her, they had isolated her and prevented proper social growth. The scene before her was obviously not one of those antics. She couldn't remember the last time she'd seen her daughter cry without dramatics.

Delriahna looked to Mordechai for support. After seeing her stare through his peripheral vision, he closed his eyes, sighed and prepared himself to enter the conversation. He was unaccustomed to emotional fragility, or how to quell it.

Books and scrolls didn't cry. Matters of state rarely involved tears. War and conflict were about unbridled passion, anger and fear. Those were the things that made sense to him. With a sigh, he decided to speak pragmatically. He could only hope that Tylee would see reason, despite her emotions.

"Laurence is a very capable man," he started. "If I am correct in my supposition, he will attain a position of authority within his class in record time. This will afford him additional liberties. Visitation to Raven's Nest happens during days of rest, which usually take place on Ris'Enliss.

"Even if he were to under-perform my estimations, he would still see you on those days, which amounts to once per week. Supposing he achieves what I expect, you will see him much more frequently," Mordechai explained.

Stifling back tears as best she could, she peered into Mordechai's eyes. Sheepishly, she asked, "Do you really think so?"

"I do," he said with a nod. He then returned his gaze to his meal and added, "Eat up. We have much to do, a great distance to travel, and we are precious short on time."

"Precious short on time? Laurence will arrive this afternoon. What's the rush?" asked Delriahna.

"With Laurence gone, I'm left with the responsibility of escorting you. I am expected at both Fel'Rechaun and Fel'Vizsiour simultaneously. There are matters upon which I must report, evidential materials to catalog, and research to be conducted. As such, I must travel quickly and report to both schools in as timely a manner as possible. If... that is okay with you, m'lady," he said with a flourish of his hand.

With a roll of her eyes, Delriahna resumed her meal.

Tylee followed her example, though with the knots in her throat and swelling of her sinuses she was barely able to force her food down.

Bronsin passed through the tavern several times carrying their luggage. When his task was complete, he returned, paid for their expenses, and grabbed a sack of food for himself rather than join them at the table. Wendy happily prepared his meal, thanking him for the group's patronage. As he headed toward the door, he paused briefly, looked over to his companions, and barked, "Coming?"

With that, they all wiped their mouths and removed themselves from the establishment. Shortly thereafter, they were back on the road.

ASPIRATION

Ris'Nammlil, Oghenfall 20th, 113 of the 2nd Era

Horror brings one's strength to light,
Another clings to hope.
It's all for naught, yet still they fight,
Their battle's not begun.

Night's Writ, Parable 12

AIR RUSHED gently past Laurence's face as he leaned around Kyrilis's left shoulder. The trees below seemed little more than weeds, and the fluctuations in the landscape across the rolling hillsides made the plains seem like ocean waves. The sun was close to setting in the west. It was blindingly bright from their elevation, casting deep shadows towards them.

Bah'Shiri was an impressive creature. He'd heard tales of griffins and seen drawings in Arcturus's books. He'd never expected to see one in person, let alone ride one. He held onto Kyrilis as tightly as her sword would allow. Occasionally she released the reins with her right hand and reached down to ensure his arms were firmly in place around her hips.

At the moment, however, none of those things mattered to him. He'd totally forgotten about the beautiful world beneath them, or the allure of the woman to which he desperately clung. The only thing that mattered to him now—the reason he was peering over her shoulder—was the tower of Fel'Rechaun in the distance.

"Amazing, isn't it?" asked Kyrilis.

The tower stood at the center of a large, complex structure.

Walls stretched across the landscape, leading away from the tower like curved spokes in a wheel. Each line of wall had a gentle curve, creating a spiral when viewed from above. The far edge of each inner wall joined the outer wall that encircled the entire complex, completing the spoked-wheel appearance. Atop each intersection stood a watchtower. The central tower and primary building of Fel'Rechaun was taller than anything he'd seen or imagined, rising more than three hundred feet into the sky.

Eight courtyards of equal size surrounded the central tower. Each had a purpose, and a unique collection of buildings. Three of the courtyards contained an arena of unique size and shape. Large gatehouses stood at each cardinal direction, providing four entrances to the school's grounds. Each gate included a nearby barracks and two watchtowers.

They began their descent in a circle above the complex. Laurence saw several people staring up from below, watching their flight. Bah'Shiri came to rest outside the northern gatehouse, next to the Western Reach, and the two of them dismounted. Laurence adjusted his armor and sword, while Kyrilis patted her mount on the maw and whispered a command.

The griffin backed away several feet and took flight. She flew up and to the top of the central tower, becoming a mere speck in the distance as Laurence watched.

∴ ∴ ∴

GAERIN STOOD atop the hill, signaling for Lyla to join him. He'd climbed up to look for a place they could rest and had instead found something else entirely. When she arrived at his side, he pointed to the north. Across the field before them, near the tree-line on the far side, a thin line of smoke was gently rising into the sky. The branches and leaves at the edge of the wood diffused the smoke, leaving very little for them to see, but see it they had.

Farmland stretched between the distant smoke and where they stood, starting at the base of the hill beneath their feet. The road lay behind them, at the other side of the hill. The field seemed well tended; rows of corn spanned the expanse to their right, beanstalks filled the center and wheat sprawled over hills to their left. It was a fairly wide variety of crop, which told Gaerin that the residents weren't likely to travel for trade.

"We couldn't see the smoke from the road because of the hill, and the trees. Wise considering the trolls less than a day's travel west. Obviously the farmers have been here a while. They might not take kindly to strangers," supposed Gaerin.

"There's no town nearby to defend them, so they're probably well armed. That means they're capable of helping us with the trolls. I'm sure they'd appreciate us clearing them out," she offered.

"Well... rather than us stand here making assumptions, why don't we walk over and find out?" he asked.

"It's that or keep going east. Telon's Respite should be nearby, and the Engle Plateau just beyond that. So... should we disturb these farmers? Or not?" debated Lyla.

"We riled the trolls. We caused the issue. I think it's best we handle this quickly, which means we can't afford all that travel if we can help it. If they can't, or won't help... then we'll make other plans," reasoned Gaerin.

"Agreed," she responded.

They crossed the field slowly, stepping carefully around sprawling bean plants tied to undersized stakes. Gaerin had a mind to stay for a while and give them a helping hand, but he knew they didn't have the time.

Lyla sighed in frustration behind him, agreeing with his sentiment.

The farmhouse was small; constructed from thick logs, chinked with black tar. Several gaps had formed between the logs as the chinking dried out and receded. Algae and black mold dotted the building's patchy hay roof in small patches.

Rusted farming implements, rotted furniture, small tufts of moldy hay, and piles of forgotten household things lay strewn about the yard. The smell of age, filth, and musky dampness permeated the area.

Viewed on its own, the state of the farmhouse and the contents of its yard suggested its owners had abandoned it long ago. The sound of erratic, repetitive thumping on the other side of the home suggested otherwise.

They crept around the house slowly, hoping not to startle the owners. They had to remind themselves that they'd just crossed a field of fairly healthy crops. All things considered, the farm as a whole seemed functional, even if its dwelling was ill kept.

As they neared the other side of the building, Gaerin could see a small balding head. It bobbed up and down, keeping pace with a small mallet that its owner was swinging. Its owner was small, barely larger than a human child.

The small man was humming a simple song to himself at low volume. He worked happily, blissfully unaware of the world around him. A tuft of wheat lay on a stump in front of him. His mallet whipped through the air in rapid little bursts, threshing the wheat and pounding the stalks.

"Excuse me, sir," said Lyla. They stopped walking a few feet behind him and waited for a response.

The small man whipped his head around and bounced on his log seat, startled. His wrinkled cheeks squished upward to make room for his wide open mouth, which lacked most of its teeth. A scruffy, mottled beard and mustache framed his mouth like an old, tattered wreath. The pink skin of his large, bulbous nose glistened with sweat in the sunlight.

Gray and black mottled hair clung desperately to the sides and back of his head, constantly at risk of falling out. His right eye opened wide upon seeing them. His left remained scrunched behind a small monocle. The tiny man stood, dropped his mallet and approached them.

"Who be ye?" he asked. His voice was small and creaky.

"I am Gaerin, and this is my wife Lyla."

Gaerin placed his right hand on Lyla's left shoulder as he spoke, in case there was any confusion.

"We're here to see if you can help... you see-" Lyla started.

"I'm Gremill, and this here be my farm. Yer trespassing," he barked.

They weren't sure if he was angry or joking. The strange contortion in his face when he tried to think of which words to use hadn't helped that impression in the slightest.

"There, um," Gaerin cleared his throat. "There be trolls up yonder, and we figured you could help us kill em," he said, mimicking the old man's pattern of speech.

Lyla stifled a laugh.

"Goll darn trolls!" belted Gremill.

He started stomping around dramatically in the dirt, making little circles with his over-sized feet. He settled down after a moment and continued, "Every time I chase em off, they come right back. I tries to keep yonder fire goin, but it don't help much."

"Well... that's why we're here, Gremill. We want to help," explained Lyla. It took all of her effort not to laugh at the small, adorable man.

"How you know my name?" Gremill asked. He leaned forward,

squinting inquisitively, and adjusted his monocle to get a better look at her.

"Um-" started Lyla.

"Nah, I'm messin with ya," he said snickering. "Come o'er this way."

As they walked, Gaerin couldn't help but ask, "Are you a halfling?"

"Aye, me pappy were a dwarf and me mama were a human. Ain't seen a dwarf since pappy gone. Ain't seen much o' anyone since I were a boy 'cept fer trips to town, come to think o' it," answered Gremill.

"How did you end up way out here?" asked Lyla.

"Mama said it were cause city folk didn't like folk o' my kind. She moved us out here to live off the land. Is fine, though. Land's fine. Trolls," he shrugged, "they not so fine."

"Well, we like you plenty," stated Gaerin.

When he reached the back of the farmhouse, he waved his little arm at a little shed. When they hesitated to open it, he sighed and yanked it open for them, then back up and waved his hand at it again.

"Ye can take what ye need. I find this stuffs when folk dies nearby. I can't use it, so I puts it here," he said, walking back to his work. "Clean up when yer done," he called back over his shoulder.

"What a strange little man," whispered Lyla.

"I don't know *what* I expected, but this *wasn't* what I expected," added Gaerin.

They looked through the small collection of rusty weapons and armor for a while, trying to decide what might help them with the trolls.

∴ ∴ ∴

THE NORTHERN gatehouse was an imposing sight. The builders had carved its outer wall into the shape of a lion's head, standing forty foot tall. The portcullis was up, its spiked feet serving as the lion's iron teeth. The eyes of the lion acted as arrow slits through which archers kept a close eye on them both.

Guards stood watch along the walls to either side. Several more stood atop a raised platform behind the center of the lion's head. Twenty feet on either side, guard towers rose into the sky.

Kyrilis looked back at Laurence, to see if he was ready to proceed. His nerves were in shambles. He could only remember one day in his life where he'd been so anxious.

Several years prior, he'd almost leaned in to kiss Tylee. It was during one of their visits to the Reincrik. He hadn't been able to muster the courage to go through with it. She had even leaned his way, sensing his motivations and agreeing with them, but a fish had saved his nerves, hooking itself on his line. He spent the next few moments awash with both relief and regret. Tylee had given him the most confused look in response. Regret was always present when he remembered that day. Regret... and anxiety.

The gates before him weren't Tylee, though. The rest of his adult life stood before him. It was his livelihood, his chance at revenge... at honor. He had to take action. No fish was going to give him an easy way out.

Smiling at Kyrilis sheepishly, he began walking as confidently as he could. As he reached her side, she joined him and matched his pace. She was nearly two-foot shorter than he was and had to move her legs much faster to keep up. That didn't seem to bother her in the slightest.

As they approached the gates, a guard stepped forward into the center of the road.

"My lady," he said, saluting. He brought the spear he was holding before him, held it at center with both of his arms firm, nodded his head and then looked back to meet her gaze.

"Dahsh," she answered, "this is Laurence Ravencrest. He is a late arrival for this year's class and has information gathered during his journey. We must speak with the Lord Commander promptly. Please send word to Karzden. He will need to collect Laurence once we've concluded our meeting."

"Aye," confirmed Dahsh. He turned on his heel and strode back toward the gate, signaling for a messenger as he approached.

"This way," she stated. She started walking again, and Laurence followed suit. "This is real, Laurence. There are structures and politics in play that you have yet to learn. If you are wise, you will listen more than you speak and focus on learning to navigate the landscape here.

"If what Mordechai says of you is true, I've no doubts you can handle the physical expectations they will have of you. So, spend your time soaking up the things you didn't learn at home," she explained.

"I will," he answered agreeably.

They passed through the gates and into the first courtyard.

Gates to their left and right passed under the inner walls. Buildings lined the courtyard, each bearing a sign describing the office within. Kyrilis strode past them all, heading for the steps on the far end. She was leading him to the central tower.

Laurence noticed several people inspecting him as they passed. He looked at Kyrilis questioningly. She paused for a moment and turned to him.

"You are wearing the armor of a Griffin Guard. I'll grant you that the armor is older and more subtly intricate, but it is Griffin Guard armor none-the-less. You also arrived on griffin back. They don't, however, recognize you. Effectively, you are dressed above your station. I suggest you strive to earn that station. For now, let them look. Let them question," she explained with a wink.

After a quick nod of assurance, she turned and continued walking. He joined her side once more and smiled as she continued. "Let the spectacle of you grow within their minds. It might give you an advantage in your interactions, if you handle yourself appropriately."

Laurence nodded in agreement. He was in the thick of things, and Fel'Rechaun was no longer just a dream. He had arrived.

As they reached the lower step leading toward the tower's entrance, the two great doors above them opened and an armor-clad figure stepped out onto the landing. His highly polished plate armor was dark gray with a slight blue tinge. A purple sash adorned his waist, hanging low and loose around the top of the scabbard at his left hip. The hilt of his sword was exquisite.

His head was balding, with only remnants of his white hair remaining. His full beard was thick, long, and well groomed. The man before them was noticeably strong, with broad shoulders. The weight of his armor did not seem to concern him, despite his obvious age.

"Kyrilis," the man acknowledged as they completed their ascent. "Do you bring word of our initiates?"

He spoke with a very direct tone. His voice revealed his age, yet expressed a hunger and drive typically reserved for younger men.

"Yes, Lord," she answered, holding her sword arm to her chest in salute. "I also bring a witness... one that is also a gifted recruit," she finished.

"Recruit?" he asked inquisitively.

He stepped closer to Laurence and inspected the boy. As he did, he touched and hefted portions of Laurence's armor. He finished his inspection with the crest upon Laurence's left breast.

"Not just any recruit, Kyrilis. You've brought me Gahl's great grandson." Looking deep into Laurence's eyes, he added, "I served with Arcturus, lad. His letter of request for Gahl's armor spoke highly of you."

"I bring unfortunate news," stated Laurence in a somber tone.

"Let's get down to it then, shall we?" suggested Fahrul. He clapped Laurence on the shoulder reassuringly and turned to enter the tower.

The guards stationed beside the doors saluted as they passed. Kyrilis nodded in response. Fahrul ignored the gesture and strode past them.

"Preita... ale, now!" he barked as they entered.

A small woman rushed off to retrieve the ale, her bare feet pattering across the stone floor of the massive room. The room was nearly forty feet in diameter, and the domed ceiling stretched twenty feet above. It struck Laurence that the room was almost a perfect half sphere.

Cedar bookshelves and cabinets lined the walls, separated at intervals by ebony doors. Twelve thick acacia beams stretch upward from the walls, meeting at the peak of the ceiling. Murals occupied the space between the beams along the dome, depicting battles from the War of the Wilds.

A chandelier hung from the center of the dome, representing the sun. Three colored glass globes encircled the chandelier, each representing a moon; Provoss, Aygos to one side, and the smaller globe for Zathos, the day moon, on the other.

Fahrul led them to a large table in the center of the room. Piles of books and scrolls sat on the far ends of the table. Various inkwells, quills, weights and small iron figures lay strewn in a circle around the space before the commander's chair. He proceeded to his side, sat, and bid them to sit across from him.

∴ ∴ ∴

KYRILIS UNBUCKLED the strap on her back-slung scabbard, slid it off and placed it on the floor next to her chair. Laurence watched her movements, then did the same. After taking their seats, they waited patiently for the commander to start the conversation. Several minutes passed before the echoes of Preita's pattering footsteps broke the silence.

The small, feeble girl brought a jug of ale to the table along with three goblets. She cast Laurence a sheepish grin under her unkempt hair as she poured the ale. The commander watched her patiently, distributing the goblets to his guests as she finished with each.

In any other setting, Laurence might have assumed she was a slave. Fahrul looked upon her fondly, though, dissuading any such thought. There was a caring air about him, despite the requirements of his station.

"I am Lord Commander Fahrul Tamrilson. I understand that you've been training your entire life to attend our school. Arcturus spoke highly of you. While he may have ruffled a few feathers as he left the King's service, I owe that man my life and have always respected him.

"If his praise is accurate, we're lucky to have you. However, we have matters to attend before you can begin your studies. Of utmost importance is the matter of Markus and Thorsten. Kyrilis," he said, turning his gaze, "what have we learned of their whereabouts?"

"Mordechai found their corpses at the Sacton River Waystation, my lord," she answered.

"That is unfortunate," sighed Fahrul.

"Mordechai found them a few nights ago. He met Laurence's group that same night. He is making use of their carriage to transport the bodies here now," she answered.

"If these bandits can best two of our trainees, the citizens nearby haven't much hope of resistance. Since our recruits are no longer involved, I think it's time the Legion takes over," he stated.

Fahrul turned and snapped his fingers to get the attention of a guard. Before Kyrilis could interrupt, he began, "Fetch Karzden. We need to send word to-"

"Pardon, sir, but the bandits are already dead," interrupted Laurence.

"Is this so?" Fahrul asked to Kyrilis, his arm still extended toward the guard.

"It is, my lord," answered Kyrilis.

Fahrul waved the guard off and returned his attention to Laurence. "Explain."

"The day after we left Mooncrest, three bandits attacked my camp. I charged and killed the one with the crossbow, and the others fell shortly thereafter. I was on high alert, thanks to recent events, which allowed me to respond quicker than they anticipated."

"I'm to believe you single-handedly killed three men where two Fel'Rechaun trained recruits could not?" asked Fahrul.

"His companions, and Mordechai, have all confirmed the tale, sire," answered Kyrilis on his behalf.

Fahrul sat back in his chair, leaning on his elbows with his hands clasped a few inches from his chin. He contemplated for a moment, studying Laurence before responding.

"Impressive, lad... very impressive. It is disheartening to have lost Markus and Thorsten. Though it seems a twist-of-fate that the same event brought us a recruit twice their better."

He leaned forward, grabbed his goblet and lifted it in a toast. After swallowing the frothy ale, he continued, "Any word on the crossbow?"

"Unfortunately, sir, the crossbow shattered under my blow as I cut down the man wielding it. As to the rest, I handed their loot to Mordechai. He brings it with him promptly," answered Laurence.

"I see why you carried the lad here, Kyrilis. Even with this letter from Andor Colvin," he said, waving a piece of parchment, "there would have been little choice but to release his placement until next season. His classmates have completed their entry duals and weapon safety training. Tomorrow, they will perform weapon handling demonstrations and begin the ranking trials. You're aware, Kyrilis, that missing those would prevent his entry," explained Fahrul.

Kyrilis nodded, acknowledging the commander's point. Laurence raised an eyebrow.

"The ranking trials define your position within the class, lad. They are, effectively, how one earns their way into the class. The rules that govern them are not open to... bending. Now... your father-in-law mentioned in this letter you'd experienced a loss in your family? He didn't go into detail. He seemed more interested that his new son-in-law maintain attendance to earn political position and favor with the King," said Fahrul.

He tossed the letter across the table in case Laurence wished to read it.

Sighing, Laurence began, "The family loss that he *glossed over* was the vicious slaughter of Arcturus right in front of me... I nearly died with him."

Kyrilis closed her eyes and lowered her head. She had heard the tale, but not yet from his lips. She could feel his emotions.

Fahrul sat back in his chair again, catching notice of Kyrilis's somber demeanor. He waited patiently for Laurence to further his tale.

"Earlier that day, uncle Gaerin presented me with this armor. Arcturus wasn't happy I was coming here to take up my father's lifestyle, but he said that he couldn't let me do so unprotected. Gaerin suggested that—since I was traveling to Fel'Rechaun alone—I should sleep in my armor and get used to doing so.

"When I went to bed that night I kept the armor on. Later that night, a disturbance in the alchemy shop downstairs woke me. I crept down to find the doors locked, and men yelling at Arcturus about a curse from within the shop. Since I couldn't get in to help him, I went back upstairs and dove out of my bedroom window. Thankfully, it had been raining since early afternoon and the ground was softer for it.

"I rounded the corner, sword in hand, heading for the front door. When I arrived, several men were standing guard. I killed the first haphazardly and got lucky with the second. Both were very experienced men," he clarified.

Fahrul raised his right eyebrow, as if in disbelief. However, he remained silent.

As Laurence continued, he removed his left gauntlet. "A third man rounded the front of the house and attacked. He was twice as fast as I, and much stronger. He quickly overcame me. I was sure that I was dead. That's when this man walked out of the shop," he stated.

He showed Fahrul the tattoo on his left palm. Fahrul's face paled.

"This man... this, Drakahl... exited the alchemy shop with my dead grandfather draped over his left arm like a sack of potatoes. He dropped my Pap's corpse on top of me, laughed, shattered my leg, and left me for dead.

"After they'd gone, I crawled into the burning building, gathered supplies and healed myself. I then buried my grandfather, leaned on his grave and tattooed that monster's face on my hand so I would never forget," explained Laurence. "As it turns out, this is the *same* man that killed my father, and possibly Gahl as well."

With his story complete, he put his gauntlet back on. The room was silent, save for Preita's sobbing a short distance away.

"It is because of Drakahl that I will never be taken unaware again. It is because of Drakahl that I will always be ready to defend myself and those that I love. It is because of Drakahl that I must train; get faster; get stronger; get wiser," he finished, his words trailing off.

The anger that had risen in him during the retelling was giving way to sorrow. He tried not to let it show on his face.

"You've been through an unreasonable amount in such a short time. You are wise to come here rather than rushing off for revenge. Few would have had the wisdom to do the same. They... would be dead right now. You... shall survive this ordeal. We'll see to your training, though in martial areas you may not need as much of it as you think. Few could claim to have killed five grown men in open combat before they arrived at our school. Hells, son, half of our students might never kill a man," said Fahrul.

"His passion, and drive, are more worthy of note, sire," offered Kyrilis.

"Indeed, Kyr. My apologies. It isn't just about the killing, and it mustn't be. Laurence... if Kyrilis feels so fondly of your character and capabilities, then I must take her seriously. She is a keen judge of character and befriends few. She took it upon herself to rush you here, to ensure your future. You should take that to heart. It proves there are people who stand by you. Even people who've just met you... and *that*... speaks volumes," said Fahrul.

Laurence nodded, not knowing what words to use in response. He looked to Kyrilis and smiled. She smiled back reassuringly.

"Do not blame yourself for the death of Arcturus. Any man who could best the mighty Arcturus is one not to be trifled with. You bested two of his men, lucky or not. That fact alone should give you confidence. You dove through a second-story window, charged into battle knowing you were outnumbered, and managed to kill two men before you were taken down. And here you sit... alive and able to talk about it.

"If that wasn't enough, you dismantled a group of three bandits on your own. You unwittingly triggered the series of events that will deliver their victims, and their plunder, to this school. You are, whether you realize it or not, a very capable man. It will be my pleasure to see to it that when you leave here, you are more than capable of defeating this... '*Drakahl*'," said Fahrul.

Fahrul stood and extended his hand for Laurence to grasp. Laurence stood, nodded at the commander, and clasped his wrist in a swordsman's greeting. It was a greeting often used to show respect to another warrior, or knight.

The commander shook Laurence's arm, and then released it, adding, "Tolrin, by the way, was a fine, fine man. We trained here together, you know. He was the best the school had ever seen."

He could see the burning questions behind Laurence's eyes.

"Don't worry, we'll talk of him later. For now, I've duties to attend and you've got a Karzden to contend with," he said, pointing toward the door.

Laurence looked over to see a very burly, black-bearded man waiting rather impatiently for him.

"Take it easy on him Karzden, it's not his fault he was late. I'll... explain later," Fahrul called out.

Karzden nodded and visibly calmed in response. He waited patiently while Laurence equipped his sword and then escorted the lad down into the courtyard to begin his schooling.

∴ ∴ ∴

LYLA AND Gaerin settled into a pile of hay, intent on resting before their return trip. A small collection of equipment lay a few feet away, organized into neat little piles. Gremill's shed had provided them with two halberds, a new shield and two torches. The rest of the items in his stash had been too rusty or inappropriate for the task that lay ahead of them.

Gremill had been kind enough to feed them and allow their use of his barn. A full belly and sleep was exactly what Lyla needed to restore her access to spells. Galrath's power passed through her when she prayed, and the process was exhausting.

Gaerin pulled Lyla into his arms and stroked her back rhythmically as she fell asleep. He was nervous about their plans to hunt down the trolls. Fighting trolls was a young man's game, and he was no longer young. He didn't consider forty-four years to be particularly old, but his joints and bones liked to remind him of his limits.

Between their journey, the previous battle with the trolls, and the long walk to Gremill's farm, he wasn't sure his body was up to their task. His other concern was the time their hunt would require. He wanted to be across the Western Reach and on their way to Pelrigoss before Laurence could find out what they were doing.

Lyla settled into a rhythmic snore that invited him to join her. He secretly hoped that they would encounter the trolls during their trip back; that the trolls would ambush them and end their trek early. As he drifted off to sleep, he mused over the various ways he might convince Lyla to help him make that happen.

Gaerin awoke to the sounds of snapping and popping. His eyes shot open.

Lyla smiled down at him and stretched again. The tension in her back and shoulders almost sounded like small twigs breaking as the tension within them released.

Gaerin rolled his eyes and sighed as his heartbeat resumed its normal pace.

It was still night when they walked into the open air. The musty smell of the barn was hard to shake. It lingered with them for hours as they walked toward the ruins. Lyla was sure it was because their clothes were still sopping wet when they'd laid down in the hay. Gaerin assumed it was because everything Gremill owned was dirty.

Dawn had come and gone by the time they reached the ruins. They stopped a safe distance away and placed their tools on the ground to get organized. Lyla stashed their satchels next to the trees on the southern side of the road, while Gaerin prepared to light a fire.

"Remember," Gaerin started, pointing toward the halberds, "we aren't to slash with these, just impale them so you can to maintain distance."

"Not an idiot, dear," Lyla retorted.

"I know, I know. It's just, if we slash them when things get frantic and a piece comes off-"

"Then we'll have worsened our problem. I know. I get it," she said. "Not it, by the way."

"Not it?" he questioned.

"I'm not the one running up to them with a torch. That's you. That's all you," she stated defiantly.

"Oh... well... naturally," he answered with a playful shrug.

Gaerin gathered a bit of kindling and started a small fire. Lyla paid close attention to the woods to the south, the ruins to the west, and the field to the north. They didn't know if the trolls were still under the rubble, stalking them, or had fled to safer lands.

He lit both torches and began walking toward the ruin. Lyla slung a shield over each shoulder and followed, brandishing a halberd. Their normal weapons, hanging from their waists, tapped lightly against their right thighs as they moved.

The musty smell of troll blood hit Gaerin like a wave as he arrived at the ruin. He silently wished the smell of the barn would return to drown it out. Lyla grimaced and mouthed the word, 'phew,' as she joined him, wrinkling her nose.

Horse carcasses lay in front of the building, half eaten and rotting. Most of the Waystation had completed its collapse, leaving piles of rubble in its place. They climbed atop the rubble near the road and looked toward the spot where they'd buried the trolls. It was the only patch of ground that was clear. The trolls had dug their way out.

"Crap," Lyla whispered.

They searched in silence for an hour, but could find no trace of the trolls. The smaller buildings had collapsed long ago, leaving few places for trolls to hide. Feeling defeated, they met up at the road again.

Gaerin dropped the torches in frustration and put his hands on his hips.

"I guess they got away," declared Gaerin.

"Hold on a second," chirped Lyla.

Something had caught her eye. She crept north between the ruins towards the bushes on the other side. As she got to her destination, she yelled, "Crap, crap, crap!" at increasingly higher volumes.

"What is it, dear?" Gaerin inquired.

He walked over to her cautiously, a knot welling in the pit of his stomach. She pointed at the broken branches and large tracks on the ground, heading toward Gremill's farm.

"Oh, no," he gasped.

She nodded grimly.

They quickly ran to gather their things and then raced off to save Gremill as fast as they could.

∴ ∴ ∴

VISIONS OF a distant landscape swirled out of existence, replaced with wisps of black smoke and a swirl of gray fog. Back creaking with the sounds of old age, she stood upright before the crystal ball, contemplating.

Everything is in motion.

She was quite pleased.

"Garoth!" she called out, her ancient voice echoing through the halls eerily.

A tall, oafish man bent his way through the door at her beckon.

The doorways of Kulgan Palace stood eight feet tall and four feet wide, yet they were a challenge for poor, witless Garoth.

"Garoth, it is time. Send Shaer'Thog to greet his master. By the time he reaches Dagoh Bay, Drakahl will have arrived," she commanded.

"Yes," confirmed the brute, in a deep, hollow hiss.

Garoth turned, ducked, and squeezed his way out of the chamber. His movement through the halls sent tiny tremors shuddering through the floor.

Many about the palace thought Garoth to be her golem; a magical construct designed to serve her without question. The reality of Garoth was much less exciting. He was merely a mountainous man of limited intelligence whom she had long ago charmed. When the charm wore off, he continued his service voluntarily.

She walked back to the crystal ball. After a moment of contemplation, she reached her left hand toward the shadows beside the table, closed her eyes and vanished. The highest room inside the tallest tower brightened as the shadows heaved and she stepped through them.

She crossed to the balcony on the opposite side of the room as a servant entered. With fear-driven urgency, the servant raced to the table beside the balcony. Fighting to stave off her trembling hand, she poured a glass of black wine and left as quickly as her feet would allow.

Nightweaver was a name first used by those she had once terrified, so many centuries ago. She preferred it to the other names she had heard, such as 'Night Witch'. The name 'Nightweaver' perfectly represented who she was, and what she was capable of. It was a name with a dark reputation. It was a name that afforded her anonymity.

There was a time when she had forgotten who she was. Cast adrift in the throes of mental chaos, she had turned to Vaxtra to attain power. 'Night Witch' had been an appropriate moniker for a time, for a witch is what she'd become; much to her regret.

Nightweaver was a more fitting name. She no longer drew on Vaxtra for power, and in fact had never needed to. Her powers extended far beyond what he could provide; it was he that had drawn upon her. As she'd regained her memories, the truth of their bond had filled her with rage.

She had lashed out upon the poor citizens of Tellrindos, rendering an entire city to dust in a night of hate-filled madness.

The affair had earned her a new name, and a vile reputation. A reputation that she now embraced and leveraged for her pursuits.

As the memories of thousands of years flooded her mind, she had realized two things. The first was that Vaxtra had twisted her to his will and taken advantage of her weakened state. He was using her, and she would have to discover a means of breaking free.

Her second realization was a product of her memory loss. As the memories rushed into her mind in an instant, she witnessed them with a new perspective. She had long fought for what was good, and right. Thousands of years seeking to protect her world and provide safety for its citizens. It had all been for nothing.

The room brightened as black tendrils of translucent, smoky energy stretched out from the witch's right hand. They encircled the wine glass and lifted it. As the glass slowly drifted through the air toward her, she raised her hand to receive it, without changing her gaze. She stood for a time in silence, staring at Zathos on the horizon while she sipped her wine.

"All is going as planned."

.˙. .˙. .˙.

MORDECHAI HAD kept them on the road for nearly two days. Whenever they complained, he waved them off and dismissed their protests by reminding them how pressing his duties were. When the horses showed signs of exhaustion, he imbued them to enhance their stamina.

Their journey took them past several towns. Gaierford, Dunforth and Ayerton all lay along their route. Every one of them was large enough to offer lodging. Mordechai had no interest in stopping.

Each town brought more travelers to the road; some arriving, others departing. The further north they traveled, the more heavily populated the road became. With travelers all around them, their complaints died down. Delriahna was the first to go quiet, her prim and proper air too fragile to suffer embarrassment.

Eventually the party gave in to his interests, and the crowd, and resigned themselves to silence. They rotated between horseback and the front of the carriage so they could sleep. Brief, bumpy, disrupted sleep was better than nothing, or so they reasoned.

The roads had been treacherous between Salvation Shire and Ayerton. That all changed as they entered the northern pass. The roads were better repaired the closer they came to Vaelin

Crossroads. The famed intersection between the Southern Reach, Western Reach and The King's Highway saw more traffic than any other stretch of road in the kingdom.

Vellen Crescent loomed high above Vellen Wood to the northeast as they passed Ayerton. The road rose and fell through the shallowest path through the foothills, bringing the forest in and out of view as if they rode atop waves in an ocean.

Arkhan Vaelin named the mountains of Vellen Crescent for their shape and location. Vellenheim, the Kingdom's capital, lay at the center of the crescent, protected on all sides. The King's Highway ran through the western pass, stretching from the Vaelin Crossroads all the way to the capital city.

They settled to a stop at the crossroads before them. A statue of Arkhan Vaelin stood at center, towering twenty feet above a small dais. Lush greenery formed a forty-foot circle around the dais. Equipped with benches and an altar for prayer, the park served as a brief respite for weary travelers.

The Southern Reach, Western Reach and The King's Highway flowed into a circular road bordering the park. Signs posted along each road instructed approaching travelers to circle the crossroads to the right. The circular road was twice as wide as the roads that joined it, allowing for easy ingress and egress.

The group watched for a short time as traffic flowed around the circle. When a gap appeared to the west, Mordechai nudged the group forward, merging into it as it passed. Carriages, horses and pedestrians traveled in unison around the circle. All merged into and out of the circle as if they were participants in a well-orchestrated dance.

As the group passed the entrance to The King's Highway, two guard towers loomed ominously above them to the east. The towers stood four stories tall on either side of road, guarding the route to Vellenheim. A stone bridge spanned the distance between the upper floor of each tower, connecting the fortifications.

Several guards stood at their posts, peering down at the travelers that passed beneath the bridge. Banners bearing the colors and crests of several prominent houses hung from the bridge. The largest banner was of House Vaelin, bearing the crest of King Orluhnd IV.

Continuing around the circle, the great cliffs of the Engle Plateau bordered the road to their right. Acting as the southern border of the great plateau, the cliffs bordered the Western Reach for over one-hundred miles.

Tylee had tired of riding her horse as they passed Ayerton. She had wedged herself onto the bench between Bronsin and Delriahna. She watched the flow of people, carriages and horses around the circle in awe.

"There are more people here than in the whole of Mooncrest," she whispered to her mother.

"Yes, my dear, and these are but simple travelers. Wait until you see Vellenheim," Delriahna added.

Tylee's eyes lit up with wonder.

The group continued around the circle and exited onto the Western Reach. Travelers stretched ahead of them for as far as they could see. Tylee could hardly imagine so many citizens living within the Kingdom, let alone traversing a single road.

"Why are there so many?" asked Tylee.

"Many of them are traders," answered Bronsin. "My father used to work as a caravan guard. They transported goods along the Western Reach. Southern destinations are smaller and less desirable for trade. That is why we didn't see these crowds on the roads before Salvation Shire," explained Bronsin.

"Your father and I traveled to Vellenheim several times before you were born. If you find these crossroads overwhelming, that city would be the death of you. Mooncrest is much more a farming community, and of no comparison to this region in terms of population. I expect that Raven's Nest is much larger," said Delriahna.

"It is, my lady," added Mordechai. "The town has tripled in size since its days as Englevauld."

He'd slowed his pace and come alongside the carriage. They'd been so enthralled by the crowds about them—and their conversation—that they hadn't noticed.

"Raven's Nest has at least five times the permanent population of Mooncrest. Many of the residents either grow crops or produce goods for Fel'Rechaun and Fel'Vizsiour. Jorilund to the north produces most of the weapons, armor and clothing. Everything bound for Fel'Rechaun passes through Raven's Nest.

"Raven's Nest has just as many temporary residents, though. There are many who live there while their family members attend one of the two schools, then move back home. Others move there for the same reason but build a life for themselves and stay. Raven's Keep lies on the northern edge of town, protecting the region and its people, with over a thousand soldiers in its garrison," explained Mordechai.

Tylee smiled and waved at many passers-by, most of which did not return her hospitality.

Delriahna sat in contemplation, studying those they passed as if trying to discern their purpose and motivations.

Bronsin casually held the reins and ignored everything but the road before him.

Time seemed to pass more quickly on the Western Reach. Hours had passed before they realized it. Complaints and thoughts of exhaustion had vanished almost completely.

"Bear right!" called Mordechai.

To their right lay a stone ramp, carved into the cliff. It veered away from the Western Reach and ascended upward, like a tunnel with one side open to the elements. The ramp was wide enough for three carriages, side by side. A three-foot wall bordered the southern edge of the ramp, designed to keep travelers from falling to their deaths.

The carriage reached level ground atop the Engle Plateau, allowing Raven's Nest to come into view. It was far in the distance, and would likely take the rest of the day to reach. The city was much larger than Mooncrest. Farms sprawled as far as the eye could see to the north, beyond the keep.

A strange, twisted spire stood far to the north. It caught Tylee's eye as the carriage reached the plateau. She stared at it, trying to figure out what it was.

Mordechai caught her attention and pointed to her left. Far to the southwest, across the Western Reach, stood Fel'Rechaun. Her heart skipped a beat at the sight. She could see where Laurence was, even if she couldn't see him, and suddenly felt as if she were next to him. She was happy again, and all was right with the world.

∴ ∴ ∴

"WE'RE TOO late," said Gaerin.

He stood in front of the wheat field for a moment as his mind filled with dread. The broken, trodden stalks stretched out before them, leading in parallel lines toward the farmhouse. There were no signs of activity. The silence was deafening.

"Maybe he wasn't home?" hoped Lyla, sadness lacing her words.

Lyla backed away and hefted her load to the ground. Gaerin

sighed and followed her lead. Satchels, shields and weapons fell to the ground in a heap.

"We can at least clean up this mess," said Lyla, defeated.

"We couldn't have known," said Gaerin.

She dropped to the ground in front of their gear, sobbing. The emotions of the past few days were catching up to her.

"Let's get organized and see if we can't find Gremill, okay? He may be fine. Maybe he's hiding somewhere," he suggested, rubbing her back reassuringly.

With a nod, she sniffed back her sorrows and went to work. They stashed their satchels at the edge of the trees, gathered wood and lit a small campfire. After shouldering their shields, they each hefted a halberd in one hand and a torch in the other.

Gaerin lit his torch and set off across the field. Lyla lit her own and followed a few steps behind. The only sound they could hear was that of their own footfalls. The utter calm about them made Lyla feel uneasy.

Gaerin went left around the front of the house.

Lyla went right toward the rear.

After circling the home, they met on the other side. There was no sign of Gremill or the trolls. Gaerin shrugged, unsure of their next step. Lyla pointed past him to the spot where they'd seen Gremill working the day before.

Gremill's bench and stump were laying on their side a few feet away. His mallet lay on the ground nearby, caked with blood and flecks of wheat. A path led into the woods beyond Gremill's work area through broken and trodden underbrush.

Gaerin began following the trail carefully and methodically.

Lyla stayed a few steps behind him, ready to act.

Just ahead of them, something small and green writhed in the underbrush. Gaerin approached cautiously, expecting the worst. Lying in the bushes and weeds was a full-sized troll head, gnawing on a piece of what he could only assume was Gremill's corpse. Extending from the head was a ridiculously small, pulsating troll body.

Arcturus had once instructed them in everything he knew about trolls. How to fight them, how to kill them, and, most importantly, how to avoid them. 'Fire or acid,' he had explained. 'They regenerate wounds far too quickly and thoroughly from any other source. You must burn their flesh to stop their regeneration. It's the only way.'

Gaerin kept that knowledge in the back of his mind for decades.

It was information he never thought he'd have to use. The sight before them was proof that the legends were true, and it was a horrible scene to behold. Laying at Gaerin's feet was the severed head of the troll from the ruins, and it was growing a new body.

The troll rolled to face them, gnashing its teeth, and emitted a tiny growl. Its lungs and chest cavity weren't large enough to sound any fiercer. Halfling blood streamed from its mouth. The tiny arms flailed as if trying to claw them. The tiny legs whipped around unnaturally in a frenzy, as if trying to charge them.

It lay there on its back, pulsating and flailing about, unable to enact whatever vengeance it had in mind.

Lyla tapped Gaerin's right calf with her halberd, signaling him without speaking. He stepped aside to let her by. She crept up and lanced the tiny troll through the head with her rusty halberd. She then backed away, turned and headed back toward the farmhouse.

Gaerin followed, walking sideways. He kept his eyes on the surrounding forest, glancing occasionally over his shoulder to check on her.

Once in the clearing, she pushed the creature off her halberd's blade with her foot. Then she gathered a handful of thrashed wheat husks and stalks lying next to Gremill's pounding stump. Finally, she covered the tiny troll with the chaff and set it ablaze.

"One down," she mouthed.

Night was upon them, and the forest was nearly pitch black.

They returned to the spot where they'd found the troll and inspected the scene. It had been chewing on Gremill's leg, and nothing more. That indicated that the rest of him was elsewhere, and that meant the rest of the trolls were likely to be nearby.

Lyla choked back the sick that was welling up in her throat.

Gaerin stayed hunched over as he moved, holding his torch near the ground to check for any signs of passage.

Lyla followed and watched over his head, keeping her eyes on their surroundings.

A twig snapped in the distance. She turned to the left and peered into the darkness. There was nothing within her field of view, so she turned back to check in front of them. Just beyond their torch light stood a massive troll body with a tiny head. It was a few feet in front of Gaerin, who was too busy searching for tracks to notice.

"Gaerin!" she shouted

Gaerin looked up just in time to face the troll and raise his torch in defense. The troll shrieked and backed away briefly, halting its attack in mid-swing. Gaerin waved his torch at the beast and jabbed with his halberd, backing it away from them for a few moments.

Lyla ran toward the troll, using the distance that Gaerin had created to gain momentum.

The troll, still reeling, didn't notice Lyla's approach. Her halberd pierced through its right side and lodged between its ribs.

The creature howled and grabbed at her weapon, trying to pull it free. Black blood oozed from the wound, coating the troll's hands, making them slip along the shaft rather than grip firmly.

It stumbled backwards, tripped on its own feet and crashed to the ground with a tremendous thud.

Gaerin sprinted forward as fast as he could, dropped to his knees and slid up to the troll between its legs. His outstretched left arm shoved the torch into the creature's crotch firmly, setting the hair about its waist and pubic region ablaze.

The creature tried to howl in fear and pain, but the blood filling his lungs prevented it from doing so. It flailed about and rolled around desperately. Gaerin ducked under its flailing legs and kicked himself backwards to safety. The halberd ripped out of Lyla's grasp as the beast rolled to its side. The shaft snapped in two and drove deeper into the beast's chest.

Gaerin regained his feet. He handed his halberd to Lyla and began using the light from the burning troll to search for the others.

Lyla heard a very low growl on her left side. It was distant enough not to be an immediate threat, as if the owner was watching them and waiting. She signaled Gaerin to circle around and flank the beast and proceeded toward the sound.

Suddenly, the medium-sized troll jumped from the bushes ahead of her.

Lyla thrust her halberd into the creature's chest, but its momentum was too great for her to resist. Pushed backward by the beast, she drove the butt-end of the halberd into the ground, wedging it and impaling the beast under the force of its own weight.

It roared in pain, grabbed and snapped the shaft.

Suddenly, the small troll leaped from the bushes to her right, tackling her to the ground and knocking her torch from her hand.

Gaerin burst through the brush to her left and shoved his torch into the mouth of the impaled troll.

Lyla scrambled for her torch, but it was just out of reach.

The troll lashed out at her, pounding with its fists. She used her arms to absorb the blows as best she could. While her maille armor softened the blows slightly, it wasn't as resilient as plate. The troll broke her arms in several places within seconds, rendering them useless.

Gaerin rushed over, drawing his warhammer as he ran. He leapt into the air and drove it into the troll's skull with both arms as he landed at its side. The creature spilled backwards, its head split open.

"Get the torch," whimpered Lyla.

Gaerin retrieved the torch and lit the remaining troll on fire. He gathered kindling and branches, piling them on the corpses to ensure they would burn completely, and then returned to his wife.

"Are you okay?" he asked, concerned. She hadn't gotten up.

"It shattered my arms. I need you to get my armor off and do a bit of surgery," she said. The pain in her voice concerned him. The thought of doing surgery on his wife concerned him more.

"I'll get you back to the farm, but before we do surgery, I need to make sure we have destroyed every piece of troll," he said.

"Yeah... just get on with it," she moaned.

Gaerin helped her to her feet, and they made their way out of the wood. Once they were back at the farmhouse, he helped her into a chair on Gremill's porch. He made several trips away from the farmhouse to retrieve their belongings, burn the trolls, and gather the pieces of Gremill's corpse.

After returning for the last time, Gaerin built a small fire next to the farmhouse. He ran his warhammer through the flames to sear the troll blood off, then hooked it into his belt.

"How sharp is your dagger, love?" he asked as he joined her.

"Not sharp enough," she answered.

"All right... let me sharpen mine and we'll get this over with," he said.

He sat down in front of the fire and retrieved a whetstone and a waterskin from his satchel. After a few minutes, he returned to Lyla and sat his dagger on the small table next to her.

"You're sure about this?" he asked.

"Don't really have a choice," she answered. The pain had lulled for a time, but had returned in full force.

She gritted her teeth against the pain as he helped her armor off. Next came her gambeson, which was far more difficult to remove. Finally he removed her shirt, then draped it back over her chest to help with the cold air.

"Cut the back of my arms—not the front or sides—so you don't hit the artery. I need you to push the bones back into place," she instructed.

"Oh boy!" he said sarcastically. "Just what I always wanted to do!"

"Stop! Just get it over with," she moaned.

"Your entire arm?" he asked.

"Yes!" she belted.

Gaerin slowly dragged his dagger down the length of her arm, from her shoulder to her hand. Lyla screamed in pain. She wasn't sure how long she could hold out.

He used the tip of the dagger to push the muscles aside until he could see the bones within. Lyla shrieked and then growled at him to move faster. She could feel herself passing out.

Carefully, he pushed his fingers inside and nudged the bones back into position, one by one along her arm. Blood had coated her arm, right leg and the entire side of the chair. Lyla had passed out.

"Wake up!" Gaerin yelled. Gently, he tapped her left cheek, trying to wake her.

She was breathing, but he couldn't get her to regain consciousness. He suddenly felt regret that they had no healing potions. His wife was a healer, so they'd assumed potions to be unnecessary.

He knew the same surgery was necessary on her other arm. Realizing the pain from surgery had likely driven her into unconsciousness, he decided to risk operating on her other arm without waiting for her to wake up first.

After the bones in both arms had been set, he tried again to wake her. When she wouldn't wake, he ran to the satchels and retrieved his waterskin and splashed water in her face. A few more slaps and a bit of heart-racing panic later, she finally woke.

"Heal yourself! The bones are set!" he demanded.

"I... I can't-"

"You have to, you're bleeding out!"

"Did... you hit an artery?" she asked, feebly.

"No, but both of your arms are wide open from shoulder to wrist. You might want to help me out, here. We don't have any potions, and this was your idea," he said.

"Idiot," she said. It was clear that she was fading in and out of consciousness again.

"Oh no you don't," he blurted.

He slapped her hard in the face. She woke up completely and gave him the evilest look he'd ever seen from his wife.

"Stay awake and I won't have to do that," he offered.

She scowled at him and kept scowling as she muttered healing prayers. Her bones mended first, and then her muscles. Next she healed her arteries, and finally her skin.

As the last bit of skin sealed up around her wrists, she raised her arms as if checking them, reared back and slapped him far too hard for a woman that had just been healed.

∴ ∴ ∴

TYLEE'S DEMEANOR brightened dramatically when they finally reached the outskirts of Raven's Nest. Being so close to Fel'Rechaun—which she could see over the southern row of buildings—had her so excited she could hardly contain herself. She tried to smile at her mother, Bronsin, and Mordechai, but none of them seemed to notice.

The only thing on her traveling companions' minds was retaining lodging, and the beds that would come with it. As they traversed the main street, lined on either side with nearly identical brown stucco buildings, Delriahna spotted the sign she'd been looking for and called for them to stop. Bronsin dutifully pulled the carriage to the side of the street.

She climbed down from the carriage as it rolled to a stop, and without hesitation passed through a doorway beneath a sign that read, 'Housing Authority.' She was inside for what seemed, to Tylee, to be hours before returning. A small, portly man wearing spectacles followed behind her, trying desperately to match her pace.

Bronsin hopped off of the carriage and joined them at the rear. He hefted a small chest out of the carriage and placed it on the ground before the short man with a thud. Delriahna knelt, used her key, and opened the chest dramatically.

Standing and pointing at the chest, she challenged him. "As I told you, we can pay you now. There is no need for lending or political scheming. We need a house with four bedrooms, and this should more than cover that. So, can we get the paperwork done or not?"

The man looked at the chest, and then to Bronsin, nodding. Bronsin closed the chest, hefted it, and then followed the pair back into the building. A short time later, they emerged and mounted the carriage once more.

"A house with four rooms?" inquired Mordechai.

"You are welcome, and we will have a room for you. I understand that you have duties. You've been invaluable to us on our journey and the least we can do is to make a place for you in our home. So, the choice is yours. The room will sit idle should you choose otherwise," she stated bluntly. She meant well, but exhaustion had stolen her tact.

"Very well, my lady. Please... lead on," he said thankfully.

As they traveled, Delriahna searched for the address of their new residence. She didn't know which house she had just purchased. The only thing she knew was that it was west along Main Street, at the edge of the row-house district.

'It'll be noisy,' the small man had insisted, but noise was not her concern. They needed residence, and only a single-family home would do. If possible, it had to be along the southern edge of town, overlooking Fel'Rechaun. Only one property had fit her description, so noisy or not it was her only choice.

Nestled between two slightly larger homes along the southern cliffs, their house was one of the first in a series of single-family homes at the western edge of town. All the previous homes they'd passed along their route had been row-houses; small attached homes with no yard in which to store their carriage or horses.

Bronsin stopped the carriage at the front of the house and helped Mordechai unload the corpses while Delriahna inspected the home. Tylee gleefully ran up the stairs and found the room on the second floor with the best view of Fel'Rechaun, which she then claimed.

After unloading was complete, Bronsin parked the carriage in the small yard on the western side of the property and Mordechai moved the horses to the rear of the home, inside the fence at the edge of the cliff. With quiet nods to each other at a job well done, they entered the home with only one thing on their minds.

Bronsin stopped in the sitting room to cover Delriahna with a blanket before heading upstairs himself. She had passed out while they unloaded the carriage, too tired to make it up the stairs and too proud to ask for assistance.

Mordechai secured the home and retired to the room Delriahna had so graciously provided him.

Even the noise of the bustling street in the morning was not enough to wake the weary travelers.

∴ ∴ ∴

THE FIRST day of ranking trials had been nothing more than a show of forms and weapon handling against mounted bundles of hay and empty air. Laurence had demonstrated longsword, hand-and-a-half sword, shortsword, dagger, axe, mace, and warhammer. His techniques included single weapon, various dual-wield combinations, and several weapons with a shield.

None of other Initiates had displayed such a range of weaponry, skill and technique. Karzden and the other instructors had given every other Initiate tips and advice for improving their forms. They offered no such advice to Laurence. Karzden's only words to him had been to say, "I'm impressed."

That had gotten the attention of every other Initiate in his class. Some acted as if they were in awe of his skills. Others whispered that he was a spy, sent to pretend to be an Initiate for one nefarious plot or another. Still others showed an outward dislike for him, considering him their primary competition within the ranks.

Karzden explained that the purpose for the demonstrations was to give the instructors a baseline for each student's skills, so they knew what each one of them needed to learn. The more a student knew, the less martial instruction they would need. It was a process that helped to optimize each instructor's time.

Laurence was certain that his demonstration had not won him many friends. He'd dined alone that night in the dining hall, whereas everyone else sat amongst friends. Part of that, he assumed, could have been because of his late arrival. Some of it could have also been his armor, or Fahrul's notice of him. While his subconscious was curious, he knew he wasn't at the school to make friends... he was there to learn.

He had resigned himself to going through training alone. So it was a surprise when, as he was scooping a pile of buttered eggs onto his plate the next morning, a slender, tan hand gripped his bicep.

"Well met," said its owner.

Laurence whipped his head around to see who was touching him. The boy was shorter than Laurence, with sharp, angular features. Pointed ears poked through his dark, almond locks and his olive eyes were shrewd and piercing.

"I am Wilwarianel of Line Cuthdra'Gah, from Ayr'Thugohn in Ekthri," the boy explained. Seeing the confusion in Laurence's face, he continued, "You can call me Wil, or Talon. My friends call me Wil, but I went by Talon as a scout back home," he said smiling.

"I'm, uh-" started Laurence still taken aback by the man's name.

"Laurence Ravencrest! We all know who you are," stated Wil. "Quite a wonderful display yesterday."

They resumed piling their plates with food and made their way to a table.

"I wasn't trying to show off, really. I just need to prove myself and show that I deserve this training. Certain... events delayed my arrival, putting me at a disadvantage. That's all," he answered as they sat.

"Oh, I meant nothing by it. Unfortunately for me, my prior training was predominantly with staff, bow or open hand, so there really wasn't much for me to demonstrate yesterday. Hopefully, today's trials are more aligned with my skills, but... who knows," he said shrugging. He smiled and took a bite of his food.

"Why train with humans?" asked Laurence between bites.

"Do you not know?" asked Wil.

"What do you mean?" questioned Laurence.

"Both humans *and* elves built this school. Back when Arkhan Vaelin was trying to unify the lands, he struck an accord with the Ekthri and Afyr. Part of their agreement demanded he build certain schools to help train their people.

"They helped to build both Fel'Rechaun and Fel'Vizsiour. They even helped teach at both schools before relations soured. My father took part in the construction efforts for Fel'Rechaun. As soon as I learned all that our schools at home could teach, he sent me here to continue my education. I am the first member of my tribe to attend this school in a hundred years," he stated matter-of-factly.

"Wait... your father built this school, and now you attend it? How is that possible? The construction was, what, over a hundred years ago?" Laurence asked, confused.

"One hundred and fourteen years, to be precise," Wil said.

"Then... how?" asked Laurence.

"How old do you think I am?" challenged Wil playfully.

"Eighteen? Maybe?" answered Laurence curiously.

"I'm closer to one hundred and five, actually. By elven standards, still a boy. By human standards... well, very few ever live as long," clarified Wil. "You've met Kyrilis, haven't you?"

"Everyone seems to know she brought me here. So... yes," answered Laurence.

"She's twice my age," offered Wil. "Elves live very long lives, compared to humans. My father is almost six centuries old, and he still has a few years in him. However, you must understand something. Because elves live so long, elven society moves much more slowly.

"After all, there's always more time to get around to the things we wish to accomplish. Human lives are more focused, because they have an instinctive sense of urgency. It's one of the things I love about your people, and a large part of why my father wished me to train here.

"My open hand combat training back home? That took nearly forty years to complete. If I gave you the same training, the elven way? You'd not likely see the end of that training. Meanwhile, those trained here are quite formidable and the training only takes six months. It truly is astounding how much a shorter lifespan becomes a motivating factor, wouldn't you agree?" he asked.

"I guess-" Laurence started.

"There you are, Wil!" interrupted a new arrival. He was a broad-shouldered, muscular boy of Laurence's height with bright red hair. He smiled excitedly at them as he slid his tray onto the table and took a seat.

"Agnar! This is Laurence," Wil said with a gesture.

"I know who he is, silly," answered Agnar. He reached his hand over in greeting. Laurence shook it.

"Good to meet you, Agnar," responded Laurence.

"I was just over there, grabbin some grub, and I was sayin to Tamill that I hoped we'd all get as good as Laurence, you know? And just as I got done speakin about that, I heard Karzden walk by talkin to that big instructor in the white armor that we haven't met yet. He was sayin that we'd have to fight each other today. Is that true?"

"Hopefully, I won't have to fight your rambling tongue," Laurence joked.

Wil nearly choked on his food, stifling a laugh.

"Yeah, I get that a lot. Anyway, ya think we have to fight?" asked Agnar.

"Well, the next few days are ranking trials, so I would expect to see duels," offered Laurence.

"Yeah, I suppose. I thought I was good and ready for that kinda thing, right up til yesterday when we saw you swingin your weapons. Hope I don't lose too bad," said Agnar.

"That was just a techniques drill. Don't worry too much about it. There are plenty of boys here that are faster than me, and quite a few of you that are stronger," admitted Laurence.

"You sound like our Marshal already," remarked Agnar.

Wil nearly choked on his food again, stifling another laugh.

Their conversation was more light-hearted as they finished their meal. Laurence settled into the idea that perhaps having friends at school wasn't such a bad idea.

∴∴∴

AFTER DAWNFRY, Karzden brought the Initiates to the southwestern courtyard. A large sunken pit, used for combat training and demonstrations, occupied most of the space within its walls. Along the outside of the pit stood three rows of benches, situated so that all could see the whole of the pit without obstruction. One end of the pit had steps leading up to ground level. The other had a small observation platform for instructors and judges.

Karzden ushered the Initiates into the pit and called them to formation. As they lined up, shoulder to shoulder in regimented rows, Wil helped Laurence find an appropriate position, since he had missed that day of training. Karzden stood on the platform overlooking them, along with several officials.

"Today begins combat trials. Each of you will fight in one duel for each of the next three days. We will not judge your battles solely on wins or losses. Though winning is important, we will score your battles on sportsmanship, finesse, technique, endurance and strategy.

"We will then combine your scores with those of the weapons handling demonstrations and measure the results against the requirements of our school charter. Should your tally fall below threshold for attendance, your time here will end.

"We will then measure all remaining students to establish your class standing and rank. Please note that these ranks are simply to establish order within your class, and ranks may change during your stay in response to your performance throughout your training. So, if you do not make Marshal, do not fret. Any ranks earned through these trials are not permanent.

"If you kill your opponent, intentional or not, we will place you into custody and the Council will judge you accordingly. We expect you to fight with respect and honor, for your opponent may one day save your life in actual combat.

"Remember, you are all here for training so you might one day serve the kingdom. The kingdom gains nothing from the selfish, or the egotistical. Neither does it benefit from those unwilling to act with honor, respect, and concern for their fellow soldier.

"Lieutenant Cozwuld will draw the opponents for each duel in a random lottery," Karzden explained, signaling toward the man at his right. "Opponents will then report to the squires at the far side of the ring," he paused, pointing. "There you will select your choice of weaponry. Be mindful that varying your selected weaponry can improve your overall score, but not if your choices result in poor performance and failure. Play to your strengths, not to impress.

"Each bout will begin at my call, and will end when an opponent is unconscious, too wounded to proceed, or submits to their opponent by yelling, 'Yield'. We will penalize strikes with a weapon or shield to the face and groin, deducting from your score.

"Once again, your goal is not to hurt your opponent, or kill them. It is to show us how well you react to live combat and how fluidly you think on your feet. Questions?" he asked.

The Initiates remained silent, many looking about nervously.

"Very well. Our first match will be between..." he paused while Cozwuld drew two tiles. After receiving the tiles, he announced, "Laurence of the Raven, descendant of Gahl... and Izabel Tamrilson of Vellenheim."

∴ ∴ ∴

"NOBODY WANTS to fight you, you know," Wil said to Laurence.

"Why would that be?" he asked, hefting the various swords on display at the weaponry table.

"Word has spread that you've killed a dozen men already. Some say you enjoyed it," explained Wil.

"Nonsense. In all cases, I was defending myself. Besides... it was five men, not a dozen," answered Laurence. Having selected his blunted longsword, he moved to the table of shields.

"That's still five more than everyone else, Laur," Wil commented.

"Aye, and each was unfortunate. How..." he started, then turned to face Wil. "How did word spread? The only ones who knew were Kyrilis, Fahrul and myself."

"Preita overheard your briefing with the Lord Commander and

talked to the other servants, which filtered through the guards and from there... pretty much every student at the school. You're already a legend," stated Wil happily.

"That too is unfortunate. I'm only here for studies." He looked at Wil and shrugged, hefting his chosen shield. "I'm here to learn, and nothing more."

Laurence walked toward the fighting pit without waiting for Wil to respond, his mind focused on the task ahead. Every battle he'd experienced had been unplanned. He hadn't had time to think about them in advance, and both of them had resulted in the loss of life.

Izabel stepped into the fighting pit first. The Initiates surrounding the pit went silent in anticipation. She had performed very well in the entry trials, and many students had wagered she would become Marshal. Those expectations had changed when Laurence arrived.

Her pitch black hair was in a long braid down her back. Her bright green eyes were striking, even from a distance. She was beautiful. A fact which stood in stark contrast to the armor she wore, and the weapons she was wielding.

As Laurence stepped into the pit, whispers started amidst the crowd. Whispers that he could only assume were more rumors being twisted and passed around. He wondered how high his fabled kill count would be by the time the duel was over, sighing in frustration at the thought.

The two met at the center of the pit, facing each other. They looked to Karzden on the platform, and then to each other, nodding their heads at one another and readying their weapons.

Karzden suddenly yelled, "Begin!"

Izabel struck first, stepping quickly toward Laurence and swinging her sword at his chest in a wide, open arc from her right side. Laurence easily parried the attack, pushing her blade away from the space between them, and then turned his blade inward. Using the rebound from the parry, and a quick twitch of his arm muscles, he sent his blade square into her breastplate... avoiding her shield entirely.

Laurence started pacing around her in circles. She followed suit, matching his pace. Raising her blade above her head, she swung downward fiercely. Laurence brought his shield up and angled it to deflect her blade away and to the side. He followed with a thrust, sending the point of his blade past the inside of her shield and into her gut.

"Keep your attacks short," Laurence offered. "Don't swing so wildly," he advised.

She yelled angrily as she swung her blade in another wild arc. Laurence blocked her blade again with his shield. Seeing her shield finally raised into a defensible position, he drove his shoulder into it as her blade rebounded.

The impact drove her backward several feet. She tucked her sword in closer and sneered at him. He smiled back, recognizing that she was taking heed of his advice.

It was Laurence's turn to attack.

Laurence strode toward her confidently, his shield held at the ready. He slashed at her with quick strikes, alternating from the left and right in rapid succession. She parried the blows, growing more confident with each.

After several rapid strikes, Laurence saw precisely what he was after. She moved with anticipation, putting her blade into position before his attack had even begun. He continued the volley, attacking from the right. When she raised her blade in anticipation of his next attack, he drove his shield up into her sword arm instead, pushing it high to her right and out of the way.

Simultaneously, he brought his sword back across his body, knocking her shield aside with its pommel. Taking advantage of the opening he'd created, he kicked her in the gut. She stumbled back several steps, gasping for breath, the wind knocked out of her.

Frustrated, Izabel went into a frenzy. She regained her feet and attacked him with quick thrusts and slashes, one after another. He parried her attacks, alternating between his shield and sword, waiting for another opening, all the while watching her shield positioning and footwork.

By her fourth attack in the flurry, she was showing her frustration. Grunts and growls betrayed her mindset, and her attacks started losing their precision once again.

Laurence saw an opening.

As her fifth attack arced in toward his upper chest he knelt halfway down, moved his sword up to parry her and then stood and stepped forward all in one motion, bracing his shield before him. He crashed into her lower abdomen, pushing through the inner edge of her own shield and doubled her over in pain.

Izabel dropped her weapons, threw her arms up and yelled, "Yield!" as best as she could while catching her breath.

Laurence dropped his own weapons, walked up to her and extended his arm in respect. She clasped his sword arm with her own and stepped in close to him.

"Next time, just fight me. I don't need your help!" she scolded.

"I meant no offense, my lady. We're here to learn, so I thought-"

"Well, don't!" she retorted and stormed off.

The crowd chattered fiercely while Laurence collected the weapons and shields. As he made his way out of the ring, Karzden called the names of the next combatants. Laurence was too preoccupied to hear who they were.

COLLUSION

Ris'Gaula, Oghenfall 22nd, 113 of the 2nd Era

Darkness stirs in kingdom's heart,
The rot shall be revealed.
Worry not, oh sons of man,
The land will soon be healed.

Night's Writ, Parable 19

MORDECHAI CLIMBED the steps of Fel'Rechaun in contemplative silence. Several men behind him carried the corpses of Markus and Thorsten. Another carried the bag of loot Laurence had rescued.

His visit was to be a serious one, and that displeased him. He hoped that his single night of rest in Raven's Nest before reporting in would cause no additional strain. Fahrul was likely to take the news poorly, he was sure of it. Just as he was sure Fahrul would disagree with his plans to return to Fel'Vizsiour and conduct additional research.

He stopped for a moment on the landing to collect himself, shifting and straightening his robes. Usually when he volunteered to help the school, he returned with good news. He had a reputation for always coming through and was sad to see that reputation tarnished. However, because of recent discoveries, the school's business was the least of his worries. Regardless, he had to make Fahrul believe it was his only concern for the sake of maintaining good relations.

Before the guards could introduce his presence, the door opened from within. Fahrul stood before him, inviting him to enter.

"We have much to discuss, Lord Mordechai."

"I fear you are correct, Lord Commander."

They walked quietly to Fahrul's desk, their steps echoing throughout the chamber. Preita dutifully left to retrieve wine, knowing it to be Mordechai's preference. Taking their seats across from one another, they waited patiently while the guards placed the corpses beside the table.

Dahsh then emptied the bag of loot onto the table for Fahrul's inspection. He took care to place the pieces of the shattered crossbow together as if assembling a puzzle.

Preita poured goblets of wine for the two of them, then promptly ushered the guards from the room. Once all was silent, Fahrul lifted his goblet before him in both hands, contemplating the evidence before him.

It was Mordechai that broke the silence.

"I trust that Kyrilis has relayed the details of the events to you," Mordechai began.

"She has," he answered, nodding. "It is upsetting, however, to think that someone of your capabilities and renown couldn't find these poor souls before they expired, is it not?"

Fahrul looked toward the corpses with obvious distaste.

"It was unfortunate, yes. However, I'll remind you that the men didn't quite expire to the circumstances you've led Kyrilis and the rest of the school to believe. In fact, the real circumstances which placed them in harm's way are the very circumstances that delayed my finding them," replied Mordechai.

"Two members of the provisional guard, freshly graduated, joining forces with disgruntled former recruits? Former recruits who murdered an officer, stole armament and fled into the countryside on some vain attempt to rebel? Do you truly think this is the information that our guards, our recruits, or the residents of Raven's Nest need be made aware of? Would that have helped our situation?" challenged Fahrul.

"I am not suggesting that divulging such details would help the citizens, the recruits, or your staff. However, *not* divulging it to me in advance affected how I approached the investigation. Instead of questioning witnesses about three bandits, or whether two school-clad recruits had asked after them, I *could* have inquired about five men traveling as one unit.

"I wasted days in Gaierford, Dunforth, and Ayerton asking for information which nobody had, because the facts I was given weren't reality. It wasn't until Salvation Shire—of all places—that the truth of the matter came to light. It was mere chance alone that led to me finding the boys, dead, by the roadside.

"The saving grace, here, is that the disagreements within their group are likely the reason good Laurence survived to become your prized student. Do you think he'd have fared better against five foes that night? Two of which, very well armed and trained?" challenged Mordechai.

Fahrul let the anger welling inside him show upon his face. "I will remind you I was not present when Karzden provided you with the information. I was in Vellenheim reporting on our... unfortunate circumstances. An official inquisition is being sanctioned by the King. These are not pleasant times.

"Karzden was told to inform you of the finer details; the truth of the matter. However, according to him, you set off on your journey before he could do so!" scolded Fahrul.

"I had seen no indication there was more to the story! Instead, he repeatedly insisted that urgency was of greatest importance. He urged me to find and retrieve two lost recruits expediently and with discretion. Need I remind you, I am helping voluntarily. I've nothing to gain by being here, aside from maintaining relations between our two schools. Which, I'll add, is a role that many could fulfill. I offered my aid because I wanted to, not because I am compelled to do so," said Mordechai.

"Be that as it may, I am still faced with an inquisition which will probably rise to untold fervor as a result of the untimely demise of all witnesses. There stands no soul which can attest to their motivations, or intentions. We do not know, and have no means with which to discover, if outside agents influenced their actions.

"All we have are corpses, random pieces of loot, and the shards of King Orluhnd's family heirloom," he added, tossing one about on the table in frustration. "The very crossbow, I'll remind you, that his namesake used in the battle for Engle Plateau. The very crossbow whose likeness adorns the royal family crest. The very crossbow that unified these lands and forged this Kingdom out of chaos!"

"There may still be a means of discovering the lost information," assured Mordechai. "I sent word to The Oracle during our rest at Salvation Shire, begging her assistance with this matter. I've been assured she will arrive promptly."

"Ayriel is coming here?" Fahrul asked, raising an eyebrow.

"Indeed! I preserved the corpses for her inspection. I, however, might not be present for her visit. I have other matters to attend," he stated bluntly.

"Other matters? Fel'Rechaun won't be the only victim of this inquisition, I'll remind you!" snapped Fahrul.

"I have research which I must conduct from Fel'Vizsiour which may have relevance. I must conduct that research now, while the evidence is still fresh in my mind. Worry not, I am not abandoning you or the school... regardless of accusations and blame that one might haphazardly toss in my direction," scolded Mordechai.

"I apologize, Lord Mordechai. I am beset on all sides these past weeks and have let my emotions win over my senses. Please do as you deem necessary. I will prepare for Ayriel's visit in your stead," stated Fahrul in somber tones.

Mordechai finished his wine, placed the goblet on the table and stood. With a brief nod of respect to Fahrul, he closed his eyes and then vanished, leaving nothing but a wisp of thin smoke where he stood. Preita was so taken aback by his disappearance, she dropped the tray she was carrying.

Fahrul called for his guards. He had preparations to make.

∴ ∴ ∴

TYLEE WOKE with excitement. She'd never been to a big city before, and Raven's Nest had seemed rather large when they arrived. She dressed happily, intent on seeing everything the city had to offer. Sparing only a moment to stare longingly at Fel'Rechaun, she burst from her room with an energy that annoyed her mother... who was emerging from the neighboring room at the same time.

As Tylee danced down the hall, ignoring her, Delriahna rubbed more sleep from her eyes and sighed.

One of those days, I see, sighed Delriahna to herself.

Bronsin stumbled into the hall still half asleep and blurted, "What's that?"

"Never you mind," sighed Delriahna.

Upon hearing her dismissal, Bronsin returned to his quarters, and shortly thereafter his sleep.

Delriahna stopped at Mordechai's door and knocked gently. With no response, she made her way to deal with her daughter alone. She had to remind herself that she'd volunteered for the task. Sighing, she readied herself and descended the stairs, each step bringing her closer to the overwhelming boisterousness that was an excited Tylee.

As she rounded the corner at the bottom of the stairs, she caught a familiar sight.

Of course she found the bay window, she mused, rolling her eyes.

Tylee would have lived in their bay window, had it not been for her interference. Andor didn't want Tylee to wander Mooncrest on her own, out of fear for her safety. While his heart had been in the right place, the result of his decision had been a very frustrated daughter and a very annoyed wife.

Tylee turned from the window at the sound of Delriahna's footsteps, released the curtains and ran over to her mother excitedly.

"Can we go shopping?"

"We've not yet dined, dear girl. We must welcome the day properly," countered Delriahna.

"We slept through dawnfry and they serve lunch right across the street! We're not at home, we're visiting a brand new place. Can't we eat their food? See their stores? Meet new people?" she pleaded.

"Fine, let me grab my-"

"Shawl!" blurted Tylee, presenting it to her proudly.

Delriahna grabbed the shawl from her overzealous daughter and followed her crazed offspring outside. Tylee stood happily beside her mother, hands clasped, rocking back and forth on the balls of her feet. Delriahna was too busy studying the crowd around them to notice.

Countless people filled the street, going about the business of their day. Horses, carriages, and pedestrians traveled in both directions in various states of distractedness. Businesses were teeming with activity, and it seemed every doorway within sight had someone passing through it.

Buildings on the southern side of the street were mostly homes, standing two to three stories tall. On the other side of the street stood four and five-story buildings with balconies on the top floors; making it easy to see Fel'Rechaun over the homes across from them. The top floors appeared to be a mixture of dwellings and small smoking or drinking rooms; those that often targeted well paying customers.

"Come!" chirped Tylee excitedly, unable to contain herself any longer.

Before Delriahna could respond, Tylee had stepped into the

street, joining the flow of traffic. She tried to follow, but it was difficult to see where Tylee was headed. A glimpse of blonde hair caught her eye, cutting through the crowd toward the other side of the street. Her daughter's playful giggle confirmed that the hair was hers. Delriahna followed suit, crossing through the crowd as best she could.

After a few moments, the two of them had weaved their way through the swarms of people and made it to the walk, in front of a row of shops. Delriahna tossed her daughter a coarse look, but Tylee took no notice. She turned and walked into a random shop and immediately began introducing herself to everyone inside.

This is going to be a long day, moaned Delriahna.

∴ ∴ ∴

THE SMALL room sprang to life as the sound of static and thin streaks of glowing smoke interrupted its natural state. Bright light pulsed into existence and then, as suddenly as it had appeared, faded into nothingness. Mordechai stood in its place, arriving as he'd done many times. Runes, etched deeply into the stone floor beneath him, glowed deep blue briefly and then slowly faded as he stepped off them.

He had arrived within his personal chambers at the school of Fel'Vizsiour. His quarters were simple, revealing no particular wealth or station, for he did not own or need for material things aside from those which would aid him in his craft or research.

His bed was small, tucked into a nook along one wall. He owned a single well-worn chair which could have benefited from simple repairs, if he were so inclined. Much of his furniture was in a similar state, for he did not concern himself with what he considered trivial matters.

A thin layer of gray particles coated the surfaces in the room. He hadn't been to his chamber in more than a year and had made no arrangements for cleaning services in his absence. It wasn't because of neglect, so much as the fact that his room had no door through which to permit entry. Even if he had arranged for someone to keep his chambers clean, they wouldn't have been capable of gaining access to perform their duties. That, too, was a trivial matter in his mind, for the cleanliness of his chamber was something easily remedied.

With a single wave of his left hand the dust about the room, on all surfaces and beneath the papers on his desk, vanished as if it had never existed. He resolved a year of dust from disuse in the time it took him to take a single step, and he had handled it as a matter of reflex.

With a flick of his index finger, the various candles about the chamber sprung to life. Flames danced and flickered eagerly, sending shadows playfully across the chamber's granite walls. As he arrived at his desk, he began the familiar motion of lowering himself into a chair. The worn chair obediently slid across the marble floor, arriving beneath him just in time. Any later and he'd have fallen to the floor.

He rifled through the papers, scrolls and books that lay on, over, and inside his desk. Each one bore knowledge passed down through many documented and undocumented ages. Some of them bore knowledge which had no known source. Among them were scrolls found in ancient tombs, books found in forgotten libraries, and coal rubbings of lost carvings from forbidden depths. He had gathered them through lifetimes of hunting, scouring, and searching where other men feared to go.

In the recesses of his mind, he poured over the information before him. He couldn't recall the specifics of what he was seeking, only that he'd collected it at some point, and that it was within his chambers. It wasn't clear if it had been a scroll, a book, or other artifact entirely. All that he was certain of was that he'd read of the effects of Paradox magic when used to counter Time, and he'd done so within his chamber.

Hours passed as he ran his hands over scrolls, papers and tomes. Each being dismissed as irrelevant to his current research, and each moving itself out of the way once he finished inspecting it. As he dismissed a piece, it returned itself to a shelf, or a drawer, seemingly of its own accord. To him, it was a normal process and one he performed as a matter of course.

He didn't struggle with magic, as many others did. Simple magics, such as those he employed to scour his personal archive, flowed from him with little effort. To him, such simple tricks offered a convenience and efficiency that made them necessary.

Others at Fel'Vizsiour disagreed.

When he'd performed these feats in the open so many decades prior, witnesses scoffed at his actions as a waste of magical energies. They'd lamented him using magic to perform trivial tasks, insisting he should do such things by hand. To avoid further conflict, he chose to seal his chambers away from the world. A side benefit of that choice had been his ability to research, and study, with complete privacy. Privacy was something he'd grown to value a great deal.

Of course, he thought in recognition.

An old tome now lay before him, opening with a creak. Like so many others in his collection, its origins were unknown. Bound in magically imbued flesh, embossed with strange runes that he'd still yet to decipher, the book was a complete mystery.

Inscriptions filled its vellum pages, written with ink laced with lapithrium dust. The details within the tome had always intrigued him, as had the exquisite nature of its construction. As intriguing as these details were, the thing that most intrigued him through the years was that by all appearances the handwriting within it was his own.

∴ ∴ ∴

WIL STOOD at the center of the pit, bo staff in hand. He waited patiently for his opponent to arrive, eyes closed and head down in meditation. Suddenly, he snapped into motion. The staff twirled about his body in a blur, while his feet danced about in defensive and offensive postures. He ended his display with a flurry of attacks, finishing with a spinning back-kick that he held for several seconds.

As Bingrolf approached, Wil returned his feet to the ground. His staff at his side, he bowed in respect. The crowd cheered his display as Bingrolf came to stand before him, snarling angrily.

Bingrolf was a large, broad-shouldered man. He stood more than a foot taller than Wil, and his muscles rippled beneath his taught gambeson. It was obvious to Wil that he'd grown up performing lots of physical labor. His red, well-groomed beard and shaved head made him look fierce.

Wil had not seen Bingrolf's demonstrations the previous day and hadn't expected the giant two-handed maul the man now clinched before him.

"Begin!" yelled Karzden.

Wil immediately took a step back and began twirling his staff defensively. Bingrolf jabbed the pommel of his maul into the path of Wil's staff and stopped its movement abruptly.

Snarling, he rotated his maul and slammed it into Wil's shoulder. Wil stumbled back a half step, his shoulder throbbing painfully, but Bingrolf advanced and pressed up against him, then grinned at him fiercely.

"This isn't a game, elf!" snarled the man.

Wil pushed off of Bingrolf's chest and twirled his staff into the crook of his right elbow, his left hand extended toward his opponent. He held the pose for a moment as Bingrolf slowly circled him.

When Bingrolf reached Wil's left side, he swung his maul into an overhand strike. Wil spun out of its path and sent the end of his staff toward Bingrolf, driving it straight into the center of the man's chest. Withdrawing his staff, Wil spun to face him again, resuming his previous stance.

Bingrolf snarled as he lifted his maul off the dusty ground.

Wil stayed on the defensive as the maul strikes flowed. Bingrolf attacked with the head and pommel of his maul repeatedly, each attack more difficult for Wil to parry, but he stayed patient... waiting for an opening in Bingrolf's onslaught.

The maul came in from the right. Wil ducked back, swung the end of his staff around and pushed the maul it along its path, then jabbed the other end of his staff into Bingrolf's shoulder.

Bingrolf redirected the maul, jabbing toward Wil with its pommel. Wil spun his staff, slamming it down into the maul, diverting its momentum and deflecting the blow. He followed that movement with another jab of the staff, striking Bingrolf's other shoulder.

One after another, Wil parried and returned Bingrolf's attacks, faster than Bingrolf could respond. The process continued until one of Wil's parries jarred the haft of the maul so firmly that Bingrolf lost his grip. As the weapon fell to the ground between them, Wil closed the distance and stopped one end of his staff mere inches in front of Bingrolf's throat.

"Would you like to continue?" asked Wil.

"Yield!" yelled Bingrolf, gasping for breath. He stared angrily at Wil for a few moments. Wil stared back, waiting for him to move; their faces mere inches apart.

A hand clapped down on Bingrolf's shoulder. Cozwuld had joined them in the pit while hushed whispers sprang to life in the stands.

"That's enough, Initiates. Bingrolf... you must learn to control your anger. It has not served you here, and it will not serve you in a real battle," he explained.

"But sir, he was showing off before the-" Bingrolf started.

"He was warming up. There was no room by the weapons table

to do so. Do you... do you know why Wil was wielding a staff?" asked Cozwuld.

"No, sir," answered Bingrolf, defeated.

"He is an expert with the Quel'Thoz, an elven weapon. Think of it as a double-tipped spear... in simple terms. Each end of the weapon is a blade, sharp as a razor, attached to a staff similar to the one Wil was using here today. How do you think this duel would have concluded had his weapon been a Quel'Thoz?"

"I'd be... dead, sir," admitted Bingrolf.

"I am sorry to offend, Bingrolf. I did not mean to insult you with my display," offered Wil. He backed up and bowed to Bingrolf gracefully.

"Let's go get those bruises and bones tended to, aye?" Cozwuld escorted the combatants from the pit, as Karzden took to the platform above.

The crowd silenced. It had been a long day, and all had fought their battles. Most were in pain, weary, and felt unsure of themselves. Even the winners were self conscious about their performance, and uncertain of their place in the school.

"You did well today, Initiates. The contests today were quite entertaining, and very informative. It has become clear that all of you deserve a place at the school. This should set your minds at ease over the next two days. However-"

The crowd roared to life as the Initiates cheered their success. He signaled for them to quiet, then continued, "However, that does not mean you should take it easy. Tomorrow will be difficult, as will the next, and again every day thereafter, so long as you attend. Now, go see to your wounds, speak with your instructors, and head to the dining hall. Today you have earned your ale," he finished.

The crowd once again roared to life.

Laurence's own cheers were interrupted as Cozwuld tapped him on the shoulder. "Karzden would see you in his office promptly," said the Lieutenant.

"Aye, sir," responded Laurence, then immediately began making his way through the crowd.

∴ ∴ ∴

THE WALLS of the northwestern courtyard extended inward, forming the outer walls of the row-houses that lined its outer edges. Two dozen buildings stood in a cluster at the center, surrounded by forty-eight two-story homes. Each home housed up to four officers, officials, and their assistants. Captain Karzden's home, even with his high rank and status, was no exception. He shared his home with Lieutenant Cozwuld, two clerics from the medical unit, a cook, and their House Steward, Helen.

Laurence sat waiting in the only office within their residence, pondering how they decided who could use it and when. Helen returned after a few moments carrying a pitcher of ale. She poured him a tankard and smiled before seeing herself out to prepare for Karzden's return.

Time passed too slowly as he sat in the office alone. The ale was a welcome relief, but he had to make sure not to drink too much of it. Cozwuld had provided no context for his pending conversation with Karzden. He assumed it had something to do with his duel earlier that day, but there was no way to be sure.

His mind raced as he considered the possibilities, making him anxious. He was just about to leave the office to find Helen when a rustling came from the home's entrance. Helen suddenly entered the room, moving with practiced grace. She quickly replaced several candles and removed a crystal decanter from a chest behind the desk. After pouring its dark contents into two small glasses, she departed without a word.

Karzden strode into the room a few moments later. He wore a plain housecoat draped loosely over a simple black tunic. He seemed relaxed, which eased Laurence's mind. As Karzden rounded the desk, he invited Laurence to join him and smiled at the boy as he took his seat.

"All this must seem very odd to you, eh lad?" asked Karzden as he settled himself in.

"Well, to be fair, I've never attended a school before, or dealt with matters of state, so I wouldn't know 'odd' when I saw it," Laurence responded, smirking.

"Fair enough, lad. I assure you, though, that the situation is, in fact, odd."

He held up his glass to Laurence in a toast. Laurence raised his own glass, then watched as Karzden gently swirled its contents and sipped them with caution and care.

Laurence studied his drink for a moment, swirling and sniffing it. He could detect the faint smell of oak behind the overwhelming vapors of the alcohol. The drink was smooth as it crossed his tongue, but struck his throat harshly. He coughed in response and found it hard to breathe for a second.

Karzden chuckled at him.

"Brandy takes some getting used to, don't worry about it. And this... this brandy is something you should never get used to. It is quite old, and very expensive. It was a gift from the royal family after my last campaign. I only bring it out on odd occasions, which, as I've already described, this happens to be," said Karzden.

"I've yet to discern what we're to talk about, but I appreciate the experience of this brandy," stated Laurence.

"Down to business then," Karzden said, resting his glass back on the desk. "You've made an impression, lad. In fact, your skills are far beyond any expectations. You're already experienced at combat and well trained in martial skills. The leadership of this school is unanimous in the opinion that there are no students here which could challenge you in combat. We've decided it best to announce you as class Marshal at the start of tomorrow's trials," he explained.

"What?" asked Laurence, shocked.

"Make no mistake, Laurence, this has never happened and in normal circumstances, it never would. However, your situation is far from normal. Trade places for a moment. Imagine yourself in my shoes, and me in yours. You've a recruit that arrives having already killed five men in open combat. He goes into weapons handling demonstrations and displays not only competency but expertise in every weapon style you teach. He then bests a prized student, the niece of Lord Commander Fahrul.

"While doing so, he also takes it upon himself to offer his opponent advice. Then, of course, is the matter of the awe and fear said student's presence causes amongst his peers. What, I ask you, would you do under such circumstances?" asked Karzden matter-of-factly.

"I'm really not sure, sir," answered Laurence somberly. It was strange to see himself through someone else's eyes.

"Precisely. So, before this day even began, the Lord Commander and I met with the other headmasters and we discussed our options. This was our decision. It isn't fair to make the other Initiates fight you, and if I'm being honest, there isn't much we can even teach you regarding weaponry. Instead, we will focus your training on leadership, discipline, and the strategic nuances of war and politics. Which means, you will train with books and tutors while your classmates are practicing swinging their swords, or maces, or staffs.

"So, it is to everyone's benefit that you become Marshal, so we can openly focus your training where it would benefit you, and our Kingdom, the most. Further, there are details of your journey to the school that we would like your help with. That help will require time that the full training regiment does not allow," said Karzden.

"You need my help?" inquired Laurence, intrigued.

"The bandits you killed weren't simple bandits. Their names were Brellin, Hamish and Ivan. They studied here a few years ago and joined the Legion as recruits. They were a bad lot and found themselves in trouble frequently while at Fel'Rechaun. The Legion was so desperate for recruits they ignored our advice and allowed them to join.

"Eventually they found themselves in trouble again, as their kind are apt to do. The Legion discharged them dishonorably; something we predicted would occur. However, what we failed to realize was that they were friends of Markus and Thorsten. Neither of them got into trouble while attending here. Neither of them had shown any signs of misbehavior in the slightest, actually.

"They left suddenly of their own accord, and none were sure where they'd gone. While investigating their disappearance, we found witnesses in Raven's Nest who had put them together with Brellin and his crew. Two days after their disappearance, we noticed that the Vaelin family crossbow was missing from our vault.

"So, considering them the likely culprits, we sent Mordechai to discover their whereabouts. Unfortunately, Mordechai did not receive all the details before he departed, and he was unaware that the five boys were working together. To be fair, it was a theory of ours, but we had no proof other than idle testimony from tavern-goers in town.

"We weren't able to verify that testimony until Mordechai had already gone, and by then it was too late to inform him. It seems the boys had a falling out somewhere near the Sacton River, and the original three killed their two new compatriots and fled south... where you gave them their end," he concluded.

"So... I almost had to fight five men, not three. And two—the ones we brought back on our carriage as corpses—would have been well armed; still using equipment provided by the school," summarized Laurence.

"Indeed. And it seems they aren't the only ones at risk of turning against us. We've had reports of strange figures approaching students while they visit The Nest. This tells us they might be part of a grander scheme," added Karzden.

"By the gods," sighed Laurence. "Is nothing ever simple?" He took another sip of his brandy and managed to only wince as he swallowed it.

Karzden smiled.

"Simple is a flight of fancy. This troublesome scenario is further complicated by your arrival and the Inquisition, which the King just sanctioned to investigate the matter. If that wasn't bad enough, the King's daughter Ayriel will arrive on the morrow to interview your corpses," he added, chuckling. He sipped his own brandy while staring into Laurence's eyes.

"Do what, now?" asked Laurence.

"She is a seer, of sorts. She is a powerful woman in many regards... and apparently one of those regards is talking to the recently deceased," answered Karzden.

"Those corpses aren't exactly fresh," mused Laurence.

"Ah, but Mordechai made them so, did he not?" asked Karzden.

"He cast a spell on them at the bridge to..." his voice trailed off in thought. "Son of a bitch," he remarked in realization.

"Aye. Then when you stopped in Salvation Shire to rest, and he had business to attend..."

"He sent word to Ayriel," continued Laurence. "Everything is intertwined!"

"Everything indeed," confirmed Karzden. He poured more brandy, and they both drank.

"I'll be blunt with you, lad. Your uncle Gaerin did quite a number on you. I find it hard to consider you a student, much like Mordechai isn't *truly* a student of Fel'Vizsiour. The training I mentioned that we feel would suit you? It's usually reserved for officers. However, only the Legion has the authority to declare or promote officers. So, we are bending the rules to train you, keep you close, and lean on your proximity to the other students to gather intelligence. You will have access to things we don't, because of who you are and your position as a student.

"In reality, if this twisted plot were not afoot, we'd graduate you now and hand you off to the Legion to begin your service, if that is what you wished. However, we find ourselves in need of you. So, Fahrul and I will see to your training personally. You will learn to think like we do in matters of war, politics, and strategy. This is a great honor *and* a heavy burden," said Karzden.

"I accept, sir. The training I need is precisely the kind you describe. That, and I must become stronger and faster. The man that I seek requires more than technical prowess to defeat. That is why I'm here," said Laurence. He sipped more brandy in contemplation.

"So be it. You are now Marshal Laurence. We'll announce it in the morning. You will stand next to me and help judge your classmates' performance through the trials. Meanwhile, you must keep your eyes and ears open, especially in Raven's Nest."

Laurence sat with a blank stare on his face for a moment. "Sorry, sir, I'm just taking this all in. It's a lot."

"It is, lad. Take the time you need," responded Karzden. He poured them both more brandy as he waited.

"You mentioned before that Mordechai wasn't a student of Fel'Vizsiour, except that he was clear that he was," said Laurence.

"That man's been around longer than the school has, if the tales are accurate. They say he was already powerful before construction was complete and only sought entrance so he could learn to control his powers more completely. He doesn't remember a time before the school, or so he claims. In fact, he claims to only remember his given name. Not his family, not his people, and not where he comes from. So, the school set aside a room for him at the top of the central spire, and he's lived there ever since.

"He comes and goes as he pleases, attending the odd class or two when he chooses. Mostly, he seems to travel the land in search of something. Though I hear he visits Ayriel in Vellenheim often, and then there are his trips here to meddle," joked Karzden. "Though I'm not close to Mordechai, and I question the truth of the tale I was told when he arrived. Other sources say he is the Archmagus to the King. But then I wonder, why an Archmagus would waste time with the business of our school."

"He doesn't seem old enough for all that," noted Laurence.

"Your own grandfather was old beyond his years, and you question Mordechai's age?"

"I never really put much thought into it, to be honest."

"Arcturus was Gahl's son. He knew his father, which means he was old enough to have memories of him. Gahl was the first graduate of Fel'Rechaun, lad. He died one hundred and thirteen years ago," said Karzden.

"Here I thought Arcturus was just an alchemist my entire life. Since his death, I've heard tales of him casting spells and curses. And now you point out the obvious nature of his long life... I have so much to learn about magic. I wonder, though, why Arcturus never taught me such things?" pondered Laurence.

"Worry not, lad. Gaerin did you right, by my estimation. Arcturus didn't leave the King's service on the best of terms, and I'm sure that event forged many of his decisions from that point onward. I wouldn't blame him for how he raised you. Instead, be thankful for your childhood. It seems *adulthood* has plans for you," remarked Karzden.

Laurence nodded in agreement, tapped his glass against Karzden's and drank the rest of its contents. It was a few hours before he left for the dining hall. Conversation was much more pleasant for the rest of his stay, revolving mostly around Tylee and Karzden's servant Helen, who apparently was much more than just a House Steward.

.˙. .˙. .˙.

DELRIAHNA AND Tylee didn't return home until after dark. In their wake were several assistants from several shops, each carrying a sack or crate of goods. Servants had been arriving and leaving packages in the front room all day long, much to Bronsin's surprise. When he'd finally come downstairs, he'd seen neither Colvin, no Mordechai, no signs of any food having been prepared, and piles of crates and clothing all over the front room.

He'd ignored the comings and goings, happily lost in his thoughts. The most relaxing part of his day was the lack of Delriahna's constant demands. It was so relaxing, in fact, that he'd passed out, woken up, and passed out again several times as the day progressed.

When they burst through the front door, arguing as they often did, his peace shattered and his life returned to reality. With a disgruntled sigh, he slowly made his way out of his chair. His joints argued with his decision, as did his legs. There were two things preventing him from complying with the wishes of his lower extremities. The first was the knowledge that he would suffer for weeks if he neglected his duties in serving Delriahna. The second was his newfound and desperate need to urinate.

"Do not expect to spend this kind of coin daily, my dear. In fact, do not expect to spend any coin at all for a great many days," scolded Delriahna.

"Yes, mother," answered Tylee, sounding defeated.

"I mean it. It will be some time before we receive anything from your father to aid us. We have to make our finances stretch for as long as they can. Unless you wish to find work as a barmaid."

"I know, mother."

"Now... I have taken you on your shopping adventure and complied with your incessant begging for material goods. I even withheld my complaints until our return, did I not?"

"Yes, mother," she answered with a sigh.

"Good. Then it is fair that you prepare our evening meal. I will have lamb, and I expect it rare with a perfect sear," Delriahna demanded. She cleared several piles of clothing off of the couch and sat.

"But, mother," retorted Tylee.

"Bronsin is no good at lamb, so don't attempt to pass this off on him. And," she added, "he will not be carrying this disaster of shopping to your room for you. This is your doing, and your responsibility."

Tylee sighed, "Yes, mother."

Delriahna removed her gloves, shawl, and shoes as she settled in. Bronsin came downstairs, fetched her book, lit a candle, and dutifully massaged her feet. Tylee brought them both tea, shivered at the sight of Bronsin massaging her mother's feet, then removed herself back to the kitchen.

The lamb was prepared exquisitely, just as Delriahna had taught her. They ate in silence, Delriahna refusing to compliment her. Afterward, they went to their separate rooms for the night.

Not long after, Tylee begged Bronsin to move her bed to the window. She spent the rest of her night lying on her stomach; staring at Fel'Rechaun and imagining what Laurence was up to.

∴ ∴ ∴

DAYLIGHT WAS giving way to Provoss and Aygos when Laurence joined the Initiates at the dining hall. Karzden's brandy was getting the better of him, and he found it hard to focus on the individual occupants of the room. Silence filled the hall as he entered. He tried his best not to wobble.

Agnar and Wil crossed the room as the conversations around the hall resumed. Leading him by the elbow, from both sides, they escorted him to their table where Izabel and Bingrolf were waiting.

Platters piled with meat, potato and bread filled the center of the table. Tankards, at various stages of consumption, rimmed the outer edge.

"Izabel, here, wishes to apologize to you for her behavior during your duel," offered Wil as he took his seat.

She rolled her eyes at him and sighed.

"I took offense where I shouldn't have, Laurence. I realize now that you meant to help. I'm used to men trying to prove they are my better and took your actions in that regard. It wasn't until later that I realized your intent," she explained.

"It's fine. Tensions were high for all of us. We've all got something to prove and have much at stake. Your reaction was purely natural," Laurence answered, trying hard not to slur his words.

"See, this is what I was sayin to Bingrolf. Laurence is just so... innocent," laughed Agnar.

"Shut it, you," Izabel said, backhanding his chest.

Her slap reminded Laurence of the way Tylee used to act back in Mooncrest. The thought made him smile.

"Always makin trouble," said Bingrolf. His voice was fairly deep, even when he wasn't growling during combat.

"Do you two know each other?" asked Laurence. He pointed at Bingrolf and Agnar, who bore a striking resemblance to one another.

"Aye, we're cousins," answered Agnar.

"That explains *everything*," Wil declared.

Everyone laughed, toasted their ale and drank. Laurence grabbed a plate and gathered a helping of meat and potatoes. He hadn't eaten since dawnfry.

"So, Laur, Izabel says you were quite a tough opponent," said Bingrolf.

"Actually, I said that he was more skilled than anyone I'd ever fought," corrected Izabel.

"Same thing," retorted Agnar.

Another round of laughter and toasts passed between them.

"I started training when I was six," offered Laurence. My uncle Gaerin was a graduate of Fel'Rechaun in the same class as Fahrul. After that, he went adventuring and helped overthrow King Pahn of Pelrigoss."

"And he's the one who taught you?" asked Izabel.

"Aye," he answered between bites.

"No wonder you dispatched me so easily," she noted.

"This man's a killer," added Agnar in jest.

The stern looks around the table made it obvious he was out of line.

"That is not something to joke about, Agnar. I simply did what I had to in order to survive. You'd have done the same," said Laurence, nearly choking on his food. He found it hard to hide his frustration under the influence of brandy and ale.

"I didn't mean nothin," offered Agnar.

"Actual combat is not a game. It's not fun, it's not rewarding, and it doesn't make you feel powerful. Fighting with your life on the line? It makes you question your training. It makes you question your worth. It pushes you to your limits, mentally.

"I mean, sure, perhaps there are those that revel in the thrill of battle after years of fighting... but I am not that person. Battle changed who I am. The boy I used to be died that night. He didn't survive. All of my daydreams of training here—earning fortune and fame—like my father... gone, in one swing of a sword," explained Laurence.

"Like I said... he's more skilled than anyone I've ever fought, and that extends to more than just his ability to maneuver a blade," Izabel remarked.

She lifted her tankard to him in a toast. All of them took part.

"That's why I tried to help you, Izabel. It wasn't pity, or that you were a woman. It was that I didn't want to see you, or anyone, graduate here and end up in the situations I've been in unprepared. Winning a battle is more about protecting the space between you and your opponent than it is hitting them with your sword as hard as you can.

"You must keep your weapons centered, ready to strike *and* defend. Wild swings—like you performed against Wil, Bingrolf—leave you open and... dead. It's one of the first things Gaerin drilled into me, and I'm certain it's what saved my life," he concluded somberly.

"We haven't had that training yet. I mean, not really. Sure, we all swung weapons around a bit back home, but... nothin compares to real training," admitted Bingrolf.

"Speak for yourself, Bingrolf. I had extensive training. However, I now realize most of my teachers were overpriced swindlers whose only skill was fooling my parents," Izabel lamented.

Agnar and Bingrolf laughed briefly, then stopped when they realized they were the only ones doing it.

"You're awful quiet," she said to Wil, leaning toward him.

Wil had been sitting in contemplation with a very stern look on his face.

"Laurence is right. I've been in real combat with very real consequences. I've never killed anyone, but I have seen people die on the field of battle. Elvish training focuses more on fighting styles and forms; positions, moves, and counter-moves. The result is idealistically the same, but not as effective as the training Laurence received. I think we've a lot to learn from him," concluded Wil.

"Will you teach us? I mean, between classes... maybe in the evenings?" asked Izabel.

"I'll see what I can do," he answered. He wanted to mention his conversation with Karzden, but knew it wasn't prudent to do so. They'd find out in the morning with the rest of the Initiates.

"So, tell us about your wife," blurted Izabel, changing the subject.

"How did you find out about that?" asked Laurence. Not that he minded, but the rumors seemed to flow about the school like water. He was a little shocked at how fast they spread.

The rest of the evening was talk of family and friends, the homes they'd grown up in, the nuances of farming marshlands, and the politics of being of noble birth but wanting nothing of noble life.

∴ ∴ ∴

BY THE time they reached Telon's Respite their feet felt like they were bleeding, their knees were shot, and it was painfully obvious they were no longer young. The street that lay before them was lit by a single lantern. All the windows they could see were dark, even those within the tower at the far end of the street.

"Hopefully that lantern is the tavern," muttered Lyla.

"There's only one way to find out," answered Gaerin.

It was understandable for a small town to be quiet so late at night. What concerned them was the absence of any notable guard. The town existed because of its tower, so the absence of guards made little sense. King Orluhnd I ordered the tower's construction following the Battle of Ehgon Ridge, which lay an hour north by horseback. Its purpose was to protect the farmers of the region.

Telon Briarthorne fought in the battle and saved the land and its people. He was a folk hero; a farmer who—with pitchfork and little else—joined the battle and turned the tide by attacking the invading Toor tribe's chieftain from behind.

"One would think, if you have a guard tower-" Lyla started.

"That you'd have some guards," finished Gaerin.

"Even in the dead of night."

"Especially in the dead of night."

They stopped in front of the single lantern. No sign was on display to indicate what the building might be. There was a table outside next to the door, hinting that it might be a tavern or inn, but it could also have been someone's patio. Lyla walked up to a small window next to the door and peered in. She turned to Gaerin and signaled, then stepped up to the door.

"I think it's a tavern," she whispered, shrugging.

"Open the door," he whispered back.

"But what if it's not?" she whispered curiously.

"What if it's a tavern, but you knocked? It'd be all... awkward," he whispered jokingly.

"Fine," she whispered in mock seriousness.

"Fine," he whispered back in the same tone, with a smirk.

Lyla opened the door and paused for a moment, staring into the room. It was a small business, but a business none-the-less. There were two tables, one of which had patrons seated at it. Shelves lined the back half of the establishment, holding general goods for purchase. It appeared to be the town's shop, tavern, restaurant, and more... all rolled into one.

The owner stared at them inquisitively from behind a small counter as they entered. After a brief pause, they walked over and sat down at the only open table. He wandered over, cloth rags draped over his left arm, and introduced himself begrudgingly.

"Welcome to Telon's Respite, travelers. Can I offer you some ale? Or perhaps you'd rather let me go to sleep?" he asked sarcastically. He made no attempt to hide his exhaustion; a decision with which they could sympathize.

"Very sorry to trouble you, good sir, but we've been walking for days without rest. We seek ale, any food you might *already* have prepared—even leftovers destined for the bin—and a place to sleep if, you've one we could rent," said Lyla.

She tried to be as polite as she could, seeing the look on his face. His other customers were likely locals that had stayed beyond their welcome, and he was ready to close shop as soon as he could.

"Anything else?" he asked, rolling his eyes with a sigh.

"Some supplies... maybe two horses, if you know where we could buy some," answered Gaerin.

The man seemed to perk up at the thought of a real sale.

"I might have just what you need," he offered. "Name's Wellick. Let me see about some ale. I think there's still some rabbit stew leftover from dinner. I have a room upstairs in my residence, if that'll do. It's not somethin I do often, but I can make an exception. And... I'll see about those supplies and mounts first thing in the morning, okay?"

"That sounds fantastic, Wellick. I'm Gaerin, and this is my wife Lyla. We can't possibly thank you enough."

"Sure thing." Wellick left to fetch their ale. He clanked around loudly in a back room for a few minutes, then returned with a tray carrying bowls of stew, spoons, two tankards, and two hunks of slightly stale bread.

It was the first meal they'd eaten since Gremill fed them, and quite a lot of troll-hunting and travel had happened since. They were halfway through their stew when the other customers nodded and walked out. That was when Lyla noticed the patches sewn to their right shoulders.

She smirked and nearly choked on a piece of bread as she stifled a laugh. After they were outside and out of earshot, she mentioned her discovery to Gaerin.

"Those were the guards," she said, chuckling.

"Are you kidding me?" asked Gaerin in slight disbelief.

"Small towns," she chuckled, shrugging.

Gaerin raised his eyebrows, feigning shock, then chuckled as he shook his head and resumed his meal.

Wellick casually walked to their table.

"Mind if I join you folk?" Wellick asked. He seemed relieved that the guards had departed.

"Um... sure," Lyla answered.

"Sorry, I know it's not a normal request, but... we don't get many visitors out this way. I mean, the occasional supply shipment or whatnot, but that's about it. Gets kinda lonely seein the same faces, day in and day out, and you folk seem... interestin."

"No, we understand. We have a farm just north of Mooncrest," offered Gaerin.

"Ah, yea? Mooncrest... I've heard of that place. Little bigger than here, yea?" he asked.

"A little bigger, yes. I wouldn't call it big, but it's bigger. We live outside of town, though, so most days the only people we see are each other," she said.

"Well, what brings ya so far north?" he asked.

"We have some family business to take care of in Port Vaelin. Thought we'd take the scenic route," said Gaerin.

"Scenic," Wellick said chuckling. "You got that right. Southern Reach woulda been quicker, yea?"

"Quick wasn't really our concern. Besides, if we'd taken the quick route we wouldn't have found all those cute, fuzzy, stinky Kobolds," said Lyla.

"Or the trolls," added Gaerin.

"Kobolds? Trolls? My, my, you folk get around, eh?"

"Oh yeah. We get around. We've been getting around on foot for days, ever since trolls ate our horses," said Gaerin.

"Trolls ate your horses?"

"Yep," confirmed Lyla.

"Where did that happen? Wasn't nearby, I hope..."

"It was at the Ekthri Crossroads, a few days west. Your town is safe, don't worry. We killed them," answered Gaerin reassuringly.

"Oh, whew... that's good to hear. I'm sure Gremill would like to hear that too. He's come to town a few times on his old donkey askin for help. Guards don't like him, so they kinda told him to deal with it himself. I felt bad for him, but I ain't no kinda warrior or nothin, *if you know what I mean*."

Lyla's food caught in her throat. She didn't know how to break the news to Wellick. Tears welled up in her eyes.

"Gremill didn't make it, Wellick. We tried, but we were too late to save him," said Gaerin.

"Gremill's dead?"

"Yes," confirmed Lyla, with tears in her eyes.

"That ain't good. He was a good fella... his farm supplied a lot of our wheat, corn and beans. Heck, he made most of my flour. Most of the other farmers in these parts sell their goods to Raven's Nest to feed the schools. They pay more than I can." Concern washed over Wellick's face.

"Well... I know it isn't much, but we could put in a word in Grellenheim to inspire more trade. We'll be passing through and it wouldn't be any trouble. Or maybe we can talk to one of the local farmers for you," she offered.

"Whatever you think might help. I just... I don't know how I'll be able to feed the guards, myself... or anyone if we can't replace what he supplied. It's not like folk come here spendin lots of cash. They just buy what they need, which doesn't leave me much to resupply. Vicious circle, yea?"

"We completely understand... you get a cut if we buy those horses, though, right? Isn't that why you cheered up when we mentioned it?" asked Gaerin, looking toward Lyla as he spoke. She nodded, agreeing with what he was thinking.

"Yeah, I get ten percent. Local ranch has horses to sell, and Raven's Nest turned em away; said they was too scrawny. But, 'scrawny horses ride the furthest', he told em. Didn't matter. They wanted 'war horses', and that ain't what he's got. So he told me, 'Hey, Wellick, you help me sell some horses and I'll get ya ten percent'."

"Well... how about we pay you an extra five percent as a finder's fee? Then you'll earn fifteen percent total. Just... keep the extra five percent quiet, so the rancher doesn't take some of it, okay?" offered Lyla, continuing Gaerin's thought.

"You ain't gotta do that for me, no ma'am."

"We insist," offered Gaerin. "We met Gremill; he was nice. He fed us and gave us extra weapons to help hunt down the trolls after they ate our horses. We went after them, but they circled back and killed him before we could arrive. So, we feel partly to blame for his death. If we'd stayed put, he'd still be alive. We feel like we owe you this."

"I don't think it's fair to blame you. He wouldn't blame you neither. But the extra coin might help me keep things goin a little longer. So, sure... I help you, you help me... sounds fair." Wellick nodded and stuck out his hand to Gaerin so they could shake on it. Gaerin grasped his hand and shook happily.

When they finished eating, Wellick took them upstairs to his bedroom. He changed the sheets, fluffed the pillows and presented the quarters as if they were in a high-class room in a very expensive inn. He was proud of himself.

Lyla told him how beautiful the room was and paid him twice his asking price. In all honesty, they were so exhausted that the state of the room didn't matter.

Wellick leaned a chair against the wall in the hallway and slept there, promising he would guard them and keep them safe.

It was the best night's sleep they'd had in what felt like ages.

∴ ∴ ∴

LAURENCE JOINED Karzden on the platform overlooking the pit, drawing many hushed whispers among the Initiates. Lord Commander Fahrul's arrival that morning had already caused quite a stir, and he now stood watching from the other side of the arena. The rest of the ruling Council stood at Fahrul's sides. None of what was taking place seemed normal, and the students could hardly contain their curiosity.

Karzden raised his hands to silence the crowd. "Initiates!" he yelled.

A hush fell across the stands.

"We have an announcement before the trials resume. I recognize that this is abnormal and apologize for the abrupt nature of these proceedings. However, the Council has made a decision for the benefit of all, and you deserve to know the details.

"It has become clear just how much an impact young Laurence's arrival has had upon you all; between the rumors that spread between you and his performance these last two days. Many of you have asked questions and expressed concerns to myself and my fellow officers.

"We've come to understand that many of you feel it to be unfair for a person of Laurence's skill to fight against you in the trials. Some of you even wondered if he was a spy we planted among you as some kind of test," he said.

Several members of the audience laughed. He waited a moment for them to quiet down.

"Laurence is just a student, much like you. We didn't add him to your class as a test, and he isn't spying on you. He does, however, have an advantage which we now recognize to be unfair. An esteemed graduate of Fel'Rechaun, seasoned adventurer, and hero of renown trained him for over a decade before he joined us. His uncle Gaerin, son of Arcturus, son of Gahl, is of famed descent in our halls. As a result, Laurence has already learned most of what we have to teach you about weaponry and armed combat."

Laurence looked around the crowd as they talked amongst themselves. He couldn't determine how they were receiving the announcement, and Karzden hadn't even gotten to the point. All he knew was that he didn't want to be standing on the platform. He felt like an impostor.

As the crowd quieted, Karzden continued, "We have decided that Laurence, as of today, will be class Marshal and will no longer compete in the ranking trials."

The crowd erupted as many of the students voiced their disagreement. Lord Commander Fahrul raised his hand from the other side of the pit, calling for silence.

"This is not a slight to any of you," Fahrul explained. "We believe that his continued presence in the fighting pit during ranking trials would place unfair disadvantage to those of you who have not had the benefit of his level of training and experience.

"We also feel we have much to offer Laurence that he could not learn from Gaerin, so it would be equally unfair to prevent him from attending our school. We designed this compromise to put him in a position where he could learn from us while helping you. So, please... listen with your minds, and not your egos."

Cozwuld approached the platform with Izabel following closely behind. The crowd's grumble grew to a roar as they walked up to stand beside Karzden. Cozwuld nodded to Izabel and took a step back, allowing her to address the crowd. She had earned the respect of her classmates and was of noble birth. They quieted as she approached the front of the platform.

"My fellow classmates, I ask that you cast your minds back to when we arrived. Some of us entered this school sponsored and paid in full; able to attend with no commitment to serve in the Legion upon graduation. Many of you had to earn your way into the class by dueling—proving you had what it took to attend—and swearing an oath to serve upon graduation.

"I took part in those duels, despite my family, or my station. Many of you have heard the tale. My father did not want this life for me, so he refused to sponsor my place here. I earned my right to be here, just like many of you. In that earning, you all bore witness to what I was capable of. Many of you congratulated me directly. Several of you even asked if I would teach you.

"Until Laurence arrived, there was even talk that I would become your Marshal. Agnar, Bingrolf, Wil, Darvis, Felix, Warren, Galfor... the list goes on. I could barely eat a meal in peace, for all the well wishing and congratulations I received. I even bought into the idea myself, I heard it so often.

"Then... Laurence arrived. The rumors about him shocked us all. Before you even met him—and most of you still haven't—his fame was upon your lips... and we hadn't even seen him fight," she said, feigning shock.

"After the weapons handling demonstrations, did we not discuss his capabilities at length? Did we not ponder how he might have learned what he knew? He used every single weapon combination that this school teaches, and did so with impressive accuracy.

"Who remembers the dining hall that evening? Who remembers

the debates all around the room as we tried to figure out who among us had the ability to beat him in the pit? Several of you placed bets. I recall bragging that his skills were 'all show', and that I would prove it if given the chance.

"Of course, as luck would have it... I was the first to face him in the pit," she said to a roar of laughter. "I was wrong. He handled me easily. Far too easily, actually. He knew what I was going to do before I did it. He saw through me, as I'd seen through so many of you in the entry duels."

She paused for a moment, to let the crowd drink in her words.

"What most of you *don't* know is that while he was basically toying with me, he took the time to whisper advice. He offered me tips and pointers which—because of my arrogance and frustration—I ignored. He tried to *help* me, while I was *fighting* him. He treated me like a compatriot, rather than an enemy.

"Even amid the rumors, the looks, and us talking about him constantly behind his back... *he wanted to help*. Even though losing to me would have hurt his standing, he took the risk of offering me advice," she explained. "So, I ask you. Would you rather I—who was too arrogant to heed his advice—led you as Marshal? Or someone else with aspirations towards *fame* or *power*?

"*Or*... would you rather have a Marshal that considers your interests and success above his own? A Marshal that inspires us all to succeed, *equally*. A Marshal that I trust, wholly, with my future here at this school," she concluded.

The crowd sat in thoughtful silence for a time.

Karzden studied them, looking for discontent, but found none that was obvious.

Fahrul smiled at Izabel, deciding that she had a knack for public speaking. He was sure he'd be using those skills often during her attendance. Several Council members leaned toward him to whisper the same sentiments.

"We're with you, Laurence!" yelled Wil, breaking the silence.

With a burst of laughter, the crowd applauded both Izabel and Laurence.

Izabel took a few steps back to stand behind Cozwuld.

Karzden smiled at her and nodded his approval before taking over.

"Thank you, Izabel, for that perspective. It is important that we all remember why we are here, and that is to learn. Your rank here means nothing in the Legion. Your rank here means nothing as you enter the world beyond this school. In fact, your rank here simply means you being watched, inspected, and scrutinized to a far greater degree than the rest of your classmates. Being Marshal is a *responsibility*, not a prize.

"I've tasked Laurence with even more responsibility than Marshals have had in the past. He comes to us well versed in combat and weaponry, and I will expect him to assist you all in learning these skills. Furthermore, he will receive training in leadership, tactics, and strategy... things that will push him beyond his limits; all to assist him in leading you more successfully. We will hold him to high standards, just as we do all of you," Karzden explained.

Across the pit, he could see Fahrul signaling.

"I would also like to address the rumors I've been hearing make the rounds about Laurence," started Fahrul. "I must first insist that they stop. You do not, and will not, know the circumstances of his battles. They were unfortunate events for which he is not proud and were quite out of his control. It was only through his uncle's training and his own wit that he survived them, and they are not events to be praised or envied.

"I wouldn't wish upon any of you, the tribulations that Laurence has already faced; not in your lifetime, let alone at his age. Knowing that, and seeing his display of skills, some of you might wonder why? Why would a man such as he seek to attend this school? Does he not already possess the skills he needs; the very skills you seek to learn? To that, I say, listen to Laurence. He explained his motivations succinctly to both Karzden and I," concluded Fahrul.

Laurence cleared his throat nervously. He wasn't used to being the center of attention, and it felt unnatural to him. He had also never spoken to a crowd before, and the one before him was large. Fighting in the pit had been easy by comparison. Holding a sword and shield felt natural and proper. He'd done it for so many years, it didn't matter how many eyes were upon him.

"As Fahrul explained," he began with hesitation, "I have had... experiences. Circumstances arose that I hadn't planned for, and I was forced to handle them. To settle the many arguments I've overheard, five men have fallen by my sword. Not twelve, not twenty... just five. In my opinion, that is five too many," he said bluntly.

People scattered throughout the crowd nodded and whispered to one another. Their reaction gave him more confidence.

"However, those encounters revealed my shortcomings. I was

already on my way here before those battles occurred. I grew up hearing tales of Fel'Rechaun and—like many of you—had dreamed of one day attending this school. I often laid awake at night, daydreaming of fame and glory, as I'm sure many of you did. That part of me died the night before I left to come here, leaving me with a cold, harsh reality. What I knew was not enough.

"So, I continued with my plans to attend this school. Not under fortunate circumstances or the glow of my daydreams, but under pain, sorrow, and regret. I journeyed here knowing that I had failed; that I wasn't good enough to save my family. So when anyone asked, *why do you wish to attend Fel'Rechaun*', I realized my answer had changed.

"I am here to learn, yes. That much is obvious, but... what I'm here to learn is discipline, control, and strategy; to learn to defend myself against stronger, faster opponents. Make no mistake, there *is always* someone better than you. I met several of them on my journey here. I fought several of them. Those fights showed me I was not prepared. So... I am here to become prepared. I am here to ensure that I am never again caught unaware. I am here so that when the time comes, I am capable of saving not only myself, but the ones that I love," he explained.

The crowd had remained silent while he spoke, taking in his every word. Laurence saw sorrow in the eyes of those closest to the platform. He took a moment to choke back his own feelings of remorse before continuing.

"When Karzden explained that the Council had selected me to be Marshal, he had to talk me into the idea. He had to convince me, because I didn't come here to prove I was better than any of you, or to earn a *rank*. I came here, knowing I had flaws, seeking solutions to those flaws. So... here I stand before you, a Marshal who did not ask to be one.

"I will help all of you as much as I can. If there is anything I can teach you, I will. For I know that if it comes to real combat, we only survive together," he offered to the crowd. "I only hope that real combat never comes your way, for isn't glorious or romantic. It isn't fun, or rewarding. It is something you should prepare for, but hope to never see."

After a moment, the crowd applauded. Laurence expected that it was Wil who started them chanting his name, but that was the sound that prevailed as he descended from the platform.

As he made his way past the stands, several hands reached out to pat his shoulder in support. It was as if all at once the Initiates felt relieved, shocked, and empowered. It was an emotional journey for Laurence, and he could only assume it had been the same for them.

He wondered, though, how many had taken the news poorly, and how many would be after him in the days to come. There was no time to ponder such things, however, as Fahrul and the Council were waiting to meet with him; their request had sounded urgent.

As he left the courtyard, he could hear Karzden taking charge and calling for the trials to resume.

∴ ∴ ∴

THE COUNCIL chamber was peaceful, compared to the experience he'd just had. The echo of his footsteps as he approached the meeting hall was calming, and more welcome to him than a roaring crowd and the pressures of public speaking. At the center of the room was a large table in the shape of a crescent. The center was large enough for several people to stand and interact with those seated. The opening to which lay directly in his path.

Around the table were a fourteen chairs, twelve bearing the seal of a specific Council member. Fahrul and the other members sat waiting. Kyrilis occupied the thirteenth chair. She patted on the last remaining seat, indicating he should join her. Her presence was a welcome surprise.

"It's good to see you again, Marshal Laurence."

"Already?" he gasped.

"Already," she said nodding.

Other than their quick banter, the room remained silent for a time. Laurence wasn't sure how Council meetings typically progressed, as he had never attended one. Everyone seemed to simply sit content in their silence. When he looked at Kyrilis, he realized that his confusion must've been written on his face. He tried quickly to hide it. She smiled and tried not to laugh, making it clear his efforts were unsuccessful.

He was about to ask her what they were waiting for when footsteps began echoing through the chamber. As the footsteps' owner drew closer, anticipation permeated the room. Council members—even Fahrul—perked up and straightened their posture. Someone important was coming.

Mordechai entered the room, heading straight for the center of the table. He stood for a moment, hands clasped before him, and accounted for those present; staring each one in the eye briefly. When his gaze met Laurence, he smiled and nodded a simple greeting. Laurence returned the acknowledgment in kind.

"You have returned earlier than we expected, Lord Mordechai," said Fahrul.

"Your fears of a foreign agent would appear to be well founded," announced Mordechai.

Several members whispered to one another in response.

"There is evidence that forces are at work within Fel'Vizsiour and Fel'Rechaun; possibly even the Legion itself. Three students of Fel'Vizsiour have gone missing this past week, and two the month prior. That is besides those you're already aware of. It seems... someone is recruiting from within our ranks."

"This is unfortunate news, Lord Mordechai," answered Fahrul.

"Indeed, my lord. Made more unfortunate by the timing of Lady Ayriel's visit today," Mordechai added.

More whispers echoed about the room.

"A visit you requested," stated Fahrul.

"Indeed. We only have one lead in this investigation, and that lead requires speaking to the dead. As inopportune as her presence might be at this time, I assure you that it is quite necessary," he answered.

"What of the inquisition?" asked Fahrul.

"Councilman Fehrer would know more than I," offered Mordechai.

Everyone in the room turned to look at Councilman Fehrer in unison.

"They will also arrive today. From what I've been told, Ayriel is accompanying them," he answered.

"Does anyone else wish to add to today's challenges?" remarked Fahrul sarcastically.

Several Council members laughed in response.

"Mordechai, will you be available to act as Ayriel's personal guard while within these walls?" asked Fahrul.

"I will, and I request that Laurence and Kyrilis accompany me."

"Very well," Fahrul answered, turning his attention to his left. "Councilwoman Einhart, I trust that you can handle preparations for receiving, and managing, the Inquisitors?"

"I can, Lord. I will need assistance from Councilmen Fehrer and Kargon, of course," she answered.

"Then it is settled," said Fahrul. "Kyrilis, once Ayriel's investigation is complete, please see to it that she is returned safely to the palace."

"Consider it done, sir," answered Kyrilis.

"This meeting is adjourned," declared Fahrul.

Laurence, Kyrilis and Mordechai waited for the Council members to leave before extending proper greetings and discussing their plans for Ayriel's visit.

.·.·.·.

TYLEE PROPPED herself on her pillows, lying on her stomach. She'd drawn the curtains out and around her bed, encircling herself in a shroud of linen privacy. Her tea sat upon the sill within easy reach. Small fluffs of steam rose from her cup, kissing the panes of the window before her. Watching the Reach was her new favorite pastime, she'd decided.

From her position, she could see the far edge of the Western Reach below. The road stretched to her left and right as far as she could see. She often watched as the tops of carriages crossed the view beneath her, imagining the lives of the travelers she could see; often naming them as she did so.

Paul is a simple man. He lives on a farm with his wife and a three-legged dog named Greg. He loves Greg dearly, but does not miss his wife overly much.

Thedus is an angry man and scowls at everyone he meets. He's angry because it hurts him to pee, but his pride won't allow him to speak to an alchemist about it.

Her pastime offered hours of endless entertainment and kept her out of her mother's hair. After dawnfry that very morning, mother had told her to, 'Just go. Go to your window and be... you. I've things to attend.' She didn't care what her mother's motivations were. Back in Mooncrest, staring out the window at the front of their house had caused many arguments. That was not the case in Raven's Nest, and that was all that mattered.

Her mind wandered to Laurence and their marriage. He'd grown so much as a person that he was no longer the jovial, playful boy she'd fallen in love with. She knew that she still loved him, but she also knew that her love for him had changed.

Perhaps it's time for me to change as well, she pondered.

Amidst those thoughts, she squinted her eyes, trying to discern the few people that she could make out at Fel'Rechaun. Most of those that she could see were atop the walls, or at the front gates. Places where she wasn't likely to glimpse her husband, as she was well aware. However, some of them might know of him—she fancied—and that was enough for her... for the moment.

Staring longingly at the gates which led into Fel'Rechaun, she noticed a very intriguing caravan approaching. Those traveling eastward stopped in their tracks as the caravan came to the short road which led toward the gatehouse. The caravan, coming from the east, crossed in front of the stopped travelers and spread out as it did.

Soldiers on horseback lined the sides of the road to the gatehouse, each turning to face the middle as they arrived. Three carriages followed, coming to a rest side by side in the middle of the small entrance; each facing the gatehouse. All the noise from the road below had ceased, save for the new arrivals. She imagined that she could hear the horses below whinny as the carriage drivers called them to stop.

The carriage in the center appeared to be gold. Its roof bore the symbol of House Vaelin, the royal family. Tylee perked up and slid forward across her bed, placing her forehead against the glass to get a better view. There were many more soldiers trailing back along the Western Reach in rows. Two more carriages sat waiting to approach the gatehouse. The scene filled her with excitement.

A woman stepped out of the golden carriage, the purple of her silken houppelande shimmering in the sunlight. The bottom of her robe caressed the ground gently as she walked toward those who awaited her at the gates. Servants rushed from the carriage in her wake, staying a few feet behind, but ready to attend. Her blonde hair flowed down her back like a magical waterfall, bouncing slightly with each of her steps.

The other carriages opened up, letting loose a flood of dark-robed figures. Their houppelandes stopped near their feet, seeming to float above the ground as they moved. Their garb was not the attire of common men, but they did not possess the wealth or standing of the woman who preceded them. Tylee wondered what the commotion was, and why such persons were visiting the school. She hoped that Laurence would tell her when he visited.

Among those that greeted the woman, Tylee thought she could make out a dark-skinned man in Laurence's armor. She was sure it had to be him, even though her eyes struggled to confirm her suspicion from so far away. Her excitement soared.

∴ ∴ ∴

MORDECHAI STOPPED for a moment in the courtyard. His companions proceeded while he stood, eyes closed in contemplation. He reached out to them with his senses, attempting to confirm his suspicions. There seemed a latent power buried within his young friend; a power that was familiar. Realizing that his suspicions were correct, he called out.

"Laurence! Might I have a word?"

"Certainly," answered Laurence, turning. He returned to the strange mage, right hand on his hip.

"Be on your guard in these matters. Ayriel is far above your station, as a daughter of the King, and you would do well to mind your tongue. Further, those that travel with her are here to investigate us, and you are not safe from their inquiries. We do not yet know what is afoot, and there are very few that we can trust in coming days," Mordechai explained.

"Of course," answered Laurence.

As they turned to continue toward the gate, Mordechai paused again. He became certain that future Laurence was one of the magical presences he'd detected on the other side of the strange portal at Sacton River. He didn't know how that could be, or what would transpire to cause such an event, but Laurence's involvement was clear to him.

It was quickly becoming apparent that there was more to Laurence than even he, himself, was aware. His young friend was quickly becoming his chief concern.

Bah'Shiri sighted the caravan from high above, calling down to her master with a ferocious cry as they neared. Mordechai, Laurence and Kyrilis walked through the gates to greet the new arrivals. They stood side by side, calmly watching as the soldiers carved through the traffic on the Western Reach. As they lined the edge of the entry, the golden carriage of Princess Ayriel, The Oracle, rounded the corner.

White horses, much larger than the rest, stopped a few yards in front of them. Their carriage lurched heavily as it came to rest behind them. The drivers sat upon their bench in frilled, fancy tunics and jackets; their heads adorned with purple caps bearing a single red feather. They did not acknowledge the three that stood before them and instead stayed focused on their duties.

Ayriel stepped out of the carriage, her purple houppelande flowing about her like flower petals dancing on the wind. Golden ropes cinched the robe tightly around her waist, clasped at the center with a golden buckle, engraved with the royal seal. At her left hip, a small golden dagger hung loosely from the ropes.

The bottom of her robe formed a train behind her, dragging lightly across the ground as she walked, revealing her family's extensive wealth. Even with such a display of wealth and status, the robe's wearer did not carry herself with a sense of superiority or power. To Laurence, she seemed kind, caring, and inviting. Her blonde locks highlighted the curves and features of her face exquisitely; framing it as if viewing a living painting.

The eyes that gazed back at him revealed that she knew the impression she was making. Her smile revealed that the impression was neither her intention nor concern.

"It has been too long, Lord Mordechai," she said.

Her voice was powerful and alluring, cutting through the air like a knife. Even travelers stopped along the Western Reach leaned toward her, trying to catch her every word.

"It has indeed, your Eminence," he said playfully.

He bowed and kissed her extended left hand, the tip of her sleeve resting upon the top of his boot.

"Eminence, hah!" she scoffed with a laugh. "You very well know this fanciful display before you is my father's doing. I'd be here in traveling leathers, if the decision were mine."

"Do you think that would make you any less overwhelming to behold?" teased Mordechai.

"I do not. It would, however, make nature's bidding far easier to attend," she joked.

"I can imagine," he answered.

The Inquisitors fell in behind Ayriel, each dressed in identical black robes. Ayriel and Mordechai grew serious as they approached.

"Show me to the bodies," Ayriel commanded firmly.

"This way, my lady," answered Mordechai.

The three companions led Ayriel through the gatehouse toward the tower without hesitation.

Councilmen Fehrer and Kargon stepped into the Inquisitors' path and stood their ground. Councilwoman Einhart walked between them, intent on drowning the Inquisitors with thankfulness and pleasantries; stalling them, and putting them off their defenses, being her primary concern.

$$\therefore \therefore \therefore$$

AYRIEL FOLLOWED them into the subterranean levels of the tower. The marble walls, floor, and ceiling echoed loudly at their passing. Torches flickered along the walls as they passed, causing shadowy illusions to play about them eerily. She felt a strange peace in such environments. A peace she did not experience in palaces, ballrooms or great-halls.

She closed her eyes as they passed between two gates which led to prison cells on their left, and torture chambers to their right. The essences of the deceased were about them, swirling amidst the thin wisps of smoke escaping the wall sconces. They reached out to her, pleading her with inaudible whispers to help them reach the afterlife. Many had seen the end of their days in that damp, dark dungeon.

When she finally opened her eyes, the group had arrived at the morgue. She could sense the tension from Laurence and Kyrilis as they waited on either side of the door. Mordechai stood patiently within the room beyond in silence, all to familiar with what she was experiencing.

"We will need to secure the room," she stated.

Her voice was heavy with the weight of her task, and not playful as it had been at the gatehouse. Kyrilis and Laurence looked at each other curiously before following her into the room.

Kyrilis locked the door behind them and announced, "The room is secure, my lady."

"That's not what she meant," offered Mordechai.

Ayriel lowered her head, closed her eyes, and whispered an incantation. The air swirled about the room as if stirred by a summer wind, and yet there was no source from which wind could arrive in the chamber.

Laurence and Kyrilis looked about with concern in their eyes. They could not see the power of Ayriel's spell, but could feel the air move and sense the atmospheric pressure rising.

To Mordechai, the room had become a whirlwind of magics streaking away from Ayriel. Small runes flew toward and attached to the walls, ceiling, and floor; shimmering brightly as they landed and fading to a dull, blue glow.

All at once, the spell stopped. Ayriel looked up at them and declared, "It is done."

"What was that?" asked Laurence.

"Spirits fill the halls of this dungeon. Prisoners, soldiers, and students who once died within these chambers, unable to find their way to the great beyond. I could feel them, and hear them, pleading with me as we entered," she explained.

The two looked at her with a glint of horror in their eyes.

"I cannot help them this day, but I could not have them interrupting my investigation either. So, I have sealed the room against their entry," Ayriel explained.

She made her way over to the two fallen Initiates and stopped as she arrived between them. Her hands hovered over them briefly as she explained further. "Once I open myself to speak with these boys, I will become a doorway through which any spirit might walk. Performing this task without protection is tantamount to psychological suicide."

"That is why you wanted the room secured?" reasoned Kyrilis.

"It is," she answered.

"The two of you are here as witnesses, to help remember what her investigation uncovers. I may need to assist her, in which case I wouldn't be capable of focusing on her revelations. Listen, quietly, and remember. That is your only duty," Mordechai explained to them.

"As you wish," answered Laurence with a nod.

The corpses lay atop stone slabs, each measuring seven foot long and three feet wide. Each slab sloped gently toward one end, with a small inset iron drain. Under each drain sat a small wooden bucket.

Recognizing the purpose of the slabs, Laurence hoped she wasn't planning on dismantling their bodies while he watched. He sighed in relief when she started chanting instead of grabbing tools.

Mordechai slowly waved his left hand in an arc through the air in front of him, lifting his preservation spell out of Ayriel's way. He watched as blue tendrils streaked through the air, encircling Ayriel then reaching down and caressing the bodies of the deceased.

She placed a hand upon each man's chest, and increased her chanting in both pace and volume.

Suddenly the chanting stopped. Both bodies heaved under Ayriel's touch and then sank back down onto their slabs. The air about them settled once more, as did Ayriel's hair, which had been blowing around as if in a breeze. Her head was down, facing the floor, and her eyes were glowing dark blue.

"Why did you leave Fel'Rechaun?" asked Ayriel. Her voice was hollow, echoing within her own chest, and sent chills through Laurence and Kyrilis.

Markus's mouth cracked as his jaw broke loose from the seizing of death. His chest rose slightly as it filled with air, sucking sickly into him with a faint whistle. Thorsten's corpse also began to heave with the intake of air.

"Break the pearl," Markus's corpse whispered.

"Say the words," whispered Thorsten.

"To loose them," added Markus.

"Loose who?" asked Mordechai.

"For her," Thorsten's corpse moaned.

"Who were you to set loose?" inquired Ayriel in the same hollow tones.

"The Velloth," whispered Markus.

"The Velloth," echoed Thorsten.

"For her," Markus repeated.

"Who are the Velloth?" whispered Laurence to Kyrilis.

"Shh! Not now," Kyrilis whispered back.

"Who is she?" asked Ayriel.

"Ancient one," answered Markus.

"Walks in shadows," added Thorsten.

"Is... shadows..." added Markus.

"The pearl was shadows," said Thorsten.

"Gave them shadows," said Markus.

"Won the war," said Thorsten.

"Made our Kingdom," said Markus.

There was a brief pause why Markus and Thorsten sucked air into their chests, through gaping mouths.

"Why help her?" asked Mordechai, frustrated.

"Power," answered Thorsten.

"Like The Demon," added Markus.

"Make us strong," said Thorsten.

"To save us," said Markus.

The corpses writhed atop their slabs. Ayriel struggled to keep her hands in place atop them. Mordechai rushed forward and held Thorsten down at the shoulders. He looked at Laurence, and then Markus, suggesting that he follow suit.

Laurence rushed over and reached to put his hands on Markus's shoulders.

Markus's left hand shot up suddenly and grabbed Laurence's left wrist. He pulled Laurence's hand in close to his face and whispered again, "The Demon!"

"The only way," said Thorsten.

Laurence ripped his arm free, dislodging the corpse's arm from its shoulder in the process. It flopped loosely toward the floor. Laurence took an involuntary step back.

Kyrilis arrived and placed her hands on Markus to hold the corpse down, while Laurence stared at his hand; horror and anger flushing his face.

"She comes for us," said Markus.

"She waits for us," said Thorsten.

"The time is near," said Markus.

Ayriel chanted again under her breath, completing the ritual and setting the boys free. The corpses stilled as they were released from her spell. Decay filled the air as a week of stalled decomposition caught up to them all at once.

Mordechai walked over to Ayriel and helped her get clear of the slabs to more breathable air.

"What in the hell?" challenged Laurence.

"We'll discuss this with Fahrul, Laurence," answered Mordechai. He continued leading Ayriel out of the chamber, back toward the dungeon's exit.

Kyrilis cast Laurence a concerned look. "I thought we'd find out they wanted to party, or make some quick coin with stolen loot, but this... this is..."

"Beyond what we could have expected, and we still don't have the full details. They know what these men were alluding to," Laurence answered.

They strode through the same halls, determination in their steps.

"I mean to find out," said Laurence.

∴ ∴ ∴

ENGLE PLATEAU extended from Vellen Crescent in the east to Telon's Respite in the west. The cliffs of its southern border prevented easy access to the plateau from the Western Reach, and thus very few settlements had risen upon the plateau's surface.

Of the several small towns and villages that had once existed there, few had thrived or survived. Separation from the primary route of trade was too much for their economies to survive. That was especially true when compared to settlements south of the cliff.

Without the landscape hindering access, the southern settlements' success stood in stark contrast.

What remained atop the cliff—aside from Raven's Nest and other militaristic locations which received special funding from the Kingdom's coffers—were mostly ruins, abandoned structures, and individual farms.

Grellenheim was one such city located south of the cliffs, and was the largest city west of Fel'Rechaun. It wasn't as large as Raven's Nest had grown, but it boasted lodging, amenities, and shops for weary travelers. It had once served as the Kingdom's trading hub with the Ekthri.

The city's leadership was lenient and less apt to enforce the more trivial—or easily overlooked—laws of the Kingdom. That leniency had led to the city's higher-than-normal population of personages of ill repute. The side effect of such a population was that the surrounding area was not as safe for farmers and landowners, leaving the fields and hills around Grellenheim barren, and under utilized.

Honest people seeking a decent living or any semblance of a normal life moved elsewhere—if they had the means—or avoided the city entirely. It, therefore, didn't surprise Lyla when Gaerin sat on his horse outside Grellenheim's gates, hesitant to enter.

He gave Lyla a side-long glance, attempting to discern her interest in visiting the establishments within. She shrugged in response to his unasked question. They both knew it would be more than a day of riding before they reached Raven's Nest. They also knew that their horses needed rest, and that there was no safe place to set up camp nearby.

The lack of safety provided by Grellenheim's guard meant they'd have to ride for hours to make camp, and that would put their horses at risk of severe fatigue. They also lacked enough food, water, and supplies to care for themselves or their horses properly out in the wilds. Fate—it seemed—wanted them to enter... even if they preferred not to.

Swallowing their concerns, they nudged their horses forward with their heels. The city streets were full of citizens and travelers alike, moving about in a dusty dance that revealed the town's priorities. Roads were ill-repaired, because earnings went into pockets rather than infrastructure. Protective walls had their stones ripped free for the construction of brothels and gambling halls.

There was a single establishment—according to rumor—that had a reputation as refuge for honest travelers. It was the original tavern and inn; one of the first buildings ever constructed in Grellenheim.

Gaerin and Lyla weaved their way slowly through the crowds and up the hill toward the keep that lay at the center of the city. Two buildings sat on either side of the entrance to the keep. One was a temple of Galrath—which Lyla found ironic given the city's reputation—and the other was called The Founder's Public House.

The Founder's, being the oldest building in all of Grellenheim, was a formidable structure that had survived for hundreds of years. Large stones comprised the foundation and half of the first floor's outer walls. Massive wooden beams rose from atop those stones, providing support for the upper two floors. Smaller beams ran horizontally between them, and weathered, yellowed stucco filled the gaps in between.

The clay tile roof that loomed far overhead was bare in several places, revealing that the establishment's owners either couldn't afford to replace them or—if Gaerin was correct—didn't own a ladder tall enough to do the work themselves. Lines of brown rust trailed down the stucco where each window's bars attached to the wall.

Lyla approached the massive oaken doors while Gaerin stayed with their horses. The doors moaned on their hinges as she pulled them open. Stepping inside, she took a moment to let her eyes adjust as they closed with a thud behind her. The smell of fresh-baked bread filled her nostrils, reviving her forgotten hunger. Blinking off the change in light, she approached a small woman that sat behind the counter.

"Do you have any rooms available?" she asked.

The small woman placed spectacles on her face, squinting at an enormous book in front of her for a moment before responding.

"Aye, seems we have bout three dozen. How many would ye like?" she asked, her voice revealing a lifelong habit of smoking.

"How many rooms does this inn have in total?" asked Lyla inquisitively.

"Bout three dozen," answered the woman frankly.

"So you have all your rooms available?" she asked, seeking clarification.

"Yer a bright one, ain't ye?" sighed the woman.

"I'll take one, with a large bed fit for two. And we must stable our horses where they'll be safe," said Lyla.

The small woman dipped her quill and began writing in the registry. "What be your name?" she asked, eyes focused on the book before her.

"Our family name is Ravencrest, the room can be under that name," she answered.

"Haven't seen one o' your kind in," she began. After flipping through the registry for a few moments, she concluded, "Thirty-two years." She flipped back to the page she'd been writing on and finished her new entry.

"Thirty-two years? And you remembered it?" Lyla asked.

"Yassum, he were dark-skinned like you, a little taller, gray beard, dressed like a hermit. Called himself a wizard," she described.

"That must've been my father-in-law, Arcturus." Lyla smiled at the coincidence.

"Nice feller. Helped pa with stuff round town. I cleaned the stables back then, but Keifer handles that now. Keifer!" she yelled over her shoulder.

A teenage boy entered from a door behind the counter and ran dutifully up to the woman.

"We got ourselves some guests. Why don't ye head outside and he'p with the horses. Let Gabner know to see ta their supper on yer way through," she ordered.

"Thank you, Keifer," offered Lyla.

He smiled sheepishly back at her as he scurried toward the front door to be helpful.

"Gabner works in back, Keifer'll get yer dinner goin after he stables yer horses. Hope ya like turkey, cause that's all Gabner knows ta cook. Well, that n' bread," she explained.

"That sounds splendid, actually. We haven't had turkey in some time," Lyla said. Turkey wasn't a meal they'd commonly consumed, and she looked forward to tasting it.

"Well," the woman said as she grabbed a big iron key, "that's what ya get when ya buy a Kobold to do yer cookin. But ya ain't gotta pay em much, so it works out. Keeps the riff-raff out too, cause they don't fancy a Kobold fixin their meals. Keeps the place quiet."

"A Kobold? Cooking?" Lyla blurted excitedly.

"Aw sure, they dumb n' feisty n' such, but once they get a taste o' civil life, they quiet down enough. Gabner ain't got no interest in returnin to his folk... says they smell bad," she said, laughing.

"Oh believe me, they do!" answered Lyla.

Lyla found the turn of events ironic, after begging Gaerin for a Kobold to help around the kitchen so many months prior. She was sure he'd get a kick out of it, or at least roll his eyes... which she loved to cause him to do.

"I can't wait to taste Gabner's cooking," she said merrily.

Gaerin entered as the old woman hopped out of her chair and came out from behind the desk. His wife was short, and the woman before them was even shorter. He stood blinking his eyes for a moment before proceeding. When he could focus properly, before him stood his very giddy wife. The sight alarmed him because they'd both been so somber and cautious riding into town, especially after all that had happened with Gremill and Wellick.

"Clearly I missed something," he stated.

"I can't wait for you to have dinner here," she said gleefully, turning to follow the old woman up the stairs.

"I put ya in room two, top o' the stairs. Keifer, Gabner and I live on the top floor. Gabner snores, so I wanted ya far away from his room. If ya need anything," she said as they reached a door labeled 'Tew', "just holler '*Maude*' and I'll come a runnin," Maude explained.

She handed Lyla the key and went back downstairs; stopping on each step until both feet had reached it, and clinging desperately to the railing as she went.

"She's not running anywhere," remarked Gaerin quietly.

"Stop, she's delightful. Maude remembers Arcturus staying here," she exclaimed happily.

Lyla opened the door with the key and literally jumped inside, excited to be there.

Gaerin shook his head in disbelief and followed her in.

∴ ∴ ∴

AYRIEL ALMOST recovered her strength by the time they reached Fahrul's great-hall in the tower. The steps leading up to it had sent her into a momentary dizzy spell, and she'd nearly collapsed. Mordechai continued to walk just behind her, holding her right arm with his left hand just in case.

When they reached the top landing, she stopped and smiled at him briefly before calmly stating, "I'm okay. Thank you."

Fahrul was standing behind his table, hands on his hips with anticipation written all over his face. The four of them crossed the room to join him. Ayriel was the only one of them who took a seat.

With a look from Mordechai, Fahrul realized the details of their briefing were sensitive. He took a moment to dismiss all servants and guards from the chamber, forgoing the usual ale or wine that might greet his guests.

Once they were alone, and all doors were closed, Mordechai muttered a single word and waved his hand.

"We are alone, and may speak freely. I've sealed the chamber from prying ears," he explained.

"Now will you tell me what just happened? And I mean, details, Mordechai. None of your fancy talk," demanded Laurence, much to Fahrul's surprise.

Mordechai sighed, attempting to withhold his desire to reply in a similar tone.

"How about we start at the beginning," injected Fahrul.

"I spoke with Markus and Thorsten, Fahr. The matter is far worse than we anticipated," explained Ayriel.

Fahrul noticed her dismissal of formal titles and pleasantries. She wanted to get straight to details and skip any pomp and circumstance that could muddy his understanding of the situation. He appreciated her decision.

"The boys were tempted by the promise of power and were sent to *'release the Velloth'* on some part of the Kingdom at the bidding of Nightweaver," explained Mordechai.

"The Velloth? They're a myth," challenged Fahrul.

"An elven myth," confirmed Kyrilis.

"Who is Nightweaver, and how do you know that's who they meant?" asked Laurence.

"Ayriel and I are lifelong students of the mystic arts. There are legends of a sorcerer—a witch—that can move from place to place through shadows. Similar to the teleportation spells I sometimes use, though my teleportation is limited to specific runes placed at exact locations.

"If the tales are correct, she could emerge from a shadow in this room right now, if she so pleased, regardless of my protections. And it is said that she's had this power since long before our land existed," he explained.

"If she is real," added Ayriel. "No one in our circles has seen her to confirm her existence in more than a hundred years, and even then it was pure conjecture. There are tomes about her in Fel'Vizsiour, as if she were a legend of old; studies about the effects of her magics, and musings about the power necessary to perform the feats attributed to her."

"Fine. Assuming this Nightweaver is behind whatever these boys were up to, what did she promise them? What is she looking to gain from their servitude?" asked Fahrul.

"Markus grabbed my hand and repeated that she would make them like Drakahl, yelling it at my tattoo. He called him 'The Demon'," answered Laurence. "I know from my encounter with him that he looks like a demon in his armor, and his men were talking about becoming like him... so it is within his plans to share that power, and I'd assume that includes similar armor."

"Your tattoo?" asked Ayriel.

Laurence then realized she'd never seen it. He leaned forward and showed it to her.

She studied it for a time and then placed her hands around his sympathetically. "Yet another myth confirmed," she stated, releasing Laurence's hand. "If Laurence's tattoo has done that helmet justice, I know what they were promised. I just... don't know how it's possible."

"The Skorned," answered Mordechai knowingly. "I'd expected that as possibility when I first heard Laurence's tale, but the pieces are falling into place now and I've become certain."

"What is a Skorned?" asked Kyrilis.

"Before Arkhan Vaelin made his first attempt to conquer the lands and form Arkhania, it is said that the last tribe of Toor still roamed the Warlunds to the northwest. They hailed from ancient times, back before history was being chronicled. Their legends included the creation of armor powered by Toor, Human and Elvish souls.

"It required many sacrifices to construct, trapping the souls of the victims into each piece of armor as it was forged. Then, a demonic soul would be summoned and imbued upon it to give it its final appearance and powers. This was kept from our history out of fear that some might try to create the armor themselves, which would end in all manner of horrific failure," explained Ayriel.

"The trouble is, the demonic spirit would slowly gain dominion over those that wore the armor and would eventually possess them and take over. Further, I formally discounted the legend's voracity because Toor cannot cast spells. They lack the ability to channel magical energies of any kind. It was within reason to assume the stories to be false. Clearly they must've had help in creating the armor back then, for clearly I was wrong in my assumptions," added Mordechai.

"So, if they're trying to make more of these–" started Laurence.

"Then they've found a way around the problem," continued Mordechai.

"That's a bold gift to offer a recruit," Fahrul surmised.

"Indeed! But it wasn't the only gift alluded to during the interrogation. They mentioned breaking the '*pearl*' to set the Velloth free. The pearl that once adorned the crossbow's stock. They also hinted that the same entity that wooed them had gifted the pearl to Arkhan to power the weapon. That would mean–"

"That Nightweaver was critical to the eventual formation of Arkhania," said Fahrul, completing Mordechai's thought. His face went stark white at the revelation.

"However, creating several Skorned is not so easy as a single black pearl. So I question the truthfulness of her offer. I think it was false hope; something extravagant to lure them in with no plans of fulfilling the offer. They'd probably arrive to collect, and she'd have Drakahl kill them," answered Mordechai.

"What of the Velloth, then? Why that specific thing?" asked Fahrul.

"What *are* the Velloth?" asked Laurence desperately.

"The Velloth are an ancient Elven race, driven underground by the Toor long ago; before common man and elf arrived here, or so cave drawings would lead me to believe," answered Mordechai.

"The Velloth have red, scaly skin, oily black hair and black eyes that glow red in darkness. They live underground and—if you're a bad boy or girl—they come to eat you while your parents sleep," offered Kyrilis. "The Afyr use them as fairy tales to control unruly children. They aren't real," she insisted.

"I have been to the depths of many a cave, cavern, and ruin across Arkhania and Tellrindos... yes, as rumors have it, I do indeed scour the lands in my research. In those trips I have seen mention of what Kyr describes many, many times. Red skin, black hair, elvish... even scales. Some have mentioned them by name, but the names are almost always unique to those who were describing them.

"Velloth is a name given to them by the Toor, and was adopted by both the Afyr and the Ekthri. Fel'Vizsiour's volumes on the race are extensive. The tomes were given to the school by the royal scribe of the Ekthri, Belsifor Vicaern. I have since expanded upon them through my own findings," explained Mordechai. "I assure you, they are very, very real. Though, I will admit it unlikely that they eat small Afyr children who talk back to their parents."

"Yet no one has seen them in at least one hundred years," declared Ayriel.

"Closer to two hundred, and even then it was but a small scouting party by all appearances," answered Mordechai. "They don't seem to fare well on the surface for long periods of time."

"So," began Fahrul, "we have an ancient witch who helped build our Kingdom, aiding a demonic knight plotting to *disrupt* that very Kingdom by recruiting our own troops to betray us by unleashing a fabled race of underground elves... for purposes we have yet to uncover," he summarized sarcastically.

"That appears to be the case," answered Mordechai.

"There is no chance in hell that the Inquisition will accept this explanation," lamented Fahrul.

"Not even in the slightest," sighed Kyrilis.

"That still doesn't tell us *how* they were going to release the Velloth, *if* they succeeded, or *where* it was done," said Laurence.

"No, it does not. That is just as troubling as the believability of it all," answered Fahrul.

"We might know where, actually," mused Mordechai.

"Do tell," said Fahrul.

Mordechai looked at Laurence confidently and said, "Sacton River."

"Damnit!" exclaimed Laurence.

"Explain," demanded Fahrul.

"I found the boys in the abandoned Waystation on the north bank of the Sacton River, by the bridge. Laurence fought the other three just south, as they were fleeing the area. We also experienced a magical disturbance on the south shore of the river, which is how I met Laurence in the first place. I can only assume that the magical disturbance was drawn to the location because of lingering magics left behind, from the boys breaking the Vaelin pearl and '*saying the words*' as they put it," answered Mordechai.

Laurence was happy he left out the finer details of the disturbance they'd seen.

Mordechai started pacing as he continued. "My theory is, they'd already completed the ritual to release the Velloth. Or, they started the chain of events which would lead to their unleashing. The boys then had their falling out atop the bridge, because Markus and Thorsten wanted to go see Nightweaver for their reward. However, the other boys wanted to continue looting, or were either afraid to go with them, or were unaware of her involvement. She might have even inspired them to turn on one another, just to cover her tracks."

"Then where are the Velloth?" asked Fahrul.

"That is the pertinent question," answered Mordechai, stopping beside Laurence.

"I'll start by scouting Salvation Shire, Gaierford, Ayerton, and Dunforth. Then I'll head west along the old farm roads. If that's the area they performed their unknown task, then it very well may be the area where the Velloth came to the surface," offered Kyrilis.

"Go now, we've no time to lose. Mordechai, take Laurence and scout west of the tower, toward Grellenheim. I'll send Cozwuld with word to Raven's Keep. Ayriel, we need you back in Vellenheim to speak with your father. This Inquisition will hamper both the school and the Legion as we try to discover and defeat this threat. He's the only chance we have of backing them off. He also needs to know the gravity of this situation, from you and not some Inquisitor," detailed Fahrul.

"A wise course of action," agreed Ayriel.

"If we expect to encounter the Velloth, I'd like to have a few others with me, sir," said Laurence.

"Fine, select a handful of recruits to accompany you, and see Dahsh to have them outfitted. You don't have much time, so act quickly," said Fahrul.

Mordechai waved his hand to release the seal upon the room as they exited, each party going their own way. "I'll meet you at the western gates in one hour, Laurence," he said on his way through the door.

∴ ∴ ∴

SHAER'THOG STOOD patiently awaiting his master on the docks. His hooves slowly seared the wood, sending tendrils of smoke rising into the air. Several dock workers raced about with buckets, trying desperately to keep the docks around the creature wet enough to prevent open flames. They hated the beast's visits and were thankful they were infrequent.

Ahm had summoned Shaer'Thog as a present for Drakahl from another world, where the demon inside his armor had once been its master. Nightweaver and Ahm had spent a fortnight gathering reagents and creating the circle to perform the summoning in secrecy.

Each of its four hooves were constantly alight with flames that could not be extinguished. The dark, red fur just above its hooves shone brightly in contrast to the pitch black skin underneath. Unlike a normal horse, that fur and a mane were the only hair on the steed's body. Black leathery flesh covered the rest of the beast, revealing an impressively muscular physique underneath.

Its three tails were long and serpentine, writhing in the air behind it menacingly. Its red mane served as reins, but only for its one true rider. Large, leathery wings adorned the creature's sides. Though they did not allow the creature to fly, it could glide from great heights, jump farther than a normal horse, and use its wings to protect its rider when necessary.

Bone plate armor grew naturally about the creature's head and snout, much like a horn on any other creature. Peering through holes in the black bone plate were two flaming eyes, watching with patient longing for his master to reveal himself. Small puffs of smoke escaped the bone nose holes every time the creature snorted, causing a stir among those closest to it.

The Dread Tide rounded the rocky cliffs bordering Dagoh Bay, exciting Shaer'Thog. He reared back in celebration at his master's return and kicked a dock worker in the head. As the corpse slid across the dock, splashing into the water below, the beast dropped back onto all fours and trotted towards the ship's destination; leaving burning hoof prints in its wake.

Day passed into night as the crew moored the massive ship. When the gang plank finally lowered, Drakahl was the first to descend, the plank groaning under his weight. He stood for a moment to caress his steed's mane, their heads pressed together. He smiled at the beast and gave it a small kiss on its snout before mounting.

Nothing pleased Shaer'Thog more than the weight of his master, and kick of his heels.

VELLOTH

Ris'Enliss, Oghenfall 24th, 113 of the 2nd Era

Be wary of the rising tide,
It's depths were long unknown.
In its wake doth hell reside,
Awakened now, they come.

Night's Writ, Parable 8

N LARGE cities it was often a custom for the church bells to ring at the first light of dawn. With the absence of farm animals to call out the new day, such custom was usually one born of practicality. The ringing that woke Gaerin and Lyla that morning was not that kind of ringing... it was frantic and repetitive.

They knew immediately that something was wrong, and got out of bed as fast as they could. Donning their armor in haste, they looked at each other with deepening concern. The ringing had suddenly halted, clearing the way for the sounds of combat to reach their ears.

Screams of anguish, cries for help, and the grunt of men fighting echoed throughout the main floor of the inn, pouring in through broken windows. Shattered glass crunched beneath their feet as they approached the main door, unsure of what they'd find on the other side. Gaerin lifted the bar that held the doors secure and placed it against the wall. With a concerned look between them, they each pushed a door open, revealing the scene beyond.

The town guard was fighting between the church and the inn, defending the gates of the keep in sheer desperation. Citizens ran through the streets, either fleeing from their attackers or trying feebly to fight back. Attacking them were creatures that Gaerin and Lyla had never seen or even heard of in stories. They stood taller than an average human, were more slender, and yet seemed stronger.

Their flesh was scaly and crimson red—like serpents—and their hair was oily black and shimmered in the limited light of the evening. Fierce, black teeth snarled as they growled in exhilaration at the sight of their opponents falling before them. Glowing red eyes peered at their victims through strands of black hair, adding to the horror of their visage. Elven ears poked through their hair, reveling in the sounds of anguish and fear that surrounded them.

All of them wore dark brown leather armor with a single disk of black stone at the center of their chest, and blackened spikes protruding from their shoulders, elbows and fists. They wielded several types of weaponry, all crafted from the same black stone. Their skill was unmatched among their human opponents, and they were easily tearing through the guard in a manner suggesting they were enjoying themselves immensely.

Gaerin ran down the steps to join the guard in their defense.

Lyla remained on the steps casting a banishment spell, assuming they were demons. Her spell crashed into the Velloth nearest her and dissipated, accomplishing nothing. Horrified, she jumped down the steps to join her husband.

∴ ∴ ∴

LAURENCE AND Mordechai stopped briefly atop a hill just southwest of Grellenheim, taking in the scene below. Wil, Izabel, Agnar and Bingrolf stopped their horses shortly behind, waiting for a call to action. The city below them was burning throughout its southern half. A battle still waged in the middle of the city, but they could not see the north clearly. The sound of a frantically ringing bell called to them, pleading for help.

They kicked their horses hard, sending them into a gallop. While they'd ridden through the night, their horses' exhaustion was the least of their concerns. The dead had proven truthful; they had released the Velloth. All the companions steeled themselves for battle, trying as best they could to choke back their fears.

Even Mordechai felt concern for their success, and their safety.

Burning buildings lined the streets as they barreled through the southern portion of the city. Corpses lay strewn about the city blocks in piles, most dragged from their homes and slain as if for sport. Most of the dead were still in their nightclothes, or a few haphazardly-donned scraps of armor. The Velloth had caught the city unaware, and ill-prepared for an invasion.

Laurence pulled his horse to a stop and dismounted. As his companions followed suit, he slapped his mount on the rear to send it clear of the chaos. Determination consumed him as he drew his sword.

Mordechai clasped his right hand as if holding a sword and placed it into the palm of his left. When he pulled his hands apart, a silver blade seemed to grow out of thin air. He twirled the weapon once, testing its weight, and nodded at Laurence to indicate he was ready.

A Velloth charged the group, its black swords held out to its sides in a menacing pose. It brought the swords forward, slashing sideways with both simultaneously as it closed in on Laurence.

Laurence jumped back—just out of harm's way—and swung his sword upward, parrying the blades as they crossed and sending them high above his head. Izabel stepped in from his left at the same instant, driving her sword through the creature's exposed chest.

Two more Velloth ran toward them, one wielding a two-handed maul and the other a spear.

Laurence ran straight toward the one with the maul and as the vile elf swung the heavy weapon downward to crush him, he tucked and rolled to the ground sideways... straight into the elf's legs. The maul narrowly missed its diving opponent, crashing into the ground as the elf lost his footing and tumbled over Laurence. Red elven flesh burst open, allowing skull and brain to break free as Bingrolf's maul smashed through the prone elf's head.

Agnar engaged the other, parrying a thrust of its spear as he closed the distance. Wil bounded to his side, Quel'Thoz in hand, and with a twirl decapitated the elf while Agnar distracted it.

Mordechai smiled at their prowess as he strode forward to join them.

Up the hill ahead of them, more Velloth had taken notice and were heading their way.

Mordechai raised his left hand above his head in a fist, then quickly knelt and slammed his left palm into the ground between his companions, yelling, "Tyribosh!"

Blue light burst from the ground where he struck it, slamming into his companions and sending a fresh wave of energy through them. He stood back up and urged the companions to attack.

Laurence ran toward the Velloth more quickly than he normally could have. His companions took notice and followed suit, arriving at his side with unnatural speed. Side by side they easily parried attacks and ran through their opponents, ending another dozen Velloth lives.

As their magical haste faded, they found themselves beside the cathedral. A ferocious battle was underway in the courtyard beside the church, with countless guards and citizens fighting desperately to survive.

They had no time to hesitate.

Laurence, Izabel, Wil, Agnar and Bingrolf strode into the field of battle determinedly, their confidence raised and their fears temporarily quelled.

Mordechai stayed back and began chanting another spell.

∴ ∴ ∴

GAERIN AND Lyla quickly took command of the men at the gates, who had fallen into disarray. It was obvious to them that most of the guards were poorly trained volunteers. Gaerin ordered them into formation while parrying blades, spear tips and axes... saving several of their lives in the process.

Lyla followed in his wake, bashing several Velloth about their body and skull as they reeled backward from Gaerin's defense. The Velloth were not yet dying by their hands, but neither were the guards. The Velloth onslaught had been stalled.

Forced to regroup, the Velloth shifted their forces more towards Gaerin and Lyla's positions. The guards, inspired by the new arrivals, rallied and formed up beside them. Several wounded regained their feet to rejoin the battle. Those too wounded to strike at their foes grabbed a shield in each arm and provided cover to their comrades.

Gaerin slammed his warhammer into the skull of a Velloth, ending the creature's life. He kicked the body away from them as it fell, yelling, "Stay on defense! Let them make the mistakes! Do not overextend!"

The guards took heed of his advice and yelled their agreement loudly. Up and down the line, they parried, blocked, and waited. They no longer dove through their own lines seeking a killing blow, or overreached with their attacks and exposed themselves. Instead, they stayed behind their shields to maintain their cover and keep defensive postures.

The Velloth, now enraged, attacked with greater ferocity, driven by anger and disbelief.

Just as the men had gained their footing and were holding their ground, a commotion stirred at the rear of the Velloth lines. Several of the horrid elves on the southeastern side of the battle turned to engage new foes. The guards found new strength at the sight and pressed their opponents harder.

A ball of lightning formed above the Velloth, swirling and pulsating. Powerful bolts of electricity arced through the air, striking several of them at once. Charred corpses fell sizzling to the ground, blood bursting through the air where they'd been struck. Fear grew in the eyes of the attackers, their snarls of hatred turning to gasps as realization set in.

Lyla climbed back to the top of the steps. She looked to the far side of the battle, trying to discern who had arrived to help them. Blades flurried about from several opponents, displaying a skill and determination which the guards did not possess. Their actions showed precision and coordination, often completing one another's attacks or defending their comrade as if the entire encounter were a single practiced maneuver.

Behind them stood a mage with black robes, and silvery-white hair. He wielded a silver sword, flashing through the air and leaving thin trails of blue energy as he moved his hands in intricate patterns. Another ball of lightning grew in the sky above the quagmire, arcing through the crowd and sending more Velloth to their graves.

She moved to call down to Gaerin, but before she could, someone caught her eye.

∴ ∴ ∴

LAURENCE WAS growing confident in his comrades. He had instructed them for hours during their ride to Grellenheim, warning them that coordination and patience would be their key to victory. Repeating his prior advice to Izabel, he stressed the importance of keeping their weapons and shields inside the space between themselves and their opponent, and using precise movements for most of their attack and defense.

When they first engaged the Velloth at the cathedral's courtyard, they hadn't yet adopted his advice. Agnar kept overextending, and Bingrolf was swinging in wide, exaggerated arcs, trying to add more strength to his blows. However, as the battle progressed their movements grew closer and closer to themselves, and wild aggression gave way to strategy and precision.

Laurence parried a Velloth's sword, and Agnar ran him through.

Bingrolf crushed the head of a Velloth, and Agnar turned in time to deflect a spear sent in retaliation.

Izabel's attack forced a Velloth to parry, wide and to the right, leaving an opening for Laurence to slice its throat.

Wil deflected a strike aimed at Izabel, then turned the other end of his staff to stab another Velloth in the chest.

The more they fought together, the more they acted as one.

Mordechai cast another spell above the Velloth, slaughtering half a dozen of them at once. The others backed away momentarily, fearful that the mage would destroy them all.

Laurence pressed forward, taking advantage of their retreat. His companions followed suit. They killed eight more Velloth in short order and then found themselves with a moment to breathe.

Corpses littered the ground before them; some Velloth, others human. Some were charred from Mordechai's lightning, others had been slain by various weaponry. The air reeked of death and charred flesh.

Izabel stood beside Laurence, ready to continue. He looked about the battlefield and, seeing the guards successfully defending the gates to the keep, turned the party's attention to the mass of Velloth attempting to flee north.

Without further hesitation, the five pursued their quarry.

Mordechai paused for a moment, studying the group at the gates. Seeing the other Ravencrests taking charge and rallying the troops successfully, he turned and followed the students north with confidence.

∴ ∴ ∴

LYLA MADE her way to Gaerin's side, trying desperately to stay out of sight of the new arrivals.

"Laurence is here!" she gasped between blows. "He's with a group from Fel'Rechaun and they have turned the tide of battle!"

"We can't let him see us. He can't know what we're doing!" added Gaerin as he parried and returned an attack.

"These men can handle the rest. We should go," answered Lyla.

They made their way back to the inn, slaying another Velloth along the way. Looking back at the courtyard, Gaerin felt confident that the guards could handle what remained of the enemy forces. He looked toward the northern edge of the courtyard to see Laurence and his group fighting through Velloth with coordination and focus.

"That boy is impressive," remarked Gaerin as they turned and passed through the doors.

Maude stood behind the counter, as if it were any other day. She looked up at them briefly as they entered and returned her attention to the registry as if unconcerned. Keifer was trembling in the corner behind her, overcome with fear. Gabner was on top of a table to their left, peering through broken glass at the scene in the courtyard below.

Lyla ran upstairs to gather their things while Gaerin stayed to deal with the inn's staff.

"The city is lost. Half of it's burning, and most of the citizens are dead or running for their lives. We need to get you out of here."

"I'm not going anywhere," answered Maude.

"But-"

"No buts," she interrupted. "This is my family business and I'm not leavin it behind. Sides, they're gonna need a place for workers ta sleep when they rebuild."

Keifer whimpered from the corner.

"Ye can take Keifer n' Gabner, though. Lad's no use ta me when the inn is full, he can't keep up. And the folk that build towns don't like their food bein made by no kobold," she said with a flick of her quill.

She tore the page she'd been writing on from her registry and handed it to Gaerin.

"That's all ye need anywhere in the Kingdom. Says you own Gabner, and I've sent my boy ta live with ye," she offered.

"Are you sure we can't escort you to safety?" asked Gaerin as he folded the paper.

"Just keep my boy safe and take that dang kobold off me hands. That's enough. If you're ever by again, once we rebuild, come back n' we'll see bout me buyin em back. It's fer the best," she answered, nodding.

Lyla came downstairs carrying their satchels over her shoulder. She looked at Gaerin, with Keifer and Gabner standing to his sides, and shrugged at him as if to say, '*we did our best.*'

The courtyard was clear of combat when they exited the inn. Battle still raged to the north, and many citizens were running in every direction attempting to flee. Corpses of both Velloth and human littered the streets in all directions.

They quickly checked on their horses but found them dead. As they led Keifer and Gabner to the south—around the cathedral and away from the battle—all they could smell was burning timber and flesh.

Once outside of town, they found three saddled horses. Lyla scooped Gabner up in one arm and carried him onto a horse with her. She even let him hold the reins. Exhausted, and more than a little shaken, they continued east for some time before turning north towards the Western Reach.

∴ ∴ ∴

LAURENCE AND Mordechai stood on the main road near the exit to the Western Reach. They looked around them at the remnants of the once-vibrant city. Reputation aside, only the day before it had been bustling with life.

No one deserves to die this way, thought Laurence.

He looked down at himself, covered in blood, and wondered how much of his life he would spend that way. It was a concerning thought, so he quickly convinced himself to move past it.

Looking up at Mordechai again, he asked, "And how is it *you* remain so clean?"

Mordechai smiled in response without turning his head to face him. He was studying the streets and alleyways as dawn crept over the horizon. He could still hear the sounds of skirmishes echoing through the streets. Somewhere, Wil, Izabel, Agnar and Bingrolf were chasing down and finishing the last of the Velloth which remained.

"It is an unfortunate thing, *this*," he said, waving his hand toward the bodies strewn before them. He turned to Laurence and added, "However, seeing you in action was a sight to behold, and not one I'll soon forget."

"You know full well that our success was not my doing," countered Laurence.

"Not yours alone, no. You had help, as any strong warrior does," answered Mordechai.

"I am not a strong warrior," retorted Laurence.

"You are skilled, well trained, and strategic. You did not win this battle with strength, and that is good. Strength wanes. Strength can fail you."

"Your spells made us faster than we should have been. Your spells slew dozens of Velloth and frightened them, pulling their wits out of the battle and giving us opportunity. This battle was won by you, not I," answered Laurence.

"I did as I must, just as you. Do not discount your capabilities, Laurence. Even with my help, others would likely have failed. I would have been forced to fight these Velloth all on my own and... I do not relish that thought. I am not one for combat. My spells and knowledge are more suited to other pursuits," he finished.

He placed his hand on Laurence's shoulder reassuringly.

"As to how I remained so clean, *that*... is a simple thing," he said with a smirk.

Laurence felt a tingle across his entire body as Mordechai removed his hand. When he looked down at his armor again, he was as clean as if he'd just bathed, armor and all. "*Now* you're just showing off," he quipped.

Mordechai shrugged and resumed watching the streets for their companions.

It was daylight before they returned and declared the streets to be clear of their enemy.

∴ ∴ ∴

AFTER WALKING through the city in search of stragglers, they mutually agreed that there were none left to find. No Velloth remained, and any citizens who survived had fled; most to the north along the Western Reach. The southern half of the city lie in ruined heaps of burning timber and crumbled clay.

The group remained quiet as they walked. Agnar occasionally grunted in pain, favoring a wounded right leg. Bingrolf sneered and winced, breathing heavily on account of his injured ribs. The solemn reason for their presence in Grellenheim weighed upon them all.

None of them felt much like talking.

"Of course!" bellowed Izabel from the front of the line, breaking the silence and tossing her hands into the air.

"What is it?" called Laurence.

The four hastened their pace to catch up to her.

"Our horses are gone! Not dead, just... *gone!*" she exclaimed.

"I guess we're walking," stated Laurence.

"That'll be fun," answered Agnar sarcastically.

"The healing salves and flasks were in the satchels on our mounts, Agnar!" explained Izabel.

"If we went back to the Reach," started Wil.

"We'd be swarmed by terrified townsfolk and our journey would be even more difficult," completed Laurence.

"Laurence is right," offered Mordechai.

He placed his hand on everyone but Laurence, one by one, and repeated his cleansing spell. They looked at him with both thankfulness and wonder in their eyes.

"This much I can do for you, and the cleansing extends to your wounds. Take rest and bandage yourselves. Get some sleep, if you can. Head back to Fel'Rechaun when you're rested and the journey will not be as difficult. I will send for you with fresh horses. Follow the route we took to get here," said Mordechai.

"You're not staying with us?" asked Laurence.

"No, I must report to Fahrul as quickly as possible. I'm sure you understand," he concluded. He closed his eyes, bowed his head, and vanished from their presence before they could argue.

"There's that, then," remarked Izabel.

"Let's get a respectful distance from town and set camp, then. He's right, we need rest. Daylight or not, we haven't slept in at least a day and we're all exhausted from battle," Laurence said. "Izabel, see if you can find any blankets or bedding in town before we move on. We don't want to rob or pillage, so just take the bare minimums we might need for a camp. Agnar, Bingrolf, Wil, find a flat piece of land to the east and settle in," ordered Laurence.

"Where ya goin?" asked Bingrolf.

"To find healing herbs, firewood, and perhaps some food," answered Laurence.

∴ ∴ ∴

FAHRUL WAS deep in conversation with a pair of Inquisitors when Mordechai's footsteps echoed through the chamber. He looked up at his friend and smiled in relief, then began the long process of ushering the men from his hall.

Mordechai waited in silence until everyone had left, so they could speak in private. The great doors shut, and the latch fell into place as a wave of Mordechai's hand sealed the room once again. It was a routine they were both familiar with and required no coordination to perform.

"We found a small army of Velloth attacking Grellenheim," started Mordechai.

Fahrul dropped into his chair, letting his fear and frustration show.

"We do not know where they came from, or how they arrived at Grellenheim. It could have been a target of opportunity, or their intended target. We cannot say either way. Their forces are dead, but our victory came at great cost. Most of the city died with them," explained Mordechai.

"What were their numbers?" asked Fahrul.

"I counted fifty, but I'm sure there were at least a few more. Wil, Izabel, Agnar and Bingrolf chased down the stragglers out of my sight, so I can't be certain. The total count was surely less than one hundred. The town guard was in disarray, and the citizens were ill prepared to fight in the dead of night. I cannot say for certain that the result would've been much better in daylight, though. They outnumbered the Velloth twenty to one and still... they stood no chance," explained Mordechai.

"And our enemy has done this from afar, with intrigue, manipulation and false promises."

"That would appear to be the case. I think this confirms everything we learned from Ayriel's investigation."

"How did our Initiates perform?" asked Fahrul.

"Splendidly! Laurence chose his companions well, and spent our journey educating them, just in case. His guidance provided the edge we needed to survive the encounter. I do not think the Velloth have fought recent wars against experienced foes. They seemed unprepared for our techniques."

"Perhaps we should invite Gaerin to teach here at Fel'Rechaun. He's done a splendid job with Laurence," suggested Fahrul.

"I don't think he would accept, seeing as he's presently traveling toward what I can only assume is his family's revenge," answered Mordechai.

"He's what?" asked Fahrul, concerned.

"I don't think he realizes, or knows who I am... but I saw him fighting outside the keep in Grellenheim. He organized the guards and got them fighting together, as one, and turned the tide of their battle... much like his nephew was doing with our Initiates a short distance away. I don't think Laurence noticed him, and I've not spoken to him on the matter.

"I know that family... I remember Gaerin and Tolrin from their time at this school. It was definitely him that I saw. He is a Ravencrest, and that means he will not abandon his quest," said Mordechai.

"If this Nightweaver is plotting against our Kingdom, then we find ourselves in a predicament. Drakahl, who we think she's assisting, lies wherever they have hidden themselves. Meanwhile, we are besieged within the core of our Kingdom. Perhaps we should lend Gaerin aid and let him pursue his goals. It could serve as a distraction, slowing or preventing other attacks within our borders," offered Fahrul.

"Laurence mentioned that Drakahl killed King Pahn of Pelrigoss while traveling with Tolrin, Gaerin, Arcturus and others so many decades ago. Surely he claimed the throne and has returned there by now. That is sure to be Gaerin's destination. As to Nightweaver meddling in our Kingdom's affairs? As we've learned, this isn't the first time it's happened... it's just the first time we've noticed. Why help us build the Kingdom with a gift such as the Vaelin crossbow, only to tear us down now?

"There are too many possible motivations for me to discern for certain. The simplest of which could be delaying Laurence's attempts at revenge. Though, that seems the least likely. If he were to travel there now, his vengeance would almost certainly fail. I have the feeling that these plots and schemes, though intertwined, are as yet unrelated. I believe her designs for our Kingdom are for a different purpose.

"Although... having her eyes affixed elsewhere for a time could provide us with the advantage, and give us time to investigate further," said Mordechai.

Fahrul contemplated his friend's words. "Taking direct action against her—if she's working with Drakahl—will be nigh impossible. We will never convince King Orluhnd to attack Pelrigoss directly. It's a center for trade between Tellrindos, Arkhania, Haern and many distant lands. At best, we can afford an agent or two to assist Gaerin in secret. Anything further will raise too much suspicion. Suspicion which we are already under. We need more time to devise a more... direct response."

"The nature of Pelrigoss and the benefits of their trade to this Kingdom add much complexity to this situation," confirmed Mordechai.

"I will dispatch Kyrilis to join Gaerin when she returns. She can find them on the road and travel with them to Pelrigoss in secret. I will instruct her to convince them to do reconnaissance only, and not to engage with Drakahl or his supporters. Hopefully, they will heed my advice and wait for us to send support their way," said Fahrul.

"By support, you mean Laurence," clarified Mordechai.

"If that is how matters transpire, but the boy is not yet ready. He showed great promise in Grellenheim, but our forces were small in number. To take down Drakahl, and Nightweaver, means to overthrow a King. Kings mean armies, so he will need to *raise* an army. He needs more training to even stand a *chance* of conquering an entire Kingdom."

Fahrul paused for a moment to let the thought sink in, "That *is* what we're discussing, is it not? The downfall of Pelrigoss? This isn't a simple matter of hunting down a man and his witch."

"This is to be no small feat, I agree. Nothing involving Laurence's family ever is, from what I've seen. He is passionate and skilled, but... he doesn't know the depths of the situation. He isn't aware how complicated this has become," offered Mordechai. "We cannot let him find out about Gaerin's plans. When they return... send the five of them to recuperate in Raven's Nest. Tell them I am investigating further and not to discuss Grellenheim with anyone," said Mordechai.

"A wise course of action, Mordechai," agreed Fahrul.

"In the meantime, let's use those Inquisitors to our benefit. Steer them toward Raven's Nest and Jorilund. Tell them that I told you several missing recruits from Fel'Vizsiour had been seen in those areas. That should send them scampering about," added Mordechai.

"Which will hopefully kick up the right amount of dirt to reveal other plots," agreed Fahrul.

"I will send word to Ayriel," Mordechai stated before vanishing.

The seal upon the room faded with his departure, allowing the incessant knocking on his chamber door to find his ears. With a sigh, Fahrul stood to go speak with the impatient Inquisitors.

ELUSION

Ris'Enliss, Oghenfall 24th, 113 of the 2nd Era

Victory, sweet victory,
Not yet what they think.
Averting eyes, diverting spies,
They fear that which they seek.

Night's Writ, Parable 3

BY THE time they arrived at the Western Reach, their horses had gone as far as they could. They'd ridden through the rest of the night and into the next morning, giving Grellenheim a wide berth in their passing. The horses, already in need of rest when they found them, started to fight back; unwilling to continue traveling.

Gaerin dismounted and signaled to the others to do the same. Refugees crowded the Reach, huddled together and distraught. They stood in groups discussing the devastation of their city, still burning in the distance. Families sat, defeated, both beside and on the road. Those attempting to travel past had to weave between them, a difficult task considering the deep gouges in the road's surface from decades of carts and wagons.

"There's no way we can lead these horses through this mess," stated Lyla as she joined him.

"Wa... why not?" asked Keifer timidly from behind.

"The road bears deep ruts from wagon wheels which, in normal circumstances, we'd keep our mounts between to protect their footing. The crowd is thick, demanding we weave between clusters of refugees, preventing us from doing so... not to mention the state our mounts. They're pretty much done," answered Gaerin.

"We'll leave them behind; maybe send them back into the field where we found them," she suggested.

"Let's gather our things," he said. "Might as well grab whatever they have in their saddlebags too. They aren't likely to find their owners in this mess."

Lyla turned to go back to her horse and start gathering their things. That's when she noticed the small crowd that was forming around them, all staring at Gabner and talking amongst themselves. Kobolds weren't a normal sight in civilized territories. They had a well-deserved reputation for being unintelligent and attacking wayward travelers. The sight of one in their company had made them something of a spectacle.

In Gabner's case, his appearance was just as likely to cause confusion as it was concern. Unlike the wild kobolds that cityfolk might imagine—often unclothed or wearing rusted bits of metal as armor—he wore black braies, black boots and a white tunic. His hair was combed and well groomed, and he smiled at them rather than growling, or snarling.

His little three-fingered paw-hands gripped the reins of his horse as he happily peered out at the crowd that was forming around him. By all appearances, he was a kobold pretending to be a small human. He waved excitedly at his new fans.

"We have another problem," added Lyla, returning to Gaerin.

"Oh?" asked Gaerin. He looked over his shoulder in the direction she was pointing and saw the scene unfolding. "Oh!"

Gaerin walked over to Gabner and reached up to help the little guy down off his horse. Gabner reached out to him in much the same manner a small child would, happily accepting the help. "It's fine, he's our chef," said Gaerin. He wasn't sure *why* he thought that particular explanation would suffice; it was just the first thing that came to mind.

"I chef!" yapped Gabner happily.

He waved a tiny paw-hand at the crowd again, smiling with his tongue hanging out. Keifer walked over and grabbed Gabner's hand, leading him to the side of the road and away from the crowd.

"We have to carry things now, Gabner," explained Keifer. He began unbuckling the saddlebags from the horses and handed one to the eager kobold.

"Okay," answered Gabner happily. "I carry! I help!"

After retrieving the last of the saddlebags, Gaerin and Lyla slapped the horses on their hindquarters to send them into the field.

Gaerin rolled his eyes and led them east through the crowd while Lyla happily walked beside Gabner. He held her right little finger with his little left hand, a saddlebag over his right shoulder, yipping a little song gleefully.

"Must be nice to be out of that kitchen, huh Gabner?" asked Lyla.

"Feel alive!" he answered excitedly. "I helping!"

Lyla was suddenly very happy. Holding his little hand, she found it easy to forget the battle they'd just survived.

Gaerin sighed at the day ahead of him.

∴ ∴ ∴

LAURENCE RETURNED with another armful of branches and kindling then dropped them on the ground near the fire. He stood for a moment, taking in the scene that was unfolding.

Izabel was fidgeting with Agnar's leg, who was trying to get away from her by pulling himself along the ground backwards. Bingrolf tried to laugh at his cousin, but his side sent searing pain through his torso, causing his laugh to come out as a moan instead.

"I think the first order of business when we reach Fel'Rechaun is that you all need lessons in tending wounds," he said lightheartedly, "and in resting while receiving treatment."

"She's hurtin me, Laur," whined Agnar.

"Stop whining, you baby!" yelled Wil.

"She's *helping* you... or trying to," laughed Laurence. He took a seat by the fire and stared at his friends in disbelief.

"Easy for *you* to say," whined Agnar.

"Sit *still*, you idiot!" barked Izabel.

Agnar huffed for a moment and then crossed his arms, contorted his face into a wince.

"I haven't even *done* anything yet," she replied, noticing the look on his face.

"Just get it over with," he grumbled through clinched teeth.

As she began her work, Laurence laughed heartily. "The herbs I found should help heal your leg well enough to walk tomorrow, so hold still," Laurence tried to explain as he watched. He found it amusing to see a grown man of Agnar's size act like such a child. He wondered if it wasn't and attempt to flirt with Izabel, or prolong her help as long as he could. Either way, it was a vast improvement over the combat they'd endured, so he watched for a time before resuming his duties.

After a while, Laurence left camp again to gather food for their dinner. Earlier, he had cut a bit of cloth from the sheets Izabel brought to camp and turned it into very thin strips. Using those strips, he'd set traps while collecting herbs. He hoped that at least one of his traps had snagged a small rodent, or bird, and that he wouldn't have to go hunting for meat.

He checked the traps and found that not one but three of them had snared food. Once again, Gaerin's teachings were paying off. They'd gone hunting, trapping, and fishing many times in his childhood. 'It's *important to learn to live off the land*,' Gaerin had said.

He'd taken those lessons to heart, thinking that someday he might find himself on an adventure far from home and need use of them. While his current situation wasn't precisely what he'd imagined, the memories struck him all the same.

When he returned to camp carrying two rabbits and a squirrel, the others showed their excitement. Izabel raced over and asked if she could watch him prepare their meal, because she'd never learned to cook. He agreed and showed her each step in the process carefully. She even tried her hand at skinning and gutting a rabbit, with moderate success.

The others joined them at the fire once preparations had concluded and the meat was roasting over the open flames.

"So, Laurence... a barrel roll through the legs, eh?" asked Wil.

"Hah! Yeah," answered Laurence sheepishly.

"What we wanna know is, why? You use strange tactics sometimes," said Wil.

"They were a lot stronger than me. I didn't want to take the brunt of his blow with a parry and risk injuring my arms or shoulders," said Laurence.

"What the hell are you talkin about? I've seen you run around in that armor like it's nothin!" exclaimed Agnar.

"It's enchanted to be lighter," said Laurence.

"It's what?" exclaimed Izabel. She gave Laurence an evil look, as if he'd betrayed her.

"It doesn't make me a better fighter. It's just lighter. It feels like

I'm wearing my nightclothes," Laurence explained.

"Here I am, dressed like a pauper," moaned Izabel.

Her armor, sitting across the camp on her bedroll, was very expensive by Laurence's estimation. "I couldn't afford your armor, don't be silly. I inherited mine. It was Gahl the Raven's armor. He's my great grandfather," explained Laurence.

"I want armor like that," said Bingrolf.

"Our great grandfather dug rice patties," said Agnar.

"I didn't mean I want to *inherit* it, idiot," said Bingrolf.

"We ain't rich, is all I'm sayin."

"Well, I'm rich and I don't have enchanted armor, so stuff it," said Izabel, returning her attention to Laurence. "What do you mean you aren't strong? Even lighter armor can't make someone as skilled as you."

"I'm not," he said, matter-of-factly.

"You grew up on a farm!" she said, frustrated.

"I grew up in an alchemy shop. Our farm was an herb garden. Gaerin brought us food from *his* farm, which I *occasionally* helped with, but it wasn't what I did every day. I mostly sat on the floor painting labels on flasks, or at a desk copying recipes, or reading about herbs, potions and elixirs. All of my weapon training happened when I visited Gaerin on weekends, or when I snuck out at night," Laurence explained.

"Prove it!" challenged Izabel.

"Prove what?" asked Laurence.

"Arm wrestle me. Prove your strength," she stated.

"Are you serious?" he asked.

She walked over to a large stone beside the camp, got down on her knees, put her elbow on top, and raised her hand into position.

"You're serious!"

"Yes, I'm serious. And don't hold back, either!" she demanded.

Laurence tried to hand the skewers of meat to Wil.

"Oh no, I'm not missing this!" answered Wil.

With a sigh, he sat the skewers down beside the fire and walked over to Izabel and her boulder. He knelt across from her and put his elbow down as she had, grasping her hand. She took a moment to help him get into proper position, noticing that he'd never arm wrestled.

Once both contestants were in proper position, Wil yelled, "go!"

His arm tensed in response to hers. It seemed to take all his strength just to keep his arm upright. Their hands shook slightly with the power they were both putting into the match.

Slowly, he made progress, pushing her arm downward inch by inch. The afforded him by his taller stature and longer arms were winning the day.

With a loud grunt that grew into a violent yell, she pushed back with all her strength and drove his arm back into its upright position. His arm leaned backwards, her strength more than he could resist. Gasps filled the air as their friends watched them struggle.

In a sudden movement, she powered through his resistance with a surge of strength from her tricep and shoulder, driving his arm the rest of the way down onto the stone.

Wil, Agnar and Bingrolf started laughing, slapping Izabel's shoulder in congratulations, and punching Laurence's shoulder to tease him.

"I can't believe it," she said, getting to her feet. "I got bested in the trials by a weakling!"

"Yeah, yeah. Rub it in," he said as he returned to the fire and his skewers.

"You really are something, you know?" said Izabel, returning to his side.

Laurence sighed, defeated.

"No, I mean it. Literally not a single student would have bet on me to win that. I'm a girl," she said, realizing too late how her remark sounded. "I mean, I *wield weapons* and *wear armor*; I've spent my life training to do these things. So, I'm not under any delusions I'm a *typical* girl… but I'm a girl, and you're half a foot taller than I am. You win all these fights and make it look easy… our natural assumption is that you're stronger and faster than us. But… that's not the case, is it?"

"It's not. I'm quick, but I seem faster because my armor isn't slowing me down. I seem strong, but really I'm just tactfully deciding what to parry, block, deflect, or dodge completely based on what I know of my own limitations," he explained. "Like with the Velloth, I rolled through his legs because I knew very well there was no way I could stop his maul with just my sword. I couldn't have stood toe to toe with him… not even close.

"I knew early on that I would never be physically strong. My daytime life was too sedentary. The little muscle I have was a byproduct of helping Gaerin on his farm, milking cows, and volunteering to heft heavy things for Arcturus whenever I could. Gaerin knew strength would limit me, so he taught me every fighting style he knew.

"He taught me how to attack, how to defend, how to gain advantage, how to find and create openings, and how to use terrain and circumstance to my advantage. I latched onto those things; anything I could do to strengthen my mind for war. I started approaching everything that way. Hell, I even spent an entire rainy weekend outside practicing forms in the mud to improve my footing; all on my own," he described.

"You won't live this down, you know? Being beaten by a girl? But... I have a newfound respect for you. I need to learn how that mind works," she said as she lightly tapped his temple with one finger, "And I need to master the skills you've mastered. I'm often faced with opponents, like Bingrolf, who are twice my size. So far, I've only beaten them with sheer luck and speed," she explained.

"And now you understand how frightening it is that Drakahl's men bested me so easily," he said.

They sat and talked about Drakahl again, and the nuances of fighting with the power of tactics rather than strength. Once they ate, they retired to their make-shift bedrolls for the evening.

Laurence took first watch with the agreement that he would wake Izabel after a few hours. He chose, instead, to stay on watch the entire night. It wasn't that he mistrusted his friends, he just knew they needed sleep more than he did. He was growing accustomed to staying awake for days on end.

∴ ∴ ∴

TYLEE ROUNDED the side of the couch and sat beside Delriahna. "Mother?"

"Yes, dear?" Delriahna was never sure what her daughter was up to.

"I'm... troubled," said Tylee.

"Finally! Should I seek a priest or an alchemist?" she joked.

"Oh, stop! It's just... I want to do... *more*. All my life I've been stuck in a window. You and father kept me at home, unable to go out and see the world in person. Unless Laurence came to call, there I was, bottled up like one of father's expensive brandies; like some princess. But I'm not a princess," she explained.

"Your father didn't trust everyone in town to treat you with respect and care. You're our only child, and very precious to us. Besides, the way you act? That doesn't inspire a lot of confidence in your ability to make wise decisions."

"Put yourself in my shoes, mother. My only entertainment was dusty old books about politics, government and history... or watching the world go by through a window... or getting a rise out of you," Tylee explained, her voice cracking with hints of sadness.

"You sure exploited that last one, dear."

"How else was I ever supposed to find humor? The two of you were no help; always shoving lessons down my throat. My entire life was scheduled and dictated to me. Whenever I was in your presence, I wasn't allowed to be a *kid*!"

"Humor? You found the way you behaved humorous?"

"Your response usually was."

"No. It was not," corrected Delriahna.

"It was," Tylee said, smirking.

"Ty!" Delriahna barked angrily.

"Fine... agree to disagree," she conceded.

"What is this all about?" challenged Delriahna, wrinkling her brow.

"Well... I've been watching through the window in my room. First, I thought it was so I could catch a glimpse of Laurence. I mean, we only just married and then all this happened and... it's like he was ripped away from me. However, I've realized that I was never going to see him from this far away.

"Then it occurred to me that I was only in my window out of habit. I started wondering what I'm doing with my life. After all, I'm a married woman now. I'm an adult. I can walk around town, make friends, and find things to occupy myself. So... why am I in a window *watching* instead of *doing*?" she asked rhetorically.

"I agree. You need to find a healthy way to occupy your time. Maybe you could start by reading some of those books you turned your nose up at for so long."

"Mother!" she said with a frustrated gasp. "I've read those books—many of them more than once—so stop. I want something else. I want to live. I want to be... *useful*! Laurence is down there at school becoming a warrior and, knowing him, he'll probably serve in the Legion. He's making something of himself. He won't just... *make do*, like so many of the people I used to watch from my window in Mooncrest.

"So, I was thinking maybe I would start small. Maybe I'll start by handling the shopping and cooking while we stay here. Maybe venturing out to shop for our needs will introduce me to people, or places, that inspire me or present opportunities. I dunno... it's a silly thought, but what else do I have?" she asked.

"I think that's a very mature first step, Tylee. Just... do me a favor. Keep your spending to a minimum?"

"Yes, mother. Just the things we need," she said with a nod.

"Just the things we need," Delriahna agreed.

She hugged Tylee tightly. It wasn't clear to her whether the gesture was genuine, or just another Tylee fantasy. She decided to let things play out, and give her daughter the benefit of the doubt.

"You've got shopping to do, daughter. We have little left in the kitchen and horses who've gone through all their feed."

"I've got this!" chimed Tylee, her mood visibly brightening.

She had to admit that Tylee was right. They had kept her too isolated, which resulted in interesting, often frustrating, personality quirks and social awkwardness. Perhaps letting Tylee take new responsibilities would help her mature and find purpose.

∴ ∴ ∴

MORDECHAI ARRIVED in his room with a crack of energy, having just returned from Vaelin Palace where he shared his findings with Ayriel. He flicked his finger, and the candles sprang back to life. As he stepped off the rune, thoughts of their elusive, manipulative foe filled his mind.

"What are you up to?" Mordechai mused.

Several years prior, he'd tried to find evidence of the fabled Nightweaver; proof of her existence. Her legend stretched for over a thousand years; popping up in writings, etchings, and artwork throughout many cultures across the entire eastern seaboard of Gargoa, and the whole of Xulrathia.

His efforts had been exhaustive, but ultimately fruitless. Even now, confronted with witnesses to her existence, he was unsure if she was the same Nightweaver spoken of in so many tales.

Nightweaver was human, according to legend, and a human's typical life expectancy was between half and two-thirds of a century. He knew of a few who had accomplished longer lives through magic, or alchemy, such as Arcturus. So, it was not outside the realm of reason that a powerful being, as legends purported her to be, might survive for longer. How much longer would depend greatly upon just how powerful and adept one was at whatever methods they chose for extending their life.

The oldest person he was aware of with a magically extended lifespan was Joril Herrickson, a weapon and armor smith of secret renown. His wares were only available to those the King deemed worthy, and that rarely occurred. Many had searched far and wide for another source of such craftsmanship, and they had found none.

Joril had served Lord Arkhan Vaelin during the great wars of the First Era and had crafted the Lord's crossbow, sword, shield and armor. Arkhan had been unbeatable and was very close to forming the Kingdom he envisioned. His second wife killed him in his sleep, thwarting the completion of his lifelong quest. His eldest son, Orluhnd Vaelin, took up his father's mantle and demanded a suit of armor of his own, and several for his closest men.

He knew that Orluhnd's request, and continued demands, would require more than his lifetime to accomplish, for he was already an elderly man. Orluhnd, and his wife, scoured the land in search of a way to extend Joril's life. They succeeded, but made no record of how. Many students of Fel'Vizsiour lost decades trying to discover the secret.

What mattered, in context to his current investigation, was that Joril still thrived in service to the Kingdom. According to records, he was over two hundred years old; a substantial accomplishment for a human, and nearing the life expectancy of a dwarf. Several tomes detailed the cost of such an extended life. While those findings revealed that falsely extending one's life bore many negative side effects, he knew that most would still do so if given the chance. That is why so many researched, attempting to discover the means.

Mordechai didn't know his own age. What he knew for certain was that there seemed no permanent enchantment about him, and he had no need of repeated alchemical treatments as Arcturus had once employed. Ultimately, he couldn't understand why he didn't age.

Much of his research had included attempts to find his own origins, hints of his past, or explanations to his longer-than-natural life. One thing that he'd discovered throughout the years was that while he appeared human, or as an elf without pointed ears, he was something else entirely. He wasn't an elf, a human, or a hybrid of any known species he could find.

He could not, therefore, use himself as a baseline to any life extension powers or experiments, for as far as he could tell... he was the only one of his kind... or was he?

"Perhaps she isn't human either," he concluded.

Walking over to his desk, he slowly waved his right arm from left to right. Everything atop his desk moved out of the way obediently, returning to their proper place on shelves about the room. As he arrived, he placed both hands on his desk, deep in thought.

I was looking for a human. I focused my magic on seeking someone ancient with a human bloodline. I constrained myself where I shouldn't have. I was foolish, he chided himself.

With a sudden burst of inspiration, he decided to try something new. He reached into a drawer and withdrew a small cauldron; placing it at the center of his desk. Using a small dagger—withdrawn from beneath his robe—he sliced into his left palm and let his blood drip into the iron dish.

As the blood pooled and settled in the cauldron, he retrieved a small box from the shelf above his desk and bent his knees to sit down. His chair slid across the room, coming to rest beneath him obediently as he lifted the lid of the box. Inside were dozens of shards of black glass, all of them curved and none of uniform shape.

Accompanying them was a small golden pedestal, etched with blackened runes. He removed the pedestal from the box and placed it so that its feet rested upon the lip of the cauldron—as if it were the cauldron's lid—then slid the box to the right.

As he withdrew his right hand from that motion—back towards the cauldron—the glass shards floated toward their pedestal. The shards, one by one, floated into position and re-formed themselves into their original whole. Holding his right hand above them, he closed his eyes and muttered a single word, "Ahk'vaela." The shards of glass fused, solidifying to form a black crystal ball.

It was an artifact he'd used in the past to scry other casters. If he wanted to see what someone with significant power was up to, it was the only device safe for him to use. At the conclusion of each scrying, he shattered the ball so that his intrusion would be harder to discover or trace back to his location.

Often, such scrying required an object owned by his target, or a piece of them such as hair, or a droplet of blood. However, those things were not always easy to come by. He was often forced to use assumptions, and a studied approach, when scrying certain targets; tracing them through assumed bloodlines or family histories. More often than not, his tactics succeeded.

In Nightweaver's case, he had never been successful. He'd tried everything he could think of, including samples of human bloodlines from all the known kingdoms. He had even used Arcturus's blood—donated freely—in his attempts to divine her, as recently as three decades prior. That had been the last time he'd attempted to find her, and he'd had no reason to continue to pursue what he'd concluded to be myth. Fate, it seemed, had a penchant for both drama and irony.

He closed his eyes and bowed his head, chanting words from an ancient, forgotten tongue. Pushing all thoughts from his mind, he focused on the crystal ball and the blood that lie beneath. Images swirled like fog, as if living inside the black orb in front of him. He opened his eyes as he finished the words and placed one hand on either side of the sphere, a hair's thickness away from its surface. With the twitch of a finger, he changed the image divining further.

Image after image came into view, frustrating him with each flick of his finger; the chest at the foot of his bed; the desk at which he sat; the mysterious tome he'd found in his handwriting. At first, all he could see were things associated with himself; things that he owned.

He reached out with his mind, refusing to see anything directly associated with himself. He willed the magics to show him other beings to which he connected, either through species or direct blood relation. Only once had he tried to summon such images, and it had ended in failure. He'd spent an entire week staring into the ball, trying to coax images of a father or mother... but had neglected the simple search of basic genetic alignment. He'd made the mistake of assuming he was human. Since then it had become clear he was not, but he'd never thought to returned and pursue further scrying. His mistake had been to assume he was the last of his kind.

An overhead view of a woman came into focus through the crystal, as clear as if she stood beside him. She was old; presumably ancient. Her hair was long and gray, nearly dragging the floor as she walked in her hunched posture. The staff in her left hand clanked against the ground as she used it to aid in her movement. The skin of her left arm sagged under its own weight, as if it no longer bore the strength to cling to her muscle and bones. She was decrepit and seemed on the verge of decay.

She looked up suddenly and knowingly—as if alerted to his clairvoyance—smiling a grim, deathly smile. Darkness swirled about her and clouded the crystal's view. Pain wracked Mordechai's head, causing him to grab his head with both hands and fall backwards to the floor as a single word began resonating throughout his mind.

The word echoed in reverse, growing louder with each rebound. As it reached peak volume, the crystal shattered violently, sending crystal shards flying and crashing about the room.

The reality of that single word struck as he opened his eyes. A single word, acting as a curse from, cast from untold distance. That single word haunted him, for the power required to accomplish what she'd done was beyond anything he could comprehend. She had firmly uttered the ancient elven word for 'blind'... "*Dalltash!*"

∴ ∴ ∴

PROVOSS AND Aygos shone brightly in the sky by the time they reached the western ramp leading up to Raven's Nest. Between refugees clogging the road, travelers gawking at Gabner, and the slowness of tiny kobold legs, traversing the Western Reach had been an arduous task. Dread settled into Gaerin as he realized their journey's most difficult task lie ahead of them.

Ascending the ramp, he mulled over their options, and could not think of one that was both agreeable and easy. He glanced back at Lyla and, once he caught her attention, signaled with a nod of his head that she should join him at the front of the group.

"Finding an inn will be a chore," he lamented.

"One that will accept a kobold," she added.

"We're almost out of coin, and we've not yet reached Port Vaelin."

"I'll," she started. She paused for a moment and looked back to be sure Gabner was far enough away. Deciding that he was, she continued, "I'll go see a guard at Raven's Keep on the north side of town. Maybe they'll pay for those ears," she offered.

"Good thing Gabner hasn't asked what was in the sack, eh," he joked.

"All the more reason to rid ourselves of them now."

"I really hope they still do that," he said, alluding to their previous conversation.

"What... burn bodies?" she teased.

"Bah."

When they reached the top of the ramp, the western edge of Raven's Nest stood directly before them. They moved their party aside, out of the major thoroughfare, and into the dark of the field north of the road.

"We'll wait here. I can't go dragging Gabner through town

hoping to find an inn without someone else to help look after him, and I can't very well secure a room that you can't find," said Gaerin.

"Makes sense," she agreed, nodding. She dropped her satchel next to him, along with her shield and mace. Hefting the sack, she turned and jogged toward the northern side of town.

"Be quick," he called behind her. The refugees were pouring onto the plateau in waves. Many had already begun flooding the streets of Raven's Nest, pleading for help. Gaerin knew they had a long night ahead of them.

Four long streets spanned the city from east to west, with buildings of various kinds lining both sides of each. The southern edge of town looked down on the Western Reach and Fel'Rechaun, but the Legion's military barracks and buildings bordered the north. Central to those buildings was Raven's Keep.

Lyla rounded the northwestern corner of town and jogged down the street along the first row of Legion buildings. A bell was ringing in the distance, and officers stood between several of the buildings giving orders. Men and women poured out of their barracks, some still in the process of equipping themselves. She assumed the activity was in response to the refugees who had just arrived.

As she approached the main road heading north toward the keep, she stopped and leaned on her knees to catch her breath. Soldiers and officers marched past, heading into the heart of Raven's Nest, several of them carrying tent cloths, rods and rope. Just north of the intersection stood two small towers meant to guard the road to the keep. Standing in front of the eastern tower was a man in full plate armor with a half cape pinned to his left shoulder and right hip, just behind his scabbard.

Lyla approached the knight as several soldiers turned away from him, yelling, "Aye sir!" at the top of their lungs. They marched off, heading toward town.

"Pardon, my lord, I know these are trying times. I might be of service in them," she offered. He looked at her inquisitively, as if deciding whether to take her seriously. She continued, "My husband and I were in Grellenheim during the attack. We helped defend the keep from those vile elves. As it so happens, we were also beset twice upon the King's roads on our way to Grellenheim and I've word and proof of those encounters."

"Come inside," he said, holding the tower door open for her. She nodded in agreement.

Ris'Enliss, Oghenfall 24th, 113 of the 2nd Era

The doorway opened into a small room with stairs leading up to the left and down to the right. Passing through that room brought them to a larger chamber with a table for dining and a small desk. He approached the dining table and stood behind a seat, offering it to her. She sat with a thank you and placed her sack on the table in front of them. He rounded the table, removed his sword and set it aside before sitting joining her.

"I am Centurion Vale of the Fifth Centain," he declared.

"I am Lyla Ravencrest of Mooncrest," she responded.

"Ravencrest... decades without your family presence here, and now we seem to overflow with them," he remarked.

"Oh?"

"There is a Laurence attending Fel'Rechaun who has made quite a name for himself. Several of our younger recruits joked that your family's arrival was an omen. The town and our keep are both named for your ancestor, after all. Laurence arrives, Grellenheim suffers an attack, and you bring me news of trouble on our roads... one would think these omens were bearing fruit."

She stared back at him blankly, unsure of what to say.

"So, what have you brought me?" he asked.

"Well, when we first set out from Mooncrest, forty kobolds attacked us. They'd set up camp in a ruined tower along the Elbermire Way, with several traps set in the nearby wood. We dispatched them easily enough, but others might not have been so successful," she explained.

"You dispatched forty kobolds?"

"Well, yes," she answered, opening the sack and showing him the pile of ears inside.

"You... brought me their ears?" he questioned. His face wrinkled in disgust and disbelief.

"I know that in the old days we used to turn them in for reward, but I didn't know if that was still the custom. We've been farmers for the past two decades."

"Well, no, we don't generally pay for... ears. That practice died long ago. However, I will see if we can make an exception," he said. Closing the sack and setting it aside, he mouthed, 'blech'.

"After that, we made our way to Ekthri Crossroads and camped in the ruined Waystation. Trolls attacked just before we fell asleep. It was raining and we couldn't burn them, so we fled to the east. When the weather broke, we went back to finish them, but they'd circled around behind us and caught a farmer named Gremill unprepared. He died for our mistake. Telon's Respite is suffering a lack of crops now, and may need additional supplies from the Kingdom to survive the winter," she detailed.

"Please tell me you haven't brought me troll ears," he pleaded.

"No, no. We wouldn't want fresh trolls growing from their ears in this tower," she said, shuddering.

"Thank the gods for small favors," he exclaimed. "You seem to know much... for a farmer."

"We adventured in our youth with Arcturus. My husband is Gaerin Ravencrest, a graduate of Fel'Rechaun."

"The man who trained Laurence?" he asked.

"The same."

"That explains how you defended the keep in Grellenheim. We've already heard reports of your valor, and of Laurence's at the same battle. You're to be commended," he said as he stood up. He made his way toward the door as if to signal someone.

"We don't need commendations, my lord. We were there, so we helped, and... we'd rather Laurence not know it was so. He doesn't know we are traveling, and it would not do well for him to learn of it," she pleaded.

He turned to face her again. "Explain."

"We're seeking revenge for the murder of Arcturus Ravencrest, Laurence's grandfather; the man who raised him. He... doesn't know. If he were to find out, he would surely leave school to race off and join us. That would not serve him, or the kingdom, very well. I'm sure you agree."

"Revenge on whom?" he asked.

"Our target does not live within the borders of the Kingdom. We are en route to Port Vaelin so we might set sail toward our destination," she explained, as vaguely as she could.

"Very well. However, your actions saved many lives, and Grellenheim Keep. Unfortunately, not the Keep's lord, but rebuilding a Keep is an expensive operation and one which the kingdom will not have to fund... thanks to your efforts. I can offer you a thousand silver for your troubles, if that will suffice," he offered, his gaze firmly on the sack. He begrudgingly added, "and... one bit per ear?"

"That will do nicely, my lord, and is much more than I came here seeking. Thank you," she said as she stood and curtsied.

With a bag of coin replacing her sack, she walked into town. She found the shadiest tavern she could and secured a room. Compared to other towns, the establishment wasn't very shady at all. However, for Raven's Nest it was as unconcerned for the law as they would find. Of critical importance was that the owner didn't care they had a kobold in their party, and it wasn't on Main Street across from Fel'Rechaun.

Her task complete, she set off to collect her group and show them to their beds.

∴ ∴ ∴

BAH'SHIRI SCREECHED a warning as she lowered herself to the ground outside the northern gates. Kyrilis dismounted, patting her beloved mount in thanks. She strode through the entrance with purpose as her griffin took to the sky, without a word or nod to the guards.

As she crossed the courtyard toward Fahrul's door, those in the courtyard took notice of her and cleared a path without question. She carried a Velloth head in her left hand, gripping it by its oily black hair.

Fahrul awakened to the sound of his great hall's doors slamming shut. The simple curtain that separated his bedchamber from the meeting hall did little to block the noise. Everyone at the school knew better than to wake him without reason, so he'd removed his door to make the process easier should the need arise.

He entered the main hall to see Kyrilis standing next to his table, bloody Velloth head in hand. Preita was scurrying about the room, blinking sleep from her eyes while lighting candles and trying her best to give Kyrilis and the head a wide berth. The scene almost struck him as humorous, despite the grim nature of Kyrilis's prize. Making his way to his chair, he waved Preita from the room, letting her know she'd done enough.

Preita happily complied.

"I see you found a Velloth," he remarked, gaining his seat.

"Yes," she said, sitting the head on the table between them. She dropped abruptly into the seat across from him with a disgruntled sigh.

"Mordechai has already been and gone. The Velloth attacked Grellenheim last night. Mordechai killed them all with help from Laurence, Izabel, Wil, Agnar and Bingrolf. Unfortunately, they arrived too late to save most of the citizens. Raven's Nest is overflowing with refugees, and Laurence and his group still haven't returned."

"A small group of them also destroyed Gaierford. The town only boasted twenty residents, mostly farmers and merchants. I arrived as they were finishing up and killed them, but nearly met my end. Bah'Shiri saved my life several times. They seemed to fear her," added Kyrilis.

"Great," sighed Fahrul.

"Worse, my Lord. One of them fled and as I chased him down, I saw where they'd surfaced," she added.

"Go on."

"Do you recall the old town of Kallenfall, west of Gaierford? It was a mining town. The Kallen Hills south of there contain several mining tunnels, all abandoned long ago. That is where they emerged. My guess is that a small group went east while the larger force went west. However, I have my doubts we've found all of them. In fact... I'm sure we haven't.

"I continued west for a time and saw a path cut through the marshlands heading southwest... not northwest toward Grellenheim. I don't know where they're headed, or their purpose. Once I realized I'd lost their trail, I returned here to report in," she explained.

"This just gets better and better."

"We have to hunt them down, Fahr. We can't let this massacre continue."

"We will, but you are otherwise allocated," he responded.

"What?" she challenged.

"Gaerin and Lyla Ravencrest showed up in Grellenheim, on their way to hunt down Drakahl," he said bluntly.

"So?" she questioned.

"So... we need you to work your way into their group, go with them, and keep them safe. More importantly, we need you to gather information, and find a way to get it back to us."

"I fail to see how this helps our current situation."

"By all accounts, Drakahl is working with Nightweaver. It is she that beguiled our men into setting the Velloth free. Mordechai and I believe that this is the start of her meddling, not the end of it. If Gaerin is seeking Drakahl, he is likely going directly into danger, and will potentially hasten her plans... whatever they might be."

"So I am to play spy," she mused.

"And steer them toward reconnaissance, with the promise that we will send others to support them when the time is right."

"How long do you think *that* will take?" she asked.

"A reasonable question, but one I do not have an answer for. It is unlikely the King will sanction any movement that would jeopardize our trade agreements with Pelrigoss. They are our safe harbor with the other kingdoms, being disconnected from the continent as they are, and in the middle of all shipping lanes," he explained.

"So it is complicated, and will take an undetermined amount of time. This sounds neither promising nor fruitful," she countered.

"It is all we've got. I cannot send troops; I am not the Legion. The Legion cannot act without permission from his majesty. I can't detain Gaerin and his group, because I have no jurisdiction to enforce laws outside of this school's walls... and they've not *broken* any laws. Quite the contrary, they are sure to be local heroes thanks to their actions in Grellenheim. All I can do is send an emissary in secret, collect information, help defend these territories, and play political games to win the support that we need," he said with distaste.

"Since I am, by contract, an emissary from the Afyr and not under direct command of your school, the Legion, or the Kingdom-"

"You are the perfect candidate, and one who's absence I can easily explain away."

She stood and bowed her head, saying, "Understood, sir. It shall be done."

As she left the hall, he realized how much he'd leaned on her services over recent years. He wondered how he would fill the void created by her absence. With a scowl born of both frustration and concern, he yelled for Preita. His day had begun no matter the time, and he had work to do.

∴ ∴ ∴

FAHRUL ARRIVED at Raven's Keep early in the morning, before they had even served dawnfry. The portcullis was down, as if the guards expected trouble from the refugees. The scene struck him as odd. One of the two guards posted at the gate approached him with one hand up, signaling him to stop.

"What is your business here," demanded the guard.

"I am Lord Commander Fahrul of Fel'Rechaun and I wish to speak with Commander Cricht to discuss matters of Kingdom security," he explained.

The guard put his hand down and replied plainly, "Sorry, my Lord, but Commander Cricht has been called to Vellenheim by Lord

Commander Elrend."

"Shit!" exclaimed Fahrul.

"May I be of service, Fahrul?"

The voice had come from behind him, but sounded familiar. He turned to see who it was. "Glorin Vale!" he shouted happily. "You are a sight for sore eyes."

"It's Centurion now," corrected Vale.

"Congratulations, old friend... may we speak in private?"

"Of course," answered Vale, pointing toward the doorway behind him.

Fahrul dismounted and handed his reins to the guard who'd stopped him. He ignored the guard's rebuttals as he walked away. Once they were inside with the door secure, they made their way to the dining table and sat.

"I was just about to have my morning coffee when I heard your horse outside my door. Would you like some?"

"You have blessed me further," Fahrul accepted.

"What brings you to Raven's Keep, Lord?" asked Vale as he served their coffee.

"As you are aware, Grellenheim was attacked a day ago," said Fahrul after a sip of coffee.

"Indeed it was, and the refugees have kept me busy for most of the night," answered Vale.

"A small force of fifty or more Velloth perpetrated that attack. Did you know that as well?"

"I've heard several refugees, and some warriors, describe their assailants as red elves with black eyes, but that could have been anything in the dark of night. Zathos plays tricks on the eyes, casting a red hue on a great many things."

Fahrul reached into the satchel he'd brought with him, extracted the Velloth head and placed it on the far end of the table, away from their coffee. "Is this a trick played by Zathos's light?"

Vale choked a bit on his coffee before responding. "I never wished something to be false more in my life, and I have survived a great many battles," he exclaimed.

"The unfortunate news is that this particular head is not from Grellenheim. Tell me, have you any reports from eastward? Gaierford, perhaps?"

"I have not," answered Vale, concern crossing his face.

"Likely that is due to the limited trade we send them. That

won't be a problem for Gaierford any longer, as all of them lay dead upon their streets and many of their buildings are now ash. Kyrilis recovered this head to serve as our proof," explained Fahrul.

"By the gods…"

"She tracked their origin to an abandoned mine south of Kallenfall, and followed a trail southwest through the marshes before she lost them," he added. He paused for a moment to let Vale realize the implication.

"Which means there are more of them roaming our land, and they may have already attacked other settlements," Vale responded, visibly shaken.

"As you are also aware, an Inquisition is already upon us. You've undoubtedly had several of your men questioned already—if not yourself—just as I. I assure you, the circumstances that led to their necessity have caused this very attack. Princess Ayriel gathered that information during a visit to our school just a few days ago and has already shared it with the King.

"What I have come here to ask you, therefore, is to lend aid in searching for the remaining Velloth. My recruits, thus far, have been doing your Legion's job for you. I wish to see that change. I wish to see… more experienced soldiers handle this, and remove the risk to my students," declared Fahrul.

"That is a very reasonable request born of a clever mind, as I've come to expect from you, Fahrul. Further, it would help us both save face with the Inquisition and perhaps put an end to that madness. However, I assure you that none of my soldiers have any experience with Velloth raiding parties. In fact, most of my forces never see combat. That is why so many nobles have tried to have the Legion disbanded entirely, in recent years.

"So, I will agree to send a detachment to hunt these creatures down, but I request that your men—the ones who defended Grellenheim—accompany them. While my forces generally have more training, and better equipment, they lack in practical experience. Experience your students gained last night. They can share their knowledge of our enemy, and their presence will grant our combined expedition a greater chance of success," answered Vale, regaining his senses.

"Those are agreeable terms, Centurion Vale. Our interactions are always a pleasure, even if the context of them is not," said Fahrul.

"Now… are you needed presently at Fel'Rechaun, or do you have time for me to bounce some ideas off of you regarding this recent flood of refugees?" asked Vale as he poured them more coffee.

"Keep that coffee coming and you can ask me whatever you want. I drank the last of my personal supply this morning," Fahrul said humorously.

Vale laughed with him, knowing precisely what he meant. They continued to talk for hours before parting ways.

∴ ∴ ∴

NO THREATS had appeared to disrupt his companions' slumber. For that, Laurence was thankful. The cool air, crickets singing, and view of the stars had calmed him and allowed him to reminisce of quieter, simpler times. For that, he was also thankful.

He hadn't had an opportunity to sit by himself and think since Arcturus's death. His whole life had become a whirlwind of circumstances that were out of his control, and everything seemed to revolve around him. All of the recent events seemed to be the work of the same mysterious forces, and he couldn't wrap his brain around what they hoped to gain, who was really working with who, and how he fit into their plans.

Just when he felt the familiar sadness creeping back in, Wil joined him at the campfire without saying a word. *I'll have time to think about that night, and to grieve, when this is all over. It' best I don't dwell on it now*, he decided.

The two of them sat in silence watching the stars until morning. As the sun rose to greet Zathos, the rest of their companions began to stir.

"It's time to get moving!" Laurence yelled in jest. "We've a long walk ahead of us!"

"Fuck off!" replied Bingrolf, covering his face with the edge of his bedroll.

Agnar laughed, still half asleep within his own.

Wil got up to go poke them until they got out of bed.

"You didn't wake me," mentioned Izabel as she emerged.

"You needed the rest more than I," he answered.

"Your body is as bruised and beaten as mine," she retorted, hands on hips before him.

"Perhaps, but I've been through fights with my life on the line several times. Yesterday was your first."

"True enough," she admitted.

"I've also had more practice going without sleep. Repeatedly these days, so it seems."

"That won't do for long, you need rest like everyone else."

"We'll see," he said, smiling.

Agnar and Bingrolf finally made their way out of their bedrolls and begrudgingly helped clean up their camp before setting off. They were in good spirits, by Laurence's estimation. He spent a good portion of the previous night worrying that his companions' morale would suffer after their battle, and was glad to see his worries were unfounded.

They had only walked for a few hours before a line of horses crested a hill ahead of them. Dahsh rode the lead horse and waved to them as they came into view.

"Oh thank the gods," Wil sighed.

"Well met, young heroes. Tales of your victory are being sung far and wide, this day," called Dahsh.

"Do all simple scouting missions end like this?" asked Laurence.

"Thankfully no, Marshal Laurence," he answered laughing. "Fahrul dispatched me with these horses for your party, but... you aren't to return to Fel'Rechaun just yet."

"Where are we to go?" questioned Laurence.

"Raven's Nest. You've earned some time away, and Lord Mordechai feels it is prudent he investigate further before sending you lot back to the school. It's hard enough to keep the other students focused on their studies without their heroes walking among them, and we may still need you in the matters at hand. For now, go get some rest. He will send word in due time," he explained.

"Very well," answered Laurence.

"Can't argue with that!" yelled Agnar excitedly.

"I've never had time off before," mused Izabel.

"How's that?" asked Bingrolf.

"Well," she started while mounting her horse. "I've trained every day since I was five to be a warrior. How does... one... relax, exactly?"

Laughter filled the air as they kicked their horses into action. Agnar and Bingrolf filled their entire journey with advice on the many ways one could relax, especially in a place like Raven's Nest. Laurence listened on in amused silence.

∴ ∴ ∴

IT WAS morning when Kyrilis took off on Bah'Shiri one last time.

She knew that she couldn't take her along, especially across the sea to Pelrigoss. With one more flight over the school for memory's sake, she steered her griffin for the cliffs of Engle Plateau and the refugee camps beyond. She found a clearing near the tents and brought her beautiful beast to the ground. Every eye was upon her as she dismounted, which made it easy to signal a guard. He sprang to life and ran to her eagerly.

"I'm looking for a pair of dark-skinned humans; a man and a woman. They're middle-aged, wearing armor, and have weapons stowed about their person. They likely arrived with the refugees, but were not citizens of Grellenheim," she explained.

"Aye, there was a pair as you describe. They had two others with them," he explained. "Headed into town not long after nightfall. We kept an eye on em cause one of their party was a kobold in a tunic, if you can believe that," he said, laughing.

She did not laugh with him.

Seeing the stern look on her face, he continued, "They took a room in the Wiley Fox Game House. They have a few rooms upstairs for those that don't mind the noise."

"Thank you, soldier. Carry on," she answered.

As he walked away to resume his duties, she turned to face Bah'Shiri. She removed the insignia of the Kingdom that adorned her chest and put it in the small pouch behind the saddle. "Fly home, Bah'Shiri. Fly to the Afyr and be at peace. I will return for you in due time."

With a pat on the neck, the griffin took flight and cried out to her master from above. After a few moments circling, she turned north and ascended toward the clouds. Kyrilis looked up at her longingly for a while before moving on, heartbroken that her duties had forced their separation. She'd been with Bah'Shiri for decades and already longed for their reunion.

To all appearances she was now just an elf woman in expensive armor, and not a servant to the Kingdom. It made her feel strange and out of place, but she knew she couldn't travel to Pelrigoss with Arkhania's emblem on display... not under the circumstances. Such thoughts occupied her as she crossed the town. It didn't seem to take long for her to reach her destination.

Customers, smoke, and noise filled the interior of the Wiley Fox. She stood at the entrance for a moment, deciding how to proceed. Games of cards and dice were being played at tables around the room. She saw stairs leading upward in the far right corner, and crossed the room to take a seat at the empty table beside them.

"Is there anything I can get you?" asked the young girl who approached.

"I'm looking for my companions. A dark-skinned man and woman, a clothed kobold and one other," she explained. She found it odd to voice such a sentence.

"Oh, aye. They're still in their rooms. Should I fetch them?"

"No, let them rest. I will have whatever meal you are serving for dawnfry, and some coffee," said Kyrilis.

"Sorry, miss. We ain't got no coffee, it's too expensive for our regular folk," she apologized.

"Then bring me whatever hot drink you serve in the morning," she sighed, placing a silver coin on the table.

"But... that is far too much," explained the girl.

"Keep the rest, and be prompt," ordered Kyrilis.

"Yes miss," answered the girl with a bow. She quickly scurried off to see to her new favorite customer.

Her mood improved as she ate her meal. The warmed ale served alongside it was less than desirable at first, but was likely the largest contributor to her improved demeanor, she had to admit. She soon decided she'd found a new favorite establishment in The Nest.

∴ ∴ ∴

IT WAS nearly an hour before anyone descended the stairs. Lyla was the first to come down, followed closely by Gaerin, Keifer and Gabner.

Kyrilis rose to greet them. "You must be Lyla Ravencrest," she said, smiling.

"I... I am," Lyla answered.

"And Gaerin," said Kyrilis with excitement. "Laurence has told me much about you. You trained him far too well, if that's possible."

"You are?" asked Gaerin as he shook her hand.

"I am Kyrilis of House Nandari of the Afyr and I am here to join you," she explained.

"How do you know Laurence?" he asked.

"Why don't we sit. You can eat while we talk," she offered, pointing to her table.

They agreed and approached the table, but there weren't enough seats. The excited service girl from before ran over to remedy the situation, taking two chairs from a table nearby. Kyrilis handed her three silver and said, "They'll have what I had."

"All of them, miss?"

"Yes, all of them. Even the kobold," Kyrilis added firmly.

"Yes, miss," she answered and scurried off.

Kyrilis sat down with a smile at Gabner. "I have met no kobolds before now. What's your name?" she asked.

"I Gabner, pretty elf. I cook. You eat. We friends," he said in a scruffy voice.

"I'm Keifer, my lady. Everyone forgets Keifer," he whimpered.

"And so you are, lad," she said, extending her hand. "Forgettable folk make the best spies."

He shook her hand eagerly, inspired by her insight.

"Not to look a gift horse in the mouth, but why do you ask to join us?" questioned Lyla.

"I'd say it was a simple matter but that would be a lie. The short of it is that Lord Commander Fahrul and I are fully aware of the tragedy that befell Arcturus and Laurence's desire to seek revenge on Drakahl. Mordechai saw you in Grellenheim, and we are confident in our assumption you seek revenge, likely to keep Laurence from further risk.

"Simply put, we wish to help. Fahrul doesn't have the authority to send troops, and neither does the Legion. To do so would require a lengthy political affair, and might not be possible even then. So, I am here to join you, to improve your chances of success and help keep Laurence out of the matter for as long as possible," she explained.

"We weren't aware the tale had spread so far and wide," lamented Gaerin.

"In truth, it has not. I met your nephew and his wife on the road to-"

"Wife?" interrupted Lyla. "So he *has* married Tylee!"

"Indeed, he has. He traveled here with Tylee, her mother Delriahna and their house man Bronsin. They joined up with Lord Mordechai, an esteemed Archmagus from Fel'Vizsiour, and it was my search for *him* that brought me to Salvation Shire, where I met them."

"Nothing with that lad is simple, is it?" asked Lyla.

"Not a thing," confirmed Gaerin. "How has he fared at Fel'Rechaun, then?"

"That boy is a treasure; an Initiate like none we've seen since your graduation, if I'm being honest," answered Kyrilis.

"That good, eh?" asked Gaerin.

"I speak truly. Your training has elevated him well beyond the point at which most of our Initiates graduate. In fact, the council deemed him unfairly advanced compared to the other recruits and promoted him to Marshal to continue his training in matters of leadership and tactics."

"How do you fit into all of this? Are you an instructor at the school?" asked Gaerin as their food arrived.

"The Afyr sent me as an emissary to serve the school as a Griffin Guard, as an act of good faith between the Afyr and King Orluhnd IV. As an emissary, I was the only person easily dismissed by Fahrul to aid you. It is in all of our interest that Laurence not discover your quest, and that you succeed so he can stay within Arkhania, where he's needed. Worry not," Kyrilis added, "I am skilled in my own right and will be of benefit to your pursuits."

"Welcome aboard, then," said Lyla with her mouth full of meat.

"How did you come by Keifer and Gabner?" Kyrilis asked.

"They saved us from Grellenheim, my lady. They drove back those foul beasts and pulled us from the city as it burned down around us. Luckily we found some horses outside and made it here before any more showed up," stated Keifer.

Kyrilis laughed.

"Why do you laugh?" asked Keifer.

"Those were Laurence's horses," she answered with an entertained sigh.

Gaerin and Lyla laughed while shaking their heads. They ate for a time as they got to know one another. Kyrilis stood often to send away other patrons who came over to gawk at Gabner. He appreciated her help very much. After a time, all of them had eaten their fill and Kyrilis was ready to get them moving... before any of the other Ravencrests found them.

"Do you still have those horses? If so, I'll need to acquire one of my own," she said.

"Unfortunately, no. We rode them through the night and, knowing they weren't ours, decided to leave them behind so they could rest and perhaps find their owners," explained Gaerin.

"Well, then. Shall we walk to Port Vaelin, or would you prefer mounts?" asked Kyrilis.

"Mounts," answered Lyla. She retrieved a handful of coins from a pouch at her waist and presented them to Kyrilis.

"Don't bother. Fahrul will reimburse whatever I spend on our journey, and I have credit at most of the establishments in Raven's Nest. Meet me east of town in an hour, I'll bring fresh horses."

She left the tavern before they could argue.

∴ ∴ ∴

A CRACK of energy broke the silence of the marble hallway. Mordechai stumbled out of the nook inset into the wall, set aside by Ayriel for his use in teleportation. Two guards, seeing him stumble, ran over to assist. As they lifted him up, one of them panicked and backed away at the sight of his eyes. The other led him hastily down the hall toward Ayriel's receiving room.

He knocked on the door to her chamber eagerly and waited for her to respond. Ayriel walked up behind them, alerted by the terrified guard who'd gone the other way.

"What's the matter?" she questioned.

The guard helped Mordechai turn to face her.

Her eyes opened wide with concern. "Help him into my chamber, Tavish, and tell my father I will be absent from court for a time," she commanded.

"Yes, your Eminence," he answered.

They led Mordechai into the chamber and helped him into a chair. Tavish left hurriedly to pass on the Princess's message. Once they were alone, Ayriel studied Mordechai's eyes. White cataracts had grown over them, and a faint black mist swirled about their surface.

"What happened, my dear friend?" she asked.

"Nightweaver," he muttered.

"How? How did she do this to you?"

"I discovered the secret to finding her with clairvoyance and used my crystal to do so. She... she cursed me through the crystal in retaliation." Still rattled by the curse, he was struggled to form his words clearly.

"That's not possible!"

"And yet it happened."

"How do we remove this curse? Do you know what it is?" She was deeply concerned for her dearest friend and held his face in her hands while she wept.

"She used an ancient spell that... that I do not understand how I recognize... Dalltash," he explained feebly.

"Dalltash?" she pondered.

"It is elven," he clarified.

She stood up with purpose, looked toward the servants' door at the rear of her chamber, and called out, "Silith, I have need of you!"

Silith came running, her silken dress trailing the floor behind her with a distinctive sound. Mordechai knew her well and enjoyed her presence when visiting Ayriel. He considered her as much a friend as he did Ayriel, and it was for that reason that they honored him with the knowledge they were secretly in love.

Ayriel's position as Princess and heir to the throne prohibited her from such unions, but that hadn't stopped her from finding a way to live with the person she loved. It was only in front of him, or in total privacy, that they could put aside their false pretenses and be themselves. So it was no mystery to him why she was always nearby; always a breath away from bursting through a door for her beloved Ayriel.

"I must travel to the Afyr-"

"Ekthri," corrected Mordechai.

"I must travel to Ekthri in search of answers for poor Mordechai. Please watch over him as if he were me," Ayriel requested.

Silith, with tears in her eyes at the sight of Mordechai's ailment, replied with a nod. She knelt before Mordechai and, much like Ayriel had done, put her hands to his face.

Ayriel hiked up her nightgown and left as quickly as she could. Her royal guard raced to keep up with her.

Machination

> Destiny, oh destiny,
> Doth thou bow to it?
> Oh listen ye who fight as free,
> Learn now and submit.

Night's Writ, Parable 7

AYRIEL'S INABILITY to master the art of teleportation—like Mordechai—often frustrated her. The situation she found herself in was certainly one of the times when her failings in the area truly pained her. However, he was not as adept as she in the art of enchanting.

In fact, she was the most well-known enchanter in the Kingdom, and the most powerful aside from the unexplainable skills of Joril Herrickson. If there were any situation that warranted the excessive enchanting of a mount, her current predicament was it, she decided. After all, she hadn't even stopped to change clothes or slip shoes onto her feet.

Upon reaching the royal stables, she called for the servants to bring out her horse. He was a beautiful creature selected for his rare breed, striking appearance, and impressive pedigree. His hair shone silver when struck with certain light and was unlike any other horse in the land. His name was Tegris and his fame stretched far and wide.

She stroked his mane as he arrived, whispering to him lovingly. "I apologize, sweet Tegris, for what this might do to you. But, we cannot let Mordechai suffer, and this Kingdom has great need of his services."

Tegris whinnied and clopped his right hoof into the ground. Many had wondered, over the years, if he was intelligent enough to understand when she spoke to him. Ayriel knew with certainty that he could, and that he not only understood the common tongue, but elvish as well.

Her hand upon his mane, she began chanting. The spell was so strong that everyone about the courtyard could see the magical runes come into being, glowing upon his fur. He snorted, feeling their power course through him. With no concern for a saddle, she mounted Tegris and kicked his hindquarters with her bare feet.

The stable boy looked on as a silver streak raced away, Tegris's saddle cradled uselessly over one arm.

Already faster than every horse in the Kingdom, Tegris's speed increased tenfold under Ayriel's enchantments. She steered him up the eastern ramp of the Engle Plateau and then north, to go around Raven's Nest and Raven Keep. Once clear, she rode southwest until she passed Telon's Respite and eventually met up once again with the Western Reach. She could feel Tegris's excitement at galloping so quickly across the terrain without saddle or bridle.

By the time she arrived in the Ekthri wood, only half of the day's light remained. She slowed her pace, unsure of where the Ekthri cities were located, for according to legend they moved. She had arrived in Ekthri with incredible speed, but her real chore lie ahead of her. She needed to find the Ekthri capital of Ayr'Thugohn, discover one who could help, and then bargain for that help. Her task was going to be difficult, that much was clear to her.

Tegris trotted along the Ekthri Fjord slowly, allowing his master to look about for signs of elvish civilization. A narrow bridge came into view, constructed of precision-cut stone blocks and thick iron. The bridge had stood for hundreds of years without need of repair or maintenance. It spanned the gap between cliffs that gave the road its name; trailing down hazardously to the river a thousand feet below. The view was stunning, and she couldn't help but stop to appreciate it.

With her desire for the beauty of nature sated, she continued west. All around her were sights she rarely got a chance to see. Her noble obligations and proximity to the throne had kept her trapped in Vellenheim for most of her life. She continued on for some time before reaching a fork in the road. Pausing for a moment to mull over the few details she could recall about the Ekthri and their civilization, she chose the northern fork.

After several hours with no signs of a city, she resigned herself to making camp. It didn't take long to find a small clearing in the trees beside the road. She dismounted and led Tegris into it slowly, careful to not lead him through brambles or other hazards. Inside her protective spells and wards, she slept peacefully beneath the stars on a cushion of grass... which was yet another new experience for her.

∴ ∴ ∴

IT WAS night by the time Laurence reached Raven's Nest. Along the way they'd made plans for how they would split up and who would cover which part of town searching for rooms. Laurence told them where Tylee's house was on the southern cliff and offered them all a place to stay. They agreed to return if no other rooms could be found.

Laurence stopped in front of the home and tied the horse's reins to a post on the porch. Not knowing who was awake or who he would frighten, he knocked instead of trying the door. He could hear heavy footsteps travel across the floor from the back of the house as he waited. Bronsin opened the door and immediately smiled at him.

"Lad!" he belted as he threw his arms around Laurence.

With a grunt, Laurence replied, "Good to see you too."

"So glad you could make it, sir *Laurence!*" he yelled. In a whisper he added, "She's driving us insane!"

Laurence laughed as he walked in, closing the door behind himself. He knew very well how his wife could be. Just as he knew very well that the sound of thunder coming from the stairs was his wife running to greet him with reckless abandon.

"Careful, my little klutz," he called up to her.

"Shush you!" she barked back as she nearly tackled him into a hug. She kissed him frantically, as if he might vanish if she stopped.

"Let him breath, dear," suggested Delriahna as she joined them.

Tylee backed away from Laurence, still holding his hands. She was too happy to argue with her mother.

Laurence didn't mind the attention. It was a delightful change of pace from the life he'd been living.

"How does your schooling progress?" asked Delriahna in her most unimpressed tone.

"Fine. I'm learning quite a bit," he answered, unwilling to brag and unaware what information his position duties him to share.

There was a sudden knock at the door. Laurence knew who he was likely to find, and was pleased to see not one but all of them when he opened it.

"Sorry, Laurence," Wil started. "All inns in the entire town are full, thanks to the refugees. We have nowhere else to go," he explained apologetically.

Turning to his family, Laurence introduced them. "This is Izabel, a noble from Vellenheim; Wil of the Ekthri; and finally Agnar and Bingrolf, cousins and farmers from the marshlands south of Grellenheim. They also attend Fel'Rechaun and, as we've exceeded expectations of late, we were all given extra leave together as reward."

Izabel nodded at Laurence, agreeing with his decision to gloss over their circumstances.

"Pardon, Laurence," started Delriahna, "but where do you expect them all to sleep?"

"This is your house, and that is your decision," he answered.

After a few moments of contemplation, met with patient stares from the crowd before her, Delriahna decided. "Izabel shall have my room. Agnar and Bingrolf, please share the empty room. Bronsin, I shall share your room. After all, we've known each other since before Laurence was born. Wil, I presume that as an elf you don't sleep as much, and therefore *might* be okay without a bed?"

"You presume correctly, my lady. Though I do enjoy the occasional mattress, it is not a requirement," he answered.

"Then it is settled," declared Delriahna with finality. "Bronsin," she called, ascending the stairs, "come help me move my things."

"Yes, my lady," he answered. For a moment, it had looked as if he was going to argue her decision. He chose instead to push those feelings back and simply do as he was told.

Laurence and Tylee were as quiet as they could be that night. Izabel, whose room was across from theirs, didn't get much sleep.

∴ ∴ ∴

"WHAT NEWS have you, witch?" challenged Drakahl, restraining the power of his voice out of respect.

"All has been set into motion. The Velloth have been loosed," she said, reveling in their deeds. She walked up to him and placed her old, frail hands on his chest. "Vehkstaerelliox will soon ravage their lands, my King." She smiled up at him as if being pleasured. "And you... you've brought news of your own?"

"You have already seen what I know," he whispered.

"It is always a pleasure to hear you confirm it," she retorted playfully.

"Our plans are secure. Arcturus is dead, and there is no cure for the curse he placed upon me. The gifts it imparts are permanent, and we may proceed without fear of hindrance," he explained.

He stepped back from her, turned and walked to the window to peer out at his domain.

She walked up behind him and wrapped her arms around his waist, veins showing through her paper thin skin. "What of you? Do the pains continue?"

"They have subsided, but I-" he started, placing his hand to his head. "I had to let part of it in. We have come to an accord."

"An accord? With the armor?" she asked, concerned. "That was not part of our agreement."

"I am in control, worry not. Now instead of pain, I hear a voice. I can understand it's urges and desires more clearly. That is all. The curse prevents Axvalla from fully taking over, just as we expected. For now, the demon is content to simply have a voice."

She hugged him tighter. They stood in silence for a few moments while she considered the risk he was taking.

"I have dispatched Thorgen, Grohm and Soth to the Triblunds to gather souls for our pursuits. We simply need time," he said.

He looked down at her hands for a moment. The flesh upon them appeared to decay, slowly, before his eyes. Bubbling with sickly ooze, the flesh turning black and wilted out of existence. The muscles receded as he watched, revealing pearl-white bones which then faded to gray and crumbled to dust. As suddenly as the vision began, her hands reappeared about his waist. In that moment, her hands were beautiful, revealing how she'd appeared in her youth.

The moment was fleeting. The vision of decay began anew.

"I cannot wait to watch as Vehks plays with them," he said, turning to look into her eyes.

His men would have to learn to live with the curse as he had. Its benefits were simply too powerful to overlook. He smiled at the thought of leading a legion of warriors with his armor and strength into battle.

∴ ∴ ∴

LAURENCE AND Tylee ate a leisurely dawnfry that morning, prepared quite by surprise. Wil had been in a thankful mood when he woke. He spent the remainder of the night cleaning their house and began preparing a feast for them all as the sun crested the horizon. Afterward, they found themselves alone, all of their friends and family having left for a day of shopping and leisure.

He leaned over and kissed her, staring deeply into her eyes. She smiled and blushed, simply happy to be in his presence and feel so loved. They played and flirted as they cleaned up after their meal. It was everything she'd ever dreamed of.

"How do you wish to spend our day, my love? Shall I show you around town?" she offered.

"I know I'm supposed to be here for leisure pursuits, but I'm not sure I can spend an entire day that way. Something is gnawing away at me, and I fear it must be addressed," he said solemnly.

"What is it?" she asked in a fearful tone.

"No, no, dear... it isn't you. Gods, no," he reassured. "I was in Grellenheim when the Velloth attacked. Many people died. So, I feel obliged to help those who survived; the ones who came here seeking aid. I thought we could use some of Delriahna's funds to buy them food and supplies. Maybe help shore up their tents. Anything that could make their lives a little easier for the day."

"What are 'Velloth'?" asked Tylee.

"They are vile ancient elves with red, scaly skin that were driven underground long ago," he explained.

"They sound horrifying!" she gasped.

"More than you know, love. Most residents of Grellenheim died in their attack. Very few survived, and they're here in Raven's Nest. They need our help," he added.

"Well... let's help the refugees together!" she declared. "I was just telling mother yesterday that I didn't want to waste away in my window any longer. So let's get going!" It was time she learned how the new version of Laurence spent his days, she decided. She wanted to be a part of his entire life, not just his leisure time.

"Very well, let's be on our way," he said, smiling. He hadn't expected her to be so interested in his idea.

They returned to their room to dress. Laurence donned his leather armor, deciding it wiser not to appear too intimidating. Tylee dressed conservatively as well, following his lead.

It had been a while since he'd been without his armor and sword. Walking around town, he felt very unprotected, almost naked. It was a strange sensation when combined with the fact that he could feel the weight of the armor, since he wasn't wearing the entire suit.

They stopped at several shops to buy a hand cart and several supplies. When they finally arrived in the refugee village outside of town, several of them approached and offered to buy their goods. It was a pleasant surprise to all when they began handing out loaves of bread, hunks of sausage, wine, milk and cheese while asking nothing in return.

When their cart was empty, Laurence began inspecting their tents, addressing issues wherever he could. Tylee returned to a group of women she'd helped distribute their gifts to earlier. The women sat around a small campfire, each repairing a piece of clothing or a blanket.

"Might I join you?" she asked.

"Sure, hun," offered one of the women, casually passing her needle through the garment in her lap.

Tylee sat on an empty stump, smiling at the women in thanks. The day had been exhausting, and she'd hadn't eaten since dawnfry.

"I wanted to thank you again for your generosity, my lady," said a woman. "Seems like most folk around these parts would prefer we didn't exist. The church sent a few priests to us, but they mostly just wanted to pray for the ones we lost. Prayers are all good and well, but they don't fill bellies."

"Well, my husband helped kill the Velloth in Grellenheim, so he witnessed what happened. He suggested we come and offer assistance to you, and... here we are," answered Tylee.

"Velloth?" asked another woman.

"He said they were elves who were trapped underground since ancient times. I don't think he knows why they attacked, or where they came from... or at least, he didn't explain as much. He was very upset that his group didn't arrive in time to save everyone. He feels guilty."

"Well, we're all glad he showed up at all," she said. Many of the women nodded and voiced their agreement. "He can't blame himself for those that died. Who could have predicted what happened? Surely it wasn't his fault."

"I suppose that's true," said Tylee.

"I'm Greta Stowell," said another woman, extending her hand.

Tylee stood and shook Greta's hand happily before returning to her stump. "I'm Tylee Ravencrest!"

"This is Gretchen Bamford," Greta said, continuing the introductions. "The crotchety ole crone to my left is Theresa Holloman. Don't mind a thing she says, she's still upset that she didn't win that beauty pageant forty years back," she said, eliciting chuckles around the crowd. Theresa gave her best harrumph as she tried to hide a smirk. "Between you and Theresa is miss Franny Gillsworth."

"Francesca," she corrected, extending her hand. Tylee shook it eagerly.

"Franny here will talk your ears off if you let her. You've been warned," continued Greta. "On your other side is Willamina Stoh. She's our shy one." Willamina looked up at Tylee with a sheepish smile before returning to her work. "Last but not least-"

"Saving the best for last," interrupted the woman. "I'm Cynthia Karlsberg. Anything you need, you come to me. I know everyone and everything."

"What she *means* is she's the town gossip," corrected Greta. The women all laughed in response.

"I'm glad to see all of your spirits so high in light of recent events," said Tylee.

"Make no mistake, we're all hurtin inside," answered Greta. "But at the end of the day, it's up to us to hold this camp together. We had our day to mourn on the road, and now we're faced with new challenges which require our focus. We've got to keep it together for the children... *and* our men," she said with many nods and grunts of agreement, "And we've got plenty of work to do."

"Speaking of your men, where are they? So few men are in the camp right now," said Tylee.

"My husband is helping tend a nearby farm," answered Gretchen.

"All our husbands are helping at nearby farms. There's nothing else they *can* do," corrected Greta.

"You were all farmers?" asked Tylee.

"No, dear. Not a single one of us were farmers. We're cityfolk," Cynthia answered.

"My husband, Carter, is a carpenter. I finished his pieces, and we sold them in our shop on Main Street," said Francesca.

"Gerald, is a stonemason. He worked for Lord Gemlesh and maintained the official buildings, the keep, and all that. I ran a small daycare for our children," said Cynthia.

"That's where she gets most of her gossip," teased Greta. "Children." Laughter filled the air, lightening the mood. "My husband, Aric, managed Garven's Goods, the general store on Main Street."

"What about you?" Tylee asked Willamina.

"My... my husband Rolph worked at Haven," she whispered without looking up.

"Haven was a gambling den near the north gates. It was a pretty rough establishment, so they hired men to guard the place and kick people out that didn't follow the rules, or started trouble. Rolph is a big man, well suited to the work. And he's very protective of his little flower Willamina," added Greta.

"I don't mind," said Willamina in a sheepish whisper.

"I've known Willamina since she was tiny. Watched her grow up. She was always too kind and gentle for Grellenheim. Rolph kinda... took her under his protection when they were kids and... they're just inseparable now," added Cynthia.

Willamina blushed.

"A lot of the guys in town that worked as enforcers, um..." started Greta, unsure of how to explain what she wanted to say.

"They beat their wives," said Cynthia bluntly. "Not Rolph, though. In fact, he likes to find those guys and teach em a lesson. He's a big fella, but he's really just a big ole *fluffy bundle of love*."

"Don't call him fluffy," giggled Willamina.

"He's a gift, Willie, a blessing... and you know it," said Francesca.

"Yeah," admitted Willamina.

"If I were a younger woman, I'd-" started Theresa.

"If I have to listen to you droll on about Rolph's body *one more time*," interrupted Greta.

Willamina and Cynthia laughed. It was a conversation they'd obviously had many times.

"It's just so gross," said Francesca.

"Maybe your man needs some lessons in how to treat a woman," jabbed Cynthia.

Francesca feigned shock and gasped dramatically.

After a few moments of laughter Tylee asked, "With their skills and yours, why don't you build something better than tents?" Seeing their faces, and hearing the abrupt arrival of their silence, she clarified, "I don't mean any offense. It just seems you're all very well equipped to build houses, and all that."

"We lack materials, for one thing. The Legion won't let us, for another. My husband asked if he could fell some trees to build a few small homes, but they said we couldn't touch the trees and *certainly* couldn't build any permanent structures. They don't want to expand the town's borders," answered Greta.

"I'm sorry. I didn't know," offered Tylee.

After a few moments, their conversation resumed as if Tylee hadn't asked her question. They asked about Tylee, and she regaled them with tales of Mooncrest, and Laurence, and their journey to Raven's Nest. She explained that she regretted not getting to visit Grellenheim before the attack, and that she wished they'd met under better circumstances.

A few hours later, Laurence showed up to collect her. Most of the women around the fire teasingly said, "Hi Laur," in unison and pretended to swoon. All except for Theresa, who sat in silence for a moment.

"If I were a younger woman, I'd-" started Theresa.

"Ew, gods! Stop!" yelled Francesca, playfully.

The sound of laughter was still filling the camp as Laurence and Tylee began their walk home. Tylee told him all about them, their jobs, and their husbands.

$$\therefore \therefore \therefore$$

FRUSTRATION WAS beginning to overwhelm the creature. It couldn't find a way to reach its prey, and could not understand what was preventing it from acquiring its meal. The fleshy pads of its fore-claws returned to the ground again as it resumed pacing around what seemed to be a circular, invisible barrier. It growled deeply—instinctively—in frustration.

Ayriel awoke, adrenaline coursing through her. She closed her eyes tightly and reached out with her mind, attempting to discern the state of her protective barriers. They were still intact, but their power was waning.

It must be nearly dawn, she decided.

She could hear something pacing around her clearing, and its steps were hastening and growing erratic. Whatever it was, it was growing impatient.

She rolled to her stomach and looked around the edge of the clearing. The sun was slowly rising in the eastern sky, but hadn't risen far enough to reach through the trees. As she gained her feet, movement on the other side of the brush at the northern edge of camp caught her eyes. She couldn't make out her predator in the darkness, but did her best to follow it as it paced just beyond her vision's reach.

"Krishuthris," she whispered, casting a spell that would temporarily enhance her vision. The enchantment was a simple one, designed for use in the dead of night or when deep underground. It allowed the affected being to see heat radiation. It also allowed one to see ultraviolet light, which could reach through tree cover, even when visible light could not.

It was a risky spell to cast, so close to full sunrise. She knew that if the spell was still in effect when the sky fully brightened, the result would be temporary blindness. It was a calculated risk that she had no choice but to accept, if she wished to know what threatened her before it was too late. Her breath caught in her chest as the spell took effect, allowing her to see what stalked her.

Before her loomed a creature that her extensive studies described as a Skaar. It was one of an ancient race of dragon-kin, once used as slaves by a vast Draconic empire. The Empire of Kyggathuun had spanned the eastern coast of Gargoa before the founding of the three kingdoms. Historic texts from many civilizations of the First Era had detailed the hunting of dragons to clear the lands and make them safe for races such as humans, dwarves and elves.

The Skaar, freed by the slaying of their masters, had gone into hiding; fearing their own extinction. There had, of course, been rumors, myths and legends for ages that the Skaar still wandered the Mythaeil Mountains and the woods which bordered them. Few souls were brave enough to go out in search of them, and fewer still were lucky enough to return from such hunts.

The Skaar before her had four eyes; two at the front of its head, and another on each side. Six legs held up an elongated body that ended in a long, serpentine tail. The four hind legs were close together, providing great stability and speed. The feet attached to those four hind legs each had four massive fingers, two on each side; allowing for easy passage on unstable terrain.

In front of the shorter hind section, its mid-body benefited from a highly flexible spine. It could bend backwards easily, allowing the front two-thirds of the creature to rise upright and stand taller than most men. The front of the creature was a human-like, having and extremely muscular torso that boasted humanoid arms complete with fully functional hands. Each of its fingers ended in a long claw, capable of ripping through flesh, light armor and bone. A thick, muscular neck supported its lizard-like head.

The creature confirmed nearly every detail of Skaar that she'd studied so many years prior. She could make out the razor sharp horns that protruded from the creature's spine, which revealed it as a warrior cast from the species.

Because of the lack of proper light, the color of its scales was the only detail she couldn't verify. Knowing the color of its scales would reveal the creature's immunities, and without that information she was unsure how she should, or could, proceed.

The texts describe Skaar as intelligent, yet they did not possess the means with which to produce complex sounds and form words. They could growl and hiss, which afforded them limited means of communication within their own species. However, tales and legends often described them as terrifyingly devious hunters. Further, they had been intelligent enough to take complex commands from their Draconic masters and follow those commands with a high degree of precision.

They acted as the Kyggathuunic labor force, building the complex structures and temples of the empire. One legend even suggested that the Skaar might have scribed the history of the masters, and the rise of the humanoid kingdoms; indicating that they were intelligent enough to read and write.

As the power of the first ward faded with a visible shimmer, the Skaar leaned the left side of its body toward the clearing. Its scaly skin ground against the inner ward, causing sparks of resistant magic to fill the air. It leaped back a few feet in pain, landing with its entire body in direct line with her. A hiss emanated from the beast as it reared back onto its hind legs, revealing its massive size and imposing form. She knew she only had a matter of seconds with which to prepare her defense.

She couldn't attack with spells because she didn't know the beast's immunities, not to mention she simply didn't know many attack spells. Her desire to find a cure for Mordechai had also driven her with such haste that she'd brought with her neither weapon nor armor.

Think, she demanded.

Renewing the wards would only delay the inevitable and drive the creature further into a frenzy, so that wasn't an option. If what she knew about the Skaar was accurate, it was too intelligent for illusions to have much success. She looked about her camp frantically, seeking anything that she could wield as a weapon; anything that she could enchant.

She found a branch near the southern edge of the clearing that was roughly the length and thickness of her arm. She hefted it briefly and considered its weight acceptable for wielding. It was soft from age and weather, offering little on its own in the way of a tool or weapon. That did not concern her, for to her the branch was but a vessel for her powers.

Holding the branch in her left hand, she quickly began chanting spells while moving her right hand along its length. Runes sprang to life along the branch, hardening and empowering it. Spell after spell emanated from her right hand and stretched out to envelope the branch, absorbing into it. One spell straightened the branch, another cast off its bark.

The far end came to a point, as the branch lengthened and stretched into the shape of a blade. Her right hand moved the length of the blade, fingers outstretched around it, as another spell sharpened the blade far beyond that of a normal sword.

She grasped the wooden longsword before her in both hands, with less than a second remaining before the final ward waned. As it faded from existence with a telltale shimmer, the Skaar charged her with frightening speed. She raised the sword perpendicular to its approach, above her head, to parry its fore-claws as they descended upon her.

The blow struck her blade with the strength she had anticipated, yet was unprepared to deflect. She reeled backward, pain radiating through her arms, shoulders and spine. The Skaar pulled its fore-claws back in shock, the fleshy pads of its palms bleeding and cut to the bone.

Tegris rushed to defend his master. The Skaar lashed its tail at the horse, striking him lengthwise across the body and sending him to the ground in pain, whinnying and snorting involuntarily.

Angrily, the beast lashed out at Ayriel, tearing at the air in front of her with talons alone. It was attempting to hit her while keeping its bloody palms free of further harm.

She ignored the pain in her upper body and parried the beast's attacks with unrealistic speed, severing talons from fingers with each strike.

It reared back, trying to put distance between them. The Skaar suddenly realized it had horribly underestimated its meal.

Ayriel took advantage of the beast's withdrawal and rushed forward with attacks of her own. Her wooden blade cut into the center of its chest. It reeled in pain, whipping its tail around to push the unnatural enemy away from itself. The attack hit Ayriel hard in the chest, sending her a few feet away onto her rear.

As she regained her feet and readied her blade for another volley, two arrows erupted through the creature's throat and chest from behind. Each arrow tip glowed to her eyes, shimmering with the power of enchantments. Shock and horror filled the Skaar's visage as it fell to the ground in a heap.

Her make-shift sword crumbled to ash as she released her grip on it, the enchantments having expired.

"State your business," called out a voice from above.

The sunlight was growing brighter, making it hard to see clearly when she looked up through the trees. She dismissed the enchantment and looked again, finding an elf standing on a branch high above the clearing. She took a moment to whisper a few healing words to recover from the bruising she'd suffered to her ribs before responding. The elf waited patiently, understanding her priorities without need of explanation.

"I am Ayriel Vaelin, Princess of Arkhania. First, I'd like to thank you for your assistance with this Skaar. I had not anticipated such an encounter when I journeyed here. I come to you seeking aid with a matter of grave importance, and bring news of several recently discovered happenings that might affect your people," she explained.

The elf dropped deftly from branch to branch, descending the tree. In short order, he stood before her, bow at his side.

"I am called Fox, by my team. We have watched you since your arrival in our wood. Do you have proof of your personage?"

"If you are unfamiliar with the royal family of Arkhania, then I fear there is little I could provide you as proof. Perhaps you are aware of Tegris; a gift to my father, King Orluhnd IV, from your King many years ago?" she offered, pointing to her horse.

Tegris regained his feet and walked over to her upon hearing his name, snorting questioningly.

"We are familiar with Tegris. Your knowledge of his origin should suffice, for now, as proof of your honesty. Be warned, we have eyes and ears upon you at all times. However, I will lead you to Ayr'Thugohn where you can meet with Wyk'Daienor. She will evaluate your information and offer the aid you seek, if she finds you deserving."

"I thank you, Fox, for your assistance. I wondered why I had not seen any of your peoples' structures or settlements thus far," she alluded.

"It should come as no surprise to learn that our homes are high among the trees. This," he said, pointing at the Skaar, "is but one of many reasons that our people adapted to live in such a manner. You passed beneath a small village at the fork and did not notice, which is a testament to our elders' wise decisions."

"Indeed," she said in agreement.

She walked beside him, leading Tegris, as he led her back to the road. They continued north on foot in silence.

.·. .·. .·.

WHEN LAURENCE came downstairs the next morning, Wil was pouring coffee for a guest. The man was wearing a full suit of plate armor that bore the sigil of the Legion. His shield and sword leaned against the wall behind his chair, which strained under his weight. His helmet sat on the table next to him.

"Who is our guest, Wil?" asked Laurence from the doorway.

"Ah, good, you're awake," said Wil. "This is Vinetar Kotann, leader of the First Vintain of the Fifth Centain."

Laurence gave him a confused look.

"You'll have to excuse Laurence, my lord, he's yet to learn the complex structures of the Legion."

Kotann stood and reached out his hand in greeting. "Your reputation precedes you, Laurence." He shook Laurence's hand and continued, "I've heard a great many things about you, including tales of your victory against the Velloth forces in Grellenheim."

"We may have defeated them, but I wouldn't call it a victory. Hundreds of citizens died that night, for we arrived too late to save them," Laurence lamented.

"You were right about him," Kotann said to Wil with a glance. Turning back to Laurence he continued, "I am here to collect your group. We are to meet with Lord Commander Fahrul in Fel'Rechaun. Afterward, we head out on our mission together. My Vintain is already on their way to your school, and shall be awaiting our arrival."

"A Vintain is twenty soldiers, Laurence," added Wil, without being asked. He sat down and gestured that they should do the same.

"Let us eat and get to know one another. I've been told that the two of us will lead this expedition jointly. I'd like to know the man who will share my command," said Kotann as he sat.

"Do you know where we're heading?" asked Laurence as he joined them.

"Centurion Vale has only instructed me as far as meeting with Fahrul. I do not have the full details of our mission, save that it involves Velloth like the ones you fought in Grellenheim. You and your companions have experience fighting them. The Legion... does not. So, Fahrul and Vale agreed it prudent you accompany us," he explained. "Let us not dwell on unknowns, we've still not received our briefing.

"For now, let us talk of more personal matters. I am Magnus Kotann of Vellenheim. I've never been south of Fel'Rechaun. Perhaps you could tell me of Mooncrest, and your journey here? I prefer not to rely upon rumors," he requested.

Laurence told Kotann his story while Wil prepared dawnfry for the household. It was a long, complex tale, but Kotann listened intently throughout. Laurence made sure to leave out details of Nightweaver's involvement, or the true nature of the boys they found dead at the Sacton River. Much of what he knew was secret, and he didn't want to overstep his boundaries.

∴ ∴ ∴

THEY FINISHED their meal before anyone else from the house came downstairs. Their meal had been fine, and the conversation pleasant. However, they had things to do, and a trip to embark upon. Laurence took a moment to help Wil clear their dirty dishes and set the table for the others.

"I must go fetch my armor and bid my wife farewell. I will meet you out front shortly," he said to Kotann. "Wil, could you see to the rest of our group? I'd like to leave soon. We're losing sunlight."

Wil nodded his affirmative and followed Laurence upstairs.

Laurence opened Tylee's door quietly and crept toward the bed, trying not to wake her. His plan was to crawl into bed and wake her with a kiss. However, as his knee pressed into the mattress, both Agnar and Bingrolf howled from the room next door, protesting whatever prank Wil had pulled to wake them.

Tylee blinked the sleep out of her eyes and looked up at her husband. He brushed her hair aside, caressing her cheek, and leaned in for a kiss. As their lips touched, Izabel yelled across the hall for Wil to, "Get out!"

"What's going on, my love?" asked Tylee in a whisper.

"Fahrul has called us to Fel'Rechaun. He needs us for another mission," he explained, still touching her nose with his.

"I understand," she answered. Tears welled up in her eyes.

"I will be back as soon as I can, Ty."

She reluctantly released his hand as he removed himself from the bed. Her eyes never left him as he put on piece after piece of his complex armor. As he buckled his scabbard onto his back, he turned to face her and smiled.

When he was nearly finished, she slid out of the sheets and sat on the edge of the bed with her hands held out to him. Smiling, he grabbed her hands and pulled her to her feet, into his arms. After another kiss, he wiped a tear from her cheek.

Smiling up at him, she said, "Now go. You've places to be, and people to save."

He smiled at her and considered how different she was to the girl he'd married; changed as a result of all they'd been through. She was gaining a sense of clarity and maturity that her previous life hadn't required of her. He was proud of what she was becoming and knew that she was proud of him as well. It hurt to leave her behind, but his sense of duty wouldn't allow him to do otherwise.

She followed him out of the room in her evening gown as he made his way outside. At the back of the house, he patted Onyx and got him ready to travel. He then stopped by the carriage parked on the side of the house and dug around for a moment before coming out with Wyk'Kydarian's shield, in case he would need it.

It was at that moment that she realized how serious his departure was. Drawing on the strength she'd seen in the women at the refugee camp, she cast aside her concerns. Smiling, a tear still descending her cheek, she pulled him close one more time.

With one last kiss, he mounted Onyx and left to join his party at the front of the house.

∴ ∴ ∴

KOTANN'S VINTAIN stood waiting when they entered Fahrul's hall. Karzden and Dahsh stood next to Fahrul, who rose to his feet when the door opened. Laurence made note that Mordechai and Kyrilis were nowhere in sight, which struck him as strange.

"Welcome back, Laurence, and congratulations on your victory over the Velloth," started Fahrul.

The soldiers clapped and cheered, impressed that a boy so young had been so successful on the field of battle.

Karzden walked over and patted him on the shoulder, saying, "Good job, lad!"

"I am told there is a mission before us?" asked Laurence.

"Straight to business, that's why I like this lad," joked Fahrul. Several soldiers chuckled in agreement. "We all know about Grellenheim, but most of you are unaware what else happened that night. Kyrilis, in her scouting, discovered and defeated a smaller group of Velloth in Gaierford. They slew the citizens of that town before her arrival. Much like the losses we experienced in Grellenheim, I fear."

Several about the room muttered curses under their breath. Fahrul waited for them to silence before continuing.

"She followed their trail to the west and then south. From there, she observed another trail departing toward Grellenheim. Clearly, both groups had the same point of origin. However, that is not the end of it. She lost the southern group's trail in the marshlands southwest of here and was so close to our school by then that she gave up the search to report her findings to me. That is what has transpired to bring you all before me today," he explained.

"So, this isn't over," stated Laurence.

"Do we know their number?" asked Kotann.

"It isn't, and we do not. All she was able to find was their trail leading into the brush of the Sacton Delta and nothing more. The area is uninhabited aside from a few remote farmsteads further south, none of which are equipped to seek aid or send word with any haste.

"Therefore, it is up to us to seek the rest of the Velloth out and end their insurgence before matters worsen," detailed Fahrul. "A detail that seems just as alarming is the fact that the forces which attacked both Gaierford and Grellenheim seemed perfectly sized according to their target. The smaller force went directly to a smaller town, and the larger force proceeded without deviation to Grellenheim, the larger target. By all accounts, they'd have succeeded there as well, were it not for the intervention of our Initiates and Lord Mordechai."

"So since we don't know their numbers, we can't approximate their likely targets and seek to intercept them. We must, instead, give chase," surmised Kotann.

"Indeed," confirmed Fahrul. "That is why I had an audience with your Centurion to formalize the mission. This falls well within the Legion's jurisdiction and has exceeded the purvey of Fel'Rechaun, for it is no longer a simple scouting operation." There were nods of agreement from many about the room. "However, we feel Laurence and his group's experience with the Velloth to be invaluable."

"I agree," declared Kotann, turning to address his men. "We will be traversing marshes, so Gharick and Berril will need to prepare spells for drying and treating our horses, and our feet, to prevent sickness and rot. That means they will be without attack spells during that portion of our journey. Halgar and Thax, you are to stay on high alert and ride next to them to provide extra protection and cover.

"The rest of you will need to fan out and watch both the ground beneath you, and ahead of you, as we advance to note any signs of passage. Bring extra rope so we can hold it between our mounts to keep proper spacing." Completing orders to his men, he turned his attention to Laurence and asked, "Are any in your party knowledgeable of the marshlands?"

"I am, sir," answered Agnar, "and so is my cousin Bingrolf," he said with a thumb pointing in Bingrolf's direction. "We grew up in a farmstead south of the delta."

"We'll need you to ride up front and guide us, if that is acceptable to Laurence," Kotann said.

"I'm fine with it," answered Laurence.

After the news of the attack on Gaierford and the other Velloth forces, Laurence thought it prudent to withhold his questions about Mordechai and Kyrilis and there whereabouts. More pressing matters were at hand, and he was confident wherever they happened to be, they were performing critical duties.

"Then it's settled," concluded Fahrul. "Karzden will lead you to our armory. Grab whatever you need for the mission and set out in the morning. We've no time to lose."

∴ ∴ ∴

PORT VAELIN was a sprawling city. The northern half of the buildings and streets began high on the sides of the rocky cliffs and mountains along the exterior of Vellen Crescent. From there, the city sprawled down to ground level before curving to follow the shoreline of the harbor.

To the south, the city once again met with small, rocky cliffs and hills and grew upward into the sky. From their vantage point—as Vellen Wood opened up to reveal the breadth of the city below—Port Vaelin seemed like an enormous bowl.

The engineering and construction techniques afforded government buildings and noble houses a view of the city below, and allowed for easier oversight of the goings-on therein. A tunnel through the mountains to the north provided easy access for the import and export of goods to Vellenheim without the need to travel days through the pass to go around.

The Trade Commission owned and managed most of the property to the north. It served as the governing body for all of Port Vaelin and the shipping lanes that traversed the eastern shores of Arkhania through the waters of the Hystari.

Gaerin knew that they needed to avoid the Trade Commission as much as possible. Their reputation for extreme taxation would likely drain the group of all their resources as they attempted to hire a ship to take them to Pelrigoss.

It was to his surprise and pleasure to hear that Kyrilis agreed with his plan to focus on black market traders. Given more time, he would have preferred Gusarski Cove to the Kingdom's primary port. He had expected her, being a servant of the Kingdom and an experienced soldier, to disagree and insist on using proper channels.

Kyrilis had reservations about their chances of success in Pelrigoss. She dreaded any potential confrontation with Drakahl or his forces without support from Arkhania, and many troops at her side. That did not detract, though, from her excitement at the prospect of sailing across the open waters of the Hystari.

She'd never been aboard a boat or ship of any kind and had smelled salty sea air for the first time as they approached Port Vaelin. As an elf raised in the snowy Mythaeil Mountains, everything from that point forward was going to be new to her.

Lyla pulled Gabner's hood further down to cover his face. He sat in front of her on her horse, where she intended to pass him off as their child. Their plan was to claim he had leprosy, and that they sailed to Pelrigoss to visit a fabled healer specializing in the disease. She hoped that their story would keep wary guards and Trade Commission staff at bay, for fear they might contract it.

Gabner was very excited by the idea that he was Lyla's son and seemed to have difficulty understanding that he actually wasn't. For the sake of their need for subterfuge, she decided to go along with his enthusiasm.

They rode slowly through the main gates, toward the southern half of the city. Their primary goal was obtaining lodging. After a few hours, Gaerin chose the most run-down tavern he could find and went inside to procure rooms. When he returned, he had but a single key.

"One room?" asked Lyla, concerned.

"That's all they had. They didn't even ask how many guests I had with me, or who anyone was… which means this is the right place. We'll just have to pile our bags and spare clothes about the floor for comfort and make do as best we can," he offered.

"Do they have stables?" she asked.

"No, we'll sell our horses down the street. You and Kyrilis can take everything inside. I'll take care of the rest," he answered.

"Affirmative," said Kyrilis.

Everyone dismounted and started unloading their supplies. Kyrilis helped Gaerin tie the horses in a line with bits of rope and then carried the last of the bags inside. As the rest of them carried their belongings through the doors, Gaerin walked off with their horses.

Once everything was in their room, Lyla set about dispersing the bags and bedrolls so everyone would have a place to sleep. Kyrilis stood at the door, waiting patiently. When Lyla finished, she signaled her over so they could talk.

"I'll stay in the room with Keifer and Gabner. You two can handle whatever business you need. All I ask is that you bring back food for us from time to time and make this stay as brief as possible. I don't trust this place," Kyrilis said.

"I don't either, but I trust you. We're of the same mind, as I'd planned on asking you to protect our room while we secured a ship," explained Lyla with a smile. Kyrilis patted her on the shoulder knowingly. "We also need to recruit a few mercenaries to accompany us. This is going to take some muscle, we know that. We're not idiots. That may take a few days."

"Understood. Perhaps I'll sneak out at night for fresh air whenever you and Gaerin return to the room. I just don't think it's wise to let Gabner be seen," said Kyrilis.

"Agreed," answered Lyla.

She walked over to their belongings and withdrew a few pieces of parchment, a quill and an inkwell. She'd brought them with her for precisely such a moment. Taking them to the nearby table, she made small flyers advertising their need for mercenaries, and listing the inn's bar as the place to meet any night after dinner.

"I'd like to be present when you interview those who apply," said Kyrilis. "Many of the mercenaries in this part of the Kingdom are former Legion members, or graduates of Fel'Rechaun. I may recognize them and have additional insight."

"That sounds like a wonderful idea," said Lyla. She was enjoying the prospect of having Kyrilis around.

When Gaerin returned, he and Lyla set out. They stopped by the front desk and had them post a flyer, then left to do the same across the southern end of town. As they exited the building—finally alone and without horses and equipment to keep an eye on—they took a moment to study the city.

Most of the people walking up and down the street wore dirty tan or brown braies or breeches. Some of them wore tunics, others wore simple shirts which hung loosely around them. They were in a working-class section of the city and most of the people they could see fit that description.

There were people of all colors, shapes and sizes; most were human, but others appeared to be halflings; a blend of human and another species.

Perhaps we misjudged the dangers posed by Gabner's presence, thought Lyla.

They walked for a while in silence, studying the buildings and their occupants as they passed. Several of the shops sold fish; their delightful smells tempting them as they walked by. Other shops sold equipment for sailors; clothing, rigging and the like. Very few of the storefronts offered anything other than goods relating to the sea.

"Spare a bit?" a beggar asked someone nearby.

The beggar was an elderly, feeble man with matted remnants of stark white hair desperately clinging to his head. He wore a sack as clothing, with holes worn through the seams to provide space for his head and arms. As he sat in a pitiful heap next to an alley, he held his hands toward the man in front of him pleading.

"Go back to uptown!" demanded his target.

The man stepped over the beggar's legs and continued down the street in a hurry. He didn't appear to be a wealthy man—more a working man with things to do—and was likely offended that a beggar would ask for money in the poorest section of town.

Lyla left Gaerin's side and started toward the beggar.

"Lyla, don't-" came Gaerin's protest. His wife's selective hearing and growing distance interrupted him. He huffed in frustration and followed after her.

"Spare a bit?" the man pleaded as she approached.

"I will spare several bits, if you can help me with some information," she responded.

"Oh, yes, miss! I see everything what happens down here. Most people ignore me... makes it easy to learn things," he said with a big, gaping smile. His one remaining tooth stood proudly at the front of his grin.

"We are looking for reliable men and women; those willing to fight for coin who don't care where that fighting takes place," she explained.

Gaerin, realizing what she was up to, eased his posture and his growing impatience. He felt like an idiot for not thinking of the same tactic.

Lyla handed the beggar a flyer.

"Oh, I can't read, miss," he said, shaking his head. Little flecks of mud and sweat spattered on Lyla's hand. She tried not to flinch and make the man feel uneasy. "I can show you where to find people like that, though."

"Maybe you can do us one better. Give me a moment," she said. She turned around and stood to face Gaerin.

They stepped a few feet away and spoke in hushed tones.

"This may seem... awkward, but I have an idea."

"Go on," he said.

"What if we cleaned him up, dressed him properly, and took him with us?"

"You're right, that is awkward. Almost insane, some might say," he joked.

"Stop fooling around, I mean it. He's used to staying in one place and listening, picking up information and not being seen. Kyrilis told us on the ride here that we should spend time gathering intelligence before we act, so... I mean, are you a spy? I'm not a spy. Gods know Keifer is no spy. And Gabner..."

"In an odd sort of way it makes sense," he said, shrugging. "You've had your head about you this entire trip, I'll trust your judgment."

She walked back to the beggar and knelt down in front of him, bringing herself down to his level.

"We are going on a voyage with some friends. My husband and

I are skilled in combat, but we are looking to hire others to make our job easier, and ensure our party's safety. As you say, you are often unnoticed and can gather information easily," she said as he nodded in agreement, "so I have a proposition for you.

"Rather than give you a few bits now, how about you join us? We'll get you cleaned up and provide you with some real clothes; some nice traveling attire, perhaps? We'll feed you, and you can help us find this place to recruit more fighters. Afterward, we'll charter our ship and you can come along with us.

"Where we're going, we need skills like yours. We need someone who is used to blending in and going unnoticed. We don't need you to fight anyone, and we don't intend to put you in harm's way. However, we could certainly benefit from your ability to listen, learn, and report back to us with the things you discover," she explained.

"I spent my entire life on these docks, hoping to find adventure; hoping to sail the seas and see new lands. Now I'm but a beggar on the street, homeless and shamed... and a strange woman arrives to grant me my lifelong wish?" he asked, weeping.

"Will you join us?" she asked as she put his hand in hers reassuringly.

"Yes, miss. I'd be honored. You have just given me more than I could have asked the gods to provide... not that they listen," he said.

"What's your name?" asked Gaerin.

"Street folk call me Skank, ever since I showed up here. Real name's Bolrin," he answered.

"Well, Bolrin," she started as she helped him stand. "I have two questions for you. First, where is the closest bath house? Second, are you fond of kobolds?"

"What's a kobold?" asked Bolrin.

"He'll fit right in," Gaerin said, rolling his eyes at his wife.

She smiled back at him.

They headed to a bathhouse and made sure Bolrin got clean. Afterward, they took him to buy new clothes and dressed him in traveling leathers and a nice pair of boots.

Tears of joy filled his eyes when they presented him with his new clothes. He'd never dressed as nice, and could hardly believe what was happening.

Afterward, they took him back to their lodging to eat and meet the rest of their group.

∴ ∴ ∴

TYLEE LEFT before Delriahna and Bronsin woke up. With a heightened sense of her new responsibilities, she left the house before dawnfry and made her way to a farmer's shop in the center of town. She was inspecting vegetables for the day's meals when a Legion soldier walked in.

"Are you the owner of this establishment?"

Tylee turned to see who was speaking. The owner of the voice was a soldier, dressed similarly to the ones she'd seen at the refugee camp with Laurence. She perked up and got closer, trying not to seem obvious.

"Yes sir," answered the woman behind the counter.

The shopkeeper was a middle-aged woman of fair complexion and stocky build. Her skin tone spoke of long hours spent in the sun. She seemed to be a woman that prided herself on hard work.

"We are asking all shopkeepers for assistance. You are aware of the tragedy in Grellenheim, yes?"

"Aye, such a horrible thing," she answered.

"As you know, such a large city is not easily rebuilt. So, it will be some time before the citizens of Grellenheim can return. Unfortunately, that was not the only location affected by the tragedy. Gaierford was similarly attacked, and all were lost," he explained.

"Oh, no!" she exclaimed. She put her right hand to her lips in an expression of genuine shock. Tylee reacted similarly, inching closer to the conversation.

"The central buildings of Gaierford are mostly intact. So, we are asking the business owners of Raven's Nest to donate goods and services to help re-establish the town, in hopes that eventually the refugees can move there. This would help the King and Raven's Nest greatly. However, with the expenses required to rebuild Grellenheim, the King fears he cannot afford to offer assistance with Gaierford. Instead, he is offering tax relief for those who contribute, proportionate to their contributions," detailed the guard.

"Why don't we ask the refugees to rebuild Gaierford?" asked Tylee abruptly.

The guard looked at her inquisitively. "Pardon?"

"My husband and I went to their camp yesterday. We handed out food and helped them through their day; repaired some tents and such," Tylee started.

"That is all well and good, but–"

"In our time there, I met several men and women with experience in carpentry, farming, stone-laying... even a blacksmith. I'm sure that if I went to them, they'd welcome the chance to build a new town in Gaierford. It'd be a chance to start anew, rather than begging from the Kingdom," she explained.

"If they are willing to do the work, I would gladly donate some food stocks to get them started... with the tax break, of course," added the shopkeeper.

"Very well," said the guard. "I will come back this afternoon with a carriage to be filled, and the paperwork to document the agreement."

"See you then," answered the shopkeeper.

"My lady," he said to Tylee, "would you... accompany me on the rest of my visits and explain this plan to the others? Many owners are declining to donate. I think your ideas and energy in the matter could help persuade them."

"I would absolutely love to. However, I think we should talk to the refugees first, and I need to let my mother know I won't be available to cook dinner tonight. Would you care to come along?" she asked.

"If we must," he replied as they exited the shop. "What is your name, my lady? Or should I refer to you as 'my lady' the entire day?"

"Oh, I'm sorry," she offered. She turned and stuck out her hand. As he shook it she said, "I am Tylee Ravencrest. My husband is attending Fel'Rechaun."

"Another Ravencrest? Is there anything your family doesn't do?" he asked jokingly.

"Nope!" answered Tylee. She turned again and started toward the refugee camp.

"It's a pleasure to meet you, Tylee. I am Master at Arms Tillman. I've been assigned to gather materials and lead the rebuilding of Gaierford, and I believe you've just made that task far easier than it could have been."

They crossed town, weaving through the crowds, and arrived at the refugee camp and hour later. Tylee spotted a man she thought she recognized, tending his children while his wife found a place to bathe. She walked up to him with purpose and a smile on her face.

"Aric, isn't it?" she asked, extending her hand. She recognized him from Greta's description. He shook her hand eagerly.

"Tylee, right? My wife told me all about you. Thank you so much for helping the other day. Not many have been so kind to us since we arrived. I think most consider us a burden," he explained.

"Well, the man I'm with today is Tillman, a Master at Arms for the Legion. The King has ordered them to rebuild Gaierford, because it's small and should be easier to recover in these times of need. Tillman, here, has been assigned to lead the operation. We're wondering if you wouldn't mind moving your family to Gaierford and helping to rebuild it. You're a store manager, if I remember correctly, so you're experienced in managing goods and fostering trade?" she asked.

"Gaierford suffered the same fate?" asked Aric.

"It did, sir. However, most of the buildings and a few of the homes remain intact. The church has volunteers there now, burying the dead, just as they are in Grellenheim. As you are aware, more than half of Grellenheim burned down, and many of the other buildings took heavy damage. It will be some time before the King declares the city safe for re-population," explained Tillman.

"Aye, I could see that being the case. What of the others? I can't build a town by myself," said Aric.

"We'll need carpenters, stonemasons, guards, farmers... everything. I'm sure there's a place for everyone in the refugee camp, if we manage this correctly," declared Tylee.

A small crowd began gathering around them, listening intently.

"I'm sure we'd all be interested. A chance to rebuild our lives and not live in tents on the edge of town? Sure! But if we go to Gaierford, who will lead us?" asked Aric.

"We haven't selected a public official yet to act as Constable," answered Tillman.

"What's required to become a Constable?" asked Tylee.

"There are no true requirements for a town the size of Gaierford, my lady. Though, having a mind for politics would help, as would already having the respect of the people," explained Tillman.

Aric looked at Tylee and asked, "Would you do it?"

"Would I?" she started but caught herself in a laugh. She couldn't believe what she was being asked. "You want *me* to be your Constable?"

"You care about us; you've already gone out of your way to help us when you didn't need to. That's enough for me," Aric explained.

"It isn't common for a woman to be Constable, but... it's not the strangest thing I've heard this week. Do you have any experience with public office?" asked Tillman.

"My father is a Councilman in Mooncrest. My parents raised me with studies of public office, politics and history. They practically forced the knowledge down my throat. I hadn't really considered pursuing an office, but... maybe this is a sign?" answered Tylee.

"You did come up with the plan, and the people seem to love you, so perhaps this makes sense. I don't have the authority to grant such a position, but I could go see Centurion Vale. He has authority to make that decision in absence of Commander Cricht," offered Tillman.

Tylee thought for a moment and then decided that thinking was the wrong thing to do. "Go see your Centurion. I wish to help these people, and this course of action seems to be the best way to do so. I'll go see my mother now and tell her the news," she said.

Tillman nodded to her in respect and agreement before setting out. *She's already talking like a Constable*, he decided.

"Aric, will you talk with the others and explain the situation? Tillman informed me on our way here that there are currently twelve homes, an inn and a single store lying vacant in Gaierford. The inn has eight rooms, and each home has two to three. That should give us room for thirty or more families temporarily while we build new homes. I think if we all pull together, we can have everyone in their own home in just a few short months. What do you think?" she asked.

"As long as you can get us permission to fell trees in the surrounding wood, and cultivate unused land for crops," injected a man.

She recognized him as Francesca's husband, Carter.

"I will make that happen, Carter," she assured him.

His visage brightened when he realized that she cared enough to know his name.

"My lady, there are twenty-eight families here in camp and a few dozen who've not yet married. There might be room for all of us, if you can coordinate this the right way!" Aric said excitedly. "Oh, this is terrific news. Yes. Yes, I will talk to everyone for you. Go and make your plans, and we'll start packing up. Thank you! Thank you so much! You will not regret this, miss Tylee... I mean, Constable Tylee."

"Make that Constable Ravencrest," she decided.

"I like that," he said, smiling.

Aric ran off to talk to the others, stopping tent by tent.

Excitement spread across the camp as everyone packed their things.

Her final task was convincing her mother.

∴ ∴ ∴

DELRIAHNA WAS sipping tea in the sitting room when Tylee returned home. She looked up to see that her daughter was empty-handed, and yet somehow proud of herself. It was perplexing, and part of her dreaded asking what was going on, though she knew she had to.

"Did you forget something, my dear?" asked Delriahna, half of her not wanting to know the answer.

"No, mother. I'm going to be Constable of Gaierford!" she answered, as if her mother knew what was going on. Realizing she didn't, and seeing the look on her face, Tylee decided to explain more thoroughly.

"I met Master at Arms Tillman, from the Legion, while I was shopping. The Velloth attacked Gaierford, just like Grellenheim. However, Gaierford is a small town and is cheaper to rebuild. So, he was looking for shop owners to donate goods to the effort in return for tax breaks. I suggested they should use the refugees to rebuild the town; that many of them were skilled workers eager to earn their keep. After all, I met many of them the other day while helping Laurence.

"Then we went to talk to the refugees—just to make sure they'd help out—and one of them suggested I should be their Constable. Tillman is on his way to talk to Centurion Vale right now to make it official!" she explained excitedly.

Tylee talked so fast that Delriahna was having a difficult time keeping up. After a few moments, once all her words had soaked in, she looked her daughter in the eyes and said, "Please come join me. Sit... let us talk for a moment."

As Tylee sat down she retorted, expecting her mother to fight the idea. "This is something I really want to do, mother, and I'm capable of doing it. Don't you want me to use all that knowledge you forced on me for all those years?"

"I'm not disputing your chosen course of action, dear, I'm just surprised, and I need to explain a few things," she said reassuringly. "If you want to be Constable, then be Constable. However, there are some things you must understand."

She handed Tylee a cup of tea and encouraged her to drink some. After Tylee had complied and calmed her breathing, she continued.

"What you and Laurence did the other day was a very good and noble thing, and I've been meaning to talk to you about it. Frankly, I was shocked when I discovered what you'd done. I came home to find some of our silver missing and thought the worst. Nothing in your past led me to anticipate such an action. Further, the money you took to perform your good deeds... wasn't ours," she explained.

Tylee's face contorted, revealing that she was worried.

"Fret not, it wasn't truly stealing. However, you should know that the money we brought with us was donated by the Council of Mooncrest. Understand that Laurence's attendance at Fel'Rechaun puts noble eyes on our town; a town that the Kingdom has mostly forgotten, in a portion of the Kingdom that is mostly ignored.

"We decided that this was an opportunity that shouldn't be passed up; an opportunity to show the strength of our people and inspire the King to increase trade through our region... maybe even build a Legion fort nearby. Anything to bolster our town, improving the lives of all Mooncrest citizens.

"That may seem selfish, or as if your father was looking to improve his own standing somehow, but I assure you our intentions are always guided by what we think is best for Mooncrest. This path you've volunteered to pursue? It's not something we could have anticipated, or hoped for. However, it *does* afford us an even greater opportunity.

"As Constable you'll be expected to act with authority; to resolve conflict and sway people toward actions that better the town as a whole, rather than the individual. One of the things that can make that easier to achieve is silver. So, what I propose is that we take the money that Mooncrest donated and use it to help rebuild Gaierford.

"I will act as accountant for those funds, and you will submit official requests to me when the need arises to access them. I will also act as your adviser in day-to-day operations. When anyone asks about our funding, we will be truthful and explain that Mooncrest is providing for the restoration of Gaierford. Not you, not me, not the Colvin family, not the Ravencrest family, not the King... Mooncrest."

"This is really happening, isn't it?" asked Tylee.

"Do you agree with my terms?" asked Delriahna, sternly.

"Yes, mother. You are very wise, and this all makes perfect sense. By doing this we help Gaierford, Mooncrest, and the refugees from

Grellenheim all at once. This feels very much like the right thing to do, and it gets me out of the window, like you always wanted," said Tylee.

"It only took seventeen years," scolded Delriahna with a roll of her eyes.

Tylee felt like a brand new woman, and she hoped Laurence would be proud. She realized he might get upset that she left Raven's Nest, but Bronsin assured her Laurence could visit Gaierford too, even if it would be less frequently due to the distance. Besides, 'he isn't gonna be in school his entire life,' as Bronsin had said.

Delriahna left to send word to Fel'Rechaun and notify Laurence. Tillman returned later that evening with an official document declaring Tylee as the Constable of Gaierford. The document gave her permission to oversee the town on behalf of the King and the Legion, and to act with the King's authority under the name Constable Ravencrest.

They left that evening, a full caravan of refugees and supply carriages traveling as one.

PURSUIT

Ris'Gaula, Oghenfall 28th, 113 of the 2nd Era

As terror grips the lands of peace,
Where honor never lived.
Rejoice for those whom death doth meet,
Rebirth requires an end.

Night's Writ, Parable 4

LAURENCE WATCHED as Kotann and the Legion soldiers prepared for their mission. Including Kotann, he counted three knights, two archers, two healers, two blacksmiths, twelve soldiers, three squires, two others—who appeared to be assistants—and a horse for every one of them, plus two more carrying supplies. Combined with his own group of five, their total force was a staggering thirty-one people and thirty-three horses.

Steeling himself for the task ahead, he nudged Onyx into action and rode to the head of the formation with Kotann, Izabel, Wil, Agnar and Bingrolf. Directly behind them rode the archers and healers. The rest of the Vintain brought up the rear. It was an impressive sight to behold on school grounds and had drawn quite the crowd.

"Ready?" asked Kotann.

"Aye," answered Laurence, eager to get back into the action. Every bit of downtime allowed his mind to relax and slip closer toward thoughts and parts of himself that he wasn't quite ready to confront.

Kotann raised his hand, signaled his soldiers to move, and

kicked his horse into action.

Laurence, Wil, Izabel, Agnar and Bingrolf did the same, and led the group through the southern gates of Fel'Rechaun, out into the grasslands.

They rode south for half a day, several members of the party introducing themselves and telling stories along the way.

Dozens of tributaries flowed from the Mythaeil River, most of which ended having never exited the Ekthri Wood. The Sacton River was an exception, splitting away from the Mythaiel a few miles west of the Elbermire Way and flowing across the Kingdom from west to east; eventually emptying into the Hystari Ocean. The Sacton cut harshly through fjords and crags, spilling onto the grasslands at a small waterfall as it passed beneath the Elbermire Way.

The center of the Kingdom sat atop a vast expanse of underground stone and precious minerals, raising the water table significantly. These features prevented the Sacton from flowing at its normal depth and strength, causing it to spread across the land and form the Sacton Delta. Many of Kallenfall's mines stretched beneath the resulting marshlands.

Small tributaries crossed the landscape, splitting and rejoining; overflowing and saturating the surrounding lands with standing water that, in places, seemed to sit stagnant and unmoving. Farmers had long ago settled the southern reaches of the delta, cultivating the wetlands to produce rice, sugar, and other crops that fared better when saturated with water. Further east, the Sacton reformed and rushed with renewed vigor across the land over a series of small falls before finally emptying into the sea.

The farmsteads occupied the center of the delta region, acting as a disconnected community where all helped one another; contributing to their common good. To the east—as the river coalesced and gained speed—millers processed wheat, barley, and other grains using great water wheels. In the west, tanners processed skins to produce leather. Still further west, nearer to Ekthri Wood, coal burners processed felled trees into charcoal.

If Raven's Nest was the thriving center of the Kingdom's military, the Sacton Marshlands of the Sacton Delta region were the beating heart of its infrastructure. Being centrally located, the farms along the marshlands were where tanners, coal burners, and millers often gathered to exchange goods.

Agnar and Bingrolf grew up on such a farmstead. The fact that their group was following the Velloth into the marshlands—so close to their home—concerned them greatly.

The group arrived at the northern edge—bordered by a wall of tall reeds—just as night fell. They stopped and camped on the border of the marsh; a time-consuming process with so many people. Laurence and his friends finished their preparations in short order, but the armor worn by the Legion took time to put on and remove.

Laurence pulled supplies and pots out to start a fire and cook, while the Vintain finished their preparations.

"Do not, good Laurence. We have people for that," interrupted Kotann. He walked over, still unbuckling straps on his armor.

"Pardon?" asked Laurence.

"My men are paid as soldiers, but also for performing extra duties. They volunteer for those duties as they receive training, which signifies what they will be paid. A Vintain consists of two Conroi. Each Conroi is a unit of ten soldiers trained to work together as a self-sustaining combat unit. A Conroi always includes at least one cook, so... my Vintain, therefore, has two. Let them do their jobs," explained Kotann.

"Very well," said Laurence. The structures and nuances of the Legion intrigued him. Bored, he walked back over to where Izabel and the others were sitting and joined them. "I guess I have nothing to do."

"Yeah, and you might actually have to sleep," said Izabel sarcastically.

"Maybe you should take this time to practice arm wrestlin," joked Agnar.

"Or maybe lift something heavy for a few hours," said Bingrolf, laughing.

"Maybe I will," said Laurence sarcastically.

"All joking aside, we aren't alone this time. We're with the Kingdom's best. So, relax. We might not have another peaceful night for a while," suggested Izabel.

"*You're* telling him to relax? *You*? Miss *'pent up aggression'*? Miss *'how does one relax, exactly'*?" teased Wil.

"Maybe I learned some things during our leisure time in Raven's Nest," she retorted.

"Sure, all *one day* of our break," said Wil.

"Bah!"

The smell of cooking meat and vegetables wafted toward them, interrupting their conversation. Several bellies rang out their desire to consume what they smelled.

"I've cooked at camps before, but it didn't smell anything like that!" said Laurence.

"Smells like," Wil said, sniffing the air, "lamb with an herb sauce, sauteed greens, and roast tubers."

"How can you tell?" asked Izabel, testing the smells for herself.

"I saw them pulling out the ingredients earlier," he laughed.

"Ugh," she grunted, and slapped him across the chest playfully.

When dinner was finally served, the friends devoured their food as if they hadn't eaten in days. The cooks who brought it over barely had time to release their grip on the plates before their ravenous consumption began. They both stood and watched with interest as their food vanished far too quickly.

"Let me guess... it was terrible?" asked one of the cooks as he gathered their plates.

"Do you guys eat like this every day?" asked Agnar.

"We do," answered the other cook.

"I'm joining the Legion," said Bingrolf burping.

Agnar slapped him on the shoulder, cheering in agreement.

Laurence quietly extracted himself from the group and went to his tent while they continued their banter. He was fast asleep before he realized he was laying down.

∴ ∴ ∴

GAERIN SAT next to Lyla and looked at her with wonder in his eyes. Had he set off on their quest alone, he'd still be alone. He would probably have run straight off to Port Vaelin and on to Pelrigoss, dying horribly with no support of any kind. His wife, by contrast, continuously found every way possible to garner support and draw a crowd around her.

When Laurence was growing up, they helped Arcturus with him constantly. While Gaerin didn't mind, her idea of 'help' was far above and beyond what he would have done. Any time he'd ask her if they were doing too much, she'd always responded, *'it takes a village!'* He hadn't realized that her philosophy extended to every single part of life. He was certain they'd have a complete village following them by the end of their adventure.

His eyes caught Bolrin grinning, mouth wide open, on Lyla's left side. "I'm going to have to ask you not to do that," he said.

"Do what?" asked Lyla.

"Him. Grinning. He can't do that while we're talking to mercenaries," Gaerin clarified.

"He's right," said Kyrilis.

"Bolrin, don't grin. Act... angry," Lyla said.

"Yes, miss!" he barked in a much too slobbery way. His face contorted into a grimace and stayed that way.

Gaerin rolled his eyes.

"Are you sure Keifer is okay up there with Gabner alone?" Lyla asked Gaerin.

"He'll be fine. Gabner's a kobold, remember? Not our actual son?" teased Gaerin.

"Ugh," Lyla grunted.

Two men walked up to their table and sat across from them. One of them was wearing battle-worn brigandine armor with a thick, studded pauldron over his left shoulder. His black, unkempt beard barely concealed the scar that ran across his neck. Piercing blue eyes peered out at them from beneath thick, scraggly brows, and his hair was tied back as if he were ready for action.

The other man, in contrast, wore brand new armor that was a mixture of scale and leather. He kept himself well groomed and bore no visible scars. Gaerin couldn't decide if he was more or less imposing than his counterpart.

"Gellix, Dagha... what brings you to our table?" asked Kyrilis.

"You know them?" asked Lyla before they could answer.

"Oh yes, I most certainly do," she answered. She leaned forward so they could see her better. She paid particular attention to the one wearing new armor.

"Hello, Kyrilis. I didn't expect you to be the one hiring mercenaries," exclaimed the man.

"Well, Dagha, it's a good thing that I am, wouldn't you say? Otherwise you'd murder these fine folk on the road and rob them blind just like your last victims!"

"Hold your tongue, foul elf!" yelled Dagha. "Commander Cricht cleared me of those charges!"

"Commander Cricht wasn't there to see the evidence, was he? You claimed that bandits attacked your group and killed them, and yet... you somehow came out of the encounter without so much as a scratch; not even on your armor," she scolded.

"Clearly we don't want your services, Dagha," injected Lyla.

"Leave!" said Gaerin.

Dagha shot angry looks at all of them, but stared long and hard at Kyrilis as if deciding whether he could best her. Without another word, he stormed through the bar and out into the street, knocking several patrons around as he passed.

The group took a moment to let the air settle before proceeding.

Gellix looked around nervously. "Does that mean I need to leave too?" he asked.

"Gellix is a simpleton but a fine warrior. He always does what he's asked, when he's asked, and nothing more. As long as you don't require him to make critical decisions, you can't go wrong by hiring him," said Kyrilis.

"Well, Gellix, what do you ask in return for your service?" asked Lyla.

"Will we be fed?" he asked.

"Yes," she answered.

"Do we get to kill things?" he asked.

"Eventually. Not right away, but we plan to once we have answers."

"Three silver now, fourteen when we return... for each of my crew," said Gellix. He was fidgeting and kept glancing at the area to Lyla's left side.

"How many in your crew?" asked Kyrilis.

"Kellum, Oben and Gareg... uh... four, including me," answered Gellix.

"Very good math, Gellix," teased Kyrilis.

He did not smile.

"Do you know them?" Lyla asked Kyrilis.

"Yes. It's the same crew he brought to several... undisclosed missions for the Legion last year. They're fine warriors and trustworthy. It's worth noting that Oben is a halfling; half human and half orc. Some find that off-putting," she answered.

"That doesn't concern Gaerin and I, we just need men of action that we can trust. We don't want a repeat of... Drakahl," said Lyla, turning to Gaerin.

"I trust Kyrilis. If she says they're fine, then I'm fine," answered Gaerin.

Lyla considered for a moment, then decided she agreed. "Okay, Gellix. We'll pay your crew five silver each right now, and twenty silver each upon our return," offered Lyla.

"I said we wanted three silver now and fourteen when we

returned," Gellix said, getting angry.

"She's offering you more, Gellix. Take it and go gather your crew," said Kyrilis.

"Okay. Will be back in the morning," he said. After second guessing himself, he added, "Do we leave in the morning?"

"No, we hope to leave the day after, so come back then. And... here's your silver," said Lyla. She placed the twenty silver for the crew's up-front portion on the table and slid it over to him.

"Okay. I will go now... be back with the crew day after tomorrow," he said with a nod.

"At the docks," said Lyla.

"At the docks," confirmed Gellix. He collected the silver and stood abruptly, leaving without another word.

Gaerin and Lyla looked at each other in slight bewilderment. That's when Gaerin caught a glimpse of Bolrin, still grimacing. He couldn't help but laugh.

"Kyrilis, why don't you bring the others down. Let's have a bit of celebration before we set sail. Who knows when we'll be back, or how trying our times will be where we're going," suggested Lyla.

"Lyla, I don't think-" started Kyrilis.

"I think that's a fine idea," interrupted Gaerin.

Kyrilis sighed and left to do as they asked. She wasn't sure it was the wisest course of action, but then she was out of her element. Most of her life had been regimented; dictated by military structures and disciplines. Perhaps it was time she entertained other ways of doing things.

The evening was filled with merriment, though Kyrilis mostly stayed back and observed. She kept her eyes on anyone that came near their table, intent on keeping the group safe. As she watched, she realized that even though most of the members of the group had only recently met, Lyla and Gaerin treated them as if they were family. She'd never witnessed such openness, love, and caring.

∴ ∴ ∴

THEIR OVERLY-CROWDED shared room had a strange scent about it that Kyrilis just couldn't place. Everywhere she stepped, she risked waking or injuring one of her traveling companions. It was painfully obvious to her just how comfortable she'd become with the life of a Griffin Guard.

Flying above the land, you didn't encounter fellow travelers and with rare exception you traveled alone. She'd grown accustomed to a life that was mostly solitary, even when she wasn't aloft. Her room at Fel'Rechaun was near the top of the tower, on a floor designed to house a dozen Griffin Guard. Being the only one in service to the school meant that she had the entire floor to herself, so her isolation and peace extended to her times of rest and leisure.

She could summarize most of her social interactions in previous years as pushing through crowds and brief conversations with Fahrul, with little else. As a result, she found social interaction to be exhausting. While she had been aware of these changes within her, the true depth of her acclimation to the lifestyle of a solitary scout had not dawned on her completely until that very moment.

She stood quietly at the window for much of the night while her companions slept. It was peaceful enough, except for Gabner's snoring and Lyla's tendency to mumble in her sleep. However, it wasn't their noise that made her feel trapped, or as if she were battling suffocation. That feeling certainly wasn't helped by the fact that the lowtown district—as it was called—had a curfew.

Everything she might have done to seek distraction or entertainment had closed for the night. The streets were eerily silent, save for the distant clop of hoof on stone as lazy guards patrolled in the distance. In the dark of night and the silence that teased and tempted her with illusions of solitude, it was easy for her highly trained elven ears to pick up the sound of a deftly manipulated door lock.

Her head whipped around to face the door, eyes squinting to adjust to the shift in light between the window she had been staring out and the darkness of the room's interior. The door's lock quietly clicked. It was a sound that would have easily gone unnoticed by those sleeping, or even a guard who was less alert. She turned her body slowly, carefully shifting her feet around Keifer and Gabner who lie beneath her under the window.

As the latch handle slowly clicked out of its closed position, she realized what the cause of the smell that had been eluding her. *Oil*, she deduced. The smell was the faint odor of a small amount of distilled fish oil; often used in coastal cities to lubricate pulley wheels, locks and other simple moving parts constructed from metal.

She remembered one of her former comrades had used such oil on his armor. Passed down for generations, some of the armor's joints squeaked as he moved. The substance had worked for him then, and someone had used the same implement on the hinges of their room's door.

When they'd arrived the day before, the door to their room creaked and groaned upon opening. She remembered the group discussing their noisy door as a good thing, as it would wake them if anyone attempted to enter. At that moment, as the door slowly opened before her eyes, she could hear no sound.

She kicked off the floor, leaping half the distance to the door in a single bound. She landed on the other side of Keifer, Gabner and Bolrin, and drew her weapons. Sword in her right hand, dagger in her left, she stood ready. Alerted to the sound of her movement, the door flung wide.

Dagha stood before her, war axe in one hand, dagger in the other. His brow lowered as anger and anticipation grew within him.

Kyrilis struck first, sending her sword's tip straight for his teeth in a thrust. He parried it aside with his axe, then carried the movement further with his dagger in a two weapon parry. His axe then turned and came in toward her neck. She parried the strike with her dagger and brought her sword back to center.

Her sword twisted between them and changed direction again, striking at his neck with an outward slash and a flick of her wrist. Dagha brought both of his weapons in to block her blade, attempting to catch it in the hook of his axe to lock it in place.

Their first volley happened so quickly that it wasn't until his second block—and the loud clang that resounded throughout the room—that Gaerin sat up to see what was happening. Lyla moaned her displeasure at being awakened, still not realizing that they were under attack.

Dagha backed into the hallway, knowing that small quarters would limit Kyrilis's ability to wield her sword effectively. She thrust again with her sword, turning through the doorway and into the hall to follow him.

Gaerin called out behind her, "Kyrilis!"

As Dagha pressed his advantage, Kyrilis withdrew into a defensive stance and focused on parrying his attacks with as little lateral movement as possible. She parried several quick, weak slashes from his axe in rapid succession with vertical movements of her sword before finally bouncing the end of his axe off the wall beside them, sending shudders through his arm violently.

He backed up a step in hesitation, just as a dagger slid to a stop at Kyrilis's left heel.

Gaerin yelled out from behind her, "Take it!"

She looked down at it quickly, then back up to Dagha with a wicked smile. He slashed again at her with his axe in a downward strike. She caught the axe's hook with her sword and ripped it from his hand with an upward strike, then kicked him in the chest. His axe fell to the floor just over his shoulder with a clatter.

As he leaned down to retrieve his weapon, she returned her longsword to the scabbard on her back and knelt to retrieve Gaerin's dagger. Dagha, noticing that he'd lost the advantage afforded him by their tight quarters, turned and ran down the stairs as fast as he could.

Kyrilis was happy to follow.

Dagha burst through the doors of the inn, out into the street.

Kyrilis followed a half second later, gaining quickly. "We can finish this now, or I can hunt you down later. It matters not to me," she declared forcefully.

Dagha knew his chances of evading a Griffin Guard were slim, with their advantage of flight. He whipped around to face her, resigning himself to live or die in that very moment. "Now it is," he growled.

He attacked with his axe. Kyrilis parried with both daggers, her left deflecting the weapon on its shaft, her right striking the seams on the underside of the bracer on the same arm. He winced in pain, withdrew his axe hurriedly and thrust an attack at her with his left-hand dagger.

She brought her right-hand dagger down fast to parry his thrust, and her left-hand dagger straight down into the space between his pauldron and chest piece, driving the blade between the plates and hilt-deep into his flesh.

His axe clanged to the ground, alerting nearby guards to their confrontation. Dagha yelled out in pain as his right arm stopped responding to his commands. He thrust his dagger toward her face in a desperate move, pain hindering his ability to put much power behind his strike.

She dipped her head to the side to avoid the blow and grabbed his left wrist with her left hand, pushing it up into the air and driving her right-hand dagger deep into his unarmored underarm.

He screamed out in pain, dropping to his knees; his metal greaves sending tiny sparks flying as they collided with the cobblestone beneath them.

"I yield!" he whimpered, pleadingly.

"No more trials!" she exclaimed. She drew her sword and sliced his throat open, all in one smooth maneuver.

As Dagha's body fell to the ground, Gaerin and Lyla exited the inn still dressed in their nightclothes. Lyla ran up to Kyrilis and hugged her from behind, yelling, "Are you okay? Did he hurt you?"

Gaerin turned and, seeing the guard approaching them at a gallop, walked over to intercept him. "Ho there," called Gaerin.

The horse came to a stop beside him, but the guard's eyes never left Kyrilis. The guard's right hand grasped his sheathed sword's hilt tightly. Gaerin could see he didn't know whether or not to engage in combat. After all, he'd just seen the woman nearly behead a man.

"It's okay now, sir," Gaerin said. "Everyone's fine, we're all fine. The dead man's name is Dagha. He tried to kill us in our sleep. Kyrilis was protecting us. That is all that has transpired," he explained calmly.

The guard eased a little, and looked at Gaerin. "Have you proof?"

"Pardon, but do murders and brigands normally do their business wearing their nightclothes?" Gaerin asked, pointing at himself and Lyla.

"He speaks true, my lord," inserted Kyrilis.

She wiped her blade off on Dagha's inner thigh and sheathed it as she approached the guard.

"I am Kyrilis, a Griffin Guard assigned to Fel'Rechaun. I am escorting these people on a mission, and we met Dagha last night while seeking to hire capable mercenaries to accompany us. He was angered when we didn't select him for our journey, so he sought revenge on us as we slept. In his outrage, he apparently forgot that elves don't need sleep," she explained.

"I have heard your name, Lady Kyrilis. What is the nature of your mission?" inquired the guard, his right hand leaving his sword's hilt.

"We are not at liberty to say. I'm sure you understand," she answered.

Two other guards rounded the corner at the end of the street, galloping down the road to join them. Kyrilis looked at them as they approached and then back to the guard she was addressing. "It would be best for the Kingdom if this went no further," she insisted.

She handed him a small token. He inspected it briefly and handed it back. Quickly recognizing what it meant, he turned and signaled to the other guards to stay back. They stopped a short distance away, both curious about what was happening.

He turned back to Kyrilis and said, "You may go back inside. We will handle this, my lady. I apologize for this unfortunate impediment. You will be troubled no further." He bowed his head in respect and rode toward the other guards to explain.

Kyrilis waved Gaerin and Lyla back inside, then retrieved her daggers and joined them. When they returned to the room, Keifer and Gabner were both awake and quite scared. Bolrin continued to sleep peacefully at the foot of the bed.

"It's okay, Keifer," said Lyla as they walked in. "He's gone, and won't be disturbing us any longer. Kyrilis protected us." She knelt down and picked up Gabner.

"It's okay now? Is he dead?" asked Keifer.

"It's fine, lad," assured Gaerin.

"No hurt?" Gabner asked as he inspected Lyla's face, neck, and shoulders.

"No hurt," she answered.

"Me cook?" he asked.

"I don't think they'll let you, little one," answered Lyla.

"I no little. Biggest in tribe," said Gabner proudly.

"I bet you are," said Lyla with a smile.

"Listen," started Gaerin, lightly touching Kyrilis's arm. "I really don't know how we can thank you. We wouldn't be alive right now if it weren't for you."

"No thanks are necessary, Gaerin. It never will be," she answered. "Try to get some rest. It's not morning yet, and you've a long day ahead of you," she added. "Both of you!" she said, raising her voice so that Lyla would hear.

"Yeah, yeah," answered Lyla. Begrudgingly, she put Gabner back down next to Keifer and returned to her bed with Gaerin. Neither of them returned to sleep that night. They both lay awake, eyes closed, thinking about Kyrilis's battle. Neither of them were certain they could've beaten Dagha as easily as she made it look.

Lyla spent the rest of her night thanking Galrath for their blessings.

Gaerin spent the rest of his night thankful for the women in his life... even the one who adopted a kobold, a random boy, and a strange beggar.

∴ ∴ ∴

KYRILIS NO longer felt out of place by the time morning came. The battle the night before made her realize the sense of protectiveness she carried inside of her. Though she'd only known them a short while, the fondness she felt for Laurence extended to all of them. Meeting Laurence had changed her life more than any person she'd ever met. Though it was not all his doing, nor intentional, he had brought with him a wave of change; a passion that she hadn't realized she was lacking.

The way he'd smiled when he first met Bah'Shiri, and how excited he was at the chance to ride a griffin. His playful smile whenever their paths crossed, and the honesty that lie behind it. He treated her with awe; with a sense of respect, as one might have for a superior or a valued equal. She wasn't a tool in his eyes; a thing to be used and discarded. He didn't look upon her just as an elf, or a woman. From their first meeting, he'd treated her as someone he respected and admired. That type of treatment had been rare in her life.

Now she stood amongst the remnants of his family, duty-bound to protect them. Yet, it was not in duty that she found inspiration when fighting Dagha. Admittedly, it was first anger at the man's audacity; the sheer nerve to attack sleeping travelers. After the initial burst of adrenaline hit, she realized that all she cared about was keeping these people safe; keeping Laurence's family safe.

One thing that had become abundantly clear to her was that his family—and he himself—were special. She yearned to get to know them better, especially Laurence. The life and passion that she saw in his eyes were things she needed to experience more of, even if from a distance. She didn't wish to see that drained from his gaze; to see the passion within him die along with the rest of his family.

He'd already lost too much.

Gaerin and Lyla getting out of bed broke her train of thought. She turned and helped them gather their armor so they could start their day. As quietly as they could, the three of them carried the gear into the hallway and shut the door. With their armor donned and weapons stowed, she hugged Lyla and patted Gaerin on the shoulder, sending them off.

She returned to the room, happy to continue guarding her companions. Happy to finally be considered part of a family.

∴∴∴

WALLS AND watchtowers separated the docks in Port Vaelin into three distinct districts, each serving a different purpose and clientele. In the north, Orluhnd's Landing had space for ten large ships which rarely left port. They served the King for ambassadorial and military missions.

The ships that docked there were some of the largest to enter Port Vaelin and were an impressive sight, but completely off limits to the public. Three towers guarded Orluhnd's Landing, making it one of the most protected locations in the Kingdom outside of the royal palace.

To the far south, Beggar's Landing allowed for up to twelve small ships to enter port and make trade. Seldom were those ships allowed to stay for longer than a day. The docks were unguarded, aside from various mercenaries brought by wealthy merchants. Each group enforced different rules, carrying out their merchants' private agenda. While that allowed for more illicit affairs, the landing had nothing on places like Grellenheim's northern district or Gusarski Cove when it came to criminal activity.

Between them was Tybir's Landing, the largest of them all. With room for up to thirty vessels, it served as the Kingdom's largest trading port. Any ships with papers under the protection of the Trade Commission could dock for free, so long as their purpose was to load or unload a certain volume of cargo as indicated by their charter. That made trade through Port Vaelin very lucrative for those that could afford Commission dues, but prohibitive for chartered ships to dock without trade to conduct.

Knowing the typical business of each district, Gaerin and Lyla headed for Beggar's Landing. Thousands of people swarmed the docks conducting business, moving goods, entering the city, exiting the city or socializing at one of the four taverns located there. Each 'Porter Pub' catered specifically to the tastes and needs of those who entered port, did their business and quickly left again.

Much of the business conducted at Beggar's Landing transpired in one of the pubs over food and ale. Their convenience and proximity to the docks allowed captains to get back out to sea before the Trade Commission could pay visit and charge docking fees.

Lyla immediately headed for one named The Briney Princess. With a chuckle, Gaerin followed her in. *Of course this is the one she chose,* he thought. He wasn't even sure she'd seen the names of the other pubs.

Its interior was exactly what he expected; lots of rowdy sailors pushing, shoving, drinking and blowing off steam before setting sail again.

Lyla stopped and peered around the room, searching for

anyone talking calmly or sitting alone. When her eyes met Gaerin's, she smiled gleefully. It was exciting for her, despite the happenings of the previous night and in spite of the task that lay before them.

Of course she's happy, he thought to himself. His wife never ceased to amaze him.

Without warning, Lyla barged through the crowd, leaving him behind. With Lyla being slightly less than average height, he lost sight of her almost immediately. He looked around for several minutes, checking every part of the crowd, looking for her.

Just as he was about to call out her name in frustration, he caught sight of her jumping up and down at the back of the room, waving at him. Instinctively, he rolled his eyes at his silly wife before making his way through the crowd to join her.

Sitting at the table across from her was a spindly, middle-aged man with a thick, scraggly beard and a black tricorne hat. With skin wrinkled and tanned from long years in the sun, it was obvious he was an experienced sailor. He smelled of both ale and old fish.

Gaerin sat next to his wife and gave the man a curious look, waiting for someone other than himself to speak first.

"Your wife says you're seekin passage to Pelrigoss," said the sailor.

"She does the negotiating. I'm just here to swing my warhammer and annoy her at night," he replied.

"He's right," Lyla agreed with a nod.

"Well, The Soggy Fool was bout to head up to Gusarski Cove but I reckon we could see fit to head over to Pelrigoss for the right price. Don't often get out that way, seein as you gotta be chartered to use Dagoh Bay."

"I hadn't considered that," said Lyla. "Is there another port we can use?"

"Depends," he answered.

"Depends on what, precisely?" asked Lyla.

"Can ye row a boat? We could let ye off on a dinghy near the western shore... but we can't dock anywhere legally, so that's bout as best as ye can get," he clarified.

"That sounds less than ideal," said Gaerin.

"Ain't nobody gonna give you a better offer, less you go talk to a chartered boat in Tybir, but... since you're here talkin to me, I figure that's not an option for ye," he explained.

"How much would this cost us?" asked Lyla.

"Our hold is empty right now, so we can carry up to thirty

people if ye don't need to lay down. You gotta bring your own food and drink, cause we only carry what we need for the crew. We were headed up to Gusarski Cove to pick up more goods for quick profit, and that's what you're interruptin. So, I figure... six-hundred silver?"

"That's a little steep, don't you think?" Lyla asked, vaguely insulted.

"Look, you're welcome to shop around, but my ship leaves in the mornin. My boys been at sea for three weeks, comin up from Haern, so we paid port taxes to stay an extra day. You got lucky findin me when you did. Most of these folk come and go so fast you can barely catch their smell, let alone buy passage to Pelrigoss. Sides, ain't nobody like goin there anyway, even the charter boys."

"How much do you make carrying goods from Gusarski Cove to here?" asked Lyla in a challenging tone.

"About a hundred to five hundred silver, depending on the load. And it's a third of the distance away. Sides I have to leave a boat with you that I'll have to replace. I *should* be chargin more," he said. His face wrinkled as he gave the idea thought.

"We'll pay it. Six-hundred silver for a trip to Pelrigoss, leaving tomorrow morning at first light. We have nine passengers total, not thirty, so there's no worry about space," Lyla explained.

"Figure you can pay me three-hundred when you board, and three more when we catch sight of land?" asked the man.

"That sounds fair," she said, nodding.

"Well then, my name's Captain Bagris, and I'll see ye out in front of The Soggy Fool tomorrow morning," he said extending his hand.

Lyla and Gaerin took turns shaking it and then saw themselves out. Once they were outside, they looked at each other for a minute with a mixture of confusion and shock crossing their faces.

"That was a little too easy," said Lyla.

"Well, with the luck we've been having lately, I don't think I want to look this gift horse in the mouth quite yet. He had a lot of valid points and seemed reasonable. Besides, most of our group are capable fighters now, especially Kyrilis. I think we're safe to proceed."

"In that case, it's time to go stock up on sea rations to cover nine people for a week," she said, smiling.

"Oh yeah, precisely my idea of excitement," he said sarcastically. Thinking for a moment as they walked, he added, "We'll have to have everything delivered to the ship directly. It'll be too much to store in our room."

"Plus Gabner would probably try to eat it all ahead of time," she said.

"What is it with you and kobolds?" he teased.

"Talking puppies!" she exclaimed.

"Why did I even ask?" he sighed.

∴ ∴ ∴

THE GROUP got an early start the next morning, waking as the sun crested the horizon. The cooks handed out dried meats in place of dawnfry, clerics treated the horses with protective spells to prevent hoof rot, and soldiers donned their armor. They were west of Kallenfall and the foothills, just about where Kyrilis had told Fahrul she saw the trail through the reeds.

When all were ready, Agnar and Bingrolf took the lead, riding twenty feet apart. Laurence and Kotann rode slightly behind and between the cousins, right next to one another. Izabel and Wil spread out on either side of them. The two other knights fell in behind the leaders, with the healers and archers to their sides. Everyone else began spreading out in a line to either side of Izabel and Wil to scout for evidence of the Velloth's passing as they moved.

"This must be the path Kyrilis saw!" Agnar called out from ahead.

"Hold!" commanded Kotann. He rode forward to see what Agnar was looking at.

"It looks like this is what Kyrilis saw from above. It was thinner where we entered, so it could've been an animal or somethin. But this-" Agnar said.

"This is a wide path, caused by many creatures. If this was animals, it was a stampeding herd. Heading into a swamp? That's not likely," agreed Kotann.

Leading south from their position was a swath of bent and crushed reeds, wide enough for six riders to travel beside one another.

"Form up by fives! Stay alert!"

The soldiers fell in behind Laurence and Kotann, riding five wide across the path in rows, one after another. Kotann returned to his position beside Laurence while Wil and Izabel drew in closer to join them. He signaled to Agnar and Bingrolf to keep going. They followed the path south for most of the day, pausing now and then to let Agnar or Bingrolf find more stable footing for their horses.

It was almost dusk when Bingrolf signaled for the group to stop.

"Kotann!" he called out.

Kotann rode up to speak with him. "What is it, Bingrolf?"

"The path turns west up ahead," he said, pointing. "If I remember right, there are old ruins west of here, still on this side of the main flow. Agnar and I used to fish out that way, on the other side."

"Aye, I remember that. Good ole catfishin spot, that was," Agnar added.

"Yeah," Bingrolf said chuckling.

"Stay focused! How far is it?" asked Kotann.

"Probably half a day or more, but we're movin kinda slow," said Bingrolf.

"Yeah, and we need to camp. No offense, but you guys camp slow, and there ain't many spots of dry ground to do that between here and there," said Agnar.

"Yeah, right here'd be best for campin," said Bingrolf, nodding.

Kotann inspected the area and decided that they were right about the spot they'd found.

"Round up and make camp! Double the watch, we'll need extra campfires to dry out!" he commanded.

∴ ∴ ∴

SOLDIERS SPRANG into action as horns broke the silence of the morning. Laurence shot upright in his tent and reached over to grab his sword, dagger and satchel. He tossed the satchel out of the tent, slid the dagger into its sheath on his right calf and made his way out of the tent. As he buckled the straps of his back-slung scabbard into position, he studied the activity about him trying to discern the cause for alarm.

People ran in all directions, gathering gear and donning armor. Most of them slept in nightclothes, unlike Laurence. He'd gotten so used to sleeping in his armor on the road that he continued to do so every night, unless he was with Tylee. Other than the soldiers who had been on guard duty, Laurence was the only one in camp fully prepared for whatever enemy was upon them.

"Agnar!" called Bingrolf from behind.

Laurence turned to see Bingrolf standing in front of Agnar's tent, half dressed and frantic. He ripped open the flap of the tent to see Agnar and Izabel emerging from their sheets.

"Close the tent!" yelled Izabel.

"Shit!" replied Bingrolf. His face was flush with embarrassment as he released the flap and jumped back. Laurence smirked and made a mental note to inquire about that turn of events later, when things calmed down.

As Laurence turned to look for Kotann, the southern sky entered his line of sight. For a few seconds he stood frozen, staring. Black smoke streamed up through the sky across the horizon. Realizing he hadn't been breathing, he caught his breath once more, grabbed his satchel and raced across the camp toward Kotann's tent.

Kotann was standing beside his tent as a squire helped to fit the last piece of his armor when Laurence arrived. The squire rushed off to retrieve his master's sword with fear in his eyes.

"Farmsteads are burning," Kotann said, his eyes on the southern skies.

"Aye, several to the south, and more southwest. They're miles away, though. I don't think we're in any immediate danger," said Laurence.

"No, but we know who the likely perpetrators are. This means they're active, and that our destination has changed."

"Has it, though? I agree we should investigate the farms, but the path they carved through this swamp still leads toward the ruins," countered Laurence.

Kotann turned to face him as his squire returned with the sword. He quietly accepted the blade and slid it into its sheath as he considered their course of action.

"If the farms are already burning, I doubt there's anyone left to save. More than likely, the damage has been done and our diversion to those locations would simply delay our finding the Velloth. We don't even know which of the farmsteads they attacked first, or last, so we can't even guess as to the direction they're traveling," reasoned Kotann.

"Assuming Agnar and Bingrolf are right about their destination, I would assume the Velloth proceeded from the ruins to the farmsteads in the southwest, and then headed east attacking the farms along their route. If we continue to the ruins, we might still find them, or at least learn what they're after," suggested Laurence.

"That's a reasonable deduction, assuming the ruins were indeed their target. I could send a Conroi southeast in hopes of intercepting them, but we don't know their number, or if they're actually in that area. I'd rather keep our forces intact."

"They're not going to like this," said Laurence, indicating the camp around them. "Especially Agnar and-" his words caught in his throat as realization crossed his face. His friends grew up on a farm to the south. One of the lines of smoke in the sky could certainly be their home. He now realized why Bingrolf had been so frantic to wake his cousin.

"What is it?" asked Kotann, concerned.

"I hope I'm wrong!" yelled Laurence as he bolted back toward Agnar's tent.

He ran as fast as he could through the throng of soldiers. Tents were being taken down and packed in haste. Horses were being brushed and saddled. Laurence glanced briefly at every face as he weaved his way through, searching for the cousins.

"Agnar?" yelled Izabel, half dressed in front of her tent.

"Where is he?" asked Laurence as he arrived, panting.

"I don't know. He and Bingrolf ran off," she explained. "Do you think it has anything to do with the smoke?"

"It has *everything* to do with the smoke," answered Laurence.

Wil ran up to them from the south of camp. "They left on foot. I ran after them, but they had a head start, so I came back to see what we're doing about this."

"Damnit!" responded Kotann, overhearing the news as he arrived.

"We have to send someone after them," demanded Laurence.

"They know this terrain, we don't," answered Kotann.

"I'm going," said Izabel.

There was a slight look of fear and pain in her eyes.

"I am too," said Wil.

"They've got to cross the river. How do you know where they went, which place is safe to cross, or which smoke will lead you to their farm? Tracking them in this swamp is only going to work for so long, no matter how good a scout you are," countered Kotann. "The best way to help your friends is to continue to the ruins. We'll keep an eye out for a safe crossing as we travel, and at such a time we'll decide who goes after them."

"I just-" started Izabel.

"Your friends acted rashly! Being just as impractical isn't going to improve the situation!" argued Kotann.

"We'll do as you suggest, Kotann, but we need to move with haste. Every minute they're out there-" started Laurence.

"I know, I know!" barked Kotann. He turned to his men and continued, "Get your asses in gear, *now*, before more problems arise!" He stormed off to find his horse and rally the troops.

Laurence turned to Izabel to calm her. "We'll find them. They're capable of defending themselves, and I doubt any Velloth are still at the farms, anyway. They'll be fine."

To Laurence, Izabel and Wil, the soldiers seemed to take hours to finish packing. They tried to help with tents, fire pits and the myriad other tools scattered about the camp but were told to stay out of the way several times.

Impatient, Laurence signaled to Kotann that his group was going to go on ahead of the rest. Kotann threw his hands up in frustration and seemed to mouth, 'Of course!'

They stayed on the beaten path of reeds and grass as it turned westward toward the ruins. The soldiers eventually showed up in the distance behind them, but Laurence's group continued onward, maintaining their pace and acting as forward scouts. There were few turns in the path, indicating to Laurence that the Velloth had known their precise route before setting off into the delta.

By the time the sun had reached its peak in the sky, the smoke on the horizon had all but dissipated. They'd ridden for hours and seen no sign of their friends, the Velloth, or a bridge of any kind. When the reeds finally gave way and revealed a short span of open river, they stopped to look around. Wil dismounted and checked if the currents were safe to cross.

A short while later, Kotann and the soldiers caught up to them. Kotann dismounted angrily and walked over to scold them, but before he arrived Thax called out from near the back of the formation. Both archers stood on top of their horses, scouting the distant terrain.

"Movement!" yelled the archer.

Kotann and Laurence raced over to get Thax's report.

"Movement to the south, sir. It appears to be two persons dragging a third," he explained as they arrived.

"How far?" demanded Kotann.

"Just outside my range, sir," answered Thax. Thax knew Kotann would understand how far he could shoot with accuracy, so it was a good way to reference the distance.

"Too far to recognize anyone," muttered Kotann.

"It could be Agnar," offered Laurence.

"Yes, it very well could be. Damnit!" he vented. "Did Wil find a way to cross?"

"Knowing Izabel, she's probably already swimming it," answered

Laurence.

The look of frustration on Kotann's face was unmistakable. He signaled to Thax and Halgar to hop down and join them. Fishing briefly in Thax's saddlebag, Kotann withdrew a rope and marched back over to the clearing with Laurence and the archers.

Wil and Izabel were preparing to swim the river when they arrived.

"Tie off," barked Kotann as he walked up. He handed the rope to Izabel first. She tied it around her waist with several feet to spare at one end. When done, she handed the rest of that end to Wil, who tied it around his waist as well.

"Fine, go. When you get to the other side, stay put and hold the line for Thax and Halgar to join you."

"Yes sir," said Izabel as she walked back to the river with Wil.

Kotann signaled for two more of his men to dismount and join them. As the friends stepped down into the deeper channel of the river, he handed the two soldiers the other end of the rope. Laurence checked the leather clasps that locked his weapons into their scabbards while they waited, revealing his intent to cross.

The river grew steadily deeper as they crossed, suddenly dropping out beneath them as they neared the center. Currents were much stronger in the middle, with a significant undertow. Forced to swim, they continued to cross but drifted eastward while doing so. They were nearly at the end of the rope by the time they could reach the bank on the other side.

Soaking wet, cold and weighted down by saturated armor, they climbed ashore and walked west to stand across from the rest of their group. Izabel sat down in the mud, her legs facing the group, and dug in her heels. Wil took notice of her idea and followed suit.

"Good call," he said.

She nodded back to him without speaking, determination masking whatever emotions she might be experiencing.

Laurence, Thax and Halgar crossed one by one using the rope as a guide. Once all had crossed, Thax drew two arrows from his quiver and stuck them down into the mud, then looped the rope around the arrows to anchor it on their side.

The five of them set off to the southeast, looking for the three people Thax had seen earlier. When they finally got close enough to see who it was, Izabel ran toward them faster than anyone had ever seen her move.

Agnar and a strange woman were ahead of them... and they

were dragging Bingrolf.

"What happened?" cried Izabel, sliding to her knees as she arrived. She came to a rest just in front of Bingrolf. Agnar and the woman lowered his head into Izabel's lap. Gasping for breath, Agnar answered as best he could.

"Our farm's gone. Just... gone. The Velloth are takin people. Takin em! Not killin em like in Grellenheim. Takin em and burnin their farms!"

The woman looked at them all with tears in her eyes.

"What the hell?" asked Laurence.

"We was runnin across the field and Mildred here was runnin toward us. She was bein chased by a Velloth. We thought we could take it, but he was different from the ones we fought, Laur. So much bigger and stronger. He had black plate armor and a big, black flamberge," said Agnar, with fear and sadness in his eyes.

He knelt beside his cousin.

Bingrolf's chest was splayed open down the center. The long gash in his face revealed that the fatal blow had struck through most of his head, neck and torso in rapid succession. The impact of the weapon had been violent, efficient, and very thorough in achieving its goal.

"How are you alive?" asked Laurence.

"Big guy saw us out in front of her, knocked her over and came right at us. Bingrolf raised his maul to block the elf's blow, but it went right through its haft and... did this," he said, pointing at the wound. "I started wailin at him with my sword. Not like you told us, Laur, but just... angry swingin. He just kept parryin and laughin like I was some kinda toy.

"Then Mildred here, she... she saved my life. She grabbed Bingrolf's dagger off his thigh, jumped up on the elf's back and stabbed him in the neck," he explained. His words were catching in his throat. "So, he fell to his knees, grabbin at his back, tryin to get her off and I walked up and stabbed him down through his amour. Nothin ever felt so good to do, but so bad after."

Izabel got up and went around to hold Agnar. Laurence walked over to Mildred and pulled her aside while Agnar wept. Thax and Halgar turned and made their way back to Kotann as fast as they could to share the news.

"You are a very brave woman," said Laurence.

"Th... thank you," said Mildred timidly.

"Did you see where the Velloth were taking everyone?"

"West, sir," she answered.

"To the ruins?" he asked.

"Might be," she answered.

"We have soldiers with us. We'll get you to safety, okay?" he said reassuringly.

"Thank you, sir."

Mildred watched as Laurence, Wil, Izabel and Agnar lifted Bingrolf and carried him toward the river. She wept for the passing of their friend, and the loss of everyone she'd ever known.

∴ ∴ ∴

LAURENCE EXPLAINED the situation to Kotann while Gharick and Berril tended to Bingrolf's corpse. When they completed their prayers, they wrapped him in a blanket and tied him over the back of his horse.

Agnar, meanwhile, was inconsolable despite Izabel's best efforts.

"So not only do we have stronger Velloth ahead of us than you faced in Grellenheim, but there are civilian hostages. This complicates an already complicated matter," said Kotann.

"Mildred says the ruins aren't far ahead. I suggest we set up camp here for the squires, assistants, horses and Mildred. Maybe leave a guard or two, and then go the rest of the way on foot," suggested Laurence.

"I think that is the best course of action. We'll need to approach carefully and hope they don't notice us. Plate armor," he said, accentuating his point with a tap on his breastplate, "isn't very stealthy. You, Wil, Halgar and Thax will have to lead."

Kotann circled up with his soldiers and explained their plans. Laurence joined his friends off to the side and did the same. Kotann selected the four that would stay behind to build and guard the camp, and the rest of them formed up and headed west on foot.

They traveled several hours before the top of the ruin was in sight. The ruin was the remnant of a half-fallen tower built in ancient times to serve as a temple. It's structure, from all appearances, was mostly intact and a credit to its builders. Weather and constant water from the Sacton river and its marshes had spent the past few centuries reclaiming the structure. Half-sunken into the ground and leaning slightly to the northwest, it was still an imposing sight.

Once it became clear to Laurence what they were looking at,

he signaled that they should enter the reeds to their right and gain cover. Wil took the lead and inched forward so slow that it was hard to tell if he was moving. His years of practice as a scout in Ekthri Wood were evident to all who watched him.

Kotann signaled his men to stay back and be ready. He didn't want their armor making unwanted noise and giving away their position. His troops complied, but tensions and adrenaline were rising. He could hear strong hands gripping leather and cord wrapped hilts all around him. They were ready, and that reassured him.

Wil reached the edge of the reeds facing the ruin. Carefully he parted the final few reeds just enough to look out and get a clear view. The tower was ringed with half-sunken, crumbling stone walls. Mossy, matted ground covered the entire area around the temple. To his far left he could see what appeared to be an old stone bridge spanning the river. It, too, had sunk slightly into the ground over time.

In front of the tilted doorway stood three Velloth, all in black plate. To their right lay a pile of broken bones and old, tattered rags. The Velloth appeared to be quietly debating something. Dusk was upon them, and the light was fading. Velloth forces were sure to have the advantage over Wil's human counterparts at night, and he couldn't tell how many were inside the ruin. The presence of shattered skeletons in a pile worried him further. He hoped they weren't what he thought they were.

Returning just as carefully, Wil rejoined the group. He signaled the number three to Laurence, who in turn passed the signal on to Halgar, then Thax and back to Kotann in a chain. Kotann nodded and drew his sword. Each man up the line to Laurence repeated the action. Laurence drew his own and nodded to Wil.

It was time to attack.

∴∴∴

ARROWS STREAKED through the early night air and ricocheted off of thick, black plate. The Velloth guards spun to face their foes, snarling behind their helms with their red eyes glowing through protective slits. They picked up the weapons that had been leaning against the outer wall of the tower and stood at the ready.

Wil, Laurence, Izabel and Agnar burst through the reeds at full speed. Wil was the fastest among them and reached the Velloth first. He leaped into the air, spun, and whipped his Quel'Thoz around with the force of his momentum. The bladed tip of his weapon crashed into the closest Velloth's right hand as it held its weapon up to deflect the attack. Half of the Velloth's hand fell in a bloody chunk as the huge weapon it was holding crashed to the ground violently.

Laurence reached the Velloth next, with Agnar close behind. He used the slippery nature of the mossy ground to his advantage, dropped to his knees, and slid mere seconds before colliding with the other two Velloth. The one closest to him swung sideways and missed, his extremely long blade cutting through the air less than an inch from Laurence's scalp.

Agnar closed the distance and veered center, just as Laurence dropped to his knees, and raised his weapon to knock the Velloth's wild swing even further to the side. Laurence gained his feet behind the Velloth and stepped back into the doorway, still facing his opponents, while Agnar turned his sword in and struck the center Velloth in the face. The blade ricocheted off of the Velloth's helm, sending waves of pain through the elf's face and neck.

The third Velloth turned to assist its friends in earnest, right as Izabel engaged, exposing its side to her; an error in judgment. She brought her sword over her head and around into a backhand swing as she slid to a stop, landing the strike squarely on the elf's right arm plates. The elf's arm lurched forward at the blow, sending its weapon in a small thrust toward its friend.

Wil spun again, dipping down low to the ground, and kicked his victim's legs out from under him. The Velloth fell to the ground, crashing into the central Velloth as it descended. Laurence thrust his blade into the eye slit on the prone Velloth's helm, ending its life.

Kotann, his knights, priests and soldiers joined the fight as Laurence's fatal blow landed, causing the remaining Velloth to question their chances of success. Izabel, Agnar and Wil ducked out of the way and slipped behind the Velloth to join Laurence as the knights' weapons and shields crashed into the two with ferocious might. With so many opponents, the Velloth fell in short order.

Kotann knelt and removed the helm from one of them. He made sure all his men took the time to study the creatures, their armor, and their weapons. Agnar spit on the Velloth before they continued, sure that he was going to see every last one of them dead before the night was through.

∴ ∴ ∴

IT WAS dusk when Ayriel and Fox reached their destination. The area near the ground was exceptionally dark, as if more shadows were being cast from above than would be normal. She looked up to see buildings and walkways high in the trees, braced between trunks and across branches. Very little of the forest's natural form had been disrupted by the construction techniques used by the elves, and the city from below was exceedingly impressive in the waning light of the evening hours.

Her escort withdrew a small whistle from his pocket and blew a single, nearly-inaudible note. Two ropes descended from a platform above in response to his call. He bid her to tie Tegris off to the side and hold on to one of the ropes. She followed his instructions and rode the rope into the trees, pulled up by an unseen force.

The city of Ayr'Thugohn was even more impressive from her view on the platform than it had been from below. Small runes and orbs of light glowed in a myriad of colors across the city. She recognized them as minor enchantments that could only be seen from small distances, and only by those that could see magic, or extended light spectrums such as heat and ultraviolet. The technique allowed the elves to light their city at night without giving away their position or number to creatures below.

The city was constructed from the same materials as the trees themselves. Wood, bark, branches and leaves comprised the whole of their building materials, allowing the city to blend into the forest canopy more successfully. She followed her escort quietly, observing everything around her.

The city was beautiful beyond what she had imagined. Everywhere she looked were small details one could easily overlook; carvings; etchings; branches, twigs and leaves bent and crafted into art. Elves of all sexes and sizes lined the walkways, stood in their doorways, or stared out their windows; watching as she passed.

Her escort came to a stop again, and blew another faint tune on his whistle. Another pair of ropes descended from above. She hadn't even thought of looking up to see if the city extended higher. Excitedly, she grasped the rope and stared upward at the next platform as she ascended.

As she passed through the opening in the platform and stepped out onto the walkway, a golden palace loomed before her. Gone were the wood and leaf structures of the lower city. The building in front of her had been constructed from expertly manipulated ancient wood, inlaid with golden runes and artwork. The palace stood three stories tall and breached the canopy of trees, giving those on the top floor an unobstructed view of the sky.

She wondered if Kyrilis ever flew to Ayr'Thugohn directly, and what it was like to take such a flight and witness the city's majesty from above.

As they ascended the steps to the palace entrance, guards lining the stairs bowed their heads and presented their Quel'Thoz in front of them in a show of honor. Her escort stopped at the top step and indicated that she should proceed alone.

Wyk'Daienor stood at the doors, awaiting her arrival. Having studied the nobility of Arkhania in preparation for just such an occasion, she quickly stepped aside and opened the great doors of the palace. Several servants, dressed in flowing silk, filtered out of the opening and fell in beside and behind her, ready to respond at the expression of any whim or desire.

Ayriel walked forward into the great hall beyond.

∴ ∴ ∴

KOTANN SIGNALED for the soldiers to proceed. The group crouched, one by one, through the doorway and continued down into the depths beneath the tower. Water slowly wept through sections of the stone walls as the swamp continued its centuries-old efforts to claim the ruin completely. The stairs wound downward in a gentle spiral, growing more and more cramped with every step. The ceiling above them—cracked and partially sunken—made some areas quite difficult to pass.

Swampy water had long ago flooded the lower landing, seeping in through cracks where it had sunk below its original position. Walls, ceiling and floor seemed sheared free of the rest of the structure and twisted at an angle, while the ruin beyond remained intact and in its original position.

Wil went first, swimming under and through a small gap in the fallen stone, mud and roots. After a few moments he resurfaced and signaled that it was safe for all to follow. Agnar, Laurence, Halgar and Thax made several trips through the narrow passage to assist their plate-wearing companions, as the waters made it difficult to pass under the weight of their armor.

Once all had completed the trip, they found themselves on level flooring, surrounded by stone brick walls and a solid stone ceiling. Support beams provided additional support at regular intervals down the length of the hall that stretched out before them. Red light emanated from runes along the top of the walls, breathing into life and fading again, slowly, in a never-ending cycle. It was a place unlike anything they'd ever seen.

Laurence looked at Agnar, wondering if he and his cousin had ever ventured inside the ruin. The look of fear on Agnar's face answered the unspoken question clearly. The sounds of combat echoed down the hall toward them in spurts. In the gaps between, they could hear distant chanting, barely audible but haunting none-the-less.

Wil pointed at their feet, then along the floor into the distance. Drag marks comprised of mud and marsh water trailed down the hallway into the deep recesses of the ruin.

"The captives were dragged through here alive. They kicked and flailed, trying to break free," whispered Wil. He started down the hallway at a slow, methodical pace.

Laurence, Agnar, and the archers sneaked behind him.

Kotann released a frustrated sigh and simply started walking. The sound of his armor echoed down the hallway, revealing their presence.

Wil turned, shocked, and looked at Kotann as if to challenge his change in tactic.

"Unless you've spells of silence to grace us with, let's face the inevitable," offered Kotann with a shrug. His men chuckled behind him.

With a sigh, Wil realized that Kotann was right. Begrudgingly, he turned and proceeded down the hall without relying on secrecy. Just as he did, two Velloth spilled into the hallway from a room on their left, brandishing swords and shields.

Wil fell back into the group, his staff-like weapon too long to fight with properly in such a confined space.

Laurence, Agnar and the archers fell back and to the sides, creating an opening for the knights that charged forward behind them, shouting, "Make way!"

Kotann and his two knights slammed into the Velloth shields with sheer, brute force. Steel blade met with black stone weaponry in a flurry of sparks. Arrows streaked through the air, inserting themselves into the eyes of one of the Velloth, sending it to the ground. The knights quickly overcame the other, ending its life with a myriad of gaping wounds about its chest.

They continued down the passage, stopping at each doorway.

Kotann signaled at a door on the right, sending a knight and two soldiers inside to attack the Velloth within. The rest of the group continued past.

The process repeated further down the hallway, with a knight and two soldiers sent into a room on the left.

At the third occupied room, Kotann ran in himself with two soldiers to handle the Velloth.

Laurence followed their example and kept moving.

When they reached the ninth room, Laurence barged in with Agnar, Izabel, Wil and Gharick.

The Velloth inside were already in combat. Crypts lined the walls of the chamber, from floor to ceiling. A stream of corpses climbed out of the crypts, one by one, and attacked. The Velloth fought valiantly, and desperately, to kill the undead assailants, and hadn't noticed Laurence or his companions entering.

Laurence froze for a moment, gazing at the fantastic, horrific scene before him. Skeletons wrapped in decayed flesh and remnants of tattered cloth stumbled toward the Velloth, lashing out with bone hands and gnashing teeth. As the Velloth blades struck them, their bones sizzled and hissed as if the weapons burned them.

It dawned on Laurence that the material the Velloth used to forge their weapons and armor was likely born of necessity; that these might be familiar foes. That idea chilled him to his core.

Clumps of rotted flesh fell to the ground at their feet, sending puffs of decrepit dust into the air. Shards of bone ricocheted off the nearby walls and columns. The Velloth grunted their displeasure at the situation. They found themselves fully engaged in combat with a dangerous foe and beset by other enemies from behind. Dying to one meant simple death, but dying to the other meant an eternity of horror.

Gharick stepped fully in the room, chanting a prayer.

The Velloth refused to change targets, intent on preventing their death at the hands of the undead.

Laurence, Izabel, Agnar and Wil moved toward the Velloth and slew them from behind with relative ease. Izabel struck one of the shambling corpses with her blade. Her sword rebounded off the skeleton's ribs without leaving so much as a scratch on the creature's exposed bone.

"Oh no," she gasped, realizing their folly.

Laurence's blade crashed into the skeleton in front of Izabel, shattering its ribs and sending the creature into a pile of dust and bone at their feet.

She looked at him in astonishment.

"I didn't know either!" he remarked. It was immediately apparent to both of them that Gahl's sword, like his armor, also bore enchantments.

Wil, Agnar and Izabel backed up a few steps and allowed Laurence to occupy the remaining skeletons.

Izabel sheathed her sword and picked up one of the Velloth blades. After hefting it in her hand for a moment to test its weight, she jumped back into the fight to assist him.

Agnar saw her new blade destroying the undead and followed her example.

Suddenly, a burst of yellow light filled the room as Gharick's prayer completed. The companions squinted and cringed, blocking their eyes in reflex. Coughing, as their lungs filled with bone dust, they waved their hands at the air and blinked dust from their eyes to look around.

The undead had turned to dust and ash.

"You could've done that sooner," joked Wil.

Laurence, Kotann, and the rest of the group reunited in the hallway.

The chanting grew louder, reaching what they hoped was not the climax of whatever spell or ritual was being performed. Realizing that they might be running out of time, the group raced down the hallway toward the source of the sound.

∴ ∴ ∴

AYRIEL WALKED across the ebony floor with a grace and demeanor befitting a Princess. It wasn't until she bowed before the King, and saw her own clothes, that she remembered leaving Vaelin Palace so quickly that she'd forgotten to change out of her bedroom attire. Cheeks flushed with embarrassment, she stood upright again and addressed the King with all the modesty and respect she could muster.

"Your majesty, I am Princess Ayriel Vaelin; daughter of King Orluhnd Vaelin IV. I have come to you under the most dire of circumstances, and regret that I could not be here under more desirable conditions, or a more presentable state. I hope that my unfortunate attire and lack of shoes properly conveys the gravity of the situation."

The King nodded to her and then looked at several servants

and wiggled his finger in their directions. They ran out of the room briefly and returned carrying an open front robe of exquisite design.

"A person of your standing should not be forced, even by circumstance, to appear below your station, my lady. This belonged to my wife, and it is now yours. Please... accept this gift and know that it is I who should bow to you. Our people have been distant for much too long. We have let our relationships stagnate for reasons that few are alive to remember. Tell me," he said as she put the robe on over her clothes, "what troubling event has brought you to my humble city?"

He stood and descended the dais, coming down to her level. He was quite tall for an elf, even taller than her. She knew this to be an extremely rare trait, as most elves were shorter than the average human. Gently, he placed his hand on her elbow and guided her toward a pair of comfortable chairs at the side of the room.

"It is a myriad of concerns, truth be told, and I fear that they may yet have an impact upon the Ekthri. I do not believe these to be human matters alone," she explained as they walked.

As they took their chairs, he bid her to continue with a flutter of his hand.

"As you know, over a hundred years ago the great War of the Wilds came to its conclusion on Engle Plateau. Many elves helped Orluhnd Vaelin win the battle that day, founding the Kingdom of Arkhania and fulfilling his father's dreams. However, that day wasn't without treachery and tragedy," she explained.

"I was there, my lady," he answered.

"Then you might recall the murder of Orluhnd's most valued hero, Gahl, and the man who betrayed Orluhnd and murdered him on the field of battle, Drakahl," she said.

"Indeed. I recall several Griffin Guard hunting him down for weeks and never finding anything."

"That is true, my lord, he was never found. We have learned in recent days that he yet lives, and has been King of Pelrigoss for nearly two decades. He was revealed to be the same person after he returned to Arkhania in secret. He killed Gahl's son, Arcturus, and has set into motion a series of events that—we believe—involves the legendary witch Nightweaver. It appears that-"

"Drakahl has returned? Nightweaver? Two things that reason dictates cannot be," interrupted the King.

"I would not be here were it otherwise, my Lord. She has

somehow beguiled several of our soldiers from afar, inspiring them to defect. They stole the Vaelin crossbow, pried the magic pearl from its stock and used it to unleashed the Velloth from their hiding place underground. Grellenheim and Gaierford were destroyed, thousands of souls slaughtered at their hands. We have troops hunting the rest of them down at this very moment in the Sacton Delta," she explained.

"Nightweaver? Velloth? Drakahl? This is all too much, my Lady, and hardly believable," challenged the King.

"Are you familiar with Archmagus Mordechai, my Lord?" she asked.

"I met him when I was a boy. We have seen him in our forest occasionally, but he is always respectful of our wood and our ways. There are some who regard him as a protector of our people. The Skaar seem to sense his presence and withdraw when he is nearby, as do a great many other threats," he said.

"We know that Nightweaver is real, and involved, because she cursed him with blindness... from Pelrigoss... through his crystal ball as he sat in Fel'Vizsiour divining her," she explained.

The weight of her statement did not hit him all at once. What she was describing sounded impossible, by his understanding of magic. Yet, the tales of Nightweaver from ancient times had always described her as having other-worldly powers beyond reason or expectation. He wasn't sure how to respond.

"That is why I have come here. First, to seek help with a cure for his blindness. Second, to warn you of the plots which we face, so you are prepared should they spill into your wood and threaten your people. We do not know what beasts or evils she will conjure next, or where the rest of the Velloth have gone. I fear Ekthri may be one of her targets," she explained.

"Why do you seek our help with a curse? Why not just send an emissary with word of these events?" asked the King.

"Mordechai said she used an ancient elven curse that he recognized, but can't remember how he recognized it. She uttered the word, 'Dalltash.'"

The King's face flushed with fear. He reached into his robes and withdrew a small medallion on a hair-thin silver chain. Slipping it off his head, he presented it to her and bid her to take it. A small, black heart glinted in the candlelight at the center of the medallion, suspended inside a circle of silver etched with strange runes. When she shifted the medallion, the light bouncing off the heart made it appear to beat as if it were functional.

"When I was a boy, Mordechai visited our village. He met with my father and they talked at great length. Afterward, he came to see me in my room. I was in the middle of my studies, but I knew how important he was to have taken up so much of my father's time. It was exciting to talk to him and meet this great man that so many of our people whispered about.

"Before he left, he handed me this medallion. He said it was a gift and that I would someday have to give it to a woman in a time of great troubles. I was to wear it at all times, and it would protect me and help me guide my people. I've worn it as a charm since that day. He told me several times how I would know it was time to pass it on," he explained.

"But... how?" she asked. She struggled for words as her mind tried to piece together this tale of Mordechai's visit hundreds of years prior.

"He was very clear and repeated his instructions to me several times and made me repeat it. '*A woman will come to you in your final days. She will herald the coming of a Time of Sorrow. You will know it is her, for Dalltash will reveal her truth.*' It was a confusing phrase, and I spent years musing on the meaning of those words.

"The medallion seemed to inspire and guide my hand, and it became a part of who I was. Dalltash, though, means '*blind*' or, more accurately, '*unseeing*'. To have the '*unseeing*' reveal truth... you can understand why this might be confusing. Now I see that it wasn't a clue at all, but a specific sign that needed no interpretation."

"What do I do with it?" she asked, turning the medallion over in her hands.

"There was one part of our wood that he warned me to never personally venture. My people could go there, but not build there. It was only I that was to avoid crossing its threshold. In the southern half of our wood there is a single blue tree. If you travel to that tree and then head west... you will reach that spot. It is a clearing," he said as he stood.

Fear and dread lined his face.

"What are y–"

"He also told me that when the medallion crossed into that clearing, my rule would come to an end. My fate, it seems, has caught up to me. I must go make final preparations for our people's new King," he said, cutting her off.

Without another word he left the throne room and, followed by a swarm of desperate servants, started preparing for his own death. She sat for a time, trying to piece together what had just happened. Deciding that only Mordechai could help her figure it out, she left the room the way she entered.

As she reached the platform, the trees around the palace shook violently.

∴ ∴ ∴

THE GREAT doors at the end of the hallway burst open violently as the group entered the ritual chamber. Draconic runes pulsed red around the room, as if breathing. An inverse dome adorned the center of the twenty foot high ceiling, covered in runes that glowed a bright, fiery orange. The concave floor beneath it descended at the same angle toward an altar.

Spears stood in a ring around the pit. The blunt ends securely planted into small holes in the floor, their tips reached up toward the center of the ceiling above the altar.

Impaled upon the spears in several stages of death, bleeding out or already dead, were the men, women and children captured from the marshland farms. Their blood ran down and into the pit along rune-lined grooves, surrounding the altar in a pool of red.

Velloth lined the rim of the pit wearing robes, their hoods drawn up around their heads. They chanted repetitively, heads bowed with their arms clasped before them. At the base of the pit, a priest stood next to the altar, leading the chant; his arms raised in worship toward the runes on the ceiling above him.

The top of the altar was a cradle, designed to hold a single item. Inside the cradle sat a single, massive horn made of black bone. The red runes engraved into the horn glowed, pulsed and heaved with the rhythms of the ritual.

As the group entered the room, the ritual concluded. The chanting ceased and the head priest bent slightly at the waist, pressing his lips to the horn.

A deep, resonating tone burst forth.

The runes around the room glowed as bright as the sun.

Red streaks of power, like lightning, arced out of the ceiling and struck the chanting Velloth, passing through the sacrificed farmers in its path.

A beam of light streamed down, enveloping the head priest.

Back at the camp, the sounding of a great horn shattered the silence of the night. A red beam of light lit up the night sky, arcing out of the distant ruin and crossing the sky as it faded into the horizon headed west.

Awakened and alarmed, the group at the camp studied the sky, trying to discern what had happened. Far in the distance, Kundarr was glowing.

The Velloth, their human victims, and the pool of blood seared into ash in an instant.

The group looked around and at each other, horror in their eyes.

"What have they done?" asked Laurence.

"We have failed," said Kotann, putting into words what they were all thinking.

∴ ∴ ∴

AYRIEL RACED to the hole in the platform. Two servants lowered her down to the under city with the same rope she'd used to ascend. As she ran across the platforms and walkways of the lower city, the shaking of the trees became a violent quake.

Art, carvings, and random belongings stored on shelves or pinned to walls crashed down all around the city.

Elvish citizens panicked and cried out.

She didn't wait for the servants to assist as she reached the final rope. Grabbing it in both hands, she swung out over the edge and let her body weight lower her to the ground.

Tegris was frantic, trying desperately to free himself from the tether.

She uttered a quick calming enchantment, soothing her beloved mount, before untying him.

As she freed Tegris, the sound of an explosion echoed through the trees, coming from the Mythaeil Mountains to the west. She wondered if the ancient dormant volcano, Kundarr, had awakened.

She repeated the enchantments she'd used to reach Ekthri wood, as quickly as her skills would allow. Runes sprang to life along Tegris's body, providing strength, endurance and speed.

The ground rumbled violently as something barreled toward her from the west, trees crashing and breaking in its wake. Fear rose up inside her, nearly breaking her concentration. Pushing past the fear, she continued her spells as a huge, reddish-brown foot, larger than Tegris, slammed into the ground a few yards away.

A fire giant—escaping whatever was happening in the mountains beyond the wood—attacked the city above her in a panic. The gargantuan creature—not known to experience fear—lashed out at the city in horror as if it were blocking its means of escape.

Barely able to complete her enchantments in time, she mounted and kicked her steed into action. As Tegris reared back, preparing to charge, Skaar came pouring into the wood beneath the city, similarly fleeing whatever was happening in the west.

Tegris lurched forward, quickly reaching a gallop, as the sky above the trees grew brighter.

An orange glow filled the sky from the west.

Kundarr had indeed erupted.

VEHKS

Dreadful fight, with tooth and fang,
Shall sunder many souls.
Your tragic deaths are not in vain,
Balance cares not the cost.

Night's Writ, Parable 10

FOR THOUSANDS of years, the chamber remained undisturbed. Sealed away from the world, the amethyst tomb kept its single, slumbering occupant safe and alive. Long gone was the era of its kind. They had once roamed the land freely and ruled with impunity.

Leathery wings once soared through the skies, casting all beneath them in shadow. Their empire rose from the ashes of the Agthari, built upon the backs of mortal servants who yearned for purpose in the absence of their former masters.

Their kind had been all too eager to fill the void, conquer the lands and take over where the Titans of old had left off. However, as they flew over their domain—reveling in their power—they had grown complacent.

They were woefully unprepared for what was to come.

When Vehkstaerelliox—the Harbinger, the Grand Seer, the Prophet—warned them of their impending doom, they shunned her in disbelief. With all their might, they could not fathom anyone, or anything, overcoming their empire and delivering unto them the same fate as their predecessors.

Much like the few remaining Agthari, Vehks resigned herself to go into hiding. She'd seen the power of those that entered their world; witnessed with her own eyes as they poured from the depths, crossing the landscape in untold numbers.

They were not the Toor, easily bent to Draconic will.

They were not the Skaar, compliant and happy to serve.

What she saw had frightened her, for she knew not from whence they came.

Each of the new races had free will, desires, and motivations the likes of which the Toor had never expressed. She knew such characteristics would spread like a virus throughout their world; infecting the Toor; infecting the Skaar; driving their servants toward rebellion.

As their arrival drove the Toor north, she warned the council of elders again.

When the Skaar fled the marshlands and forests seeking the safety of the desert, she reminded them of her warnings.

At all turns, they insisted that draconic might would prevail. They had once facilitated the Agthari fall at the talons of demonic hordes; their false sense of security ensuring their demise. She could see the pattern repeating among her own kind.

Only a few Agthari survived those horrifying times, and only a few of her kind would accomplish the same. Of that, she was certain.

So it was that she found an isolated chamber near the center of Kundarr. She breathed into it, melting the stones and causing their composition to break down. Using her magic, she reformed the molten slag into a shell of pure amethyst, trapping herself inside.

Lulled by the magics she'd imbued into her crystalline tomb, she entered an eons-long slumber. Ahava, the first Velloth, was left with instructions on how to wake her—should her predictions prove inaccurate—and was sent into hiding underground to watch in her stead.

Their call to awake never came, and as dragons died across the whole of Gargoa, she slept in quiet solitude.

Thousands of years later, she woke as the amethyst shell cracked open. Ancient, black scales trembled with the quaking of her muscles as she stretched off eons of sleep, shaking amethyst dust and shards from her form.

Her violet eyes opened into slits, peering at the chamber around her. Kundarr's fire stirred at the end of the tunnel before her.

The volcano has awakened. The call has been made, she realized.

Stiffly, she stood on her mighty talons, stretching her tail as straight as she could behind her. The chamber was too small for her to reach her full size. She needed the open air.

Gripping the amethyst beneath her, she dragged herself free of the cavern.

Vehkstaerelliox tucked back her massive wings and lowered her horned head to pass through the tunnel toward the magma. She exited the lava tube onto the molten slag at the edge of Kundarr's main vent. The magma licked and hissed at the scales on her massive claws, exhilarating her and bringing warmth to her old bones.

Once clear of the tube, she stretched her wings out to their full extent. Two hundred and thirty feet of leathery wingspan basked in the heat of the vent, warming in preparation for flight. With one last flex of her muscles, and a deafening roar, Vehkstaerelliox once again took flight.

It was a sight no one had seen in eastern Gargoa for nearly three thousand years.

∴ ∴ ∴

"THEY HAVE released Vehkstaerelliox. All is as I said it would be," declared Nightweaver. She turned to face Drakahl, who stood beside her. The vision in the crystal ball clouded, fading into nothingness.

"Not exactly as you said it would be," corrected Drakahl. He spoke in forcibly hushed tones, but was clearly angry.

"Nothing is ever exactly as it was foretold, young one," she retorted, reminding him of his place. "The Velloth accomplished their primary goal, regardless of interference. Vehkstaerelliox has been released and will fulfill her role. The wheels are in motion, and none can stop them. We need but time to watch the events unfold. Your impatience will help nothing," she explained.

"I should have slain the boy with his grandfather. Instead, your advice has allowed him to intercede," he challenged.

"He was *always* going to interceded. His presence pushes our plans further. He still has a purpose. Besides, it was my advice that made you King," she reminded him.

She stood and faced him, rising to her full height, which was something she rarely did. Hunching over and pretending that she struggled to move allowed her to seem weak, and that often made those around her underestimate the power she held. In that moment, she needed to remind Drakahl not to overstep.

"My advice brought you the curse that you covet. My advice brought you Ahm. With my assistance, Ahm made you the armor you hold so dear. Perhaps you should question my advice less and do as you are told!" she scolded.

Her voice grew to an unreasonable volume as she spoke, sending chills down Drakahl's spine as she reached her final point. Drakahl didn't feel fear, and the sensation was both foreign and concerning to him.

"You are right, Sorscha. I have much to thank you for, and will seek to better convey my respect and patience in the future," he offered.

Using her true name was a gamble, but one that he hoped would convey his understanding and appreciation for what she was doing and what they were trying to build.

"You are forgiven, Drakahl," she breathed.

Her body resumed its normal, hunched position as she patted him on the chest. His armor seemed to writhe and shrink away from her touch in fear.

Axvalla hissed in Drakahl's mind.

"See to it that Shaer'Thog receives his meal promptly. I've lost enough of my priestesses to his hunger," she said as she departed.

Drakahl stood for a few moments in silence, contemplating his relationship with the witch. He hadn't known ambition before meeting her. The concept was foreign to the Toor, who lived simplistic, nomadic lives. Her ambitions had become his own over time, driving him from his own people and putting him into the path of Orluhnd Vaelin and Gahl. Everything about who he'd become had cascaded into existence from that moment.

He wondered if he too weren't a pawn, like the Velloth and Vehkstaerelliox. Concerned that she might hear his thoughts, he buried them and set about the evening's tasks. It wasn't healthy to dwell on the witch and her motivations. So long as her ambitions aligned with his own, he would happily comply with her desires, as he'd done for hundreds of years.

We must complete the Circle of Nine. Only then will I be free of her plots. Only then will her scheming conclude, thought the man-demon.

'Will it?' hissed Axvalla.

∴ ∴ ∴

THEIR RIDE had been treacherous, and Tegris was nearing the end of his ability to keep moving. By the end of the night, they'd ridden the equivalent of four days' travel. It was an unreasonable distance without rest, even for a horse as capable as Tegris; even with her enchantments.

Ayriel pulled back on the reins, slowing Tegris to a cantor, and looked around for a place to rest.

Just ahead, her eyes caught sight of a strange tree. It didn't fit in with those around it. Most of the forest was redwood, with high branches and towering trunks. The canopy towered over the forest's floor, keeping most of it in shadow.

The tree ahead of her was small and devoid of leaves. Its white bark curled and peeled off in thin sheets all along its trunk and branches. The wood underneath was a faint blue.

"We're here," she told Tegris.

She dismounted and patted his neck reassuringly. He snorted in response, as if in thanks. She led him to the tree, tied him off so he could rest, and looked to the west. Just beyond the next few trees she could see a clearing just as King Faelrin had described.

As she crossed the threshold of the clearing, the medallion around her neck grew warm and glowed to life. Ringing pierced her ears, growing in intensity as she walked further. The sound grew to painful heights, forcing her to double over in pain, grasping at her ears. She ripped the medallion off and tossed it to the ground, fearful of what was happening and wondering if the medallion was somehow killing her.

The medallion skidded across the ground, coming to a stop several feet away. As it came to rest, the ringing in her ears stopped abruptly. She stood and looked at the medallion, still glowing with a silvery black energy amidst the underbrush and grass.

Unsure what was happening, she took a few steps back.

A black tower made of pure hematite appeared instantly in front of her, right on top of the medallion. The whole of the one-hundred-foot tall tower seemed to be formed from a single piece of stone that had grown into its shape. All along the tower's surface were tiny rings of runes that either someone had etched with unbelievable skill, or—if her eyes were correct—were a natural part of the stone.

Her heart skipped a beat as the tower materialized. She took a moment to study the exterior and then decided that the medallion's purpose must have been to summon it. Cautiously, she approached the single door at its base, which sat atop three steps, each formed from a solid sheet of hematite.

As she arrived at the entrance, the door opened of its own accord.

She entered the tower and found herself in a single, large, circular room with no obvious doors, steps or points of egress other than the door through which she'd just passed. Shelves lined the walls from floor to ceiling, each holding a collection of scrolls, books, and small artifacts. At the center of the room stood a single desk with a chair behind it, and two chairs before it.

Standing behind the desk—inviting her to join him with a hand gesture—appeared to be Mordechai. Everything about him seemed familiar... save for his chest. Black, metallic armor, of a kind that she'd never seen, covered his upper chest, replacing his familiar hardened leather padding.

She paused, unable to control the shock and horror that crossed her face. An over-sized black heart protruded from the center of his chest, beating rhythmically. Dark purple energies flowed through the arteries, leading into his flesh. A silver ring encircled the heart, acting as the inner border of the black metal armor; etched with glowing purple runes which pulsed brightly along with the rhythmic beating of the strange heart.

"Please, sit. It's been a very long time since I've seen you," offered Mordechai.

"But... your..." she stammered, pointing at her own chest.

"Ah, yes. That is something I cannot discuss. Suffice to say, the Mordechai you know cannot be told of it either, lest he risk his own future," he explained.

"Future? You're..." she started, coming to a realization as she sat.

"Yes. I am not the Mordechai you know, but rather one that you once knew. That may be confusing, but it will have to do," he said, taking his seat. "I know why you are here, and... I have engineered this meeting to dissuade you from pursuing your quest further."

"But... he's blind! I mean, *you're* blind!"

"He is. I was. Clearly there is an end to the blindness from which he suffers. There are many possible resolutions to his predicament. However, I am here to ensure you choose the most beneficial path. The one that blinded him cannot hear, see or detect my presence, and the world outside will be just as you left it when you return. Tegris will not even know that you've been gone. So, we can take whatever time you need to make sure you understand your next course of action," he explained.

"I don't understand what's going on," she said in frustration.

"I was once him. I have been through much in my time since those days... your *present* days. He has powers he does not understand and has forgotten that he knows. I went in search of answers, and that is what led to both this," he said indicating his chest, "and the tower in which you now sit. There is much, much more at play than I could possibly convey to you.

"If I were to explain everything it would neither make sense, nor come to pass. There are things you would seek to prevent—or cure, such as this blindness—that would dramatically change the future in ways that you could never comprehend.

"So, I am here to insist that you let Mordechai's future unfold along the path he is already on. I calculated that there was a chance he'd send you to find a cure and planned for that eventuality. The fact that you are here tells me which history you are experiencing. Everything will indeed work out for the best if you simply stay the course," he said.

"I don't understand why. Why must he be blind? Why would it hurt to cure him now?" she begged.

"If he was not blind, then he would not learn to see," answered Mordechai.

Her face contorted further into confusion.

"If you cure him now, he will use his eyes, no? That will prevent him from... using *other* senses which he has yet to fully develop. He must develop those senses, and he must do so without guidance or assistance."

What Mordechai was trying to explain started to make sense. She still didn't understand the motivations or the precise details about what he was saying, but she'd caught on to the fact that this stage in Mordechai's life—his blindness—was necessary and that it would lead to something critical to their future.

"His path will take him on a journey. Let it. Do not stand in his way and do not intercede. When you return, explain that the Ekthri knew of no cure, and that their city was lost; that you barely escaped with your life. In other words, tell him the truth. Simply leave out the details of the medallion, Faelrin's prophecy, and your visit with me. I have seen how that future unfolds, and it is the least desirable of all outcomes," he explained with a dramatic roll of his eyes.

"If there is such risk in helping me, or curing him, why intercede? Why did you give the medallion to the Ekthri hundreds of years ago, knowing it would draw me here?" she asked, clearly frustrated.

"When it comes to Time, and free will, nothing is ever certain. Any little flutter from any number of infinite sources can change the entire course of history. I learned these things the hard way, and have caused ripples through time that I am still atoning for. Planting the medallion when and where I did was a preparatory measure, and one I hoped would not be needed.

"Leaving the medallion with Faelrin and planting that seed would cause no harm if my prophecy never came to pass. However, should events deviate and cause Mordechai to send you out in search for a cure, I knew that my involvement would become an inevitable necessity.

"You are... closer to one another than you were in his original fated journey. And so, should you continue this path he will wait for you to return with a cure for however long it takes you to find it. That will prevent him from leaving your palace, and... well, I've already said too much," he concluded.

"So all of this is your doing?" she asked, growing angry.

"No. However, what happens next will get far worse thanks to my attempts to prevent... this," he said, pointing generally to the world around him. "I lived through everything that is taking place right now; several times, in fact. I tried to go back and prevent it. That failed. Horribly. It led to much worse results, and many thousands more died as a result of my meddling. I am here to right the course and ensure that history resumes its normal path."

"Very well," she said with a sigh. "I still do not understand everything that is going on, but I think I comprehend enough to trust you and do as you ask," she said, standing to leave.

"I am truly sorry for putting you in this position, sweet Ayriel. You will struggle with this for years before everything becomes clear. If there was any other way-"

"I will return to Vaelin Palace promptly," she said.

Joining her, he gently lifted her hand with his own and kissed it. Mordechai had only ever done that once before; when they'd first met.

With a smile, she exited the tower. Once outside, she turned around to get another look. The tower had vanished, replaced once again with the amulet.

Ayriel picked up the amulet and considered what she'd just experienced. As she walked back to Tegris, she slipped the necklace back around her neck.

I'll have questions when this is over, she thought.

∴ ∴ ∴

VEHKSTAERELLIOX FOUND herself inexplicably drawn toward the east, in the direction of her former roost. She'd once lived between rocky crags south of her lord Hahrfurgadhen's crescent mountain fortress. Memories of the clanging of tools upon stone—as her servants worked the eastern quarry—brought happiness to her briefly.

Her enjoyment was short lived as the nagging sensation at the back of her mind drove her onward, insisting she waste no further time. Angered by the subconscious forces that she could not deny, she roared her displeasure at the fields and marshes of the wetlands beneath her.

She drove her wings down with all of her strength as she crossed over the ruins of the temple Ahava had built for her. Several snacks—descendants of the invaders that had slaughtered her kind—ran about on the ground below. As hungry as she was, the incessant voice inside her would not let her stop to dine.

∴ ∴ ∴

THE SUN shone brightly in the sky, in stark contrast to the darkness of the depths they were leaving. Soaking wet and exhausted, the group exited the ruin feeling defeated and lost. They knew not what the Velloth had done, nor what action to take next. It was unfortunate for many reasons when the answer presented itself moments later.

Massive, black, leathery wings flapped once from overhead as a deafening roar echoed off the surrounding landscape. The air about them rushed downward with such intense force that many of them were unable to hold their feet and fell to the ground.

A great dragon soared past the ruin, heading east.

Terror and shock filled the soldiers.

"What the fuck was that?" shouted Thax.

"It can't be!" exclaimed Laurence. Arcturus's library contained several tomes dedicated to the study of ancient dragons and according to all of them they were extinct. He couldn't believe his eyes.

"We must find out where it's headed!" barked Kotann.

"They summoned a dragon?" yelled Izabel in a panic.

"We weren't fast enough! We could have stopped them!" lamented Agnar as they broke into a run.

"We couldn't have known," reasoned Wil.

"What of your people? It came from the west!" exclaimed Izabel.

"I can't think of that right now," stated Wil, hastening his pace.

They ran as fast as they could back to camp. When they arrived, the camp was still in a frenzy. Their horses took nearly an hour to calm.

Kotann was so insistent they move quickly that he abandoned their tents and belongings.

The blacksmiths and squires that traveled with them stayed behind, with instructions to report to Fel'Rechaun and escort Mildred to safety.

With no need to move slowly looking for Velloth tracks, Laurence, Kotann and their soldiers raced out of the marsh and eastward across the plains as fast as their mounts could carry them.

∴ ∴ ∴

KARZDEN WAS fast at work teaching one of his students to create opportunities with their parries when a distant roar echoed between the walls of the courtyard. Guards atop the southern wall called out frantically from above. Too many of them called out at once to discern what they were saying.

Students and staff nearer to the walls screamed, fainted, or grabbed for weapons.

Unable to discern the cause for commotion, and disturbed by the sound of the roar, he left his student and ran across the courtyard toward the stairs that led up the wall. By the time he reached the stairs he'd already tired of yelling, "Move!", and "Clear a path!"

Once atop the wall, he approached one of the guards. "What is it?" he asked.

"A dragon, sir," responded the guard, pointing.

Karzden followed the guard's finger toward the southeast. A huge, black dragon flapped its wings as if on queue. After taking a moment to close his jaw and compose himself, Karzden turned back around and bounded down the stairs to inform Fahrul.

As he made his way across the courtyard, he repeatedly muttered the phrase, "This is bad, this is bad, this is so bad."

∴∴∴

SETTLEMENTS LIE in every direction she looked. It was as she feared; the invaders had taken over their world. They built out in the open, seemingly unconcerned about attacks from above. It was a clear sign that she might be the last of her kind.

Anger swelled within her.

She caught sight of a group of traveling fodder in her path. Straightening her wings to glide on the breeze, she bent her tail upwards and slightly tipped her wings forward. Descending, she let loose a great roar in anticipation. Incessant nagging or no, she would dine before continuing further.

Her hunger, and anger, had grown to uncontrollable heights.

∴∴∴

DELRIAHNA'S CARRIAGE turned onto the road leading toward Gaierford. The merchant and refugee caravan behind her was near the point of total exhaustion, but they had made great time on their journey.

As she looked up in the sky, Tylee saw what she assumed to be a raven. Its black form slowly approached, gliding on the winds with a sense of freedom that she was feeling within herself. She thought it fitting that a raven would appear over Gaierford upon their arrival.

She considered what sort of omen or sign it might be; contemplating whether the raven was ominous or beneficial. When she turned to ask Delriahna, she noticed the look on her mother's face. Returning her gaze to the sky, she realized the raven was growing larger; much too large to be a bird.

The dragon roared and dove toward the caravan with shocking speed. Everyone in the caravan dismounted horses, climbed off of carriages and ran in the most convenient direction they could.

Draft horses panicked, kicking and tugging, trying to break free of the weight they pulled.

Livestock, trapped in cages, went into a frenzy trying to break free.

Tylee and Delriahna crashed to the ground, diving to avoid the dragon's massive wing as it dipped its maw to scoop up two horses at once.

Both horses leading the livestock carriage disappeared into the beast's mouth simultaneously. The leads and rigging which had bound the horses to their carriage snapped with a loud crunch. The carriage tumbled through the air, landing on the other side of the road.

Vehkstaerelliox heaved upward with a flap of her wings, slamming the ground and those upon it with a rush of air that knocked some unconscious, and stole the breath from many others.

Distraught, injured, and terrified, the travelers watched in desperation as the dragon continued east, up and over the trees. None knew what to make of the horrific event. Most were unaware what the creature was.

Tylee was the first to shake off her feelings of shock and horror. She got up and ran from person to person, checking them all for injuries and organizing them to move out of the road, in case the beast returned.

∴ ∴ ∴

GAERIN STOOD waiting on the docks in front of The Soggy Fool while Lyla orchestrated the delivery of their goods. Gellix and his mercenary band helped carry the crates over, piling them like a make-shift wall along the edge of the dock.

Keifer and Gabner stood a short distance away, hiding behind Kyrilis.

Gaerin decided the scene perfectly described what his life had become; the eclectic mix of disparate souls his wife had collected to join them in a quest for vengeance, where everyone felt out of place, and oddly unified in purpose.

Captain Bagris stepped up to the edge of the ship, overlooking the small crowd and all their supplies. He removed his tricorne hat. As he lifted it, the scraggly tufts of hair went with it. He scratched his bald head for a moment, puzzling over the sheer absurdity of the group he was about to welcome aboard before returning his hat and its sewn-in mop of hair to his scalp.

"Lower the plank," he called out.

Several crewmen ran over to the side of the boat and lowered a feeble gangplank down to the dock. Gaerin boarded first, not willing to wait on the dock for them to load all the supplies.

"Thank you again, Captain. Your help with our journey means the world to us," he said, extending his hand.

"Aye, it would appear to be quite an affair," replied the Captain as he shook Gaerin's hand.

"That is the wonder of being married to my wife," joked Gaerin.

"Aye, I've known the sort. Special, but they have a way," agreed the Captain.

"A way of driving a man slowly insane," completed Gaerin.

"Aye!" agreed the Captain.

Gellix and his men loaded the crates into the hold. Gareg and Oben seemed exceptionally strong, often carrying twice the load of the others.

Lyla stayed on the dock to coordinate until the last crate of supplies made it onto the ship. The process of receiving the goods and loading them into the hold took nearly half the day, much to the displeasure of their Captain.

As the crew raised the gangplank, an officer of the Trade Commission approached on the dock.

Captain Bagris seemed frustrated by the man's arrival. "What be the trouble, tax man?" yelled the Captain.

"Your ship is several hours late for your scheduled departure and has exceeded its allotted use of the docks. According to statute six-fourteen of the Port Vaelin Decalogue, you are required to pay for additional port fees, including taxes and penalties for your overage... as I am sure a man of your position is keenly aware," explained the frail man.

"You can take your port fees and shove it up y-" started the Captain.

A deep, resonating roar interrupted them from the west.

Everyone looked toward the source of the sound. To their disbelief and amazement, a massive dragon was razing the town. It swooped low over the city, breathing fire down on the buildings and citizens in its wake. As it pulled up, back into the sky, arrows ripped through the air. The arrows either missed entirely, or feebly bounced off the dragon's thick scales.

"Time to go!" yelled Bagris to his crew.

The crew raced to prepare the ship to sail. They released the moorings, raised the anchor, and cranked the rigging into position in what Gaerin could only assume was record time. Port Vaelin slowly went up in flames as the dragon dove toward it, time and time again, breathing fire and causing devastation.

"I don't know what's going on, but I fear for our kingdom. Drakahl, those nasty elves, and now this?" said Lyla, distressed.

"These are troubling times, indeed," agreed Gaerin.

As the ship started moving, the dragon swooped down for another attack. A series of blue streaks raced through the air and smashed into the dragon's chest. Blue tendrils of power raced across the dragon's form, gripping it and causing excruciating pain. The dragon crashed to the ground, destroying an entire city block and several surrounding buildings.

"They're winning!" yelled Lyla gleefully.

"Perhaps, but at what cost?" asked Kyrilis.

With a roar, the beast reared back and released another bout of flame, directed at the source of the magical attack. After a few moments of devastating exhale, it took flight again. Several rips were clearly visible in its wings, and its power of flight was waning.

As their ship rounded the rocky boundaries of the harbor's inner opening, the dragon retreated over the western horizon... thousands of the Kingdom's citizens lie dead in the aftermath.

∴∴∴

VEHKS SAW the sprawling city beneath her as an abomination. Gone were the glorious members of her kind; her servants; their structures; the quarry; her home. Feeble buildings, docks and ships had replaced everything she held dear.

Even the landscape had changed. The once glorious mountain to the east had somehow disappeared; replaced with an ocean. Her roost was no more.

Small, insignificant creatures scurried about the streets, fleeing her might and majesty.

She could no longer feel the fear and dread she'd once had for such beings. Gone was her hesitation. Unwavering rage replaced every emotion and drowned out the inexplicable urges which had driven her toward her home. She felt nothing but the need to wipe the pitiful things below her from existence.

With a great heave of her massive chest, she dove toward the city below and exhaled with all her might. The glands in her chest injected particles of volatile mucus into her breath, while the glands in her mouth generated heat and ignited them. Molten fire lay waste to a swath of city as she swooped down and back up again, circling for another pass.

She crossed the city time and time again, breathing fire upon her victims. With each pass, the flames engulfed the city, spreading quickly to surrounding homes and businesses. The burning mucus in her breath clung to the ground, the buildings, and the people below, ensuring the fire would take hold and spread wildly. Arrows filled the sky around her, bouncing harmlessly off her armored scales.

Suddenly, magic bolts streaked through the air and collided with her chest. The energies spread around her torso, constricting and preventing her from taking a breath. Pain coursed through her at a level she'd never before experienced. Unable to breathe, her muscles gave way, and she lost control of her wings, sending her toward the ground in a gentle spiral.

The city shook with her impact as she crashed into buildings, homes, horses, carts, carriages and fleeing citizens. Once a bustling city block, the area crumbled into nothing more than a smoldering debris field, trapped beneath the weight of a hundred-foot-long dragon. She pushed herself off the ground onto her talons.

Whipping her head toward the source of the magical attack, she focused her vision. Six humans stood on a ledge at the northern edge of the city, high on the side of the mountain. Each wore black robes, and they were chanting another spell.

She raised her right talon, palm upward, and focused on the side of the mountain above their head, chanting a spell of her own. With the final word of the spell crossing her draconic lips, she clinched her right talon into a fist and yanked it downward, slamming it into the ground.

The rocky slope above the wizards ripped free of the mountain and crashed violently down atop them, crushing and killing them all. Vehks reared up, inhaled, and blasted the same ledge with fire, making sure of her kill.

Fighting through the pain that wracked her entire body, she pushed herself to take flight. Her torso had suffered severe damage, inside and out. Cracked ribs sent pain shooting through her with every breath. Fragments of peaked roofs, wedged beneath her scales, cut deep into her flesh from the impact of her crash.

The flesh of her wings—torn, swollen and bleeding—could barely hold her aloft. She knew she didn't have long before she would be forced to land, and she no longer knew the terrain; too much had changed. She knew she had to find somewhere to rest—and to heal—before the creatures could gather their forces to retaliate.

∴ ∴ ∴

AYRIEL HAD not provided Tegris enough time to rest before re-enchanting him. His body had almost reached the point where he could no longer continue, and the spells were likely to cause serious damage. She'd ridden him through the rest of the night and most of the next day, intent on reaching Vaelin Palace and Mordechai.

Tegris slowed against her wishes, rearing back and coming to a stop at the Vaelin Crossroads. She dismounted and tried to comfort him. To those in the crossroads upon her arrival, the silvery horse and its rider seemed to appear out of nowhere. Surprised, curious, and a little afraid, many of them drew closer to the pair.

Ayriel turned her attention to them, trying to assure them that all was well and that they should go about their business. Just when she had almost accomplished that task, screams and cries of alarm rang out among them. She followed their gaze and looked southeast... catching sight of a great dragon rising over the distant forest and heading further south, out of sight.

The shock of such a sight, on any normal occasion, would have frozen her where she stood. With everything that had occurred recently, she found she was growing numb to the idea of fabled or extinct foes rising up to confront her Kingdom.

With a sigh, she resigned herself to what she needed to do. Mordechai would have to wait.

She turned back to the crowd, found a man on horseback and approached while he sat staring toward the south, expecting the dragon to return.

"Pardon, good sir, but I am in need of your horse," she said.

He jumped at the sound of her voice, startled. "Excuse me?" he asked rudely. After looking at her, he recognized who she was and shame crossed his face. "I meant nothing by it, your Majesty. Of course! Of course! Take it!"

He climbed out of the saddle and held the reins out to her.

"Your apology is unnecessary, I assure you," she responded with a smile. With a thankful nod, she accepted the reins. "Please take Tegris back to the palace. Inform the guard that I sent you, and that I said you were owed coin for two horses."

"Your majesty, no, I-"

"Nonsense. It is not my place to take from my people," she interrupted. "Now, take Tegris directly to the palace. He is near exhaustion, and will not last for much longer."

"Yes, your Majesty. As you wish," he answered humbly.

His horse was far less powerful than Tegris, so rather than risk enchanting it, she simply mounted. She didn't know what she was going to do about the dragon, but she had an inclination that somehow Laurence was involved and would be there to assist.

It was time she joined the fight.

∴ ∴ ∴

TYLEE WAS in the middle of helping several refugees calm the horses when the dragon re-appeared on the eastern horizon. Screams and cries of concern rang out across the area. They watched in stunned silence as the dragon turned south and flew down toward the horizon, appearing to land some distance away in the southeast.

"Okay, we need to hurry," instructed Tylee.

"How do we know Gaierford's gonna be any safer?" demanded Greta.

"We don't, but standing out here on the open road sure makes us look like a convenient, tasty snack, wouldn't you say?" challenged Tylee.

Several of the refugees heard her and voiced their agreement. The group sprang to life with purpose, shoring up the carriages that remained and getting the horses ready to resume their travels. Delriahna moved ahead with those that were on foot or horseback.

The sun had nearly set when they reached the gates of Gaierford. A large, arched sign proudly announced their arrival in the small, run-down village. Tylee led her carriage to the center of town and pulled it to a stop. She climbed up on top of the carriage and signaled for everyone to gather around. Her mother watched with interest.

"I know that times have been difficult, especially today. However, we made it. We're here, and we're all alive. Half of our battle is won. From this point forward, we are building a new Gaierford. This is our town, and we're going to make it the best town along the Southern Reach!" she began.

Several among the crowd sounded their agreement. The rest kept checking over their shoulder.

"What we need to do for the rest of the day is find a space for everyone to sleep. But before you begin, I want to remind you we are building *new* homes for everyone. None of the houses that currently exist in Gaierford belong to anyone. None of them. Once each house is emptied—as you move into your new homes—they will be converted into businesses, schools and public buildings like libraries and offices.

"So for now, I want families to pick a house, pick a room, and move your family into that one room. Yes, you must share a room with your whole family for now. Together, the families in each home will share the responsibility of upkeep to that home, its property and the shared facilities, such as the kitchen. Be fair, be nice and remember... we're all in this together.

"If you do not have a family with you, find a room in the inn and pick a bed. Be prepared to share your room, as there are barely enough beds to go around. Again, we will be building more appropriate housing for everyone and that includes those of you who do not yet have your own family. Before you question this, I have received word that Gaierford," she said, pausing for effect, "now includes all properties up to and including the town formerly known as Kallenfall. So there is plenty of space to go around!"

Cheers erupted throughout the crowd as her audience realized she wasn't all talk and was going to get things done. Many of them had wished for her type of leadership in Grellenheim.

"Tomorrow I will be inspecting the lands around our new town, and will be working with Aric and Delriahna to parcel the land for homes to be built. The rest of you will spend the day cleaning up the town, moving our supplies into the general store, and other such matters. By the end of the week I hope to hear from each of you what your chosen profession and experience is, so we can allocate farmland to farmers, houses with workshops to blacksmiths, and so forth."

She climbed down from the carriage as the crowd dispersed. Several families walked together, talking about the houses and making plans. The general mood seemed to have improved, though she caught many of them casting a glance southeast to watch for the dragon.

"You've received word, have you?" asked Delriahna as she approached.

"It's better to ask forgiveness than permission," said Tylee with a nod.

"Those are your father's words, dear," scolded Delriahna.

"Kallenfall has been abandoned for decades. Why not claim it and turn this into the next Raven's Nest?" said Tylee.

"Well, we have our work cut out for us."

"Yes we do, mother. Yes, we do."

∴ ∴ ∴

OVER HALF of lowtown and a third of uptown lay in ruins. Fire raged across the city, while those that were capable ran to and from the docks with buckets, attempting to douse the flames. Now and then another piece of a building would give way, crashing to the ground. Each time, several people nearby jumped and hurriedly studied the horizon, fearing the dragon had returned.

Word of the destruction spread quickly to Vellenheim. Workers from the Vaelin Pass—the tunnel that connected the cities—fled quickly when several Trade Commission wizards died horribly to the dragon's retaliatory magic.

The tunnel—a marvel of engineering that none remembered building—allowed for easy transfer of goods through the use of specially designed carts and rails. The central corridor was as wide as the Southern Reach and allowed several carriages to traverse side-by-side down its length. It also boasted a series of taverns and inns at the center, because it was much too long to cross on foot in a single day.

The outer corridors sloped from one end to the other, in opposing directions, allowing carts to cross the entire distance in just a half day, rather than several.

Seeing the destruction of Port Vaelin, and the death of the commission's famed wizards, the workers quickly emptied several carts and escaped at tremendous speeds. Their arrival, and the news they brought with them, sent Vellenheim's warehouse district into a frenzy.

Guards at the trade tunnel's northern gates sent riders to Vaelin Palace, and the Legion fortress high on the northeastern quadrant of the city. Citizens went into a panic, many of them running home to pack their most precious belongings and flee. Chaos ensued on the streets of lower Vellenheim, causing the deaths of nearly a hundred citizens; trampled beneath horses, carriage wheels, and the feet of their neighbors.

Vellenheim's central Wayfarer's Respite boasted no less than twelve inns, so that those crossing the city could rest along their journey. On foot, the city was several days' walk across. As a result, many residents who grew up in a particular section of the city rarely found need to venture elsewhere.

Vellenheim's size made enchanted horses a matter of necessity for the city guard. Never had they been more essential than that day. The riders accomplished their task quickly, considering the staggering size of the city.

Lord Commander Elrend immediately dispatched aid to Port Vaelin and gathered his council of advisers to decide their next course of action.

King Orluhnd IV declared the attack a tragedy and ordered the palace Quartermaster to send immediate financial aid and supplies to those affected.

News did not take long to spread throughout the palace and find its way to Mordechai.

"That must be why the Velloth were loosed," he surmised. "Silith!" he called out.

"Yes, Mordechai? What do you need?" she answered, silently weeping at the tragic loss of life.

"Lead me to Ayriel's desk. Please," he requested, trying to phrase his words gently to avoid distressing her further. Silith came to his side and, like she had done many times during his stay, placed her hand under his right elbow. Once he had arrived at the desk, she moved the chair for him and helped him sit.

"Is there anything else, Lord?" she asked.

"I will need a small cauldron, or bowl. It needs to be metal, and have an opening this size," he said, gesturing with his fingers to form a circle. He listened as her feet pattered across the floor and back to his side, followed by a small 'thunk' on the desk as a small, but heavy, bowl came to rest before him.

"Thank you, precious Silith. Now, please leave the room. I must have silence."

"Yes, Lord," she said.

Her demeanor had brightened at the sound of Mordechai calling her precious. He was not one to show emotion often, and she knew that he was suffering. Those facts made his words mean more to her than he could know. Smiling, despite her tears, she left the room and closed the door.

Mordechai reached into his robe and withdrew the small box whose contents he'd used to divine Nightweaver. He was about to try something he had never done before, and could feel fear creeping in. Pausing for a moment, he considered the ramifications of scrying an ancient dragon. He'd lost his sight divining an ancient witch, so there was no telling what the outcome of his plan would be.

To make matters more challenging, he'd never attempted to divine while blind. With enough focus and a known target, he'd been able to bring forth both images and sounds in the past. However, he'd never tried to use sound alone. He wasn't sure it was possible.

He hoped to divine the dragon's name or age; anything that could help determine where it came from, and why it attacked. The dragons of eastern Gargoa had long been extinct, by all accounts.

He knew dragons still lived in the western territories of Gargoa, and the northern half of Xulrathia. However, a dragon approaching from the far west would have attacked more targets along its flight path. One arriving from the far east would have approached from the direction of Pelrigoss. All indications pointed toward a dragon rising from within Arkhania.

He needed to do something he had only read about in one place; the same place he learned his form of teleportation from; the ancient tome written in his own hand.

Most wizards who accomplished teleportation spent most of their lives learning the art. In addition, their form of teleportation had limited range, drained them of every ounce of power they could muster, and often caused severe, undesirable side effects. He'd once studied those same methods, attempting to achieve teleportation. After discovering the tome in an ancient crypt, his entire approach toward magic had changed.

He accomplished his own teleportation through Time magic. Through extreme mental focus, he could picture a location, calculate its position upon the world, the world's position in space, and then push himself through Time. The effort required to accomplish the task was tremendous, and prohibitive for normal use.

The tome suggested placing unique runes at common destinations. Using those runes, he could focus his mind on their position in relation to the world's magical weave and simply will himself to be there. Placing runes across Arkhania allowed him to cross the Kingdom in the blink of an eye, with very little effort.

Effectively, his techniques made his form of teleportation illegal according to the laws imposed and enforced by Fel'Vizsiour. He wasn't teleporting, in the mythical sense, so much as time traveling.

The task before him involved similar powers. He needed to divine the beast's history until he found another dragon speaking its name. He needed to scry through Time.

Carefully, he prepared the crystal as he'd done before. Leaning back in the chair, he considered what he was about to do. The tome contained several pages detailing the process of scrying through Time, but he didn't have it with him, and of course had no vision with which to read it.

No living soul knew that simple magics derived from the Weave required no effort from him. He could cast those spells through sheer force of will. The power behind them derived from the Magical Weave that surrounded the planet, and it simply did his bidding.

There were limits to how strong a spell he could cast that way. Anything stronger, or anything having to do with elemental powers, such as Time, took actual effort. If he tried to do too much, those greater powers could hurt or even kill him.

Steeling himself for whatever may come, he leaned forward and began to chant.

Hours later, Silith found him passed out on the floor, dried blood in a trail down his cheek from one of his ears.

∴ ∴ ∴

AGNAR SPENT most of the day riding at the very rear of the formation. The loss of Bingrolf weighed heavily on him, as did the destruction of his family's farm and their capture by the Velloth. He ran the events of the ritual chamber through his mind over and over, trying to recognize any of the humans they sacrificed to summon the dragon. No matter how hard he tried, he couldn't identify any of the people he'd seen as someone he knew.

There was a nagging sensation lingering beneath his every thought that told him he had missed them in the group. However, his conscious mind told him that both his and Bingrolf's parents still lived; trapped somewhere as prisoners of the vile elves.

Laurence slowed his pace halfway through the day to ride beside his friend. He could see the sadness in Agnar's eyes and understood better than anyone the pain his friend felt. Knowing that words would not suffice to ease his pain, he rode in silence to offer support and remind Agnar that he wasn't alone.

As the day lengthened—sunlight casting long shadows in front of them—the lines of mounted soldiers in front of them came to an abrupt stop. Soldiers dismounted and guided their horses off a distance to the south, returning to the formation with swords and shields prepared for battle. Seeing the event unfold from a distance, Laurence and Agnar had no idea what was going on.

Thax and Halgar stood high atop their saddles, calling out their findings to Kotann and pointing northwest. Laurence stood in his stirrups, peering in the same direction. Descending a hill in the distance was a series of mounted individuals leading several riderless horses behind them. They appeared to be heading on an intercept course with their own group.

Laurence settled back into his saddle and looked over at a very confused Agnar. "We're being joined by riders from the northwest. Fel'Rechaun, the Legion or something else entirely. I can't be sure from this distance. Let's catch up to the others and find out what's going on," he suggested.

"Aye!" barked Agnar in agreement.

A few moments later they stood with their group, weapons ready. Tensions were high, after all they'd been through. None of them had slept and many were still sore or suffering from minor injuries from their battle with the Velloth. Their horses were on the brink of exhaustion, and none of them had eaten all day.

"It's Karzden!" announced Thax. He and Halgar dropped to the ground and walked over to the others.

Sighs of relief echoed through the crowd as they sheathed their weapons and stowed their shields. Several of the younger soldiers patted each other on the shoulder.

Laurence knew at the back of his mind that their arrival changed nothing. He needed to see the situation through, and he dragon was getting further away.

"You are a sight for sore eyes!" yelled Kotann as they neared.

Karzden arrived with a dozen guards and two dozen students from Fel'Rechaun. Trailing behind them was an equal number of horses, allowing for his group to travel farther distances between rests by swapping mounts. It didn't appear to Laurence as if they planned on camping.

Karzden dismounted and greeted Kotann. "Clearly you've kicked a dragon's nest," he joked.

"We've much to discuss," answered Kotann. He waved Laurence over to join them as they left the group behind. After reaching enough distance to talk in private, Karzden's demeanor shifted from one of greeting to one of distress. They picked a spot atop a small hill and stood watching the eastern sky while they talked.

"As you might assume, we found the Velloth," started Kotann. "Their path cut through the marshes just as Kyrilis described, bearing west after a time and ending at an ancient ruin located there. Several raiding parties departed from the ruin and razed the farmsteads along the southern border of the delta," he explained.

"So many deaths," said Karzden, sadness lacing his words.

"Oh, but it gets better. They didn't kill the residents of those farmsteads. Because, of course, why would they? No, they dragged them back to the ruin and completed a ritual, deep underground," explained Kotann.

"They what?" Karzden exclaimed.

"We fought our way into underground chambers beneath the ruin, through Velloth and undead. There was a ritual chamber deep inside where they sacrificed the farmers and then blew some kind of horn," explained Laurence.

"It's a simple deduction, and perhaps inaccurate, but it could be that this ritual was specifically to wake, or summon, that dragon," added Kotann.

"That would indicate that the dragon was the entire reason for Nightweaver unleashing them upon the Kingdom in the first place," said Karzden. "Which would make Gaierford, Grellenheim and the farmsteads collateral damage."

"More likely the cities were meant to disrupt the Kingdom's stability and cause distraction," corrected Laurence. "Each location seemed to be specifically targeted. They didn't wander or search for something to attack. In fact, they avoided Fel'Rechaun on their way to Grellenheim and arrived with great haste. Not only that, but they sent only the forces they needed to each location.

"Had we not arrived in Grellenheim when we did, the fifty or so Velloth they sent would've easily overwhelmed that entire city. It's as if they somehow knew exactly what they needed based on the defenses of each location," Laurence explained.

"In the end, they actually won. We didn't arrive in time to stop their ritual, and the dragon was loosed upon us. Who knows what damage that beast has already caused as we blindly charge across the plains. We've not had sight of the foul thing for hours, and even then it was but a speck on the horizon," lamented Kotann.

"We saw it on the southern horizon from Fel'Rechaun. Fahrul sent me out to intercept the beast with whoever we could find in the courtyard at the time. Not that I was looking forward to fighting a dragon, mind you, those arts are long lost to tales and legends, but we couldn't just stand by and watch further destruction from afar. He also sent word to the Legion, but we didn't wait for a response," said Karzden.

"Do you think they could see it from Raven's Nest?" asked Laurence, concerned for Tylee.

"I don't think so, lad," Karzden said. Suddenly realizing why Laurence had asked, and remembering that Laurence wasn't up to speed on recent events, he grabbed Laurence's shoulder. "Tylee isn't in Raven's Nest now, Laur. She took your assistance to the refugees to heart and has volunteered to be Constable of Gaierford. She's leading them all there now to rebuild the town," he explained reassuringly.

The news did not reassure Laurence as Karzden had hoped. In fact, his previous curiosity had changed to desperation. "She's in its path!" he yelled as he turned and ran.

"Crap!" exclaimed Karzden.

Laurence ran over to the fresher horses which hadn't been carrying riders and hastily mounted one. Without a word to anyone, he kicked his mount into action and raced eastward. Izabel, Wil and Agnar took notice and raced over to fresh horses themselves. Kotann and Karzden, headed back to the group and watched as three more horses raced off trailing Laurence.

"That man inspires loyalty, I'll give him that," said Kotann.

Karzden grunted his agreement, and disapproval.

∴ ∴ ∴

VEHKSTAERELLIOX LAY atop the ashes of felled trees, craggy bits of rock, dirt, and sand. Salty waves lapped up and over her tail, calming her as she attempted to enter the dream world. The island was barely big enough to hold her, but she hadn't had many options. She hoped that her distance from the mainland would provide her enough time to recover before the tiny invaders could make it to her.

As she'd left the mainland, dozens of ships had dotted the sea. Unlike the Toor, these creatures had conquered the waters, so she knew they would be capable of reaching her eventually. Also unlike the Toor, they had spread far and wide building permanent homes, cities and ports.

The Toor had been easy to control. Driving nomadic tribes to relocate, and twisting them to their will, had been easy for her people. Easier still when one considered the Toor's lack of magical capabilities. The pain in her ribs reminded her that these invaders, though small and feeble, were far more powerful than they seemed.

Landing on the shores of the island had revealed even more injuries along her legs, talons, and hindquarters. Scales had fallen off in her flight, exposing the bare flesh beneath. She'd bled substantially while pulling up the trees on the small island to craft a make-shift nest. Breathing fire on the carefully placed logs had been an excruciating experience; one that nearly caused her to pass out.

After removing chunks of debris and pieces of buildings from her flesh, she laid atop the pile of ash with a groan. She yearned for Hahrfurgadhen and his healing ways, for they were arts she never learned. Why would she have? She had him to aid her. She would always have him to aid her.

Finally falling asleep, she lamented the accuracy of her prophecies.

∴ ∴ ∴

TYLEE STOOD in the fields west of Gaierford, waiting for Delriahna and Aric to join her. The three of them had skipped dawnfry and headed immediately to the fields with plans to inspect and parcel the land for future construction.

Milling around impatiently, she glanced toward the west and something caught her eye. Several travelers were approaching from the plains on foot.

"Who do you think it is?" asked Aric as he arrived.

"I don't know," answered Tylee.

They watched as four figures walked toward them, studying as best they could in an attempt to discern their intent. After what seemed like an hour, Tylee jumped and squealed. "It's Laurence!" she belted.

Before either of them could respond, she ran across the field to greet him.

∴ ∴ ∴

"TYLEE!" YELLED Laurence as she approached. The group stopped walking as she closed in. Adrenaline coursed through his veins, giving him fresh energy. His companions sunk to the ground, desperate for rest.

Izabel looked up at him as if he were magical, and not just equipped with enchanted gear.

"I've missed you so much!" Tylee yelled as their bodies collided into an embrace.

"Are you okay?" he asked, gently pushing her back to inspect her.

"Yes, yes. I'm fine. A big ole dragon ate some of our horses and gave us a scare, but everyone's fine," she answered. "A dragon! Can you believe it?" she exclaimed excitedly.

"We're chasing that dragon. Karzden came out to join us and said you were in Gaierford. That was the direction we saw the dragon heading, so I left our forces behind and raced here to check on you," he explained.

"On foot? How far have you been running?" she inquired.

"No, dear. We departed on horseback but eventually had to release them and continue on foot. I didn't want to stop for camp and risk your death, if I could get here fast enough to prevent it," he answered.

"We're fine. It looked like the dragon flew over to Port Vaelin and attacked, but it's in the southeast now. Or at least that's the direction we saw it fly," she explained.

"What's this, then?" asked Delriahna, walking up to them.

Aric followed closely behind, excited to meet their visitors.

"We came to check on you after we heard about the move to Gaierford," explained Laurence. "Right now... we need fresh horses. We've a dragon to find, and a countryside to save."

"What you need, dear, is rest," insisted Delriahna. She could see their exhaustion clearly.

"Let's get you all back to town and fed," offered Tylee.

Begrudgingly, Laurence's companions got to their feet and followed. Delriahna noticed Agnar's depression and felt for him. She walked beside him on the way back to town and listened as he explained all that had happened.

By the time they reached Gaierford, Izabel, Delriahna, Tylee, and Agnar were quietly crying.

∴ ∴ ∴

AYRIEL HAD ridden through the night, and it had taken a toll on her borrowed horse. Frustrated and exhausted, it buckled its knees and dropped to the ground, refusing to go any further. She understood how it felt. She'd been on the road for days without rest. With a reassuring pat on its neck, she climbed out of the saddle and continued on foot.

Dawn approached, and the sky was crystal clear. A cool breeze blew in from the west, hinting at the coming winter. Autumn had always been her favorite season, but she feared such trying times would taint those feelings. She knew it was her sense of duty that had brought her into the situation.

What do I know about fighting dragons, she wondered.

She decided to walk south to Salvation Shire before turning East. It wasn't clear to her where the dragon had gone, but there was a chance the cities along the southern reach might have suffered from its passing.

Besides, I might be able to procure another horse in Salvation Shire, or the Legion could catch up with me there, she decided.

As sunlight cleared the eastern terrain, casting better light on the road, a pile of debris caught her eye. Sitting on the eastern side of the road lay the remnants of a wagon and several cages. The animals in the wreckage seemed to have died recently. Inspecting the area, she determined that a large caravan of travelers had passed through recently, leaving deep channels in the muddy road. On the western edge, directly across from the wrecked wagon, a large swath of the ground was dug out toward the center like a trench.

It was clear that something had happened, and the road toward Gaierford lie directly beside the evidence. She accelerated into a jog and turned toward Gaierford. She was certain that the dragon had attacked someone on the Reach, and that they'd taken to Gaierford seeking shelter. As a princess, it was her duty to care for her people. Even if she didn't have a horse, coin, food, supplies or an army to help defend them.

The detour would delay finding the dragon, but part of her wanted to stall for others to join her fight with the dragon, anyway. She didn't relish the thought of facing it alone, but would die trying if it meant saving lives.

As she jogged, she really hoped it wouldn't come to that.

∴ ∴ ∴

LAURENCE, IZABEL, Wil and Agnar sat on the steps of the general store as they ate, watching the new citizens of Gaierford. Every one of the refugees, including their children, worked to repair the town, organize building supplies and help Tylee parcel the land for optimal distribution of goods and services.

He found it refreshing to see the excitement and hope for the future that they possessed. Laurence couldn't help but be proud, and in awe, of the woman Tylee was becoming. Somewhere deep inside, she was still the little girl he met on his first trip to town as a boy.

Standing at the apple cart in front of town hall while waiting on her father, she'd held her little apple like it was the most spectacular thing in the world. At first, he felt jealous of her apple, but when he caught sight of her face and her deep, blue eyes… he forgot about everything else. Even at the age of five, she had instantly become the most important person in the world to him.

When she noticed him, she gasped and dropped her prized possession. In hindsight, her initial reaction seemed appropriate. His family had relocated to the area and lived outside of town. He was likely the first dark-skinned child she'd ever seen, and just as much a novelty to her as she was to him.

Excitedly, he ran over to her apple and picked it up, rescuing it from the dirty street. After brushing it off on his shirt, he handed it back to her and asked, "Are you an elf?" drawing quite a bit of laughter from her in response.

"No, silly, you are!" Tylee had responded, drawing an equal amount of laughter from him.

They were friends from that moment on, and Laurence remembered asking to visit 'tie-wee' many times in the months that followed. As he stood and kissed his beautiful, brilliant wife, he thought how strong and wonderful a woman she had become.

A disturbance from the east interrupted their moment, as people all around them called out, "Tour Majesty!" and "It's the Princess!" in various degrees of respect and shock.

Laurence separated himself from his wife's embrace to see Ayriel running into town.

"Horses just aren't what they used to be," joked Laurence.

"Tell me about it!" returned Ayriel, coming to a stop in front of him.

"What brings you to Gaierford?" asked Laurence.

"Long, long story. The short version is, I was at the Vaelin

Crossroads and saw a dragon crest the horizon and fly southeast. So, knowing I couldn't just *leave that* for someone else to handle, I-"

"Charged south, exhausted your horse and had to run the rest of the way here in your nightclothes," completed Laurence.

"Well, of course! What else does one fight a dragons wearing?" she joked.

"Armor," said Agnar. "Usually armor."

"Your Majesty!" exclaimed Delriahna, bursting out of the store.

"I appreciate your recognition, my lady, but there's no time for ceremony," responded Ayriel, still gasping for breath. "What I need right now is something to eat, a horse and maybe a change of clothes. Anything more fitting for a battle than my nightclothes and this elvish robe," she finished, laughing.

"I'll see to it, my lady!" answered Delriahna with fervor. As she turned to go back into the store, something caught her eye at the western edge of town. Pointing, she called out, "It seems your army has caught up to you, Laur!"

Considering for a moment, she stepped back into the street and yelled, "Quickly! I need cooks and anyone skilled with horses to come with me *right now*! We have a literal army to feed!"

"Thank you, mother!" exclaimed Tylee as her mother walked by.

Delriahna and several volunteers poured into the store to prepare for their guests.

Kotann, Karzden and their forces came to a stop at the center of town, filling the street with horses and men.

Several citizens ran over and volunteered to take the reins of their horses while they dismounted and found a place to sit and rest.

"You can't go running off like that, Laurence!" chided Kotann as he walked up.

"I know, I just had to check on-"

"Your wife. I get it, but you're a soldier now, or *training* to be. You have a duty, and that duty must come first," scolded Karzden.

"Go easy on him," said Ayriel.

"Your Majesty!" said a shocked Kotann with a bow.

"Stop with the pleasantries, we've work to do," said Ayriel.

"You are joining the hunt?" asked Karzden.

"I'm not here for the biscuits," answered Ayriel with a smirk.

Karzden turned to Kotann, grabbed him by the shoulder and shouted, "our odds improve!"

"Why don't we all rest for a bit? My mother-in-law and several townsfolk are seeing to your meal as we speak, and we all deserve a moment to shake off the journey we've had. There will be plenty of time later to plot and plan the destruction of a dragon," suggested Laurence.

"If there's anything our town can do for you, just say the word," offered Tylee. She smiled and stuck her hand out toward Kotann and Karzden and added, "Constable Ravencrest at your service."

One at a time, they shook her hand with a nod of respect to her position.

Ayriel walked up to Wil, sadness in her eyes. With a nod, she signaled that they should walk away from the rest to talk in private.

"You are Ekthri, are you not?" she asked.

"Yes, my lady," he answered, unsure what to expect.

"Then I have the unfortunate duty of sharing ill tidings. I'm afraid that the dragon's arrival brought additional consequences. Giants and Skaar fled the Mythaeil Mountains and, due to their path, your capital city Ayr'Thugohn suffered for their panic," she said, placing her hand on his shoulder.

Tears welled up in his eyes. "What of my father, King Faelrin?"

Ayriel's face went stark white. She hadn't known Laurence's friend was a Prince. In fact, she wasn't sure that anyone at the school knew his status. Thinking this might have been intentional, she continued, "I am more sorry than I can possibly convey. I was in Ayr'Thugohn when everything started and was below the city when the creatures arrived. A fire giant destroyed the palace before I could even think to respond." Her eyes filled with tears at the memory.

"Thank you for informing me, your Eminence," he replied, unable to think of anything else. Without another word, he walked off to deal with the news.

∴ ∴ ∴

AFTER EATING and getting a short nap, Laurence met with Karzden, Kotann and Ayriel. Tylee showed them to a table in the common room of the inn with coffee that Delriahna had prepared.

"I've made sure the inn is empty, so you won't be disturbed. If you need anything, I'll be right outside," she said. Tylee sent a wink and a nod toward Laurence as she left the room and shut them in.

"She's pleasant," Ayriel said to Laurence as she pressed a mug to her lips, blowing gently across its hot contents.

"I think we've had enough pleasantries. We don't know where the dragon is, how to find it, or how long it will be there. We need a plan, and a good one," said Karzden.

"How do you propose we kill it, Karzden? Dragons are legends. Nobody in this Kingdom has ever seen one before. Ever," declared Ayriel.

"That thing passed right over our heads at the ruin. It's larger than anything I've ever seen," said Kotann.

"Where did it even come from? You'd think we would've *accidentally* run into a sleeping dragon by now," said Laurence.

"Kundarr, the volcano in Mythaeil Mountains. It erupted, driving giants and Skaar through all of Ekthri Wood, destroying their capital city and gods know what else," said Ayriel.

"So this isn't just a problem for our Kingdom," Laurence surmised.

"Lad, the Ekthri people *are* a part of our Kingdom. They are a city-state within our Arkhania's borders, just like the Afyr. King Orluhnd III ruled with an iron fist, and strained relations with them; causing them to threaten to secede. When Orluhnd IV took the throne, he made peace with them by allowing them to act with autonomy as their own city-state within our borders. Kyrilis was assigned to Fel'Rechaun in fulfillment of part of those treaties," explained Kotann.

"Wil must be devastated," said Laurence. Suddenly it felt as if his friend was more important to him than the dragon.

"He is, but he will overcome it," offered Ayriel.

"Back to the task at hand, we need to figure out our options. We're not getting any younger here, and if you want my help, we're going to have to get a move on," said Karzden.

"By its flight path I assume it was leaving Port Vaelin," said Ayriel.

"Aye, and that means we won't be receiving any help from the Legion any time soon. They'll have their hands full," said Kotann.

"Tylee said it flew southeast from there," added Laurence.

"That is what I saw as well," said Ayriel.

"There isn't much southeast of Port Vaelin. It doesn't seem likely that the dragon attacked any other towns. Perhaps they wounded it at the port?" asked Laurence.

"That would stand to reason, considering this town and the others to the north are still standing... though I don't know how they managed to injure it," answered Ayriel.

"Well, the only thing I'm aware of in that direction is farmland and fishing villages," said Kotann.

"Cragenfell," said Karzden with a nod.

"Pardon?" asked Ayriel.

"Best oysters in the Kingdom. The fishermen of Cragenfell harvest them in the channels between the small islands that dot the coast," offered Karzden. "It's east of Salvation Shire, right on the shore. It's a small fishing town with not much else around. More importantly, getting to the dragon if it's on one of those islands is going to be a real pain in the ass with our forces. And if it hit Port Vaelin as we suspect, we won't have a navy to assist us."

"Dragons are thought to be quite intelligent. If they injured the beast badly enough to stop its attacks and drive it away, then it stands to reason it had the wisdom to seek those isles to rest in relative safety," discerned Ayriel.

"Well, it's a better plan than sitting around here, waiting for another attack. Let's round up the men and get moving," said Kotann.

With nods of agreement, the rest of them threw back what they had left of their coffee and got to work.

∴ ∴ ∴

MORDECHAI SHOT upright in bed. The pain in his head pulsed and throbbed from the motion, making him dizzy. With his hands on his temples, trying to fend off the pain, he called out, "Silith!"

"My lord!" she responded, running across the room to him frantically.

"How long was I out?" he asked.

"An entire day, my Lord," she answered.

"Don't call me 'my lord', Silith. I consider you a friend," he said. "Besides, the sound of it makes the pain worse."

"Very well, but... what happened?"

"I was a *moron*," he answered.

"I find that impossible to believe," she laughed.

"You know that I cannot remember my past."

"Yes, Ayriel has explained such to me."

"My memory goes back as far as our history does. Everything prior is but legend," he explained.

"What do you mean?" she asked.

"We are living in what some scribes refer to as the Second Era of Man. They call it such, because it's beginning marks the rise of Arkhania. All history before that is, as might seem obvious, the *First Era of Man*," he said.

"I have heard of such things. My father enjoyed the study of our history," she said proudly.

"Do you know of any history prior to the First Era? Anything further back than around twelve-hundred years?" he inquired. He was already sure of the answer, but wanted her to think about what he was about to say.

"Well, um... no? I mean, there are legends, but-"

"Precisely. There are only legends; no written history; no living soul that remembers anything of that time. It's as if we all just appeared out of thin air and yet... our cities already existed; people knew how to live their lives; we clearly had a civilization prior to the First Era. In fact, we've *thoroughly* documented the First Era. And yet... we still know nothing of the time before it," he explained.

"How is that possible?" she asked, clearly intrigued.

"I now know why we cannot remember that time; why no history exists with which to learn of it. Something is blocking us. Some *force* caused all living creatures to forget their past, aside from the few carvings, cave paintings and legends that remained. Legends that, it would appear, were left intact to serve as a warning. As for everything else, we are apparently forbidden from knowing," he said in frustration.

"But how-" she started.

"I tried to divine the dragon. To do so, I had to listen and feel into the past. No matter how hard I tried, I could not breach the barrier. Twelve-hundred and thirty-three years and I was stopped. I pushed and pushed to no avail. The harder I tried, the more it hurt... until eventually, I woke up in this bed. I have failed to learn what I was after, but I have learned two things in its place.

"The first is that my memory was lost twelve-hundred and thirty-three years ago whenever this 'barrier' was put into place. It wasn't an accident, as I originally thought. The second is that whatever event caused my memory loss affected the entire world. For now, I must focus on resolving these troubles that have beset the Kingdom, so that I might then turn all my powers toward finding out what this barrier is, and why it exists."

∴ ∴ ∴

THE NEXT day, northbound travelers filled the Southern Reach as the army made its way south. Many of them were fleeing Salvation Shire and Cragenfell, pleading for help as soldiers rode past them. As soon as the crowds cleared and it was safe to do so, Kotann hastened their pace. Several eye witnesses had confirmed the location of the dragon and all that remained was to get there before the beast flew somewhere else.

Night fell just as they reached the eastern edge of Salvation Shire. Kotann called for a full stop a few hours later, knowing that what lay ahead of them would push them to their limits. Their journey was nearly complete, but he knew exhaustion would doom them if they pressed on.

"Camp here for the night! We must be rested when we face this beast!" ordered Kotann.

"No campfires, and I want six guards at all times!" added Karzden.

With nods to each other, Kotann and Karzden dismounted and their forces followed suit. The road beneath them was a simple, dirt farm road that weaved between fields of wheat, corn, soy, potatoes and other crops. Small side roads were frequent, each leading to a farmhouse, barn and small out-buildings.

"Try to camp on the roads, not in the fields!" yelled Ayriel. "It is almost harvest, and our people have lost enough to this calamity! The last thing we need is a ruined harvest and starvation to add to our kingdom's troubles!"

"How far to Cragenfell?" Laurence asked Karzden.

"A few hours, more or less. Kotann thinks we should leave before sunrise. So, get some rest while you can. We won't be here for long," explained Karzden.

A short distance away, Ayriel approached Wil, who was still depressed and hadn't spoken. Izabel had watched him the entire day with sadness in her eyes.

"Will you help me, Wilwarianel?" Ayriel asked. He responded only with a nod, his eyes still facing his horse. "I need to gather some beans. Not a lot, mind you, but enough to enchant our horses for tomorrow's task." Turning to Izabel and Agnar, she asked, "would the both of you collect every bow and arrow our archers possess? I will enchant them as well."

Izabel and Agnar handed their reins to a nearby soldier and ran off to do Ayriel's bidding. Ayriel calmly took Wil's reins and passed them off as well. Holding his hand in hers, she led him into the soy field nearby and began their collection efforts. As they walked, she found herself grateful for the use of Delriahna's traveling leathers, and the many pouches and pockets they came with. She made a mental note to wear such clothing whenever she wasn't in court.

That night, while most of the forces slept, Ayriel stayed awake and prepared for the next day's challenge. With Wil as her assistant, she cast a series of enchantments on their collection of soybeans, and then proceeded to the bows and arrows. By the end of the lengthy process, dawn loomed on the distant horizon, and she struggled to stay awake.

"What will these accomplish?" asked Wil, breaking his silence.

"We will feed each horse one bean. It will allow them to run three times faster than a normal horse, and it will cost little effort for them to do so. The effects will last until they pass the bean, and the bean will collect toxins as it passes through them to limit any side effects.

"I have enchanted the bows to give them extra force. Any arrow that flies from them will travel twice as far as normal, in the same span of time... meaning they will be faster. I have enchanted the arrows to pierce scale and hide, specifically.

"They wouldn't have any additional strength against an armored foe, like a knight. However, most animals will be exceptionally vulnerable to them. I have made a few assumptions in the casting, though. The toughest hide or skin I've ever faced was a Skaar, and I assume a dragon's scales to be several times tougher than a Skaar's. So, I have attempted to make the arrows strong enough to pierce through scale that is three times stronger than a Skaar's," she explained.

"That will certainly help," said Wil.

"Truth be told, I wish there was more I could do to prepare us. The enchantments on the bows and arrows will only last half a day, at most. That is why I waited to perform those spells last. However, I must rest if I am to be of any use during the fight. I don't know many attack spells, but I won't even have those if I don't get some sleep.

"I've already done more spellcasting this evening than I've ever done in a single day, and I feel hollow inside, as if stripped bare within the core of my being," she said.

"I will watch over you, my lady," said Wil.

"Thank you," she answered.

Ayriel only managed to get a few hours of sleep before Wil woke her. Blinking the sleep out of her eyes, she looked up at him and whispered, "Thank you," before standing. She could feel that she wasn't at full strength, but her time was up and whatever power she could muster would have to do.

"I already passed out the beans, bows and arrows. Everyone's packed up, and most have already mounted. I waited to wake you until the last moment I could, my Lady," said Wil.

His tone was still somber, but his mood seemed to be improving. "Have all the horses eaten their beans?" she asked, steadying herself with a hand on his shoulder.

"Yes, my Lady. Even your own," he answered.

"Very well, let's be underway."

∴ ∴ ∴

SEVERAL SOLDIERS yelled in delight at their horses' new pace. Karzden barked at them to quiet down, seeing their destination ahead of them.

As a result of Ayriel's enchantments, they reached Cragenfell in under an hour. Kotann signaled for them to stop and dismount. The gravity of the situation set in as they followed his instructions. All wonder and cheer experienced on their short ride instantly faded, replaced with a looming sense of dread as they focused on the task at hand.

Cragenfell was a small fishing town, as fishing towns go, with fewer than a dozen buildings in total. All but one of which was a fisherman's family home, each laid out in a row from north to south. To the east of the homes stood the fishery, standing twice as tall as any other building and several times as long.

The fishery jutted out over the water on a massive pier, with small docks sticking out of each side. Several offices inside the building's second floor offered a commanding view of the surrounding waters, allowing officials to more easily coordinate the comings and goings of the town's many vessels.

The building's first floor provided storage for their catch and equipment for production of several fish-related byproducts. Many fishermen commissioned fishery workers for the production of fish oil, one of the chief exports of Cragenfell, whenever they caught fish unpopular for dining.

Several boats of varying sizes knocked rhythmically against the docks as the morning tide sent waves toward the shore. Cool, damp, salty air permeated the town accompanied by hints of old fish and oil.

Beneath it all was a smell none of them could quite place. It came and went as the air shifted about them, smelling of rot and sulfur.

As the soldiers joined Thax and Halgar on the shore, the dim light of early dawn revealed to them a terrifying sight. Across the water were several islands, on the largest of which appeared to be a massive, sleeping dragon.

"How can we defeat such a thing," muttered a soldier.

Ignoring the soldier's fearful pondering, Kotann said, "we're going to have to row out there, Karzden."

"There aren't enough boats," answered Karzden. "The larger ones would take too long to rig, and couldn't go ashore once we arrived. Besides, our men aren't sailors. That leaves us with a random collection of dinghies."

"With the archers you brought, and the ones in my Vintain, we have six men that might be capable of fighting from here," said Kotann. "It's unlikely the entire battle will take place on the island. It's far too small, with that thing taking up the whole of it."

"So, we're going to split our forces? Are you hoping to stir the beast and drive it off of the island? If we use arrows and whatever spells Ayriel, Gharick and Berril can muster, then the whole of our forces can engage her when she comes over to fight back. It'll take all of us," countered Laurence.

"What would stop her from just attacking us from a distance? We need to drive her off the island, not attempt to lure her to us," answered Kotann.

"It could work," said Ayriel, joining them.

"Fine. I'll lead some men to the island," said Kotann. "Laurence, you stay here with the archers and casters on the beach. Be ready to draw her over to the mainland. Karzden, hide the rest of our forces behind the homes in town and bring them out to assault her when she lands."

"But-" started Laurence.

"Listen, kid. You're going to make a fine warrior, but this is something that is beyond us. I'll take Wil and a few of Karzden's men. I'd rather have our best combatants here for the most dangerous part of this plan," Kotann said firmly. Realizing how he had sounded, he turned back to Laurence with an apologetic expression. "Look, I mean no offense but... fucking dragon," he finished, pointing at the beast.

"Alright, you heard the man! Archers! Casters! To the shore with Laurence and wait for his order to attack!" belted Karzden.

Kotann walked through the crowd, telling Wil and eight of Karzden's Initiates to join him.

As Karzden led the rest of the soldiers out of sight, fear gripped most of the combatants.

Five boats began making their way toward the island a few minutes later, the soft slap of the occasional oar reaching Laurence's ears. One of the boats suddenly scraped against a rocky outcropping just below the water. Oars crashed into the water in response, as those on the dinghy attempted to free the boat and correct their course.

Vehks raised her head and turned to peer in the sound's direction.

The men in the boat yelled out in fear.

"Attack!" yelled Laurence. Thax and Halgar looked at Laurence, hesitating. "Now! Draw the beast here before it kills them all!"

Arrows streaked across the sky faster than should have been possible, two burying themselves deep into Vehks's right side, the others falling just short of their target. She reared back in pain and rose to her feet, turning to face her oncoming foes. Logs snapped against rocks as she stood on her hind legs, readying her fiery breath.

Three arrows pierced her neck, sending waves of pain through her.

She abandoned her plans to set the boats ablaze and decided, instead, to get out of harm's way and take to the sky. With a forceful flap of her wings, she jumped into the air and took flight. The gust of wind from her ascent blasted down on the boats, capsizing three of them outright and sending the others into the rocks.

Ayriel, Gharick and Berril began to chant as the dragon took flight. One by one, their spells slammed into the dragon.

Gharick's spell attacked the beast's right wing, exploding with holy energy and tearing the wing further open.

Berril's spell sent a holy bolt of energy straight for the beast's chest, sending searing pain throughout its torso, but doing little else.

Ayriel's spell ripped a pocket of air from beneath the dragon's wings, changing the air pressure and sending her into a downward spiral.

Several arrows pierced her flesh as she tumbled through the air, crashing to the ground north of the row of houses.

Karzden, Laurence and all those on dry land raced to engage the dragon as she came to a stop and scrambled to her feet.

She peered back toward the casters, now running toward her, and raised her right front talon in their direction, two claws pointed directly at Gharick and Berril. With a horrific roar that sounded vaguely like words, she uttered a spell and clinched her fist.

Gharick and Berril fell to their knees, screaming, as blood erupted from their chests; their organs spilling to the ground.

Six more arrows streaked through the air, piercing the great beast's chest.

Karzden and two of his men raced past the dragon and attacked her back legs.

Mucus ignited as it left her throat, covering a dozen soldiers in molten flames as they approached.

Screams of anguish and death filled the air.

Vehks kicked her left leg at the two attackers that wailed on her harmlessly from behind, sending them both flying dozens of feet.

Karzden jumped back and rolled out of the way as she kicked with her right.

Ayriel finished chanting her second spell, changing the air inside Vehks's throat to ice.

The great dragon gasped for breath, dropping to the ground in panic.

Laurence, Izabel and Agnar raced in, attacking the flailing dragon's head and neck as best they could.

Four more arrows streaked through the air, hitting the dragon's left shoulder.

Izabel's blade grazed the dragon's left eye, but appeared to have no effect.

Agnar, wielding the same Velloth blade he'd picked up in the ruins, stabbed the dragon in the snout, breaking through scale and deep into flesh.

Vehks slammed her nose into him, tossing him aside and knocking his weapon free. The ice in her neck began to crack and break loose. She took a deep breath that whistled between the shards of ice as it entered.

Laurence thrust his sword toward the dragon's throat, finding purchase and ripping a gash in her neck as he pulled it free.

Izabel picked up Agnar's Velloth blade and sliced the dragon's throat from the other side, as it rolled in response to Laurence's attack.

Crushing the ice in her neck, Vehks got back to her feet and reared back for another blast of fire.

Laurence, Izabel and Agnar ran in opposite directions to get clear of the dragon's mouth.

"Take cover!" yelled Karzden, but his call was too late.

Molten fire rained down on the soldiers that wailed on the beast, attacking the wound she'd sustained in Port Vaelin on her chest and sides. Seven soldiers melted beneath her as she crashed back to the ground, her talons digging deep trenches.

Vehks stretched out her wings, testing to see if they were capable of flight. Her right wing sent searing pain through her body as it flexed. Infuriated, she looked at Ayriel, and began to rumble another spell with her deep draconic voice.

Ayriel started chanting, circling her hand in front of her. Protective wards sprang to life around her, just as the Vehks summoned a bolt of lightning from the sky to strike her.

Arcs of electricity bounced off of Ayriel's wards and slammed into those around her, sending Thax, Halgar and two other archers flying backwards.

Two more arrows streaked through the air, puncturing the dragon's neck.

Vehks roared, stretching her neck out of reflex and lowering her head closer to the ground. She scooped up a soldier, biting him in half in the process. His legs fell to the ground by Agnar's feet, while Izabel ran back into the fight.

Laurence waited patiently for the dragon to lower its head again. He locked eyes with Izabel briefly and pointed to his neck with his left hand. She nodded back and smiled wickedly.

As the dragon lowered its head to bite another soldier, Laurence and Izabel ran toward each other, stheir swords held high above their heads, gripping with all their might. When they crossed under the dragon's neck, their blades sliced deep into its flesh. A wide gash opened in the wake of their passing, sending blood pouring out and pooling onto the ground below.

Vehks's eyes opened wide in shock; she couldn't believe what was happening. Terror filled her, as three arrows struck between her eyes.

As she gurgled and spat—trying desperately to breathe while blood filled her throat—Laurence and Izabel climbed on top of her head and drove their blades deep into her eyes.

With a final, bubbling gasp, Vehkstaerelliox's life faded.

RESOLVE

Ris'Gaula, Arran'Hael 4th, 113 of the 2nd Era

I beckon thee come and see.
See that which pride hath wrought.
For those who valiantly fought,
Desolation be thy prize.

Night's Writ, Parable 18

AS VEHKSTAERELLIOX fell, Axvalla fueled Drakahl's rage; as he'd begun to do in recent weeks. The vile demon fed on his anger, and seemed to relish every action he took which could be construed as wicked, or reckless.

Drakahl felt the demon's rage coursing through him and succumbed to it willingly, enjoying the adrenaline rush that it gave him. He grabbed the extra chair beside Nightweaver and threw it across the room, screaming in anger. It shattered into splinters as it slammed into the wall.

Nightweaver ignored him and whispered into the crystal, "*Velloth, ukthir. Garthakru etmu. Jakkar, gukkin, trivah, epskjen unpryzentur.*"

Completing her spell of influence, she turned to face the King of Pelrigoss. The crystal darkened, its view of Vehks's lifeless body fading into nothingness.

"They've slain our dragon," said Drakahl firmly.

"She was always going to die. Not precisely there. Not precisely then, but her death was always a part of my plans," she said bluntly.

"Why would we want her dead?" he asked.

"You have your duties. Let me handle mine," she challenged. "She has served her purpose in life, and now the Velloth will ensure she serves her purpose in death. I will simply have to redirect them to her new location."

"What did you say to them just now?" he asked.

She could see the frustration contorting his face and decided to placate his curiosity. "Velloth, come. Gather these things unto me. Scale, tooth, claw and leather; bring for your reward. Roughly. Their language is difficult to translate, but that's close enough."

His growing anger subsided at her words.

She reached up and placed a hand on his wrist. "What have I always told you?"

"All things in due time," he answered.

"Keep that in mind, rather than questioning me. Trust that if you have difficulty understanding my goals, our enemies will find the task impossible," she explained.

"Everything and everyone is but a pawn to you!"

'Yes!' hissed Axvalla in his mind.

Drakahl pushed the thoughts back, and resisted the growing ire inside him. *She is an ally, fool, and far beyond my power to overcome,* he reminded the demon.

"Even you, my dear," she said slyly. As she rose from her chair and left the room, she repeated her statement to be sure he understood it. "Even you."

Why did you deviate, Ayriel? You were meant to be seeking his cure, she mused.

∴ ∴ ∴

LAURENCE AND Izabel climbed down from the great dragon's head. The ground still burned in places. Small piles of ash lay strewn around the area, each marking the remains of a fallen comrade.

Ayriel, Izabel, Agnar, Karzden, Laurence thought, accounting for the survivors as he looked around. *Thax, Halgar, four more archers...*

Only six other soldiers stood among them, several wounded and burned. There was no sign of Kotann, Wil, or anyone from the boats. Laurence sheathed his sword and ran for the shore as cheering rang out behind him. He could hear Karzden yelling at them to stop cheering just as the beach came into sight.

As Wil rowed the only surviving boat ashore, Laurence jumped into the water to pull it onto the sand. The boat was empty, save for

Wil and Kotann's corpse.

"I pulled him into my boat off the rocks, but I couldn't save him. His head bashed open when he was thrown from his boat and I-"

"I'm just glad you're okay, Wil," said Laurence, tears running down his cheeks.

The emotions of the past few days finally hit him. He extended his hand and pulled his friend out of the boat and into a hug.

"How many did we lose?" asked Wil.

"Only Thax, Halgar and two knights from Kotann's Vintain survived. Karzden lost sixteen of those that came from Fel'Rechaun. All told, this battle cost us thirty-three lives," he summarized.

"By the gods, when will it end?" asked Wil, a tear cascading his cheek. "Grellenheim, Gaierford, Bingrolf, my father, Ayr'Thugohn, Port Vaelin and now thirty-three brave souls give their lives to slay an ancient beast of legend... and for what? Some *asshole's* revenge on your family?" said Wil, angrily.

Karzden ran up to them, noticed Kotann's body and the lack of other survivors. "Kotann," he said with sadness. He looked at Laurence, "This is a fucking tragedy, and it's all your fault."

"What?" gasped Laurence.

"If you hadn't called the attack early, Kotann and his men might still be alive. In your arrogance, you've cost countless lives!" Karzden yelled. He stormed off before Laurence could respond.

"I do not blame you," offered Ayriel. "I might have made the same decision in your position. This battle was going to be costly no matter what we did. Karzden... is just upset and needs someone to blame. I will explain everything to Fahrul, and my father. However, there are things to which I must attend. They shouldn't take long, but-"

The sound of horses departing interrupted their conversation.

Izabel and Agnar ran up to them, concerned. "Karzden just took everyone else and left. We're all that remains," said Izabel.

"He blames me for our losses. I'm sure he's racing off to tell Fahrul right now. I'll be expelled, or worse," said Laurence as realization hit.

"I've no home to return to," said Wil.

"You have a kingdom to rebuild and to rule," corrected Ayriel.

"I can't. Not right now. If this bitch is going to keep coming after us like this, nothing I do back home is going to matter. We must put an end to this madness," Wil said sternly.

"If this is going where I think it's going, count me in," said Izabel.

"All that's waiting for me at home right now is a bunch of I-told-you-so's, politics and matchmaking. I just killed a dragon, I'm not giving this life up just yet."

"Yeah, I've got no family left either. If you're goin to Pelrigoss, I'm comin. I wanna see this through... for Bingrolf," said Agnar.

"First, I suggest you take Kotann to Gaierford and have Tylee see to his burial. Then come see me in Vellenheim. I'm sure-" said Ayriel, but Laurence interrupted.

"I'm sorry, your Majesty, but I don't think Vellenheim would be wise if Fel'Rechaun seeks to punish me for this mess. It'd probably be best to avoid anywhere with any significant Legion presence. And if Port Vaelin has been destroyed—as we assume—that leaves only one port with ships that sail to Pelrigoss," he said.

"Gusarski Cove," Ayriel agreed, nodding. "Fine. If this is to be your path, I will not stand in your way. To get to Gusarski Cove, you must go back to Engle Plateau and head north, which will take you through Jorilund. That city is heavily guarded, so be very careful. Once you reach Gusarski Cove, find lodging and lie low for a time. I'm sure there's someone else who would like to accompany you."

"Mordechai," said Laurence, recalling their previous conversation.

"Yes, Mordechai. I will see that he finds you there," she said. "For now, see that Kotann is treated with respect. Meanwhile, I must be off. I was on my way to meet with Mordechai when this dragon appeared, and I've much to tell him."

"Aye, my lady. Thank you for everything you did to help us. Without you, we would all be dead," said Laurence.

After she left, they carried Kotann to their horses and tied him on top of one. It was a brief ride to Gaierford with their enchanted horses. When they arrived, Izabel and Agnar took Kotann into town and made an excuse for Laurence's absence.

Laurence loved Tylee more than anything, which is why he knew he could not go to see her. He was sure she would try to talk him out of his plans, and Delriahna would help her do it. He was also certain that every delay he allowed would mean more deaths, and that was something he could not abide.

When Izabel and Agnar rejoined Laurence and Wil on the Southern Reach, they kicked their horses into a gallop and rode as fast as they could toward Engle Plateau, hoping to make it past Raven's Keep before the enchantments faded.

∴ ∴ ∴

KARZDEN BARGED into Fahrul's hall, angry and distressed. Several pigeons took flight as he entered, giving him pause. Preita, frantically trying to recover them, sent a scowl in his direction. Fahrul looked up from a paper in his hands and sighed, frustrated.

"So, you're back. This dragon better be handled, we're in a world of shit right now," Fahrul said, pointing at the pile of messages on his desk. "Ayr'Thugohn has been destroyed, along with three other Ekthri villages. Over half of Port Vaelin is in ruins, and every ship that could set sail has withdrawn into the Hystari, seeking safe harbor elsewhere.

"Citizens died in Vellenheim trying to flee the dragon. Ayerton and Dunforth are requesting aid because they've been overrun by refugees from Salvation Shire and Cragenfell. Gaierford has been handed over to Laurence's *wife*, of all people. The engineers sent to evaluate Grellenheim have declared the town unlivable... I swear, if there is any more bad news!" exclaimed Fahrul.

"There's more bad news," said Karzden matter-of-factly as he sat down.

Fahrul gave him a stern look, revealing his displeasure.

"We joined up with Kotann, Laurence and their forces, chased down the dragon in Cragenfell and killed it," explained Karzden.

"That's splendid news. So, why do you look so upset?" asked Fahrul.

"Laurence called the attack early, which alerted the dragon and caused it to attack before we were ready. Thirty-three of our people died. I returned here with barely a third of what I left with, and Karzden's Vintain is down to only four men. Total. Kotann himself was among the casualties," said Karzden, anger lacing his every word.

"Thirty-three dead," sighed Fahrul, frustrated.

"The dragon was sleeping on an island. Kotann took a group out to attack it, but there weren't enough boats for everyone. So, he left the archers and casters with Laurence and had me hide the bulk of our forces as a trap for when the creature came to the mainland and landed.

"Suddenly, Laurence called for attack, the archers woke the beast up, and it took flight early. All the boats crashed under the wind caused by that foul beast's wings, and our entire force was in instant disarray," barked Karzden.

"There could have been something else that triggered the dragon, forcing Laurence's hand. Were you honestly close enough to say otherwise?" asked Fahrul.

"I... perhaps not," admitted Karzden.

Fahrul sighed and shook his head, obviously displeased at how Karzden had handled himself.

"Thirty-three men," lamented Fahrul. "I knew killing the beast would cost lives but... this is too much-"

"Fuck!" shouted Karzden as realization set in.

"What now?" asked Fahrul.

"I scolded the boy for attacking early and raced off to see you in anger, without another word. If I were him, I-"

"Would be on your way to Pelrigoss this very moment, sure that Fel'Rechaun would expel you or put you on trial," finished Fahrul. "Gods damnit, Karzden!"

"I'll send scouts to Port Vaelin and Gusarski Cove to find him. They can bring him back here and-"

"We don't have the resources for a man-hunt. Furthermore, unless it's you that finds him with an apology already on your lips the moment he sees you, how are they going to convince him that *everything is okay* before he either ends their lives in presumed self defense, or flees again?

"Are you confident that our guards or Initiates can handle Laurence? I'm not... the boy's more skilled than both of us. Finally, our Kingdom can't take anything else right now. We simply won't survive another attack. If he returns of his own accord, that will be wonderful, but... *perhaps* it's for the best that he races off to face his destiny," explained Fahrul.

"You said yourself that he can't handle Drakahl yet, or Nightweaver for that matter," reminded Karzden.

"I may have been wrong. He's better than anyone at this school; he's taken down Velloth invasions; he hunted down and killed a dragon. Who are we to say what he's capable of? Look at how many people flock to his side and put themselves in danger to help him. Hells, look at the way Mordechai *clings* to the boy. The most powerful caster in the land... if he leaves for Pelrigoss, he's already surrounded by support," said Fahrul.

"What do you mean?" asked Karzden.

"Izabel... Agnar... Wilwarianel... and probably Mordechai when he finds out."

"Yes, I think you're right. Those kids act like family... they aren't going to leave his side," said Karzden.

"If he hurries he might even meet up with Gaerin, Lyla and Kyrilis... If they joined forces, I shudder to think..."

"He still doesn't know they've gone," said Karzden.

"Well, we will have to leave it to fate. As fond as I am of that boy, he's out of our hands now. We've been ordered to assist the King with all the political and social turmoil the recent attacks have caused. The Legion is stretched thin. The rebuilding of Port Vaelin will probably bankrupt the Trade Commission. Half the Kingdom's crop supplies are in jeopardy. People across the land are without homes and starving. We've got *plenty* of work to do," said Fahrul.

"So it appears," said Karzden.

Fahrul and Karzden reviewed the messages for hours, plotting their response and how to send aid. Amidst their discussions, they agreed that training their students was going to have to stop. The students would have to learn in the field while helping provide security at Port Vaelin, Grellenheim and the other affected cities.

It wasn't a scenario either of them found desirable, but they didn't have many options. For the first time in Fel'Rechaun's history, no students would be on its grounds.

∴ ∴ ∴

AYRIEL DISMOUNTED in front of the palace steps, as throngs of people swarmed around her. Several guards raced down to meet her and cleared a path so she could ascend. As she reached the upper landing, she took a moment to study the courtyard and its occupants.

Refugees from Grellenheim and Port Vaelin crowded the courtyard. Tents and piles of hay lined the walls, indicating that many had set up camp awaiting word from their King. They shouted for assistance, pleading with her to speak to the King on their behalf. With a sigh, she turned back toward the palace and made her way to the throne room.

The central structure of the palace was far too large for human occupants; a detail that most overlooked. Popular tales suggested that Arkhan Vaelin constructed the palace during the War of the Wilds; the palace's architecture designed to act as a show of strength, or power.

Her family knew the truth of its construction, but had kept such information secret. The fabricated version of the palace's construction played to the family's advantage, so they let the rumors persist. The truth was far less inspiring.

The core of the palace already existed when Arkhan Vaelin claimed it for his purposes. It started life in the distant past, built by an ancient empire, long before the rise of man. Constructed by highly skilled workers, it survived for eons. They had built it for a race far larger than any human could hope to be.

After her encounter with the Skaar in Ekthri Wood, she walked the halls leading to the throne room with a new perspective. The doorways leading off from the main hall were tall enough for a Skaar to pass freely. Several side halls were tall enough for a giant. Rooms and quarters in the wings, like her own bedchamber, were large enough for Skaar or Toor slaves. The palace had been home to a powerful dragon; she was sure of it.

Arkhan had commissioned construction in and around the palace, but it had only been to adapt the palace for human use. He had workers lay new flooring over much of the old. They split taller rooms into lower and upper levels. He had the steps and stairs of the palace altered for a human's stride, and a facade constructed on the outside of the palace to mask the gargantuan exterior doors.

The central hall of the palace was the largest room in any structure in the Kingdom. Six-foot-wide columns stretched upward toward the great, vaulted ceiling over a two hundred feet above the floor. Upon each flat section of wall hung one-hundred-and-thirty-foot tapestries depicting the rise of Arkhania and the unification of Human, Ekthri and Afyr.

As she entered the throne room, the heels of her riding boots echoed throughout the chamber. Her father stood in front of the dais, talking to several of his counselors. As she neared, her footfalls attracted their attention.

Pushing through his subjects, the King walked over to greet his daughter.

King Orluhnd Vaelin IV was an old man, by human standards. He was nearly eighty years old and had survived longer than nearly all his human subjects. The current generation of Arkhania's human population had no memory of a time before their current King. Even still, the task of recovering from his father's tarnished legacy had been a lifelong burden, which showed in the lines on his face, and how he moved.

"Ayriel!" he said, embracing her. "Wherever did you go? I received word that you would be absent from court, but no explanation why.

Here you are before me wearing rags, looking exhausted. Your assistance would have been invaluable in recent days."

"These are not rags, father, they are traveling clothes and cost our people quite a lot of their meager earnings. Furthermore, while you've been discussing these trying times within the safety of the palace, I've been out slaying a dragon," she explained, her voice revealing her irritation.

"The dragon is dead?" he questioned, surprised.

The council members walked up behind him, their interest piqued by mention of the dragon.

"It is, but at great cost. I joined with forces from Fel'Rechaun, led by Laurence Ravencrest and Karzden Mahrer, and forces from the Legion, led by Vinetar Kotann. We lost thirty-three souls fighting that dragon at Cragenfell, but managed to slay the beast. Laurence Ravencrest and Izabel Tamrilson struck the fatal blow," she explained.

"You have saved this kingdom, my dear!" he yelled excitedly. "Where are these heroes that I might reward them for their efforts?"

"Kotann died in battle, Karzden has returned to Fel'Rechaun, and I believe that Laurence and Izabel have already set off on another mission," answered Ayriel, avoiding the finer details of Laurence's departure.

"We have much to do. The Kingdom is in turmoil, and I would appreciate your input on-" he began.

"I will certainly help as much as I can, Father. However, Archmagus Mordechai has been awaiting my return for some days now. You know what he's like when kept waiting for too long," she said, interrupting him. She was the only person in the kingdom, besides Mordechai, from whom he tolerated such behavior.

"Oh! Do not keep him waiting. However, I expect to see you in the council chambers promptly," said the King.

"Yes, Father," answered Ayriel.

As she left the hall, she could hear the counselors debating her ability to slay a dragon, and her arrogance for interrupting the King. Her father yelled at them for their insolence as she entered the hallway, bringing a smile to her face. The King was nothing if not a loving, supportive father.

It had been his idea to hire Silith as a servant. 'Keep her close,' he had said. It was unfortunate that the nobility and clergy of the Kingdom expected their ruler to produce legitimate heirs. That was the only thing which kept her from marrying Silith and publicly declaring their love. 'Save face,' he insisted. 'Have your love in secret, find an understanding suitor, and wed him to appease the nobles.'

It wasn't a plan she necessarily agreed with. Telling Silith about it had caused the expected wave of tears and depression. However, Ayriel knew that the Kingdom would soon lean on her for leadership. Her father wouldn't live forever, and there were no other suitable candidates to rule. Mordechai had even agreed to marry her for appearances, which had endeared him to Silith.

∴ ∴ ∴

"OH, MY love!" yelled Silith as Ayriel entered. She ran across the room and embraced her returning Princess as fast as she could, kissing her frantically.

"I was beginning to wonder if a dragon had eaten you," joked Mordechai from the bed.

"Mordechai, it's so good to see you. I have so much to tell you," said Ayriel.

He got out of the bed and slowly walked toward Ayriel, hands extending before him. She watched with interest as he rounded the bed and navigated between Silith and a chair before coming to her side. He then reached up and pulled her into a hug in greeting. Releasing her, he backed up a few steps, adjusted the chair and sat down.

"How did you do that? You're blind!" Ayriel blurted.

"The mind is an odd thing," he answered. "I've come to learn that my abilities allow me to move around in the palace without much assistance, even though I cannot see. Sit, and I'll explain."

Ayriel pulled up a chair and sat down in front of him. She signaled Silith by pretending to hold a teacup and tipping it to her lips. Silith nodded and left the chamber to fetch them something to drink.

"We both know the nature of this palace," he said. "What I didn't realize until *now* was that there is faint magic resonating within the original structure; binding it together and keeping it from deteriorating. I assume you failed to notice this as well, because unless you were looking for it, you'd never detect it. It is faint, but it is present.

"There are many who claim I am powerful. I don't deny that. Compared to a common wizard, I am. You know that I have a distaste for the title your father's father bestowed upon me; Archmagus. It is something I've often refused to discuss. In fact, you're well aware I don't enjoy discussing my abilities in general, or admitting to how skilled I might be.

"I learned over a century ago that it was wiser to appear as an equal to those I encountered, lest they attempt to leverage my abilities for their personal gains. We've briefly discussed as much on several occasions, often as I warned you to be wary of the same," he said.

"Yes, I remember those conversations."

Silith returned and handed them both a cup of tea. She sat the kettle on the desk behind Mordechai and perched on the edge of the bed to listen.

"What I've never admitted—not even to those at Fel'Vizsiour—is *how* I cast spells. I am what you might call a Leyweaver, a Thought caster, and—to a lesser extent—an Initiate Timewalker. *Before you react*, I realize that the Primal forces of Time are forbidden. I do not actively pursue such powers, I simply have them. I've always had them, at least to the extent that my memory serves," he detailed.

"What is a Leyweaver? I have heard of Leywalking, but never this?" asked Ayriel.

"I do not require the use of spells. Through Leywalking I can see and access the magical weave directly, and need not store power within me as a Wizard would, or draw it from a material source like a Sorcerer. I can simply pull magic out of the air around me and—using my ability to Weave spells—twist it to my desired outcome.

"This is, again, something I've always been able to do for as far back as my memory serves. I do often use words when casting spells, sometimes out of habit and others because I've no mastery of the area of magic I'm attempting to employ. For example, attack spells are not a field which I've spent much time attempting to master, so I use verbal components to help focus the energies. However, for most spells that I cast, I simply need to draw power from the magical weave and... think about what I want to happen," he said.

"That is... astounding. If I weren't already familiar with your capabilities, I'd call you mad," said Ayriel.

"This is all relevant to my two recent discoveries. The first is that I can sense magic around me and, to a limited extent, use it to navigate the world without sight. This is easier to accomplish when in the presence of higher quantities of magic, such as within this palace or when approaching you. For example, when I crossed the room I could sense where you were, and the fact that a human form was blocking my path. So, I knew where I could step, and that I had to navigate around Silith to reach you.

"I couldn't see anything with my eyes. However, I've started to learn how to interact with my environment by simply sensing latent energies, or even by radiating them from myself and sensing the echoes as those energies interact with what's around me," he explained.

"That is incredible!" she exclaimed.

"The second discovery is more grave. When news of the attack on Port Vaelin reached the palace, I attempted to divine the nature of the dragon. I tried to use my limited access to Primal Time to reach back through history by feel, and by sound. I was trying to learn the dragon's identity, where it had been, and how it came to be here. That's when I discovered a barrier."

"What do you mean 'barrier'?"

"You know well that I cannot remember my past, and that I have been alive far longer than a human should be... yet I appear human," he said rhetorically.

"I do," she confirmed.

"I have been alive for twelve-hundred-and-thirty-three years according to what I can remember. That is to say nothing of a time beforehand."

"H... how could that be?" she asked, confusion lacing her words.

"That much I still do not know. However, I have studied this barrier at length and its existence coincides with all the research I've done over the past few centuries. You might also recall that most of my research involved digging into our collective past, trying to find evidence of my origin or birth. With my age, you now understand why I am so highly motivated to do so."

"Certainly."

"One of the constants in that research is that written texts only go back to a specific point in time, with very rare exceptions; twelve-hundred-and-thirty-three years. From every culture in every land, the story is the same. It's as if everyone woke up all at once, with no memory of anything prior. Every single culture seems to have spawned out of nothing, able to speak, able to write, able to perform tasks and live within different variations of civilization.

"This is a factor that has always confused me. I should have found history stretching back to varying degrees in each culture; some longer and others shorter. I should have found evidence of the creation of written languages, as civilizations developed and evolved. I should have found records of places like Vaelin Palace being constructed, or of its original inhabitants.

"That's just not the case. It has always, literally, been as if every single sentient humanoid on this planet just popped into existence, fully developed and ready to contribute to the cycle of life from day one. It makes absolutely no sense... unless one considers the barrier.

"When I regain my sight, I am going to catalog my findings in great detail. So, please pardon my ramblings. However, this barrier, I believe, is the product of a singular world-spanning event. It affected everyone, not just me. I simply happen to have lived long enough to realize what was occurring, or *had* occurred.

"Some event—which I'm calling the Grand Awakening— occurred over twelve-hundred years ago and caused everyone to forget everything about our world's history, all at once. This barrier I've discovered sits between us and our discovery of the past, preventing us from relearning what was taken from us," he concluded.

"Not even elves live as long as you have. So, that would mean you are the only one still alive who can attest to this Grand Awakening, if it is real," she responded.

"It is real... but I'm not the only one," he said.

"Who else could there be?" she questioned.

"I believe that Nightweaver is also from the time before the Grand Awakening," answered Mordechai.

"That is concerning. Why would you think that?" she asked, growing concerned.

"I also learned something of myself when I divined her. She is a distant relative, and she is my ancestor," he explained.

"That cannot be! Surely you're mistaken!"

"No, I am quite certain. Long ago I discovered that I am not related to any known bloodline that is human. I don't know what I am, but given that discovery and the incredible lifespan I seem to have... I am most certainly not human. Neither is Nightweaver.

"I succeeded in scrying her with the use of *my own* blood, searching for an ancestor or relative on a whim. We are not human, and we are not elves. We are of no known subspecies I've studied. We are, from all I can discern, our own species... and she is my ancestor. We are of the same bloodline," he explained in grave tones.

"Do you think she caused this Grand Awakening?" asked Ayriel.

She was having a hard time processing all of the information and was very concerned for her friend. Perhaps his discoveries were part of the learning that his future self had alluded to.

"I cannot be certain, but her behavior since that time would certainly mark her as our primary suspect. She has manipulated world events across various cultures for centuries. My fear is, everything she's ever done has been toward a singular goal that we've not yet realized. Hell, she powered the Vaelin ancestral crossbow with a black pearl that was later used, under *her influence*, to summon the Velloth so that they might release a dragon upon us. To say she is a master of manipulation would be an understatement," he answered.

"And you learned all this by using forbidden magics," she reminded him.

"My dear Ayriel, I teleport through use of Time magic," he stated bluntly. "That is how I came to the realization that one might scry into the past."

"So you routinely use Time magic? Even though discovery of this would mean your death?" challenged Ayriel. Her concern for her friend was growing.

"As I stated, I already had those skills when I awoke. I have put no effort into learning them, and the little I have used is easily disguised as Leywalking to the learned. The uninitiated cannot fathom what I do when they see it, so they do not think to question my methods or means. I have been safe," he assured her.

"I fear what may become of you if you persist along this path," she stated bluntly. Her mind raced with images of his future self, alone in that magical tower, the black heart beating atop his chest.

"I have shown for twelve centuries that these powers do not entice or control me. My magic has always been at the service of the common good, and never for personal gain. These things you well know," he assured her.

"I will always be concerned for you, Mordechai," she stated. Placing her teacup on a side table, she slid forward in her chair, leaned over and grabbed his hand between hers. "You have been a part of my life since I was born and mean as much to me as my father. I love you as I love myself, and will always trust and support you.

"However, I am allowed to be concerned for the powers within you, and how they might someday change you. You have given much to our family and this kingdom; more than anyone could ever ask. I am simply sad that I was not able to return some of your generosity and kindness. There is no cure for your blindness among the elves," she explained. She sat back and grabbed her tea for another sip, trying her best to hold back tears.

"I feared as much," he said.

"Furthermore, the awakening of the dragon caused panic among the fiends that live in the Mythaeil Mountains. Giants and Skaar rampaged through the wood in terror at the beast's rising and destroyed Ayr'Thugohn and several small villages throughout the wood. The beast arose from Kundarr, the ancient volcano," she explained.

"Vehkstaerelliox," he stated as his face contorted in frustration.

"Pardon?" asked Silith, unsure if he was saying an actual word or simply mumbling.

"There was a stone tablet in a Toor cave in the Warlunds. I found it in the year one-twenty-nine of the First Era. It was etched with Draconic runes, which took a great deal of time to decipher. In fact, I had to travel to Xulrathia to find a translation. The tablet was small and didn't say much that seemed relevant until now. It was the prophecy of a dragon named Vehkstaerelliox predicting the coming destruction of her empire, and her plans to withdraw to Kundarr.

"The inscription was informing her slaves among the Toor that she would be absent for a time and that they should not look for her," he explained. "By the gods, why didn't I realize that earlier?"

"What the hell? I thought you said the Grand Awakening affected everyone around the world, and that no history was preserved?" challenged Ayriel.

"I said 'humanoids' and 'civilizations'. Whatever the event was, it had no effect on dragons. Dragons still live in northern Xulrathia, as do their subjects. It was they who helped me translate the tablet. They knew of Vehkstaerelliox and referred to her as the Harbinger of Omens. Their empires were at war in ancient times. Sadly, they knew little of our history.

"This palace was the throne of her emperor, Hahrfurgadhen. That is why it is so large and grandiose," he explained.

"Well, that explains why she headed this way when she woke up. Seeing her is what caused my delay," she said.

"You fought her?" asked Mordechai.

"We slew her. It was not easy, though. There were severe casualties on our side, and she was already injured from her attack on Port Vaelin. I doubt we'd have won otherwise," she explained.

"Who else was with you?" he asked.

"I met up with Laurence, Karzden and Kotann at Gaierford. They had a force of over fifty with them. Thirty-three died fighting her. As I said, our casualties were severe."

"Is Laurence... did he-"

"He's fine, Mordechai. Laurence and his friend Izabel struck the fatal blows but... that leads me to my other piece of critical news. Laurence and his friends are abandoning Fel'Rechaun and heading for Pelrigoss," she explained.

"They're what?" barked Mordechai, alarmed.

"Karzden blamed Laurence for their losses and raced off to report to Fahrul. So, he and his friends have departed for Gusarski Cove to find passage to Pelrigoss. The boy has a good head on his shoulders. I think he sees that these attacks are only escalating, and not likely to stop until Drakahl and Nightweaver are dealt with," said Ayriel.

"He must pass through Jorilund, I can meet him there and-"

"They are riding enchanted horses, Mordechai. They may already be there."

"I do not have a Focus in Gusarski Cove. I will have to try to intercept them," he said. Before Ayriel could respond, Mordechai bowed his head and vanished in a puff of energy.

"I have to learn how to do that," remarked Ayriel.

∴ ∴ ∴

IZABEL HAD taken the lead during their journey, being the most knowledgeable of the plateau. Certain that their horses wouldn't make it all the way around the Vellen Crescent to Gusarski Cove, they'd decided to risk lodging for the night in Jorilund. She'd known precisely how to get them there in a hurry, without being noticed by any guards or Legion soldiers from Raven's Keep.

The first half of their journey had been on, or alongside, the roads of the Southern and Western Reach, weaving around travelers and desperate refugees seeking aid. After cresting the ramp onto the Engle Plateau, she'd led them directly through farmland on a northern path that skirted the Vellen Crescent. Their horses were already beginning to slow down by the time they reached that point, and they still had many miles to ride.

They rode for hours in the shadows of the Arkhan Cliffs, crossing rocky terrain that bordered the outlying farms. The cliffs stood at the western edge of the Vellen Crescent, a ring of mountains that surrounded and protected Vellenheim. Riding beside the sheer rock walls had been both breathtaking and intimidating.

By the time they broke free of the cliffs—as the mountains began to recede toward the east—Jorilund was within sight. Their horses had reduced to normal speed, and signs of exhaustion began to show themselves. It wouldn't be long before they could ride no further.

In total, their journey had taken only half the day, which was impressive considering the distance they'd covered. Any normal horse would have taken several days to make the journey. The abilities of Mordechai and Ayriel continued to impress Laurence, causing him to wonder what Arcturus had hidden of his own talents. After all, both of them held Arcturus in high regard, as had Kyrilis.

Could Arcturus have done this for our horses, Laurence pondered.

Just as they reached the gates, Izabel's horse stopped, buckled its legs and dropped to the ground, whinnying in frustration.

"Oh, come on!" yelled Izabel. "Ten more feet, you dumb mule!"

The guards at the gatehouse laughed at the scene before them as, one by one, the group's horses followed suit.

"Looks like you've got a rebellion on your hands," remarked a guard smiling.

"Could we, maybe, tie them up here for now? Come back for them later, after we find lodging?" asked Laurence.

"Certainly, lad. Just don't be too long, aye? Anything for the future of our Legion," said the guard, recognizing their equipment came from Fel'Rechaun.

"Thank you, sir," answered Laurence.

With nods of thanks, the group dismounted and drove small stakes into the ground, tying up their horses before setting off on foot. The town was very different from Raven's Nest, Grellenheim, or anywhere else most of them had been. It seemed to be much older, and much more robustly constructed. The buildings were several stories tall, each made from stone slabs with iron supports.

Izabel was familiar with Jorilund. As a child, she had traveled there from Vellenheim several times with her father. She led them through the city, weaving between residents in their path, heading straight for her favorite inn.

∴ ∴

WITH THE crashing and tumbling of crates, Mordechai arrived in Jorilund. His Focus was in Joril's shop, tucked back in a corner. He had placed it there with permission from the old smith, but word had apparently not passed to his assistants.

He could only blame himself, as he hadn't visited very often. Thankfully, his style of teleportation created space for him to land, pushing aside the crates that occupied the corner. If he had been Leywalking, parts of his body could have fused with the obstructions.

Old Joril turned slowly on his stool to see what the ruckus was about. Upon seeing his old friend, he made his way across the room for a proper greeting. Yellowed, broken teeth peeked out beneath his dense, white mustache and beard as he gave Mordechai the biggest grin that he could muster. He wasn't aware that Mordechai could not see him.

Musty, matted hair pressed against Mordechai's cheek as the old man embraced him. The smell of sulfur, coal and oil filled his nostrils, nearly causing him to cough. Old as he was, Joril's grip was still quite strong and his hug was painful. Mordechai hugged him back, enduring the pain that clearly showed the happiness his presence brought to an old friend.

"What brings you to this old man's shop, eh?" asked Joril. It wasn't in the man to judge his friends. He was far too kind to think ill of Mordechai's lack of visitation.

"I come seeking a very important boy and his companions. I mean to join them on their journey to Pelrigoss," answered Mordechai.

"Ah! They are in Jorilund, are they? So, I am just a convenience, then?" teased the old man.

"I think you'll find the lad interesting, old friend. He wears the armor and sword you crafted for Gahl the Raven."

Joril's ears perked up. He enjoyed revisiting his previous work, and to see a piece he had crafted so long ago was exciting. "Oh my! Well, where is he? We must find him! I had hoped to see it earlier this year, but apparently my assistant quoted a repair fee beyond the owner's means or desires... such a pity."

"Yes, that is a pity," confirmed Mordechai.

"It's a pity because that armor does not *need* repairs. One must simply touch the damaged parts and say the proper word," he said, laughing. "Youngsters these days just don't have any imagination. When a King pays you to make a suit of armor, you *make a suit of armor*, am I right?"

"I suppose so!" said Mordechai. "Now, can I escape this alcove and leave your shop to find my friend?"

Joril realized he'd been standing so close that Mordechai still stood in the corner that held his focus, unable to move. "Oh, my. Yes!" he blurted as he hopped out of the way.

"Can you guide me? I can manage, but it's easier to walk when I have a guide," said Mordechai.

"Why do you need a guide?" asked Joril.

"I have been temporarily blinded. It is a matter I trust will be resolved, but for now I am at your mercy," he admitted.

"Well, then... take my elbow," said Joril, extending his right arm.

Mordechai reached for and gently gripped the bony elbow, his fingers nearly getting tangled in the bushy white hair of Joril's forearm in the process.

Joril led Mordechai through the stifling heat of his workshop.

Sweat covered Mordechai's brow, neck and torso almost immediately as they entered. Several apprentices brought hammers down on glowing, hot steel at intervals as they passed, sending sparks shooting forth with each impact. Oil hissed as they quenched forged metal, sending foul odors into the air.

Without the benefit of sight, everything was a surprise and amplified his growing anxiety. Once they were finally out in the street, the cool rush of autumn air across his damp skin sent chills down Mordechai's spine. The sensation was both unexpected and refreshing.

"There's really only one inn where travelers feel much at home in town. The others tend to watch their guests like a hawk, expecting them to steal or what-not. We'll check there first," offered Joril.

People moved out of the way as the pair approached. Joril was famous, respected, and considered royalty by the city's residents. Jorilund bore his name, and he had been a presence since before any of them were born. He rarely left his shop, or his home above it. So, when he did, they made sure to give him space.

The walk to the Ironworks Inn was brief, thanks to both its distance from Joril's forge and the parting of crowds as they passed. Its only distinguishing feature was the sign above its door. Everything else about the building was the same as every other building on the street.

The heavy doors swung wide as they entered, allowing the faint smell of roasted meats and butter-roasted potatoes to greet them as the air rushed past.

Joril walked up to the counter and addressed a very nervous attendant, "We are here seeking... um," he paused for a minute, then lurched his right arm forward to drag Mordechai fully to the counter, "You tell him."

"We're seeking a group of travelers who would have just arrived today. One of them is a tall young man with brown skin, wearing a striking suit of armor," Mordechai explained.

"Ye... yes, we have received guests fitting that description. B... but I fear they've left again to see to their horses. I could send someone for them?" the attendant stammered.

"We'll wait, actually. I'm starving," said Mordechai. "Find us a table and fetch us a good meal. When they return, send them over to us. Make sure our table will seat all of us."

∴ ∴ ∴

MORDECHAI AND Joril had finished their meal by the time Laurence returned. They sat slowly sipping the most expensive brandy the Ironworks Inn could offer discussing the old days. The attendant frantically ran from behind the counter as the companions entered and hurriedly ushered them into the dining room. Upon seeing Mordechai, Laurence's confusion subsided and joy filled his demeanor.

"Mordechai!" he yelled as he walked to the table.

"I am coming with you, Laurence, and I'll not take no for an answer," said Mordechai bluntly.

"Straight to the point, for once! Some might say I'm rubbing off on you," joked Laurence. When he caught sight of Mordechai's eyes, stark white with swirling black mist on their surface, he panicked.

"Worry not, Laur," said Mordechai, realizing what Laurence was seeing. "This will not hinder my ability to assist you on your quest, and I have confidence it is only temporary."

"How did it happen?" asked Laurence as he sat down across from his friend.

"That is a story for another time. I believe introductions are in order," Mordechai responded. "The man beside me is Joril. He made your armor and sword."

"Oh, come over boy and let me see," said Joril. As Laurence approached he added, "How did you come by Gahl's armor?"

"I am his great grandson," answered Laurence.

"Ooh! That is wondrous!" chirped the old man.

Izabel, Agnar and Wil took seats at the table and waited patiently for the others to notice them.

Izabel bit back on the jealousy that was slowly growing within her. Laurence, no matter where they went, always seemed to be the center of attention. It wasn't that she wanted people to dote on her, or anything, she just wanted people to take her seriously. She wanted to be included in decisions, plots and plans. However, she knew that those thoughts would not aid her, or their quest, so she pushed them aside.

"The armor has held up quite nicely, wouldn't you say?" asked the old man.

"Absolutely. It's fantastic, actually. It doesn't even feel like I'm wearing it," said Laurence happily.

"Oh, my dear boy. You have only learned part of what this armor can do. Sit, sit! I shall explain it to you!"

Laurence sat beside Joril and turned his chair to face him. *Perhaps stopping in Jorilund was the right idea after all*, he thought.

"I crafted this armor for your great grandfather at great expense... oh yes. It took months to work the Skaar hide, forge the metal and make the rings. That's not the half of it, though. I used melrithium instead of steel. It's a special metal in very limited supply. In its natural state, it's softer than steel, *but* it's far superior at holding enchantments!

"Not only does it bear no weight when you wear the full suit, but it has added magical defense and resilience to counter the softer nature of melrithium. It also protects you from extreme weather, somewhat, by lessening the feel of warmer and colder climates. It won't protect you from extremes, like a volcano, but you can safely travel this world, or high into the clouds, without fear of the natural temperatures of the air around you. Oh, oh! It can also repair itself!" exclaimed the excited old man.

"It can what?" asked Laurence. His head was reeling from the flood of information. He hadn't noticed the extra abilities of the armor at all.

"Yes... let me see where Gahl was run-through," he said. He leaned forward and removed a few of the plates from Laurence's chest. Running his finger along the seams in the chain, he said, "Some fool has done a very poor job of fixing this."

"Well, Arcturus said you charged too much to repair armor, so he sent it to someone else. I don't think he knew it could repair itself... it hadn't repaired itself, even after all those years," said Laurence.

"Oh, well... his request was answered by a good-for-nothing apprentice that has been scolded *quite* thoroughly for sending a quote without talking to me first—let me assure you of that. I sent a messenger with a correction, but all he found was a pile of rubble and ash. So-"

"Arcturus was slain the very night I put on this armor and set off for Fel'Rechaun," Laurence interrupted.

"That explains it, then. The armor does repair itself, but it requires a command. You touch the damaged portion like this," he said as he stroked the area with two fingers, "and say 'Deisiuth'."

As the word escaped his lips, the steel links which had been used to repair the maille fell out of position, clinking to the ground. The melrithium chains pushed together, reforming their missing counterparts and closed together to repair the armor to its original state.

Izabel's eyes grew wide. She couldn't believe what she was seeing. Laurence, Agnar, and Wil gasped in wonder.

"The same will work for your sword, should it need repair or sharpening," added Joril.

"I... can't thank you enough!" exclaimed Laurence.

"Do you have any more of this stuff?" asked Izabel.

"Oh, hello dear. We haven't been properly introduced, have we?" asked Joril, extending his hand.

"I'm Izabel Tamrilson," she answered while shaking his hand.

"Ah, Tamril. He was such a kind man. Many questioned his intent when he separated his line from the Vaelins. I knew better, though. He wanted his reputation to be of his own making and not ride in the wake of Orluhnd the first. A wise decision, if you ask me, for a man whose family would never be given a chance to take the throne," he said.

"You knew him?" she asked. "I mean... there are those that know the history, certainly, but... you actually knew Tamril Vaelin?"

"I did, indeed. He was a brilliant man and less prone to being swayed by power or station. His values were more... honorable, and that relegated him to servitude. It's hard to claim power when you are unwilling to play the 'game', you see. He knew this, and it did not bother him. He was a great man to know. You should be proud of your heritage," explained Joril.

"I am. Though I doubt my family is as proud of me. All my father cares about is improving his station by marrying me off. He only allowed me to train as a warrior to placate me and keep me from rebelling," she said with sadness in her voice.

"Well, unfortunately, I do not have any enchanted armor available right now. It takes quite a long time to make, and I am held back by *lazy* apprentices who refuse to dedicate themselves properly to such work. However, I do have a shield," he offered.

Her demeanor brightened noticeably.

"Why don't I send the bill to your father?" he asked with a smirk.

"I think I love you," she giggled. "That would be perfect."

"I will send my lousy apprentice, Darrish, over with some things for you all promptly. For now, I must return to my work. Those lazy sods are probably throwing a party in my absence," he said.

Joril stood and made his way around the table. He stopped for a moment, patting Mordechai on the shoulder, before leaving. Once he had gone, Mordechai turned back to the companions with a grim look on his face.

"Izabel, Wil, Agnar... nice to be with you all again," he said.

"You missed a big'un, Mordy," said Agnar.

"Don't call me that," said Mordechai with a sigh.

"We killed a dragon!" blurted Izabel.

"Where is Bingrolf?" asked Mordechai.

"The Velloth got him," answered Agnar angrily. "Red-skinned pricks took everyone I ever knew an killed em to bring out that dragon, Mordy."

"I am sorry for your loss, Agnar, but please don't call me Mordy," Mordechai insisted. "That dragon's name was Vehkstaerelliox, and she was the last of her empire. She was thousands of years old, and had gone into hiding because of the arrival of... people like us," he explained. "Nightweaver released the Velloth, the dragons' former servants, to summon her.

"Other than trying to disrupt our Kingdom, I can't figure out what she hoped to gain. There are far easier ways to cause turmoil than summoning a dragon," he explained.

"If you are joining us, we'll need to find you a horse," said Laurence. "We're headed to Pelrigoss to deal with this once and for all. We could certainly use your help."

"I'll handle it," said Wil.

He had remained silent, quietly coping with the destruction of his homeland. Mordechai joining their party was a turn for the better and gave him hope. Without another word, he left to purchase a horse.

The rest of the party shared the details of their journeys with Mordechai.

∴ ∴ ∴

WHEN WIL returned to the inn, a small cart sat outside waiting for them. The cart only had two wheels and leaned forward on its rails. A very tired young man wearing a thick leather apron stood in front of it with his hands on knees, panting. "Are you Darrish?" Wil asked as he approached.

"I am," he answered, gasping. "I've got to deliver this stuff to some travelers inside."

"They're with me. I'll go get them," offered Wil.

"Oh thank gods," said Darrish as he slid to the ground.

Wil returned to the cart a few moments later with a very excited Izabel and Agnar in tow. Laurence followed shortly behind, smiling with happiness for his friends. He leaned against the outside wall of the inn, arms crossed and watching the scene unfold.

Izabel picked up the shield, hefting it on her arm. The shape was fairly standard from the front, being flat on top and tapering to a point at the bottom. However, it had a much more pronounced curve when viewed from the sides, the corners and tip bending backward toward the wielder. It was made from melrithium, with an extra layer of banding around the edge; forge-welded and bolted into place. Devoid of the typical crest, the entire shield was silvery and seemed to shift colors faintly as it moved.

A longsword lay next to the shield, including scabbard and belt. It matched the shield, so the boys let Izabel take that too. In addition, she found a suit of plate armor with black leather under-armor similar to Laurence's, although non-magical. The breastplate was slightly more convex around the chest, allowing more room for her bosom.

He thought of everything, she mused as she gathered her new equipment.

Agnar stepped to the rear of the cart and stood for a moment, trying to decide which of the two remaining suits of armor he wanted for himself.

Wil looked on in confusion before chiming in. "You do realize that only one of those suits of armor will fit me, right? The other is clearly sized for an oaf like you," he explained.

"Maybe I don't *want* scale armor," said Agnar.

"Maybe it's better than the stuff the school supplied and you should be happy to wear it," insisted Wil.

"Yeah, I like scale better than leather anyway," said Agnar, smirking. He collected the suit of finely crafted armor and walked away to inspect it. He ignored the two-handed sword that lay in the cart, preferring to keep his Velloth blade instead. Agnar turned and walked directly inside to try his new gear on.

Wil shrugged, grabbed the black leather armor and returned to the inn as well.

Izabel smiled at Laurence, ecstatic. "Can you, possibly, help me carry some of this?" she asked.

"Of course, Izzy," Laurence answered with a smile.

"I'll just wait here, then," said Darrish.

"For?" asked Laurence.

"Your old armor and such. Joril likes to take old armor and weapons and remake them into something new, or give them to poorer folk who need them and can't afford better," Darrish explained.

"Ah, that makes sense. We'll bring it right back in a bit," said Laurence with a nod.

After a few minutes, the friends returned from their rooms wearing their new armor and feeling proud of themselves. Laurence decided they looked like a professional military unit, all with a similar style and gear. He was happy they'd come to Jorilund, and that Mordechai brought Joril to meet them.

It wasn't long before they tired of watching Agnar pose and flex in his scale. With the rolling of eyes and many sighs, the others picked up their old gear and returned it to the cart for Darrish.

Agnar was still flexing when they returned, transitioning from one pose to another every few seconds.

Darrish grunted and moaned as he hefted the weight of the cart and began pulling it back to Joril's workshop. He hated his job.

∴ ∴ ∴

AS THE group rode through the northern gates of Jorilund, the cool, damp air of morning greeted them gently. The sensation reminded Laurence of more peaceful times. He thought for a while about all they'd been through, comparing it to everything he had dreamed this kind of life would become.

Gaerin and Arcturus's warnings about the dangers of an adventurer's life, and the trouble one would find while living by the sword, echoed back at him. Silently, he wished that they were with him so he could admit they were right.

He realized that his life had become a mission. No longer did he have a choice of what to do, or where to go. Everything lay out before him in such a way that he had only one option; take care of things now, or suffer the consequences later. He was firm in his decision to seek resolution to the troubles that had beset his family, and the Kingdom.

It wasn't that he couldn't trust others to do what needed to be done, it was that he needed to see things through for himself. Obligation was a new feeling for him, but one that had become a driving force since he left home.

Beneath all that was a yearning that grew in intensity with every moment he spent in Tylee's presence. As much as he'd dreamed of travel and adventure in his youth, he realized that those flights of fancy were not truly what he desired. Instead, his battles were an impediment to what he'd come to realize he truly wanted; a normal life.

Is that something I can ever have? How long until this is resolved, he wondered.

Deep inside those thoughts, he realized that he yearned to raise a family with Tylee. Seeing her in Raven's Nest with the refugees, and taking the mantle of Constable of Gaierford, had shown him her caring spirit; something he had somehow missed during their childhood. He could only imagine the kind of mother she'd be, and the life they could provide for their children with both of them home—safe—to care for them.

The sound of laughter broke him from his thoughts. Izabel seemed to be succeeding in her efforts to brighten Agnar and Wil's mood.

"See? He doesn't even know!" barked Izabel, pointing at Laurence.

He looked toward her quickly, curious as to her meaning. His movement caused something small to fall out of his lap, grazing his right arm on its way to the ground. As the three friends laughed even harder than before, he looked to see a dead squirrel rolling to a stop behind him.

"What in the hell?" asked Laurence, flabbergasted.

"I put that thing in your lap an hour ago, ya dolt!" laughed Agnar.

"What were you thinking about?" asked Wil.

"I was thinking that we should use our time trapped on the ship sparring, to hone our skills," he lied.

"And that had you so distracted you didn't see, or *feel*, Agnar pranking you?" laughed Izabel.

"I guess," chuckled Laurence with a shake of his head.

"We've gotta stop lettin him think, I tell ya," joked Agnar.

"You guys are too much," Laurence teased.

He looked at Izabel again and smiled. She smiled back and nodded once, confirming that his assumptions about her intent were correct. He slowed his horse briefly, falling behind to join Mordechai.

"You haven't said much," said Laurence.

"There isn't much to say at the moment. Our situation is about to become very serious, and we still don't know what we're walking into," answered Mordechai.

"It's all connected. My great grandfather, my grandfather, my father, the Velloth, the dragon... everything is leading somewhere," said Laurence.

"It is, I just can't piece together what their motivations are. Your revenge might stave off whatever is coming, and it might not. We could be doing precisely what they want... I could be delivering you to them on a silver platter," mused Mordechai.

"If they wanted me dead, I'd already be dead. Drakahl could have ended me with no trouble at all. I was wounded, disarmed and prone."

"There's something about you that's different. I met Gahl and Arcturus. They were great men, to be sure, but they were just men. In you, I sense... something more. I fear that Nightweaver has sensed this too."

"I don't think I'm special. I'm just caught up in... whatever this is. It's certainly not what I expected when I planned to leave home," said Laurence.

"There's something else... I've been wondering how to tell you."

"Well... just say it. Spit it out," offered Laurence.

"When we were in Grellenheim, I saw your uncle Gaerin fighting the Velloth."

"What?" Laurence asked, angrily. "Why didn't you tell me sooner? What was he doing there? He-"

"He's heading to Pelrigoss, just like you," explained Mordechai.

"Drakahl killed his father, not to mention his brother and grandfather. You aren't alone in your need for revenge."

"But why didn't you tell me?" demanded Laurence.

"Fahrul and I agreed that you weren't ready yet. We didn't know about the dragon, or how deep this plot went," answered Mordechai.

"That wasn't your decision to make!" yelled Laurence.

The conversation between the friends in front of them stopped abruptly.

"Actually, it was *precisely* our decision to make. You are... or *were* a student at Fel'Rechaun," corrected Mordechai.

"I spent almost no time at that school," Laurence complained, worried and frustrated. Not only did he have to deal with Drakahl and protect his friends, he apparently had to find Gaerin.

"You were schooled through experience in the field. Your battles taught you more than sparring in a courtyard ever could. You entered the school a young boy full of dreams and anger, and now you have people flocking to you, eager to follow you to other lands and risk everything... *for you*. The school presented you with challenges, which you embraced. I'll concede that the circumstances weren't *typical* instruction, but these aren't typical *times*."

"I can't believe you didn't stop him, or send me with him," said Laurence.

"We sent Kyrilis to join him. Sending you... well, I've already said we didn't think you were ready. I'm not saying you're ready now, but you're certainly more prepared than you were at that time. We also couldn't send you, or Izabel, or Agnar, or Wil without causing political turmoil on top of the destruction our Kingdom is facing.

"Something—I might add—your current actions have forced the school to contend with," Mordechai explained. "I know it wasn't ideal to hide this from you, or to send Kyrilis. None of this is ideal... and besides, do you really think we could have stopped Gaerin? You know your family."

"Well, now we have *another* reason to get to Pelrigoss quickly," said Laurence calmly.

∴ ∴ ∴

"WHAT ARE they doing?" asked a soldier.

"I have no idea. Keep watch while we do what we came for," answered his superior.

"Should we attack?" the soldier inquired.

"I *said* keep watch. They outnumber us three-to-one, and we don't have the resources in this region to defeat them. Right now, they aren't attacking anyone. The most we can hope for is that they continue doing whatever they're doing and bother us no more," insisted the officer.

The officer returned to the rest of his men. Fahrul had sent them to gather the horses and supplies that Karzden abandoned after the battle, and that's what he intended to see happen. The nearby activities of the Velloth concerned him, but he knew attacking them would mean death for them all.

Unfortunately, the horses Fahrul sent them to retrieve had scattered about the town and surrounding areas; a great many of them were riddled with anxiety and unwilling to cooperate. What should have been a simple task had become a source of frustration laced with danger.

This is just what I need, thought the Junior Commander sarcastically. He was thankful that their operation confined them to the southwestern areas around Cragenfell; far enough from the Velloth to flee at a moment's notice.

To the northeast of Cragenfell, close to the shore, lie the massive dragon's corpse. A large group of Velloth clamored around and on top of the beast. They'd posted a dozen guards around it, standing quietly in black armor with halberds held at the ready. The rest of them, wearing simple leathers and scraps of clothing, seemed to be harvesting pieces of the dragon's carcass.

Do they plan to eat it, wondered the commander.

Shaking the thought out of his head, he resumed coordination of his men and made his best efforts to keep them focused on their task. He wanted them out of the area as soon as possible. Once they gathered, tethered and prepared the horses for travel, the Junior Commander walked back over to the guard he'd posted.

The Velloth were still busy harvesting parts from the dragon across the field.

"Has anything changed?" he asked the guard.

"No, sir. Their guards just stare at me, and the workers keep carving things off the dragon," he answered.

"Well, it's time to go. Mount up," said the Junior Commander.

"But-" started the guard.

"We are ten men. They clearly have more than thirty, probably closer to fifty. I don't like this any more than you do, but we don't stand a chance and you know it," said the commander.

"Laurence Ravencrest led six people to victory over fifty in Grellenheim, sir," retorted the guard.

"Well, when he shows up we'll attack... but he's not here, is he? So, get your ass moving, soldier," ordered the commander.

After the human soldiers left, Ahava emerged from the fishery and returned to Vehkstaerelliox's body. She towered over the other Velloth, though they were similar in every other way. She was the first of her kind, and the only one as tall and strong as a Toor.

As she approached Vehks's maw, the others stopped working and knelt to show their respects. She ignored them and continued to her fallen master. With her eyes closed, she rested her head on Vehks's nose and gently stroked the magnificent creature's scales with one hand.

You saw the value in me when the gods, and my own people, did not. We have been diligent these past eons, and have learned much about the creatures you feared, and their gods. You were right to fear them. I wish that this day had not come, that you could continue to sleep peacefully in your eternal slumber. Fate has demanded differently, and a great evil is coming. Your sacrifice will ensure that we continue, that the world survives.

Please forgive me.

Ahava kissed the great dragon one last time, then turned to her people.

"Continue the harvest. We haven't much time."

Dark energy swirled around her. The ground opened, allowing her to pass through to the tunnels beneath. When the ground returned to its natural state, the workers continued their harvest as their Queen commanded.

∴ ∴ ∴

CAPTAIN BAGRIS stomped on the doors to the hold, waking his passengers. "Time to disembark!"

Gaerin rolled onto his back and answered, "We'll be up presently!"

The group went to work putting on their armor and gathering their things. Gaerin and Lyla were the first to go up on deck. They went to stand at the rail, peering out at the land in front of them. Oben came up shortly after and dropped a heavy load of equipment on the deck behind them.

"That is our destination?" asked Oben. His voice was very deep and quite distinct.

"Not quite," answered Gaerin as he turned his head and looked up at the tall half-orc. "Legends say that long ago Pelrigoss was adjoined to Gargoa from Tellrindos to Cragenfell. Nobody knows if that is true, or when it changed, but there are several local tales about the sundering of the land. None of them agree with each other, as you might expect of local legends. However, Pelrigoss is split into 5 distinct isles.

"The one that lies before us is either Aegir or Drog'na. Both lie to the west of the Triblunds; Aegir to the north and Drog'na to the south. If we were to take port, we'd be headed south around Drog'na, then east past the Triblunds toward Dagoh Bay; on the southeastern shores of Caierthor. In other words, we'd still have a long way to go. The palace of the King lies in northeastern Caierthor," explained Gaerin.

"Why don't we dock in Dagoh Bay? Would it not be quicker?" Oben asked.

"We can't. We don't have the proper trade papers, and no cargo to load or unload. There are no other safe harbors in Pelrigoss for larger ships," answered Lyla.

"Then we row," said Oben bluntly.

"Yes, we row," confirmed Gaerin. "We'll also have to carry our dinghy, if possible, or find a way to procure another on the other side. Or, we can row around the western isles and straight to the Triblunds. From there, we'll have to cross the land and find a bridge.

"Nobody crosses the Odvodi rivers to Caierthor without a bridge. It flows fast and, in contrast to normal rivers, towards the center of the main body of the isle, draining into a phenomenon known as the 'Well of the World'. It's a massive whirlpool that pulls the waters of the Hystari inland along the Odvodi, separating East Caierthor from the Triblunds."

"If that is Drog'na, I would rather we go around. My grandfather fled to Gargoa after being exiled by the Daulga who live there," explained Oben.

"That is very good to know, thank you Oben," said Lyla with a smile.

He relaxed at the sight of her smile, realizing that she was not judging him.

"Did I hear ye right? Ye plan to row all the way to the Triblunds? Are ye mad?" asked Captain Bagris.

"Do we have a choice?" asked Lyla.

"The waters aren't safe, lass. That there be Aegir, not Drog'na. I figured when I saw your companion here," he pointed at Oben, "that ye'd want to avoid Drog'na. Ye can cross Aegir fine, if you mind your business and stick to the shore. Just don't hunt. The Aegra that live there... they don't like those that hunt or harm nature," explained Bagris.

"I've never heard of the Aegra," said Gaerin.

"They be small faun; a nomadic folk with strange powers. Folk don't land on Aegir, out of fear. Legends tell of those who tried but ne'er returned," said Bagris.

"Then why would we want to land there? If others never returned, then-" started Lyla.

"Ye have little choice. The sea's too rough, and the shoreline's too riddled with rocks. Tide's worse here than Gargoa, so rowin round on a dinghy ain't your wisest choice. Course... y'all do as ye like. Once I lower ye down, t'ain't my problem no more," said Bagris.

"Couldn't you sail around to the north and drop us off on-" started Gaerin.

"Not happenin. We've business to attend in Gusarski Cove, and ye delayed us long enough."

"What business could be more important than our silver?" asked Gaerin.

"Ye seen the dragon. We need to pick up our families and get down to Haern. Already detoured enough for your coin."

Noticing that the rest of his group was on deck and ready, Gaerin said, "Fine. Let us be off, then."

"Here's the rest of your silver," offered Lyla, extending her hand.

Bagris accepted the purse full of coins and tipped his hat in thanks.

∴ ∴ ∴

GUSARSKI COVE was a sprawling city, roughly half the size of Port Vaelin. The buildings, constructed from wood and stucco, appeared in need constant repair. The southern border of the city sprawled up and onto the side of the northern face of the Vellen Crescent. Extending north, it spilled loosely across the landscape following the shoreline, in a relatively haphazard and ill-planned fashion.

The town's main thoroughfare wound up the side of the southern mountains like a coiled snake. The cross streets were erratic and not often interlinked. The combination of construction and engineering made the city difficult to traverse in haste and easy to hide evidence of skirmishes or even murder. That suited the purposes of its residents and visitors well.

If one could fly, Vellenheim was less than a day south. Though that did not make enforcing laws from the sky, such as with Griffin Guard, any easier. Almost every building in town was the same style, shape and color. Finding specific locations amongst the repetitive structures from above was a task that few willingly performed more than once. By horseback, one could only reach the Kingdom's capital by going around the crescent mountains and descending Engle Plateau; a trip that took several days.

The sandy shoreline led into water with a shallow table, a series of rocky outcroppings, and constantly shifting sandbars. Ships with a deeper draft had great difficulty traversing the nearby waters, resulting in the many wrecks that littered the port's exterior.

The city only boasted one dock, reserved for repairs and the transfer of high ranking passengers. A single channel led around the cliffs of Vellen Crescent from the Hystari to the dock, limiting speed of entry and egress dramatically.

The builders had erected stone walls along the northern side of the channel to hold back the ever-moving sandbars, making it a tight fit for larger vessels. Most ships anchored off-shore and used pulleys to transfer their goods into dinghies, which then brought them to shore.

The combination of city engineering, difficult waters, limited ability to dock ships, and distance from the capital by horse allowed those with lower inhibitions to operate with relative ease and very little risk of being caught. As a result, Gusarski Cove quickly became the 'pirate capital of the north'. Most of its residents happily embraced that title as a badge of honor.

Anything imported or exported through the black market passed through the city's port. Anyone seeking secret entry or exit from the Kingdom always ended up in Gusarski Cove. Of most importance to the companions, Port Vaelin lay in ruins and difficult port before them had become their only option.

The final hours of their journey had taken them through the village of Menshe and the forest of Prell. By the time they exited the wood and rounded the corner to see Gusarski Cove down the hills, night had fallen. The faint glow of torches and lanterns posted on doorsteps, posts, and being carried through town, revealed the size and scope of the city.

"Let us head directly to the shore, and look for empty dinghies preparing to head out to their ships. We might be able to acquire passage relatively quickly if we're lucky," explained Mordechai as they descended the hills. "It would be best if we did not spend time in Gusarski Cove. There is no law here, no constable, no mayor, and no one to enforce the Kingdom's rule."

"I agree," said Laurence. Thinking for a moment, something critical dawned on him. "Mordechai? How do we get our horses home? I can't leave Onyx here for weeks or months. And... how are we going to pay for this journey?" He'd been in such a rush to get there, he hadn't considered the pertinent details.

"Oh, crap!" blurted Izabel as the same realizations struck.

"I will simply inspire your horses to return to Gaierford. We'll send a note on Onyx for Tylee. As for passage... leave that to me," said Mordechai.

"I am forever in your debt," said Laurence.

"I do not put any effort into recording or remembering debts that might be owed to me. I simply do as I must, when I must," Mordechai stated bluntly.

Unlike their trip through Menshe, the residents of Gusarski Cove didn't stop to gawk at them as they passed. Everyone they rode past kept their heads down and hurried their step to avoid the group. The companions—many of them were uncomfortable in such an environment—maintained their silence out of respect for the privacy of the citizens.

"Why don't they just build piers?" Izabel asked as they came into view of the shore.

Dozens of small dinghies lined the beach, transferring goods.

"Those piers would need to be over a mile long, and their footing would be rather difficult to stabilize. The shelf and sand bars shift constantly. Besides, the amount of effort it takes to load and unload in this fashion discourages chartered ships from attempting to use the port, which keeps the Trade Commission out of the way," explained Mordechai.

"So this is how the black market survives," she surmised.

"More importantly, this is how one ships goods and avoids the Trade Commission's laws and taxes. Most of the goods that come through here are the same products you'll find in legal market stalls all across the Kingdom. The difference is, their prices can be lower. Believe it or not, the King is very aware of what happens here, as was his father. He turns a blind eye to it because it fosters competition, ultimately bolstering the economy and keeping goods within reach of the poor.

"The Commission detests it, because they lose their portion of the profits. However, there isn't much they can do once a ship reaches this port. They've tried, but again... the difficulties of this port limit their ability to interject. It's not that the King prevents them from doing so, it just isn't cost effective," Mordechai detailed.

"We're here," said Laurence as they reached one of the dinghies. His announcement was more for Mordechai's benefit than the others.

"Stay here," said Mordechai.

"But, you're–" started Laurence.

"Stay here," he repeated.

Mordechai dismounted and stood for a moment with his eyes closed and head down. He focused on the surrounding area, sensing for magical energies. Some of his group's equipment radiated behind him. Laurence's inner being glowed in his mind like a beacon. Reaching out further, he could feel the strands of the magical weave above them, twisting and writhing in the sky like a living net.

Slowly, he drew from the weave. Thin tendrils of energy descended from the sky, filling him. He pushed with his will, causing the energies to emanate from his body, creating an aura about him. He could sense the aura around him, shimmering and pulsating in what his mind pictured as a bright blue hue.

Where the aura touched objects in its path, he could see the energies bending to reach around them. The horses behind him, his companions in their saddles, the dinghy a few feet away... as he extended the aura further he could sense the position of everyone working on the beach, one by one.

He kept his eyes closed as he started walking, concentrating on what his mind could sense around him. Up ahead, he found an empty dinghy, and its passenger preparing to depart. Methodically, he strode toward his target, deftly weaving between those moving crates along his path. As he reached the dinghy, he turned to face the man hunched in front of it, preparing to push it into the waters.

"What do you want?" asked the man in a gruff voice.

"We are seeking passage to Pelrigoss." Mordechai's aura licked about the man, caressing his face. His lips curled in anger.

"We aren't a passenger ship. Now, go!" barked the man.

"You are emptying cargo at night and returning none to your

ship. Where are you headed?" asked Mordechai.

The man's face contorted further as he stepped up to Mordechai, their chests nearly touching. The man's breath was hot upon Mordechai's cheek. "That is none of your business, weakling," challenged the man.

Power rolled out of Mordechai in a wave, sending unnatural warmth through those nearby. He tickled the man's brain with it, triggering his sense of fear and dread. A chill ran down the man's spine as Mordechai opened his eyes, revealing the black wispy smoke that swirled above them.

He could hear the man's breath catch in his throat. "I will not ask again," said Mordechai, his voice magically enhanced to resonate deeply and echo through the man's very being.

"I'll... I'll see what the captain says," whimpered the man, now terrified.

"We will board and explain for ourselves," said Mordechai, his voice still amplified by magic. "We will pay your captain for our passage, and you will keep out of our way. Wait here," he finished, turning.

"Y... yes, my lord," said the man as a tear rolled down his cheek.

Mordechai walked back to his companions, all of whom stared at him in shock. Everyone in his path parted before him, each in varying degrees of panic. All of them had sensed the power he was radiating.

"Dismount. I will send your horses to Gaierford as we discussed," said Mordechai, calmly.

"What in the hell was-" started Laurence.

"I do as I must. We do not have time to seek lodging and spend days bartering with every ship that graces the port with its presence," offered Mordechai.

"We could feel that from here," said Izabel as she dismounted. Her voice trembled slightly as she spoke.

"I will have to master the technique. It was new to me. I apologize," offered Mordechai.

"Must you?" asked Izabel.

"I don't think this is the last time that trick will be useful," answered Wil.

Mordechai handed Laurence a piece of parchment and a small bit of coal. "Write your letter."

Laurence used Onyx's saddle to support the paper as he wrote. 'I apologize for not saying goodbye, my love. I do not think I would

have had the strength to leave had I seen your eyes. We set sail for
Pelrigoss now, to deal with Drakahl. Worry not, for I am surrounded
by close and capable friends. When I return to you, we will build our
life together. I am proud of the woman you have become, and will
miss you greatly during our time apart. Please care for these horses
and consider Onyx your own. I love you.'

After placing the parchment into one of Onyx's saddlebags, he
turned to Mordechai and handed back the remainder of the coal,
saying, "Thank you."

Mordechai walked between their horses, touching each one on
the neck. He pushed with his mind, concentrating on Gaierford,
and the route they would need to travel. As he left each horse, they
turned and trotted toward their destination.

Once his task was complete, he joined his companions and led
them back to the dinghy. The dinghy's owner waited anxiously for
them, pacing back and forth.

"Are you... are you ready, my Lord?" whimpered the man.

"We are," answered Mordechai calmly.

"I'll help push us out," said Agnar.

Agnar handed Laurence his weapon as the group got into the
dinghy and helped the man push the boat into the water. Laurence,
Izabel, Wil and Agnar grabbed the oars and started rowing quietly.

"What is your captain's name?" asked Mordechai.

"Fraeg," answered the man. "I... I'm Lauden, my Lord. Anything
you need, I can handle it. Just don't-" said Lauden.

"Don't worry, we mean you no harm. We simply don't have time
to wait around for pleasantries and debate," explained Mordechai.

"Captain Fraeg's not gonna like this, my Lord. He's not fond of
passengers."

"I'm sure my coin will change his mind," said Mordechai.

"I dunno, my Lord. We make plenty of silver runnin the coast."

"We aren't paying silver."

"Copper bits won't do, Lord. Not to offend, but-" he started.

Mordechai interrupted by presenting him with a gold coin.

"I'm sure it won't be no problem, Lord," Lauden said, gladly
palming the gold coin.

Once they reached the ship, the crew lowered rope ladders.
It was a fairly small ship; small enough to navigate less-than-
favorable coasts while being large enough to handle short distances
in the open sea. As the group climbed onto the deck, Captain Fraeg

scowled at them and stared down at Lauden. He was unhappy with the turn of events.

"Interestin cargo ye grabbed while ashore, Lauden," said Fraeg.

"My apologies, Cap'n, but they pay in gold," offered Lauden.

The handful of crew aboard the ship stopped in their tracks and turned toward the conversation with piqued interest.

"Is that so?" asked Fraeg. He walked up to Laurence, squinting with his one available eye, his other hidden behind a patch.

"We do," answered Mordechai.

Fraeg turned to face him with a whip of his head. Oily, black locks of hair slapped gently against Laurence's chest as he turned.

"Where am I to take ye?"

"Pelrigoss," answered Mordechai.

"Fifty gold!" barked Fraeg.

"Thirty, no more," Mordechai retorted firmly.

"Not enough. We're all wanted men in Pelrigoss. Made a mess of Dagoh Bay, we did. Not too fond of returnin."

"Forty, and you send a man to shore to acquire food and drink for our voyage," answered Mordechai.

"Forty five, and we drop you off on Aegir," said Fraeg.

"Forty five and you drop us off on the Triblunds east of Aegir," countered Mordechai.

"Done!" barked Fraeg.

Mordechai handed nine stacks of five gold coins to Fraeg one at a time as he extracted them from a fold in his robes. Fraeg counted them eagerly, his eye growing wide with pleasure.

"I've never seen gold coins," Agnar whispered to Izabel.

"They're rare, that's why. Nobody pays for goods from a farm in gold. Each coin is worth two-hundred and fifty silver," she whispered back.

"By the gods, Mordechai is rich!" whispered Agnar a little too loudly.

"He's been around longer than our Kingdom, hun," offered Izabel quietly.

Fraeg offered them his quarters for the voyage and had his men bring up several small mattresses for their comfort. Lauden went back to shore and returned after a few hours with a load of fresh meats, vegetables, water and rum. The crew pulled the dinghy out of the water and tied it to the side of the ship, then Fraeg ordered his men to raise the anchor and hoist the sails.

Wil cooked dinner for everyone on board as the ship took to the sea. It was nearly dawn before the companions settled into their quarters, having spent most of the evening getting to know the crew and sharing their tales of chasing down and slaying a dragon. By the end of the night, the idea that they were transporting dragon slayers had the crew excited and eager to serve.

SUBTERFUGE

Ris'Anyu, Arran'Hael 7th, 113 of the 2nd Era

Sleep thee now, oh silken one,
For soon you will awake.
Know ye now what must be done,
It's you who'll raise the stakes.

Night's Writ, Parable 20

GAREG AND Oben slowed the boat by shifting the oars to create drag. Kellum rode at the prow, poised to leap off to help drag them ashore. With nine people on board, each sitting on a crate, the dinghy rode low in the water. All the occupants were eager to step onto dry land once again.

Gaerin and Lyla shared a knowing glance. None of their companions suffered from the growing sense of doom they did.

As Kellum leaped from the prow, splashing waist deep into the water, Gellix and Keifer followed suit. The three of them dragged the boat closer to shore as Oben and Gareg continued to steer and manipulate their speed with the oars.

Once the boat was far enough onto dry land, Gaerin helped Lyla and Gabner out of it. Kyrilis joined them while Bolrin started moving their few remaining crates of supplies toward the front of the dinghy. Oben and Gareg jumped out and began carrying the crates up to dry land while the rest of the party went to take a look around.

Gaerin and Lyla climbed through the rocky crags and boulders above the shore where the beauty of Aegir stretched out before them. Fields of grass flowed into the distance, dotted in places with trees, bushes and patches of flowers. To the northeast stood a forest of pine and spruce, surrounding a single, distant mountain.

A small dusting of recent snow clung desperately to life in the shadows of boulders, bushes and trees. A short distance to the east they could see what looked to be a small group of green and brown spheres.

Lyla looked at Gaerin with wonder in her eyes.

Kyrilis smiled at the two of them. She was glad to see them find beauty along the way to such a dark destination.

"Pretty!" chirped Gabner from Lyla's side.

She giggled and looked down at him. "Yes, Gabner. Yes, it is," she confirmed.

"We should probably investigate those spheres," suggested Gaerin.

"They're intriguing, but why?" asked Lyla.

"My guess is it's a camp full of Aegra. If they're this close, we don't want to just set up our own camp. In fact, we should throw any meat we have with us into the sea," Kyrilis suggested.

"Oh, good call," she responded. She turned to face the others, still down on the shore. "Open the crates and throw any remaining meat into the sea. We don't want to insult or offend the Aegra!"

"Are you certain?" questioned Gellix.

"I don't like this," grumbled Oben.

"Do as I ask!" demanded Lyla.

"Leave it to me!" yelled back Bolrin.

"Climb up and stay here once that's done... Lyla and I will return shortly!" declared Gaerin.

Gellix saluted in response.

Gaerin, Lyla, Kyrilis and Gabner set off toward the strange spheres. As they closed the distance, they noticed that the Aegra had made the spheres from bent branches, pine needles and long grass. Each sphere included a small hole, through which tiny creatures could enter.

"Oh, my gods... those are homes they can just roll along when they move!" exclaimed Lyla.

"It's impressive, really," said Kyrilis.

"You know... I just realized, we're dressed like we're about to slaughter a village... and we're approaching a village," said Gaerin.

"We're just gonna have to hope for the best," said Lyla.

"We approach with weapons stowed, shoulders slumped to seem less imposing, and hands held up at shoulder height to show we are submitting to their inspection," suggested Kyrilis.

"Will that work?" asked Gaerin.

"Would you rather walk up, shoulders upright and proud, with your weapon hand swinging at your side within inches of its hilt?" asked Kyrilis.

"Good point," answered Gaerin.

As they approached the small orbs, the group grew quiet. Other than Gabner, they each made an attempt to be as unimposing as possible. Gabner was skipping happily, thoroughly enjoying the entire affair. Lyla looked down at him and rolled her eyes.

Suddenly, roots reached out of the ground and entangled Gaerin, Lyla and Kyrilis's feet. The roots wrapped around their lower legs as they watched in shock and horror.

Gabner continued skipping toward the spheres, happily yipping a song. He stopped a dozen feet ahead of them and waved at something amidst the spherical homes.

"Don't struggle," Kyrilis whispered, putting her hands out to indicate her companions should stop.

Gaerin and Lyla complied, begrudgingly.

A small creature, barely taller than Gabner, came into view from behind one of the spheres. It stood upon goat-like, furry legs and had a head much like a goat. Its torso and arms looked like a human child. In its right hand was a gnarled, wooden staff topped with a crook. His left hand was making symbols in the air.

The roots stopped growing as his hand stopped moving. "Why are you here?" he asked. His voice was animalistic, and he seemed to struggle to form words that they would understand.

"We are traveling to Caierthor and only wish to pass through. Our ship couldn't continue the journey and dropped us off on your shores. We are sorry to intrude, and mean you no harm," said Kyrilis, speaking slowly.

"Why go to Caierthor? Their people not welcome here," said the faun.

"We have come to fight Drakahl, the King of Pelrigoss," said Gaerin bluntly.

Kyrilis shot him a frustrated look.

"Why kill King?" asked the faun.

"He murdered our family," answered Lyla. "Do you *mind* if we kill the King?" she asked, concerned that the faun would try to stop them.

"He is bad King; demands too much tribute. We are a simple people—live one with nature—cannot offer tribute to his liking. He sent troops to claim our lands, but they stayed on the sunrise coast. Can you make them leave? Will killing the King let us be free?"

"We will do what we can to help you," said Lyla.

Kyrilis sighed. *These people can't stop helping everyone and just stay on task*, she thought to herself. *Perhaps that is one of the reasons I love them?* They were unlike everyone she had served with in the Legion or Fel'Rechaun.

The roots receded and withdrew into the ground. Free to move, they walked over to the faun cautiously. He looked up at them patiently, his head no higher than Gaerin's waist.

"You come now and feast with us. We plan for the attack on their fortress," said the faun. He turned and walked back into the tiny village without waiting for a response.

"Gabner, go and get the others," said Lyla.

"Go get friends!" barked Gabner. He turned and ran as fast as he could back toward where they had come ashore.

The rest of them entered the little village and sat down in the center. Small fauns began climbing out of the spherical homes to join them. Many of them stopped to caress and inspect their armor and weapons. Gaerin settled in for what he expected to be an awfully long night.

∴ ∴ ∴

"THIS COURSE of action is going to come back to haunt us," said Kyrilis. She stood next to Gaerin sipping the Aegra's strange tea, watching the sunrise.

"We have little choice. By helping them, we earn safe passage through their lands. Then, of course, there are the docks on the far eastern coast that they told us about. It's guarded by Drakahl's men, so we have to kill a few of them anyway... this saves us the hassle of attempting a week long portage," said Gaerin.

"You're right. I know you're right. Doesn't ease my concerns, though. By the time we're done here, Drakahl will know we're coming," said Kyrilis.

"Oh, I'm certain he already knows we're coming. He probably knew we'd come after him before he attacked Arcturus. I'm sure he has a grand scheme to deal with us," said Gaerin.

"Worse... he has a witch that can cause the Velloth to rise and wake an ancient dragon from another continent," said Kyrilis.

"Yeah, there's that too," sighed Gaerin. He sipped the rest of his tea and walked back into camp to retrieve their companions.

Kyrilis continued staring into the distance, trying her best to bury her concerns.

Lyla was in the middle of the small camp, transferring supplies from various crates into small packs constructed of vines, leaves and grass.

Gaerin walked up to her and knelt down to help. The packs that the Aegra supplied stretched and conformed to their contents and were in many ways superior to their own cloth satchels. However, they couldn't hold anything that was too small, as those contents would spill out of the pack through gaps between the materials.

Gellix, Oben, Gareg and Kellum stood a distance away, talking amongst themselves. They hadn't seemed comfortable around the faun the night before and had stayed apart from the group; even going so far as sleeping outside of the Aegra camp.

As Bolrin, Keifer and Gabner ran over to help Lyla, Gaerin got up and walked over to the mercenaries to figure out what was going on.

Gaerin considered the men as he approached. They seemed capable, but he hadn't seen them in action yet. Still, their skills appeared perfectly designed to complement one another.

Kellum was half human, half elf and wore black brigandine armor. He was slightly shorter than Gaerin, lean, strong, extremely agile and had impressive vision and hearing. Kyrilis had discussed the man's skills at length and sounded impressed with him. His quiver hung low at his right hip, its belt interconnected with the bandoleer of throwing knives he wore diagonally across his chest. Completing his armament, two daggers rested in sheaths on the outer edge of each thigh.

Gareg the Berserker was taller than Gaerin. His brown leather vest left his arms exposed, the muscles of which were thicker than Gaerin's legs. He carried a single weapon, leaned across one shoulder; a two-handed greatsword with a five foot blade. Runic tattoos covered his cleanly shaved head. He was not a man Gaerin would ever want to face in combat.

Oben the half-orc was taller than Gaerin by nearly a foot. He wore scale armor mounted to brown leather; the scales of which had been unskillfully painted black. His skin had a pale green tinge, and the tusks emerging alongside his teeth from his bottom jaw prevented his mouth from remaining closed without effort. His oily black hair hung in a thick plait down his back. At his waist hung a pair of large battle axes.

Gaerin was confident that the Aegra were just fine with the idea of this group of hardened warriors sleeping outside of their camp. However, their motivations were unknown, and that was cause for concern. He couldn't allow another betrayal, like Drakahl so many decades prior.

"Everything okay, Gellix?" asked Gaerin as he joined them.

"Yes, boss. We're just… nervous around their magic," answered Gellix.

"By 'we' he means me. I can feel their power. It's… not like other wizards we've met," said Gareg in a surprisingly soft voice. "It's closer to what I feel when I rage."

"Wouldn't want Gareg losing his cool at the wrong time," added Kellum.

"Two of them are traveling with us. Is this going to be a problem?" asked Gaerin.

"I'll find a way to deal with it. Two might be fine. A whole group of them, though… it's too much all at once," said Gareg calmly.

"Very well. We're meeting with our guides in a few minutes on the northeast edge of camp. I expect you'll be ready?" asked Gaerin.

"Yes, boss," answered Gellix.

Gaerin and Lyla finished packing the things they decided were most important and gathered everyone so they could leave. After a few moments, two fauns walked toward them. Both held small bows and had a little green quiver on their right hip. They looked identical to each other.

"I am Wehrenel," said one.

"I am Ahrwie," said the other.

"Wehrenel? Ahrwie? Wehrenel Ahrwie? You're joking, right?" laughed Lyla.

"I don't get it," said Wehrenel.

"Me either," said Ahrwie. Their gruff little voices expressed genuine confusion.

"I don't think their names mean what they sound like to us," chuckled Gaerin.

"Appropriate names for scouts, I suppose," said Kyrilis.

Lyla couldn't stop herself from laughing at Kyrilis's remark. It took a second for her to compose herself. "We, um... well, first, we're sorry. We don't mean to offend. However, we can't tell you apart," said Lyla. "We don't want to call you the wrong names."

"He's a weevil shorter than me. Should be obvious," said Ahrwie.

"Yeah, no. We can't tell the difference," said Lyla.

"Actually, he's right," said Kellum. "I didn't notice until he pointed it out. Wehrenel is the short one."

"Okay, fine. Most of us can't tell the difference," corrected Lyla.

Wehrenel sighed and walked over to a tuft of wildflowers. He pulled up a handful of them and twisted their stems around in his hands. After a few seconds, he reached up and fastened a tiny, make-shift wreath of wildflowers around one of his horns.

"There. Wehrenel has flowers on his horn," said Ahrwie.

"Does this help?" asked Wehrenel.

"Indeed, it does. Thank you for being so understanding," said Lyla.

Gabner moaned, "Ooooo," with glee and awe as he walked up and touched Wehrenel's flowers.

Wehrenel shooed him away with a swat.

Gabner frowned and stepped back, fidgeting with his hands.

"Okay, valiant scouts. Which way to the fortress you want us to clear?" asked Gaerin.

Wehrenel and Ahrwie looked at each other for a moment and discussed their route in a language that sounded like a series of barks, yips, grunts and throat clicks. Ahrwie clopped his tiny hooves into the ground as Wehrenel nodded, apparently signaling they had come to an agreement.

"This way," yipped Ahrwie as he trotted through the group toward the forest.

"That way," agreed Wehrenel, pointing at Ahrwie.

The rest of the group hefted their satchels and vine-sacks, then turned and followed. They walked in silence for most of the day, biting back against the cold air that was slowly building in intensity. They didn't reach the woods until it was almost time to set camp.

Oben offered to collect firewood, drawing evil glares from their Aegra scouts. Wehrenel grunted, walked to the center of the camp and held his hand to the ground while muttering a few strange words. The ground glowed a faint green and warmth began to radiate from the spot in small waves.

"You don't need fire," said Wehrenel.

"Okay, then," answered Lyla with a hint of shock.

Most of the group was fairly unhappy with their meal that night, consisting of nuts and berries that the faun had collected. Lyla, however, was thoroughly enjoying their new companions.

Of course she likes this, thought Gaerin as he munched on a very bitter handful of berries.

Their sleep that night was surprisingly comfortable, huddled around the small patch of glowing green ground.

∴ ∴ ∴

AYRIEL SLID out of her saddle and handed Tegris's reins to Silith. She studied the debris strewn about the forest floor with tears in her eyes. Seeing the beautiful city of Ayr'Thugohn in such a state was heartbreaking.

The souls of the many elves that died that fateful night called out to her, pleading to tell their tale. It was a tale she was already familiar with, but she promised them with all her being that she would make time for each of them.

She turned to the fifty men and women from Vellenheim and signaled that it was time to begin. Workers ran into the clearing with small tables and laid them out as quickly as they could. Engineers and architects approached and laid out their plans.

Over a hundred displaced survivors had joined them during the trip through Ekthri Wood. The elven men, women, and children slowly began the process of building temporary housing at the edge work site. Walking into and out of the clearing, crossing paths and causing confusion, they gathered materials from the fallen city for their purposes.

The human engineers, carpenters, stonemasons, and blacksmiths trying to build their stations were getting frustrated at the elves constantly interrupting their efforts. Assistants and general tradesmen unloading the twenty wagons of cargo dropped goods as elves got in their way, throwing up their arms in frustration.

Ayriel stepped in, seeking to put a stop to the confusion.

"Everyone, stop! Listen for a moment! We are here to help these poor citizens of Ekthri Wood. I know that today's efforts were supposed to be about surveying and planning our operation, but it is clear that the pressing needs are temporary housing for all those that have joined us. If you notice, their efforts also serve a secondary purpose.

"We must clear the debris of Ayr'Thugohn eventually, no matter how much we plan or strategize. Assisting them with their homes not only provides a place for all to sleep, but accomplishes that task as well. Further, it will allow them to assist their fallen into the afterlife. Many died here that night, and the longer we delay in recovering their corpses, the more horrid that task will be.

"So, drop what you were doing. I don't care what your job is, or what you imagined this day would entail. Stop everything, and assist them in clearing the debris, and using those remnants to build temporary homes. Help them carry their loved ones to a safe place, so they might deal with their losses in their own way. Once that is accomplished, you can resume your planned activities without the debris and elves in your way."

A young elven man ran up to her as she finished her speech. She watched for a second as the human workers dropped what they were doing and started assisting the elves. The elves cast many nods of thanks in return. The chaos temporarily resolved, she turned to address the man before her.

"I am Raz'Fetheil of Line Cuthdra'Gah, second in line to the throne. Have you any word of my brother, Wilwarianel?" he asked.

"He is presently occupied with his efforts to hunt down those that caused the awakening of Vehkstaerelliox. When his task is complete, and we are safe from further attacks, he will return," answered Ayriel.

"Then we are without a leader," said Raz, not wanting to make assumptions as to his own rights to the throne.

"Nonsense. King Orluhnd and I recognize your situation and will honor your position on the throne in Wilwarianel's stead until such time as he is able to return. We recognize that King Faelrin wished his eldest son, Wilwarianel, to succeed him. However, we also understand that unfortunate circumstances have prevailed against his wishes. So, please, feel free to speak on behalf of your people," she explained.

"What are your plans for rebuilding, if I might be so bold? We appreciate your assistance, surely. However, I have questions after seeing the materials you've brought along," he said, indicating the wagons full of stone.

"Ah, well. Our engineers and fortification experts have decided that, for Ayr'Thugohn, it would be best to rebuild on the ground as well as in the trees," she answered.

"That is not the way of our people," said Raz.

"No, it is not. However, your people are part of the Kingdom of Arkhania. Building on the ground will serve multiple purposes. The first is that it will allow us to more easily re-establish trade with your Kingdom. This will foster better relations and allow us to support your rebuilding efforts with goods and supplies.

"The second is that we plan to build fortifications at ground level capable of thwarting any future assaults by the Skaar or the giants. The stone you see is but one of many shipments that will follow in the months to come. The purpose of the structures on the ground will be to serve as a staging area for defense of our mutual western borders.

"At any time when your forest or the western borders of Arkhania beyond are threatened, we will send forces here to help defend your capital city and to act a central location from which to orchestrate our joint efforts in overcoming those threats," she explained.

"There will be no permanent occupation of the lower city by Arkhanians?" asked Raz.

"Not unless you, or Wilwarianel, wish it," clarified Ayriel.

"Then I agree with your plans. Where shall we begin?" asked Raz.

Ayriel spent the next few hours going over the plans with Raz and directing engineers, architects and foremen. When the workers had cleared enough of the debris to unload their supplies, she redirected a few of them to begin that task.

They unloaded the twenty wagons into organized piles off to one side, while the rest of the workers continued clearing the area. As they recovered corpses, the elves carried them beyond the clearing to the south, lining them up in preparation for burial rites to be performed later that evening.

It quickly became Raz's job to manage the elven survivors, to keep them productive and organized. His people were unfamiliar with working at the humans' pace, and building on the ground. He soon realized that keeping them out of the way was just as important as keeping them from standing around watching.

He now understood why humans had expanded across the land as quickly as they had. Seeing them work was an impressive sight. His confidence for the future of Ayr'Thugohn was rising.

We'll be done in no time, he thought, proudly. *I will make my brother proud.*

∴ ∴ ∴

GAERIN AND Lyla's group traveled through the woods for a day and a half.

Several Aegra had visited them as they passed. As each group arrived, Wehrenel and Ahrwie explained their purpose, and the visiting Aegra cheered at them; clearly happy at the prospect of being free from Drakahl's rule. The process repeated several times throughout their travels, delaying their progress and causing much frustration.

Finally reaching the other side of the wood, they set camp along the northern shore. Cool air wafted in from the north, hinting at the coming of winter. The three moons, Provoss, Aygos and Zathos, joined each other in the sky as the night began its transition into dawn. Warm gusts of wind mixed with the cool air, swirling about the camp, as warm rain began to fall.

Wehrenel and Ahrwie woke the group and urged them to move into the forest for shelter from the storm. The rain increased until they could barely see beyond the trees, covering the night sky in a thick sheet of gray. At the height of the storm's fury, a crashing sound came to them from the northeast.

"Thunder," remarked Bolrin.

"No, there was no lightning," said Lyla.

"What be it then, miss?" asked Bolrin

"We'll find out when this clears," answered Lyla.

The group stayed awake for the rest of the night, unable to return to sleep due to the storm and their concerns over the noise they'd heard. When dawn came, and the storm had abated, they left the safety of the trees and started north, seeking the source of the disturbance.

Far in the distance, Kellum spotted a concerning sight. "A shipwreck!"

Everyone ran toward it, intent on finding any survivors. A small ship—barely large enough to sail the open sea—had smashed into the rocks during the storm. Small pieces of debris littered the sand, and larger pieces of the vessel poked up through the waters along the shore. Several bodies lined the beach, many with visible gashes, protruding bones, caved ribs or smashed heads.

Lyla ran to each, checking for signs of life. One body, in particular, struck her as odd. The woman lie face down in the sand and her body was fully intact with few visible wounds. What remained of the woman's garments were but a few scraps of silk, wrapped loosely around her body; the rest had been shredded by rocks and violent waves.

Countless scars lined the woman's back, shoulders, arms and legs. It was apparent she'd been whipped and beaten many times in her life. She was fairly small, thin and muscular with pale skin; similar in many ways to Kyrilis.

Kyrilis ran up beside Lyla full of concern, wondering what she could do to help.

The woman lay on her stomach and didn't seem to be breathing. By the looks of the sand behind her, she had clawed and crawled her way out of the sea and passed out.

Lyla rolled her over to check for a heartbeat. Her elven ears, previously hidden by locks of silvery-white hair, came into view as Lyla moved her.

Kyrilis's heart skipped a beat.

The Afyr were a solitary people, not known for world travel. Kyrilis was an exception to the rule and only traveled because her kingdom demanded she do so. The woman they'd just found, whoever she was, had lived an intense and painful life, and had somehow washed ashore on Aegir. Too many questions were racing through Kyrilis's mind for her to be of any assistance.

Lyla leaned in and placed her ear next to the woman's mouth. A faint puff of air lighted upon Lyla's cheek.

"She's alive!" she yelled. She quickly pulled the bedroll out of her Aegran pack and laid it atop the woman. Once she was covered, Lyla pressed on her chest, sides and stomach; feeling for softness or rigidity where those sensations shouldn't be.

"Several of her ribs are fractured. Her left shoulder is dislocated, and her right collarbone is shattered. There seems to be a fair amount of internal bleeding. I'll need to relieve the pressure on her lungs and heart before I administer any healing magics. Someone purify a dagger... a *sharp* dagger," ordered Lyla.

Ahrwie trotted up to her and handed over his blade. "It is purified by the essence of nature, Lyla. It should suffice for your needs," he explained.

The dagger was tiny in Lyla's hand, but would offer greater precision, she decided. Carefully, she rinsed the woman's torso clean with the contents of her waterskin and selected a spot between two of her lower ribs. With great care, she sliced into the woman's flesh with the tiny blade. Far more blood gushed forth from the wound than should have been possible.

As the pressure on her internal organs released, the woman gasped for breath. Lyla placed a few more cuts around the woman's ribs, each one relieving more pressure, and each followed by heavier, healthier breathing.

The woman moaned in pain.

"Why so many cuts?" asked Kellum.

"I have to pull her ribs back into position," said Lyla, grimly.

Lyla began chanting a healing prayer under her breath. Reaching through the cuts she had made, one by one, she lifted the broken ribs as best she could with two fingers. As the edges of the rib bones met, her prayers fused them back together.

The woman, though unconscious, screamed out in pain.

"I'm so sorry, dear," said Lyla as she cut open the skin around the woman's right shoulder. She reached in and pushed as many shards of bone as she could find back into place to reform the collarbone. With one last prayer, Lyla's hands glowed with a visible yellow light as she placed them gently on the woman's chest.

The woman lurched upward, as if in pain. The cuts across her body sealed shut, each emitting a faint yellow glow. After a few moments Lyla's prayer ended, her healing prayers exhausted for the day.

"Will she be okay?" asked Kyrilis.

"I think so, but we can't know when she'll wake up," said Lyla, covering the woman's body with a blanket.

"Can you do anything to help her?" Kyrilis asked, turning to face Ahrwie.

"Our magic requires sacrifice. To heal a thing, we must consume a thing. Healing such wounds would require injuring something else, perhaps even killing it. That is why we do not fight the King's men on our own. To do so would mean the death of the forest, and perhaps our own people, as we consumed life to power our spells," explained Ahrwie.

"Holy crap!" responded Keifer.

"Druidic sorcery," explained Gaerin for Keifer's benefit.

Gaerin had heard of such magics, but never seen them in action. He found himself wondering what the shaman at the Aegra village had destroyed in order to trap them with roots, or what had died to allow the twins to create a heat source when they camped.

"I'm sorry, but we can't leave her," said Kyrilis.

"I've no plans to," answered Lyla.

"I guess we camp here for the night," said Gaerin. He turned to the rest of the group and said, "Okay, men. Let's get the rest of the bodies gathered and buried properly. If you find anything of worth, bring it back here. Especially if it will help us identify the ship, their origin, or their destination. I'm sure they have loved ones who would like to know what happened to them."

"Aye, boss," answered Gellix.

The men laid their weapons down near the unconscious woman and set about gathering the dead. Wehrenel and Ahrwie went up to the edge of the forest and began digging graves. Gaerin knelt beside the woman with concern in his eyes. He looked up at Lyla and noticed she was crying.

"Did you see those scars?" she asked. "Can you imagine living such a life? Those weren't wounds from swords... she's been whipped... many, many times. I think she was a slave."

He placed his hand on her back and pulled her into his arms. His wife was the most compassionate person he knew. They sat for a time, waiting for the woman to wake.

Kyrilis sat by the woman's head, gently stroking her cheeks with a finger and fixing her hair. "Who are you?" she whispered.

After a few hours, the group made camp and moved the woman into a small lean-to. With their evening meal prepared, the faun left to find herbs for the woman. The sound of waves lapping up onto the shore became the dominant sound; many of them began to nod off.

∴ ∴ ∴

THE INJURED Afyr sat up swiftly, knocking her head into the branches of the lean-to, which she hadn't expected to be under.

Lyla heard the noise and rushed over to her, followed immediately by Kyrilis.

"Who are you? Where am I?" asked the woman. Her voice was exceptionally light, almost delicate.

"You are on the shores of Aegir. Your ship crashed into the rocks during a storm, and we found you injured on the beach. I am Lyla, and this is Kyrilis."

"Who are you?" asked Kyrilis.

"I am Vaelys," said the woman, after a moment of thought.

"Where were you headed?" asked Lyla.

"We sailed from Tellrindos, destined for Port Vaelin," said Vaelys.

"Why are you on Aegir? Doesn't this land belong to the Aegra?"

"Yes, we are helping the Aegra," answered Lyla.

"That explains why you aren't dead," said Vaelys. She pushed herself upright, carefully holding the bedding in place upon her breast. "Do you have any clothes I might borrow? I seem to be missing mine."

"I have a simple tunic and breeches in my pack. I keep them for general use around town when I don't want to draw attention to myself," offered Kyrilis.

"That would be just fine," said Vaelys. "Far better than the eyes of so many men upon my bare flesh."

"I will be right back," said Kyrilis.

"Are you Afyr?" asked Lyla.

"I was... a very long time ago," answered Vaelys.

"Do you mind if I ask about your scars?" asked Lyla.

"You ask too many questions. I only just met you," said Vaelys, sternly. She winced in pain as she moved her arms.

"You were severely injured when we found you. I had to heal several of your ribs, and your right collarbone. Internal bleeding had compressed your lungs... you were nearly dead," said Lyla.

"That explains quite a lot of what I'm feeling. Thank you for saving me," said Vaelys. She smiled at Lyla as best she could through the pain. "Will you be able to heal me further tomorrow?"

"I will. Absolutely, I will," said Lyla.

"She's awake?" asked Gaerin, walking up from the beach.

"She is. Vaelys, this is my husband Gaerin," Lyla said, introducing them.

"We will have time for proper introductions once I'm clothed."

Kyrilis returned with her spare clothes and handed them to Vaelys.

Lyla and Kyrilis then held up the bedroll to block everyone's view while Vaelys dressed. After she finished, they helped her to the center of camp.

The Aegra had not complained when they used parts of the ship to start a fire. It had taken some effort on Lyla's part to dry the wood enough with her prayers to allow it to burn properly. However, the companions were happy to have an open flame for the evening. Vaelys joined them at the fire and took a seat next to Kyrilis.

"Thank you again for the clothes. Everything fits nicely, even the boots," she said.

"If I could do more, I would," said Kyrilis. "Anything for a fellow Afyr."

"There are few of us," said Vaelys.

"Too few," confirmed Kyrilis with a nod.

"Does anyone have any daggers I could borrow? You seem to be in the middle of a mission. I would offer my services in thanks for saving my life," said Vaelys.

"How skilled are you?" asked Kellum.

"I will not spar with you to prove my capabilities, if that is where this is leading," said Vaelys.

"Why not? Are you scared to fight a man?" teased Kellum.

"I do not wish to kill you," she said bluntly. "I do not spar. Those I fight never live," said Vaelys.

A chill ran down Kyrilis's spine. She didn't sense that Vaelys was bragging, merely stating fact. Concern crept into her mind for the safety of her companions. What kind of woman, covered in scars, was so confident in her fighting abilities? What kind of woman had they let join them? If there was an Afyr so deadly with a blade, why hadn't she heard of her? Her mind raced with the possibilities.

Kellum withdrew a knife from his bandoleer and threw it at Vaelys, yelling, "Catch!"

Vaelys caught the blade point first, heading directly for her face. She didn't flinch. "You walk a very fine line, archer," said Vaelys.

Gone was the delicate nature of her voice. Anger laced her words. Lyla's eyes grew wide.

"I... I'm sorry," said Kellum, taking a step back.

Everyone who saw the act displayed their disappointment in Kellum, and shock at what they'd seen Vaelys do. Kyrilis wasn't sure she'd be able to catch a blade so easily, and she considered herself very skilled in the arts of war.

"You can have my daggers, my lady," offered Kellum.

He removed the sheaths from his thighs and placed them at her feet. She handed his throwing knife back to him with an evil smirk upon her face. Vaelys stood and linked the belts together to position the sheaths at the small of her back sideways, the handle of each facing outward. Drawing them with blinding speed, she twirled them about in her hands, swinging them in mock combat before returning them to their home. She made little effort to hide the pain she felt as she tested her new blades.

"The left one is a hair off balance, but they'll do," said Vaelys as she returned to her seat.

Kellum gulped, realizing she was the last person he wanted to infuriate. Gellix got up and pulled Kellum away from the camp, yelling at him for his stupidity. Gaerin walked over and joined them, anger lacing his every word. Meanwhile, Bolrin and Gabner went to work reheating their evening meal of wild root vegetables, onions and herbs.

Kyrilis leaned over to Vaelys and whispered, "Are you... from House Fa'Rezlin?"

Vaelys's face tensed. "Why would you think that?"

"The Fa'Rezlin lived outside a small town at the edge of our southern borders long ago. They were attacked by Toor, but their daughter was never found. I just wondered if-"

"Well, stop wondering... that was me. I was five, and my mother told me to run. So, I ran, and I kept running. I found a cave and I went in to hide. Before I knew it I was lost. A few days later, I found myself so deep underground that I stumbled into a Velloth scouting party. I was their slave for over eighty years," said Vaelys.

"By the gods... I-"

"Shouldn't have asked, but now you know. Not all Afyr are blessed with a life of luxury. I learned a lot from the Velloth, and even more when I fought my way to freedom. After I returned to the Afyr, I was shunned and exiled. I didn't fit into their perfect little society any longer. I've been on my own ever since," explained Vaelys. "So, you'll have to forgive me if I don't see you as kin."

"I am so sorry, Vaelys," said Kyrilis.

"Did you say Velloth?" asked Lyla.

Vaelys sighed. "Yes, I said Velloth."

"They attacked Grellenheim a few weeks ago, and a dragon attacked Port Vaelin right as we were leaving," said Lyla.

"What the hell?" asked Vaelys, surprised.

"It's true," said Kyrilis. "In fact, the Velloth attacked several locations, and performed a ritual to wake an ancient dragon that attacked Port Vaelin."

"Fuck!" said Vaelys.

"What?" asked Kyrilis.

"We left Tellrindos because the Velloth attacked the entire northern border of Arkhania and spilled into the villages, including Port Gandraias where I was staying," Vaelys explained.

Kyrilis's face went stark white. "What of the Afyr?"

"I didn't receive word of their fate, but I assume they were attacked as well," said Vaelys.

"Oh no," said Lyla.

"I killed three dozen of the fuckers on my way to the docks. Two of the men on the ship were traveling merchants who paid for passage to escape. I saved their lives, so they brought me along. They talked at great length about the burning villages along the southern roads," she sighed. "I thought it was just happening in Tellrindos."

"You cut your way through thirty-six Velloth? Alone?" asked Lyla.

"More or less. Not all at once, mind you," said Vaelys. "They terrify me, still. All I could think of was getting away from them... here I was about to sail right into more," said Vaelys.

"No, we killed the ones that attacked Grellenheim. Well... me, Gaerin, a few city guards, our nephew and several students from Fel'Rechaun," said Lyla.

"I killed the ones that attacked Gaierford, and then Laurence, her nephew, led a group to hunt down the rest. As far as we were aware, Arkhania was free from them," added Kyrilis.

"Clearly central Arkhania was equipped to handle the invasion, but Uldenheim and Tellrindos failed miserably," said Vaelys. "I need to travel to Dagoh Bay and seek passage on another ship."

"We are traveling to Caierthor, you could accompany us," offered Lyla.

"I will do that," said Vaelys.

Not all of her story had been true, but they hadn't seemed to notice. She decided they didn't need to know her true past, her true destination, or why she'd been wearing silk. The less they knew, the easier it would be to learn more about them. Besides, if they realized her true identity she'd be forced to kill them all. She normally disliked doing that to people who seemed so nice and genuine; especially those that saved her life.

Gaerin returned to the group and changed the subject.

Everyone took time introducing themselves to Vaelys while they ate. Conversations were much more jovial for the remainder of the night.

∴ ∴ ∴

LYLA PRAYED over Vaelys for more healing in the morning while the rest of the group packed and prepared to move. Rolling her right shoulder around in its socket, she nodded at Lyla in approval and thanks. Her shoulder still hurt, and her ribs ached, but she had proper mobility and felt confident that she'd be able to contribute in a fight.

The mountain to the east occupied much of the horizon; its peak flat, as if cut off by some unknown force long ago. Many members of the party stood on the shore watching as the sun crested the peak, setting the sky ablaze in a spectacular display.

"What is the name of this mountain?" asked Lyla as Ahrwie approached.

"Krierga is an ancient volcano," he answered.

"There are legends that it once flowed with wondrous might, creating Aegir for the Aegra," added Wehrenel.

"A gift from Kaggarha," said Ahrwie.

"Now it gives life," said Wehrenel.

"What do you mean?" asked Lyla.

"It flows with water, the essence of life," said Wehrenel.

"Boiling pools up top with many geysers," said Ahrwie.

"Eastern side is sheared off, flattened over a thousand years by a series of waterfalls," said Wehrenel.

"That's why ships don't use the channel," said Ahrwie.

"Too turbulent," Wehrenel clarified.

"That's fascinating," said Lyla.

Lyla stared at Krierga for a few minutes, wondering where its waters came from. As she was about to ask more questions, Gaerin walked up adjusting his gauntlets.

"How much further to the fort?" asked Gaerin.

"Is along the western face of Krierga," answered Ahrwie, pointing.

"Wouldn't it have been faster to cut straight through the forest?" asked Gaerin.

"Yes, but many villages along the way which would have slowed us down," said Ahrwie.

"And patrols, which could alert them to our presence," added Wehrenel.

"Fair enough," said Gaerin. Turning to the rest of the camp, he yelled, "Let's get moving!"

∴ ∴ ∴

THEIR JOURNEY along the shore lasted nearly the entire day. As the shore became more and more littered with mossy rocks and boulders, they turned southeast into the woods once more. As day turned to night, they reached a field of old stumps from trees felled many years prior.

Ahrwie stopped beside one of the stumps and signaled for the rest of them to do the same.

"It's not far now," said Ahrwie.

"We need to be careful," added Wehrenel.

"How many did you say were in the fortress again?" asked Lyla.

"We don't know. It changes frequently," said Wehrenel, shrugging.

"They come and go... twenty to thirty perhaps," added Ahrwie.

"Soldiers, archers, servants... all will defend," said Wehrenel.

"All must die," confirmed Ahrwie, nodding.

"They will," answered Gaerin.

"Only those who will be fighting should proceed from here," said Ahrwie.

"Have the rest set camp here," said Wehrenel.

"Without campfires," added Ahrwie.

Gaerin nodded in agreement. He gathered Keifer, Bolrin and Gabner and gave them instructions for setting up camp. Everyone else gathered and prepared for battle, leaving their satchels behind in a pile. With their preparations complete, they returned to Wehrenel and Ahrwie.

"With these stumps, and the forest is thinning, we have less cover... they'll see us coming," said Gaerin.

"Yes, but we have a plan," said Ahrwie.

"We will sneak ahead of you. Since we are small, and at one with our forest, they will not catch sight of us," assured Wehrenel.

"We will make a distraction, and provide a way to climb the front wall of the fort," said Ahrwie.

"Someone should sneak in from the east, behind the keep," suggested Wehrenel.

"I'll go," said Vaelys.

"Me as well," added Kyrilis.

With their crude plan decided, the group set out slowly and carefully. Night had fallen, and the forest canopy limited the amount of light provided by Argos and Provoss, casting great shadows.

Gaerin, Lyla, Gellix and Gareg found it difficult to navigate the woods without torchlight and had to rely on assistance from Oben and Kellum, both of whom could see fairly well in dim light due to their orcish and elven blood.

Vaelys and Kyrilis split away from the group, heading directly east toward the edge of the wood and the mountain beyond. Afyr were more at home in the cold climates of the north; a detail that was common knowledge. The villages that most travelers visited were located along the border to Tellrindos amidst the foothills of the Mythaeil Mountains.

Most did not know the capital city of the Afyr, Vey'Thugohn, sat high in the cliffs on the side of Mount Feyr. Afyr were at home on mountainous terrain, which allowed Vaelys and Kyrilis to move rather quickly up the rocky slopes and crags to a small ledge above the keep.

Two layers of log walls surrounded the wooden fort, bound by rope and chinked with brown clay. Three feet of dirt filled the space between the walls, making the fortifications six feet thick. Rough planks lay atop the dirt core, allowing guards to walk their length and keep watch.

From their position, they could see four outbuildings around the courtyard and a keep at the rear that stood three stories tall. A small tower sat atop the keep at the northeast corner.

Vaelys made her way to a spot on the cliff directly across from, and slightly higher than, the roof of the keep and waited for the distraction to occur.

Kyrilis joined her, waiting to see what Vaelys planned to do so she could follow.

They watched as soldiers dined in the courtyard, laughing around tables full of food and mead. Three guards paced the wall, quivers on their hips and bows at the ready.

Candlelight flickered gently in the top room of the keep's tower, drawing Vaelys's attention. She focused, waiting, and decided on her first target.

∴ ∴ ∴

WEHRENEL AND Ahrwie split up. They each selected a large tree in the second line from the edge of the woods. Their selected trees were half as tall as the distance between where they stood and the edge of the wall. With a simple prayer for forgiveness, they both placed their hands on their respective trees and began to chant.

Gaerin, Lyla and the other companions huddled up a short

distance away and watched with curiosity as the faun cast their spells.

Kellum whispered to them, describing what he could see with his night vision.

The underbrush, moss, grass and clover around the faun turned brown, withered and shriveled into dust in a matter of seconds. The trees they were touching absorbed their own bark, revealing the white wood underneath as the tree bodies swelled and grew larger. Pine needles shrank back into their branches, and the branches shrank back into the trunks of the trees as each tree grew taller.

Several trees around each faun began to wither and die, as they consumed their essence to push the growth of their chosen trees further and further. After a few minutes, their trees grew tall enough to extend over the top of the fort's walls if they should fall. The trunks increased in width, becoming square to provide a flat surface to walk on.

"By the gods, they're making tree-sized planks so we can run over the walls," gasped Kellum.

"Do we need to help chop them-" began Lyla.

The trunks of the two trees broke clean through, their loud snap interrupting the group's discussion. They fell toward the fort; the air rushing around them with a great whoosh.

Kellum and Oben urged the companions to hurry toward the trees.

Gaerin and Lyla followed Oben to the closest tree, while Gareg and Gellix followed Kellum to the furthest.

Ahrwie and Wehrenel passed out from exhaustion as the trees crashed through the front line of the woods and down onto the wall.

The sound of the impact was so loud that it ruptured the eardrums of a nearby archer atop the wall on the north side of the compound. As the trees crashed down between the poles of the outer wall, embedding themselves firmly into the clay and dirt core, the guard planks ruptured, sending splinters and shards flying in all directions.

Kellum and Oben climbed on top of their respective tree ramps and ran their length, headed for the fort.

Gaerin, Lyla, Gellix and Gareg followed as quickly as they could behind them.

.˙ .˙.˙.

THE SOUND of the trees crashing through the walls echoed off the cliff where Vaelys and Kyrilis perched.

Vaelys clung to the wall with her fingertips, her back to the keep. She raised her feet parallel to her waist, released her grip and kicked off as hard as she could, launching herself through the air.

She twisted mid-air to put herself face down as she crossed between the cliff and the keep. Her elevation had been just enough to allow her to dive straight through the open window, tumble across the floor and rise to her feet in one motion.

Kyrilis choked back her fear and prepared to follow, unsure if she could perform the same maneuver.

The fort's commander had been reviewing papers when the crash occurred. Rushing to the window facing the courtyard to inspect the cause of the noise had unwittingly placed his back toward Vaelys, making him an easy victim.

Kyrilis crashed into the wall of the keep, clinging desperately to the window Vaelys had passed through. Vaelys slid her daggers deftly through both sides of the commander's neck. She climbed through the window just as Vaelys vanished down the stairs.

Who is this woman, thought Kyrilis?

Kyrilis considered herself quite agile and skilled in combat. Seeing Vaelys in action made her feel inferior, and that was not a feeling she enjoyed. Not only was she more agile, she was apparently much stronger.

As impressive as Vaelys's speed and lethality were, Kyrilis also couldn't recall hearing any noise as she slew the commander, or brought him to the floor. Vaelys had somehow managed to kill the man without making a sound, despite the notoriously noisy plate armor he wore.

Steeling herself for the battle at hand, she ran down the stairs behind Vaelys as quickly as she could.

∴ ∴ ∴

THE SOLDIERS in the courtyard scrambled to retrieve their weapons. Several arrows whizzed past his head as Kellum ducked and weaved his way to the end of the log. Another ricocheted off his brigandine, careening harmlessly away but ripping the cloth that covered it.

Kellum fired two arrows before he came to a stop, killing two of the three archers on the wall with shots to the face.

Oben closed the distance across his own log, cleaving the third archer through both shoulders with his twin axes as he arrived. He jumped from the wall and raced toward the soldiers in the courtyard, many wearing partial suits of armor and still without their weapons.

Kellum stepped aside to make room for Gellix and Gareg to pass and began peppering the soldiers in the courtyard with arrows, injuring one after another.

Gareg jumped to the ground without hesitation, running straight toward a very terrified soldier who was ill-prepared for such an attack. Dragging his greatsword behind him as he ran, he brought it around as he closed the distance with his target. As he ran by, the sword cleaved the man in two at the waist. Gareg roared angrily as he continued toward a group of three men.

Oben raced across the grounds, heading for another archer who had just retrieved his bow. Desperately, the archer tried to turn and fire at Oben. The half-orc dipped to his right, allowing the arrow to fire harmlessly over his left shoulder. He stood quickly, driving his heels into the ground as he drew the axe in his right hand up into the archer's exposed chin, splitting the man's face open to horrifying effect.

Gaerin and Lyla descended the stairs from the wall and immediately engaged a group of five nearby soldiers. Gaerin lowered his posture and braced behind his shield as they closed the distance, driving it into two of the men on the left. Lyla followed suit, driving her shield into the man on the far right.

As if on queue, an arrow struck the man in the middle, piercing through his neck.

The man on Lyla's left attacked, reaching around her shield. She dipped to her right, causing the blow to glance off her pauldron.

Gaerin shoved hard to his left, pushing the man on the outside of the fray back, while he brought his warhammer in toward the other man's side with all his might. His weapon crashed into the man's left forearm, shattering the bones inside as he attempted to deflect Gaerin's blow.

Kellum released another arrow, killing the man to Lyla's left. He looked back across the courtyard, and watched as Gareg swung his massive sword at a soldier, missed, and crashed through one of the tables they'd been eating at.

With another arrow, Kellum killed the man that dodged Gareg's blow, giving his friend a chance to pull his blade free of the mess he'd created.

.·.·.·.

KYRILIS ROUNDED the corner of the stairs, entering the second floor of the small keep. Two corpses lie in the hallway before her, necks sliced open with deadly precision. She leaped over them and continued her sprint, trying to catch up with Vaelys. A door slammed open in front of her as a soldier barreled out of his chambers.

Upon seeing Kyrilis, he turned and attacked with his longsword. She parried his blow easily with her dagger, sending it high and into the wall. Pressing her parry to hold his blade aloft, she stepped into his reach and slipped her sword through the armhole in his brigandine, deep into his chest. Gasping for air and groaning in pain, he dropped to his knees with a resounding thud as his sword clattered to the floor.

She pushed him aside and stepped around the door, continuing to the next set of stairs. The clash of blades rang out from below.

Kyrilis bounded down the stairs in a hurry to assist. As she rounded the corner at the bottom, she could see Vaelys standing in the middle of six men in the central chamber.

One attacked, and she parried with a dagger.

Another attacked her from behind, but she spun to parry his blade just in time.

A third thrust his blade toward her. She spun, stabbed the man between the bones in his forearm and pulled his arm across the opening, driving his sword into the fourth.

Pulling her blade free, she spun to face a fifth man. Raising her weapons in unison, she caught his downward slash with her crossed daggers and kicked him in the chest, sending him backward several feet.

Her maneuvers happened so fast it was hard for Kyrilis to keep up with what was going on.

Shaking herself free of her astonishment, Kyrilis raced forward to help. *Not that she needs my help*, she thought. She charged the sixth man, weapons at the ready. Her target turned and braced to meet her charge.

Vaelys smirked evilly and took the opportunity to drive a dagger through the man's neck from behind.

Kyrilis changed targets and ran to the rear of the first man she'd seen Vaelys parry. As he turned to face his new opponent, she slid her sword through the neck of his brigandine, driving it down into his chest, then ripped it free violently.

Vaelys spun and parried blows from three opponents in a blinding flurry.

The man she'd stabbed in the wrist backed away from the battle, grasping his sword arm eagerly with his other hand. His sword still planted firmly in the chest of his unintended victim; he was unprepared to defend against Kyrilis as she spun around the rest of the group.

Her sword came around in an arc as she turned, slicing through his neck just as he noticed her.

∴ ∴ ∴

GAREG HAD drawn a crowd; something his friends had come to expect. Seven men gathered around him in a wide circle, each attempting to duck in for an attack whenever his back faced them.

Gellix and Oben took advantage of the soldiers' frantic attempts to control their berserker comrade, and dispatched three of them before the others caught on to the trap they'd fallen into.

Kellum chuckled at the sight as he turned his attention back to Gaerin and Lyla.

Gaerin deflected one man's sword with his shield and stepped backwards to dodge the other man's downward strike.

Lyla deflected her opponent's slash to the outside and took advantage of the opening to send her mace upward into the man's chin, shattering his jaw and sending him to the ground. She jumped over his body to assist Gaerin, taking one of his opponents off his hands.

Gaerin winced as his opponent's sword glanced off the top of his shield and sliced open his left cheek. Angry, he lifted his shield higher, pushing the man's sword out of the way. Without hesitation, he stepped forward and drove his warhammer into the man's groin.

Lyla ducked under her opponent's wild swing, and crashed her mace into his left knee, sending him to the ground.

Kellum put an arrow into each of their opponent's heads to finish them off, then nodded to them as they looked up in thanks.

Vaelys and Kyrilis burst through the doors of the keep, racing into the courtyard.

Vaelys turned on her heel and, in one fluid motion, threw her daggers at the backs of the two men fighting Gareg.

After Gellix, Oben and Gareg finished the last three soldiers, the companions gathered at the center of the courtyard.

"Well, that was intense," observed Gaerin as he stowed his weapon.

"Exhilarating!" exclaimed Vaelys with a wicked grin.

"You are impressive!" Kyrilis remarked.

"Not so bad yourself," offered Vaelys.

"How many were inside?" asked Lyla as she stowed her mace.

"Ten," answered Kyrilis, "including their commander." Kneeling, she cleaned her weapons on the pants of one of their victims, then sheathed them.

"Eighteen outside," added Kellum.

"Twenty-eight total... sounds about right," said Gaerin. "They said between twenty and thirty."

"Leave it to Kellum to steal my kills," joked Gareg as he walked up. "Can't let a man kill in peace."

"That wasn't me, Gareg," Kellum retorted, pointing at Vaelys.

"My apologies," offered Vaelys.

Oben walked over to Vaelys, offering her the daggers she'd thrown. "These are yours."

"Thank you, Oben."

"What do you say we make camp here for the night?" Lyla asked Gaerin.

"We'll clear the bodies," offered Gellix.

"I'll, um... collect our friends," offered Kellum.

After an hour of dragging corpses, the courtyard's center was clear and the keep was empty. Kellum returned with Bolrin, Keifer, Gabner and the faun while the others were working.

Bolrin, Keifer and Gabner entered the keep in search of a kitchen, expecting everyone would be hungry after such an affair.

∴ ∴ ∴

GAERIN WAS sitting in the commander's office reviewing documents and maps by candlelight when Lyla approached. He was completely unaware of how long he'd been sitting there, and her sudden presence startled him. When she touched his shoulder, he jumped in his seat and whipped his head around so fast it sent a wave of pain shooting through his face, making him wince.

"You know... this would be funny if it weren't so horrific. You should have let me fix that cheek of yours before you disappeared," she mused.

The wound on Gaerin's left cheek nearly exposed his teeth. Blood was caked on his face, his neck and down into his gambeson. Coupled with the dirt from their travels, and his recent lack of shaving, he looked like a homeless man, fresh out of a bar fight.

"I-" he retorted. The pain that shot through his face as he attempted to talk was excruciating.

"Yeah, don't do that," she said, reaching for his cheek with a wet cloth. "Let me clean this up and heal it for you, *then* you can get all snarky."

Gaerin sighed and clenched his jaw, biting back against the pain as she worked. She carefully cleared away the blood and dirt that crusted in and around the wound, inspecting the damage to know the extent of healing he would need. After a few seconds, she chanted a simple prayer and placed her hand over the gash, sealing it and repairing the muscles underneath.

"There, now you can-"

"You should see what I found," interrupted Gaerin.

"What's *that*, love?" she asked, sighing and rolling her eyes.

"This garrison arrived years ago on orders to build this fort and wait. They demanded tribute from the locals, alright, but that wasn't their real purpose. It seems the commander has been communicating with the mainland by pigeon this whole time, asking if they could proceed to the next step of some... *plan*."

He showed her a few of the papers containing responses from someone named Ahm Stonehawk, High Priest of Pelrigoss. She studied them for a moment, before handing them back in frustration.

"Why don't you just give me the relevant bits. Don't make me read the-"

"This fortress was phase one in an expansion plan, but... they aren't just claiming territory. They're claiming *souls*. More importantly, they want the souls of the Aegra that live on Aegir. That's not all... they appear to be doing the same thing across the Triblunds, and Drog'na."

"Why do they want souls? How does that even make sense?" asked Lyla, exacerbated.

"Apparently, the commanders of each garrison were promised armor like Drakahl's. To make that armor, they have to consume souls in ritual sacrifice. The more magical the souls, the more powerful the armor."

"That doesn't even sound possible."

"Well, it's happening. The last message he received clearly stated reinforcements would be arriving within the month, and that his unit should relax while they could... that they wouldn't get another chance to rest once the 'Gathering' began."

"How long ago did he receive that message?" Lyla asked, even more concerned.

"Two and a half weeks," answered Gaerin with worry lacing his words.

"Fuck!" blurted Lyla.

"Indeed. They could almost be here. We could run into them before we hit the docks, at the docks, after we cross to the Triblunds..." Gaerin's words trailed off as his thoughts turned to the worst possible outcomes. "This garrison wasn't prepared to defend an attack, because the Aegra haven't put up a fight, and outsiders don't come to this island. We took them by surprise, and that's-"

"The only reason we defeated twenty-eight men with our small group. We need to get out of here!" she exclaimed.

"We can't. Not tonight, anyway. Everyone's exhausted, the night's half gone already, you're probably out of healing spells," reasoned Gaerin.

"Well... this just went to shit, didn't it?" Lyla asked rhetorically, throwing her arms into the air in frustration.

"We're in the thick of it now, my love," he answered.

Gaerin stood and embraced her for a moment. She sighed and turned to leave. He rolled the various papers and maps together and went down to the barracks level with her.

The rest of the party were fast asleep already, except for a simple guard rotation. Aside from their anxiety at the information they'd discovered, the night was fairly peaceful, even if short.

∴ ∴ ∴

VAELYS RARELY slept. As an elf, her body only needed a few short hours of meditation to feel fully rested. However, as she meditated—perched atop the keep's tower—dark shadows climbed up her body as if living things, encircling her head, and drawing her into a deep slumber.

For hours—which felt like years—she dreamed of fighting battles where surrender was her only option. Time and time again, she envisioned herself fighting for her life and dying, or surrendering and going on to achieve greater glory. As she twisted and lurched on the roof of the keep, the shadows about her writhed and shifted, bringing her dream after dream.

Hundreds of miles away, Nightweaver leaned back in her chair and the vision within her crystal ball went dark. Drakahl stood beside her, impatiently waiting for news of her recent manipulations. When he could wait no longer, he broke the silence and interrupted her train of thought.

"So you send her to aid our enemy? Why did I free her from the Velloth decades ago, only to fight against her now?" asked Drakahl.

'She's betraying you,' hissed Axvalla. Drakahl pushed back, driving Axvalla out of his conscious thoughts.

"You assume too much, young Drakahl," chided Nightweaver. "I brought her to them so they might carry her to where she needs to be."

"She is to join us?"

"Control yourself and exert some patience, for the sake of my sanity as well as your own. She has a task to perform, and she is on a path towards it. Much like you have a task to perform," she stated. "How does your task proceed, with your constant presence at my side?"

"Ahm is handling it," answered Drakahl. "What of our garrison on Aegir? Why allow them to destroy it?"

"A necessary turn of events, nothing more. The Aegra were never to be touched by our plot. Freeing them does nothing to prevent us from reaching our goal. Who was it that sent forces to Aegir without my blessing, I wonder?"

"Ahm," answered Drakahl, turning to leave.

"See that he does not continue to lose focus and overreach," she instructed as Drakahl departed.

He strode out of the room, angry and frustrated. How she could know so much of the future, and their path, was beyond his ability to reason. It wasn't in his nature to be comfortable following others, especially when he couldn't see the breadth of their plan. If she hadn't proven herself time and time again, he would have handled her just like every other frustration in recent years.

Intent on proving his worth and regaining the favor his impatience had cost him in recent weeks, he set off to search for Ahm.

ADVENT

Ris'Anyu, Arran'Hael 13th, 113 of the 2nd Era

Come they will, to the sundered isle,
And bring their might to bear.
They come to take the Demon down,
But still they must prepare.

Night's Writ, Parable 11

MORDECHAI STOOD alone at the railing for a time, puffing gently on a pipe and musing over what would come of their journey. Try as he might to avoid it, his mind kept wandering back to the Grand Awakening. Relief came when Laurence joined him, providing a much-needed distraction.

"You've been out here a while," Laurence mentioned. He leaned his elbows on the rail at Mordechai's side, looking at his friend for a moment before casting his gaze toward the stars.

"There isn't much else to do on a ship for days on end." Mordechai took another long drag on his pipe before tapping it out on the railing; small embers fizzling as they drifted into the waters below.

"You could spar with the rest of us," joked Laurence.

Mordechai chuckled at the thought. "I'd have a better chance of accidentally killing myself with my own blade than besting the likes of you," he quipped.

"Oh, I'm nothing special."

"I beg to differ," retorted Mordechai. "Besides, I'm blind."

"True enough," admitted Laurence.

"I've heard the others lamenting your progress. You're no longer ducking out of the way when Agnar strikes. You're faster than you were before... Izabel won't shut up about how frustrating you are to fight. It is, perhaps, time to drop the modesty and face what you are," said Mordechai.

"Arcturus drilled modesty into me as far back as I can remember."

"Be that as it may—and while I'm not suggesting you brag—constantly speaking with that level of modesty while displaying such skill is insulting to those you spar with. So, do your friends a favor," suggested Mordechai.

"Will do, Mordy," said Laurence, chuckling.

"Sometimes I hate Agnar," sighed Mordechai.

Laurence laughed, drawing a smirk from his friend. "Tomorrow marks one month since Arcturus died," said Laurence.

"A lot has happened since then."

"A lot more combat than I expected, if I'm being truthful. I've seen and learned a lot. Being with you, I've also been exposed to a lot of things I never imagined. To that end," began Laurence, hesitating, "I've been meaning to ask what you are."

"What do you mean?" asked Mordechai.

"I mean... my grandfather was an alchemist, and apparently some kind of wizard. Karzden told me two versions of what you were, seeming to be confused as to your past and your station. Fahrul led me to believe you work directly for the King. So, what are you, precisely? I know you're not just a student, but I can't just go around calling you 'mage' forever," inquired Laurence.

Mordechai took a few moments to withdraw a few pinches of tobacco from his robes and pack his pipe again. He produced a tiny jet of flame from his right pinky finger and used it to light the pipe as he gently puffed. Once the pipe was burning properly, he removed it from his lips and turned to face Laurence.

"I am Archmagus to Arkhania, that much is true. And I am no more a student of Fel'Vizsiour than you are. As for what kind of 'mage' I might be, I am both a Timewalker and a Leyweaver," he answered matter-of-factly.

"A what and a who? Look... I've seen you do some crazy things, but those terms make little sense to me."

"Leyweaver means two things. It is a combination of Leywalking and Weaving. Leywalkers can sense, see, and interact with the magical weave that surrounds Ayrelon. It looks like a blue net made of lightning—if you will—but on a much grander scale. It crosses the world east to west, north to south, and diagonally. The points where those Leylines cross are called a Nexus.

"With normal Wizardry, the caster memorizes spells, meditates on them and pulls the power for those spells into themselves. They hold those spells in reserve and then release them when they wish, by calling them forth. With Leywalking, one learns to pull power right out of the air, drawing directly from that magical weave at the time of their casting.

"While being a much more powerful form of casting, it is also more dangerous to the caster. The energies—while not stored—still flow through the caster, but there are no safeties. With a stored spell, there is a prescribed and pre-defined limit. When you pull directly from the magical weave in real time, the powers coursing through you are unconstrained by the structures of a spell and can overwhelm you.

"However, this opens up so many more possibilities than normal Wizardry, because you aren't bound by written spells. This leads to a technique most casters strive for but never achieve... Weaving," he explained. He stopped for a moment to puff on his pipe before continuing.

Laurence waited eagerly, his interest piqued.

"Weaving is the art of casting without casting. Or rather, casting without the use of defined spells. A Weaver learns to draw magical energies and form them into their desired effect freely. The limits of such a manner of casting are the imagination of the Weaver, their experience in bending those energies to their will, and their ability to act as a conduit for the energies required to produce the result. It is a difficult method of casting that few ever master. I'm so old that I do not remember learning it," he explained.

"So you can just... make things happen?" gawked Laurence.

"To an extent, yes. I have not had reasonable motivation to learn or push my limits in recent centuries. I've been too caught up in researching my origins and scouring the lands for any bits of history I could find," he answered. "Most of what I use my Leyweaving abilities to do are conveniences. Though, I did use them in combat with you in Grellenheim when we fought the Velloth."

"I heard you cast spells in Grellenheim," corrected Laurence.

"Yes, but no. I am a Thought caster, meaning I can usually think of what I want done, and then bend the Magical Weave's energies to make it happen. In areas where I have less experience, such as combat magics, I use Verbal and Somatic gestures to help me channel those energies and focus them. Think of me speaking when I cast, or waving my arms around, as a funnel you might use to fill a particularly small flask with fluids in your grandfather's shop. It's a tool that isn't always necessary, but helps in certain situations," explained Mordechai.

He casually lifted his pipe and took a deep drag, exhaling the smoke over his shoulder toward the sea.

"Okay, so what about Timewalker? I thought you said—when we first met—that Time casting was outlawed?" asked Laurence.

"It is. I don't remember learning it, so clearly that occurred before Arkhania existed, and therefore prior to the laws you refer to. The only thing I normally use it for is teleportation. In truth, I didn't originally know that was how I accomplished that feat. I woke up twelve-hundred and thirty-three years ago simply knowing and doing these things, and only recently pieced together how I did them," he answered.

"So, what you're saying is that you are immensely powerful!" exclaimed Laurence.

"I suppose... as I stated, I don't push myself to see how far I can go. If I need to do a thing, I do that thing. Other than teleportation, chores, or moving scrolls around my office at Fel'Vizsiour, I rarely use magic. In fact, Ayriel casts spells far more often than I, and she's a princess who spends most of her time at court," Mordechai explained.

"In truth, magic brings both power and risk. I don't know my limits, and that terrifies me. I don't know how I learned what I can do, and that also terrifies me. When I used that spell on the shores of Gusarski Cove, I didn't know if it was going to work or be my undoing. In fact," Mordechai stated firmly, "I have cast spells far more recklessly since I came to know you than the sum total of my prior life's memories combined."

Laurence contemplated the gravity of Mordechai's words. He hadn't realized the risks involved in magic, or the danger Mordechai was in every time he cast a spell. The world of magic was far more complex than he'd been led to believe in his upbringing.

"How do you know that you 'woke up' twelve-hundred and thirty-three years ago? And what do you mean by that?" asked Laurence, attempting to change the subject.

Mordechai sighed, realizing the distraction was over.

He didn't minded talking about magic, and how spellcasting worked. It had been a welcome change from the revelations he was trying to avoid thinking about. Begrudgingly, he spent the next several hours explaining his discovery of the Grand Awakening to Laurence.

∴ ∴ ∴

THE NEXT morning, Lyla discovered that Wehrenel and Ahrwie were no longer in the fortress. Frantic, she sent everyone in the group scouring the compound. After an hour of searching with no signs of the faun, Gaerin finally convinced her to give up.

As they completed packing up and made their way toward the gates, a stream of faun poured over the wall over the fallen trees. The group froze, watching the fauns' actions intently.

Vaelys's hands instinctively went to her daggers, ready to act.

Aegra scattered throughout the courtyard, each taking a position next to a corpse along the walls. They knelt and placed one tiny hand on a corpse and the other on the wall, chanting. Wehrenel and Ahrwie approached the group hurriedly.

"It is time to leave," said Wehrenel.

"Before they finish," added Ahrwie.

"What are they doing?" asked Lyla.

"Consuming the corpses to burn the fortress down," said Ahrwie.

"So that the forest can reclaim the land," finished Wehrenel.

"Oh! Well... let's get going then!" exclaimed Lyla.

The group traveled southeast along a well-worn path through the woods as the fortress burned behind them. Thick streams of black smoke drifted into the sky.

Gaerin looked back and noticed the smoke, then turned to Lyla with concern. "I don't think that was the wisest course of action."

"Why's that?" she asked.

"Someone's going to see that smoke," he pointed out.

"Crap," she responded. "Everyone listen up!" she shouted. "That smoke is going to draw attention, and Drakahl's forces made this path we're using. Kellum scout ahead, please. Everyone be on alert!"

"Nicely handled," said Gaerin.

"That's because I handled it," she said, smirking.

"Oh, come o-"

"Nuh-uh. You could've handled it yourself, but you chose to whine. You get no say in the matter," she teased.

Gaerin sighed, then chuckled quietly. He knew she was right; he should have just organized the group himself. The group was larger than he was used to dealing with, and he simply was not a social creature like his wife. *If we get through this, it will be her doing,* he thought.

Kellum ran ahead, using the forest for cover.

Kyrilis, Gellix and Oben formed a line at the front of the group, leading their way along the path.

Vaelys and Gareg fell to the rear to protect against any attack from behind.

Gaerin and Lyla watched as the members of the group went into action without needing to coordinate their positioning, as if they had been traveling together for years.

The group traveled in that formation for nearly an hour with no sign of trouble. However, just as Gaerin, Lyla and the others in the center of their group were about to relax and assume they'd overreacted, shouting rang out ahead of them.

Kyrilis, Gellix and Oben ran as fast as they could toward the noise. They rounded a bend in the path to see two corpses on the ground, wearing full armor, with arrows protruding from their throats. Several voices called out from their right.

The rest of the soldiers searched for their unseen assailant.

The trio turned and ran through the forest, intent on assisting Kellum. When they arrived at the scene, they could see Kellum sitting on a tree branch, gleefully waving down at three soldiers below him.

Kyrilis stifled a laugh as she ran in from their rear, sword and dagger at the ready.

Hearing them approach, the soldiers spun around to defend themselves. The one in the middle stepped forward and slashed his sword toward Kyrilis. In one maneuver, she parried his blade aside with her dagger, thrust her sword through his throat, ripped her sword to the right, and parried an attack from the man next to him.

Oben closed in, axes twirling, and caused the third man to panic, step backward and trip over an exposed root.

Gellix engaged the man on Kyrilis's right, driving his sword into the man's side, while Oben finished the prone soldier.

With the soldiers slain, Kellum hopped down from his branch. "Thought I'd leave you guys something to play with," he joked.

"Did you kill the two on the path from here?" asked Kyrilis as she cleaned her blade.

"Of course he did, he's a show-off," said Oben.

"You're just jealous," retorted Kellum.

"That's enough boys," said Gellix in his gruff voice. "We got a boat to catch."

The four of them returned to the path to see Gaerin and Lyla waiting eagerly for some sign leading to the rest of their enemies. Upon seeing Kyrilis and the others walking calmly toward them, Gaerin put away his weapon and gave them an inquisitive look.

"It's handled, sir," offered Gellix.

"Five scouts... or messengers," said Kellum, shrugging.

"Which is it?" asked Gaerin.

"I didn't ask," laughed Kellum.

Gaerin sighed and shook his head. After sparing a few minutes to look for messages tucked into the soldier's pouches, the group resumed their journey toward the docks.

.· .·. .·.

AFTER NEARLY a full day of walking, they reached the outskirts of the small dock town. In the waning light of dusk, it was hard to tell how many soldiers were present from their vantage point along the tree line. Kellum tapped Gaerin on the shoulder and pointed up, signaling that he was going to climb the tree next to them for a better view.

Gaerin looked up at Kellum after a few moments. He signaled how many soldiers he could see by holding out five arrows. Nodding in acknowledgment, Gaerin passed the information to the rest of his group.

"Charge in?" whispered Lyla.

Vaelys and Kyrilis unsheathed their weapons.

Gaerin shrugged and retrieved his warhammer from his hip, then nodded.

With a quick gesture to Bolrin, Keifer and Gabner to stay back, Lyla turned, stood, and charged toward the series of small shacks around the docks.

Vaelys and Kyrilis split left and right, making room for their slower companions to fill the center.

Gaerin and Lyla struggled to keep up as Gellix, Oben and Gareg passed them.

Wehrenel and Ahrwie trotted alongside them, tiny bows in

hand, ready to help.

Kellum, still sitting in his tree, killed a guard at the front of the small town with two shots to the chest, alerting the rest of the soldiers that something was amiss.

Four guards ran into the open field to see what was going on, saw the party charging them with weapons at the ready, and fled back into the center of the small ring of shacks.

A horn sounded from the middle of town as the party split and ran around opposite sides of the nearest shack.

Vaelys cleared the left side of the shack and entered the open ground in the middle of town, just as two archers fired arrows in her direction. In a move that was nearly too fast to believe, she sliced one of the arrows out of the air. The second arrow made it through her parries, striking her in the right shoulder.

Vaelys yelped in pain, but kept moving toward the archers; standing on a small platform near the docks.

Kyrilis rounded the right side of the shack and diverted course to intercept, heading straight into the four soldiers waiting at the center of town.

Outnumbered, Kyrilis focused on fighting defensively. It took everything she had to deflect one attack after another in a never-ending barrage. Additionally, each of them were using a shield, making counterattacks difficult. She backtracked slowly, hoping that occupying the soldiers would be enough to help Vaelys survive until their companions arrived.

Gellix, Oben and Gareg rounded the right corner of the shack shortly after and engaged the four soldiers with Kyrilis.

Gareg focused his attacks on thrusts, so he would not harm his friends with swings of his massive sword.

Oben and Gellix, both dual wielding, went into flurries of attacks, driving their opponents frantically backwards.

As Gaerin, Lyla, Wehrenel and Ahrwie rounded the left side of the shack, Vaelys had just reached the archers.

Lyla, seeing that Vaelys had three arrows protruding from her, raced over to heal their newest companion.

When Gaerin saw where Lyla was heading, he noticed four more soldiers running toward them from the dock to the left, and a pigeon fluttering into the air from a shack near them.

"Fuck!" blurted Gaerin as he raced to join his wife.

Oben hacked his right axe at the top of his opponent's shield, latching it securely to the top after many such attempts. He pulled downward with all his strength, lowering the man's shield. His opponent retaliated with a sword attack, but Oben easily parried with his left axe. As their weapons collided, Oben turned his axe inward and jabbed it tip first into the man's nose. Blood erupted from the man's face.

Reeling backwards, the man failed to defend against Oben's next flurry of attacks and within seconds met his end.

Gellix attacked his opponent higher and higher, forcing him to raise his shield. Suddenly, he turned his weapons sideways, crossed them over each other and drove both fists into the man's shield with all his might.

He stepped into the punch and kicked down onto his opponent's left shin, shattering the bones with his hardened riding boot heel. As the man crumbled to the ground, Oben turned and buried an axe into the man's skull.

Kyrilis forced her opponent backward and began a flurry of quick strikes to the left side of his shield. As the man parried and blocked, she drew closer and closer. Occupying his weapon with left-handed strikes, she turned her right shoulder inward and jumped with all her strength, driving her shoulder and the full force of her weight into the shield, sending him backwards.

Gareg, fighting his own opponent next to her, noticed what she was doing and followed suit. He pressed his attack to drive his opponent backward, causing the two men to crash into one another.

As they collided, Kyrilis attacked Gareg's opponent with her longsword.

He raised his shield to deflect her strike, and Gareg used the opening to drive his greatsword through the guts of both men at once. After pulling his weapon free, the four of them raced over to help Gaerin, Lyla and Vaelys.

On the other side of the small town, Vaelys arrived at the archers with anger contorting her face. Her right shoulder, right thigh, and lower left side each had an arrow sticking out of them. Using her left arm, she slashed at the first archer's bow, shattering it in a single, powerful strike. She then tossed the dagger at the floor of the platform, burying the blade in the floor. With her left arm, she reached in and grabbed the terrified archer's wrist.

In the heat of the moment, she forgot where she was, and who she was with. Without proper concern for her identity, she used her true strength and wrenched the man's wrist around on itself, shattering the bones within. She stepped into the maneuver, bending his forearm at an unnatural angle perpendicular to the rest of his arm, driving the bones of his shattered forearm through the skin and the simple cloth sleeve that adorned it.

In a horrid display of strength, she drove the bones of his wrist across the gap between his arm and torso, burying them deep into his liver; strands of flesh and blood left streaming between the remnants of his arm and his torso. It was an attack that her true identity was famed for, and she had used it errantly in a moment of hate-fueled rage. The only thought on her mind prior had been, *how fucking dare you?*

The second archer dropped his bow instantly, absolute horror depriving his face of proper blood-flow. He tried to take a step back to avoid the insane elf before him, but found himself unable to move; his fear gripping him thoroughly. He watched in terror as she calmly knelt, retrieved her dagger, and slit his throat.

Lyla slid to a stop in the dirt as she witnessed Vaelys's attack. The horrific nature of the maneuver, the technique involved, and the sheer strength required to execute it shocked her to her core. Suddenly, she didn't feel comfortable around the strange woman. A rush of fear and regret filled her, momentarily preventing her from moving.

However, her dedication as a healer pushed past the hesitation in her conscious mind. After a few seconds, she regained her composure and pushed her fears aside enough to get moving. As she walked onto the platform, hands glowing with the power of healing magics, she looked Vaelys in the eyes and said, "We will talk about this later."

Gaerin missed the scene on the platform, focused instead on the new group of soldiers. Right as he engaged, two tiny arrows crossed over his shoulders. Each arrow found a home in one of the soldiers' eyes, giving him hope that he had not made a wrong move by running toward them so blindly.

He parried and blocked their attacks stepping backward, trying to bring them closer to his forces.

Kyrilis and the others joined Gaerin, ready to end the battle and claim the docks.

Outnumbered, the two men backed away from the fight as best they could. A dagger flipped quickly through the air from the direction of the platform, landing hilt-deep in the side of a soldier's skull. The other died shortly after, overcome by the rest of the group.

Vaelys stood silently as Lyla pulled the arrows from her flesh and applied small heals. She stared at Lyla constantly, waiting on judgment or recognition. Eyes still locked on Lyla, she noticed the two men fleeing out of the corner of her eye and, with a flick of her wrist, sent a dagger into the skull of one of them.

When the battle concluded, everyone gathered around Lyla and Vaelys, who still stood atop the platform.

Lyla's hands stopped glowing their yellow light, and she looked up at Vaelys, disbelief in her eyes.

"No, it will not be discussed," stated Vaelys firmly.

"Did I see what I think I saw? Are you-" began Kyrilis.

"*Who I am* and *what I am* are of *no concern to you!* For now, our paths align. I need to get to Dagoh Bay, and your group is heading to Caierthor, within which *lies* Dagoh Bay. My presence here means *nothing more than that.* So, I can keep assisting you, or I can continue on my own. Either way, I'm boarding that boat in the morning, and..." Vaelys continued angrily, turning to face Lyla again, "no, we will *not* discuss this."

Vaelys winced in pain as she stepped off the platform. Lyla's healing had been enough to keep her alive, but had not fully restored her movement, or healed her completely. She didn't have much concern for what the group thought of her. While she appreciated their assistance on the beach, she had no need of their approval. Feeling both anger and disappointment in herself for losing control, she walked off to find a quiet place and recover her composure.

As soon as she was outside earshot, Lyla mouthed, 'What the fuck?'

Kyrilis signaled for everyone to follow her toward the docks. Once they were further away from Vaelys, she whispered, "If she's who I think she is, *do nothing to upset her.* I can't stress that enough. I-"

"Who do you think she is?" whispered Gaerin.

"I've only heard of two people dying to the technique she used on that man. One was a prince in Tellrindos, the other a lord in Haern. Both deaths were considered assassinations," whispered Kyrilis.

"She's an assassin?" whispered Lyla with shock and fear in her voice.

"She's *the* assassin. And if she knows we know, she'll kill us all.

Nobody has seen her face in hundreds of years," explained Kyrilis in a fearful whisper. "I doubt Vaelys is her name, and somehow I doubt that's her real face. But make no mistake, her good will is the only reason we're still alive." Kyrilis was visibly trembling; filled with both adrenaline and fear.

"Who is-" started Gellix.

"She's Sylk. Founder and leader of the Hands of Death. Why she's here, in person, I don't know. Maybe she was being truthful? Maybe she was just traveling and got caught in a storm?" said Kyrilis. Whispering was becoming harder for her to accomplish.

Gaerin's eyes went wide at the mention of the name Sylk. He'd heard Arcturus speak of her.

Lyla wept, despair getting the better of her. She felt like it was her fault they saved Vaelys and brought her into the group, putting everyone at risk.

"Assassin or not, we've benefited from her presence... have we not?" suggested Gareg calmly. "She's not here to kill one of us, or we'd be dead. If she is indeed the most powerful assassin in the world... who are we to turn aside such good fortune as to have her fighting alongside us?" His cool, calm delivery helped drive his point home.

Realization crossed the faces of everyone present, one by one.

Lyla wiped the tears from her cheeks, sniffling as she did so. Firming herself for her next course of action, she turned to go find Vaelys.

"What are you doing?" whispered Kyrilis frantically.

"I'm going to go welcome Vaelys to our group. Again. The right way. And I'm going to tell her we are thankful for her help, and that we're here for her. You saw her scars. You heard her past. She needs someone in her life that cares. I'm going to tell her that as far as I'm concerned, she's family," said Lyla with newfound certainty on her face.

"You're going to what?" asked Gaerin.

"Gareg's right! What right do we have to act as if we're above her? Were we not killing the very same soldiers that she was? Have we not taken the same lives these past few days? How are we better than her?" demanded Lyla.

"I... suppose your right," answered Kyrilis.

"With what we're facing, we can't afford to turn away her help. Besides... if any part of her story is true, she needs love more than anyone here," she said with finality.

Lyla turned before anyone could respond and walked off.

As the rest of the group composed themselves, Kellum walked up with Bolrin, Keifer and Gabner.

"What did I miss?" asked Kellum.

.·. .·. .·.

LYLA FOUND Vaelys on the dock the next morning watching the sunrise. As she approached, the elven woman turned her head ever so slightly, then returned her gaze to the east.

"Lyla," Vaelys said, acknowledging her visitor.

"I am so sorry we reacted the way we did last night," she apologized. "We talked after you left and decided that we need you, and value you. It doesn't matter who you really are, where you came from, or what you've done. I don't want to know your past... I just want to welcome you into our group."

"I am not a social person... I never have been, and I never will be," answered Vaelys. "However, I accept your invitation until such time as my path takes me elsewhere."

"Will you help us defeat Drakahl?" asked Lyla.

"I am afraid I cannot," she answered firmly.

"May I ask why?"

"I do not involve myself in politics. Killing a King is political, whether you feel it is justified or not. It doesn't matter what your reasoning or justification is... that is a game I choose not to play," she explained.

"If it's a matter of-" started Lyla.

"Money? You are treading close to a line I suggest you not cross. My services are not simply purchased," stated Vaelys.

"So... there's a moral code, or something?"

"Let this be the last time this is discussed," barked Vaelys. Calming herself, she continued, "Not everything in this world is black and white. There are those who feel an abundance of either is problematic, and over time disrupts the freedoms of individuals... which in itself could be seen as evil.

"As for your hint at hiring me... if I am what you think I am, you are not the kind of person to hire me. Don't become that person," she suggested.

"I... I won't. We're happy to have you along for as long as you can stay," said Lyla.

There was clearly more to Vaelys, and being an assassin, than she had assumed.

"Shall we?" Lyla asked, pointing back toward the group. "We need to pack and get going."

Vaelys nodded and followed her to where the others had gathered.

Kellum walked over at the same time, coming from the platform the archers had used.

"Good thing they had archers; I was nearly out of arrows. Half the ones I took from the goons at the fortress were useless, handmade crap," he noted.

Lyla kept walking past the group to Wehrenel and Ahrwie on the other side. They stood a short distance away, yipping to each other in their native tongue, Ahrwie's forehead wrinkled in what Lyla could only assume to be frustration.

"What's the matter, guys?" asked Lyla.

"I think we should go with you," said Wehrenel.

"I think we should go home," said Ahrwie angrily.

"You're welcome to come along, but we didn't expect you to. You're free to go if you like."

"If we don't help you kill the King, he'll just come back," Wehrenel explained.

"If we don't go home, father will be angry!" exclaimed Ahrwie.

"Father will be angrier when more soldiers arrive!" argued Wehrenel.

"Father will", started Ahrwie. He paused for a moment, considering Wehrenel's point, then admitted, "he will be angry if the soldiers return... yes. Fine! We can go with," he agreed, still angry.

"Well, that's wonderful. Gabner enjoys your company," she said, smiling.

"Gabner's a simpleton," said Wehrenel.

"He smells funny," agreed Ahrwie.

"Well, he thinks you guys are the best. So, maybe play nice a wee bit, okay?" she asked.

"Fine," agreed Wehrenel.

"Fine," agreed Ahrwie.

The group split up, packed their supplies and gathered a few useful tidbits from the slain soldiers and the shacks. Afterward, they made their way to the two dinghies, loaded up and embarked on their brief journey.

The currents were strong, flowing south between Aegir and the Triblunds. Oben and Gaerin rowed hard to the northwest to keep their direction of travel relatively westward. Gareg and Gellix did the same in their own dinghy, following closely behind.

Gabner sang a little tune for them as they rowed, helping them to keep a rhythm.

Wehrenel and Ahrwie listened for a few moments and eventually joined in. All three of them sang in the kobold tongue, while the fauns' little hoofed feet kept the rhythm on the bottom of the boat.

Their journey was fairly uplifting compared to the trauma they'd experienced the night before.

* * *

AFTER NEARLY two hours of rowing, the group finally made it to a set of small wooden ramps on the other side of the channel. To their left and right rocky cliffs rose up to meet the land above, making the ramps the only possible place they could come ashore.

The boat ramps granted access to a small, pebbled beach which stretched thirty yards before meeting with the face of a sheer cliff. To the north and south of the beach, small rock-strewn dirt paths led up to the lands above.

Kellum leaped out of the first dinghy and helped pull the boat onto the ramp. Vaelys leaped out of the second dinghy and did the same. As the boats made firm contact with the wooden planks of the ramps, those rowing hopped out and helped pull them far enough for everyone else to disembark safely.

Gaerin, Oben, Gareg and Gellix's upper bodies were on fire from lightly torn muscles and a healthy dose of fatigue. They stood on the shore watching as the others retrieved the equipment from the boats and made small piles on the shore.

Gaerin was so exhausted he had Lyla help him remove his armor, placing it on the sand beside him. He collapsed onto his rear, massaging his sore muscles through his gambeson. Lyla knelt beside him and took over the massage, helping to ease her husband's burden.

Gareg, seeing Gaerin, looked over to Oben longingly. Oben shook his head ferociously, indicating that he had no intentions of massaging Gareg's muscles. Gareg let loose a hearty laugh... just as an arrow slammed into Oben's left shoulder.

"To arms!" yelled Gareg, as a horde of goblins rushed down the dirt ramps toward them.

Vaelys sprang into action, drawing her daggers and running toward the goblins to the south.

Kyrilis drew her weapons and raced to meet the goblins from the north.

Kellum jumped to his feet, nocked an arrow, and fired at a hobgoblin, standing at the top of the south ramp.

"Oh, no!" yelled Lyla.

She got to her feet as fast as she could and ran back to the equipment piles to grab her weapon and shield. As she bent over to grab her mace, an arrow whizzed past her head.

Gaerin grabbed his warhammer, got up and ran toward the fray without his shield. He hoped that adrenaline would carry him through the battle.

Green-skinned, four-foot-tall creatures swarmed down the ramps. Their tattered, mud-caked, fur loin cloths slapped disgustingly against their thighs as they ran hunched over. Matted, black hair adorned their heads, dripping with oil and leaving dirty streaks down their horrid faces. Their beady, red eyes sneered happily at the prospect of slaying their victims.

A quick glance at the field of battle told Kellum there were over twenty of the beasts descending each ramp. He fired again at the hobgoblin, again missing because of a deft dodge on the part of his target. As he nocked another arrow, red streaks arced through the air, descending from the ridge above them toward the dinghies they had arrived in.

Flaming arrows struck the small boats, oil-filled vials at their tips bursting open and setting the craft ablaze.

Kellum looked up at the ridge to see a dozen humanoid figures looking down at them, watching. Several held bows, while others held swords. The one in the middle stood much taller than the rest and held a shield.

"Fuck!" he yelled.

Vaelys crashed into the first of the goblins, daggers slicing in all directions as fast as she could move. Goblin after goblin fell at her feet, while Gareg and Gaerin rushed to join her.

Kyrilis arrived at the bottom of the north ramp and began slaying her own stream of goblins, one after another, while Oben and Gellix ran to her position.

Lyla stood with Wehrenel, Ahrwie and Kellum to protect them

while they used their bows to pick off goblins along the ramps. As the others collided with the goblins, more and more poured down the ramps from above in what appeared to be an endless stream.

Three hobgoblins now stood atop each ramp, waving their arms in the act of casting spells

Lyla alerted her archers, yelling, "Stop them from casting!"

Wehrenel, Ahrwie and Kellum fired arrows at the casters as fast as they could. Several shots found their target, leaving one per ramp alive.

Fire erupted at the base of both ramps, setting several party members ablaze, including the goblins they were fighting. The flames were short lived and went out quickly. However, Vaelys, Kyrilis, Gellix and Gareg suffered mild lung injuries from inhaling the searing hot air and had to back away from the fight for a moment.

The four men who had rowed them ashore struggled to stay in the fight but were holding their own. As the battle raged on, the tide of goblins slowed to a trickle.

Everyone's spirits lifted.

We might just make it out of this, thought Lyla.

"Enough!" echoed a voice from above.

The tall figure in the center of the group on the cliff raised his sword. Archers took aim at the group below. As he lowered his arm, they released their arrows.

Bolrin and Keifer, cowering beside the flaming dinghies, died instantly as arrows pierced their skulls.

Another struck Gellix in the head. He fell sideways and smashed into Kyrilis, knocking her over.

Gareg, Gaerin and Oben were each hit in their dominant arm, forcing them to drop their weapons.

Vaelys took an arrow to her right collar, re-opening her recent wound and shattering the bone within. She had flashbacks of the dreams she had been having recently, quickly identified them as prophetic guidance, and dropped her blades. She lowered herself to her knees and put her left arm in the air in an act of surrender.

Gabner ran toward Lyla, terrified but intent on saving her. He jumped into the air in front of her just as he arrived. They locked eyes as an arrow pierced through his neck, and two others landed in his back. As he crashed to the ground, he reached his hand toward her. He struggled to force one last word past his lips as he felt his life fading.

"*Mama!*" said Gabner. Though the damage to his throat made the word nearly inaudible, Lyla heard it clearly.

She watched in horror as Gabner and her other companions either died or suffered terrible injuries. In one dreadful moment, what was left of her world came crashing down around her. Trembling, she dropped her weapons and fell to her knees.

The last few arrows narrowly missed Kellum, Wehrenel and Ahrwie.

"Yield!" yelled the same voice from above.

The companions that were still standing looked at Lyla, saw that she was on her knees, and submitted to their surrender. Cackling rang out among the remaining goblins as they went about the task of collecting the group's belongings.

The hobgoblins forcefully tied their hands behind their backs, then ran a long rope between them. As they finished tying the companions to the lead rope, the leader of the group descended the north ramp. He smiled as he inspected his catch, his few remaining yellowed and rotted teeth on full display.

"Welcome to the Triblunds! I am Grohm... and we are going to become very close friends," he barked, snarling wickedly beneath his knotted black beard.

* * *

IT HAD been a week since Bronsin left to deliver the horses back to Fel'Rechaun and the Legion. Tylee had initially resented Laurence's decision not to visit when his group dropped them off. However, she understood that something important was taking place, and knew it would be hard for them to say goodbye, yet again.

Managing Gaierford's citizens and their rebuilding efforts kept her too busy to worry over why Laurence left the way he did. The refugees were making excellent progress and had even begun restoring the abandoned buildings in old Kallenfall, a few miles to the west.

"Twenty-two more refugees arrived this morning from Port Vaelin," said Delriahna as she approached.

Tylee handed her the list of materials she had been drafting all morning with Aric. "This is what we need if we're going to keep up this pace for much longer. I'll have Aric help assign the new refugees living quarters, and work to do, but... why are they coming here? We've received no official word on the matter."

"According to one of them, a Thomas Caliburn, the Legion has sent them here to fortify Gaierford as a hub for the rebuilding efforts in the entire eastern region," explained Delriahna. "You've made a huge impact, and it's only been a little over a week."

"Well, it's easy when everyone is motivated and working together. If we keep getting flooded by newcomers, that motivation might wane. Some of the Grellenheim families are already concerned they'll lose the parcel of land I promised them," stated Tylee.

"There's plenty to go around between Gaierford and Kallenfall. I'm sure those rumors are easy enough to dissuade," said Delriahna.

"With new refugees arriving daily, I've had to pull Rolph Stoh off the construction efforts and make him Marshall. So, if you see him wearing a terrible, hand-carved, wooden badge... you know why. Meanwhile, Aric has asked if we can send an emissary south to Mooncrest to request volunteers to assist us, or provide resources in trade for debt," detailed Tylee.

"That's a good idea. Andor used to lament how the town had to pay farmers to produce fewer goods because we couldn't export them fast enough to compete with the Sacton Marshlands. Now that the marshlands are in disarray and unable to produce, perhaps it's time Mooncrest steps up," said Delriahna.

"As soon as Bronsin returned we can send him. He's bored sitting around with us anyway," said Tylee.

"Wise choice," agreed Delriahna.

A knock rang out across their small office above the former general store. Tylee, still standing, walked over and opened the door to greet their visitor. Standing in the doorway were two men in dark gray Legion plate armor.

"Good afternoon, Constable. I am Lord Commander Elrend and this is Commander Clendon, of the Fifth Command at Candohr Keep. Do you have time to meet with us?" asked the elder of the two.

His white hair and beard stood in stark contrast to the dark tan, wrinkled, and scarred skin of his face. A dark scar ran from above his right brow, down his face, and disappeared into his beard.

The other man was younger, but still much older than Tylee. His hair was black and pulled into a tight ponytail. He seemed much more clean-cut and well groomed. His chiseled features were striking, and his gaze was shrewd; as if he studied everything in great detail.

"Of course," answered Tylee, inviting them to enter.

The four of them gathered around a small table on the far side of the room. Delriahna retrieved the morning's kettle of coffee, still nearly full, and placed cups around the table. As she poured, the soldiers stood behind their seats, waiting for Tylee and Delriahna to sit first.

Once all had taken their seats, the men nodded their thanks for the coffee, hefted their cups and gently blew the faint wisps of steam away. After a few sips, Elrend sat his cup down and looked Tylee in the eyes, smiling.

"You have surprised us," he said. "In times like these, it is amazing to watch to see which citizens will step forward, take charge of the situation, and drive positive change. I dare say, no one expected a seventeen-year-old girl from Mooncrest to be our people's heroine."

"I was raised into politics by my parents, Andor and Delriahna," she said, indicating her mother with a gentle wave of her hand. "My husband is also an inspiration to me. I decided it was time to use all those years of boring, laborious study and perhaps live up to the standards set by Laurence."

"Well, you're certainly of right mind, my lady. Too often, men of my age will take charge and... we admittedly move too slowly, if I'm being blunt. We get stuck in our old ways, political banter, or gaming the system... and that limits actual progress. You took charge, rallied the refugees behind a cause, and made your own declarations without waiting to seek approval.

"It's a breath of fresh air; the very kind we need in the kingdom right now. In times of peace you would've ruffled a great many feathers with your actions, but in times such as these? I think you've done a splendid job," stated Elrend.

"Which is what brings us here today," added Clendon. "How much do you know of the Fifth Command?"

"I know nothing of Legion structure, I'm afraid," admitted Tylee.

"Well, then... It's time for a crash course in Legion politics, because you'll be dealing with us quite a lot in the coming months. The Arkhanian Legion is split into five commands," he began.

He took a sip of his coffee before continuing.

Elrend leaned back and smiled at Tylee again.

"First Command is headquartered at Vaelin Keep. Commander Landis and his men guard the palace and offer policing services to Vellenheim and Port Vaelin. The keep is also home to Lord

Commander Elrend's offices and staff.

"Second Command is headquartered at Raven's Keep, on the northern edge of Raven's Nest. It is operated by Commander Cricht to protect both schools, their supply towns and farms, and the trade routes between them.

"Third Command lies at Northwatch Keep in Uldenheim in the north. Commander Gipstein is tasked with guarding our border with Tellrindos and protecting the trade routes across the northern territories.

"Fourth Command is based in Southwatch Keep, along the southern border of the kingdom at the furthest point of the Southern Reach. Under Commander Halrund, it acts as our defense against any forces that might seek to enter the kingdom from the Bo'Lari Wastelands to the south. Those lands are populated by all manner of creature, bandit, and ruffian that would seek to harm decent folk.

"Fifth Command is based in Candohr Keep on the western edge of Vellenheim, near Vaelin Pass. Our purpose is more... clandestine. We send operatives to other kingdoms when needed, or even distribute them across Arkhania to gather intelligence or assist the other commands.

"We have determined that the best course of action for the Fifth Command—in light of recent events and their consequences—is to build a small keep between Gaierford and Kallenfall. The keep and its forces will provide protection and guidance to the region while you rebuild," Clendon explained.

"Let us be blunt," started Elrend. "Port Vaelin and Grellenheim will take years to restore. Both cities are old and constructed mostly of stone. While Grellenheim can rebuild faster, it is not along any major trade routes and is of less importance to the sanctity of the Kingdom and its economy.

"In fact, Grellenheim's reconstruction is to be bartered with the Ekthri after Ayriel's contingent helps them with Ayr'Thugohn, so it will be some time before those efforts even begin. Port Vaelin... while it's critical to the economy of the Kingdom, nearly two thirds of the city was destroyed by the dragon's attack. That is going to take time and resources. Much of the First Command's forces are engaged in assisting with those efforts as we speak.

"Our citizens need somewhere to go. Further, they need food to eat and we need materials to help these locations with their construction efforts. To that end, we must reopen the mines in

Kallenfall, and provide jobs and housing for a thousand or more displaced citizens. What you're doing here must extend to all the cities of the Southern Reach, and the marshland farming communities.

"These efforts must also produce enough goods to help with Port Vaelin, Grellenheim and the Ekthri. And since you are the one who stepped up, took action, and began the work in earnest-" said Elrend, trailing off.

"You want me to help oversee the efforts of the entire region, not just Gaierford," realized Tylee.

She felt overwhelmed, and it showed in her voice.

"The people rally behind you. They've grown weary of the Legion and—try as he might—King Orluhnd still hasn't overcome the foul legacy of his father's rule. We lack the support of public opinion. This dragon attack is seen as our failing by most of the residents of Vellenheim, and we must assume that extends to the rest of the Kingdom," explained Elrend.

"So, you want my daughter to be the public face of Arkhania's rebuilding efforts while you control things behind the scenes?" asked Delriahna.

"Not at all. We want her to be in charge of the efforts, and work in coordination with Clendon and his men," corrected Elrend.

"Typical politics would require the assignment of a council of elders to govern such an effort, and they move too slowly. The Fifth Command is known for taking action first and seeking approval later, much like your daughter has done for Gaierford. We agree with her motivations *and* her approach. I would not stand in her way. In fact, I would like to work in coordination with her and continue directly on the path she has already established," added Clendon.

"Think of Clendon as your personal political agent; able to accomplish things which you cannot," added Elrend.

"If we are to open the mines, we'll need to double our efforts on Kallenfall's dilapidated structures. We will also need to re-pave the roads between Kallenfall and the Southern Reach, through Gaierford. The dirt and mud are simply not sufficient to support heavy carriages loaded with stone and other mined resources," said Tylee.

Elrend smiled at her and looked to Clendon. "Isn't that the same thing you were lamenting on the way here?"

"Indeed," agreed Clendon, smiling as well.

"I've been on those roads quite a lot these past few days. I'm just calling it like I see it," she admitted.

"Well, I've brought two hundred of my men. They are presently waiting west of town, in the fields, for you to indicate our best location for constructing a keep. We also have nearly a hundred refugees, and several dozen stonecutters ready to work the mines," said Clendon.

"Well, let's head out to the field and I'll show you a great hill where we'd already planned to erect a watchtower. You can build your keep there. I assume you've tents for your forces?" she asked.

"We do," he said, standing.

She joined him, and they walked toward the door together.

"We'll have to open the mines first and use the stones to pave a road toward the keep. Then we can build the keep and continue paving the road through Gaierford toward the Reach," she explained.

"This will all be easier to coordinate from our new offices in the keep once we construct it," he said.

"Our offices?"

"You'll be getting one too, Duchess Ravencrest," he smirked.

"Du... duchess?" she asked, stopping cold in her tracks at the doorway.

She turned and looked back at her mother in shock.

"Did we forget to mention that? Duchess Tylee Ravencrest of the Eastern Reaches, I believe the King declared. This whole affair was his idea," offered Elrend, smiling.

"My daughter is a duchess?" gasped Delriahna.

"The reality is, such titles long ago became nothing more than a name. Those who possess them live near Vaelin Palace and clamor for the King's attention, rather than doing anything for the people. So, the King thought it high time such titles go to people who deserve them, earn their place through action, and put the needs of the people above themselves. He's bringing back those titles of old, to inspire our citizens... much like you have done," said Clendon.

"When times are as trying as these, the Kingdom must embrace those who rise to the challenge of pulling us through to the other side. Your daughter is one of those people. Once we find Laurence, the King plans to knight him into his elite guard, as reward for his help with the Velloth and that dragon," explained Elrend as Tylee and Clendon left the room.

"Well, this day certainly brightened," gasped Delriahna.

"Let us talk of Mooncrest, Lady Delriahna. The King would like to name Andor and yourself as Duke and Duchess of that region. Of course we'll also need to see an increase in farm production for the sake of the Kingdom," explained Elrend, leaning toward her.

"Oh, my!" exclaimed Delriahna. "And... certainly. We were just discussing Mooncrest's farms, right before you arrived."

"A messenger is already on the way to Mooncrest with word of his decree. I'd like to discuss whatever else you think needs to happen in order to support that effort. Port Vaelin and Vellenheim need resources badly," he explained.

They spent the rest of the afternoon discussing the politics and logistics of Mooncrest and the surrounding farms.

∴ ∴ ∴

"THIS IS as close as we can get, lads," apologized Captain Fraeg. "The channel, as you can see, is too turbulent here for safe passage."

Laurence stood at the railing with Mordechai, staring up at Mount Krierga's western face. A series of waterfalls dotted the face of the mountain, trailing down into the channel between Aegir and the Triblunds. Laurence gasped at its glory and placed a hand on Mordechai's shoulder.

"I am so sorry that you can't see this," said Laurence.

"Don't be," corrected Mordechai. "The waters that flow from Mount Krierga are laced with magical energies. It is I that should apologize to you for your inability to see it as I do."

"Sorry to be interruptin, but we must be goin. There's an old smugglin trail up to the Triblunds along the cliffs if ya row east," said Fraeg nervously. He didn't want to upset his militant passengers, especially after seeing them duel in the hold below. However, he also didn't want to get caught at an improper port by Pelrigoss's fleet.

"We're on our way," said Laurence, tugging at Mordechai's sleeve to get moving.

The group collected their things as quickly as they could while the crew lowered a dinghy into the water. After they climbed down a rope ladder, Agnar pushed the dinghy free of the ship and grabbed an oar. Laurence, Agnar, Izabel and Wil rowed in shifts for a few hours, searching the shoreline for a place to go ashore.

"There!" yelled Laurence, pointing to a relatively flat section of beach.

After running the boat ashore, they retrieved their gear and climbed out into the waist-deep waters. The rocky slopes that loomed over them stood only twelve feet tall, allowing them to climb relatively easily up to the grasslands above. Once they had all completed their climb, Laurence turned to Mordechai.

"Okay... where to now?" he joked.

"Well, we don't know where they landed. However, if you give me a few moments to find a flat place to set up my crystal ball, I can try to divine their location," Mordechai answered.

"No, I was joking," laughed Laurence.

"I was not," said Mordechai frankly.

Izabel found a boulder nearby that was flat on top, and guided Mordechai to it. The rest of the group went to task preparing a leisurely lunch while they waited on Mordechai to give them a sense of direction.

∴ ∴ ∴

GAERIN AND Lyla's group walked for the rest of the day, dragged behind their captors' horses by the long rope that ran between them. Those with open wounds continued to bleed as their constant movement and the tugging on their arms wrenched their bodies about.

They traversed a worn path surrounded by rocks and boulders. Grassy plains dotted with acacia trees, small bushes, and various forms of underbrush extended in all directions from their path. The grass was yellowed, and the land underneath was dusty and dry. Their captors dragged them east along the path for half the day before turning north.

Injured and past the point of exhaustion, the group felt both relief and dread when black and red flags came into view. As they drew nearer, they could see black tents lining the western edge of a massive pit. Small reed-and-branch huts that seemed stable—but ultimately temporary—lined the far side.

Their captors dragged along a path toward the tents. As they got closer, the prisoners below them came into view. Nearly a hundred elven women huddled at the far end of the pit; dirty, starving, and terrified. Dust covered their bronze skin, tear streaks lining several of their faces.

All of them had red hair, styled to symbolize their uniqueness yet matted with dirt and signs of mistreatment. Only a few of them had clothing; simple scraps of tan leather, hanging loosely about their shoulders and waists.

The sounds of weeping drifted up to the companions as their captors yanked on their leads, pulling them into the midst of the black tents.

∴ ∴ ∴

THE GUARDS forced Gaerin, Lyla, and their companions to kneel in front of the largest tent. To the west, a series of poles rose into the sky, dotting the landscape.

Gaerin looked at Lyla with fear in his eyes.

When Grohm emerged from his tent, he paced up and down the line of captives, as if trying to choose one.

"I think you'll do," he said, staring down at Oben. "Bring him," he barked to his men.

Several soldiers in a mixture of leather and brigandine ran over and disconnected Oben's ties from the line that connected the captives. Grabbing his large arms, they forced him to his feet and pushed him along behind Grohm, through the tents and toward the poles. They half pushed, half dragged him to one of the poles.

When they released his bonds to re-tie him to the pole he shoved one of the soldiers as hard as he could with his left hand, sending the man back several steps. As he punched another, a mace slammed into his head, knocking him unconscious.

When he regained consciousness, he found himself tied to the pole in a forced-upright position.

Grohm stood in front of him, grinning.

"You'll do nicely," he said.

A small human walked up beside him, dressed in a black robe and cowl. The robed man began chanting strange words as he withdrew a palm-sized, beautiful piece of lapis lazuli from a pouch about his waist. He extended the rock, its gold streaks glimmering in the sunlight, toward Oben as the chanting intensified.

White wisps, like smoke, began streaming from the surface of Oben's body, drawing into the piece of lapis.

Oben screamed in pain and horror as he felt his life force draining.

Lyla broke out in tears as Oben screamed.

Several of them grew angry and wrestled with their binds.

One of the guards hit Gareg in the head with the pommel of his sword to quiet the angry barbarian.

Oben's skin dried and shriveled, splitting open at points to reveal the withering muscles underneath.

Grohm stepped forward and unsheathed his knife.

As the priest's chanting reached its peak, Grohm sliced Oben's throat releasing a small stream of blood that turned to dust and drifted away as it ran down his neck.

When the process was complete, Grohm turned to the priest with his hand out. The priest handed Grohm the lapis and walked away, his task complete.

"That's enough for the day. Strip the rest and toss them in the pit. We'll drain a few more tomorrow and then we return to Kulgan Palace," Grohm ordered.

They knocked out the companions, one by one, and undressed them. When the soldiers threw them into the pit, the elven women attempted to catch them to soften the impact of their fall. Grohm's men didn't seem to care what happened to them.

Several of the elven women shed their tattered remnants of clothing to dress the new captives, crying sympathetically in the process. The women carried the companions away from the piles and puddles where they often relieved themselves, and leaned them against the eastern wall.

Kyrilis was the first to wake. She looked around hastily, studying her situation. Despair hit her like a wave.

The elven women stood around them in a small circle, providing them shade from the late afternoon sun. Many of them wept.

"Where... where are we?" asked Kyrilis.

The women looked around, as if deciding who would answer. One of them stepped forward and knelt before Kyrilis. Her green eyes shown as bright as emeralds glinting in the sunlight.

"I am Saerasha. You are in what remains of our holy site of Thu'Brin. We come here once a year to worship," she explained.

Her voice was silky and alluring, a stark contrast to the harshness of their surroundings.

"Your people... you are Tryn, yes?" Kyrilis asked.

"We are. You are Afyr, very far from home," answered Saerasha.

"I am, yes. We came to hunt Drakahl, but it seems they cut our journey short," lamented Kyrilis.

"His generals are scouring the Triblunds for soul sacrifices, disrupting our natural order and slaying many of us. Otherwise, we would have welcomed you and aided your mission. Sadly, we can offer nothing but shade from the afternoon sun," said Saerasha.

"Where are your men?"

"We are a nomadic people. The Kalmesh, our men-folk, and Tulmesh, the women-folk, are different tribes. We meet here, once a year, to celebrate our goddess, Yshna, and form union. That is why you find us skyclad. We were ill-prepared for their attack, and most of our men were slain. I fear this may be the last generation of Tryn to walk these lands," said Saerasha somberly.

"Most of my companions are injured. Would any of your people be skilled in healing?" asked Kyrilis.

"I am tribe Shaman. However, my healing ways require the sacrifice of life and nature, much like the fauns which travel with you. In this dusty pit, I can do little to aid you," she lamented.

As the rest of the companions woke, Kyrilis and Saerasha helped them and explained the situation. It was hours before Lyla woke, and each of her companions were eagerly waiting to see who, if anyone, she would be able to heal. With little debate on the matter, Lyla got up and walked straight to Vaelys.

"If anyone is going to get us out of here, it's you. I only have enough energy to pray over one person for now, and I don't know how much rest I'll get in the evenings here with all the people and the noise," Lyla stated.

"Very well," accepted Vaelys.

After a few short prayers, Vaelys's wounds had healed enough that she could move freely without pain.

The group then gathered and tried to come up with a strategy for escaping.

∴ ∴ ∴

AFTER NEARLY a half day of meditation in front of the crystal ball, Mordechai reached up and disassembled it, placing the pieces back into their box. Laurence walked over, waiting patiently to hear what Mordechai had discovered.

"They are south by southeast of us," he offered.

"How far?" asked Laurence.

"On foot? If we walked through the night, we could meet them before they break camp in the morning," answered Mordechai.

"Alright guys, you heard the man! We're walking through the night!" yelled Laurence to his friends.

"That's not what I said," clarified Mordechai.

"It totally is," joked Laurence.

Mordechai sighed and held out his left arm. "You're going to have to lead me, if you want me to stay focused on their position. We're following a magical glow on the horizon, in my mind. I won't be able to see terrain, rocks, trees, bushes... you get the idea."

"We'll take turns leading you around," said Laurence, nodding.

Laurence's friends didn't mind the idea of walking through the night, not after being trapped on a ship for the better part of a week. They were all happy to be back on solid ground, and they had more than enough adrenaline with the anticipation of their adventure building.

LIBERATION

Ris'Kitthu, Arran'Hael 15th, 113 of the 2nd Era

Free her from the chains that bind,
Her soul's not yet unleashed.
Free her from a tortured mind,
Her destiny's with me.

Night's Writ, Parable 14

LAURENCE AND his companions lay on the ground atop a hill looking down at a field of poles bearing corpses, and a series of black tents beyond. They could see wooden structures behind the black tents, but they were too far away to see much detail.

"You're sure they haven't moved?" asked Laurence.

"They're moving now, but very little," Mordechai answered. "We should wait and see if they leave the camp or not before we head down. They could be among friendlies or hostiles; we simply have no way of knowing."

"The mere chance that they've been captured tells me we should move as quickly as possible," said Izabel.

"No, he's right. We don't know who we're up against, and that's a lot of tents. There could be thirty or forty men down there, ready to help us or hurt us. We just don't know," clarified Laurence, biting back on his own fears.

"So, we wait?" asked Agnar.

"We wait," confirmed Wil.

∴·∴·∴

THE PRISONERS awakened to the sounds of shouting above. Several soldiers stood in the pit, having lowered ladders and climbed down to retrieve their sacrifices.

"Grab the black ones!" yelled Grohm. "They remind me of that shitty alchemist we killed on Gargoa."

"Lyla!" yelled Gaerin as the soldiers grabbed the two of them.

"Gaer!" she yelled back.

"Do something," Kyrilis demanded to Vaelys as soldiers dragged the couple away.

"We're outnumbered quite dramatically, and as far as I'm aware I'm the only one of us who is skilled in unarmed combat. We'd be slaughtered," said Vaelys.

"But-"

"It's pointless, and you know it. They're watching us at this very moment, waiting for us to do the very thing you're suggesting. Look," said Vaelys, pointing at the archers on the far end of the pit. "We'd make it ten feet... twenty tops."

"Gods damnit!" yelled Kyrilis.

∴ ∴ ∴

"SOMETHING IS happening," said Wil.

Off in the distance they could see several figures emerge between the tents, dragging two others toward the poles. Laurence grew nervous, unsure what was going on and if he should act. His gut was telling him to move and move fast.

"Go, Laurence!" yelled Mordechai, confirming Laurence's instincts.

They got to their feet and ran as quickly as they could down the hill toward the scene. By the time they entered the field of poles, they could hear two people screaming horribly.

Laurence cursed his inability to run faster. He felt as if everything was happening in slow motion.

As they drew closer, it became obvious that the victims in the scenario ahead of them were his aunt and uncle. He felt panic rise in his gut. That panic was quickly overcome with anger as he closed the distance.

∴ ∴ ∴

GROHM SNEERED fiercely as his last two victims' souls drained slowly into their lapis lazuli prisons.

The priest chanted fiercely, holding a stone in each hand, as Gaerin and Lyla screamed in horror.

Gaerin struggled to break free, but his body did not respond to his commands. While he screamed involuntarily at the pain that coursed through him, his mind raced with thoughts of Lyla. Loss and regret filled him thoroughly, underscored by a complete inability to accept his fate.

Lyla reached out to Gaerin in her mind, unable to move or resist what was happening to her. She knew he blamed himself for their situation. However, she also knew they couldn't survive it. She felt the peace of Galrath rush through her and prayed for her husband to feel the same. Not a single part of her wanted to leave the world, or her husband's side, but she trusted that they would reunite in the afterlife.

One of Grohm's lieutenants yelled out, "To arms!" to signal everyone to prepare for an attack.

"Finish it!" demanded Grohm.

∴ ∴ ∴

VAELYS HEARD the soldiers shouting defensive alerts from the tents. She quickly turned and signaled for Kyrilis, Kellum, and Gareg to follow her to the side of the pit. As they'd planned the previous night, Gareg locked his hands together and placed them down low. As Vaelys placed her right foot into his hands, she jumped as hard as she could while he lifted with all his strength.

Vaelys landed on the edge of the pit, twelve feet above them.

Kyrilis and Kellum landed next to her soon after. They followed as she raced toward the black tents.

Saerasha ran to Gareg and pointed to the same ledge. He quickly repeated the maneuver, sending her up to join the others.

Vaelys reached the first tent and ripped open the back of it, jumping inside in a flash. She grabbed a sword she found inside and exited the front of the tent. She drove the sword into the ground for Kyrilis to retrieve and kept moving, entering another. As she exited the second tent, she tossed two daggers toward Kellum and kept running.

A soldier jumped out and blocked her path suddenly, raising his sword and shield in a defensive stance. Vaelys jumped into the air while running full speed. She drove her heel into the man's shield with the force of her momentum, sending him back a few steps. He slashed at her with his sword, but she stepped into his reach, grabbed his arm and fractured the bones inside with a twist.

As he screamed in pain, she continued her run toward the poles and the woman who had saved her life.

∴ ∴ ∴

LAURENCE WAS only twenty feet away when he saw Grohm's priest raise a knife and slice Gaerin and Lyla's throats. "No!" he screamed at the top of his lungs. His eyes filled with tears of rage and sorrow as he ran the last few feet and brought his sword around toward Grohm in a violent strike.

Grohm drew his sword and parried the fierce blow in one motion. "You?" he sneered, then laughed.

Laurence began a flurry of attacks. He recognized his opponent from his last, tragic night at home. The man before him was the one who'd urinated on his face before departing.

He slashed from the left, and Grohm parried it easily.

He twisted his sword and brought it back from the right, and Grohm parried that attack as well.

As he continued to slash in opposing directions, he sped his attacks more and more. He attacked so quickly that Grohm had no choice but to anticipate Laurence's movements, if he wanted to defend himself.

When Laurence noticed Grohm falling into the pattern, he swung again as if striking from the right, twisted his blade three-quarters of the way through the swing and redirected into a thrust toward the man's face.

Grohm corrected his parry at the last second and managed to deflect enough of the thrust to save his own life. Laurence's blade slashed open the right side of Grohm's face, causing him to back away for a moment.

Laurence took advantage of his brief retreat and pressed the advantage, thrusting his blade toward Grohm's waist, and then arcing with the momentum caused by Grohm's parry into another slash attack. Once again, he pressed Grohm into a defensive posture.

Wil, Izabel and Agnar ran past the pair and engaged the soldiers that were running toward them. Within what seemed like seconds, a dozen soldiers surrounded the three of them.

Grohm's priests took the opportunity to flee.

∴ ∴ ∴

VAELYS EXITED the tents and ran straight for the backs of the twelve soldiers. Kellum and Kyrilis ran as fast as they could behind her, while Saerasha struggled to catch up.

As she reached the first soldier, he raised his sword for a downward strike at Izabel. Vaelys grabbed his wrist, twisting and splintering the bones within. His sword fell from his grasp as he shrieked in pain. She caught the weapon's hilt, spun to her right and drove the blade into the back of the soldier beside him, breaching his brigandine armor like it was simple cloth.

Kyrilis stabbed the neck of a soldier attacking Wil and turned to defend against the one beside him when he spun to face her.

Kellum ran up to a pair of soldiers on the other side of the line and drove his daggers through the necks of each simultaneously, saving Agnar in the process.

In short order, the six of them easily overwhelmed the remaining soldiers, and turned their attention toward Laurence.

∴ ∴ ∴

LAURENCE SUCCESSFULLY twisted another attack, driving the tip of his blade through the leather on Grohm's left shoulder. As he pulled his blade free, Grohm pushed him back and kicked him in the chest.

"You've learned a lot, boy! Pity you couldn't save that pathetic old man when you had the chance!" growled Grohm. He spat blood on the ground from the wound in his cheek. His teeth showed through the bloody flesh as he grinned back at Laurence.

"Fucking die!" yelled Laurence, feeling more anger than he ever had in his life.

Grohm rushed to attack, putting Laurence on the defensive. His sword moved quickly, but Laurence could tell he was tiring. Having the advantage of youth, Laurence chose to bide his time and make Grohm work for a bit.

It was then that Laurence realized Grohm was fighting with the same techniques Izabel often used. So, he started using the same tricks and techniques that always confused Izabel, and caused her to fight recklessly. As the fight progressed, Grohm started falling into those same traps and Laurence gained confidence.

As the last of the other soldiers fell, the companions looked over at Laurence and Grohm; watching the battle but allowing Laurence his chance at justice. Izabel watched Laurence's tactics intently. His approach felt familiar. She quickly studied Grohm's technique and realized he was a student of the same Endril Faierthorne techniques she'd learned growing up. A smile crept across her face.

"Oh, this guy is *fucked*," she quipped, placing a hand on her right hip and cocking her head to the side.

"He fights like you do," laughed Agnar.

"Precisely," she confirmed. She smiled as she watched, adding, "Laurence is playing with him."

Saerasha joined them quietly. She had a sheet folded and wrapped around her, soaked in the priest's blood. None of the companions seemed to notice.

Grohm slowed noticeably, fatigue setting in. The boy before him was frustrating. Every technique he attempted was easily deflected and turned against him. *Drakahl should have killed you on the farm*, he thought.

Laurence smiled wickedly, causing Grohm to growl with rage.

He lashed out with his blade again, but Laurence parried the blow, twisted his blade, and jabbed him in the shoulder with the tip. Frustrated, he attacked again, and Laurence performed the same trick.

Anger set in, driving Grohm to attack more ferociously. He abandoned technique, expecting his strength to win the day. His sword twirled around for a downward strike. Laurence lithely stepped to the side, drove his sword through the man's stomach, twisted, and pulled it free.

Grohm lifted his sword again, frantically. As he swung again in desperation, Laurence easily parried the attack away with a flick of his wrist.

Stepping into the man's reach, Laurence grabbed the front of his leather jerkin with his left hand, raised his sword in the other and slowly pushed the blade through Grohm's neck. He smiled at the look in Grohm's eyes as realization set in.

Grohm crumpled to the ground.

Laurence retrieved his blade and cleaned it on the man's pants before putting it away. It was only then that he noticed his friends cheering him on.

∴ ∴ ∴

LAURENCE FELL to his knees beside Gaerin and Lyla, sobbing uncontrollably.

Kyrilis sat next to him, put an arm around his shoulders, and pulled him close. Their deaths hurt her just as much as the pain in his eyes. She wanted nothing more than to whisk him away and save him from the life that destiny laid before him, but she couldn't. She wept because Gaerin and Lyla were dead, because he was hurting, and because she couldn't take his pain away.

Wil returned to the hill to retrieve Mordechai while Saerasha led the others toward the pit to free her tribe.

Vaelys, meanwhile, broke off from the group and started going through the tents looking for their gear.

After an hour, Gaerin and Lyla's companions had reclaimed their belongings and freed the rest of the prisoners.

The Tryn split up and went to their respective huts to get cleaned and dress, while the companions began lowering the corpses off the poles around the field.

After Gaerin and Lyla lay safely on the ground, Laurence went over to the pile of gear that Vaelys was making and started retrieving their clothing and armor.

Kyrilis joined him, and put a hand on his arm, indicating that he should stop. "Let us do this," she offered.

He sat for a moment, looking into her eyes. "I can't believe they're gone," he wept.

Kyrilis folded him back into her breast as another wave of sadness overtook him. She wished that Tylee were with them, to offer him peace and comfort. The love that flowed so freely from Gaerin and Lyla had taught her the value of its presence. What she felt for Laurence, and the love that lay behind it, was something she couldn't properly share.

She had never known love before meeting his family, nor the loss of having it stripped away so violently. The pain in his eyes was more than she could bear. As he gently sobbed into her chest, she hugged him tighter and placed her cheek on his head.

After seeing Laurence's pain, the fauns began carrying the rest of Gaerin and Lyla's gear over to their bodies.

Kellum helped to dress them quietly while Kyrilis continued to comfort the young man. He didn't know the party that had showed up to help them, but he knew pain. He'd seen more pain in

Laurence's eyes than he'd ever wish on anyone.

Saerasha returned from her lodge and joined Laurence, sitting cross-legged in front of him. She wore a brown leather shirt, pants, and boots etched with the black runes of her order. Black sinew lacing lined the outer edge of all three pieces. The neckline of her shirt lay open in the front, black lacing hanging from the collar, ready to use should she choose to close it.

"What is your name, my lord?" she asked in a calm, silky voice. She reached out her right hand, placing it on Laurence's left knee.

"I am Laurence Ravencrest," he answered, lifting his head out of Kyrilis's embrace to look her in the eyes.

"I am Saerasha Raivene, Shaman of the Tulmesh tribe. We are a race of elves known as the Tryn who follow nomadic traditions. I've never been to Gargoa and have interacted with few humans. As such, I am unfamiliar with your customs for handling the deceased," she explained.

"Traditions vary based on location, societal class, religion, and family preference," said Kyrilis.

"Are you asking what I want done with Gaerin and Lyla? I... I don't want them buried in Pelrigoss soil. Too much pain has come to my family in these lands," he said. He calmly wiped a tear from his cheek and sniffled lightly, trying to compose himself. Kyrilis laid her head on his shoulder and wrapped her arms around his waist, trying to comfort him.

"Would you prefer a sky burial, or a pyre?" she inquired.

"What's a sky burial?" he asked.

"We would build a platform to raise them up for the gods to claim. As carrion birds feast upon them, they ascend to the heavens," she explained. "Though that effort seems fruitless, considering..."

"Considering what?"

She presented two lapis lazuli to him, indicating that he should hold them. "Grohm and his men were here to drain souls through horrid, ritual magic. We don't know why, but when they did so... the souls entered these stones. The larger of the two, I believe, holds your uncle Gaerin. The smaller, Lyla."

Laurence could clearly discern the remorse in Saerasha's voice. He didn't know what to do with the information, and couldn't believe what was happening. The situation felt surreal. "Is there any way to free them?" he asked desperately. His hands trembled as a new wave of remorse hit.

Kyrilis pulled him closer. He could hear her weeping and feel her gentle sobbing. It was he that now felt the need to comfort her.

"There may be a way, yes. We will need to visit the Inok, a tribe of Minotaur to the northeast near Mount Skain. They have tales of such horror and may know a way to release trapped souls safely. Shattering the stones is said to damn their occupants to eternal torment," she explained.

"We?" asked Kyrilis, raising her head.

"Yes. I would like to join you. Last night, Lyla explained that your purpose on Pelrigoss was to slay Drakahl. I would see that task completed for the protection of my people," said Saerasha. "If his rule has escalated to such events as these, I fear what might come next."

A thought dawned on Laurence suddenly. He wasn't sure where it had come from, or what it would mean, but he couldn't resist the urge to voice it.

"You are a Shaman... would you... be able to summon ravens to a sky burial?"

Kyrilis perked up, intrigued at the proposal. "Where did that idea come from?"

"I... I don't know, it just came to me," he answered, turning to face her. Her face was closer to his than he'd anticipated, and their lips nearly touched. He didn't know if losing Gaerin and Lyla had caused him to be more vulnerable to such urges, or if part of him truly yearned to be with Kyrilis. Reminding himself of Tylee, he focused his attention back on Saerasha.

"I certainly could. May I ask why?" Saerasha asked.

Calmly, he placed Gaerin and Lyla's stones in his belt pouch and retrieved the ring he had obtained from the mysterious event at the Sacton River. He presented it to her, pointing out the raven at the center of the crest. "I am a descendant of Gahl the Raven. That's where we get our name and our crest. Somehow, I feel this would fit for a new tradition, or at the very least to honor Gaerin and Lyla who gave their lives defending our family bloodline."

"Very well, I will see that it happens," Saerasha agreed. She handed the ring back to Laurence and got to her feet, then walked away to instruct several Tryn in burial proceedings for the numerous dead.

Mordechai joined Laurence and Kyrilis shortly after. "She's quite intriguing," he said.

"How so?" asked Laurence.

"She claims to be a Shaman, but I sense strong latent magics within her that exceed what a shaman should be capable of," he explained. "In fact, Shaman do not typically possess magic within them."

"I think she's rather genuine, and very grateful that we arrived when we did. Her people were on the verge of being slaughtered. In fact, most of their men *were* slain," Kyrilis stated.

"I wasn't questioning her motivations. I was simply suggesting that she's more than she appears to be, and perhaps more than she is aware of herself," he clarified.

"Well, she's coming with us," Laurence decided.

"We need all the help we can get," agreed Mordechai with a shrug. "Who do I detect walking back and forth with... has magical implants," said Mordechai.

"Magical implants?" asked Laurence.

"Magical energies emanating near the bones of their ribs, shoulders, wrists, thighs, and ankles," Mordechai detailed. "Whoever it is, they aren't magical of their own accord. I see no attachment to the weave; which would appear like faint tendrils reaching into their person. I see no stored spells, so it isn't wizardry or priesthood.

"I, therefore, surmise the most likely source of the strategically placed magical energies is enchantment. However, since enchantments on living flesh are temporary, and can cause severe side effects long term, I deduce that the energies are coming from inanimate objects buried beneath the flesh to provide permanent enchantments indirectly," he explained.

"You must be talking about Vaelys. She's an Afyr," said Kyrilis. "She is unreasonably strong, and fast. Perhaps that is the purpose of the enchantments you sense." She didn't know if it was wise to divulge her theory that Vaelys was actually Sylk to someone as powerful as Mordechai.

"Vaelys of the Afyr? Why does that name sound familiar?" mused Mordechai. He thought for a moment, and then blurted, "Ah! Vaelys Fa'Rezlin... I knew the name was familiar."

"How did you know?" Kyrilis asked.

"Surely that's not the name she gave you," stated Mordechai.

"It is," she confirmed.

"I buried Vaelys Fa'Rezlin hundreds of years ago. Poor girl was trapped in a cave system under Mount Feyr, heavily wounded and nearly dead. She claimed that she was escaping a group of Velloth which, at the time, I believed to be a myth. Before I could get her to the surface, she expired. I returned to the surface with her body and she was buried by her uncle in their family crypt under Vey'Thugohn," he explained.

"In truth, she is far more than she seems to be. However, I would not press the issue. She has made it clear that her true identity is off limits... though I have my suspicions," said Kyrilis.

"I have my own suspicions, and if I am correct you are very accurate in stating that her identity is off limits; we should not press the issue. She fights alongside us?" he asked, intrigued.

"She does," answered Kyrilis. "At least for now. She's traveling to Caierthor, destined for Dagoh Bay."

"Then we shall let her and be thankful for her assistance as long as she is willing to grace us with it," he said.

"I have no idea what you guys are talking about," chimed Laurence.

"Nor should you. I will explain once she is no longer in our company. For now, she is Vaelys, and she is a trusted and worthy ally," instructed Mordechai.

"Very well," answered Laurence.

∴ ∴ ∴

THE TRYN constructed the sky burial platforms from the poles that Grohm's men had used in their rituals. Once complete, Laurence and Kyrilis undressed Gaerin and Lyla so the Tryn women could anoint their bodies with oils and herbs. Afterward, Gareg, Agnar, Laurence and Vaelys lifted them onto square sheets of woven branches and then to the top of the elevated platforms.

Wehrenel and Ahrwie joined Saerasha between the platforms, chanting prayers to nature and bidding ravens to come and take the fallen. After a time, black birds came into view on the western horizon, heading toward the platforms.

Saerasha stood and bid those that were watching to leave, so that the ravens could do their duty.

With one last look, Laurence joined the others in finishing the burial rites for the murdered Tryn males. They placed each of them in a shallow grave and covered them with mounds of small rocks. The Tryn women had spent most of the day digging the graves, collecting the rocks, and making piles next to each of the fifty-two graves.

Gareg and Kellum, meanwhile, walked into the northern fields and built a pyre for Oben. They stood and reminisced about their travels with Oben while his body burned. Neither of them knew what was appropriate to say. Kellum—the half-elf with his extended lifespan—had assumed Oben would outlive them both.

It had been night for several hours by the time the last stone settled into place in the field of buried Tryn. Several of the Tulmesh held torches to light the final hours of their ceremony. When their task was complete, they spread out toward the wooden lodges and took up positions to light the way for everyone else to return in safety.

When Laurence and his companions moved to walk toward the black tents instead, Saerasha signaled him to stop. "We will feast tonight, in memory of the fallen and in thanks to you and your companions. Without your assistance, we would have died this day and the Tryn would be all but extinct. Join us, and let us share our thanks," she invited.

"That is very kind of you," said Laurence.

The outsiders watched as the Tryn dismantled several of the small wooden lodges and quickly pieced together a series of small tables from their parts. It seemed as if the task was something they performed often, as every one of them fell into a rhythm and did their part without speaking.

∴ ∴ ∴

THE TABLES crafted by the Tryn were low to the ground; designed for attendees to sit cross-legged. Saerasha guided her guests to the center table, indicating that they should sit together.

Laurence lowered himself to the ground at the center. Mordechai and Kyrilis sat on either side of him; Mordechai on his right and Kyrilis on his left. The rest of the companions joined them at the table shortly after. Saerasha took her place across from Laurence, joined by the two fauns; one on either side. She smiled as they sat beside her and patted them on their scruffy heads.

"Please don't," requested Wehrenel.

"We are not pets!" exclaimed Ahrwie.

"I'm sorry, small ones. You are just too adorable," chimed Saerasha.

"We are not!" barked Wehrenel. His little flower jiggled on his horn when he spoke.

"My apologies," said Saerasha, bowing her head. After a moment, she looked up at Laurence and addressed him directly. "I am sure you've noticed that most of my sisters do not speak. They can, but it is our custom not to waste time with words. I am our Shaman, which means I do the speaking for all of us in most matters.

"Our daily lives are fairly simple. We hunt, we gather, and we move to where the best hunting or harvest presents itself. As you've witnessed, we construct and dismantle our shelters for many purposes. We rarely stay in one place for very long. This has been to our benefit in recent years, as King Drakahl has sought to impose his rule on our lands more sternly.

"Times have become progressively more difficult since he took the throne. King Pahn—for all his faults—ignored the Triblunds. That is why we declined to aid the citizens of Caierthor when they sent emissaries to our lands seeking to overthrow him. To us, he was a fine King, for he stayed out of our way.

"However, with the recent assault on the various tribes of the Triblunds by Drakahl's forces, we cannot afford to sit idly by when a group such as yours arrives to dethrone him. The Inok have also suffered his tyranny. As I mentioned earlier, they may hold the key to freeing the souls of those we've lost," she explained, holding up a bag full of lapis lazuli for them to see.

"Grohm and his priest slew fifty-two of our men and women. We come here once per year for three days to celebrate Yshna, our goddess of love and fertility. We spend those days skyclad, experiencing one another and praying for the coming of the next generation. Grohm was well informed, for he knew to come here and attack us while we were unprepared to defend ourselves. Unclothed and without weapons, we were easy prey.

"The Inok have similar rituals to their god of the hunt, G'nok. I have no doubt that they were beset similarly. While we feast tonight, we must prepare ourselves for a speedy journey to their lands, to free them as you freed us. If we heard Grohm's men correctly, Thorgen was the general Drakahl deployed to the Inok.

"He is much more powerful than Grohm, and far less forgiving. That is suitable, since the Inok are much more formidable than we Tulmesh in physical combat. The Inok do not take kindly to outsiders; even us Tulmesh. We maintain peace with them by avoiding their lands, as do all other tribes who are wise," she detailed.

"We will do all in our power to free the Inok. Killing Thorgen and his men will weaken Drakahl's defenses, and deprive him of the souls they have collected. If they can help us free those trapped in these stones, all the better," agreed Laurence.

"You will also need a weapon more suited to defending against Drakahl's sword," she stated. "The Inok may have information that could lead us to one. More importantly, saving them should earn us safe passage through their lands. That will allow us to visit the Deepfolk Clan," she explained.

"It has been far too long since I visited the Deepfolk," said Mordechai as memories flooded his mind. He turned to Laurence and explained, "They are mountain dwarves that live deep within fortified structures carved inside Mount Skain. They are famed for their craftsmanship. Knights and adventurers from across the realms used to seek them out; most were turned away."

"It is said they still hold many treasures. What we should seek is a blade that lives only in legend. Our history is passed from generation to generation through our shaman. My mother instructed me in our ways, and one of the tales she told was of the sword that sundered Pelrigoss and created Zathos from its pieces," explained Saerasha.

"I have heard of no such legend," said Mordechai.

"In truth, it is hard to believe. Such is the way of legends. It is said that in the olden times—before we forgot—two casters arrived in our lands seeking the assistance of the Deepfolk to construct a blade. The blade was to be strong enough to allow them to focus their powers to fight the gods themselves. As the tale goes, they used that blade to tear Pelrigoss in two, trapping a god within the chunks of land and stone, and sending it into the sky to form Zathos.

"The legend says that is why Zathos is red; colored by the anger of the god trapped within. The sword is said to be deep under Mount Skain within a forbidden vault, buried hilt-deep in an obsidian altar," she said, finishing her tale.

"The thought of this blade's existence intrigues me," said Mordechai.

"More critical is the nature of the sword. It is not very powerful on its own, mind you. It was specially enchanted to channel its wielder's powers, and binds to their soul. The sword must bond with a single owner, and after the bond is complete, no force may separate its wielder's soul from their body," she explained.

"Drakahl's sword drains souls," added Mordechai, following her line of thinking.

"A sword like that would let me fight him without dying to random cuts and scratches," Laurence realized.

"If it doesn't exist, we could even ask the Deepfolk to help us make something similar. As long as they can craft a blade strong enough to hold the enchantments, I could retrieve Ayriel and together we could impart the enchantments ourselves," said Mordechai.

"So, whether or not the legend is true, we're headed to Mount Skain," said Laurence.

"Indeed," agreed Mordechai.

Wooden platters full of herbs, root vegetables, and small pieces of meat arrived at their table. Several Tryn placed wooden plates in front of each guest, and Saerasha indicated that they should take whatever they wanted from the platters in the center.

When Saerasha noticed that Mordechai wasn't grabbing any food of his own, she leaned forward and peered into his eyes.

"You are cursed," she stated bluntly. "Can you not see?"

"I was cursed with blindness by Nightweaver," he answered.

"The Shadow Witch?" she asked.

"The same."

"Come with me," she said as she rose to her feet.

Laurence took Mordechai by the arm and helped him navigate through the myriad of diners sitting at the tables all around them. They followed Saerasha into the fields to the south, arriving at a small paddock; fenced off and filled with goats.

Saerasha unlashed a small bit of rope and opened the gate, bidding them to enter. Once through, she followed and lashed the gate closed again. She led them into the center and bid them to sit, then sat in front of them.

"My mother once removed one of the Shadow Witch's curses from a traveler. I will now attempt to do the same for you, in further thanks for saving my tribe. I am not sure if I will succeed, but I cannot allow you to risk your lives hindered by that witch's foul curse.

"These goats serve a single purpose. We do not eat them or milk them. To perform my magics, I must tap into the life-force of nature around me. These goats travel with us so I might use them as a source of power to grant healing to our tribe. That may seem cruel, but we revere these goats as treasures and treat them fondly throughout their lives. This is their only purpose.

"I explain these things so that when you see harm come to them during my casting, you will understand what is happening. Should I become unconscious, please have me returned to my lodge so I might rest," she requested.

"Please be careful," requested Mordechai.

∴ ∴ ∴

SAERASHA SAT cross-legged before Laurence and Mordechai, placing the backs of her hands onto her knees. Closing her eyes, she bowed her head and meditated for a time on the task before her. As she began chanting, she raised her head and pointed her eyes, still closed, toward the sky.

Her soft-spoken words drifted on the wind that swirled about them, overlapping in strange, echoing patterns.

The goats cried out, circling the paddock nervously.

She raised her right hand, pointing her palm toward Mordechai. She placed her left palm down against the ground. Unseen power raced across the ground from her hand, streaking toward the animals.

To Mordechai, the power surge seemed to glow a fierce green, moving like lightning across the ground.

The grass and weeds died instantly in its wake, wilting and crumbling to dust. As the streaks of dead grass reached a goat, the animal froze in its tracks and fell to its knees. Crying out in pain, the goat fell onto its side and decayed to nothing in a matter of seconds.

Visible green energies glowed around Mordechai's eyes.

Laurence watched in amazement and horror as the process repeated, one goat after another. Saerasha could sense the witch's powers unraveling, bit by bit. She pressed harder, focusing her energies with every ounce of her strength; casting more powerful magics than she'd ever wielded in her life

Saerasha reached out to every goat left in the paddock, seizing their collective life-forces all at once.

The energies crossing through the air between her right hand and Mordechai's eyes glowed to life, becoming strong enough for Laurence to see. Her active chanting ceased as she screamed out in pain, while the remnants of her spoken words continued to swirl about them on the winds created by her spell.

Mordechai screamed out in pain, his mind blinded by the powers involved in her casting. He shut himself off from the weave out of reflex, saving himself from the magic-induced agony he was experiencing. The pain in his eyes, forehead and cheeks became evident, no longer drowned out by the pain his visions were causing him.

All at once the winds died down, the echoes of her chanting faded away, the green energies vanished, and the remaining goats died.

Saerasha fell backwards.

Mordechai blinked rapidly, trying to adjust his vision.

"I can see!" he declared.

"She did it!" blurted Laurence.

"She..." Mordechai started. He noticed a horrible consequence to his returned vision and alerted Laurence, "She's not breathing!"

Laurence lurched forward, closing the gap between them as quickly as he could, and checked her for signs of life. No breath escaped her lips; her chest wasn't heaving; there was no pulse when he placed his fingers on her neck.

"She's dead," he said somberly as he looked back at Mordechai. That was when he noticed the small crowd of tribal women that had gathered outside the paddock, watching the event unfold.

Several Tryn reached out to Saerasha from the other side of the fence, tears in their eyes.

∴ ∴ ∴

THE ELVEN women carried Saerasha to her wooden lodge, laid her down on the small pile of furs and stepped outside to mourn. Mordechai ducked into the small pyramid-like structure and got down on his knees beside her. He placed his hand on her chest and whispered, "I'm sorry."

Laurence watched from the doorway while his friend suffered, blaming himself for the shaman's death. It was inspiring for the prospects of their quest that Mordechai had his vision back, but the cost was too great.

Wehrenel and Ahrwie, standing by his side at the doorway, hadn't been able to heal her as she lay in the paddock. Their failure upset them. They stood silently, torturing themselves for being too weak to help.

Saerasha's torso arched upward suddenly, then dropped back onto the furs.

Mordechai withdrew his hand quickly, his eyes wide with surprise.

"What did you do?" asked Laurence.

"I did nothing. There was a surge of energy," Mordechai

explained.

Her chest heaved again, this time a faint blue glow accompanied the movement. It was as if something was colliding with her body from underneath, forcing her chest upward and then retracting.

"What the hell is going on?" pleaded Laurence.

Several nearby women ran over to see what was happening, knocking the faun aside to get a better view.

"I don't know, Laurence," belted Mordechai as her body once again surged with power.

He backed away from her hurriedly.

Saerasha's body rose into the air as a stream of faint blue energy streamed out of the ground and passed through her. The women outside the tent shrieked and covered their mouths. Laurence stepped closer, feeling drawn to the powers that coursed through her.

"Don't!" yelled Mordechai, holding out his hand to stop him.

As suddenly as the event had begun, it ended. Saerasha's body dropped to the ground, landing atop the furs with a thud.

She gasped for air, and began breathing frantically, looking around her in confusion.

"It's okay! Calm down! Breath normally!" ordered Mordechai, coming back to her side and placing his hand on her stomach reassuringly.

"I... what? How am I-"

"I think I know what has happened, but I need you to calm down before I try to explain," offered Mordechai.

∴ ∴ ∴

IT TOOK almost an hour for Saerasha to get control of her breathing and come to her senses, and nearly another hour to calm the rest of her tribe. Once things settled down, Mordechai and Laurence walked her a short distance away from the camp and sat under the stars.

She looked at Mordechai and studied his eyes. "So, it worked. My spell worked," she declared.

It did," said Mordechai.

"But you died in the casting," added Laurence.

"Then how am I alive? What happened?" she asked.

"Before I answer that, I first need to confirm my suspicions. Can you... do something for me?" Mordechai asked.

"What more would you ask of me, after what I've just been through?"

"It is a simple thing. You have a great connection to nature, and excellent control of your spellcasting abilities. What I ask of you should be a fairly simple task, and will place you in no danger," he clarified.

"Fine. What would you have me do?" she sighed.

"Hold out your right hand and... without reaching out to nature, produce a small flame."

"What?" she gasped.

"Reach within yourself for the power, not outward to the sources you are used to consuming. Rather than transfer energies from without, draw your power from within. Produce a simple, small flame at your fingertips," he explained.

She sat for a moment, staring blankly at him. "That is not how shamanistic magics work," she declared bluntly.

"I am fully aware of that. Please... indulge me."

"Fine," she said.

Complying with his odd request, she held out her right hand, put the tips of her fingers together in a cluster and focused as best she could.

"Sense within yourself. Feel for a power, an energy, growing deep inside you. Pull that energy into your hand, and tell it to produce a small flame," he encouraged.

She sighed, closed her eyes, and focused on reaching down within herself, as he'd suggested. Much like she was used to doing with nature, she pushed her senses inward, seeking power. To her surprise, she felt something. Drawing from that power as she'd learned to do from nature, she pulled it into her fingertips and imagined a flame.

When she opened her eyes, a small flame danced upon her fingertips, flicking in the light breeze that drifted past them.

Laurence stared at her in amazement.

Mordechai smiled.

Releasing the flame, she stared directly into Mordechai's eyes, bewildered. "What did I just do? How did that work?"

"You are a Celestial," Mordechai stated frankly. "I have a very special tome in my collection at Fel'Vizsiour that speaks of such magic, but I've never seen or heard of anyone being able to use it. There was a cult in southern Haern a few hundred years ago that committed suicide, one by one, trying to become Soulfyr casters. One of the requirements to become a Soulfyr caster is unfortunately what prevents most people from succeeding. You have to die first," he explained.

"What the hell?" blurted Laurence.

"I'm not sure how it works, to be honest. The tome speaks of three kinds of Soulfyr magic; energies produced by one's own soul or some form of internalized magical weave. Once mastered, the tome suggests that it leads to power of untold magnitude.

"Celestials are such casters who are good of heart and aligned toward the betterment of the world, and its people. Diabolists are those who seek power, and what we would consider evil pursuits. Cosmists seek balance in all things, and will do good or evil as it suits their perception of balance in each moment.

"As you are a good and kind soul who gave her life to restore the sight of another, it is fairly easy to surmise that you are not evil, and not overly concerned with balance. That would make you a Celestial, rather than a Diabolist or Cosmist."

"So... I can produce my own magical energies now? I need not drain life from the world around me?" she asked, both confused and intrigued.

"Once you master your new skills, yes. You'll be able to do everything you did before, and more. You will still be able to cast the same magics you once did, and in the same manner. However, I believe that once you learn to control your newly unlocked abilities, you will abandon your old ways as unnecessary.

"In fact, this may even provide you access to other sources of magical energies you could never tap into before," he explained. "However, this will take some time for you to learn and master. Don't push too hard, it will come with patience and practice."

"I... should go prepare the tribe for my departure," she said, rising to her feet.

"You're still coming with us?" asked Laurence.

"Yes. We still need to be free of Drakahl's rule, regardless of what has happened to me," she answered.

"Can I help you prepare?" Laurence asked, standing up.

"Sure," she said, smiling.

As they walked away, Mordechai closed his eyes. He focused on the pair of them with the magical sensitivities he'd learned while he was blind. Saerasha glowed like a beacon in his mind's eye. Laurence, walking to her left, showed a faint glow that slightly resembled her newfound powers in structure.

I thought so.

∴ ∴ ∴

LAURENCE AND Saerasha walked at the front of the line as the group departed the next morning.

Mordechai followed closely behind with Kyrilis and Izabel, debating the state of Arkhania after the attacks.

Agnar and Wil walked further behind with their newfound friends Gareg and Kellum, telling war stories.

Wehrenel and Ahrwie walked with Vaelys at the rear, teasing her occasionally by tickling one hand or another with small wild flowers or grass. She did not mind their antics; she welcomed the distraction. The group's journey had taken an unwelcome detour, and her mind raced with thoughts of where she would rather be.

Several hours into the day, Gareg removed a satchel from his shoulder and signaled to Wehrenel and Ahrwie. They ran up to him and held out their hands. As he handed each of them handfuls of nuts and berries, they raced up and down the formation distributing snacks to their companions. This process repeated several more times during their trek, allowing them to walk with very infrequent stops.

It was nearly nightfall when Saerasha signaled for them to stop on a hill. The savanna had given way to foothills. Acacia grew in dense patches, faintly reminiscent of a forest. Once atop the hill, she signaled that they should rest and eat a proper meal.

"Not much further," said Saerasha. "We should let the others rest here while a few of us scout ahead."

"We need to see if the Inok were attacked as we suspect," he agreed. "A count of Thorgen's men wouldn't hurt either."

"My thoughts exactly."

Laurence collected Vaelys and Kellum for the scouting mission and told the others to stay and rest. He looked toward Kyrilis for a moment. She smiled back at him and nodded.

The four scouts set out shortly after, continuing northeast from the camp.

∴ ∴ ∴

TYLEE WAS standing atop a hill talking to a worker when Delriahna approached. The worker was holding a rough map before them while Tylee pointed out some of her concerns. When she finished, the worker rolled the large parchment and jogged back toward his tent. She crossed her arms and stood for a moment, tapping her foot.

"Rough morning?" asked Delriahna.

"I'd call it stressful," Tylee answered. She looked over at her mother and smiled. "Things are going okay, there's just so much going on... it's hard to keep track of everything."

Standing beside each other, they turned their attention to the landscape below them. In the distance to the south lay the remnants of Kallenfall, several buildings in the middle of being repaired.

Clendon had ordered his men to stow their armor during the build and work construction for the road and keep. Tylee and Delriahna watched as the base of the road was being dug below them by dozens of soldiers. Others carried gravel from the far side of Kallenfall, near the mines, and scattered it into the base.

The sound of hammers on stone rang out through the air from afar. As they brought the stone up from the mines, workers smashed it into gravel for use on the road project. The activities carried out like a grand performance below them, each worker playing their part dutifully.

"It's a sight to behold," said Delriahna.

"If they were villagers, they'd be moving so much slower, and complaining non-stop," stated Tylee.

"They would," agreed Delriahna.

"What brings you to the hill, mother?" Tylee asked. She did not mind her mother's visits, but there was always a reason she made the trip.

"Aric has left for Mooncrest. Rolph had to arrest two men for fighting last night in the new tavern. Cynthia has asked for help running the daycare out of the first floor of the inn. Greta... well, she's just being pushy about everything under the sun," vented Delriahna.

"Surely those aren't the reasons for your visit," surmised Tylee.

"No... no they are not. We have a problem back in Gaierford," she admitted. "Several of the new arrivals from Port Vaelin are squatting in the fields we'd previously allocated to refugees from Grellenheim."

"That won't do," said Tylee.

"That's why I've come to you. I don't have the authority to force them to relocate," she said. "While the King has decreed that Andor and I are Duke and Duchess, these are not our territories."

"What we need is a new constable," decided Tylee. "Someone who can run Gaierford while I'm otherwise occupied. In fact, we also need a constable for Kallenfall."

"Where are we going to find two worthy constables in all this mess?" gasped Delriahna. "These people are-"

"Homeless, scared and suffering. They're acting out of desperation, trying to make sure they don't get left behind," Tylee interrupted.

"Well, yes, but-"

"Announce a town meeting tonight. I have to travel through Gaierford tonight on my way to join Clendon in Cragenfell. I'll announce our need for constables and give them a few days to come up with candidates. We'll hold a vote upon my return. In the meantime, can you have someone prepare Onyx for me? I don't wish to walk all the way to Cragenfell, and Onyx is back in Gaierford," said Tylee.

"I will have him sent to you. See you back in Gaierford tonight, Duchess," said Delriahna with a smirk.

"You too, Duchess," retorted Tylee with a giggle.

∴ ∴ ∴

MINOTAUR CORPSES, each over eight feet in height, stretched out as far as the eye could see; tied to the poles that littered the valley below. Many of the corpses had their horns sawed off, and their brown fur had faded to gray at the center of their chests.

Laurence slowly descended the hill, entering the field of dead Inok. Vaelys, Kellum and Saerasha followed closely behind. They stayed as low to the ground as they could, using the standing corpses to disguise their movement.

It wasn't clear where Thorgen's camp was located. The layout of the hills and placement of the poles obscured their view of the surroundings. Creeping through the field, weaving between the corpses, they came to a bend in the valley and the sounds of Thorgen's camp reached them.

"Psst!" whispered Kellum.

The group stopped and peered at him. He signaled for them to wait a few moments and climbed up one of the poles. Once at the top, he looked around and then climbing back down.

"Tents up ahead. Bonfire on the far side. They appear to be celebrating," he whispered.

"Any guards?" whispered Vaelys.

"Not that I could see," he whispered back.

Vaelys nodded and moved to head toward the tents.

"This is a scouting mission," whispered Laurence.

"Then *scout!*" Vaelys whispered back forcefully. Without another word, she slipped into the shadows.

"Where the hell did she go?" whispered Laurence.

"Oh, shit... she's going for the camp alone," said Kellum.

"She'll die!" retorted Laurence.

"Uh... yeah, about that," said Kellum.

"Stop talking, then! Let's go stop her," suggested Saerasha.

They moved toward the camp with increased urgency while trying to remain cautious. If Vaelys intended on attacking stealthily, they didn't want to alert their quarry. As they crested the top of a neighboring hill, fire sprang to life in the tents below.

∴ ∴ ∴

VAELYS CREPT behind two rows of black tents, listening intently. A group of soldiers talked, laughed and cheered beside a bonfire on the other side of them. She heard someone moving inside the tent beside her and paused. After a few moments when the noise stopped, she determined that the occupant was likely trying to sleep.

Silently, she slipped around to the front. Moving the tent flap aside with the tip of her dagger, she crept inside and approached the wooden cot at the rear. A burly man lay on the cot, curled up under woolen blankets.

"Damned idiots," he grumbled under his breath. He pressed his eyelids together angrily, trying to force himself to sleep. "How do they expect to set out tomorrow with all that racket! Can't get no rest!"

He opened his eyes as her dagger slid silently across his throat.

"Sleep," she whispered wickedly.

Vaelys tugged the blanket off the man while he gasped for breath and held his throat, desperately trying to hold in his blood. She smiled at him and turned to the gear at the foot of his bed. After wrapping his longsword with one end of the blanket, she exited the tent and proceeded to the next.

Three more men died by her blade in silence as she moved from tent to tent, collecting five longswords and a mace. She wrapped each in the blanket so that none of them touched, to keep them hidden and silent.

Deciding she'd found enough, she proceeded with the next step of her plan.

She entered the second largest tent; a supply tent at the end of one row. After a few short moments, she found what she sought. Using a bit of rope, she bound the bundle of collected weaponry to her back. Next, she pocketed a small piece of flint. Finally, she grabbed the small wooden barrel of torch oil she had entered the tent to find.

Once outside, she moved to the near end of the line of tents and uncorked the barrel. She splashed each tent with oil as she moved toward the far end of camp, trailing oil in her wake. After she reached the far end, she ducked behind a tent and waited for the soldiers at the bonfire to make more noise.

At the outburst of a round of laughter, she struck the flint with her dagger, but the sparks missed her target. After each strike, she waited for another outburst before trying again. Following her third strike, she looked up to see what had caused the movement in her peripheral vision.

Laurence, Kellum and Saerasha had come into view on top of the hill.

"Amateurs," she whispered.

As the crowd roared to life again, she struck the flint a fourth time. The sparks landed in the oil in front of her, setting it on fire.

Flames streaked across the ground in a zig-zag pattern, setting each tent ablaze in its path. She dropped the flint and ducked around the edge of the last tent, moving out into the shadows beyond.

After a few moments, the tents were fully ablaze, and the soldiers' party was over. Several of them cried out for water to douse the flames. Many more ran to their tents to retrieve their belongings, or save sleeping friends. Calls of alarm rang through the camp as they discovered her victims.

The chaos that followed served as the distraction she hoped it would.

She crept to the other side of the bonfire, to the minotaur tied to the trees beyond. Two guards stood in front of them, staring at the chaos amidst the tents apprehensively, their hands on the hilts of their weapons.

She hefted a dagger in each hand, flipped them in the air so she could catch them by their tips, and then threw them at the guards. Each dagger buried cross-guard-deep into the throat of a guard. As they fell to the ground, she crept up in front of the minotaur and placed the roll of weapons on the ground.

Vaelys held the bottom edge of the blanket in place and pushed the roll away from her. The weapons rolled out in a line before the minotaur. They looked at the display then back at her inquisitively.

She nodded and smiled in response, then retrieved her daggers.

As she cut them free, several armed themselves from the bundle. Others ran to a nearby pile of sawed-off horns and grabbed them to use as weapons.

The minotaur freed, she ran back toward the soldiers. All the minotaur fell in behind her, happy to see their enemies slain. By the time the soldiers realized what was happening, the minotaur and Vaelys were already upon them.

Laurence, Kellum and Saerasha raced down the hill, witnessing the mayhem that played out in the camp.

"She's clever, I'll give her that," said Laurence.

"She released the minotaur," added Kellum.

"You could see that?" asked Saerasha.

"You couldn't? You're an elf, right?" asked Kellum.

"Well, with all the heat from the fire, I had to focus on using normal vision," she explained.

"Try squinting next time," Kellum joked.

Saerasha sighed in mock frustration as they closed in on the flaming tents.

Laurence and Kellum ran ahead to engage the soldiers while she hung back a short distance.

Vaelys collided with the soldiers in a flurry of steel. She parried a man's overhead strike and stabbed him in the underarm, ripping her blade through his chest.

The man to her left slashed at her head, so she ducked and stabbed him with both daggers in the groin.

A sword dove downward toward her back, so she rolled out of the way, spun and kicked the man's legs out from under him.

The first minotaur ran over the man, crushing his chest with a massive hoof.

He grabbed the next man's sword-arm in his left hand as he came to a stop. Lifting the man into the air, he drove a sword through the man's torso and roared with delight.

Most of the soldiers wore simple tunics or gambesons, their armor stowed for the evening's festivities.

One soldier stood in the back of the crowd wearing deep red brigandine armor and pauldrons. As he watched the minotaur warriors and Vaelys dismantling his men, he backed away and turned to run.

Laurence ran between the rows of burning tents and turned into the opening which led to the bonfire. A dozen minotaur were fighting the soldiers a few yards away, but they didn't concern him. As he entered the opening, their leader turned to flee. It was Thorgen; holding a longsword and wearing brigandine.

"You killed my grandfather!" Laurence growled.

He recognized Thorgen as the man who had been inside the alchemy shop with his grandfather.

"You're that pathetic kid that killed Ulger and Dison at that farm, aren't you?" questioned Thorgen. "You brought this down upon me? *For what...* some pathetic attempt at revenge?"

Kellum listened to their exchange and then slipped past to help Vaelys, leaving Thorgen for Laurence to handle. He'd seen the boy dismantle Grohm, and expected Thorgen would be just as easily handled.

"You brought this on yourself!" Laurence yelled as he attacked.

Laurence's sword sliced through the air, aimed at Thorgen's left side. Thorgen blocked the blow, and then another as Laurence started his volley. After a few attacks, Thorgen locked their blades between them and leaned in close.

"You're out of your league, boy," he muttered.

Laurence pushed himself free and began another volley of attacks.

Thorgen deflected each attack easily.

Laurence took a step back and paced sideways, circling his opponent and waiting. He needed to see more of what his enemy was capable of, which meant he had to let the man attack.

Thorgen thrust his blade toward Laurence's chest. As Laurence knocked it aside, Thorgen turned the deflection into an uppercut.

Laurence deflected the uppercut away, leaving both of their blades away from center.

Thorgen stepped into his reach and grabbed his right forearm, then punched him in the head with the hilt of his sword.

Laurence stumbled back a few steps, released from the man's grasp.

Thorgen charged in, his sword slashing through the air from right-to-left toward his head.

Laurence dropped to the ground as fast as he could, interlocked their legs and rolled over, sending Thorgen crashing to the ground. Mid-roll, he switched his sword to his left hand and slashed down toward Thorgen's prone form.

The blade bounced off of Thorgen's brigandine armor, but enough of it met his unprotected tricep to leave a gash on the back of his left arm.

Both men got back to their feet and faced each other, pacing in circles.

Thorgen favored his left arm, wincing in pain.

"You've grown in skill, boy, but this will soon be over," said Thorgen.

As they paced, Laurence looked past Thorgen to the scene beyond. The soldiers were dead. The minotaur, Kellum, Saerasha and Vaelys all watched their fight.

Kellum nodded at him and smiled.

"You're right. This *will* soon be over," Laurence responded.

Ignoring the throbbing pain in his head, Laurence attacked again with his sword still in his left hand. He thrust his blade toward Thorgen's chest, but withdrew it just in time for Thorgen's parry to miss.

Thorgen's movements resulted in his blade being high above his shoulder.

Laurence turned his withdrawn blade vertical, reached up and locked Thorgen's blade in place with its quillon.

He jumped into the space between them and punched the man in the throat with a knife-hand strike. Feeling the pressure on his sword release, he brought the sword down hard and fast, slicing through the inner part of Thorgen's right forearm, severing the tendons; making Thorgen unable to maintain a grip on his weapon.

As General Thorgen of the Pelrigoss Guard fell to his knees, shock washed across his face. Laurence kicked him in the chest, sending him onto the ground.

Laurence looked across the clearing toward the minotaur. "Which one of you is in charge?" he asked.

"I am," grunted the tallest of them. His cracked left horn was shorter than his right. He looked as if he'd seen many battles.

"He's yours to do with as you please," offered Laurence. He bent over and collected Thorgen's blade, then walked over to his friends while the minotaur leader lifted Thorgen into the air and bashed the man's face in repeatedly with his bony brow.

Kellum took off to retrieve their companions.

∴ ∴ ∴

KELLUM RETURNED with the rest of their group a few hours later. The minotaur hadn't spoken since the battle for their freedom and had spent the night burning the dead soldiers and pulling corpses out of the field behind the camp. They'd almost completed their burials before the rest of Laurence's companions arrived.

When Laurence approached their leader to speak, the nine-foot-tall minotaur shook his head as if to say, 'not now,' and went back to work.

Saerasha, Wehrenel and Ahrwie scoured the minotaur huts for food and put together a feast for everyone while they waited.

∴ ∴ ∴

"I THOOL," said the minotaur leader. He sat down on a hunk of log in front of Laurence, a bowl of buttered eggs in hand. After a few sloppy bites he continued, "I leader Inok. We like you save us. But ask why?"

"My friends and I are passing through the Triblunds in search of a weapon that will allow me to kill Drakahl," answered Laurence.

"You kill King?" asked Thool as bits of food dropped out of his mouth. He stopped eating abruptly, his spoon still hovering halfway between the bowl and his face.

"That is the plan, yes. We encountered a similar prison camp with the Tulmesh and saved them. Their Shaman brought us to you. She was worried you were also in danger," explained Laurence.

Thool looked over at Saerasha. "Tulmesh save Inok?"

"Yes, mighty Thool. The Inok are a majestic people and I could not sit idly by and watch as you suffered the same horrors as we Tulmesh," she answered.

"We thank you," Thool said. He placed his bowl and spoon down on the dirt in front of him. "We like Drakahl die. How help?"

"We are seeking a blade of legend; the one that ripped open the lands, and separated us from Caierthor," explained Saerasha as she moved to sit beside Laurence.

"Blade, no real," said Thool.

"If it was real, we assumed it would be beneath Skain," said Laurence.

"If real, yes. But no real," stated Thool.

"We need to travel to Skain to make sure, if it's all the same," suggested Saerasha.

"Fine. You save Inok. You kill King. I help," he belted. He stood up and faced his tribe, saying, "I help little ones. Back soon. Ugher lead."

"Just like that?" Laurence asked Saerasha.

"Just like that," she answered, shrugging.

"We leave morning," said Thool as he turned back around. "Now rest, mourn dead."

After their meals, the companions helped the Inok clear the rest of the camp and chop down the posts behind it. Before the day was over, Ugher had introduced herself as Thool's mate and brought mead for them all to share.

Vaelys stayed on watch the entire night, silently musing the possible existence of the blade of legend she'd heard them discuss. She decided it was wise to stick with them until she knew the truth of the matter.

∴ ∴ ∴

NIGHTWEAVER ENTERED Drakahl's throne room, her staff clanking into the stone floor and echoing throughout the chamber.

Ahm took a step back from the throne, turning to watch her approach. As she drew closer, he smiled and nodded in respect. Once she reached Ahm's side, they looked up at Drakahl, seated in his throne on the dais.

"It is time to take my leave," she stated.

"What of those who approach?" asked Drakahl.

His red armor seemed to shimmer and writhe at his words.

"They are proceeding as expected, and the pieces are falling into place. General Soth returned with his share of souls, and the Velloth are on their way to our meeting place. It is time for Ahm and I to begin the process of creating more Skorned," she explained.

"I am eager to begin," said Ahm.

"After your battle with the last Raven, Soth will bring you to me. He is aware of our destination, and knows which route to take in order to reach us in secret," she added.

"Shall I leave Thorgen to guard the throne in my absence?" asked Drakahl.

"Grohm and Thorgen have been slain," she answered. "They were inconsequential to the rest of our plans, so their deaths matter not. Your throne is unimportant. It has served its purpose, and you will soon occupy another."

"Very well," he agreed, pushing Axvalla's incessant nagging out of his mind as best he could.

"Leave this kingdom in disarray and madness. Let the people scramble to fill your void, and battle over rights to the throne. We will leave chaos in our wake, as always," she proclaimed.

"For the Nine!" he belted.

"For the Nine," she agreed with a nod.

Ahm turned and followed Nightweaver as she walked out of the chamber. When they crossed through the massive doors, he asked her, "Why do you keep this form? I have seen you younger... why do you not keep that younger form permanently? It would certainly allow us to travel more easily."

"I am not yet free of Vaxtra's control. Once I am able to sever his connection to me, I will permanently return to my normal form. Until then, I may only force my body into that state with great effort. You will thus be traveling with an ancient, feeble woman for many months to come. I suggest you get used to the idea," she explained with a tinge of humor in her tone.

"Where are we headed?" asked Ahm.

"We go to Dagoh Bay. She will meet us there," answered Nightweaver.

"Very well," said Ahm. "Once she joins, that makes seven," he added.

"Three more will join, two will depart, and then our final member will follow shortly after."

"And then the Circle of Nine will be complete?"

"For a time."

Ahm smiled in anticipation. For years he had dreamed of constructing the armor of the Skorned and expanding their power under Nightweaver's guidance. All his years of subservient support, planning, and preparations were about to come to fruition. Besides, he couldn't wait to meet their newest member.

ACCORD

Ris'Uttyr, Arran'Hael 17th, 113 of the 2nd Era

Mountain man creating smog,
Your destiny doth call.
Set aside your fear and see,
Work as one, for all.

Night's Writ, Parable 17

A S THE sun rose over the hills and mountains to the east, Laurence and Kyrilis sat staring at Mount Skain to the north, deep in thought.

Saerasha joined them after a while, accompanied by Wil, Thool and Mordechai. They sat in silence beside him for a time, waiting for him to complete his thoughts. During the festivities the night before, he had withdrawn into himself. They weren't sure if he'd gotten any sleep.

"I'm sorry," he said, breaking the silence. "I know we have a lot to discuss, but everything is just weighing so heavily on me all of a sudden."

"I understand," offered Mordechai.

It had been a while since he'd been able to study his friend's face. They'd been so busy the past few days, he'd barely had time to consider what Laurence might be going through.

"I originally planned to leave home and become a soldier in the Arkhanian Legion; to work my way up through the ranks and restore our family's position in the Kingdom of Arkhania. I grew up hearing tales of Gahl the Raven, and how he was selected to become Lord Commander of the Legion under King Orluhnd the First. That never came to pass, and I never understood why.

"Then Drakahl returned, killed Arcturus and brought all our family history out of hiding. His intervention changed the entire course of my life. I feel like... nothing is my own doing anymore. I'm a pawn in fate's game of chess, and I don't know if I'm on the winning side or not.

"At every turn I watch people die. Grellenheim, Sacton Marshlands, Cragenfell, and now Pelrigoss. Arcturus by Drakahl's hands, Bingrolf to the Velloth, dozens of soldiers to Vehks, Gaerin and Lyla to Grohm's priest... I can't save anyone," he explained. Tears rolled down his cheeks, glistening in the light of dawn. "And now when I enter combat, I'm confronted with a side of me that I detest. I no longer fight with passion or honor. Anger overcomes me—and maybe that's giving me the edge I need to defeat guys like Grohm and Thorgen—but... is that who I am now?"

"You still fight with honor, it's just that your motivations have changed. The situations you're facing are more dire. It's understandable to feel the way you do. But you must know, we wouldn't follow you if we didn't believe in you," offered Kyrilis, rubbing his back with one hand.

"What you are is a leader. You continue to gather followers everywhere you go. Your cause is just, and people see that," said Mordechai.

"I have only known you for a short time. However, in that time, I've been nothing but impressed and inspired. You talk of honor? You could have killed Thorgen yourself, but you let the Inok claim their justice instead. Mordechai has explained to me what Grohm and Thorgen helped Drakahl do to your grandfather. You would have been justified in claiming him yourself.

"A lesser man would have done just that. I do not know of any Tryn who would have sacrificed their own need for vengeance for the good of a competing tribe. I followed you because of your cause and motivations. After seeing you in battle against Grohm, I felt you were capable of seeing this through. Once I saw you fight Thorgen, I knew I had chosen wisely," explained Saerasha.

"Inok suffered. You help. Saw you fight good. Puny human surprise me. Not see other human fight good. I join. We save Inok. Help fight. Help win," said Thool.

"I should be home right now, helping my people rebuild. Instead, I am here with you; helping with your quest. Everyone else in Arkhania is wallowing in the aftermath of someone else's whims and desires. You are the only one who is fighting to save us from them. So, regardless of my responsibility to my people, I choose to address the greater threat. I choose to be here with you," said Wil.

"Thool also knows what we need to do about the souls trapped in the lapis lazuli," she mentioned.

"Oh?" asked Laurence, perking up.

"Yes. Once was lich travel Triblunds. Lord Whun. Inok forced work with Deepfolk, drive him off. He trap souls in stone. Inok try break stone, set free. It no work. Deepfolk bring stones, place under Skain. Old place have thing that free souls," Thool explained.

"Over a thousand years ago, a lich named Lord Whun ravaged our lands collecting souls. We never discovered his motivations. The Tulmesh and Kalmesh fled, unable to defeat him. When he confronted the Inok, they were able to resist his undead army, but were driven back to Mount Skain. The Deepfolk formed a truce with the Inok and joined forces to defeat Whun's army. Afterward they used an ancient ritual chamber beneath Mount Skain to free the souls from the lapis lazuli," Saerasha elaborated.

"That what I said," chided Thool.

"So, we now have two reasons to head to Skain and visit the Deepfolk," surmised Laurence.

"Well, it's going to be a complicated endeavor," said Mordechai. "The Inok and Deepfolk do not get along, and we're bringing the Inok Chieftain with us."

"Are the Deepfolk aligned with Drakahl?" asked Laurence.

"Not that I'm aware of," answered Saerasha. "Though they supply his forces with armor and weaponry, I do not know if it is by choice."

"Let us hope that it's not," said Laurence.

After a brief discussion regarding their plans for the journey to Mount Skain, the group left the hilltop. Vaelys and Kellum had taken it upon themselves to get their group ready for travel while they talked. Within the hour, they were headed north toward Mount Skain.

∴ ∴ ∴

MOUNT SKAIN loomed ominously, reaching into the dark clouds above. Red and black smoke billowed into the sky from vents at the top of the mountain, casting shadows across the land. The foggy haze of smog thickened the air, reducing visibility further.

The southern and eastern slopes came to a sharp corner in the southeast, making it seem as if only a quarter of the original mountain remained. Below the eastern face lie the western edge of the Well of the World, into which flowed the northern and southern branches of the Odvodi river. The southern face continued below ground into a deep fissure, across which spanned the great bridge known as the Dark Expanse.

Surrounding the southern tip of the Dark Expanse stood the city of Skainhold; its walls, buildings, and roads constructed primarily of obsidian. To the north, the obsidian bridge ended on a massive obsidian ledge. Great columns of granite descended deep into the fissure, providing support for the bridge. Granite corbels shaped like claws gripped the side of the fissure, reaching up to support the thick obsidian ledge.

Atop the ledge stood a two-hundred-foot tall statue representing a titan holding a greatsword before him, tip buried into the obsidian floor. Discolored from age, the bronze plating upon the statue was missing at points, revealing the black stone beneath. Travelers had to pass beneath the titanic statue's legs to enter Skainfall, the great dwarven city beyond.

∴ ∴ ∴

THE GROUP had traveled for nearly two days with Mount Skain growing ever larger ahead of them. They decided to rest for a short time before confronting the Deepfolk.

Laurence stood next to a thirty-foot-tall ring of iron, protruding from a slab of solid stone. Similar interlocking rings of iron lay strewn haphazardly across the landscape to the west, forming a chain. Its size prevented clear passage to the north, but he doubted that was the chain's original purpose. The chain was daunting and raised many questions in Laurence's mind.

"What do you think this is?" he asked Mordechai.

"Clearly it's a chain," teased Mordechai.

"Yes, but... a chain with thirty-foot links? What the hell for?" he asked.

"With the way it ends in the ground, I'd say something was once anchored here. To be more specific, something that floated above the land," Mordechai answered, cryptically.

"That makes little sense," Laurence countered.

"One of the draconic tablets I translated centuries ago spoke of the Agthari; a titanic race which lived in floating cities that were anchored to the ground. The tablet was small and did not offer much detail. I saw this very chain once long ago, when I visited here. But my studies took me in other directions, so I never delved far into its origins.

"However, it does suggest a validity in the tablet's claims. Clearly the Agthari are long gone, so it's not like I can just find one and ask questions. The only way to prove the theory for certain would be to find such a city, but... I've yet to come across one in my travels. There are rumors one might exist somewhere in the southern isles, but times have been demanding, of late. Perhaps I'll go there on vacation when this is over," said Mordechai.

"You mean a titan like that?" Laurence asked, pointing at the titanic statue that loomed over Skainhold in the distance.

"I would presume so," said Mordechai. "Vaelin Palace existed before Arkhan Vaelin claimed and re-purposed it. I bring that up, because the palace is ancient and bears magic that binds it together, allowing it to last much longer than it should. Skainfall, Skainhold and the Dark Expanse all contain similar magics, which tells me they were here before their dwarven occupants.

"If Skainhold had been constructed by dwarves, you'd expect their homes and doorways to be dwarven in scale. After all, dwarves are typically no taller than five feet. However, their structures accommodate beings as tall as nine," he explained.

"So this place has existed-"

"Since long before we can imagine," Mordechai said, completing Laurence's thought.

Saerasha walked up behind them. With a smile, she asked, "Should we get going?"

"This is fascinating," said Laurence.

"Yes, it is, but we have pressing concerns," she explained.

With a sigh, Laurence began his descent down the last of the foothills. His mind returned to the task at hand, broken free of its temporary and welcome distraction.

Wehrenel and Ahrwie skipped ahead of the group, leading them toward the great obsidian archway that allowed entry into the city of Skainhold.

∴ ∴ ∴

"THE LATEST estimate produced by the agents from Fel'Vizsiour is nine hundred dead in Grellenheim and nearly eight thousand more between Port Vaelin and Vellenheim," explained Clendon.

Tylee took another sip of her tea as a tear rolled down her cheek. She hadn't realized the devastation was so extensive across the Kingdom. Clendon's report was eye opening and brought the full scope of the Kingdom's troubles to light.

"Vellenheim was flooded with refugees from the northern regions of Port Vaelin almost immediately. Those that could work were sent to Ekthri with Ayriel to help them rebuild. They lost thousands in Ayr'Thugohn as well," he continued. "The families of those workers were sent to Dunforth, Ayerton, Raven's Nest and Fel'Rechaun.

"Those displaced from the southern half of Port Vaelin were sent to you in Gaierford, Salvation Shire and Cragenfell. A few expressed interest in moving further south and accompanied our emissary to Mooncrest. We've received word that Andor's efforts to increase farm production are going smoothly, but they'll need help from Fel'Vizsiour's druids to accelerate growth," he explained.

"Our recent count in Gaierford is seven-hundred-forty, between your soldiers and the refugees. That's a lot of mouths to feed. We're also trying to determine where everyone's going to live. Much of the housing we need can be constructed of wood and stucco, but we need more carpenters to get that moving, and a lot more wood than we have on hand," she said.

"Ayriel has informed us the Ekthri will begin shipments of wood in the next few weeks. They are quite pleased by our progress with Ayr'Thugohn and have selected a patch of their wood to contribute to Arkhania's rebuilding efforts; specifically the woods surrounding Elbermire Way. We should have the road from Kallenfall completed as far as the Keep by then," said Clendon.

"Cragenfell doesn't seem to have been harmed much by that beast," she mentioned, pointing at the rotting carcass of the great dragon.

"Thankfully, you are correct. Though the citizens were hesitant to move back at first. We're in the process of clearing several of the outer isles and building new docks to allow trade outside of Port Vaelin while we rebuild. King Orluhnd wants Cragenfell to become the new home of the Kingdom's fleet, and our new trade hub... for a time," he said.

"What's that going to do to their crabbing and fishing

businesses?" asked Tylee.

"That's the issue. We need to preserve those industries while we expand into the sea for navy and trade. More than their business health, we need to preserve their constant supply of food to the neighboring cities. I foresee a lot of fish on our future diets."

"I don't think I'm the right person to figure out how to preserve those industries," she lamented.

She walked to the window and looked out at the string of islands to the east. The second story offices of the fishing warehouse offered a commanding view of the region.

"Nor am I. I brought you here so we could figure out if there are any refugees who might have the expertise we need. Constable Haim of Cragenfell also wanted to meet his new Duchess and coordinate resources. His population has more than tripled in recent days, and he's struggling to accommodate them all," he explained.

"I've been meaning to ask you about that," she said, turning to face him. "I mean, don't get me wrong, I'm flattered by the title and what it means. It just seems-"

"Abrupt? In truth, there is more to the story. During the battle over Port Vaelin, several mages from Fel'Vizsiour managed to pull the dragon out of the sky. Unfortunately, when it crashed to the ground, it landed on Saint Bouldohn's Cathedral in mid-town. Guess who was attending services inside at the time."

"The previous Duke and Duchess?"

"Precisely. Several, in fact. The cathedral was the oldest building in Port Vaelin, and many of the noble families used it for birth rights and naming ceremonies. Six dukes, their wives, children, cousins... all dead. Duke Falhurst governed the eastern coastal regions, albeit poorly. His father moved their estate into Vellenheim to get closer to the King, and since that time the management of the region has fallen into almost non-existence," he explained.

"What of the estate now?"

"Converted into a home for the displaced; mostly children," he answered.

"Does the region bear a name, other than 'the eastern coastline'?"

"It used to be called Gulthara, before Arkhania was formed. It was one of the four city-states unified by Orluhnd Vaelin to form Arkhania," he explained.

"So, would I be free to name it?" asked Tylee.

"You're free to do as you wish. That includes naming the region, and even selecting a location for your estate," he answered.

"I don't want an estate. I may be Duchess, but I'm of the people and that's why they trust me. I will live among them. I'd rather have small homes in each city within my region, and travel between them as needs dictate," she explained.

"Now that's a different spin on tradition," he said with a smirk.

"Well... the people trust me, and I don't want that to change. The moment I act as if they are beneath me," she said, leaving him to finish the thought.

"They'll lose faith in you and assume you're just like the rest of nobility."

"Precisely," she confirmed. "So my duchy encompasses Dunforth, Ayerton, Salvation Shire, Cragenfell, Gaierford and Kallenfall?"

"And the surrounding regions, yes. From the edge of Vaelin Crossroads, south to the Sacton River. From the coast to the west, just past Kallenfall."

"Let's name the region after Arcturus," suggested Tylee.

"Interesting proposition," mused Clendon. "Though, that's a strange name for a province or region."

"Hmm... how about Tolrin? Laurence's father?" she suggested.

"Tolrin Province could work."

"Duchess Ravencrest of the Tolrin Province?" she proposed.

"Or just Duchess Ravencrest of Tolrin," he countered.

"There we are. I like that," she agreed.

"I'll send word to the King. Now... about those crabs," Clendon said, returning to the task at hand.

She thought for a moment and then suggested, "Perhaps we should build a long pier from the shore to the northernmost island, and extend docks north and south of it for their fishing vessels. Leave the space between the islands and the mainland untouched, and extend a series of bridges, buildings and small roads across the islands. Docks from the islands eastward into the sea for the navy... I don't know, we should consult with Haim and see if that makes sense," suggested Tylee.

"That would leave waters between the inner islands untouched, and hopefully not disrupt their crabbing and fishing overly much. I'll go get Haim, though. You're right, we could use his expertise," he said as he stood.

They spent the evening debating the pros and cons of various plans with Haim. They finally agreed on a modified version of

Tylee's suggestion.

∴ ∴ ∴

THE GATES of Skainhold inspired wonder among the companions. Standing eighteen feet above the road, ominous and black, they had no equal in Arkhania.

As they passed under the great obsidian arch, several dwarves ran onto the road and joined in a defensive formation. Each of them wore lustrous plate armor, highly polished and exquisitely crafted. From multi-layered breastplates and articulating pauldrons, to interlocking leg plates and sleeves; it protected every inch of their stocky frames.

Laurence could see no vulnerabilities in their armor. He hoped their arrival wouldn't end in conflict.

The group stopped in front of the line of dwarves.

Several dwarves stepped forward, pointing their halberds at Thool.

Thool growled at them and lowered his head, his bony brow on full display.

"He's with us! We seek an audience with your leader," said Laurence.

"The Inok have no business here!" barked one of the guards.

A black half-cloak hung from his left pauldron, reaching halfway around his back. Laurence determined he must be their leader. He stood four-and-a-half feet tall, but his shoulders were two-and-a-half feet wide. His raspy, deep voice seemed odd in comparison to his stature.

"My companions and I came to Pelrigoss to kill Drakahl, self-proclaimed King of these lands. His treatment of the tribes across the Triblunds inspired Saerasha of the Tulmesh and Thool of the Inok to join our crusade. We seek assistance from your people as well, and wish to speak with your leader to that end," said Laurence.

"Thool must stay outside! Only you may enter!"

"I will not leave my companions behind. Just as I would not leave you behind, if the situation was reversed. These are important matters, and ones that your leader-"

"King Drell," interrupted the dwarf.

"These are matters that King Drell will benefit from. This should be of great importance to him."

"Skifvald, is that you?" asked Mordechai. "You've grown an inch,

I nearly didn't recognize you."

The leader of the dwarven guard removed her helm. Long, silvery locks unfurled and cascaded across her shoulders as she tucked the helm into the crook of her left arm.

Laurence looked on in stunned silence. Based upon her figure and the sound of her voice, he had errantly assumed the dwarf to be male. He realized he had much to learn about dwarves, just as he still had much to learn about elves.

"Mordechai? You've been gone for far too long. How long has it been?"

"Two hundred and twenty years, give or take a decade."

"I was a wee lass last I saw you. Times have been... unkind."

The other dwarves backed away from Thool and returned to the formation upon hearing Skifvald's recognition, and the relaxed tones that passed between them.

"Will Drell see us?"

"He sees few, even among his people. He is quite old now; living beyond his years. With no blood heir, tensions are high and every day brings dread to the people. Chaos looms on our horizon; a void awaits in the aftermath of his death."

"I know all too well how difficult these times are. Drakahl and his witch have assaulted Arkhania, the new human Kingdom directly west of Pelrigoss. They use subterfuge and blatant trickery to dismantle us from within. Their generals have waylaid the tribes to the south, using evil magics to drain the souls of their victims; like Lord Whun in your grandfather's time."

"We, too, have had encounters with Drakahl's forces these past months. Walk with me, I will see that the King gives you an audience, though I cannot promise he will agree to assist you."

Skifvald turned on her heel and strode toward the Dark Expanse. Her regiment parted down the middle, making room for the group to pass. After Laurence and his companions had walked past them, the guards fell in behind and followed in silence.

"Where did you find the pup?" asked Skifvald as they walked through Skainhold.

"Ah... Laurence Ravencrest is grandson of Arcturus of House Raven, son of Gahl the Raven."

"I have heard of Gahl. His fame reached our lands, though I've difficulty believing the tales. How does one ride a... griffin?"

"I am a griffin rider, my lady," offered Kyrilis from behind them.

"Do its wings not buffet your sides, knocking you about?"

"They must be trained to fly differently to their nature, and the rider must learn to occupy as little space upon their back as possible. It is an art, to be sure."

"I would like to see this someday," said Skifvald. "But while Gahl's fame is filled with glory and honor, Arcturus is known as the usurper by our people. He helped Drakahl kill King Pahn and claim the throne. Why would we wish to assist Arcturus's grandchild?"

"Arcturus was tricked by Drakahl and his witch. He had no intentions of placing Drakahl on the throne, and had been misled into thinking Pahn was an evil ruler," explained Laurence. His voice betrayed his frustration at Skifvald's words.

Skifvald stopped in her tracks and turned to face Laurence.

"Who is to say you are not being tricked the same as he?"

"Drakahl came to my home and murdered Arcturus last month. His witch summoned Velloth to attack our Kingdom, and woke Vehkstaerelliox—the ancient dragon—to destroy our cities. If there was ever an evil King, Drakahl is it," said Laurence.

Skifvald nodded once, turned and resumed her walk.

"You have been through much. I understand your motivations, and your presence here."

Their procession moved in silence through the city of Skainhold. From the hills outside, it had been difficult to discern the true scope of its buildings.

The front of each building along the central thoroughfare contained nine-foot-tall, fix-foot-wide double doors made of cured, hardened acacia; complete with bronze handles, banding and bolts.

Most of the buildings had seemed utilitarian when they'd looked down on them from above. Walking so close to them allowed their detail to come into view. Nothing about the buildings seemed utilitarian from their new perspective. Each had a distinct style and bore intricate carvings of Agthari and Toor. Most of the buildings seemed to tell a tale with their artwork.

Mordechai lamented his failure to return and study the carvings, as he'd promised himself he would do on his previous visit. One of the challenges of living so long, something he constantly fought to overcome, was a growing sense of complacency.

Wil, Izabel, Agnar and the rest of the companions gasped in awe and pointed out different carvings to each other. Their wonder over locations like Fel'Rechaun seemed shallow compared to the grandeur of Skainhold.

Wehrenel and Ahrwie skipped along next to Saerasha, happily inspecting the massive structures around them. The buildings' doors alone towered nearly three times as tall as their tiny frames. They made sure not to get too lost in the surrounding sights and constantly glanced back at the dwarves that followed their party. They weren't sure if they could trust dwarves and had no plans to find out the hard way that they couldn't.

Kyrilis hastened her step and joined Laurence at his side. She cast a smile up at him as she matched his pace. She didn't know why her infatuation with him had increased so dramatically. Was it his passionate spirit, his incessant drive to do the right thing, or that he shared Lyla's propensity for loving those around him? She wasn't sure, but she liked the way it made her feel. Even if she could only love him from afar, she decided it would be enough.

Laurence looked back at her and smiled in return. He found her presence intoxicating and had to admit that he'd felt for her since the first time they met. His love for Tylee was unwavering; of that he was certain. However, he also had to admit that he felt inspired, comforted, and loved whenever Kyrilis was near. With another smile in her direction, he pushed his worries and doubts aside and resigned himself to enjoying her companionship without guilt.

There's no harm in us being close friends.

∴ ∴ ∴

THE BRIDGE loomed high above them, sloping high into the sky. It blocked their view of the lower half of the Agthari statue on the other side of the chasm. Thin lines of diamond-shaped etching repeated across its surface at intervals; designed to improve the footing of any travelers that might attempt to cross in the rain on foot.

As their trip across the Dark Expanse progressed, the dark clouds and smog created a shadow-laden haze that made it difficult to see the distant terrain.

"How much blacksmithing takes place on a given day in Skain? It seems as if you'd run out of things to create, after a while," said Laurence.

"A majority of the clouds and smog you see are a byproduct of our smelting, tanning and coal-burning operations. Our miners constantly find new veins of ore, and we process it in a series of stages. Refining ore into precious metals at high grade requires tremendous heat. The process must be repeated multiple times and takes a great deal of effort. We keep a stockpile of every kind of metal we work, so any contract we sign can be fulfilled without waiting for us to gather resources.

"In addition, our armorers and weaponsmiths are constantly refining our equipment. Once or twice a year, we melt down our current stock and replace it with whatever they've newly designed and crafted. Most of our operations run around the clock; our people working in shifts. So, yes, we stay very busy," explained Skifvald.

As they crested the top of the bridge, the Agthari statue came fully into view. It towered so high above them they could barely see its face. Bronze plates, several inches thick, covered most of its surface, glinting faintly in the few rays of sunlight that managed to reach it through the clouds.

Walking between the titan's sword and under its legs made them feel insignificant. None of them were sure if the Agthari had ever existed. Not all legends had their roots in reality. However, several of the companions found themselves happy that the titans no longer walked the lands.

The entrance to Skainfall stood before them. Thirty-foot-tall, six-foot-wide columns of granite straddled its twenty-foot double doors. Whoever constructed the structure, whether Dwarf or Toor, had carved the exterior of Skainfall directly into the mountain itself.

As they approached the doors, the guards behind them ran forward and formed lines on both sides, surrounding them.

Skifvald stopped and turned to face the companions.

"Most visitors make it no further than Skainhold. You are about to enter Skainfall, our home and holiest city. I urge you to act accordingly. Do not wander. Do not touch. Damage nothing, and hurt no one. We will escort you to the King's antechamber, and I will proceed in to request your audience.

"If you stray, or break one of our laws, your actions will be your last. Also know that by bringing you here, the lives of me and my soldiers are on the line. We have put our faith in Mordechai as a trustworthy and welcome friend. That is the only reason you are allowed to enter. Do not betray that trust," explained Skifvald.

When she finished her speech, eight guards exited small rooms on the outside of the columns. They ran up to the door on the left and inserted bronze bars through small rings along the bottom edge. Chanting in rhythm with one another, they pulled the door open with great effort.

Contrary to what the companions expected, no sound came from the door or its hidden hinges as it slowly swung wide for them to enter.

Once the door had opened completely, Skifvald stepped forward and guided them into the chamber beyond.

∴ ∴ ∴

GRANITE COVERED every surface of Skainfall's interior. Its builders carved into the mountain, forming its halls and chambers directly from the materials of the mountain itself. Wherever granite naturally existed and suited their design, they carved it into the shape they needed and left it in place. When carving or digging through other substances, they removed enough material to make room for slabs of granite to come flush with the surrounding surfaces.

As a result of those building techniques, the granite walls, floor and ceiling of the interior had an erratic pattern. In places, the granite was seamless, stretching for a distance and weaving in various directions. Four-square-foot granite slabs interrupted the seamless surfaces at odd intervals. Some surfaces seemed completely constructed from slabs, while others held none at all.

"What are those?" asked Laurence, pointing to strange, wavy objects that clung to the ceilings and walls.

"They displace sound, limiting echoes. Without them, your footfalls in this hallway would be too loud for us to have this conversation," answered Skifvald.

"Were they there originally?" he asked.

"When I asked my grandfather about them, he said they'd been there since before he was born. In truth, we do not know who placed them. They are made from dried and pressed plant matter, bonded together with glue. Their surface is soft and porous, leading to the excessive collection of dust. Cleaning them is a full-time job for dozens of our citizens."

"Must use big ladders," remarked Wehrenel.

"Or stand on several shoulders?" asked Ahrwie.

"Yes, we use ladders," answered Skifvald with a sigh.

The guards kept them walking past side halls and doorways. Several of the companions gasped or remarked at the contents of the rooms, but none dared venture past their dwarven escorts.

They descended two stairways, their steps re-cut to accommodate a dwarven stride. At the end of their third long hallway, they came to a large chamber decorated with gold.

Life-sized statues of dwarven heroes lined the walls. Gold crown molding lined the ceiling. Several paintings, framed in gold, lined the walls.

Skifvald brought them to one side of the room and invited them to sit on dwarf-sized chairs and couches. Sitting on them felt like riding a cushion of air, their overstuffed surfaces giving under the weight of each guest; cradling them.

"I must speak with King Drell and announce your presence. Do not be surprised if he turns you away, though I will make every effort to press the importance of this meeting," said Skifvald.

She turned and walked away, stopping near the great golden doors to whisper to her guards before exiting.

∴ ∴ ∴

SKIFVALD RETURNED the next morning and escorted Mordechai, Laurence, Kyrilis, Izabel and Wil to the King a short while later.

Agnar, Gareg and Kellum stayed behind to keep Saerasha, Thool and the Aegra company.

Vaelys declined to meet the King, explaining that she felt uncomfortable around royalty.

The companions entered and stood side by side before the king. They bowed in respect and waited for Skifvald to tap her halberd on the floor, as she'd instructed them.

Drell's melrithium throne sat on a dais made of gold, in a circular room paved with silver. Columns lined the walls at eight foot intervals, providing support for the forty-foot-high domed ceiling. Murals adorned the walls, reaching up to the domed peak, depicting former kings and Drell's lineage.

Laurence felt certain Drell's display of wealth was worth more than any King in any other land. He remembered Joril explaining the rarity of melrithium. To see so much of it forged into a throne seemed wasteful and arrogant.

Mordechai knew that the metals about the room were nothing more than an elaborate facade. A display of wealth to shock and impress; putting Drell's visitors off guard. Carpenters made the throne from acacia and covered it in the thinnest layer of melrithium their blacksmiths could produce; using barely enough to forge a few long-tooth daggers. They'd constructed the dais and covered the floor using similar techniques. What impressed him most about the chamber was how often the ruse succeeded.

King Drell sat on his throne with a grimace, clearly uncomfortable with the audience before him. His platinum crown did little to hide his balding head and scraggly gray locks. He wore chainmaille made from silver decorated with platinum, gold and rubies. The chain around his neck, made from melrithium, clasped a single fist-sized diamond.

"What brings you before me?" asked Drell, pretending, or forgetting, that Skifvald had just explained their motivations. His voice belied his age, escaping his lips only slightly louder than a whisper.

"We seek assistance in our quest," answer Wil, taking the lead. "King Drakahl has deployed subterfuge and witchery to undermine the sanctity of the Kingdom of Arkhania. His actions resulted in the destruction of several cities, including our primary port, as well as the loss of thousands of lives. We seek to dethrone him, and kill him, so that another, more reasonable ruler might take his place."

"Who are you to address me?"

"I am King Wilwarianel Cuthdra'Gah of the Ekthri, from western Arkhania."

The rest of the companions shot Wil a glance, unaware until that moment that he held the position of King.

Drell nodded in respect.

"What, specifically, did Drakahl do to your people?"

"He used his witch, Nightweaver, to summon the Velloth, an ancient subterranean race of elves. They razed two cities, Gaierford and Grellenheim, then summoned Vehkstaerelliox, an ancient dragon. When Vehks awoke, giants and Skaar tore through Ekthri Wood, destroying Ayr'Thugohn and killing my father. Vehks continued east and destroyed Port Vaelin. Between those events, nearly ten-thousand souls were lost, human and elf alike."

"What help can I possibly provide?"

"We seek a sword only spoken of in legend. It is said to be trapped within an obsidian altar, deep beneath Skain in a forbidden ritual chamber. We ask permission to seek that blade, and if we see that it does not exist, we will pay for the construction of a similar blade, for which Mordechai and Princess Ayriel would perform the enchantments."

"What of Drakahl's throne?"

"It will be up for the taking, unless someone of noble blood were to offer their military support. In which case, we could ensure that person reached the throne and was in a position to lay claim to it," answered Mordechai.

"So, you wish my permission to look in a chamber which may not exist, for a sword which may not exist, and you seek military assistance in overthrowing Drakahl... but only if I wish to claim his throne?"

"In summary... yes," answered Wil.

"The chamber you seek, if it exists, would lie deep within Vuhl, the labyrinth beneath our city. We no longer visit those halls. Many of our ancestors lost their lives exploring the wretched place, and our priests keep the keys in secret vaults. I do not mind if you risk your lives on a fool's errand, but it will take some time to orchestrate your entry.

"As to the rest, we shall discuss your plans if you survive Vuhl. I will send word to the priests to retrieve the keys. In the meantime, Skifvald will escort you to our forge so you might view the pride of our city while you wait. Everyone should have a chance to see such wonders before they depart the living world," said Drell.

The group bowed again, waiting for Skifvald's signal. When it came, they humbly turned and exited the chamber.

∴ ∴ ∴

SKIFVALD BROUGHT them down a series of stairways toward the forge. At the base of the stairs, they turned down a long hallway and down a series of ramps. After passing under an obsidian archway, a room as large as Skainhold stretched out before them.

"Welcome to the forge," said Skifvald.

Laurence looked up, but couldn't see the ceiling. He was certain the whole of Mooncrest, cliffs and all, could fit within the chamber.

One hundred anvils stood in lines down the walls, small forges set into the wall, glowing orange in front of each. Shirtless dwarves, of both sexes, swung their hammers, dutifully working hot metal wearing leather boots, pants and aprons. Each of them covered in layers of sweat and dirt; speckled with oil.

At the far end of the chamber, a forty-foot-high furnace occupied the entire wall. Ten-foot tall buckets, made of iron, hung from the ceiling on chains as thick as Laurence's forearm. The chains attached to rails, allowing the buckets to move in a circle around the center of the room and down its entire length.

Raised platforms allowed other dwarves to scoop slag out of

the buckets as they cooled, removing impurities before sending the molten contents back to the furnace in a loop. Several casting stations sat on lower platforms, where other workers tipped the buckets to pour their contents into molds.

Still more workers moved the molds, attached to carts, to a corner of the room to cool. Others removed the cooled bars of purified metal, stacking them on other carts, destined for the storage vaults.

The operation impressed them beyond words. Never in their lives could they have imagined such a sight.

"You may walk around freely. When the whistle blows thrice in rapid succession, come back to the archway and I will retrieve you for your journey. However, please do nothing to disturb the workers," said Skifvald.

Skifvald walked back down the hallway and proceeded up the ramps, leaving the companions to their own devices.

Laurence smiled at Kyrilis briefly. She walked over and joined him with a smile. They turned and walked together down a row of anvils, quietly watching the dwarven masters at work.

Saerasha, Gareg, Thool, Kellum and the Aegra walked to the other row of anvils, asking questions of Kellum and musing at how such an operation could exist.

Izabel grabbed Agnar's hand and gently dragged him toward the iron steps that led to the raised platforms. She giggled playfully as he pretended to resist.

Mordechai walked over to Vaelys, who had withdrawn in recent days, avoiding conversations entirely.

"You've been quiet," he remarked.

"I've had no reason to speak."

"I know who you are, and it does not concern me. Everyone has a role in life, and I know that your association is necessary. I hesitate to say evil, for much of your work leads to good. While I may not agree with the methods, it is clear you select your contracts with care and thoughtful insight."

Vaelys remained silent. She knew quite well who Mordechai was, and how capable he was famed to be. In normal circumstances, their conversation would already be over; as he lay dying in a pool of his own blood. However, he could not see her normal form, and knew not her normal face. Her identity remained intact, even though he'd realized the truth of her nature. She decided to let him live, or rather she decided not to die herself in the attempt.

"I hired you once, though you didn't know it was me. I knew that if I handled the target myself, our battle would cost the lives of hundreds, or thousands of bystanders. I could not have that weigh upon my conscience, but I also couldn't let the man live."

"Who?"

"A certain necromancer in Gulthara, long before Arkhania. He butchered his wife for disobeying him and returned her from the dead a subservient monstrosity. His subjects feared him, and with good reason. When I discovered the field-"

"I remember."

"My thanks to you, for your assistance in the matter. His thirst for power would have spread across the region and eventually overtaken Tellrindos and Haern. You became the tool I needed to save the lives of thousands. I learned the value of your line of work in those days. So... know that I do not judge you."

She remained silent again, unwilling to admit the motivations of that time. He didn't need to know that the man in question had married her sister, and that her corpse had become the catalyst for his rise to power. She knew the man he spoke of well, and would have killed him, contract or no.

A great horn sounded, startling the companions. The workers stopped their duties and rushed toward the archway.

Mordechai and Vaelys stepped back to make room as hundreds of workers flowed past them in a hurry.

The companions gathered near the steps to the platforms, curious about the turn of events.

"What's going on?" asked Izabel.

"This isn't normal," said Mordechai.

"Is it shift change?" asked Agnar.

"They don't change shifts like this. Workers cycle in groups, and they never abandon the furnace," said Mordechai.

They tensed and drew their weapons as the sound of marching footfalls echoed down the ramps.

∴ ∴ ∴

"WELL, WELL, well... what have we here?" asked a woman from the ramp. "Come to kill our King, have you? Well, we can't have that."

Two dozen soldiers came into view, each wearing blackened scale armor. The woman in front stood taller than the rest and appeared to be far stronger.

503

"Ravencrest, isn't it?" she asked. "Your family just won't die," she said with a dramatic shrug.

The soldiers passed through the archway and formed up in front of the group.

"Who are you?" asked Laurence angrily.

"I am Bratha. I'd invite you to tea, but only one of us is leaving the Forge alive," she said, adjusting her gauntlets.

"Handle the rest!" belted Laurence to his friends.

Laurence charged forward, gripping his sword in both hands.

Kyrilis and Vaelys nodded at each other and split to the left and right flanks.

Izabel, Agnar and Gareg charged forward to the right of Bratha. Agnar and Gareg followed a step behind her, letting her lead the charge with her shield.

Wil and Thool ran to the other side, Quel'Thoz and great-axe twirling into position.

Saerasha stood with Mordechai, waiting to react should a companion need their assistance.

Kellum took the Aegra up to the platforms to improve their view of the battlefield.

The soldiers surged forward.

As Laurence engaged with Bratha, she lashed out at him with a synchronized slash using both of her shortswords. He blocked both blades as they crossed at center and shoved with all his strength. Bratha smirked at Laurence's failed attempt to shove her backward.

Kyrilis met the left-most soldier. He thrust his sword at her midsection, expecting to end her quickly. She parried his blade high with her sword while pushing into the space between them, drove her dagger into his sword-hand, and brought her sword down across his exposed face. She stepped over his falling corpse to engage the man behind him, smiling as if the affair were pleasant. He hesitated upon seeing her smile, taken aback by her apparent enjoyment.

Vaelys tossed her daggers into the faces of two soldiers just as she neared their reach. As they fell, a third soldier swung a greatsword, meaning to cleave her in two. She dropped to the ground and slid between her victims, ripping the daggers from their faces as she passed. She stood and sliced the third man's neck from behind, severing his spine.

Thool braced his great-axe before him and charged through four soldiers at once. Two of their swords bounced off his bony brow, splitting the skin but causing no serious damage. He drove them into the wall behind them, crushing them and fracturing many ribs in the process.

Wil split to Thool's right and leapt into the air. As he spun, he brought his Quel'Thoz around in an arc at full extension, slicing across the upper chest and shoulders of two soldiers. The momentum of his maneuver pushed his blade through their scale armor, cutting them open and sending blood through the air. He finished the move with a twirl of his wrist, severing their heads from their necks, and turned to find new opponents.

Izabel barreled into a soldier, clashing shield against shield and driving him back. Agnar swung his maul over her head, splattering the man's brains across the soldier beside him. Gareg swung his greatsword at three soldiers to Izabel's left, knocking their parries aside as if they were twigs. Izabel thrust her sword to the right, stabbing the brain-splattered soldier through the gut.

Kellum shot two men in the face, while the Aegra killed two others with shots to the throat.

Laurence moved his sword as fast as he could, parrying one attack after another from Bratha. She alternated her attacks between her swords with a series of slashes and thrusts, making it difficult for him to understand her techniques or patterns. He knew a change in tactics was necessary; she would eventually find a way past his defense.

Suddenly it occurred to him that letting her past his defenses was just the tactic he needed.

He waited patiently for her to thrust with her right-hand sword. When the attack finally came, he quickly released his grip with his left hand, stepped into the attack and caught her sword in the crook of his left arm. He curled the arm at the same time, locking the blade in place between the plates in his armor as they attempted to lock into the make-shift shield.

Frustrated, she tried to wrench her blade free. She attacked with her left-hand sword, slashing toward his head, trying to force him to break free. He stepped closer, dropped his sword and grabbed her left forearm in his hand.

Sliding his hand up her arm as quickly as he could, he slammed his right hand into the crossbars of her sword as violently as he could, jarring it free from her unsuspecting grasp.

Desperately she grabbed his right elbow with her left hand, his arm now high above her head. She released her right-hand sword, leaving it clenched between the plates on his armored left side.

As the rest of her soldiers fell dead all around them, Laurence loosened his grip on her sword, letting the tip fall toward her face as the hilt slowly twisted in his palm. She reached up with her right hand, trying to defeat his maneuver, just as he flicked the sword aside. The move had been a distraction.

She reached desperately for the falling sword, in an attempt to recover. He dove his right hand down and grabbed the sword lodged in the crook of his left arm. Just as she recovered the falling blade, he brought her other sword up past her midsection, slicing deep into her chin and cleaving her face in two.

The companions looked around, making sure everyone was dead. Laurence knelt and picked up his sword, dropping Bratha's atop her, as she flinched and lurched about the ground in the throes of death.

"Why didn't you help?" asked Saerasha.

"I didn't need to," answered Mordechai. "Let's pay a visit to Drell!" he yelled to the group angrily.

∴ ∴ ∴

"I DIDN'T know!" blurted Skifvald as they barged past her.

None of the dwarven guard dared get in the party's way. They parted to make room as the companions passed, fully aware of what had just transpired. Advanced dwarven smithing protecting them or not, none of them wanted to test their skills against the outsiders.

Thool charged into the throne room doors, breaking them off their hinges and crashing them to the floor. The noise caused by their entry woke King Drell, who had fallen asleep on his throne.

"Care to explain yourself?" demanded Laurence as the party filed into the room, weapons still at the ready.

"You live?" asked Drell, surprise evident in his tone.

"You want I kill now?" asked Thool.

"No, Thool. Not just yet," answered Laurence.

"I... I didn't have a choice. Bratha was already here when you arrived, waiting for our next shipment of armor," he whimpered.

"You handed us over to Drakahl's forces, after we explained our reasons for being here?" asked Laurence.

"King Wilwarianel, please, you must understand, I-"

"Don't speak to *him*, speak to *me*!" demanded Laurence.

"If I helped you in front of Bratha, she would have had her troops kill my people. Drakahl's generals killed *two dozen* of our soldiers when they arrived two years ago. I couldn't sit by and watch that happen again, could I?"

"You claim you were under duress?" asked Mordechai.

"Yes! I am an old King, and not what I used to be. I can't fight beside my people, and couldn't ask them to risk their lives standing up to Drakahl and his demands. I made an agreement to protect my people and keep our city safe. You *understand*, don't you?"

"You tried to have us k-" started Laurence.

"Laurence! Put yourself in his situation!" yelled Mordechai, interrupting him.

Laurence paced side to side, sheathed his sword and walked up onto the dais. He bent over in front of the King, bringing his face to the man's level.

"You're getting those keys and letting us into the labyrinth. You. *Personally*. Not your priests. That way, if there is any more trickery, you fall prey to it right alongside us. We will talk to Skifvald and your soldiers, and if they believe in our quest and want to be freed from Drakahl's rule, then we will be taking them with us to defeat him."

"So I am to be pressed *further* into duress?"

"You endangered my friends, and I do not take that lightly. You dug this grave... now *lie* in it," Laurence said. He made no attempt to hide the extreme anger that welled up inside him.

"Very well," said the King sheepishly.

The companions put away their weapons and left the King's chamber, more intent on their purpose than ever.

∴ ∴ ∴

WHEN TYLEE returned to Gaierford, she saw hundreds of people in the streets, clustered near the inn and the general store. She sighed in frustration, realizing their number had nearly doubled.

"The Duchess is back!" yelled a man near the inn.

"Make way!" yelled Delriahna.

Tylee steered Onyx through the crowd toward the store. Delriahna waited on the steps, standing next to Rolph and lamenting her frustration at the crowd's refusal to follow her instructions.

Rolph pushed into the crowd, yelling, "move!" Upon reaching Tylee, he grabbed Onyx's reins and bid her to dismount.

She walked over to her mother as the people yelled their concerns and demands.

"How many?" yelled Tylee.

"Nearly two thousand!" yelled Delriahna.

"What the hell? When did this happen?" asked Tylee as she arrived at her side.

"The day after you left, a stream of newcomers arrived. They said the King sent them and plopped down in the road making demands."

"I need to have *words* with that King!"

"You need to have words with these *people*."

Tylee barged inside the store and climbed the stairs.

Delriahna stared on in confusion for a moment until she saw a pair of shutters upstairs whip open.

"People of Gaierford!" yelled Tylee at the top of her lungs. She leaned out of the window so they could all see her clearly.

"We're not all from Gaierford!" yelled a man in response. Several among the crowd laughed at the man's quip. While she didn't appreciate the man's attempt at levity, the crowd fell silent once the laughter cleared and for that she was thankful.

"No, you are not all from Gaierford. None of you are, in fact. The original citizens of Gaierford are all dead. You are all here because hundreds, if not thousands, of the citizens of your cities are also dead. We are doing our best to help you all in these desperate times, but you have to work with us.

"Crowding the center of town, rather than taking up tools and helping us to build a new city for you all. What good can come of your choice of actions? Or rather, your choice of inaction?"

"Where are we going to live? The King kicked us out of Vellenheim and Port Vaelin. There aren't enough houses here for us all!" shouted the same man.

"What is your name, sir?"

"Ahgon Thurnbul," he answered.

"Well, Ahgon, I agree. There aren't enough houses in Gaierford. There weren't enough houses in Gaierford when I arrived with the refugees from Grellenheim, either. Did they whine and cry, crowding the streets with their hands out? Or were they working, tending fields, and laying new roads when you walked into town?"

She waited for a moment, but Ahgon didn't respond.

"You know what there's plenty of? Land! Three square miles of open field and hills lie between here and Kallenfall. Do you know what we were in the middle of when you arrived? Did you bother to ask?"

Ahgon remained silent.

"Parceling that land for all our new arrivals. We expected more of you... not so soon, mind you, but we did. I have plans in this office behind me for one-thousand-eight-hundred parcels of land, each one acre in size, to be divided amongst you all equally. We need but distribute them and build the roads between them.

"Had you calmly asked, rather than stirring dissent, you would be on that land right now, building a temporary shelter for yourself and contributing to the future of our soon-to-be-great city. Our plans, when fully realized, will turn the Gaierford Kallenfall region into a city to rival Raven's Nest.

"The Fifth Command of the Legion is even building a keep between the cities, to provide protection for you all. So my question to you, is... are you willing to work for your survival? Or do you simply expect handouts? I didn't take the people of Port Vaelin for lazy."

"We aren't lazy! We worked the docks, the stores, the streets... we were the backbone of the Kingdom's trade network!" Ahgon said.

"Then let me consult with Duchess Colvin, and we'll distribute parcels to all of you over the next few days. It would be faster but... there are many of you, and only two of us. Which brings me to the concern we hoped to resolve upon my return. Gaierford and Kallenfall need Constables. Who would like the job?"

Delriahna joined Tylee in the office and bid her to step back from the window. The people in the streets talked among themselves, going over the information she'd shared, and who their Constables should be.

"We don't have that many parcels of land," said Delriahna.

"We physically do, we just need to divide them," said Tylee.

"Look, I've been thinking," Delriahna said.

"*Again*?" quipped Tylee with a smirk.

"Stop it. Listen, this whole Gaierford versus Kallenfall thing? It's just going to cause conflict. I think this needs to be one city. Make the Fifth Command's keep the center and call it what it is."

"And what... rename it? I've been doing a lot of that lately."

"What do you mean?"

"Oh, yeah... welcome to the Tolrin Province," said Tylee with a flourish of her hands.

"My daughter, the eighteen-year-old Duchess Ravencrest of Tolrin, disrupting the nobles and saving the people," said Delriahna with a smirk.

"Eighteen? But I'm... oh shit, really?"

"Happy birthday?"

"I've been so busy, I wasn't even paying attention to what day it was."

"This is the nineteenth day of Arran'Hael in the year one-thirteen of our great Kingdom. The year my daughter woke up, stepped out of her window, and started living in the real world... like the rest of us."

"Stop. We don't have time for a birthday right now."

"I'm proud of you. We'll get through this."

Tylee returned to the window. An idea popped into her head. "Ahgon, come up and join us!" yelled Tylee.

"What are you doing now?" asked Delriahna.

"You'll see," said Tylee, turning back into the room.

Ahgon walked up the stairs nervously. He didn't know what the Duchess wanted from him, and could feel his anxiety rising. When he entered the room at the top of the stairs, the two most powerful women in the southern regions stared back at him. He instantly regretted his outburst in the street.

"Come in and join us. We've much to discuss," said Tylee.

Delriahna stepped forward and guided Ahgon to their table, retrieved a chair, and urged him to sit. Tylee walked to a cabinet on the far side of the room and withdrew three small glasses and a bottle of liquor. When she returned to the table, she poured and served a glass for each of them and then sat.

"I'm sorry for my outburst, your Eminence, I-"

"Oh gods, don't call me that. No, no. That won't do at all," said Tylee.

Delriahna chuckled.

"Listen... we have a pretty complex situation before us. You're outspoken, and stood up to your Duchess, which tells me you have the right take-charge attitude to be Constable."

"I, what?"

"Don't get me wrong, this isn't a reward. The job is thankless, exhausting, and fraught with difficulties. Ultimately, you will be required to uphold my decisions, enforce the Kingdom's laws, and treat people with fairness, regardless of previous social standing. I want it made clear that in this city, we work for our place. Family history and previous financial superiority mean nothing here.

"You will not get an estate, and I am not taking one either. You will get a one acre parcel of land like everyone else. You will build your own home, like everyone else. You are still one of the people, and should not carry yourself as if you are above them. Can you handle these things?" asked Tylee.

"I led a dock-workers' union back in Port Vaelin. My entire section of the city was destroyed by the dragon. I was lucky enough to be on the docks when it attacked, and my wife just happened to be in Vellenheim visiting her father. I know well the burden of leadership, and that is what inspired me to be so outspoken earlier.

"I see now that I'd jumped to conclusions about you, and for that I apologize. I will accept this position and assist you in saving these people from the dire circumstances before them... and from themselves. But which city am I to be Constable of?" he asked.

"We're going to combine them, and the surrounding area. Duchess Colvin raised a valid point; keeping the cities separate would only lead to contention between the Constables."

"What will it be called? Gaierford? Kallenfall?" asked Ahgon.

"Kotanndale, after the hero of Cragenfell who died fighting the dragon. He was a Vinetar of the Legion. He led dozens of men and women to their deaths to save the Kingdom. His name is already upon their lips," said Tylee.

"That is a wonderful idea, hun," said Delriahna with a smile.

"Now, then... the job of controlling and convincing the people is yours. Everyone must work. I need them all to move to their parcel of land. They can set up tents, build small shacks, or even start on permanent homes. However, they can't salvage from existing buildings, or steal from the supplies we've set aside for our roads, offices or stores.

"The weather is their problem, we simply don't have enough existing homes and rooms to go around. We're working with the King to acquire more resources, but that will take time. They can fell trees, harvest reeds from the swamps to the west, or if they have coin, they can feel free to travel and buy supplies themselves.

"If they wish to build homes of stucco, or earth, we have several artisans who can assist them with the proper knowledge and techniques. We will need the names of each family, so that we can walk the lands over the next few days and allocate their land. We'll also need rope and stakes to mark the borders of each parcel.

"Finally, I'll need a cartographer to map the whole affair and ensure everyone is accounted for fairly. Make sure you coordinate with Rolph and establish a team to work under him to enforce our laws and decisions. He is your Marshall," explained Tylee.

"I've got a lot to do," said Ahgon as he stood.

"We've all got a lot to do, Constable Thurnbul. Commander Clendon won't be back for a few weeks, so I'm off to keep charge of his men in his stead," said Tylee.

"I'll find our cartographer, and the supplies for marking parcels," offered Delriahna as they parted.

∴ ∴ ∴

THE NEXT day, Skifvald brought Laurence, Kyrilis, and Mordechai to the barracks. Fifty soldiers stood in formation, waiting for their arrival.

"I see your talks went well," said Laurence.

"Make no mistake, we love our King. He did a lot for us over the past few centuries. But we must be free from Drakahl and his madness. The fifty soldiers present will follow you into battle, under my command," said Skifvald.

"Valiant soldiers of the Deepfolk Clan, I am Kyrilis Nandari, Griffin Guard of the Afyr and the Kingdom of Arkhania. I have helped defend our Kingdom for over one-hundred years. I stand before you now, having made the choice to follow Laurence Ravencrest into battle against the malevolent King Drakahl.

"Many of you are as old as I, and may find yourselves wondering why an elf, or a dwarf, might follow a human boy—barely old enough to be considered a man—on such a grave mission. What you will come to learn is that Laurence is a man of honor, integrity, knowledge, and skill. He cares for his people as if they were his own family, and will put his own life on the line before he risks yours.

"He is an inspiration to me, and will become one to you. We do not ask you to follow us lightly. In truth, if this were a matter Laurence could handle on his own, I am confident he would seek to do so, rather than risk the lives of others.

"What we embark upon will change everything in Pelrigoss, whether we win or lose. While we freely admit that we need your help, we also prefer that the citizens of Pelrigoss have a hand in their own future," explained Kyrilis.

"We are about to descend into Vuhl to retrieve an ancient artifact; one that should let me face Drakahl and defeat his soul-drinking blade. Skifvald will lead you all to Daegon Bridge, where you will defend the bridge from any further incursions by Drakahl's forces. Once we have achieved our goal, we will join you at the bridge and march into Caierthor as a unified force," said Laurence.

The dwarven soldiers cheered.

"Wehrenel and Ahrwie have been dispatched to the Tryn, Inok, Aegra and Daulga. They take word from King Drell, asking them to join forces with us to face Drakahl's armies. If all goes according to plan, our numbers will quadruple before we cross the Odvodi."

More cheering erupted.

"Expect reinforcements over the next few days and please... set aside old animosities and work together for the greater good of all; for the sanctity of Pelrigoss's future!"

As the soldiers rallied behind them, the companions followed Skifvald back through the halls.

"Thank you for speaking to them," said Skifvald.

"We're all in this together. I'd rather they see us as equals. It will go a long way toward fostering peace across Pelrigoss when our task is complete," said Laurence.

"Humans, Elves, Faun, Orc, and Minotaur banding together to save Dwarves from a ruthless Toor ruler? Nothing like this has ever been attempted," said Skifvald.

"This will be a tale for the scribes," remarked Mordechai.

∴ ∴ ∴

SKIFVALD LEFT the companions at the entrance to Vuhl and returned to the barracks to collect her small army.

King Drell stood beside the twelve-foot diameter round iron door. Three keys clinked together in his hand as he trembled with old age.

"Are you certain this is what you wish?" asked Drell.

"We have no choice," answered Laurence.

"We must lock the door behind you. The risk is too great to leave it open," said Drell.

"Gareg and Agnar will stay here to guard the door. Gareg will hold the keys," demanded Laurence.

"Which one of you is Gareg?" asked Drell.

Gareg stepped forward, towering above the King. His arms bulged dramatically as he lowered his greatsword tip down to the ground before him.

"I... I suppose that will be fine," said Drell.

Two dwarven soldiers chuckled in the distance.

Drell inserted the keys into small slots at the center of a crank in the middle of the door. He turned each of them and then backed away, inviting Gareg to turn the crank.

Tales among the Deepfolk Clan said that the crank required six dwarves to turn. It was a great shock to all of them when Gareg accomplished the task without assistance. Gasps and whispers sprang out around the room as the great iron crank groaned into action.

Gareg hunched down and drove his shoulder into the door, pushing with all his might. Dust blew into the room as the door cracked open, trapped air escaping with a hiss.

"It's going to be dark in Vuhl. Laurence, give me your sword. Izabel... your shield," said Mordechai.

"Why?" asked Izabel.

"You are the only two of us who can't see in total darkness. I'm going to enchant your melrithium weaponry to emit light when you will it to happen. Since your sword and shield are made from that metal, the enchantments will last a fairly long time."

"They're already enchanted, though," said Laurence.

"Those enchantments were applied when their forging was complete. I'll be pushing my enchantments into the center of their mass, underneath what is already there," he explained.

"That will blind the rest of us," said Kyrilis.

"The enchantment will radiate neither heat nor ultraviolet, so your eyes should be protected," he answered. "This allows us to travel without torches and keep our weapons at the ready at all times."

Mordechai applied the enchantments one by one as Gareg continued to open the door. Once he finished with each, he handed them back to their owner.

Laurence hefted his blade and willed it to shed light. It glowed to life with a soft white radiance, brightening the surrounding area. Smiling, he strode forward; leading his friends into the depths beyond.

LABYRINTH

Ris'Kitthu, Arran'Hael 21st, 113 of the 2nd Era

Come thee to the endless well,
And see what it doth drink.
Opened up, the sky must fall,
Not all is what you think.

Night's Writ, Parable 13

THE CHAMBER beyond the door turned almost immediately to the right, toward a spiral staircase. Unlike the smooth surfaces about Skainfall, the floors, walls and ceiling of Vuhl were roughly hewn, as if never properly finished.

Patches of moss clung desperately to the walls, indicating a possible water source in the depths to perpetuate its humid environment. The floor's rough-hewn surface offered just enough grip for the party to pass without slipping on the patches of slimy mold that grew in the crevices. The air smelled an odd mixture of musty, dirty and stale; a stark contrast to the smoggy interior of Skainfall.

Laurence led the way down the stairs, the footfalls of his companions echoing behind him. After a few hours with no end in sight, they stopped hunching and moving slowly. By the time they reached the chamber at the bottom of the spiral, half a day had passed and everyone needed to rest. The room at the bottom of the stairs contained nothing but a single door.

"Let's rest here for an hour before we proceed," whispered Laurence.

"Why are we whispering?" whispered Saerasha.

"I've fought undead in a place like this. I'd rather we not be attacked just yet," whispered Laurence.

"Why do you think the stairs went so deep? Who builds something like this, anyway?" whispered Izabel.

"I'm not sure we'll find, or want to know, the answer," whispered Mordechai.

Laurence slid to the floor along a wall. Kyrilis joined him, smiled, and put her hand on his knee. He smiled back at her, welcoming the company. He slouched down a bit, leaned his head against her shoulder and calmed his mind, focused on getting to sleep.

The other companions settled in and tried to nap, knowing their adventure had just begun. Wil, Kyrilis, Vaelys and Saerasha stayed awake to keep watch.

∴ ∴ ∴

AYRIEL WALKED out of the engineers' tent and surveyed their progress. The mortar between the stones for the foundation of the lower city had almost cured. The elves had nearly completed the lower platform of the upper city.

"Princess Ayriel!" yelled a man in the distance.

She turned to find a messenger running frantically through the crowd of workers. He ran up to her, panting, and leaned over with his hands on his knees.

"Sorry, your Majesty, my horse twisted her leg, and I had to run the rest of the way," he gasped.

"Take your time, good sir," she said with a smile.

"I'm sorry, but I bring unfortunate news. Your father is sick. The royal necromancer has confined him to his bed," he said as he stood.

"Did Karthas provide any details?"

"Karthas, your Majesty?"

"The royal necromancer!"

"I did not speak with him, your Majesty. I was sent by Silith," he answered.

"Find Raz'Fetheil, he's somewhere in this camp. Tell him I leave the rebuilding efforts in his capable hands and explain where I've gone!"

Ayriel ran toward Tegris, intent on reaching her father as

quickly as she could.

Enchanting Tegris and racing off... that's what I do now, apparently.

∴ ∴ ∴

WHEN LAURENCE woke, he found himself laying on his side. At some point he had slid sideways, and his head lay in Kyrilis's lap. He sat up and rubbed the sleep from his eyes, breaking her from her meditation.

"How long have we been here?" he whispered.

"A few hours," whispered Saerasha. "You needed the rest."

"Let's get going," he whispered.

He got up and went to each of his sleeping companions, waking them. After a few minutes, they all stood behind him as he prepared to open the door. Their rest had been necessary; he realized that. However, he hadn't planned on them resting for so long.

The door creaked on its hinges as he pushed it open. The hallway beyond led to several turns before ending forty feet ahead. He walked into the hallway and inspected the passageways. No clues presented themselves as to which direction they should proceed.

"Well... Drell *said* it was a labyrinth," sighed Laurence.

"If we have to explore every passage, this is going to take ages," lamented Izabel.

"I good track," grumbled Thool. "Look for altar yes?"

"Yes, we're looking for the obsidian altar," answered Laurence.

Thool closed his eyes for a moment and focused his mind. He walked to the entrance of each hallway and stood for a moment, evaluating what he could sense. He tasted the air and felt for differences in air pressure and moisture.

"This way," he barked, and stepped into a hallway.

"Wait, how do you know?" asked Laurence.

"This way water; colder air; deeper path. Others thin air; short path; taste dust; dead ends."

"Were these tunnels built by minotaur?" asked Izabel.

"Don't know. Don't care," answered Thool.

"Probably," answered Mordechai.

He walked down the hall, leaving it up to them if they chose to follow. The group fell in behind him, trusting his instincts to guide them through.

They followed Thool for several hours, twisting and winding their way through the labyrinth. Even the most robust among them grew tired. There'd been no sign of an end, no rooms to explore, just miles of endless pathways.

"We've been at this for four hours," said Mordechai, no longer concerned with whispering.

"I feel that... but how can you be sure?" asked Izabel.

"I am very attuned to the passage of Time," he answered.

"Thool, let's take a break," said Laurence.

"I haven't walked this much since I was a scout back in Ekthri Wood," complained Wil.

Thool was still walking.

"Thool! Let's take a break!" yelled Laurence.

Everyone stopped. Thool turned and looked at Laurence, angry at the interruption.

A deep grumbling sound echoed down the halls, coming from the direction they'd been heading.

"I think you woke something up," whispered Kyrilis.

Thool sniffed the air. "It big; scaly. Big room... we rest there," said Thool.

"Big and scaly? Like a dragon? And you want to rest in its lair?" gasped Izabel.

"Yes," said Thool frankly.

"Are you-" started Wil.

"Kill thing, then sleep," said Thool, shrugging.

"I doubt it's a dragon," said Saerasha.

"Still!" barked Izabel.

A deep rumbling growl echoed down the hall again.

"Nothing says it can't hunt us down here, whatever it is. So, let's go fight it in the big room with space to maneuver," said Laurence.

Vaelys strode past the group and continued down the hall. Thool followed.

"I guess that settles it," sighed Izabel.

The group ran up behind Thool and Vaelys and fell into line. A few minutes later, they found themselves at the entrance to a very large cave. Cautiously, they slowed their pace and entered, prepared for an attack. The grumbling sound suddenly repeated to their right. Alarmed, they whipped around and faced the unknown source, deep in the shadows beyond their source of light.

"Oh, fuck!" belted Kellum.

"This isn't good," gasped Vaelys.

"A hydra!" yelled Kyrilis.

Ten glowing eyes opened in the distance, all in a line, side by side. They slowly, dramatically raised into the air in pairs as a series of roars rattled the chamber, loose stones falling from the ceiling high above.

"Spread out!" yelled Laurence.

Mordechai muttered, "*Thootosh*," and pointed his right hand upward. A ball of light flew from his palm, shot into the ceiling and splashed across its surface. The whole ceiling began to glow, lighting the room as if it were dusk.

The massive creature came into view. Dark green scales, four massive legs, five long necks and five ferocious heads; all on horrid display. The creature's back rose twelve feet above the ground, and its necks stretched twelve feet in length. Its ten-foot tail lashed about behind it, frantically.

Laurence charged forward, not content to wait around to become a snack.

Kyrilis, Vaelys, Izabel and Wil ran toward it as well, each moving toward a different head.

Thool charged in, quickly overtaking all of them with his massive bull legs.

Kellum fired arrows over their heads, aiming for the creature's eyes. The creature was moving too rapidly, and each of them careened off its scales harmlessly.

Saerasha summoned the power within her, right as the group clashed with the beast, and started to craft a spell.

"Save your spells, we're going to need healing!" belted Mordechai.

Laurence slashed upward, hoping to hit the neck above him. Izabel and Wil did the same, all three missing entirely.

Vaelys kept running, and jumped onto the base of the beast's neck, sticking her daggers in as grips. She started climbing the beast, making it around to the top of the neck.

Kyrilis reached one of the heads, just as it dove to bite at her. She slashed with her sword, nicking its tongue, causing it to reel back in pain.

Mordechai summoned an orb of fire above the creature, lowered his fist and drove the orb into the creature's body.

The beast roared in pain, reared back its necks and breathed in

Mordechai's direction. The five heads fired a stream of red flame, shards of ice, a bolt of electricity, poison spit and a stream of blue flame, all aimed at the casters at the far end of the room.

Mordechai raised his hands and caused a bubble of Time energies to spawn on the spot where he stood, large enough to encompass Saerasha and Kellum. Time passed more quickly for those inside the bubble. Everything else around the room seemed to stand still.

"Run!" he yelled.

Mordechai and Saerasha ran to the edge of the bubble and looked back for a moment. Kellum stood still for a moment and fired all twenty of his remaining arrows, then ran to join them. "Go!" he yelled as he passed.

The three jumped out of the sphere, and watched as the jets of flame slammed into it, combining as they swirled about its surface to terrifying effect.

Thool slammed into the center of the beast's body as it breathed, his bony brow bouncing off of its scales. Laurence, Izabel and Wil joined him and they attacked the beast in a frantic series of blows. Only Laurence's blade appeared to be doing damage.

Twenty arrows arrived at their target, mere seconds after the Time bubble faded. Six of them found purchase in the creature's eyes, blinding two heads and partially blinding two others.

The blinded heads reared back, roaring toward the ceiling.

Vaelys continued to climb up the neck she'd chosen. The head from the neck beside it snapped around and began trying to bite her off. She rolled to the side, moving her daggers to hang from the neck's side, rather than climbing across the top.

Kyrilis slashed again at the neck just above her. The neck coiled back, bringing the head to her position. It bit down at her with haste. She attempted to stab the roof of the creature's mouth with her sword, but her response came a second too slow. The creature bit down on her, shook its head from side to side, and flung her away from the battle. She rolled to a stop several yards away.

Saerasha started running toward Kyrilis, but two of the hydra's heads breathed again, chasing her back.

Mordechai noticed where Vaelys was, only a few feet from the creature's head. Knowing her enchantments made her capable of hurting the beast where the other companions couldn't, he focused magical energies toward her, granting her Time elemental haste.

Laurence continued to slash with his sword, carving a swath of flesh from the beast's body. Thool, Izabel and Wil backed away and encircled him to provide defensive cover.

The heads lashed out, trying to reach Laurence. His friends swung wild, bouncing weapons off the heads as they drew near.

Vaelys felt Mordechai's spell enhance her. The beast seemed to move in slow motion. She smiled wickedly and climbed back atop the neck, got to her feet and ran along its surface to the head. Using the full force of her strength, she drove her daggers down, through the sides of its skull, and ripped upward. The skull split open, brains erupting into the air.

She looked back and leapt, aiming for the neighboring head that had been trying to reach her.

Laurence stepped back, exhausted, as blood and brains rained down from above.

"Thool!" yelled Laurence.

Thool spun around, saw Laurence extending his blade, and smiled. He dropped his great axe, grabbed the tiny sword and turned back toward the beast's body.

Laurence noticed Kyrilis's body, crumpled in a bloody heap near the wall. He screamed out in fear and ran as fast as he could toward her, hoping against the worst.

Vaelys landed on the second head and repeated her maneuver, then ran down the neck toward the beast's body.

Mordechai reached up and summoned power from the weave. Streams of energy passed through the mountain above, streaming through the room as bright blue bolts of electricity. They absorbed into his flesh, growing in intensity.

Laurence dropped to his knees and slid the final few inches toward Kyrilis. He grabbed her by the shoulders and rolled her into his lap, weeping and stroking her hair. Another violent burst of blood and brains erupted in the room behind him.

Thool cleaved into the beast's body with ease, carving a path through the center of its body. The beast dropped to the ground, trying to crush him under its weight. He stepped into the gash he and Laurence had created, and let the impact drive him in. Within seconds, he began carving his way out of the body, as chunks went flying into his friends.

Mordechai released his spell. A bright beam of light streaked across the room, burrowing into the creature's body. As Vaelys destroyed the last of the beast's heads, the energies exploded the beast's body from the inside, destroying its heart, lungs and stomach.

As the beast collapsed to the ground, the companions beneath it dodged and rolled, trying desperately to avoid being crushed.

Saerasha ran immediately toward Kyrilis and Laurence, hoping she'd make it in time.

Kellum ran toward the corpse to help the other combatants.

Vaelys rolled to the ground in front of the final head, quite pleased with herself.

"We need to burn its organs!" yelled Mordechai, as he began walking toward the corpse.

Saerasha arrived at Kyrilis, laying in Laurence's lap. Her torso bled profusely from several gaping wounds.

Laurence was in tears, calmly stroking her hair.

Saerasha summoned all the power within her. She'd felt it building since the mysterious event at Thu'Brin. She focused the sum of it on healing Kyrilis. As the power streamed into the fallen Afyr, she imagined it drawing her blood back within her and repairing her organs. She focused on the repairing of arteries, capillaries and veins.

After those, she focused on muscle tissue and skin. Finally, she stimulated the heart and lungs, pushing fresh blood throughout her body and stimulating breathing.

Kyrilis inhaled deeply as the energies faded, gasping for breath.

As the hydra's corpse burst into flame behind them, the companions watched as Kyrilis revived and Laurence pulled her into an embrace. Sighs of relief passed among them, as Kyrilis moaned, "oh my gods," pain coursing through her.

Saerasha passed out from the effort, completely drained of all energy.

Mordechai walked up to the group, saying, "if you don't burn a hydra's organs, they just come right back."

Nobody seemed to notice or care.

"Okay. I vote we make camp for the night. Any takers?" asked Kellum.

∴ ∴ ∴

LAURENCE PICKED Kyrilis up in his arms and stood as the party walked away.

"What... what happened?" she whispered, her pain slowly

pulsing.

"You almost died," he answered. "Any longer and you would have. Saerasha saved you at the last moment."

"Thank you," she whispered.

"For what?" he asked.

"For being there."

"I can't lose you," he said somberly.

When they reached the rest of the party, he lowered himself to the ground, shifting her so she'd arrive in his lap with her head next to his shoulder. She nuzzled in as waves of pain pulsed through her.

"So much pain," she whimpered, fresh tears streaming down her cheeks.

Thool carried Saerasha over and laid her beside Laurence. The rest of the group set about making camp.

"Mordechai? Is it safe to eat Hydra meat?" asked Izabel.

"Yes, actually. Just not the organs," he answered.

Izabel borrowed Laurence's sword from Thool and ran back over to carve off meat for the party.

After cooking the meat and dining, the party laid down to sleep. Vaelys volunteered to stand guard, too full of adrenaline to meditate.

∴ ∴ ∴

KYRILIS SAT upright, extracting herself from Laurence's lap. She tried to stand, but the pain shooting through her torso stopped her.

"Are you okay?" he asked, turning to face her.

Saerasha groaned, rubbing sleep from her eyes.

"Everything hurts," whimpered Kyrilis.

Laurence knew Kyrilis as a strong, capable woman. She had a fun, whimsical side that she rarely brought out; which she usually leveraged to tease him. He had never seen her show signs of pain or weakness. Even in the face of unreasonable odds, she'd carried herself confidently; ready to face everything head on.

He knew a little of her past; that she'd fought back against the men in her life that sought to exploit her abilities. She'd even confronted those who refused to take her seriously, rising through the ranks of the Afyr despite their claims she would never succeed.

Seeing her in so much pain, after nearly losing her the night before, made him more concerned than he thought possible. He stroked her cheek gently as she grimaced in pain, just as Saerasha joined them.

"She lived," sighed Saerasha.

"Yes, but she's not well," said Laurence.

"I passed out before I could fuse and heal her bones. She's got several broken ribs, and gods know what else," said Saerasha. "Move out of the way."

Saerasha sat in front of Kyrilis as Laurence stood and backed away. With a sigh, feeling useless, Laurence stepped further away and paced. All he could feel was panic; panic that he might lose her. He didn't understand how their connection had grown so strong.

Am I projecting the way I feel about Tylee onto her?

Saerasha focused her energies, burrowing them deep into Kyrilis's tissue, reaching for the bones within.

Kyrilis screamed as the power surged through her, shifting shards of bone into place. The rest of the companions woke from their slumber at the sound of Kyrilis's cry.

"Laurence," called Saerasha. "Come sit with her, she's whispering your name. I can't do anything else for her right now. Her bones are healed, and the pain should subside in time."

He walked over, knelt before Kyrilis and grabbed her hands.

"How are you f-"

"To arms!" yelled Vaelys.

"What is it?" asked Laurence, his eyes still on Kyrilis.

"Dwarves in full plate armor... not like the ones upstairs. These don't radiate heat," said Vaelys. She pointed down the hallway opposite where they'd entered the cavern.

Thool, Wil, Izabel and Kellum ran to the entrance and stared at the horror approaching them. Three dozen dwarves marched in formation; their armor thicker and heavier, encompassing their bodies fully.

"I don't see any weak spots," said Izabel.

"Only enchanted weapons can hurt them if they're undead," said Laurence.

"Yeah, well, we only have one of those to go around!" yelled Izabel.

"Saerasha and I will handle them, you just hold them off and give us time," said Mordechai, rising to his feet.

Saerasha nodded to Mordechai with determination as she joined him.

"Izabel!" called Laurence, presenting his blade to the side.

She raced over and retrieved it eagerly, a wicked smile on her face.

Thool, Vaelys, Wil and Kellum focused on keeping the dwarves at the entrance to the hallway. Their weapons couldn't penetrate their ancient armor, but the impact of their blows pushed them back enough to hold the position.

Izabel stood in the middle of her companions, bashing with her enchanted shield and attacking with Laurence's enchanted blade. Her strikes slowly chipped away at their opponents' armor, leaving gashes and cutting away small fragments.

"I am going to convert their metal armor into wood. You will warp and twist that wood to crush them and create gaps, then I will transmute it back into metal. We must execute the three spells in rapid succession, or this will not work. When you warp the wood, their magically reinforced bones will resist, causing the wood to rebound. So, I must land the second transmutation almost instantly," Mordechai explained.

"I don't know how to do any of that with my new powers. I was a healer for my tribe. I never learned to attack, or defend," Saerasha responded.

Mordechai and Saerasha walked closer to the dwarves.

"Do you understand my instructions?" Mordechai asked.

"I will try," answered Saerasha.

Mordechai pulled magic down from the sky, through the mountain and into himself. It streamed out of him violently, colliding with the armored dwarves and clinging to their armor.

The melee combatants parried and blocked as they backed away, giving room for the spell to do its work.

Saerasha drew upon the power of her soul, preparing to unleash her own spell. As the dwarves' metallic weapons and armor creaked and groaned under Mordechai's spell, she released her magics.

As the armor changed to wood, it twisted and warped. Ribcages bent under the pressure, some breaking, others shattering entirely. Spines crunched and twisted, pushed at unreasonable angles by Saerasha's will.

One of the dwarves lurched forward, lashing out at Vaelys with its now-wooden greatsword. Thool jumped toward it, parrying the blow and shoving it back atop the pile.

Mordechai unleashed his second spell at them, shifting the wooden armor back into iron. The arms and legs of those still standing shifted out of place, or broke into uselessness. The dwarves lay on the floor, unable to attack or defend. Still bound to the world through magical undeath, yet unable to fulfill their purpose.

Thool stepped back and considered his great axe. Its haft converted to iron by Mordechai's spell, he tested its weight. He turned to Mordechai and smiled, pleased with the results.

Izabel walked around the pile of crumpled dwarves, still writhing upon the ground. She used Laurence's sword to pierce each of their skulls, ending the threat.

Off in the distance, Laurence still sat holding Kyrilis's hands, trying to comfort her.

"I know... you're married to Tylee. I just... I want you to be happy, and you're happy with her. I'm not asking for that to change. But... when that thing bit me last night, and I nearly died? All I could think about was you, and your family. I've never known love like that before. Everyone in my life treated me like a tool, or judged me for being a woman," explained Kyrilis.

"I understand, I-" started Laurence.

"Listen to me. I... I love you. And I know that won't change anything. It can't change anything. But I was never exposed to the love of a family. Fahrul was more a father to me than my own flesh and blood. I also never knew love of a personal nature. Love is... dangerous for elves. Childbirth can be fatal or change a woman's body in disastrous ways.

"I watched my mother die during the birth of my sister, so I learned from a young age to avoid... love. I've never been close to anyone... and I find myself wanting desperately to be close to you. So, I want to be. Not close enough to disrupt what you have with Tylee, I would never want that, but... I have to be near you; to be in your life. I wasn't afraid to die last night... I was afraid to leave you," said Kyrilis, a single tear falling down her cheek.

"Look... I... love you too. I love Tylee, and I won't do anything to jeopardize our marriage. But... somehow, some way? I love you too. I don't want to lose you. You're an amazing woman, an impressive warrior, and I trust and respect you more than almost anyone I've ever met. Never in my life could I have dreamed of anyone like you. But whatever this is? Let's just... stay focused on our enemies and the challenges before us. I'm here for you, you're here for me... that's enough for now," said Laurence.

"Can we go now?" asked Vaelys from beside them.

"Try to stand," said Laurence. He stood and pulled her hands with his.

Kyrilis got her feet underneath her and used Laurence's assistance to stand. She didn't like feeling vulnerable, but felt relieved she'd admitted her feelings. In some way, she felt more connected to him after their conversation.

"Most of the pain is gone," said Kyrilis. "I should be fine now."

"We've been in this room for almost six hours now, I think it's time we get moving," said Mordechai.

Laurence and Kyrilis nodded their agreement and joined the rest of the companions at the pile of dead dwarves.

Izabel walked over and presented Laurence with his sword.

"Thanks for that... I love that thing," she said with a smile.

"It suits you," he said as he sheathed it.

After climbing over the corpses, they followed Thool through the halls, continuing their search for the ritual chamber.

∴ ∴ ∴

BRONSIN RETURNED to Gaierford with the mid-day sun, his mottled gray horse grumbling his need for rest beneath him. He was a little surprised to see the arched sign over the road read Kotanndale, but then again, with Delriahna and Tylee in charge, abrupt changes were around every corner.

He dismounted next to the gates and handed his reins to a very eager young lad. The boy raced away, leading the horse to a nearby stable which hadn't been present when he left town.

Every building seemed under construction. Workers toiled on the road, removing the dirt so they could replace it with stone. As far as he could tell, ten times as many people occupied the town as when he left.

Shaking his head at the turn of events, he walked toward the general store and the offices above. After shoving his way through the crowd in the store, and stomping his way up the stairs, he barged into the office with a frustrated sigh.

"Bronsin, thank the gods," said Delriahna as he entered.

"What the hell is going on in this town. Kotanndale? Have you both finally lost your minds?" he grumbled.

"The glorious King Orluhnd, in all his wisdom, decided we were doing such a fine job that we had room for another twelve-hundred souls... give or take a few hundred. In truth, we've lost count," she answered.

"That's just brilliant," he said sarcastically.

"I was just about to take some of them south to the marshland farms, and onward to Mooncrest, and you're coming with me," she said.

"I just got back to town! I've been on the road since," he paused, trying to do the math in his head.

"It doesn't matter how long... you will do as your Duchess requests," she said, raising an eyebrow.

"How many people are we draggin along with us?" he sighed.

"One hundred destined for the farms, to rebuild and get them producing again. Two hundred destined for Mooncrest, to expand into the surrounding areas and provide labor for our farms. Thirty more to pick up goods in Mooncrest and bring them back to Kotanndale."

"Three hundred and thirty-two of us traveling south... all at once."

"Yep! And you get to drive the lead carriage."

"What about Tylee?"

"She's Duchess Ravencrest now, and she's overseeing the rebuilding efforts of Tolrin Province. She's splitting her time between Kotanndale and Cragenfell... and if I had to guess, she's currently meeting with Commander Clendon of the Fifth Command over near the mines."

"This has just blown way out of proportion, hasn't it?"

"Dragon," she said.

"Yes, but-"

"Dra-g-on."

"Fine... let's get this over with," he grumbled.

"One more thing."

"Yes?" he asked, sighing.

"Go speak to Rolph about the guards he allocated for staffing the two Waystations along the Reach."

Bronsin barged out of the room before Delriahna could complicate his day any further. He spent the next few hours searching for Rolph, then collecting the guards he'd been told to take along.

By the end of the day, sixteen carriages lined the Reach, moving slowly amidst hundreds of travelers. Bronsin sighed as he settled into his bench, certain that he'd never again find rest.

∴ ∴ ∴

THOOL SET a grueling pace at the front of the group. The rest of the companions followed closely, but their concern over caution had waned. His frustration neared the point of boiling over. He couldn't understand why they didn't bask in the glory of the labyrinth around them. Grunting his disapproval, he hastened his pace.

"So when you pull that power forward, if you focus with more precision you'll be able to cause your desired effects using less of it, causing less exhaustion and healing your patient more efficiently," explained Mordechai a few feet behind Thool.

"Which means I need practice," said Saerasha. "So... I need more of them to get injured," she teased.

"No. You can practice with other effects. Produce flame, make a stone emit light, or something even simpler. Maybe make your hair smell nicer," he suggested.

"I think her hair smells wonderful," said Wil a few feet behind them.

Saerasha whipped her head around and smiled. "You do, do you?"

"I... um," responded Wil, taken aback.

"I wasn't suggesting it smelled bad. I was just trying to suggest something simple you could try with your magic," sighed Mordechai.

"How old are you, my woodland kin?" asked Saerasha, a hint of playfulness in her voice.

"One-hundred-and-five, fair lady," Wil said.

"Barely old enough to make such comments," she said with a smirk.

"I'm a creature of the woods, used to seeing the wonder of nature around me at all times. Stuck down here in these dark stone tunnels, where else should I look to quell my desire for beauty... except to you?"

"I'm old enough to be your mother," she answered with a blush.

"I doubt that very much," he said.

Sighing, Mordechai slowed his pace and fell in alongside Izabel, Kellum and Vaelys. He looked over at the three of them, and they responded with a series of shrugs.

"It's no better behind us," said Vaelys.

"We should've brought Agnar with us," lamented Izabel.

Kellum looked over at Vaelys and winked.

"No," said Vaelys.

Laurence and Kyrilis walked a few feet behind the rest, discussing swordplay and battle tactics.

"I've seen you do a maneuver a few times where you try to get your opponent to anticipate your next move and move early, before your sword is there. That's fine for slower opponents, but I fear you might lean on it too much," said Kyrilis.

"Oh, I know. I fear the day I fight someone significantly faster than I am," answered Laurence.

"I could teach you a few tricks... once we're out of here," she said.

"I'd love that," said Laurence.

Suddenly, the group found themselves in a large room. Thool spun around and slammed the pommel of his great axe into the floor, staring at them in anger. None of the companions had been paying attention to where they were.

"You no take serious," scolded Thool.

Laurence moved to the front of the pack.

"I'm sorry, Thool. We shouldn't allow ourselves to be distracted," said Laurence. "But, we've been walking for-"

"Six hours," injected Mordechai.

"We've been walking for six hours through miles of endless hallways," said Laurence.

"You don't know way," said Thool. "No pay attention. I die, you die. Never get out."

"Straight, left, left, right, left, right, right, straight, straight, left, right, left, left, straight, right, left, straight... should I go on?" said Kellum.

Thool looked back at him confused, then thought for a moment and smiled. "You good elf."

"What's that?" asked Izabel, pointing. She walked past Laurence and Thool to the other side of the chamber.

Everyone turned to see what she pointed at. On the opposite side of the room, six-foot wide metallic beams crossed each other diagonally atop the wall. At their center, a fist-sized ruby glowed to life as they approached.

Kyrilis was the last to enter the room. As she crossed the threshold, a three foot slab of stone shot down from the ceiling of the hallway, and another shot up from the floor. As they collided in the middle, another pair of metal beams formed across the seam, sealing the companions in the room and startling most of them.

"Damnit!" yelled Kyrilis.

"Okay, so that happened," said Izabel.

"Let's just try to figure out how we get out of here," said Laurence.

"Stand back," said Mordechai.

Pulling energy from the weave, he sent a beam of fire into the ruby attempting to shatter it. He stopped almost immediately when the room began to quake. Sharp shards of stone extruded from the walls, ceiling and floor, pointing toward the center of the room.

Everyone dodged and ducked, avoiding the shards as best they could. Thool had to stand hunched over and looked furious.

"It seems specifically designed to counter magic. There has to be a mechanical way out, or some other alternative. Perhaps something to appease the binding on the room? This was built specifically to stop people like me," said Mordechai.

"Guys, this isn't good," said Kellum, alone on the far side of the room.

"Are you hurt?" asked Saerasha.

"Oh, I'm fine. But I know how those dwarves died," he said.

Kellum picked something up and turned to face the group. He held up a small burlap sack, rotted with age. Several lapis lazuli tumbled through small holes on the side.

"Didn't you say that the Deepfolk Clan helped the Inok free the souls that Lord Whun trapped hundreds of years ago?" asked Laurence.

"It's the thought that counts, right?" asked Kellum.

Saerasha walked over and took the bag from him, adding the stones to the ones in her satchel.

"They never made it. They brought the stones down, but they couldn't get through this room. They died here," said Izabel.

"So when you die in this room, you become undead?" asked Kyrilis, concerned.

"I'm not sure that's how it works. At the very least, I think the room re-opens when it no longer detects life," said Mordechai.

"So we have to die to get out of here?" asked Izabel.

"That's not what I said. Besides, that would only open the way back out, not the path leading deeper. Our mission takes us deeper," said Mordechai.

"How do you know it would only open one door?" asked Izabel.

"Because the dwarves were on this side of the one we need opened."

Laurence worked his way around the spikes and the crowd toward the sealed doorway Mordechai referred to. He studied it for a moment, asked, "well, what about the ruby? Other than the spikes and the big x covering each door, it's the only thing distinct in here."

"It's got to be the way through, right?" said Izabel.

"I'm not touching that thing," said Vaelys.

Saerasha joined Laurence at the door. With slight hesitation, she reached for the ruby. As her hand drew near, she howled in pain and withdrew her hand as quickly as she could. The spikes in the room shook, as if attempting to grow.

"What? What is it?" asked Laurence.

The rest of the group leaned closer.

"Searing pain... I could feel it draining my energy... sapping my will."

"You're a spellcaster. It drained my magical energies and raised the spikes when I cast that spell, and the spikes shook as you drew near to it. I think it feeds on our abilities, on our attachment to the weave," said Mordechai.

"So we can't touch it? And it might be our way out?" asked Kyrilis.

"I touch," said Thool.

"No, we need to be smart about this," said Mordechai.

"I touch! No scared!" said Thool.

"Just... wait a second!" insisted Mordechai.

He closed his eyes and focused on the magical vision he'd learned while blind. The room sprang to life in his mind, tiny lines of runes coursing across its surface, all flowing into and out of the ruby's setting.

"The ruby definitely controls the room," said Mordechai, his eyes pressed tightly closed.

"What is he-" started Kyrilis.

"He was blind on our journey here. Saerasha cured him after we found you guys. While he was blind, he learned to see by detecting magical energies in vast detail," explained Laurence.

Mordechai studied the ruby, stepping closer and pushing his vision to its limits. The runes flowing into the ruby came into focus. He gasped as realization struck.

"I... can't believe what I'm seeing," he said.

"What is it?" asked Laurence.

"I'm usually alone in my study at Fel'Vizsiour when this kind of discovery presents itself. Normally I have time to formulate my thoughts, and-"

"Just spit it out!" barked Laurence, exacerbated.

"I made this room."

"Come again?" asked Vaelys.

"I don't remember doing it, which means it was more than twelve-hundred years ago. However, I recognize the rune structure and phrasing. It's a combination of Leyweaving and Time magic, and clearly my own doing."

"Why would you make this trap?" asked Laurence.

"Because the legend is true, and he was protecting the blade we seek," answered Saerasha knowingly.

"It must be," said Mordechai.

"Great, so how do we open the door?"

"Funny enough, the runes specifically block *me* from opening it. I guess... in case I changed my mind? All it says is that 'only the blood of The Rainbow Cutter' may open the way. Not that I understand what *that* means," said Mordechai.

"So it's a riddle?" asked Izabel.

"It wasn't meant to be read, so it can't be a riddle. It's part of the definition of the barrier. The ruby was attuned to a bloodline capable of wielding the sword buried deeper in the labyrinth. So, only one who is capable of wielding it can touch the ruby without harm."

"Luckily we know who that is," said Kellum sarcastically.

"A blade of legend, buried in an ancient vault by a mad wizard... no offense," said Wil.

"None taken," said Mordechai with a smirk.

"A boy who carries the blood of legends, fighting against great evils intent on destroying the lands," said Wil.

Several members of the group pointed at Laurence.

"I think it's clear who—if any of us—that message refers to," said Wil.

"I'm not a prophet. Laurence's family line didn't exist when this place was built. There's no way I attuned the ruby to just him," said Mordechai.

"No... but I don't know anything about my mother, save that Tolrin met her in Hoalfast," said Laurence.

"I touch," said Thool, stepping forward.

"I've got it, Thool," said Laurence.

Everyone watched as Laurence raised his hand.

Izabel lifted her shield higher, to give better light.

Laurence sighed as the extra light reached him. Rolling his eyes, he continued moving his hand toward the large crystal.

With a shudder and a series of clicks, the spikes withdrew into the walls, ceiling and floor. The metal bars covering the path forward slid out of the way, and those blocking the way back dissolved back into the stone. The ceiling and floor of each hallway retracted, and a gust of air rushed into the room from both directions.

"Hell yes!" belted Izabel.

The creature behind the sealed wall suddenly came into view, cutting their celebration short.

∴ ∴ ∴

AS THE door leading deeper into the Labyrinth opened fully, a man came into view. His leather pants and shirt had grown dry and brittle with age, cracked open and crumbling in places. Tattered remnants of a red silk sash clung desperately to his left shoulder, flitting like a wisp of spiderweb as he moved.

A small metal coffer in the shape of a coffin dangled from a strand of sinew, gently slapping his right thigh with each step. His flesh still clung to his undead form, missing in places, and stretched too thin in others. His feet had long ago worn down to the bone; his heels scraping eerily as he took his last few steps towards them.

A small ruby amulet, set in silver, lay at the center of his chest, attached to a thin silver chain. It glowed bright with power, pulsing in rhythm with what should have been his breathing.

"I am free," said the man, his voice deep and ethereal.

He raised his left hand toward the party, his right stayed clinched at his side.

A black bolt of energy shot out of his palm, streaking down the hallway and through the room as the party jumped to the sides. His amulet grew brighter as he cast the spell.

Laurence charged down the hallway, his sword ready.

A black blade covered in bright red runes appeared in the man's left hand, just as Laurence's sword cut toward his side.

Their blades clashed repeatedly as Laurence's flurry of attacks failed to penetrate the man's defenses.

Izabel, Kyrilis and Vaelys charged into the hall, running toward the combatants.

"Come forth!" yelled the man.

Black orbs of energy sprang to life behind him, blinking in and out of existence rapidly. Strange, demonic creatures sprang forth from the orbs as they burst. Each stood five feet tall with brown, leathery skin, glowing yellow eyes, black oily hair and black claws and horns. Their incredibly powerful muscles rippled as they moved, tensed with anticipation.

"I've got him, Laur!" yelled Kyrilis, stepping in front of the undead mage.

Laurence backed away as Kyrilis attacked, turning to engage their new foes.

Izabel and Vaelys arrived at his side just as the first one reached them.

It swatted Laurence's blade aside with one of its clawed hands and slashed at his chest with the other, tearing through the plates and rings of his armor.

Izabel braced her shield and absorbed the impact as two demons collided with her to Laurence's left.

Vaelys stood at Laurence's right, parrying attacks from two other demons.

Wil arrived just behind the trio and thrust his staff over their shoulders towards the strange foes.

Thool and Kellum stayed back to defend Mordechai and Saerasha, knowing the hall was too small for all of them to stand at the front lines.

Four claws rapidly careened off of Izabel's shield, pushing her backward and out of position. Laurence thrust to his left, forcing the pair that attacked her to jump back, giving her just enough time to get back into position.

"This is fucked!" yelled Izabel.

Vaelys focused for a split second on the speed-granting gems embedded near her wrists. She went into a frenzy, parrying attacks from Laurence's demon, the two in front of her, and several lunges from the next line behind them.

Mordechai pushed energies toward his companions, reinforcing their armor and hastening their attacks, hoping to give them an edge versus the demonic foes.

Saerasha started forming a spell of her own, intent on stopping the mage.

Kyrilis parried another attack from the undead mage, her sword sending his blade downward. She attempted to lock his blade in place with her dagger, but he moved too quickly and punched her in the chest with his hilt.

She repeated her downward parry as she stepped backward from the impact of his punch, driving his sword down once more. When her blade rebounded off his, she turned it upward, sliced through his chin, then stepped forward to re-claim her position in the fight.

The undead mage roared. A wave of red energy spewed forth, pushing Kyrilis, Izabel and Laurence backward.

Laurence slid backward across the floor on his feet, ignoring the pain to stay focused on the combatants in front of him. He stopped just beside Wil and parried three blows, but the fourth slipped through. He growled against the pain as the demonic claw tore through his right shoulder.

Izabel slid backward into Wil, who caught her and pushed her forward. She slammed into the advancing pair of demons, her shield driving through one while her sword slid through the neck of the other. She almost spared a moment to express her excitement until the stream of demons jumped over their fallen comrade and charged straight for her.

Kyrilis threw her off-hand dagger toward the mage's throat as she slid backward. It missed her intended target as he lurched his head backward mid-howl, landing instead in the crease of his right shoulder. He dropped his blade, reached up with his left hand and pulled the dagger out as she ran forward. With one motion, he threw the dagger at her and clinched his left fist.

His sword reappeared in his hand instantly.

Kyrilis caught her dagger in mid-air as she ran toward him and started another flurry of attacks as she got back into position.

Vaelys parried claw attacks from two demons at once, stepping backward to coax them closer to the right wall. As the right-most demon reached her destination, she changed tactics. When their next flurry of attacks came toward her, she stabbed them in the palms of their hands, rather than parrying.

As they reeled in pain and surprise, she jumped toward the wall, kicked off of it with her right foot, and flipped over their heads; driving a dagger through the skull of each on her way over. When she landed, she retrieved her daggers and charged toward the next pair of foes.

Saerasha and Mordechai unleashed their spells simultaneously. A bolt of electricity shot out of Mordechai's hands, striking the mage in the neck. A bolt of fire streamed out of Saerasha's right fist, striking the mage in his face.

The mage reeled backward from the impact of their spells.

Kyrilis took advantage of his stumble and cut through his left wrist with her sword. The hand, and the sword it still held, fell to the floor with a clatter. A split second later, she buried her dagger cross-guard deep in his skull.

As Laurence thrust his blade toward the demon he was fighting, sure he would end the beast's life, the remaining demons vanished in a puff of smoke.

As the tattered remnants of the undead mage's clothing dropped to the floor, a small white crystal skittered across the floor and bounced off of Izabel's boot. His sword had vanished, and his corpse had turned to dust.

Saerasha rushed down the hall to offer healing.

Laurence turned to her, desperately clutching his left shoulder in his right hand.

Kyrilis knelt before the pile of dust and clothing, studying the mysterious remains. As she poked and prodded with the tip of her dagger, Vaelys calmly walked over and picked up the mage's ruby amulet.

"Hey, what're you-" started Kyrilis.

"Consider this payment for my assistance on this journey," said Vaelys.

"It's fine, Kyrilis," said Mordechai, interrupting Kyrilis's rebuttal.

With a sigh, Kyrilis returned to the pile before her. She picked up the strange coffer and opened it. Rosewood filled the interior. A hole had been carved into the center in the shape of a small crystal. A small piece of vellum fell out when she opened it.

"I think this belongs in there," said Izabel, walking over with the small white crystal.

Kyrilis unfolded the vellum. Faint writing covered the vellum's inner surface. She read it aloud for the group.

> *Dearest Kishina,*
>
> *My entire life is full of regret, the most painful of which is my constant failure to free your precious soul. I do not know if the Soul Obelisk will free you, but I fear it is our last hope. I do not know what this will do to me. I set out tomorrow to travel to Vuhl and know not when I'll have a chance to speak with you again... I do not even know if you can hear me.*

Dearest reader,

If my plan does not succeed and you have found this note, I fear you will become Kishina's only hope for freedom. I can give you nothing for your efforts, save for my undying gratitude. I pray that you find it in your heart to help Kishina where I have failed.

Yours in eternity, Maerik.

"So he came down here to free her soul from a crystal?" asked Wil.

"This crystal," said Izabel, sadness in her voice. She held the crystal up for all to see.

Kyrilis handed her the coffer and the note. Izabel put the coffer's contents back inside, closed it, and slipped it into her belt pouch.

"What do you plan to do with it?" asked Kyrilis.

"She's going to take it to the only woman we know who can speak with the dead," said Mordechai.

"Ayriel," said Izabel with a nod.

"If he came down here to free her soul and didn't succeed-" started Saerasha.

"Then likely the device that frees souls doesn't exist, or is cursed," finished Mordechai.

"You don't remember him?" asked Wil.

"No?"

"It stands to reason he got in before that trap room existed. Otherwise he wouldn't be here; he couldn't have gotten through. So, if you made that trap room, either he was here when you did, or-" suggested Wil.

"Or I brought him here. Interesting thought, but I have no way to prove one way or the other. My memory stretches back over twelve-hundred years, and I don't remember making that trap. So, clearly, if his arrival happened prior to that, I'd similarly lack the memory of it."

"What are these?" asked Izabel.

She pointed out a pair of strange grooves in the floor to the rest of them, leading down the hall and around a corner.

"Drag marks from his heels, I'd wager," said Laurence.

"He's been down here a long time, pacing between the door and some other location," said Kyrilis.

"Let's follow them. They probably lead to whatever device is fabled to free trapped souls," suggested Saerasha.

An hour later they arrived at a small alcove set into the wall. In the center stood a black obelisk that nearly reached the ceiling seventeen feet above, its surface completely covered in runes.

"Stand back," said Mordechai.

The group made way so he could inspect the obelisk. He knelt before it for a few minutes and studied it with his eyes, then closed his eyes and studied the magics that swirled about it. With a knowing sigh, he stood and faced his companions.

"The physical runes declare the obelisk a gift from Xxrandus to the Inok, to aid in their fight against G'nok," he explained.

"That no true! Inok follow G'nok. He god of hunt. He favor Inok," said Thool angrily.

"That's what the stone says, Thool. Please remember, this has been here for more than twenty Inok lifetimes. Things may have been very different back then," said Mordechai.

"No true," said Thool defiantly.

"The magical runes paint a very different story. While the physical ones you can all see claim that the stone frees trapped souls, the runes of power swirling about it seem to be designed to separate souls from those who touch it... effectively making the hapless victim undead," explained Mordechai.

"Poor Maerik," said Kyrilis. "All he wanted to do was free the woman he loved."

"Well, that part of our plan is a bust," said Wil.

"We'll have to find another way to free your aunt and uncle, Laurence, as well as the Tryn and Inok that Drakahl's men claimed," said Saerasha.

"We'll find a way. Perhaps Ayriel can help," said Laurence.

Mordechai nodded in agreement. "If anyone can, it's her."

"Best not to waste any more time. We've another purpose for being here," said Laurence as Saerasha finished her healing. He took a moment to mend his armor, as Joril had taught him.

"I lead now. You watch. Learn. No is playtime," said Thool sternly.

"Yes, Thool, we'll pay attention this time. Thank you," said Laurence.

∴ ∴ ∴

AFTER AN hour following Thool, the group entered another large chamber. In contrast to the rest of the labyrinth, the room's walls, ceiling and floor were obsidian. At the far end of the room stood a small dais, atop which sat an obsidian altar.

An exquisite hilt rose into the air above the altar, the rest of the blade buried within.

"It's real," gasped Saerasha.

As the group cautiously moved toward the altar, several of the companions bumped into a strange, invisible barrier.

"What the hell?" asked Izabel.

"Yeah, I can't get any closer," said Wil.

Laurence walked right past them, paused at hearing their words, and turned back to face them.

"Hold on for a second," said Mordechai. He closed his eyes and focused on the magical energies about the room... and was nearly blinded. A glowing sphere of power surrounded the altar, serving as the barrier which prevented them from proceeding; yet allowed Laurence to pass through.

"It seems that this barrier works much like the ruby trap. Only one of the proper bloodline can approach the sword," explained Mordechai.

Mordechai looked Laurence in the eyes and nodded.

"This is apparently your birthright, young Laurence. Proceed with caution."

With wonder and confusion, Laurence turned and walked toward the altar. He could feel a warmth radiating through his mind, both inviting him to continue and warning him not to proceed.

He stepped onto the dais, and the warm sensation grew hotter.

The hilt of the weapon appeared to be platinum, wrapped in a dark red leather, with a single crystal affixed to the pommel. The crystal shimmered with all the colors of the rainbow, shifting and swirling as if its interior was mist.

The quillon sat flush with the obsidian. One side of the crossbars curved backward, forming a hand guard. The other stretched out a few inches and seemed to disappear into the stone along with the blade. After a few moments of hesitation, Laurence climbed onto the altar and grabbed the hilt in his right hand.

Pulling with all of his might, Laurence wrenched the blade free. As the long, elven-style curved blade rose into the air above the altar, the magical barrier fell and the whole of Mount Skain shook. The sound of a massive explosion echoed throughout Vuhl, causing the companions to cover their ears in pain.

∴ .∴. ∴

HIGH ABOVE the continent of Pelrigoss, Zathos shattered. The world's smallest moon sundered abruptly, sending most of its debris along its orbital path.

Several small pieces rained down from the sky, falling like a meteor shower into the upper atmosphere, leaving flaming streaks through the early dawn sky.

A larger piece streaked through the air, hurtling toward the undiscovered continent of Syndrilos.

∴ ∴ ∴

DELRIAHNA LOOKED up at the sky, wondering how she'd gotten herself into such a position. Traveling with hundreds of displaced citizens, spending hours each day setting up and tearing down camps; the frustration of it all exhausted her. She had come to understand Laurence's distaste for tents while traveling.

Their camp stretched over the fields and hills on the western side of the Southern Reach below her. The sound of the Sacton River barely reached her position, sitting atop a hill and dreading the morning's task. The sun slowly crested the horizon to the east, and song birds had just begun to greet the day.

All was peaceful, save for the tension slowly knotting her upper back. She looked to the northeast and stared at Zathos, envious of its simple existence. Zathos didn't have to wake hundreds of people, force them to stow bedrolls, make sure they ate dawnfry in a timely manner, or push them to start an all day march to the south.

Delriahna had just resigned herself to the day before her when Zathos exploded toward the east and west.

She gasped in horror at the sight; small chunks of moon stretching in a line where Zathos had previously orbited.

Small streams of fire filled the sky in the distance as the sound of a devastating explosion echoed across the landscape.

The camp went into a frenzy; the sounds of panicked citizens drowning out the peaceful signs of morning.

A streak of fire cut through the sky, moving south along the horizon.

It took a few moments for her own terror to fade. Bronsin joined her atop the hill, his hands wet from the tea he had spilled on his way back to her.

"What the hell was that?" he asked.

"Zathos is gone," she said, pointing at the sky with a trembling hand.

"By the gods," gasped Bronsin, following her gaze.

"I don't even-"

"You've done it now, lad," interrupted Bronsin, shaking his head.

∴ ∴ ∴

THE PAIN *overwhelmed him. How long had he been there? Trapped within stone, bound by immense magics, the wave of pain returned, washing through him. He tried to scream, but no air escaped his gaping mouth.*

Laurence stumbled backward and fell off the altar. The sword fell out of his grasp, clattering to the ground and dissolving into the crystal embedded in its pommel. The crystal skittered across the floor, coming to a stop a few feet away.

Kyrilis rushed over to him.

"Are you okay?" she asked.

"I'm... I'm fine," he answered, lifting himself to a seated position. "When I touched the sword, I was flooded with visions."

"Where'd the sword go?" asked Izabel, walking over to the crystal. "There's just this crystal now."

"I don't know. I had the sword in my h-" started Laurence. His words cut short, his train of thought interrupted as the sword reappeared in his right hand.

Kyrilis jumped back.

"Whoa!" gasped Izabel.

"That's a nifty trick," remarked Vaelys.

"Did the sword just-" wondered Wil.

"I just thought about holding it, and it appeared in my hand," said Laurence.

"Let me see it," said Kyrilis.

As Laurence handed her the sword, it dissolved back into the crystal, reappearing at its previous location near Izabel's foot.

"Whoa!" gasped Izabel again.

"No one can hold the blade but you, Laurence," said Mordechai, walking up beside them.

Izabel bent down and tried to pick up the crystal. Her fingers passed through it.

"I can't even touch the crystal!"

Laurence got up and walked over to her. He retrieved the

crystal from the floor and considered it briefly before putting it into his belt pouch.

"Let's try something," he said.

He drew Gahl's sword and handed it to her, then took a few steps back.

"Attack me," he told her.

Izabel unstrapped her shield from her shoulder and put it onto her left arm. She charged him, thrusting Gahl's sword toward his midsection.

Rainbow Cutter appeared in his hand in an instant. He deflected her thrust with ease and followed with a series of quick attacks. She struggled to keep up, deflecting blows with her shield and parrying whenever she could with the blade.

"Stop!" she yelled.

Laurence backed off and dropped his new sword. It vanished as it fell.

"How the fuck did you do that?" she asked in frustration. "You were so much faster than normal, I could barely keep up!"

"Seems I won't be needing this anymore," he said. He unbuckled his back scabbard and offered it to Izabel.

"Are you serious?" she gasped.

"Like I said before, it suits you."

"So we're done here?" asked Vaelys.

"It would appear so," said Mordechai.

"I've gotta be honest, I expected a lot more combat creeping through a dark, evil labyrinth," said Izabel.

"We had the benefit of Thool's guidance. Most would have been lost down here for weeks, and might never have even reached the hydra, let alone the trap room," said Mordechai. "To say nothing of the fact that only Laurence could have gotten through that room, or retrieved this sword."

"Well... get us out of here, mighty Thool," said Izabel.

"We won't need to be as cautious on the way out, so I suggest that perhaps Saerasha provide us with energy and sustenance through enchantment to hasten our journey," said Mordechai.

"I'll try," said Saerasha.

After a few moments, her spells took hold and the party began their ascent.

∴ ∴ ∴

AFTER TWO days of non-stop travel, the group passed through the great iron door back into Skainfall. Saerasha re-applied her spells several times during the journey, and her last application had run its course. None of them had the energy to be as excited as Agnar was upon their return.

He rushed forward as soon as they came into view and collided with Izabel, lifting her off the ground into a hug.

"When Skain shook, I feared the worst. You can't be doin me like that!"

He kissed her repeatedly on her lips, cheek and forehead.

"Put me down, you oaf!"

Laurence and Wil laughed at the display as they squeezed past.

As the companions filtered into the room, Drell rounded the corner, assisted by several worried priests.

"What did you do?" asked Drell, panicked.

∴ ∴ ∴

"IT MUST have happened when I retrieved the sword," said Laurence, looking up at the morning sky. The fragments of Zathos were difficult to make out through the smog and dark clouds produced by the forge, but what he could see gave him a sinking feeling.

"The explosion we heard was likely Zathos rupturing. Clearly the sword was the key to a spell of binding, and we broke that spell when we retrieved it," lamented Mordechai. "I should have known."

"None of my people will leave Skainfall. Those left guarding Skainhold ran here when that happened. And you've taken my royal guard from me," said Drell angrily.

"Skifvald has taken them south?" asked Laurence.

"Yes. Fifty of my best soldiers, gone to follow your disastrous plot. First you disrupt my peace with Drakahl, then you take my soldiers, and now you sunder Zathos... what next? Will you bring Skain down upon my head?"

"Go back to your people and pretend you know how to rule. Be a leader, for once. These lands will need leaders in the months to come," said Wil.

"We'll camp in Skainhold before we head out," said Laurence.

ASSAULT

Ris'Nammlil, Arran'Hael 26th, 113 of the 2nd Era

War and suffering come to all,
Yet this is not the end.
Hear ye, soon the peace shall fall,
And chaos' reign begins.

Night's Writ, Parable 16

CLENDON WALKED up beside Tylee and handed her a cup of coffee. "I'm sure he's fine," said Clendon.

"He won't be fine until he's back in my arms," said Tylee.

They stood together on the new foundation of the Fifth Command's keep in Kotanndale, overseeing the construction efforts below. The elevation of the hill was the perfect vantage point for organizing the workers and leading their project.

Tylee kept losing focus, staring up at the fragments of Zathos. The long ring of red rocks stretched across the entire sky, from east to west. The daytime moon, known to creep into the sky as if tailing its brethren in secrecy, now revealed its presence at all times of night and day. To Tylee, it seemed as if Provoss and Aygos dragged Zathos's shards across the sky in their wake.

"I feel like we're on the verge of something terrible," she said.

"I have to admit, a moon shattering like that certainly fits the definition of an omen," said Clendon.

"My love is in some far off land fighting gods know what. Our kingdom is in tatters. The King is ill. Zathos's fragments are strewn across the sky. I'd say we've exceeded our quota for omens."

"Let's just stay focused on what we can control. Which, right now, is Aric *getting in the way of our workers!*" yelled Clendon, catching sight of Aric's actions over Tylee's shoulder.

Tylee giggled at Clendon's reaction and walked down the hill to deal with Aric.

∴ ∴ ∴

AYRIEL SAT on the edge of her father's bed looking down at his pale skin with concern. He looked haggard and faded, as if he were a shell of his former self.

"It will pass," said Orluhnd, followed by a raspy cough.

"Why did he not heal you?" she asked, dabbing his forehead with a damp cloth.

"He did, but the illness keeps coming back. It must run its course," said the old man.

"How is that possible?"

"Because the illness is part of him," said Karthas as he walked in.

Ayriel turned to face the necromancer.

"The cough is but a symptom of something lesser. He is sick because his body lacks the strength to fight off common illnesses. That is not something that can be healed," said Karthas.

"So there's nothing we can do?"

"He will overcome the cough, and the exhaustion that accompanies it. However, it will probably be the last time his body is capable of fighting such things," said Karthas, reaching her side.

"There must be something," she said, sobbing.

"I'm afraid that what you are asking is akin to granting him immortality. The kind that I can offer is not something you wish for your father."

"You must rule," said Orluhnd. "I cannot sit upon the throne like this."

"Karthas, can you give us a few moments alone? I'll call for you when we're done," said Ayriel.

"Of course, your Majesty."

Karthas walked out of the chamber and shut the doors. Once they clicked into place, Ayriel turned back to her father with tears in her eyes.

"Do not cry, my child."

"I can't rule Arkhania. I'm not ready... I'm not ready to lose you," she sobbed.

"It is not your decision. I have lived beyond expectations and watched you grow into a powerful woman. A woman I am proud to call daughter, though..." his words trailed off. She expected him to cough, but none came.

"Though what?"

"I once told you that you would have to find a husband to appease the nobles."

"Yes. You told me to keep Silith close, and have happiness, but that they wouldn't support my ascension to the throne without a husband to produce heirs."

"Ignore that advice. Those were the words of a man who was flailing to maintain support, clinging to old ways and the senses of witless nobles."

"What are you saying?"

"I'm saying that these trying times have shown me the error of my ways. The people crave progress, action and decisive leadership, not indecisive councils of elders clinging to outdated traditions."

"But-"

"What came from all these attacks, if not clarity? Who do the people follow now? You, Tylee, Clendon, Delriahna... rebellious minds that stand in contrast to the old ways. They seek passion and compassion. They seek to be treated as equals and feel that their lives have value. You cannot give that to them if you follow my advice. You must follow your heart."

"If I follow my heart, I would never produce an heir. I love Silith, and she would become my queen."

"Do not concern yourself with an heir. You will have no need of one," he said.

"What are you saying?"

"I... I am not your birth father."

"What? Don't speak such nonsense."

"I am sterile. I was injured in battle before you were born, helping my father quell an uprising in the north. Our healers all died in the conflict, and by the time I was brought back to Vellenheim it was too late to repair the damage that had been done.

"I spent years trying to find someone to fix me, and all failed. Eventually I gained favor with Mordechai and he too tried to help, but alas... I could not produce an heir. I pleaded with him, not wishing to leave my throne to any of the nobles I detested so much.

"He only knew of one way to help; have someone else lay with my wife, and hide that fact from the outside world. The mere thought of it broke my heart, but I only knew one person I could trust. He refused for many years. Eventually, he gave in, took my form and lay with her. It was only once, and it still pains me to think I tricked my wife, or that another man... slept with her...

"But that trickery brought me you; the most wonderful woman in all the land. A woman I've been granted the privilege of calling daughter," explained Orluhnd with tears in his eyes.

Ayriel sat in shock, struggling to comprehend the gravity of what her father had just told her.

"I didn't want to pass before you knew the truth. Mordechai would never admit to it himself. But you are his blood. I have lived long enough to see that he does not age. You are still young beyond explanation, so you do not need an heir... for you clearly age similarly to your birth father."

Ayriel stood up, not sure how to react. Her entire world had just been tossed into disarray in her mind. As she walked out of the room he called out behind her, but she was too angry and perplexed to hear his words.

Silith ran to her side as she reached the door. They embraced in front of the guards, without a care how the public would respond once news of their love spread.

It was time the Kingdom knew the real Ayriel.

∴ ∴ ∴

AFTER DAYS of travel, the companions reached the western end of Daegon Bridge. The mile-long structure spanned the Odvodi river. Made from granite, it had offered safe passage across the dangerous waters for centuries.

Skifvald's forces had camped on a hill overlooking the bridge for several days, waiting for Laurence to arrive. As the group approached, several guards shouted their arrival and Skifvald ran out to greet them.

"Did you retrieve the sword? Was it real?" asked Skifvald.

Laurence raised his right arm and formed a fist, Rainbow Cutter appearing in his hand as it closed. He waved it around briefly, leaving trails of rainbow-colored energy in the air as it moved. When he released his grip on the blade, it vanished again, returning to its crystal.

"Well, at least that's going in our favor. It took everything to keep the soldiers here when Zathos exploded. The Inok and Tryn arrived this morning, but we've heard nothing from the Aegra, Daulga or the human tribes."

"No other forces have tried to cross the Daegon?" asked Laurence.

"No."

"Wehrenel and Ahrwie were given instructions to proceed to Hoalfast if we weren't at the bridge. Let's gather our forces and set out," said Laurence.

"The Tryn and Inok traveled through the night to get here. I suggest we let them rest and leave in the morning," said Skifvald.

"Very well. Let's settle in," said Laurence.

As the companions walked with Skifvald into the dwarven camp, Laurence hung back and stared up at the sky. Kyrilis walked over to him and placed her hand on his arm.

"You've been screaming in your sleep these past few nights," she said. "Are you okay?"

"I keep getting visions from the sword. I think they're of the previous owner suffering. They must have been linked the entire time it was in the altar," he answered, looking into her eyes. His heart started racing. Feeling a tad uneasy at his heightened emotions toward Kyrilis, he turned to look at the sky again.

"I will stay with you tonight, to help should you need it," she offered. When he looked back at her, she could see the uneasiness in his eyes. "I am not suggesting we do any harm to your marriage, young Laurence. I simply wish to be there for you in your time of need."

He nodded and pulled her into a hug in thanks.

∴ ∴ ∴

VAELYS SLIPPED out of her tent that night and kept to the shadows. She snuck through the camp, her mind on a singular task. After dodging guards and traversing the maze of tents, she reached her target. She listened at the side of the tent for a time, waiting on its occupants to settle in. After a few minutes, once all had grown quiet, she snuck to the front of the tent and slipped inside.

Wil and Saerasha sat cross-legged in the center, eyes closed and meditating. The satchel she sought lay on the ground on the other side of them.

Carefully and quietly, Vaelys moved through the tent and

retrieved Saerasha's satchel. She opened the flap to ensure its contents remained and then left just as quietly as she'd entered.

Once she cleared the tents, Vaelys stood upright and moved confidently down the road. As she passed the halfway point of the bridge, she focused her mind on her body. Magical energies seeped into her flesh, drawn from one of the crystals buried deep within her chest.

The woman who stepped off the end of the bridge was human, and no longer Afyr. She stopped for a moment and pulled her amber hair back behind her head, tying it into place with a small silk ribbon.

Still hiding her true appearance, Tristiana adjusted the satchel on her shoulder, turned south, and started her walk to Dagoh Bay.

∴ ∴ ∴

SAERASHA SMILED at Wil as they broke out of their meditation, just before noticing that her satchel was missing. Her eyes went wide with surprise, startling him.

"The satchel is gone," said Saerasha.

"The one with the soul stones in it?" asked Wil.

She got to her feet and looked around the tent, making sure she hadn't misplaced it.

"We have to tell Laurence," she said.

Saerasha ran out of the tent as fast as she could, followed closely by Wil. The camp had not yet sprung to life with the chaos of morning preparations, making it easy for them to cross in a hurry.

Kyrilis sat by Laurence's side, stroking his hair while he slept. She turned to look toward the entrance when Saerasha and Wil barged in, intent on urging them to keep quiet. The urgency written across their faces changed her mind.

"What's wrong?" asked Kyrilis.

"The soul stones are gone," said Wil.

"The entire satchel," confirmed Saerasha.

Kyrilis turned back to Laurence and shook his shoulder gently to wake him.

"Laurence... the satchel of soul stones is missing, and I'm pretty sure I know who took it," she said.

"What?" he asked, blinking sleep from his eyes.

"Vaelys stole the satchel of soul stones," said Kyrilis as she stood.

"How do we know it was her?" asked Saerasha.

"Because she's Sylk," answered Kyrilis.

"Should we go after her?" asked Wil.

"Yes, we-" said Laurence as he pushed himself off the cot.

"No. We can't," said Kyrilis.

"Why not?" asked Saerasha.

"She's Sylk. Do you not know who Sylk is?" Kyrilis asked. Looking around, she could tell none of them did. "She's the founder and leader of the Hands of Death, the assassin's guild."

"What?" gasped Laurence. "Mordechai said we should value her being along with us, but-"

"When I was traveling across Aegir with Gaerin and Lyla, we found her shipwrecked on the shore. We didn't realize who she was until several days later. However, her prowess in combat saved our asses twice. Had she wanted any of us dead, she could have done it at any time. Hell, she could've killed all of us at once.

"She also helped you free us at Thu'Brin, almost single-handedly defeated Drakahl's men at the Inok camp, and saved our asses against that hydra in Vuhl. I don't like the idea of traveling with an assassin any more than the rest of you, and I certainly don't like what she's done, but... I'm just thankful she took none of our lives," said Kyrilis.

"Shouldn't we check the rest of the camp before we decide she killed none of us? Besides, she took the stones, so she's clearly helping Dra-" started Wil.

"Nightweaver," Laurence interjected. "She killed Drakahl's men, yet she stole the stones. I'd bet anything she's taking them to Nightweaver. Either she doesn't know they're working together, or she considered those men expendable."

"That or Drakahl and Nightweaver aren't actually working together," said Wil.

Laurence felt a sinking sensation at the thought of never freeing the souls from the stones. While he was happy to have kept Gaerin and Lyla's apart from the rest, every part of him wanted to rush out and hunt down Sylk. He knew he wasn't capable of defeating someone with her skills, so he resorted to pacing instead.

"We'll talk to Mordechai when the camp is ready to move. Maybe he can track her down," suggested Kyrilis.

"We don't have time for that right now. If she's gone, she could be anywhere," groaned Laurence.

"They probably already know we're coming. If we leave to chase her now, they'll just replace the men they've lost," said Kyrilis.

Laurence stormed out of the tent. He hated the position he found himself in. Every part of him wanted to go get the satchel, but every part of his strategic mind told him to stay focused on his mission.

As the sun crested the horizon, tent flaps flung open across the camp. Laurence immediately strode toward Mordechai, leaving his friends behind in the crowd. "Why didn't you tell me she was an assassin?" Laurence blurted as he barged into Mordechai's tent.

"Good morning," said Mordechai.

"She's taken off with the soul stones," said Laurence angrily.

"No she hasn't. Everything is fine," said Mordechai.

"Saerasha said the satchel was missing," said Laurence.

"I assumed she would try something like that. When we camped in Skainhold the other night, I created a teleportation focus. When Saerasha and Wil entered meditation, I grabbed the satchel and took it to Fel'Vizsiour. I was back before anyone knew I was gone. Most importantly, I was back before *Sylk* knew I was gone."

"You what?" gasped Laurence. "Then what did she steal? What was Saerasha carrying on our walk here?"

"Lapis lazuli, of course. Just not the *same* lapis lazuli."

"You just keep a pile of those sitting around?"

"The school has a vast store of many reagents," answered Mordechai.

Laurence looked back at him in both confusion and frustration. Mordechai could tell he wanted to say more.

"Yes, I knew who she was. However, I also knew that she had no interest in anyone in our group. If she did, we'd have died before we figured out her identity. By playing along with her ruse, we avoided a massacre. As powerful as you think I am, I'm not confident that even *I* could handle her once she unleashed her true abilities. Trust me, you haven't seen what she's capable of."

"So... we played along to take advantage of her capabilities," sighed Laurence.

"For as long as she was willing to travel with us, yes."

"I'll tell the others to stop worrying," said Laurence.

Laurence watched from atop the hill as the three separate camps packed up to leave. The process took far too long for his liking. Saerasha, Wil and Kyrilis joined him for a time and brought him dawnfry. They discussed the situation with Sylk, the missing soul stones, and the plans for their journey.

"Why Hoalfast, anyway?" asked Wil.

"According to my aunt and uncle, Hoalfast is a town that prefers to stay out of politics. Hopefully that's still the case, and we can hole up there in safety and give the others a few more days to join us," said Laurence. After a moment he added, "it's also where my father met my mother."

"We'll have to establish a serious guard rotation to keep us all safe," said Kyrilis.

"I think an extra few days might also help me finish bonding with Rainbow Cutter," said Laurence.

"Those nightmares are really taking a toll on you," said Kyrilis.

"Maybe we can spar while we're there... go over those tricks you've been trying to tell me about," said Laurence.

"Absolutely," said Kyrilis with a smile.

"Looks like they're moving out," said Wil, pointing down the hill.

"Right... let's get this over with," said Laurence.

The four of them descended the hill and moved to the front of the formation with Mordechai. With a signal to the small army behind them, they set out across Daegon Bridge.

After crossing, Laurence steered them off the Daegon Way across the plains, heading northeast.

"Why do we cross the plains? Why not stick to the road?" asked Izabel.

"Hoalfast is on a cliff overlooking the Ayrduhn Forest to the east," explained Mordechai. "It's up a mountain road, barely wide enough for carriages and wagons to pass each other. Few travel to Hoalfast without specific purpose, which makes it perfect for our needs.

"However, we have to cross the Einfrid Way to get there, and that means travelers, or armed forces. Since the Einfrid stretches from Dagoh Bay all the way to Drakahl's home in Kulgan Palace, it's a heavily traveled road.

"Since our other armies haven't arrived yet, we don't necessarily want to cause alarm or find ourselves in an unwanted battle. So, we're cutting through the plains for now. We'll wind through the western half of the Ayrduhn and camp early. Just before morning we'll cross the Einfrid and start our ascent of Mount Litha."

"And we'll be safe from attack in Hoalfast?" asked Izabel.

"The people of Hoalfast stay out of politics and make no open effort to support their King or any nobles. Furthermore, there's only one safe way to reach the town. The northern edge of the village is sheer cliffs and Mount Litha. The eastern edge is also bordered by Mount Litha, and the rest of the Tagha Mountains. The southern edge is sheer cliffs descending into Ayrduhn Forest.

"So, yes, we should be safe in Hoalfast. We'll have guards posted outside of town along the mountain pass the entire time we're there," he explained.

"Does it even have room for us?" she asked.

"There's an abandoned keep there, which the locals use for excess food storage. They don't have a constable, lord or leader of any kind; just a few small cliff-side farms, a tavern and general store, and a smattering of houses," he said.

"If it's so secure, why was the keep abandoned?" she asked.

"Looking to move in?" he asked with a smirk.

She scoffed at his question in response.

"The keep was built long ago, before our recorded history. Some historians speculate the land was divided into warring kingdoms, and the noble who laid claim to the Tagha and its resources built a keep there to protect his claim. Of course, there's no way to be sure. All I'm certain of is that the residents of Hoalfast are kind and value equality and fairness, not rule or power. So, they use the keep for storage and nothing more, out of fairness to each other."

"That's... rare," she remarked.

"Indeed," said Mordechai.

"We need more of that in this world," said Kyrilis.

The mixed forces of the Inok, Tryn, Deepfolk and Laurence's companions continued their journey following Laurence and Mordechai's plans for two days. They used no tents or campfires when they camped and crossed the Einfrid just before dawn on the second day.

Thanks for their careful planning, they encountered no travelers or soldiers in their travels.

When they arrived in Hoalfast, just before the evening meal, Mordechai bid their forces to stop just outside of town while he and Laurence entered to explain their arrival. The locals were nervous, but accepted their presence and agreed to their plan of utilizing the keep.

After a few hours of organization, guards stood at their posts and the rest of the forces took a much-needed rest.

∴ ∴ ∴

LAURENCE DID not sleep well during their first night in Hoalfast. He woke with his head in Kyrilis's lap and his body drenched in sweat. He tried to tell her thanks, but no words escaped his lips. She giggled at his attempt to speak.

"Don't bother trying. You were screaming in your sleep again, so Mordechai silenced you to allow the others to rest. It should wear off when the sun rises," she explained.

He sighed and sat up, spinning to face her.

"Fret not. You just need to form a bond with the sword which should identify you as its new owner and break the bond it feels with its original owner. Let's go outside and spar for a bit. I'll borrow Izabel's new sword so you don't destroy my non-enchanted blades."

He nodded in agreement, got to his feet and made his way outside. She joined him a short time later, and they sparred until the sun came up.

When Mordechai entered the small courtyard, Laurence and Kyrilis put away their weapons and walked over.

"Thanks for your assistance last night. I don't want to be a burden on those that are helping us," said Laurence.

"We need you to use that blade as much as possible over the next few days. Spar with it, meditate while holding it, anything you can think of," said Mordechai.

"Well, now that you mention it... I did have an idea."

"What would that be?"

"You said that Sylk had gems implanted next to her bones that offered enchantment. Can you and Saerasha put Rainbow Cutter's crystal inside me? Maybe in my right arm?"

"That's... an intriguing idea."

"If it was there, I'd still be able to use it, but I'd also never lose the crystal, couldn't be disarmed, and couldn't have it stolen from me. Plus, it might force the bond to take hold faster?"

"Let's get Saerasha and find a secluded place to do it. I like this idea," said Mordechai.

"Kyrilis, can you spar with Izabel and Agnar? I'm sure they'd value your training as well," said Laurence.

Mordechai, Laurence and Saerasha walked into The Bloated Goat an hour later.

"May I help you?" asked a woman behind the bar.

"We need a room for one hour; one where we will not be disturbed," said Mordechai.

"Just one hour, eh?" said the woman, winking.

"We need to perform a medical procedure, my lady," said Saerasha.

"Call it whatever you like. We only have two rooms and we charge six bits for either of them," she explained.

"Fine," said Mordechai, handing her a silver.

"That's far too much, my lord."

"The rest is to ensure no one disturbs us, no matter what you hear."

"Very well," she said.

She pocketed the coin and led them upstairs. Their room was at the back corner of the inn, overlooking the Ayrduhn Forest below. Mordechai nodded and accepted the key she offered him, then locked the door as the three of them entered.

"For this to work, I must cut your arm open down to the bone," began Saerasha. "I'll also need to dig into your bone and use my magic to cause it to grow around the crystal. If I do not, your body may push it out over time; rejecting it, as it might a splinter. Once that is complete, I can heal you and the task will be complete."

"I will cause your right arm to experience time more slowly, which will allow her to work without too much loss of blood. It may also reduce the pain that you feel during the operation. However, once the spell wears off, all the pain will hit you all at once. More importantly, we cannot touch Rainbow Cutter's crystal, so you must be the one to place it when she is ready. That means you must remain awake for the entire process," said Mordechai.

"Very well," said Laurence. He unlaced his armor and removed all but his pants, and carefully placed the pieces to the side of the room.

Saerasha bid him to sit on the bed, his back against the headboard. She pulled a chair across the room and sat beside him.

"Where do you want the crystal placed?" she asked.

"Right here," he answered, touching his upper right arm where the shoulder muscles joined with his bicep and tricep.

Mordechai touched Laurence's forearm, sending a wave of Time energy into it. He nodded to Saerasha to indicate she could proceed.

Saerasha pressed her dagger against Laurence's skin, grasping it with both hands. She pressed as hard as she could and dragged the blade through his flesh. The blade hitched slightly as it contacted his bone, the extra resistance sending small vibrations through the steel.

Laurence couldn't feel her blade pass through the meat of his arm. It was an eerie sensation, seeing the damage she was doing but feeling none of it.

She placed her dagger on the table next to the bed and pried his muscles apart with the fingers of both hands, seeking the bone underneath. Once she revealed it, she picked the dagger back up and placed it point-first against the bone.

Saerasha held the dagger in place with her left hand, and pounded against the pommel with her right, slowly chipping the bone with each impact. Each hit bumped Laurence sideways, forcing him to lean toward her and offer greater resistance.

Satisfied with the damage to his bone, she set the dagger aside again and nodded to Laurence.

"Place the crystal now and hold it in place," she said.

He did as she asked, holding the crystal against the gouge in his bone with one finger.

Saerasha focused her healing energies on the bone, causing the chips and shards she'd created to grow over the crystal, forming a knot of bone where it had once been flat. When the formation grew close to Laurence's finger, she pulled his hand out of the way and continued her focus on healing.

After a few moments, his arm was fully healed, and their task was complete.

"It is done," said Saerasha.

"Are you ready for this?" asked Mordechai.

"No, but do it anyway," said Laurence.

As Mordechai waved his hand, the Time magics holding Laurence's right arm in stasis receded. The pain hit him all at once and his vision went dark.

Laurence woke up hours later with Kyrilis sitting beside him in bed waiting patiently.

∴ ∴ ∴

LAURENCE SPENT the rest of the day sparring with Kyrilis, Izabel and Agnar; each taking turns using his old sword. Whenever he took a break to cool down and catch his breath, he meditated with Rainbow Cutter sitting across his lap.

Each meditation brought fleeting visions of a man trapped in stone, screaming in pain and crying out for release. However, the visions grew fainter the more he repeated the cycle, so he pushed himself to the brink of exhaustion to force the bond to complete.

Whenever Laurence sparred a small audience gathered. A mixture of onlookers from their forces and the citizens of Hoalfast looked on as his blade cut through the air, leaving trails of multi-colored energy in its wake. As the day grew longer and his bond with the sword grew stronger, the power of the blade glowed brighter and the magical trails of energy became more vibrant.

By the end of the day, he could barely lift his right arm. His muscles refused to cooperate any longer, forcing him to conclude the day's training.

"You've improved already," said Kyrilis.

"Your training is superb," said Laurence.

"You didn't need much, to be fair. Gaerin taught you well. However, the weaknesses I saw in your form earlier in our travels are almost gone. You take to swordplay like no one I've ever seen," she said.

He released his grip on Rainbow Cutter and allowed it to return into his arm.

She started walking toward the tavern, then stopped for a second and looked back at him. "Are you coming?"

"Oh! Yeah, sorry. I was just going over all I've learned today," he said. As he started walking, she joined him at his side and he continued, "I'm pretty sure you could still hand me my ass, if it came down to it."

"Don't count on that," she laughed. "I was the best in my village, and the best among the Afyr. When I started my service to the Legion, I was the best in my Conroi. When I was transferred to Fel'Rechaun and given Bah'Shiri, I became my own unit, and none has matched my skill since. At least, none that I've fought.

"You... you're a different matter entirely. Tolrin and Gaerin were the two best students at Fel'Rechaun when they graduated. They traveled through Arkhania, saving towns and villages, cleaning up the northern reaches and driving away monsters and ne'er-do-wells.

"Then they came here, to Pelrigoss, and dismantled a King's rule and overthrew him. You benefited from all that experience for over a decade before you went to Fel'Rechaun. You've defeated an army of Velloth, a dragon, and several of Drakahl's best men. Not to mention our trials in Vuhl.

"Many men carry a sword for their entire lives and see little combat, especially within the safe borders of a kingdom like Arkhania. They might spar and practice, but most of them never gain practical experience... let alone survive trials like you've faced. Like it or not, young Laurence, you're a hardened warrior now," she said.

She opened the door to the tavern and invited him to enter first.

"Let me buy you a drink," she said with a wink.

"I don't know... after inflating my head with talks of skill and grandeur, drinking alcohol might not be the wisest-"

"Shut up and get inside, you," she ordered playfully.

The Bloated Goat grew quiet when they entered. Peering about the crowd, they realized the tavern was completely full, and every patron was staring in their direction.

"Perhaps we should-" started Laurence.

"Take our table, me lord," yelled an old man near the bar.

The old man stood up with his wife, inviting them to sit. Whispers rang out across the room, as many of the patrons mentioned Laurence's name, or talked about his magical sword.

When they reached the old man's table, he and his wife helped them into their chairs.

"Thank you," said Laurence with a nod.

"Anything for the Hero of Pelrigoss, me lord," said the old man.

"Hero of Pelrigoss?" asked Laurence, perplexed.

"Yes! Ye came here to free the land from Drakahl's rule, didn't ya?"

"I did, but-"

"And ye've already bested two of his generals in single combat?"

"Yes. How did you-"

"Oh, word spreads, me lord, word spreads," said the man.

"Well, I thank you. I've been training all day and I could really use some relaxation before we set out. So, tonight you are *my* hero," said Laurence.

"You are simply gorgeous, my lady," said the man's wife.

"Oh, um... thank you?" said Kyrilis, blushing.

"I saw you fighting in the courtyard earlier and couldn't believe my eyes! I think you're picking up our Hero's training quite well," she added.

"Actually, she was training me," said Laurence.

Kyrilis smiled back at him.

"Is that so?" said the old woman.

"Yes," said Kyrilis. "I am a Griffin Guard from Arkhania, and I've been serving our Legion for over a hundred years."

"Oh, my!" gasped the woman.

"Let's leave the Hero and his companion alone for the evening, eh Grenda?" suggested the man.

"Of course, dear," agreed his wife.

After the couple walked away, Laurence and Kyrilis looked at each other and laughed.

"Is it always like that?" asked Laurence.

"Well, when you barrel through a Kingdom killing their famed generals, you're sure to leave a few tales of grandeur in your wake," she answered.

"No, I meant how they treated you," Laurence clarified.

"Yes, unfortunately. Women tend to be intimidated by me, and men tend to underestimate me. Not all of them, mind you, but it seems to happen frequently enough. Then there are those that see me fight and decide they can leverage my skills for their own gain."

"I am so sorry you have to deal with that," he said.

"I've gotten used to it. But that's also something I love about you and your family. You don't see me that way."

"As beautiful? I assure you, we do," he said with a smirk.

"That's not what I meant," she said, blushing.

"I know what you meant, I was teasing. I was raised to treat everyone as equals, no matter their station in life. Arcturus often said that any noble who didn't respect equal treatment wasn't worth my respect or adoration, and that those less fortunate deserved to be treated better than they usually are."

"Arcturus was a wise man," she said.

"Back when he served the King, nobles used to fawn over him. He hated it, and refused to cater to their whims. Eventually he lost favor with them, and they helped push him out of the King's court. He saw a lot of citizens in Vellenheim being treated poorly, simply because they were lower class. He spoke out about that often, which also contributed to his removal.

"He was just... always one of those people that didn't see the point in treating people that way. Our whole family inherited that from him; as he probably inherited the same from Gahl," he explained.

"Well, he was an amazing man. I knew of him, and we interacted a couple times at court, but we never got very close. Had I realized what kind of man he was, I probably would've been involved in your life much sooner."

"I can't imagine you meeting me when I was a child," he chuckled.

"I think it would've been-" started Kyrilis.

A waitress walked over and interrupted their conversation, carrying two tankards of ale.

"We haven't ordered anything yet," said Laurence.

"On the house, Sir Laurence," said the waitress with a wink.

She sat a tankard in front of each of them, collected the old couple's dishes and left the two of them to their drinks.

"Don't let this go to your head," said Kyrilis with a smile.

"Yeah, this whole fame thing makes me uncomfortable," he said.

"Well, that's what you're in for. It's not going to stop here. You'll be hailed as a hero almost everywhere you go for the rest of your life, so you better learn to just let it roll off your back."

"You think?"

"You killed a dragon. I'm sure the whole kingdom knows it by now," she said.

"But-"

"A! Dragon!"

"Yeah, I guess. But it's not like I did it by myself."

"That doesn't matter. Ayriel's not going to take credit for any of it. I'm sure the King heard all about Laurence and Izabel, first thing."

"Yeah, I suppose so," mused Laurence. He drank a bit of his ale and decided to change the subject. "Tell me about where you grew up?"

"You don't want to hear about that," she sighed.

"On the contrary, I want to know every little detail about you."

"I've never really talked about it," she said.

"You don't have to. I'm sorry to pry."

"No, it's alright. Nobody's ever been interested before. I... was born in a village named Kydari on a plateau halfway up Mount Feyr. My father, Tevyn, served Lord Jaidus and oversaw our village's militia. My mother, Wystari, died when I was twenty-three; still a child by elven standards. Tevyn resented raising us by himself, so he passed us off to other members of the village."

"Who is 'us'?" asked Laurence, placing his elbows on the table and leaning towards her in interest.

"I forgot you didn't know," she said, blushing. "My sister, Brytha, was born when I was six. I remember helping my mother through the process. It was a difficult birth, but they both survived. Elven women don't respond too well to the birthing process; our bodies tend to give out in ways I'd rather not discuss. That is why you don't see a million elves walking the land.

"Anyway, my father was growing distant and spending far more time with the town guard than he was with us. My sister and I grew close over the next seventeen years. Then my mother gave birth again, but... she didn't survive the process—despite my efforts—and my father abandoned us completely. Brytha died that same day to an accident across town, because I was too busy helping my mother and unable to keep an eye on her.

"Tevyn blamed me for both deaths. So, at the simple age of twenty three I was left to raise little Fryja all on my own. An impossible task, in hindsight. Things did not go as well as one would hope, so we were taken by the town council and split to different homes. I... didn't see Fryja again for decades.

"I resented my father for abandoning us, especially after watching my own mother die. So I rebelled against him, the town council; everything really. I fought against the standard training given to women in my village and started picking fights with the boys in town. Eventually, I started *winning* those fights. One of the royal guard, a man named Felerix, decided to train me in secret.

"Queen Nilanna had decreed that no women would serve in the guard, and I felt that was foolish. Toor attacked from the south regularly, humans were invading our lands to the east... it was not a good time to limit our available resources, and put our armies at risk of depletion. So, Felerix—a veteran of many battles—trained me to be the best.

"By the age of eighty I was able to defeat every militia member in our town. I eventually challenged and defeated our Wyk; our village's Defender; my own father. The village council, and Lord Jaidus, granted me his position. All of this was happening at the same time Arkhan Vaelin was amassing forces to push the Toor from our lands and unify all the people into one Kingdom, to be named Arkhania.

"I went to Vey'Thugohn to plead for Nilanna to contribute to the efforts, but she refused and had me tossed out of court. I was also removed from my position. Tevyn resumed his role as Wyk and banished me from Kydari, so I stayed in Vey'Thugohn. I met Gahl twice during my stay in the capital. He was imposing, to say the least. Rumors suggested his father was a half Toor, and his size and strength seemed to confirm them."

"You met Gahl? Why didn't you say so before?" asked Laurence.

"Would it have changed anything? We never spoke. I was in the room with him twice. Once as he convinced Queen Nilanna to reinstate the Griffin Guard, and to train him alongside elves. The second time was when he convinced her to join forces with Orluhnd Vaelin to finally create Arkhania. I'd spent years working my way back into the favor of Vey'Thugohn's nobles, and didn't have the station, or arrogance, to speak on either occasion.

"When he eventually fell in battle, it was Orluhnd who met with Nilanna requesting new Griffin Guards. He wanted them to join his service and protect the schools, as a way to help maintain unity between our people. I volunteered, and that is how I ended up serving at Fel'Rechaun. My service ended under the rule of Orluhnd III, but eventually resumed under his son, the present King.

"During my years in Vey'Thugohn, I was quite often used as a tool in the hands of nobles. I would be sent on missions only to find out later what they were really about. I grew more and more guarded during those times, and had to learn to speak little; so that I could hear and understand more of their plots and schemes. I found that the less I spoke, the more speakers forgot I was present.

"Just before I was admitted into the Griffin Guard, I was sent on a mission that ultimately put someone in danger that I never wanted to harm; my sister Fryja. She was, apparently, in love with a noble's son. He wanted to protect his family line from 'filth', so I was sent to dispatch his son's mistress. You can imagine how I felt, and probably what I did to that noble. I barely escaped being thrown in prison," she explained.

"So I'm not the only one with a tragic past," said Laurence.

"No, but I've had time to cope with mine. Yours is more recent," she said.

"Maybe we should talk about something more lighthearted. I'm sorry, I didn't mean to dredge up bad memories."

"You expected flowers and puppies, didn't you?" she asked with a smirk.

"Well... I mean, that's the life I would've *hoped* for you to have. You deserve to be treated so much better than you have been."

"Fahrul and Mordechai treat me with respect. Gaerin and Lyla showed me what family love feels like. And you... well, we've talked about how I feel about you. The course of my life is being corrected, worry not," she said.

After a few more hours of ale and conversation, Laurence stood up from the table. "I think it's time for bed," he said.

"Do you expect more visions?" she asked.

"I've had them all day, every time I meditated, but they've gotten weaker. So, maybe not... or maybe just one more time, I can't be sure."

"Then I shall join you," she said as she stood.

"That is fine. I'm sleeping here tonight. We rented a room earlier to embed the sword's crystal in my arm, so I figured I'd use that instead of bothering our army with my screams again."

She nodded in agreement and followed him to the stairs.

Once they reached his room, he locked the doors behind them. He took a few moments to remove his armor, save for his cotton pants, and climbed into bed.

She removed her outer armor and joined him, resting her head upon his chest.

Laurence fell asleep rather quickly, exhaustion and ale getting the better of him. He dreamed again of the man trapped and screaming, but unlike previous dreams, the vision wasn't accompanied with pain. He could clearly see the man was being tortured by chaotic magics, ripping him asunder and repairing him simultaneously.

Time seemed to reverse, suddenly shifting to a vision of the man standing before the obsidian altar in Vuhl. He was a tall man with pale skin and long blonde hair. He was wearing purple robes with blue runes along the hems. Rainbow Cutter was in his right hand.

"Are you sure about this?" asked Mordechai, walking up next to him.

"There's no other way. This is why we made the sword. If we don't do this, the next Agthari war will end life as we know it," said the man.

"We made a pact with them," said Mordechai.

"A pact they've broken twice already," retorted the man.

"Are we sure this is going to work?" asked Mordechai.

"Your Time magic and my Paradox magic, channeled through Rainbow Cutter in a binding ritual. Magics beyond their capacity. We agreed this was the only thing that could stop them. We can't kill them, or the other gods will retaliate. If we bind them instead, the world can continue on its present course, safe and sound."

"What of the risks?"

"We're out of options," said the man.

Laurence awoke at dawn. He could feel the sword's power coursing through him.

Kyrilis was gently snoring on his chest.

∴ ∴ ∴

WIL AND Saerasha stood at the northern edge of a crevice, looking down on the rear courtyard of a stone fortress. They'd wandered west out of Hoalfast along the mountain road the night before, talking and passing the time. Along their walk they'd discovered an old path that led to a cave heading north, hidden by brush and small trees.

After following the cave network for several hours, the stone ceiling opened up to reveal the sky, and the path led into a crevice. A few hours later, as the sun crested the horizon, they discovered the overlook and the fortress beneath.

A series of small ledges offered unsafe passage into the courtyard below, if one were daring enough to risk it. The courtyard was home to stables and food storage, nestled against the cliffs below them. The central keep of the fortress was four stories tall, but had no windows facing the rear.

"We could bring all our forces right through this mountain pass and drop down into the courtyard from here. No need to siege the walls from the outside, just drop right into their laps without warning," said Wil.

"How would we get down? For us it might not be a problem, but if the other armies arrive as expected, we could have well over three hundred troops to maneuver. Those in the courtyard would be under attack before most of the forces made it down to join them," said Saerasha.

"Well... we could have a smaller force distract them from the front gates, perhaps. Or we could bring rope and drop five or six lines into the courtyard from here, drop down in teams?"

"That's a lot of rope, Wil."

"Six ropes... around one hundred and twenty yards each should do. We can anchor them up here."

"We can't even fit six people side-by-side up here."

"Okay, so we'll bring four."

"Let's just take the information back to Laurence and Mordechai, and let them figure it out."

"Sounds like a plan," said Wil.

∴ ∴ ∴

LAURENCE EXTRACTED himself from Kyrilis's embrace and got out of bed. He mused for a moment at the oddity of seeing a sleeping elf before putting on his armor.

A cool, damp morning breeze greeted him when he walked out of the tavern. Turning east, he walked toward the keep in search of Mordechai. When he arrived in the courtyard, he found the ancient mage talking to Skifvald.

"Mordechai!" yelled Laurence as he approached.

Skifvald nodded at Mordechai and walked off just before Laurence arrived. Mordechai turned to face his friend.

"Are you bound to Rainbow Cutter yet?" asked Mordechai.

"I am. The binding brought one final vision that I think you'd find interesting," said Laurence.

"Oh?"

"You were, indeed, in Vuhl before that chamber was sealed. You and another man performed a Time and Paradox ritual of binding to seal two Agthari away from the world and prevent a war between the gods. And if I'm not mistaken, the man wielding the sword was trapped along with them," explained Laurence.

"Gods damnit," sighed Mordechai.

"Oh, it's worse. The nightmares I kept having? They were of that man trapped inside red stone, as if he'd been merged with it, while chaotic magics ripped him to pieces and reformed him in an endless loop."

"Red stone?"

"Yes."

"You mean like Zathos?"

"That's what I'm thinking," answered Laurence.

"So... if you're reading the visions correctly, then we trapped two Agthari titans inside Zathos and this man, my partner in said endeavor, was trapped alongside them."

"And we just set them all free," added Laurence, nodding.

"If they survived for this long."

"The way our luck's been going lately, I'd bet they survived. There is a price here, and we're going to have to pay it eventually," said Laurence.

"Hopefully we'll have time to prepare. If they were trapped inside Zathos for over twelve hundred years, being ripped apart by Paradox and Time magics, then perhaps they'll be too weak to act for some time. Also, if that is indeed what happened, we can't be sure what state their minds are in, or if their motivations remain intact. They could very well return to Ayrelon with no memories of a time before Zathos, or with changed hearts."

Laurence gave Mordechai a look that seemed to ask if he believed his own words.

"We don't have time for this right now," said Mordechai.

"No. We don't."

"We don't even know which Agthari were trapped, or what their powers are."

"Nope. But we should probably find out," said Laurence.

"We can't. The Grand Awakening stands between us and that answer."

"Well, can't you do your little crystal ball thing and search for Agthari?"

"Not without Agthari blood, or one of their possessions," answered Mordechai.

"A problem for another day, then," sighed Laurence.

"Let's just hope we find out what's going on before it's too late," said Mordechai.

"If you were powerful enough to create a moon-sized prison and trap two gods inside," mused Laurence, letting his words trail off.

"I should probably stop holding back, eh?"

"If Nightweaver lies in our path, I don't think we can afford for you to hold back."

"Another problem for another day," said Mordechai.

Kyrilis walked into the courtyard, heading for them. She smiled at Laurence.

"You two are getting close," smirked Mordechai.

"She's intoxicating," gasped Laurence. "But, I love Tylee, so... we're just friends."

"Very close friends," added Mordechai.

"Yes," agreed Laurence.

As Kyrilis arrived, they quieted. Laurence hugged her and led her away from Mordechai.

"We should probably train the Tryn, Inok and Deepfolk, don't you think?" suggested Laurence.

"That would be wise... if for no other reason than to get everyone on the same page," she agreed.

Gareg and Agnar gathered the Inok in front of the keep and shared tactics with them for fighting alongside Laurence, Kyrilis and other non-minotaur.

Kyrilis and Kellum grouped the Tryn women at the center of town and trained them how to use their superior agility against heavily armored foes.

Laurence and Izabel gathered the Deepfolk at the edge of town and trained them on working as a single unit, defending one another during battle and anchoring the front lines so that the Tryn and Inok could fight more effectively.

Halfway through the day, Wil and Saerasha interrupted Laurence's group, running through their ranks from the west.

"We're trying to train here," said Laurence.

"Your training is over," said Wil.

"A sizable force is ascending the mountain road," said Saerasha.

"They look to be our reinforcements. But... we also found a secret passage to the back courtyard of the first of Drakahl's fortresses while we were scouting last night. So, let's go fetch Mordechai and get our core group together to strategize," said Wil.

"Izabel, can you greet our newcomers and join us in the tavern with their numbers?" called out Laurence.

She nodded her agreement and went to task organizing the Deepfolk into a protective formation at the gates.

Laurence sent Wil and Saerasha to disperse the other trainees and gather Mordechai, Kyrilis, Gareg, Agnar, Thool, Kellum and Skifvald. As they ran off, he proceeded to the tavern alone and approached the proprietor.

"I'm sorry to do this, but my council has a rather abrupt need for a place to meet and strategize in private. Would you be opposed to closing up for a few hours?" he asked.

"Anything for you, my lord," she agreed with a nod and a smile.

A few minutes later, the companions began pouring into the establishment. Once Izabel joined them with three new arrivals in tow, they barred the doors, cleared a few of the tables out of the way and gathered their chairs in a circle at the center of the room.

"Why don't we have the leaders of each group introduce themselves one by one. Please let us know how large your forces are when you do so," suggested Laurence.

"I Thool, leader Inok. Bring forty strongest warriors," said Thool eagerly.

"I am Skifvald, Commander of the Deepfolk Clan's Royal Guard. We number fifty." She nodded at the collection of tribal leaders around her in appreciation and respect.

"I am Saerasha, Shaman of the Tryn. We number thirty."

"I am Kiffren," said a small Aegra. "I brought eighty of my people, and we are eager to destroy the evil King Drakahl."

"I am Uehm, King of the Daulga," said a very large Orc. "My entire army has come to aid in this war."

"How many?" asked Izabel.

"One hundred and ten," said Uehm.

"Holy shit!" belted Kellum.

"We take this very seriously," said Uehm.

"I am Wexen, tribal leader of the Greenfolk. However, all three human tribes sent forces under my command. I bring sixty-three for the cause."

"I'm Laurence Ravencrest and these are my companions Kyrilis the Griffin Guard, Archmagus Mordechai, King Wilwarianel of the Ekthri, Agnar and Izabel. We hail from Arkhania. The others are Gareg and Kellum, former mercenaries who have joined our cause," said Laurence, pointing to each of the companions as he mentioned their name.

"Is it true you wield the sword of legend?" asked Uehm.

Laurence clasped his right hand in front of him. Rainbow Cutter appeared instantly in his hand, shimmering and casting a glow about the dark tavern. Gasps rang out among the newcomers as he dropped the sword, and it vanished into nothingness before their eyes.

"I never would've believed it if I hadn't seen it myself," said Wexen.

"With the addition of your forces, we should have the numbers to challenge the King's army," said Mordechai.

"By my count, we now number three hundred and eighty-four," said Izabel.

"Our first order of business is organizing how we'll attack. We know that the Aegra specialize in archery and Druidic sorcery. Kellum is our master archer and will organize your forces, Kiffren. You'll stay at the rear, firing at our enemies and ready to offer healing assistance to any of our wounded," said Laurence.

Kiffren nodded his agreement.

"The Deepfolk will form the front line of any martial assault. Their armor is superior to anyone else that we have with us. They will fight alongside me and my companions at center.

"The Inok will act as cavalry, charging weak spots in enemy formations and wreaking general havoc. The Daulga will fight just behind the Deepfolk, and to both flanks. With the height of your people, Uehm, they should be able to attack over the heads of the Deepfolk easily with spears, lances or greatswords. Have those with smaller arms form up at the flanks," explained Laurence.

Uehm nodded his agreement.

"Wexen, Kyrilis will introduce you to the Tryn. You will lead them along with your forces. They received training today in stealth and subterfuge tactics. Our plan was to have them attack weakened targets, or targets of opportunity, selectively while the enemy forces focus on our main group."

"A wise decision," said Wexen.

"Mordechai and Saerasha will have ultimate control over the battlefield, as they will remain at the best vantage point during any conflict. They'll provide magical support however they can and issue any urgent commands as events unfold."

"What is our first target, and when do we set out?" asked Uehm.

"There is a fortress just north on the other side of Mount Litha. Saerasha and I found a hidden cave last night that lets out into a crevice part-way up the northern face of the mountain. It overlooks the southern courtyard, and the Keep has no rear-facing windows," said Wil.

"Wil thinks we can sneak in from the rear and drop down into the courtyard using several lengths of rope, surprising them with an internal attack while other forces distract them from the front gates with a fake siege," said Saerasha.

"How large is the regiment at this fortress?" asked Mordechai.

"No clue. The keep is four stories tall, but we have no idea if there are underground chambers. As far as the area within the walls, I could see no more than twenty or thirty men. The keep didn't look large enough to bed more than a hundred," said Wil.

"So we outnumber them three to one?" asked Laurence.

"Probably more," said Wil.

"And they're all human warriors. They aren't expecting Minotaur, Dwarves, Elves, Orc, Aegra and the Archmagus of Arkhania to attack as a unified force," said Uehm. "No offense, puny human," he said to Wexen.

"None taken?" said Wexen, confused and slightly offended.

"Here are my thoughts," said Mordechai, leaning forward with his elbows on his knees. "I'll take the Inok, half the Daulga, the Tryn and Wexen's forces through the secret passage. Saerasha will take the rest around the mountain and up the Einfrid toward the fortress.

"She and I will prepare enchanted ale to hasten the movements of the group, so we arrive at approximately the same time. Once the exterior forces are in place and the alarm has been sounded, I will enchant everyone in the crevice so that they can drop down into the courtyard safely. The forces inside the walls can then have their way with the army," explained Mordechai.

"I will fight through the fortress toward the front gates and open it from the inside with my elite guard," said Uehm.

"I like this plan," said Izabel.

"Sounds familiar," said Kyrilis to Kellum.

"Same basic tactic, fewer tree ramps," joked Kellum.

"When do we set out?" asked Uehm, obviously eager to get started.

"Give us a few hours to enchant a couple kegs of ale for the siege forces and we'll depart. We should be ready just after dusk," said Mordechai.

"In the meantime, spread word to your forces about our plans, so they know their roles. And Uehm, you need to decide which of your forces are traveling with Saerasha, and which are traveling with Mordechai," said Laurence.

"I'll go with you too, Mordechai, since I've navigated the route before," said Wil.

With nods of agreement all around, the group split up to fulfill their roles. For Uehm, night could not come quickly enough.

∴ ∴ ∴

MORDECHAI STOOD at the edge of the crevice, staring down at the fortress. One hundred and eighty-nine members of their new army stood behind him, cramped tightly into the confined space within the crevice.

Night had fallen and torches were alight atop the walls. Several soldiers were on guard duty, some on top of the walls, others milling around the courtyard. The windows at the side of the keep flickered with torch and candle light, revealing that most of the fortress's occupants remained awake.

A man stumbled out of the rear door of the keep and down the steps, vomiting as he went.

"Arr, that be rancid, Thomas. You tryin ta make me sick?" he yelled back through the door.

"I *did* make ya sick, ya daft bastard!" came a voice from inside.

As the man stormed back through the door, slamming it behind him, Wil chuckled. He looked at Mordechai with a smile on his face.

"They don't expect an attack at all. They're just in there goofing around and playing pranks on each other," said Wil.

"Pelrigoss hasn't been attacked in nearly two decades. And when it was, Laurence's father and his group skirted around these fortresses and went straight to Kulgan Palace. They've no reason to be on edge. Drakahl probably sent orders to shore up their defenses, and I'd bet that's the only reason anyone is on guard duty at all," said Mordechai.

"I expected Drakahl's men to behave more... dutifully? I mean, serving a man like that, you'd expect them to be terrified of upsetting him."

"Those that have met him, sure. I doubt he's spent time at this keep, and most of these men have only heard stories about him. Any stories they've heard are probably so unbelievable that they just shrug them off."

"Fools," said Wil.

"Well, *you* know better because you know Laurence. But imagine growing up in Caierthor, where your economy was prospering and everyone lived in relative peace."

"So the terrible things they've heard–"

"Are just propaganda; stories told to defame their benevolent leader," interrupted Mordechai.

"I almost feel bad we're about to slaughter them."

"Don't," said Uehm from behind. "Given the chance, they'd run through our tribes without a second thought. We're all beneath them, as far as they're concerned; barely more than animals."

Mordechai raised his hand to silence them.

Laurence's forces were arriving at the gates.

∴ ∴ ∴

LAURENCE MARCHED up to the fortress, one hundred and ninety-three soldiers from all across Pelrigoss in his wake. He stopped thirty yards from the gate, Kyrilis and Saerasha at his sides.

The rest of Laurence's core group of companions formed up just behind them. Skifvald formed her dwarven guard in a line behind the companions. The fifty-five Daulga took positions behind the dwarves and to their flanks. The Aegra hid behind the Daulga to keep out of sight.

Several guards atop the wall scurried into position and called for their commander. After a few minutes, a man in plate armor with a red-plumed helmet stepped onto the wall above the gate and looked down at the force below him.

"What's the meaning of this?" yelled the commander.

"We are but weary travelers, seeking lodging!" yelled Laurence in jest. His confidence had never been so high.

"The fuck you are!" countered the commander.

"Let us in and we promise to play nice!" said Laurence.

"You must be joking. Do you know who's fortress this is?"

"Drakahl, right? Is he here? Please tell me he's here. Bring him out."

"You wish to challenge our King? With what, that pathetic militia you've got with you? A bunch of orcs and women? Be gone with you!"

"He didn't just say what I think he said, did he?" whispered Izabel.

"He's mine, Laur," whispered Kyrilis angrily.

"I'd pit my women against any of your men. In fact, send several... they'll need the help!"

∴ ∴ ∴

THE COURTYARD below swarmed with warriors, rushing toward the gates and getting into formation.

Mordechai turned to the forces behind him and said, "Everyone touch the person next to you, just as I instructed."

Once the men in back had complied, they sent the call forward that all were touching.

When word reached Mordechai, he nodded and then put both of his hands on Wil.

A burst of energy descended from the sky, clearly visible to those standing near Mordechai. The power surged through his body, along his arms and began coursing through each person in the crevice one by one. He felt with his mind, waiting for the power to indicate it had touched one hundred and ninety souls.

He imagined the power shifting to each of their legs, reinforcing and silencing them; providing the forces unnatural resistance to falling from great heights. The power complied.

Mordechai removed his hands from Wil and said, "Let's go."

Mordechai turned and jumped off the ledge, landing safely in the courtyard below.

Wil and Uehm followed immediately after, then signaled to the rest of their forces to follow.

In short order, nearly two hundred souls leapt from the ledge, two at a time in a constant stream, moving aside as they reached the bottom to make room for the next pair.

Wil imagined the sight as a waterfall of living flesh and bone, nearly causing him to laugh.

∴ ∴ ∴

"I CAN get you up there, Kyr," said Saerasha quietly.

"Please do," said Kyrilis eagerly.

Saerasha took a step back and reached over toward Kyrilis. She placed her hand on the Griffin Guard's shoulder and pushed a stream of power into her, strengthening her legs.

"Jump," said Saerasha with a smirk.

"Be careful," said Laurence.

Kyrilis looked at him sternly.

"I meant... have fun," he said with a smirk.

Kyrilis ran forward in a flash and jumped just before she reached the wall. Before the commander knew what had happened, she was standing beside him.

"Draw your sword. I don't wish to slaughter an unarmed man," she growled.

Frantically, the commander drew his sword and took a step back.

Six guards rushed across the wall to defend their captain, three from each side of the gate.

"Five each!" yelled Kellum to his archers.

"Loose!" yelled Laurence at the same time.

Thirty Aegra stepped out from behind their Daulga protectors and fired their arrows at the running guards. Each guard fell to the ground inside the courtyard, three to five arrows protruding from them.

When the guards inside the courtyard turned to see their fallen comrades, several of them caught the horrific sight of countless minotaur and orcs charging them from behind.

A horn sounded as the men inside the walls were beset by the other half of Laurence's forces.

Kyrilis snapped into action.

She thrust her sword at the commander's face.

He moved his sword as quickly as he could to intercept her thrust, barely managing to parry her blade to the outside. Instantly regretting his comments, he took a step back.

She brought her off-hand dagger racing in toward his sword arm as he returned his blade to the space between them, burying it deep into his right wrist.

He shrieked and dropped his weapon, pain coursing through his arm, as his forces in the courtyard below were trampled by minotaur and run-through by horns and orcish blades.

Kyrilis twisted the dagger, wedging its blade between the bones in his forearm. She shifted her grip and used the leverage offered by her dagger to pull the man closer. She could see the fear and pain in his eyes clearly as their faces drew near.

"What was that you said about women? I can't quite remember," she said angrily.

"I-"

She cut his response short; sliding her sword slowly through his chin and the roof of his mouth, deep into the soft brain beyond.

As the commander dropped to the floor, the gates below Kyrilis opened; Uehm and his men having achieved their goal.

Their overwhelming forces easily cleared the rest of the keep.

∴ ∴ ∴

LAURENCE STOOD atop the gates with Kyrilis and Mordechai, watching as Thool and the Inok impaled Drakahl's dead soldiers along the road outside the fortress.

"Are we okay with this?" asked Kyrilis.

"Not particularly, but I understand why they're doing it. After seeing what Drakahl's men did to the Inok and Tryn... I say let them have their revenge. I may not like or agree with it, but it's not my place to stop them from easing their pain," said Laurence.

"The Inok are a proud people and follow the eye-for-an-eye philosophy. Trying to stop them would lose you their trust. That is why the other tribes are inside ignoring their actions," said Mordechai.

"It sends a powerful message, I suppose," admitted Kyrilis. "But I can't watch any more of this."

The three of them descended the stairs and entered the keep. Cheering erupted from the crowd inside as they stepped through the door. As the cheering rose in volume, several voices could be heard chanting Kyrilis's name.

Seeing the displeasure on her face from being singled out, Laurence raised his hands to signal them to stop.

"I appreciate your motivation and our high morale, but I encourage you to keep the gravity of our undertaking in mind. While we may have easily succeeded today, our fortune may turn. Rest up, we head north at dawn," he said after they quieted.

Laurence went up the stairs, seeking the highest floor of the keep. Upon finding the commander's bedchamber, he dropped into the bed with the intent of sleeping.

Kyrilis walked in and shut the door, then turned to him.

"Thank you for letting me take care of that foul man," she said.

"Oh, of course," said Laurence.

"I didn't want to take him out to prove anything to him or his men... it was for the benefit of our forces. I wanted them to see that none of us should be overlooked, especially us women."

"I completely understand."

"After all, most of Skifvald's guards are women."

"They are?" asked Laurence, surprised.

"They are," she said, taking a seat on the bed. "Are the visions over now?"

"Yes," he answered.

"I guess I'll go meditate on the wall, then. I'm glad you're better," she said, her face revealing her disappointment.

Laurence could feel a yearning for her contact growing within him. He'd grown accustomed to their nights together and didn't want them to end. They only had a few nights remaining before he'd be back in Tylee's loving arms and suddenly realized he'd never spend another night with Kyrilis once that happened.

"I... I don't mind if you stay," he said sheepishly.

"I want to, more than I should."

He sat up on the bed and slid over next to her, placing his arm around her back.

"I'm as torn by this as you are. I... I can't explain why I feel the way I do. I didn't know this kind of love was possible. It's... different with you than it is with Tylee. I've known her my whole life, and I couldn't imagine being without her. But when I'm with you... I feel alive. I feel a peace I didn't know I was lacking," he said.

"I saw the wonder and lust in your eyes the night we first met in Salvation Shire. You tried to hide it from Tylee, and even yourself. She could see it, though. She knew. And I thought you'd be just another man trying to bed me; that I'd hate your touch as we flew to Fel'Rechaun that next morning, still smelling of your wife.

"But that wasn't the case. I... kept pulling you closer. Every part of me wanted you closer," she said.

"I remember you checking my arms constantly, making sure I held you tight. I thought it was just so I wouldn't fall," he laughed.

"That was part of it, yes. The way you handled yourself that night, the stories Mordechai shared of your bravery and passion, the way Tylee hung on your every word like you were the only important person in the entire world... and then feeling your embrace that morning...

"I just. I couldn't let myself feel that way. So, I pushed it down. And then I met your aunt and uncle, and the wall within me crumbled. I can't get that wall back into place, to block such emotions. I-"

"You know I'm going home to Tylee and it's... oh my gods, I'm so sorry," he said as realization struck.

He wiped a tear from her cheek and kissed the spot where it had been. She turned toward him, sadness in her eyes. Seeing her in such a state made every part of him want to take that sadness away.

"I love you, Kyrilis. I'm never going to stop loving you, not even when I return home to Tylee. But I've made a commitment to her, and I am a man of my word. This... is breaking my heart more than you can possibly know."

"What should we do?" she asked, her voice barely above a whisper; her breath lighting upon his face, drawing him closer.

Laurence thought back to their embrace at the Tryn camp, when she comforted him through Gaerin and Lyla's deaths. There had been a moment when their faces nearly met, and they'd almost kissed. It had been an accident, but he knew deep inside that he'd wanted that kiss to happen. He'd seen in her eyes that she'd wanted it as well.

He lifted her chin with one finger and kissed her.

"I can't change what will happen when this is all over," he said, his forehead pressed against hers. "I just know that I want every second with you that I can get until that time comes."

"As do I," she admitted.

Laurence kissed her again, then stood and removed all but his cotton pants. When she stood to do the same, he helped her remove her armor, piece by piece.

He laid back down on the bed and invited her to join him. She laid her head and arm on his chest and wrapped her legs around his. He could feel her tears on his skin as he gently stroked her hair.

After what seemed like hours, they fell asleep in each other's arms one last time.

∴ ∴ ∴

THE ARMY walked north the next morning, following the Einfrid toward Kulgan Palace. Several trade caravans encountered them, heading south along the road. As each saw the army, they either fled the opposite direction or calmly pulled off the road to make room.

They passed half a dozen roads leading toward small cities and villages, and at each an Inok placed the severed head of a soldier as a sign to the residents to stay out of their way.

Halfway through the day, the road turned gently to the west around a small forest. As the army rounded the bend in the road, arrows cut through the air striking several of them in the arms and legs, and a few in the torso.

"To arms!" called out Izabel.

Another volley of arrows cut through the air toward them. Mordechai raised his right hand and a pulse of energy burst through the air, incinerating the arrows; rendering them into ash in mid-flight.

The Inok and Daulga rushed toward the trees from the center of their formation.

Soldiers ran out of the trees toward the front of the formation, heading straight for Laurence and Mordechai.

Laurence summoned Rainbow Cutter and ran toward them, willing his magical blade to grant him speed. He could feel the power course through him, fulfilling his desire.

Laurence beheaded one of the soldiers as he arrived, parried a reckless attack from another, and stabbed a third through the heart; piercing through the man's brigandine as if he were naked.

"Wait," said Mordechai, putting his hand out to stop the rest of Laurence's friends from advancing.

"But he's-" started Kyrilis.

"He's one with the blade, and he's learning to use it."

"There's too many of-" she began again.

"Do you want him to defeat Drakahl, or not?"

As the rear of the army handled the rest of the ambushers hiding in the trees, twenty soldiers surrounded Laurence.

Kyrilis twitched, barely able to control herself and follow Mordechai's request.

Laurence parried one attack after another, each coming from different directions.

Mordechai watched with his magical senses as power surged within the core of Laurence's being, empowering the blade as it empowered him.

There is something very special about this boy.

A soldier slashed downward at Laurence's head. Laurence spun and deflected the blow, cutting through the man's sword with ease, and continuing his swing through the neck of the man next to him.

Another soldier thrust his blade to Laurence's back. Laurence spun back around, drove the man's sword downward and slid Rainbow Cutter along the blade, through its quillon, and the man's fingers behind them.

Laurence turned again and cleaved another soldier's head in two, ripped his sword free and cut through another man's sword and neck in one swipe.

The soldiers started to back away.

"Now," said Mordechai.

Laurence continued to kill one opponent after another while his friends rushed in to help him. After the battle was over, he released the blade and allowed it to return to the crystal in his arm.

Laurence's army sprang to life, cheering their leader's capabilities.

He ignored them and walked back to Mordechai.

"What was that about?" demanded Laurence.

"I had to know."

"Had to know what?" asked Laurence, anger still lacing his words.

"You are somehow empowering that blade to be stronger and sharper. You have a power within you, and I don't know what it is. But I had to be sure it was there."

"Why?" asked Laurence, slightly confused.

"Laurence, you just killed twelve men by yourself while surrounded!" shouted Izabel.

"I... what?"

"She's right," said Kyrilis. "I can hardly believe what I just saw."

"That sword isn't supposed to be able to do that," said Saerasha. "The legends said it was only extraordinary in that it channeled the power of its wielder. It's a sword designed for those who wield magic... and you don't."

"If it lets me do what I just did, I don't care how it works," said Laurence.

"If I had any doubts about your chances versus Drakahl, they're all gone now," said Wil.

"Your skill combined with a sword like that? That was amazing," said Izabel.

"I only wanted this weapon to protect my soul from Drakahl's sword," said Laurence. "I wasn't seeking power."

"Let's move out!" yelled Mordechai, urging Laurence to resume walking while they talked.

As their forces continued along the Einfrid, Laurence thought about the sword and its previous owner. He tried to focus on the man he'd seen in the vision with Mordechai.

Why was he wielding the sword, and not Mordechai?

'Blood,' whispered a voice in his mind.

"What?" said Laurence aloud.

"Nobody was talking, Laur," said Izabel.

Laurence thought about the sword again and focused on the man once more.

Do we share blood?

'Yes,' answered the same voice in a whisper.

"So... the sword can speak," said Laurence, frankly.

"What?" asked Mordechai.

"Yep. Its original owner? Somehow I'm related to him. I asked in my thoughts, and a voice answered yes."

"I wonder if Gahl could have wielded it? Or Tolrin?" asked

Kyrilis.

Laurence thought the questions to the sword.

'No,' it answered.

"It says no," he repeated for the group.

"Then whatever allows you to wield the sword came from your maternal bloodline, and we know nothing of your mother," said Mordechai.

"Just her name," added Laurence.

"What was her name?" asked Kyrilis.

"Myrindia," he answered.

"Remind me when all this is over and I'll investigate her; see what I can find out," said Mordechai.

"What's your sword saying now?" asked Izabel.

"It only talks when I think at it, and I don't think it can give more than a one-word answer," said Laurence.

"What about now?" she asked, teasingly.

Kyrilis giggled at their banter.

"Every time I'm quiet you're going to think I'm having a conversation with my sword, aren't you?"

"Yep!" answered Izabel playfully.

Laurence sighed.

∴ ∴ ∴

THEY REACHED another fortress just before dusk, its gates ajar and its walls devoid of torchlight. After searching the fortress for nearly an hour, they came to the conclusion that its troops had been called elsewhere.

"I wonder if these were the forces that ambushed us earlier today," said Laurence.

"I'm sure they were, which means Drakahl absolutely knows we're almost at his palace," said Mordechai.

"Think you and Saerasha could enchant us all to skip sleeping tonight and keep marching?" asked Laurence.

"My mind was going to the same place," answered Mordechai. "Saerasha, you reinforce everyone's sustenance and I'll handle their exhaustion?"

"I can't do that to nearly four hundred people all at once!" she gasped.

"How about this," said Mordechai, thinking. "You pull the spell into your core, I'll have everyone touch the way I did in the crevice, and I'll push your spell into them all, and amplify it with my own magic."

"Will that work?" she asked.

"We're about to find out," said Mordechai. "Everyone gather around! Get close to one another and touch the person next to you! I need you all connected so that we can enchant you all at once! We're going to keep marching!"

Several of them looked around confused. Those that had been with Mordechai in the secret pass explained what he was about to do and eagerly complied. Once they were all touching, Mordechai signaled for Saerasha to generate her spell. He then placed one hand on her, and another on Laurence.

Saerasha summoned the powers within her and focused on forming a spell that would sate a person's thirst, hunger and need for rest. She held the power within her chest, ready to unleash it.

Mordechai used his magical senses and could see the ball of energy form within her. He focused his mind on the magical weave, coursing and writhing like a living net high above them. He pulled with all his might, ripping power from the sky in a volume he'd never accessed before.

He focused his mind on Saerasha's suspended spell as the power of the weave crashed into him. The energies pouring out of the sky appeared like white lightning; clearly visible to their entire army, and brightening the courtyard in which they stood.

Pushing with his mind, he forced the powers to race through Saerasha, pick up her spell and carry it into every member of their army. A sensation of warmth and peace washed over them as the spell took hold; taking away their need for food, water or rest.

Mordechai dropped to one knee as his spell completed, his entire body in pain from the energies he'd just channeled.

"Are you okay?" asked Laurence.

"You told me to stop holding back," he answered.

"You just enchanted almost four hundred people at once!" remarked Izabel.

"Don't remind me," he said, standing and clutching his head in both palms.

"Should I heal you?" asked Saerasha.

"Oh, no, no, no. No more magic for a bit," he answered, waving her off.

"Right. Well, we're losing valuable time. If Drakahl is withdrawing his men to prepare for an attack, it's best if we catch him off guard," said Laurence.

Laurence led his forces out of the fortress and back onto the Einfrid Way, continuing north toward Kulgan Palace.

∴ ∴ ∴

"SHE HAS arrived, as I said she would," said Nightweaver, pointing down the road.

Ahm followed her finger, peering down the street toward what seemed to be a simple human girl.

"Are you certain?" he asked.

"You question me?"

"I–"

"That is her, but do not call her by her name. She goes by Tristiana in that form."

"She doesn't look like much," said Ahm.

"Never let her hear you say that, or I'll be finding a new priest," said Nightweaver. "Now, help me aboard. We'll be departing soon."

Ahm grabbed Nightweaver's extended elbow and helped her up the gangplank to the ship's deck. They waited patiently for their new companion in silence.

When the young woman stepped aboard, Nightweaver turned to her and smiled. "Welcome, Tristiana. We've much to discuss."

"You know me?" asked Tristiana.

"I know all your forms," said Nightweaver.

Tristiana tensed, her hands slipping to the small of her back in preparation.

"There will be no need for that, dear. We are of like mind. You hide who you are, as do I. More importantly, you've brought me an offering," said Nightweaver, extending her hand.

"Have I, now?"

"It hangs from your shoulder," she said, pointing to Tristiana's satchel.

"You? You're the one who's been sending me visions?"

"Indeed."

"You better explain what's going on, and quick," demanded Tristiana.

"Let us find somewhere more private to discuss our matters," said Nightweaver, heading toward the captain's quarters. "I am...

building something, and I think you'll find that it suits you."

"I'm not looking to join anything, I just want answers," said Tristiana, following the old woman.

As Nightweaver stepped into the dark room beyond the door, she turned to face Tristiana. The room grew brighter as she drained it of shadow, and her form changed into that of a young, beautiful woman.

"We are far more alike than you think, young one, and our motivations align quite nicely. Why don't you come hear my offer before declining?" said Sorscha, inviting Tristiana to enter.

As Tristiana crossed the threshold, her hair shifted color; becoming stark white. Her skin turned black, and her body shrank to proper elven height. Sylk, the Dynar assassin, shut and barred the door, intrigued by the witch's proposition.

∴ ∴ ∴

LAURENCE'S ARMY walked through the night and into the next day. They passed two abandoned fortresses on their way to the palace, and several empty road-side villages. It was as if the whole of the northern province had withdrawn to the palace to defend Drakahl from Laurence's wrath.

It was late afternoon when the palace came into view, its gilded peaks glistening in the fading sunlight. The palace sat in the middle of a series of four walls, each encircling a higher tier than the one before it. Five towers stretched into the sky above it, one from each corner and another at the center.

The grounds around the palace contained many small buildings; housing the many servants and guards of the King and his immediate staff. In times of peace, the palace might have been a desirable location for travelers to visit; its architecture was striking, made even more so by the setting sun.

What concerned the companions, as they looked out across the valley before them, was the army stretched out along the outer walls, and the additional forces gathered on each tier's courtyards.

They backed away from the hill and rejoined the rest of their army to discuss strategy.

"They appear to have more than ten times our number," said Laurence.

"Indeed. I see at least three thousand, perhaps more," said Mordechai.

"We need to let Mordechai rest for a few hours before we attack. That should give us plenty of time to strategize," said Laurence.

"I need rest, do I?"

"Yes, because you're going to enchant the living shit out of everyone and use our forces as a distraction. Meanwhile, I'm going to find another way into that palace and kill Drakahl, once and for all."

"You're going to what, now?" asked Izabel.

"There is another way in, I'm sure of it. Arcturus and his group used it to get to Pahn all those years ago," said Laurence.

"I'm not letting you go in there by yourself," said Kyrilis.

"He's not. I'm going with him," said Wil.

"So am I," said Izabel.

"We started this with him, and we're finishing it with him," added Wil.

"I'm going too, then," said Kyrilis.

"You can't. I need you outside leading this army," said Laurence, placing a hand on her shoulder.

"Attacking that force head-on is a suicide mission," argued Kyrilis.

"Not with my enchantments, it's not. Especially with Saerasha's help," said Mordechai. "Besides, now that I'm no longer holding back... our forces have the advantage."

"What if Nightweaver is here? What advantage do you bring then?" demanded Kyrilis.

"Look, Kyr, this is something I have to do. If we stand around outside fighting the army, with Drakahl safe in his palace... we'll lose. When he fought Tolrin, he waited until my father's entire party was exhausted and at their limits, then attacked and ended them swiftly. If we don't engage him promptly, he'll do the same to our entire army."

"I'll scout ahead and find us a way through. You stay here and come up with a plan," said Wil. He walked off and slipped into the nearby trees.

"I don't feel good about this," she said, her concern for his life depriving her of tactical thought.

Laurence guided her away from the rest. Once they were alone, he said, "look, I understand how you feel. I have the same sinking feeling in my gut over the thought of leaving you outside to face that army. But you're the most experienced soldier here, and by far our best combatant. I need you to take charge of these forces and push them to their limits; drive them to victory. You're the only one that can."

Determination crossed her face as she pushed herself to focus on the task and recover the pieces of herself that she'd abandoned in recent days. He was right; she needed to be the person he'd known her to be at Fel'Rechaun.

She'd always carried herself with a calm, reserved demeanor; always watching, and waiting, for someone nearby to make a move. That discipline and control had served her well for over a century. She'd come to be known as a force to be reckoned with. She couldn't understand why she lost that part of herself when she was near him.

Is that what love does? Or is it because I know I can't have him?

"Let's do this," she said. Without another word, she turned on her heel and marched back toward the army.

RETRIBUTION

Ris'Gaula, Amaethur 4th, 113 of the 2nd Era

Final blood of Raven calls,
The Demon stands to fight.
Asunder will the kingdom be,
Torn from their peace this night.

Night's Writ, Parable 15

Wil returned later that night, anxious and eager to share what he'd discovered. He ran through the camp, searching for Laurence, bumping into random people as he passed.

"Slow down," Laurence called out.

Wil spun around and raced up to his friend.

"I'm assuming you found a way in?"

"Yes! There's a river running down from the eastern mountains. Part of it passes right through a small gap under the wall. It doesn't seem large enough for anyone to fit at first glance, but it's been there for so long that the ground underneath has eroded. We should be able to push through, one at a time."

"Let's go tell Mordechai. Are you ready to lead us there now?"

"Yes!"

Laurence and Wil walked over to Mordechai, collecting Izabel on their way.

"We have our way in. Are your plans complete?" asked Laurence.

"They are," said Mordechai.

"One last thing before we leave. Wil needs an enchanted weapon," said Laurence.

Mordechai pondered the idea for a moment and then stood and walked over to Wil.

"If I apply enough enchantments to last the night, your weapon is likely to be consumed by the magics before they fade. Is that acceptable?"

"Whatever it takes," said Wil.

"Hold out your Quel'Thoz."

Wil complied and held his elven weapon in front of him, as if putting it on display. Mordechai placed his hand on the center of the weapon's haft and closed his eyes in concentration.

Purple energies rippled down the length of the weapon. Wil could feel the wooden haft strengthen in his grasp as the powers took hold.

"No normal weapon will break it for the remainder of the night, and it may even stand up to Drakahl's sword," said Mordechai.

Wil stepped back and twirled the weapon around, testing its new weight. With a nod of thanks, he turned to Laurence and signaled that he was ready to proceed.

"Start your preparations, Mordechai. It will probably take us a few hours to reach our entrance. We'll wait for your attack before we make our way in," said Laurence.

"Good luck," said Mordechai with a nod.

∴ ∴ ∴

AS MORDECHAI marched the army down the hill toward the palace, horns sounded in the distance; calling Drakahl's forces into position. The armies in front of the outer gates and in each tier formed up and readied their weapons. Archers took their positions atop the walls, ready for the signal to attack.

When his forces reached bow range for the Aegra, Mordechai raised his right arm and called for them to halt.

The Aegra lined up behind the Deepfolk dwarves and waited patiently.

With a signal from Kellum, an equal number of Daulga stepped forward and picked up an Aegra, setting the small creatures on their shoulders to give them additional elevation.

Kellum nodded to Mordechai that all were in position.

Mordechai raised his left arm, causing a bubble of Time magic to envelop the entire army. Everything outside of the bubble seemed to stop moving instantly.

Kellum yelled, "Loose!"

Each of the eighty Aegra fired thirty-six arrows into the air, filling the sky at the edge of the bubble with arrows; suspended in mid-air on their way toward their targets. As each Aegra emptied their quiver, the Daulga holding them placed them back on the ground.

When their process was complete, two thousand, eight hundred and eighty arrows trembled in place at the edge of the bubble, blocking the army's view of the palace entirely.

"Ready?" asked Mordechai.

"Like never before," said Kellum wickedly.

As Mordechai lowered his arm, the bubble dissipated. The arrows streaked through the sky as if they'd been fired simultaneously, released from their state of suspended animation.

Mordechai called down power from the heavens, sending it directly into the gates of the walls surrounding the fourth tier, far in the distance. He clinched both hands before him, as if grasping the bars of the gate as their arrows rained down upon their enemies.

He yanked his hands toward him violently as nearly a hundred of Drakahl's men fell to the ground, and hundreds more were wounded by the shower of arrows.

The fourth gate ripped free of the stone wall and flew down the steps toward the third, crashing through dozens of soldiers in its path.

When the fourth gate slammed into the third, it erupted through the wall and continued its path, carrying the third gate along with it.

The process continued, tearing the second and first gates through their walls as well, before finally crashing to the ground outside the palace grounds.

As hundreds of Drakahl's forces lay dead, wounded or dying from their initial attack, Kyrilis led the army's charge down the hill.

Terrified, Drakahl's army scrambled to regain defensive positions and brace for their enemies' arrival.

∴ ∴ ∴

THE SOUND of immense stone walls exploding as massive iron gates crashed through them followed only seconds after the horns of war sounded. Screams of anguish and terror filled the night, echoing off the surrounding hills.

"Fuck me," gasped Izabel.

"Remind me never to piss off Mordechai," said Wil.

"Let's go," said Laurence calmly.

Without another word, he pressed his body to the ground beneath the waters and pushed his way under the wall. Wil followed quickly after. Once on the other side, the two of them pulled Izabel through, her armor and shield barely able to fit through the gap.

Safely inside the outer wall, the group ran to the northwest, heading for a small servants' door next to a series of small farms on the first tier.

∴ ∴ ∴

SHAER'THOG KICKED the door off his stable and galloped into the upper courtyard, riled by the sound of crashing gates and walls. As he reached the upper step leading down to the third tier, he stretched out his massive leathery wings and leapt into a glide.

He soared toward the invading army, fire streaming from his flaming hooves in his wake.

His eyes burst into flames as anger overwhelmed his beastly senses.

∴ ∴ ∴

SHAER'THOG CRASHED through a dozen of Wexen's men, sliding to a stop atop their corpses. The demonic steed galloped forward, barreling through the line of tribal soldiers violently.

Uehm, Gareg and Agnar, fighting together at the right flank, looked to each other and then back at the beast. They charged in unison, driven by purpose.

Shaer'Thog stopped abruptly, extended its wings and spun in a circle, beheading several human warriors and a few of Drakahl's men.

Gareg leapt into the air, his sword high above his head. Arriving at the beast just as his descent brought him to the ground, he drove his blade several inches into the creature's back.

As Gareg wrenched his greatsword free, Uehm arrived at Shaer'Thog's head and attacked with both of his war axes.

Shaer'Thog whipped its head to the side at an angle, allowing the axes to glance off its black bone armor. He stepped forward, driving his chest through the orc, crashing it to the ground several feet away.

Agnar jumped over Uehm as he arrived, bringing his Velloth blade down in a strike as he landed. The demonic steed attempted to block the blade with its bone armor just as before, but the blade broke through and cut into his head.

Shaer'Thog reared back and kicked with his front two legs, hitting Agnar in the center of his chest.

Agnar crashed to the ground as Gareg lunged with his greatsword, the blade glancing harmlessly off of the creature's wing.

Uehm rolled out of the way as Shaer'Thog charged toward Agnar.

As Agnar gasped for breath, he looked up to see a spout of flame erupt from Shaer'Thog's mouth.

The flame burst into Agnar's face violently, splashing about the area in a fiery plume.

Gareg dropped his greatsword and retrieved Agnar's black Velloth blade. As the creature finished exhaling its fire upon Agnar's corpse, Gareg brought the stone sword down onto the creature's neck with all his strength.

The blade cut deep into Shaer'Thog's flesh, nearly decapitating the beast.

Shaer'Thog flailed, trying desperately to be free of the terrible enemies that surrounded it.

Gareg pulled at the sword, trying to wrench it free as the beast flailed, whipping its head to and fro. The black blade snapped under the pressure, leaving Gareg holding nothing more than a hilt as the creature's head knocked him to the ground.

Uehm jumped onto the creature's back and grabbed the black blade, still buried in its neck, with both hands. He gripped the horse's sides tightly with his legs and pushed down as hard as he could on the blade.

As the blade broke through the cartilage between the spine in the creature's neck, it severed the beast's spinal cord.

Shaer'Thog crashed to the ground.

∴ ∴ ∴

"SHAER'THOG BROKE out of the stables and attacked them, your Majesty. He has been slain!" yelled a soldier as he entered the room.

'Shaer'Thog!' screamed Axvalla.

Drakahl stood, picked up his throne, and threw it across the room. His rage was uncontrollable. He could feel his flesh getting hot, and adrenaline coursing through his veins.

Axvalla surged its influence and power into Drakahl, intent on inspiring vengeance for the death of its once-prized steed.

"Are your men so pathetic that they cannot win when they outnumber their opponents ten to one?" yelled Drakahl. The floor cracked beneath his feet at the power of his voice.

"My lord, they have a very powerful wiz-"

"I care not for your excuses! A wizard cannot cast spells with a sword through his heart!" His last word was full of blood and spit. His anger had risen to such heights that the gnashing of his teeth as he yelled caused his gums to bleed from the force of their impact.

Flying spittle and blood, spraying from his masters mouth, sent shudders through the soldier. He found it hard to speak, or to move.

"Yes, my lord!" answered the soldier.

He fled from the chamber as quickly as he entered, terrified of both the army outside and the King that he served.

"Nightweaver will suffer for this betrayal."

'She must pay!' spat Axvalla.

∴ ∴ ∴

THE DEEPFOLK marched forward at the center of the line, their armor nearly impenetrable. The Daulga spear-men slaughtered those who dared charge them.

Kyrilis and the Tryn women fought at the left flank alongside half of Wexen's forces, pushing their enemy back and stepping over the corpses of the fallen.

Uehm and Gareg re-joined the right flank, cutting through their enemies far too easily with the rest of the Daulga.

The Inok wreaked havoc behind the enemy lines, having charged through at the start of the battle.

All seemed to go as planned as Mordechai surveyed the battlefield from his position on the hill.

Movement caught his eye atop the wall. Several robed figures stretched out in a line in both directions.

"We're up," he said to Saerasha.

Saerasha signaled the Aegra and knelt down. As she focused her energies, all eighty Aegra knelt in a line beside her and touched the ground, chanting.

A surge of energy raced across the ground, turning stone to soft mud as it passed. The walls softened as the magical energies arrived, causing the casters to sink to their knees.

The vegetation in the surrounding area died as the Aegra completed their spells. A second wave of energy burst forth, converting soft mud to stone in its wake.

As the casters tried desperately to free themselves, the wall re-solidified, trapping their legs and many of their hands.

Mordechai pushed a wave of energy at the top of the wall. As it collided with the casters, the energies attempted to push them backwards with tremendous force. Trapped by the stone, the lower half of their bodies stayed in place.

The army inside the first tier shrieked in horror as the torsos of their mages fell to the ground, ruptured by the power of Mordechai's blast.

∴ ∴ ∴

THE GROUP reached a small door at the side of the palace following a series of paths and doors used by servants and grounds keepers. Laurence slowly pulled the door open and crept inside. Several servants screamed in terror and fled as they entered the storage room. Wil grabbed a woman as she tried to squeeze past them.

"Show us to the throne room," he demanded.

"We are here to kill Drakahl, not you," said Laurence.

The woman nodded the affirmative, taking great effort to do so despite her fear.

"Take.... take the stairs just beyond the door, to the right. Then... then take a right at the end of the hall," she said, trembling.

"We don't want the front doors to his throne room. There must be a servants' entrance in the rear of the room," said Laurence.

"I... I can show you," she whimpered.

She led them down the hall a short way, then up a flight of wooden stairs tucked back in a dark corner. The stairs were barely wide enough for a single person to ascend comfortably.

When they reached the next floor, she led them to the right and down a dark hallway. Several small doors lined the walls, allowing servants to enter the various rooms in secret to service the palace's officials and guests without disrupting them.

∴ ∴ ∴

MORDECHAI STARTED walking toward the palace as his forces pushed through the outer wall into the first tier.

Saerasha and the Aegra started moving across the battlefield outside the walls, searching for any of their fallen to offer healing.

The Inok charged ahead, barreling through the forces gathered at the second gate.

Uehm, Gareg and the Daulga from the right flank charged forward with them.

As the army battled on two fronts, several of Drakahl's soldiers attempted to block Mordechai's path on the first tier. He waved his hand at them, pushing them aside with a wave of energy.

Terrified, they ran to find other foes, leaving the mage to his business.

Mordechai continued his ascent of the palace grounds, power rolling off his robes like wisps of smoke.

∴ ∴ ∴

AFTER A series of hallways and sharp corners, the trio found themselves in front of a large oak door.

"Is this the throne room?" whispered Izabel.

The woman nodded sheepishly and attempted to back away.

"Let her go," whispered Izabel.

Wil released his grip on the woman's arm. She turned and ran as fast as she could, the patter of her bare feet echoing in the distance.

Laurence looked at Wil, then Izabel, nodding to each of them. He could feel his adrenaline rising. Arcturus's face flashed through his mind. Gaerin and Lyla's screams echoed in his memories. Anger overtook him.

With a violent shove, the servant's entrance to Drakahl's throne room flung open, rebounding off the wall with an echoing thud.

∴ ∴ ∴

MORDECHAI ASCENDED the steps to the palace. Several guards presented their swords and shields, as if ready to defend the entrance. He smiled in response.

He raised his hands in front of them, placing their backs against one another. Closing his hands as if gripping the inner edge of the double doors, he ripped his hands to his sides violently.

The doors crumpled to the outer walls in an instant, as if ripped open by a titan.

The soldiers dropped their weapons and ran down the steps past him.

Mordechai resumed his walk toward Drakahl's throne room.

∴ ∴ ∴

LAURENCE, WIL, and Izabel walked into the throne room.

Drakahl turned around at the sound of the door slamming into the wall behind him.

"I should've killed you along with Arcturus!" growled Drakahl. Stone dust shook free from new cracks in the ceiling and peppered the room as he spoke.

'*Kill him now!*' screamed Axvalla, pleading him to draw blood; pleading him to give in to his rage.

Izabel nearly froze in terror. She'd never seen a man so large, or powerful. His armor seemed to writhe and squirm atop him, as if made from living flesh. The black sword in his right hand would have been a greatsword to any normal human, yet he wielded it in one hand as if it were a normal sword.

Laurence's story hadn't done their enemy justice.

"Yes, you should have," said Laurence, stepping toward him.

"Why didn't you?" asked Wil, pacing toward the far side of the room along the wall.

"It doesn't matter. You all die today," growled Drakahl.

∴ ∴ ∴

DRAKAHL STRODE toward Laurence, meeting him at the center of the dais where his throne had been before his outburst.

As Drakahl's sword arced through the air toward Laurence's neck, Laurence raised his right hand to parry. Rainbow Cutter materialized in his grasp. The two swords met and locked in place, both men pushing with all their might, magical sparks bursting through the air at the impact. Laurence slid backward under the power of Drakahl's strength, but his sword did not give, and his form did not sway.

Surprise crossed Drakahl's face as the small, weak boy resisted his strength. His eyes drew to the sword in the boy's hand.

"It's not going to be that easy this time," said Laurence, hatred lacing his words.

Drakahl shoved Laurence back with both arms as Izabel arrived at his side.

Izabel attacked, thrusting her blade toward the crease in the armor at Drakahl's waist. He flicked his wrist, twirled his sword downward and deflected her attack, sending her into a spin with the power of his strike.

Wil leapt forward, thrusting his Quel'Thoz at demonic man's face. Drakahl brought his sword around just in time to deflect the attack, grabbed the haft of Wil's weapon with his left hand, yanked it free from Wil's grasp and tossed it across the room.

∴ ∴ ∴

MORDECHAI WALKED down the great-hall toward the throne room. Several of Ahm's disciples stepped into the hall, exiting the rooms along its side.

Bolts of black energy slammed into Mordechai's chest and back, dropping him to his knees in pain.

The priests started chanting a ritual that Mordechai recognized. They intended to rip the soul from his body.

Mordechai pulled on the leylines above the castle with all his might, splitting the power into twelve distinct lines of energy; one for each priest. As he clenched his right fist, magic surged down from the heavens as streams of fire as hot as the sun.

The bolts tore through the priests, driving through their heads and down into their torsos.

Mordechai stood and resumed his walk to the throne room as the priests' smoldering corpses fell to the floor.

∴ ∴ ∴

WIL RACED across the room to retrieve his weapon.

Laurence attacked with a flurry of alternating, quick slashes. Drakahl parried them, but seemed surprised by Laurence's speed.

Izabel stepped to Drakahl's right flank during the flurry and thrust her sword into the weak spot at his right hip while he was distracted.

Drakahl kicked Laurence in the chest, spun and slashed his sword at Izabel violently. She barely raised her shield in time to stop his blade from rending her in two. She slid backward a few feet from the power of his strike as she braced her shield with both arms.

He tossed his sword into his left hand and ripped her sword free with his right. As he tossed it aside, Laurence charged in with another flurry of attacks.

Laurence attacked with alternating diagonal strikes, using a technique Kyrilis had taught him. He focused on moving faster and striking stronger blows. His sword complied, sending a surge of energy into him as it fed upon his own.

Drakahl parried the first three attacks easily, but barely deflected the fourth. His opponent was moving at unreasonable speeds and only growing faster. The fifth attack knocked his own weapon aside, and the sixth cut through his armor and into the surface of his flesh beneath. Horrified, Drakahl stepped backward.

Axvalla screamed in pain. Never before had an opponent harmed it. *'What does he wield?'* the demon pleaded.

Laurence pressed his advantage. As his sword arced toward his foe's left shoulder, Drakahl dropped his own sword and jumped forward. He caught Laurence's wrist mid-swing and tried to wrench the sword from his grip.

Laurence let go of the blade. Rainbow Cutter slipped through Drakahl's hands and disappeared, only to reappear in Laurence's grip again.

Drakahl punched Laurence in the chest, sending the boy back several feet and onto the ground.

'Get away from his sword! Flee!' begged Axvalla.

He knelt, picked up his sword, and walked toward his prone opponent; ignoring the pleas of the demon within his armor.

He is prone, and my sword can drink his power. This will all be over soon!

"This is the end, boy!"

∴ ∴ ∴

MORDECHAI STOOD before the throne room doors for a moment. The doors were made of iron and barred from within. After pondering his options, he reached into the weave again and grabbed the metal doors with his magic.

The doors fell into a pile of rusty flakes on the floor at his bidding. He stepped over the pile into the room just as Wil charged

Drakahl from behind.

∴ ∴ ∴

WIL RACED back over to Drakahl and Laurence, his Quel'Thoz twirling through the air violently.

Drakahl turned just in time to parry several attacks from the elven weapon's blades as they whipped through the air toward his face, neck, chest and legs.

Wil pressed his attack, creating a blur of whirling steel and ebony wood before him. Every half second, one end of his bladed staff entered Drakahl's space, forcing him to defend.

Drakahl roared in anger. He jumped backward and swung his large blade upward with both hands. His attack had been perfectly timed.

The massive black sword cut through the haft of Wil's Quel'Thoz, shattering the weapon.

Drakahl turned his strike mid-air and sent it back down toward Wil's head.

Izabel arrived just in time and dove between the two of them, her shield held high to deflect the incoming blow. Both of her forearms shattered under the force of Drakahl's strength.

He kicked her in the chest, sending her backward into Wil, and the both of them to the floor below the dais.

Laurence regained his feet.

∴ ∴ ∴

"WE'RE NOT done yet," said Laurence angrily.

Drakahl whipped his head around to face Laurence, then took a step back as he turned to face the boy.

"This ends here. Right now," said Laurence.

Drakahl attacked first, snapping to action faster than Laurence anticipated.

Laurence raced to parry Drakahl's attacks; first from the left, then from the right, then overhead.

Drakahl raised his sword quickly as it rebounded off of Laurence's parry, and with a flick of the wrist cut Laurence across the forehead.

He backed away as if his victory was assured, pride showing in the grin on his face.

"Your soul is mine now, boy," he sneered.

"Is it?" asked Laurence, mockingly.

'It's *not working!*' yelled Axvalla.

Drakahl looked down at his blade. No black tendrils raced across the room. No power was entering his body as it drained from his victim. Axvalla was terrified, and so Drakahl was involuntarily terrified.

"How?" Drakahl stammered.

"What would be the point in telling you, when you won't live to benefit from the knowledge?" remarked Laurence.

Mordechai smirked at the lad's wit from across the room, watching with pride as the last Raven claimed his vengeance.

Laurence stepped forward but remained ready to defend. He began sidestepping around Drakahl, waiting for the beast-of-a-man to attack.

Drakahl screamed in rage, shaking the room with the power of his voice. He begged Axvalla for reinforcements, but none came.

He spun to attack Laurence in a downward strike, desperate to overtake the surprisingly well equipped, well prepared foe.

Laurence deflected the blade to the side and drove its tip into the floor, then whipped his sword back toward Drakahl in blistering speed, striking his right shoulder with a counterattack. He resumed his sidestepping circle around Drakahl, waiting for another attack.

Drakahl turned the opposite direction, bringing his sword around at waist-level in a powerful strike; intending to cleave Laurence in two.

Laurence pointed his sword toward the attack, just under Drakahl's sword's elevation. As their blades dragged across each other, he lifted with all his might and escorted the black sword up and over his head.

As the sword completed its journey upward, Laurence stepped into the space between them and brought his sword down into Drakahl's right shoulder, cutting through the man's armor, down to the bone underneath.

Rather than wrench his blade free, Laurence jumped backward and let go of it. Rainbow Cutter re-materialized in his hand, leaving a deep gash in his victim's shoulder.

Drakahl howled in pain and transferred his blade to his left hand.

"Your strength can't win this time, and your sword is all but useless against me," taunted Laurence.

"I will end you!"

"I'm not a defenseless old man, you pathetic sack of shit," growled Laurence.

Laurence pushed his will into his magical blade as Drakahl ran forward, urging it to cut deeper than it ever had before.

Drakahl charged with his blade in front of him, thrusting toward Laurence's mid-section.

Laurence held his blade upright in both hands and stepped into the maneuver. He deflected Drakahl's attack to the outside, stepped into his reach, and released Rainbow Cutter from his grasp.

As their bodies collided, Drakahl moved to grab Laurence with his good arm, but it was already too late.

Laurence shoved his left hand into Drakahl's right underarm, clenched his fist, and summoned Rainbow Cutter. The sword appeared in horrific fashion, its hilt in Laurence's left hand, and its blade crossing through the top of Drakahl's chest.

Drakahl's sword clattered to the floor as he lost the ability to maintain his hold of it.

Laurence stepped back, releasing his hold on Rainbow Cutter.

The wound in Drakahl's upper chest gushed blood as the sword dissipated. His lungs slowly flooding with blood, he gasped for breath but none came.

As he dropped to his knees, Axvalla pleaded with him to get up and run.

Laurence walked up and leaned down to look him in the eyes.

"Gahl. Tolrin. Arcturus. Gaerin. Lyla. You have killed your last Raven, and now the last Raven kills you," said Laurence.

He summoned Rainbow Cutter and slowly slid it across the man's throat, then pushed him backward onto the floor.

When Laurence looked up, Kyrilis, Mordechai and several of his companions were staring back at him.

The battle outside had concluded.

The day had been won.

∴ ∴ ∴

KYRILIS RAN up to Laurence and hugged him with all her strength.

"You beat him!" she gasped.

"I wouldn't have without the help of everyone here," he said.

"No great deed is accomplished in isolation," she said.

"What do we do with his corpse?" asked Wil as he walked over.

"I'll send it to the sword chamber in Vuhl," said Mordechai.

"You can do that?" asked Kyrilis.

"I left a translocation rune behind for this very purpose," he said. "I'll return in a few days and seal the ruby chamber as before. Then only Laurence will be able to retrieve the corpse, and of course he'd have no reason to."

"Sounds fine by me," said Laurence.

Kellum joined them, picked up Drakahl's blade and placed it atop the man's corpse.

Mordechai shot him a look, curious how he was able to touch the blade without pain.

"What?" asked Kellum. "You want to leave the sword here? Send it with him."

Mordechai nodded, realizing at that moment they knew nothing of Kellum. He placed his hand on Drakahl's chest, closed his eyes for a moment, and the corpse vanished.

"Right. That's over... now can we return home?" asked Izabel as she joined them, testing her wrists. Saerasha had just completed healing her arms.

"The voyage back is going to suck," said Wil.

"Finding a ship to take us is going to suck more," said Kyrilis.

"I'll teleport us back," said Mordechai.

"You can do-" started Izabel.

"Yes, I can do that. Will everyone stop asking me what I can do? I'm asking that enough for all of us these days. Besides, I have no time to waste with travel. We learned more on this trip that needs to be investigated, and while Drakahl may be handled, we've much bigger problems afoot."

"Like Nightweaver," said Kyrilis.

"And the gods we freed from Zathos," said Laurence.

"Gods?" asked Kyrilis, alarmed.

"Yeah... apparently Zathos was made by Mordechai and the original wielder of Rainbow Cutter as a prison for two gods, to prevent a war that was destined to destroy all life on Ayrelon," explained Laurence frankly.

"Ah... well, at least it's nothing serious," joked Izabel.

Laurence and Wil laughed and rolled their eyes.

"One problem at a time," said Mordechai. "For now, we head back to Arkhania and report to Ayriel and the King, then we figure out which problem to tackle next. More than likely that'll have to be Nightweaver. The real issue is, whether it be Nightweaver or a god, I can't track them magically. So whatever we're about to face, it's going to be difficult."

"Let's gather the rest of the Arkhanians and head out then, shall we?" suggested Laurence.

"Hey, where's Agnar?" asked Izabel, scanning the room.

Kyrilis walked over to her with a somber look on her face. She placed a hand on Izabel's shoulder, as Izabel's face contorted in confusion, and then fear.

"He died valiantly, fighting Drakahl's demonic steed," said Kyrilis.

Izabel's eyes went wide as she sank to the floor, shock depriving her of tears.

Laurence suddenly felt defeated. He'd lost yet another friend in his journey for revenge and hadn't even noticed.

REUNION

Ris'Uttyr, Amaethur 5th, 113 of the 2nd Era

In Ravens' blood will destiny bathe,
To bring forth what must come.
No peace for those with Raven's name,
Their job is far from done.

Night's Writ, Parable 1

MORDECHAI SENT the companions to his rune in Fel'Rechaun one at a time. As each appeared, they walked out of the alcove into Fahrul's meeting hall at the base of the tower. Several of them vomited due to the experience.

Preita was far from pleased, and proceeded immediately to fetch a mop.

∴ ∴ ∴

LAURENCE AND Mordechai were the last to arrive in Fel'Rechaun.

Fahrul rushed over and picked Laurence up joyfully as he entered the great hall.

"Lad! You've done it!" said Fahrul as he put Laurence back on the ground.

"By the gods, Fahr, I didn't realize you were so strong for such an old man," teased Laurence.

"The King's been looking for you these past few weeks. He wants to knight you for slaying the dragon in Cragenfell."

"Knight me? I didn't kill it by myself."

"He's knighting you and Izabel for your service and leadership. He planned on knighting Agnar as well, but," said Fahrul, letting his words trail off.

"He was killed by Drakahl's demonic steed as we assaulted the palace. There wasn't enough left of him to bring home for burial," explained Kellum.

Izabel started crying.

"Well, I must be off," said Kellum. "I've got places to go and people to see. You coming, Gareg?"

"No. I must go home to Tellrindos. I have been gone for far too long," said Gareg.

"Thank you both for your help," said Laurence.

"Here," said Kyrilis. She offered each of them a handful of silver coins. "Gaerin and Lyla promised to pay you. I feel it's only right that I pay you in their stead."

Both of them accepted the coins and left, heading their separate ways.

"Gaerin and Lyla are dead?" asked Fahrul.

"They were killed by Grohm in the Triblunds of Pelrigoss," said Laurence.

"I am so sorry, lad," said Fahrul, casting a glance to Kyrilis.

"That's not on her. Their group was ambushed, and all of them were taken captive or slain. It was blind luck we arrived just in time to save the ones we did. No, this is on you for sending them ahead without me," barked Laurence.

"That's not fair, Laurence," said Mordechai.

"Let's just get this meeting with Ayriel and Orluhnd over with so I can return home to Tylee," said Laurence angrily as he walked toward the door.

Kyrilis stepped in his way and placed a hand on his chest.

"It was as much my choice as it was Fahrul or Mordechai's, okay? We all thought it was best, and we were wrong. We couldn't have known what was going on in the Triblunds," she said.

Laurence forced himself to calm down. He looked down at her hand, then back to her eyes.

She could tell how much pain he was in. Drakahl's death hadn't resolved as much as he'd hoped.

"I'll go get Tylee and bring her to Vaelin Palace. Fahrul told me Bah'Shiri was in her roost just before you arrived, so I'll be quick. Make your apologies to Fahrul, gather your friends and finish this journey the right way," she said.

He nodded in response, a tear cascading down his cheek. All the death and loss was catching up to him. As she walked away, the realization that his time with her was over was nearly too much to bear. At the same time, his feelings for Tylee flooded back in; knowing he was about to be reunited with her, and would have more than a day with her before they parted ways again.

Confused about how he should feel, he turned back to Fahrul and pulled him into a hug, weeping gently on his shoulder.

"It's okay, lad. You've been through too much," said Fahrul, patting him gently on the back.

∴ ∴ ∴

"HOW THE fuck did she know he'd be all the way down here, sir?" asked a soldier looking down at Drakahl.

"You'll learn in time not to question anything that woman does," answered Soth.

He stood for a moment, studying his former master's corpse.

That kid really did a number on you, Soth mused. *Hopefully this puts your ego in check.*

"Alright. Get him onto the stretcher and let's get this show on the road. We've a ship waiting, and I hate labyrinths," said Soth.

∴ ∴ ∴

THEIR JOURNEY to Vaelin Palace took nearly two days, even using the horses Mordechai had enchanted for the trip. The city was in an odd mix of disarray and bustling with business, portions of it seeming completely abandoned while others seemed overcrowded.

Laurence wondered if the state of Vellenheim's population was indicative of the rest of Arkhania.

Laurence, Tylee, Izabel, Wil, Mordechai, Kyrilis, and Fahrul walked into the throne room as trumpets blared and the crowd around them cheered. Several citizens called out to the Heroes of Cragenfell, others called out Laurence and Izabel by name.

They stopped a few yards from the dais, looking up at the King and his daughter, then bowed in unison. When they returned to an upright position, Ayriel smiled and invited Laurence and Izabel to approach.

"You've had quite an adventure these past months. Part of that adventure resulting in the death of a dragon, and the saving of countless lives. It is with honor and respect that your King wishes to bestow the title of Sir Laurence the Raven, Knight of Arkhania, and Lady Izabel the Stalwart, also Knight of Arkhania," she said.

"The people thank you for your-" started the King, his words interrupted by a coughing fit. After taking a few moments to collect himself, he continued, "for your service."

"We apologize that this ceremony is not more lavish, but you understand the trying times we are faced with," said Ayriel.

"No ceremony was necessary, your Majesty. We did not take action with thought of reward," said Laurence.

Ayriel stood and applauded, setting off a round of applause and cheers around the room.

Wil stepped forward and put his arms around their shoulders. "Now I'll never deflate that head of yours," he said to Laurence.

"Do I call you Sir, Lord or Duke now?" asked Izabel.

"Just Laur, Lady Izabel," he laughed.

Ayriel walked to each of the companions and hugged them, thanking them individually for their efforts before they departed.

"Go get some rest, you've earned it. When you're ready to return, the Kingdom has great need of you," she said to Laurence.

He nodded his thanks and made his way out of the palace.

∴ ∴ ∴

OUTSIDE, THE small group of friends gathered away from the crowd.

"Tylee and I are going to stay at Gaerin and Lyla's farm for a while. We need some time alone, now that Drakahl has been handled," said Laurence.

"I'll bring him back to Kotanndale with me after we've recovered a bit. I'm sure Clendon will have plenty for him to do while we rebuild," said Tylee with a smile, clinging to Laurence's arm as if he would float away.

Kyrilis smiled at them and nodded her understanding. "Take the time you need. The Kingdom has already gotten more from you than it could ask for. I'm sure they'll understand you taking a much-needed vacation."

"And I'm off to Ekthri. I've a Kingdom of my own to rebuild, and I'm sure my lazy brother is making a mess of things," said Wil.

"See you later, King Wilwarianel," teased Laurence.

"Ugh, don't call me that, Lord Ravencrest," Wil groaned sarcastically.

"I've been assigned to Northwatch Keep in Uldenheim. They're giving me a Vintain to lead," said Izabel proudly.

"I'm sure your father *loves* that idea," laughed Laurence.

"I really don't care what he thinks," she said, sticking out her tongue as if to punctuate her point. "Mother is proud, and that's what matters."

"Thank you again for all of your help, Kyrilis," said Laurence.

"Yeah, you're the best!" chimed Izabel.

After a few last hugs and handshakes, the group went their separate ways.

∴ ∴ ∴

AFTER A week of travel, the couple had finally reached Gaerin's old farm north of Mooncrest. The journey had been uneventful, aside from Tylee's insistence that Laurence continuously retell the story of his adventure.

As they reached the house, Laurence dismounted and helped Tylee from her saddle.

"You know, I was so happy to have you back, I didn't even realize you no longer had a sword on your back," she said as he lowered her to the ground.

"Yeah, it's... in my arm," he answered.

"I know you told me that, but it's rather hard to imagine," she said.

He summoned Rainbow Cutter into his hand and held it in front of her at waist level so she could inspect the blade.

"Careful, it's extremely sharp," he said.

"It's magnificent. And you always have it on you?"

"In me, actually," he said.

"That's amazing!"

"It's the reason Drakahl rots in a grave. Well, aside from the three hundred and eighty-three people who helped me," he said as he returned the blade to its crystal.

She chuckled and stepped to his side, putting an arm around his waist. "How does it feel to be back in Mooncrest after what you've been through?" she asked.

"I'm not sure," he said. He walked around the back of the house and peered at the kitchen door for a few moments. Memories of the last time he stood there flooded his mind, followed by Gaerin and Lyla's horrific death at the hands of Grohm's priest.

Overcome with a fresh wave of sadness, Laurence sank to his knees.

Tylee knelt in front of him and pulled him into her breast, kissing the top of his head.

Several hours passed before he recovered himself enough to move again. She stayed with him the entire time, kissing his head every few minutes and telling him to, "Just let it out," and, "it's over now."

∴ ∴ ∴

A WEEK later, Laurence sat at the table waiting for Tylee to finish cooking. She stood over the stove, happily stirring a pot full of greens while the meat she'd roasted rested on the counter under a cloth.

"So that's when Clendon told me I was a Duchess," said Tylee, finishing her story.

Laurence had enjoyed their week together, but he knew it was going to end in the near future. The brilliant life she'd created for herself would come calling, or a new threat would confront the Kingdom; either way, they were relaxing on borrowed time.

She brought two plates over to the table and sat them in their proper places. Sighing, she repositioned the silverware Laurence had been fidgeting with and then took her seat.

Laurence looked down at the meal she'd prepared. Tylee had been spoiling him with food the entire week, and the dinner before him was no exception. A small game hen sat on his plate, perfectly roasted and smelling faintly of garlic. Next to it sat a pile of butter-wilted greens and roast potatoes.

"Okay, now I'm ready," she said, tucking a cotton napkin into her lap.

Laurence picked up his utensils and carved into the hen. He placed a bit of meat in his mouth. It seemed to melt away, buttery and delicious.

Tylee watched as he hastily ate her meal. The sight of his enjoyment brought her great pleasure. *Mom was right about those lessons paying off.* "My mother was thinking of visiting tomorrow," said Tylee.

"Is that what the messenger brought today?"

"Yes, but I didn't want to disturb your practice," she said.

"This is amazing, by the way," he said, pointing at the meal he'd almost finished.

"So, other than helping me rebuild Tolrin Province, what do you want from our future?" she asked, carving into her own hen.

"I want a family," he answered frankly.

"You want what now?" she gasped.

"Not right away," he laughed. "But eventually, yes. I want little Tylees and Laurences running around, giving us headaches," he said, smirking.

"Let's give that a few years, okay? I've got too much going on to be all porked up like a pot-belly pig," she remarked, waving her knife at him playfully.

"I was thinking maybe next month?" he said jokingly, one eyebrow raised.

"Stop!" she said, nearly choking on her dinner.

∴ ∴ ∴

LAURENCE DRIFTED in and out of sleep that night. His concern that their vacation would be interrupted by bad news had been growing over the past few days, and his mind wouldn't let him cast the thought aside.

He woke again, refusing to open his eyes. Try as he might, he couldn't push away the growing sense of panic. Something was wrong. His brain insisted something was wrong.

Tylee lay with her head on his chest, much like Kyrilis had done their last few nights in Pelrigoss.

Is that what's bugging me?

'No,' answered Rainbow Cutter.

A warm sensation washed over his chest.

Tylee gasped, her breath gurgling in her throat.

His eyes shot open. Standing over their bed was a figure dressed head to toe in black silk.

TO BE CONTINUED IN...

ENVELOPED BY
DARK'S EMBRACE
A DESTINY OF BLOOD & MAGIC: BOOK 2

HTTPS://AYRELON.COM

PRONUNCIATION GUIDE

Aegir	-	āy-jēr
Aegra	-	āy-gräh
Agnar	-	ăg-när
Agthari	-	äg-thar-ē
Ahava	-	ä-hä-vä
Afyr	-	äh-fēr
Ahm	-	ähm
Ahrwie	-	är-wē
Andor	-	än-door
Arcturus	-	ärc-tur-us
Arkhan	-	är-kähn
Arkhania	-	är-kähn-ēä
Ayriel	-	air-ēal
Ayr'Thugohn	-	air-thoo-gôn
Axvalla	-	äx-vä-lä
Bingrolf	-	bēng-rôlf
Bolrin	-	bōl-rĭn
Bronsin	-	brôn-sin
Daegon	-	day-gôn
Delriahna	-	dell-rēänä
Drakahl	-	drä-cäll
Dynar	-	die-när
Ekthri	-	ehk-thrē
Inok	-	ē-nähk
Fahrul	-	fä-rool
Fel'Rechaun	-	fell-rish-ôn
Fel'Vizsiour	-	fell-viz-jor
Gabner	-	gab-ner
Gaerin	-	g-air-in
Gahl	-	gäll
Gaierford	-	guy-er-ferd
Galrath	-	gäll-räth
Gargoa	-	gär-goä
Galeg	-	gāy-lĕg
Gellix	-	gĕll-ix

PRONUNCIATION GUIDE

Gnok	-	g-nôck
Grellenheim	-	gr-ĕll-in-hīm
Grohm	-	gr-ôm
Gusarski	-	goo-sär-skē
Haern	-	hair-n
Hahrfurgadhen	-	här-fur-gäd-hĭn
Hoalfast	-	hole-fast
Hystari	-	hisstär-ē
Izabel	-	is-a-bĕll
Kaggarha	-	kä-gar-ä
Karzden	-	car-z-den
Keifer	-	kēy-fer
Kellum	-	kĕll-um
Kotann	-	kō-tăn
Krierga	-	krēer-gä
Kulgan	-	kull-gĭn
Kundarr	-	koon-dar
Kyrilis	-	kēy-rill-iss
Laurence	-	läur-ĭns
Lyla	-	lie-la
Maerik	-	mair-ĭk
Mordechai	-	mor-de-kai
Mythaeil	-	mith-ā-ill
Oben	-	ô-bin
Pelrigoss	-	pĕll-ri-gôss
Saerasha	-	sair-äshä
Shaer'Thog	-	sh-air-thôg
Skaar	-	skär
Skain	-	skay-n
Sorscha	-	sor-shä
Soth	-	sôth
Sylk	-	silk
Tellrindos	-	tell-rĭn-dôss
Telon	-	tell-ôn
Thool	-	thool

PRONUNCIATION GUIDE

Thorgen	-	thor-gen
Tolrin	-	toll-rĭn
Triblunds	-	trĭb-lunds
Tryn	-	trĭn
Tylee	-	tie-lee
Uldenheim	-	ōll-dĭn-hīm
Vaelin	-	vāy-lĭn
Vaelys	-	vāy-lĭss
Vehkstaerelliox	-	ve-k-stair-ell-ē-ôx
Vellenheim	-	vell-ĭn-hīm
Velloth	-	vell-ôth
Vey'Thugohn	-	vāy-thoo-gôn
Vuhl	-	vool
Wehrenel	-	wair-ĭn-ell
Wilwarianel	-	wĭll-wair-ēan-ell
Xulrathia	-	zool-räth-ēä
Xxrandus	-	z-ran-dus

Months

1	Luthentyr	-	loo-thĭn-tēr	Winter
2	Djacenta	-	d-jä-sĭn-tä	Winter
3	Brighanfjor	-	brĭg-än-f-yor	Winter/Spring
4	Nyevantyr	-	nyev-än-tēr	Winter/Spring
5	Caer'Nuun	-	k-air-noon	Spring
6	Gwyddinfyr	-	g-wĭd-dĭn-fēr	Spring
7	Bloedden'Vasche	-	blud-ĭn-vä-sh	Spring/Summer
8	Aiengust	-	aīn-gust	Summer
9	Danufyr	-	dănoo-fēr	Summer
10	Oghenfall	-	ôg-ĭn-fall	Summer/Fall
11	Arran'Hael	-	air-ran-hāl	Fall
12	Amaethur	-	ä-mā-thur	Fall
13	Ahr'Antaerwyn	-	ärr-änt-air-wĭn	Fall/Winter

Days of Week

1	Ris'Anyu	-	rĭss-än-yoo
2	Ris'Nammlil	-	rĭss-näm-lĭl
3	Ris'Kitthu	-	rĭss-kĭt-thoo
4	Ris'Gaula	-	rĭss-gä-oo-lä
5	Ris'Uttyr	-	rĭss-oo-tēr
6	Ris'Enliss	-	rĭss-ĭnlĭss

THE CURSE OF KISHINA

The unfortunate tale of Maerik

THE SOUL of his beloved rest peacefully in his palm, trapped within its crystalline prison.

Too long had he carried the burden. Too far had he traveled in search of a way to release her. The hopes of bringing her back to his side had long since faded.

As he stood in front of Xxrandus's Gift, the Soul Obelisk of Vuhl, his only remaining hope was to free her; his only desire to find a way for her soul to attain its long-awaited rest.

He didn't know if she could hear him, or if she knew of his tribulations; whether she'd gone mad after being trapped for decades, or lacked all capacity for thought. He'd often looked to her crystal as a reminder of his motivations; his humanity. Deep down inside, he was sure he could feel her presence; guiding him; loving him.

He'd only once found a way to free himself of the ruby necklace and had abandoned that endeavor to continue pursuing Kishina's release. The ruby gave him power, and power was necessary to save his love. Trapped by one crystal while carrying his trapped lover in another; he was a tortured man with few associates, and even fewer friends.

He spared a moment to think back on his life; to reflect on what had brought them to that moment.

* Ris'Kitthu, Bloedden'Vasche 3rd, 69 Years Before the 1st Era *

ACCORDING TO his father, life in Delohr, a small village on the coast of the Hystari, had been simple but fair. Lord Thalish ignored the town, which suited its residents fine. He didn't offer his protection, even though they lived within the province he governed. However, that also meant he did not tax them. For the poor farmers and businessmen of the region, his absence was a blessing for which they were all thankful.

Thorim had made a name for himself as an up-and-coming scribe, and his future seemed promising. Dylara's father conducted most of his business with the assistance of Thorim's quill, so it was of no surprise to anyone when the youths fell in love and made plans to wed.

A year passed as their love blossomed. On the eve of their wedding, everything seemed to be going as planned.

Dylara sat at dinner with her father that night, discussing the morning's affair. Thorim would return from Vellenheim and head straight to the church for their wedding. She made her father repeat the list of things he needed to bring, so Thorim could prepare for their ceremony.

Suddenly, the night brightened just outside the front window, interrupting their conversation.

"More gifts?" suggested Dylara. Visitors had come and gone the entire day, leaving presents for the soon-to-be newlyweds. The light beyond the window struck her as torchlight, though she couldn't imagine who would visit at such an hour.

As she opened the front door, reality shattered her assumptions. The light playing across their dining room, causing shadows to dance upon their evening meal, didn't come from well-wishers. The buildings across the street were burning and screams echoed from the distance.

Several men rushed past the door, wielding pitchforks, wood-axes and kitchen knives.

An orc came into view across the street, chasing her friend Sirana. She cried out, blood spurting from her chest, as the vile creature's sword cut her down from behind.

Dylara slammed and barred the door, trembling with fear.

Her father ran up the stairs and retrieved an old necklace, hidden away since her mother had died. He gave it to her and explained that only a member of her bloodline could use the powers within.

"I hoped it would never come to this, but it has... I fear you won't survive the night without it," he explained sadly.

The necklace bore a single ruby, pulsing with a faint black energy. He bid her slip it over her head, though his trembling hands suggested she should hesitate.

"What will this do?" she asked.

"It doesn't matter. It will save you," he said, choking back tears to sound confident.

With fear in her heart, she donned the necklace as he requested.

* Ris'Uttyr, Caer'Nuun 17th, 68 Years Before the 1st Era *

HIS FATHER, Thorim, returned the next morning as scheduled, however, the town was not how he'd left it. With her house in ruins, most of the town burned down, and corpses littering the streets, he panicked. He searched for hours but never found the woman he loved.

Eventually he encountered a few survivors, all of which were men. They formed up and entered the forest, searching for the town's missing women. Over the next few months, they continued to find remnants of orcish bandit camps and occasionally caught sight of the orcs themselves.

However, as none of the men had any experience with combat, they found themselves constantly at the mercy of whichever mercenaries they could scrounge up enough coin to hire.

Finally, after months of struggle, Thorim managed to free Dylara from her captors. By the time he got her home, it became clear she'd suffered another fate while in captivity.

The orcs had beaten and raped each of the women they'd taken from Delohr. Only Dylara had survived, aided by the powers within her ruby necklace. Withdrawn, emotionally fragile, and with child, she was no longer the same woman he'd once known.

Refusing to let her suffer additional indignity, and still in love with whom he knew her to be, he married her and found a home outside a nearby village.

* Ris'Uttyr, Luthentyr 23rd, 64 Years Before the 1st Era *

THEY LIVED a relatively peaceful life in the few years that followed. Thorim re-established his business, providing scribing efforts for local clerics and public officials. Dylara focused on raising Maerik, their halfling son.

He had no complaints regarding those early years. Kept isolated from the public, for fear of their outcry at his mixed human and orcish blood, he never knew other children. His mother had been kind and attentive, and Thorim made time where he could.

It wasn't until Maerik turned four that things soured. By then, Dylara had grown distant from Thorim. If his parents argued or fought, he knew nothing of it. They either kept their animosity to themselves, or had become adept at hiding their outbursts from him. Either way, the disappearance of his mother came as a shock.

Nothing obvious led to her departure. To his four-year-old mind, she was simply there one day and gone the next. After a few days she returned and life proceeded as normal for a time, neither parent acknowledging what had happened.

It wasn't until many years later that he learned what she'd done. Dylara had used the powers in her amulet to hunt down and slaughter the rest of the orcish tribe. She'd apparently used those years of peace to master her gifts. If only he'd known sooner, perhaps he could have prevented what was to come. Then again, what could a four-year-old have done?

Ris'Enliss, Luthentyr 30th, 64 Years Before the 1st Era

NOT LONG after her return, the arguments started. Or rather, the arguments entered the open. It wasn't long before Thorim drove Dylara away. In a dramatic final argument, he threatened to kill her if she ever returned. His father had yelled something about 'corrupting Maerik', but he'd been too young and upset to hear it all clearly, or decipher his intent.

They continued to live in that house for years, as he grew older and ultimately rebellious. All he could remember of his mother at that time was Thorim chasing her away. He resented his father for doing it and had been intent on never letting him forget.

It was clear, so many years later, that he was at least partially to blame for Thorim's next decision. Though, at the time, it had only made him hate his father more.

Ris'Gaula, Bloedden'Vasche 10th, 59 Years Before the 1st Era

HIS FATHER, clearly at his wits' end, sold their small house and committed them both to the Church of Dyxatohr, the god of life. He hadn't been old enough to flee from his father's decision, though he always wished he'd followed his heart and done so.

The next few years at the church amounted to slavery. Cleaning behind lazy priests, washing the privy by hand, mucking stalls, tending gardens; any activity the priests considered beneath them became his responsibility. He still didn't know if that had been due to his birth, the tales of his mother, or by request of his father.

It wasn't until he met her that things changed.

Ris'Anyu, Gwyddinfyr 13th, 55 Years Before the 1st Era

KISHINA ARRIVED in much the same manner as he; dragged along by her mother to join the church, against protests to the contrary. He remembered exactly what they'd been doing when their eyes first met.

She stood under the trees, trying desperately to reach the fruit thereupon, while an elderly cleric insisted she use the ladder he offered.

He froze in his tracks, carrying buckets of human waste from the privy; her beauty striking him straight through the heart. As their eyes met, and his buckets' contents sloshed onto his feet, they both knew instantly that neither would stay for much longer. They both decided right then and there that they'd escape some day in each other's arms.

Their courtship happened in secret; a stolen kiss here, or a hidden embrace there. Before long, they were sneaking out at night to be with each other under the stars.

She hadn't cared about his bloodline, or his mother. He was a kindred spirit and a kind soul; exactly what she needed in that moment in time.

He didn't care that her mother had been a brothel maid, or that she knew nothing of her father. She was the most beautiful person he'd ever met, both inside and out.

Before long, he ached when not in her presence; constantly yearning to be with her. That pain slowly replaced the absence of his mother, and the hate he felt for his father. She became the only thing that mattered.

Ris'Nammlil, Danufyr 14th, 54 Years Before the 1st Era

AS THE next year passed, and the lovers became inseparable and Thorim began to travel. A strange priest had joined the order; a man named Father Aggrend. The two of them traveled constantly, only returning to the church to resupply and return to the road.

The turn of events suited him just fine for a time. After all, his father no longer mattered to him. The only thing that mattered was biding his time until he could leave with Kishina and marry her.

However, just as suddenly as Thorim's months-long travels began, they ended. The man that returned no longer seemed like his father. He'd grown distant. He slept during the day and only left their room at night.

That was when Maerik felt the sinking feeling in his gut; he didn't trust the turn of events.

* Ris'Anyu, Caer'Nuun 7th, 51 Years Before the 1st Era *

WHEN HE and Kishina turned sixteen, they started making plans to elope. However, his father's strange activities weighed on him. He couldn't shake the thought something terrible was about to happen.

So, he started following his father at night. Each night he grew closer to Thorim's destination, but his need for cautiousness prevented him from completing the journey.

Every time he lost track of his father, he went back to meet with Kishina. They'd try to spend time together, reveling in each other's presence, but his fears over his father ultimately took over. Every night he failed to discover his father's destination or purpose, he grew less and less able to focus on Kishina and her desires.

Finally, he'd summoned the courage to ask Kishina to marry him, with the promise that they'd leave in the morning. He swore to her that he only needed one more night to discover his father's motivations, and that it would all be over. He'd end it, whether or not he succeeded.

* Ris'Enliss, Caer'Nuun 24th, 51 Years Before the 1st Era *

HE FOLLOWED his father that night, as he'd done many nights before. Whether driven by a newly acquired sense of urgency at his pending departure, or by the will of the gods, he finally succeeded in following Thorim for the length of his journey.

Deep in the depths of the tombs beneath the church, Thorim entered a hidden chamber.

He snuck to the opening in the wall, listening intently.

What happened next would haunt him for his entire life.

∴ ∴ ∴

"ONE LAST time, how do we take it off of you? Your mother found a way!" demanded Thorim.

"I don't know! You've searched for months... you've tortured me for months... my answer hasn't changed! Just... end this now," sobbed a familiar woman.

He leaned forward to see who spoke, and fear took hold. Thinking back so many years later, he regretted not moving quicker. He'd told himself for decades that it wasn't his fault. He'd tortured himself over that night, running it over and over in his mind. Even standing in front of the Soul Obelisk decades later, he knew through every fiber of his being that nothing could have been done in that dark, distant moment... and yet he suffered for his inability to act.

Thorim stepped forward angrily and slit his mother's throat. Chained naked to the wall, ripped nearly to shreds by the whips and chains they'd used to beat her, she gasped her last breath staring directly into the eyes of her son.

He raced into the room, screaming his mother's name.

Thorim spun on his heel, just as he arrived. They collided and fought, anger filling both of them. For decades he'd imagined fighting his father, but never for the reasons that fueled him that night.

∴ ∴ ∴

HE DIDN'T know, at the time, that Kishina had followed him. Her gentle, delicate frame traversed the hallways of the tombs much more quietly than his own. Had he known, he would have whisked her away right then and there; terrified for her life, and unaware of his mother's fate.

When she heard his outcry, and the noise from their brawl, she barged in to save him.

He could still hear her voice calling out, so many decades later. It was the last thing she ever said; the last thing she ever did.

"Don't hurt him!"

Looking back, the panic in her voice overwhelmed him with sadness. He'd much preferred to have died that night than for those to be her last words.

∴ ∴ ∴

AS HE turned to face his lover, his father shoved past him, knocking him into his mother. When he crashed to the floor at her bloody feet, her ruby necklace fell into his lap.

Father Aggrend stepped into the room at the same time, grabbed Kishina and covered her mouth.

"Not so loud, young one... you'll wake the dead," said the old man in a whisper.

Thorim sighed in frustration and turned back to his son, just in time to see him put on the ruby necklace. Still trembling with a mixture of fear and hate, Maerik got to his feet.

"You killed my mother!" he growled. He'd been so angry that the words hurt his throat. Every time he remembered the scene, he could feel hints of that pain.

"She needed to die, so that I could have her amulet. And now, you need to die too!" said Father Aggrend.

His father turned to the old man in disbelief. Thinking back, he liked to imagine that his father considered the old man's words for a moment before acting. Part of him wanted to think that his father still had an ounce of humanity at that time.

Unfortunately, that simply wasn't reality. Thorim turned just as quickly as he'd hesitated, and with a nod of agreement, he charged his son.

That's when he felt the power of the amulet. A voice passed through his mind, welcoming his soul to eternal damnation; growling as if from deep within a cavern; echoing as if born of all time.

A surge of power rolled out of him, filling the room and exploding as it collided with each surface therein.

Thorim crashed to the floor, his own knife blown out of his hand and into his throat.

Kishina landed atop Father Aggrend, both thrown backward by the blast.

Father Aggrend released his grip on her, rolled her aside and stood.

Maerik stepped forward, focused on the priest. Nothing else mattered to him at that time; the man had to die. How he wished he'd focused on Kishina instead.

∴ ∴ ∴

FATHER AGGREND started chanting a spell.

Looking back, after all he'd learned, he recognized what that spell had been. The priest had planned the spell for many, many years. Most of Thorim's journeys with the priest had been to find reagents to create a phylactery; a target for that very spell.

The man knew he was near the end of his lifespan and had sucked Thorim into a plot to extend it.

As he chanted his spell, the white crystal he held glowed to life. Kishina reached her feet just in time to see the crystal grow brighter. Fearing for her lover, she rushed the priest in hopes of disrupting the spell.

He'd reached out to his lover, but his efforts had come too late.

The priest's spell took his own life, draining his soul and with the intentions of placing it within the phylactery. He had imbued the crystal in such a way that his soul could command it, animate his corpse, and perpetuate himself through un-life for eternity. Had his spell succeeded, he would have become a Lich.

With all that he'd learned in his life, Maerik knew, looking back, that the man's casting had been flawed. Instead of casting a spell to drain his soul into the phylactery, he cast a spell to drain the nearest soul into the crystal.

Kishina's body fell to the ground as the crystal sprang permanently to life. It still glowed and swirled in his hand as he stood before the obelisk; forever moving on the inside as her soul fought to break free.

He'd stepped forward that night and committed his final mistake. He knelt down, picked up his father's knife, walked up to the stunned priest and killed the man without a second thought. As tears streamed down his face, he then knelt and picked Kishina up.

He buried her that night, not realizing until decades later than if he'd only kept the priest alive, the priest could have freed her. Instead, he'd spent nearly fifty years trying to find another way to achieve her freedom.

* Ris'Kitthu, Nyevantyr 21st, 1 Year Before the 1st Era *

MANY YEARS later, his journey to free her had brought him to the city of Hoalfast on Pelrigoss. He'd heard a rumor of a special place, a place of legend, that could finally end his quest.

Lord Mordechai, a Leyweaver of infamous renown, had told him of it. All he asked in return for the information, and the guidance to reach it, had been a single item. It hadn't taken much effort for Maerik to acquire the item. The cursed amulet upon his neck gave him powers and created a close bond to the forces of darkness. He could touch things and go places that good men could not.

Mordechai located the item, but could not enter to retrieve it. In trade for completing the task, he would be taken to Vuhl and shown to the Soul Obelisk within.

'A *ruby as large as your fist, trapped within the catacombs beneath Necropolis*.'

The task had been so easy, he'd feared Mordechai would go back on his word. It had been a pleasant and welcome surprise when Mordechai upheld their bargain. Few in his life had been so trustworthy.

He thought for a moment at the irony of it all. He'd been forty-one when he found a way to break the curse imparted by the amulet. Something had told him not to go through with it. As fate would have it, keeping his forced bond with Vaxtra had led him to Mordechai, and allowed him to retrieve the magical ruby he desired.

At least he had made one good decision in his life... or had fate forced his hand?

* Ris'Uttyr, Nyevantyr 29th, 1 Year Before the 1st Era *

THE JOURNEY to Mount Skain had been long and arduous. Mordechai had set an unwavering pace and refused to let them rest. Maerik's mind approved of that decision, though his body had barely survived the journey.

Their walk through Vuhl had seemed longer. The only respite had been their conversation.

"This labyrinth was built by the Inok, a tribe of minotaur. You know of the war of the gods, yes?" asked Mordechai.

"It only recently ended, did it not?"

"At great cost, yes. G'nok, the great titan and god of the hunt, created the Inok thousands of years ago. After our arrival on Ayrelon, the Inok, like the Toor, learned what freedom was, and yearned to have it for themselves. Few of the Agthari remained, so it was easy for their creations to break free.

"When the Inok rebelled, Xxrandus, the god of death, sent them a gift. He buried it deep within Vuhl where G'nok could not see. The gift was said to allow them to free their slain from G'nok's grasp, as he trapped and siphoned their souls to empower himself," explained Mordechai.

"That is the Soul Obelisk?"

"Yes."

"Does it work?"

"Nobody knows. The war started soon after, and we trapped G'nok and his conspirators away," said Mordechai.

"You?"

"I had plenty of help, but I had a hand in it. Sealing them away stopped the war before it could get started, and likely saved most of the mortals of Ayrelon."

"Just like that? You just sealed away a god?"

"Two, actually. And at great cost, as I said."

"If you can do all that, why are you here? Why do you need this ruby that you cannot touch?"

"I can't touch the ruby because it drains the life-force of those who draw power from the weave. Your powers come from Vaxtra, who lives upon Melthax... not Ayrelon. Only one other type of caster could have touched the ruby and lived. But since I know of no willing Celestials," said Mordechai.

"You had to choose me."

"Tell me, what other witch or warlock have you encountered that would willingly assist me in sealing this place?"

"Is that what the ruby is for?"

"I can't have random mortals waking hateful gods, can I?" asked Mordechai.

"I suppose not," answered Maerik.

Another day passed before they reached the chamber that Mordechai planned to seal. After a small ritual, he placed the ruby into an iron setting. The iron fused to the ruby as he performed the simple task, locking it into position for all time.

"That's it?" asked Maerik.

"That's it. Now we see to your task. I'll take you to the obelisk and you can perform your ritual while I finish my own duties. Once I'm done, we leave and I finish the spell of sealing as we exit."

* Ris'Kitthu, Caer'Nuun 3rd, 1 Year Before the 1st Era *

HE ALWAYS found it difficult to think clearly after thinking back on his life and remembering Kishina's beauty. As his mind returned to the present, he found himself unsure of how long he'd been standing there.

'It's time I set you free, my love.'

He knelt in front of the obelisk, its sixteen foot high surface covered floor to tip in runes. Upon his touch, the runes sprang to life, glowing purple upon its pitch-black surface.

With crystal in hand, he stood back up and focused his mind.

He chanted a prayer to Xxrandus, pleading for Kishina's release.

He chanted the names of the runes that danced upon the obelisk's surface.

He pushed with his mind, sending every ounce of power Vaxtra's amulet of power granted him coursing into his right hand and into her crystal prison.

Then he touched Kishina's crystal to the obelisk.

Maerik fell backwards, shrieking in pain as if his cries required no breath. The sound of a thousand souls, screaming out in unison, spewed forth from him as he stared up at the ceiling.

His soul drained by the very obelisk he'd hoped would free Kishina, he stood back up and shambled through the halls.

∴ ∴ ∴

A HORRID scream broke Mordechai's concentration. He quickly finished his task and returned down the hall to see what had happened.

Maerik's wretched corpse slowly shambled toward him; devoid of life and doomed for all eternity. The amulet upon his neck, the key to the power he received from Vaxtra, glowed to life as he raised his left hand.

Mordechai latched on to his control of the primal forces of Time. He sent out a wave of energy, freezing Maerik in place in an instant. With a sigh of regret, he walked up to the man.

"I'm sorry, Maerik. I should have stayed to guide you. I am sorry that I cannot free you from this prison, but I've fought enough gods for one century. Besides, soon we will all forget. You will stand as eternal, unwitting guardian to the chambers that lie beyond. You will prevent hapless mortals from unleashing the evils beyond and bringing our destruction full circle.

"Know that I am sorry... but that you serve a purpose," said Mordechai.

As Mordechai departed, he sealed the ruby's chamber, locking Maerik away for all time.

When his spell later faded, Maerik released a bolt of energy into the empty hallway, and then shambled on, seeking his non-existent prey.

∗ Unknown Date, 113 of the 2nd Era ∗

AYRIEL STOOD next to the corpse that lie on the bed, a new sadness overtaking her. First the loss, and then her refusal; it was nearly too much to bear. What good were her powers if she couldn't save the ones she loved?

'I *can save you*,' Ayriel had said.

Ayriel walked over to the desk and retrieved the small iron coffer. Its shape, that of a coffin, seemed fitting considering its contents. Izabel had brought it to her from Pelrigoss, knowing it was special but not understanding why.

The companions' journey to Pelrigoss seemed so long ago, though she knew it had only been a few months. So much had happened that she'd learned nothing of the box's contents, save that a soul lie within.

Walking back to the corpse, she considered the woman's final words.

'*Someone more important is waiting.*'

Ayriel opened the coffer and peered within. People across the land knew her as the Oracle of Vaelin; famed for speaking with the dead and receiving prophecies. She'd just talked to the corpse and its spirit didn't want to return. Instead, she'd suggested this crystal, with a hint and a glance.

'What makes you so special?'

Ayriel reached toward the crystal with her mind. She couldn't speak to the spirit within, no matter how hard she pushed. What she did find disturbed her. She felt love; endless, bottomless love. The sensation overwhelmed her. It was a woman's spirit; trapped for a very long time.

'You're right... I'll bring her back. You've lived a wonderful life... and she has not. I loved you, as you loved me. While I do not wish you to go, I will not force you to stay. I do not know the soul within this crystal, but it is clear her story has reached you in the afterlife. I will abide by your wishes. I will bring her back.'

As the most famed Enchantress in the land prepared her mind to unravel the spells that bound the poor soul to its prison, she walked over to the corpse of her lover and dumped the coffer's contents into her hand. She focused all her power on releasing the soul within; trapped for nearly thirteen-hundred years.

A soul, once beloved, lie peacefully in her palm, waiting for release from its crystalline prison.